The Signers

The Adventures of the Cushman Family

Jim Bollenbacher

Copyright © 2020 Jim Bollenbacher
All rights reserved
First Edition

PAGE PUBLISHING, INC.
Conneaut Lake, PA

First originally published by Page Publishing 2020

ISBN 978-1-6624-1382-7 (pbk)
ISBN 978-1-6624-1384-1 (hc)
ISBN 978-1-6624-1383-4 (digital)

Printed in the United States of America

Chapter 1

Where Liberty is, there is my country.
—Benjamin Franklin

Early May 1776
Atlantic Ocean, five miles east of Delaware Bay

The boatswain entered the captain's quarters quietly, keeping a sharp eye on the mysterious passenger. *I've got better things to do than look after this lubber,* he thought to himself. *Must be someone important. The captain wouldn't have given him a bed in his own cabin.* Fingering the brand-new pistol he kept tucked into his waistline, the crewman edged closer to the sleeping stranger. He grabbed his shoulder, gently attempting to awaken the last-minute arrival when it happened.

Suddenly he was suspended in midair, followed quickly by his entire body crashing hard to the cold wooden floor. The muscular stranger was on top of him, one hand gripping his throat, the other brandishing a six-inch knife. His grip tightened around the sailor's throat, the knife pressed below his left eye. The twenty-six-year-old sailor struggled for breath; there was fear in his eyes. "Don't move or you'll need a glass eye, you understand?" the lubber asked calmly.

The boatswain nodded as the stranger released his iron grip.

"Now, why are you sneaking around the captain's quarters? Didn't your mother ever teach you any manners?"

"The...the captain..." The boatswain struggled to speak as he gasped for air.

"I'm listening. The captain..."

"The captain wants to see you on the quarterdeck, immediately."

"Is there trouble?" the stranger asked, unable to hide his concern.

"Yes—"

But before he could finish his sentence, the mystery man was gone, bounding from the cabin like a tiger ready to pounce.

"Captain Gray, I understand there is a problem," the passenger demanded more than asked, darting onto the quarterdeck less than twenty seconds later.

Without saying a word, Captain Jonas Gray handed over a powerful telescope and pointed. "There, off the port stern, just showed up about fifteen minutes ago," the captain declared, removing what remained of an unlit cigar.

"Can you identify her?" the stranger asked while continuing to track the ship.

"Certainly British. It's a war frigate, probably fifth rate," the captain stated confidently, still chewing on the cigar.

"Ship of the line? We should be able to easily outrun it," the stranger said hopefully.

"Wish that was so," proclaimed the captain. "She's a fast scout, newer version." The captain pointed toward the approaching ship. "She's a fast one, all right. See, there are no gunports. A few years ago, they began to build the newer frigates without the gun decks. They were too close to the waterline, couldn't operate them in heavy seas. Not much good if you can't fire 'em. The higher-rated ships of the line still have the gun decks, some of them two, but they are bigger and *slower*." He put a heavy emphasis on the word *slower*.

"You're right, no gunports. How many guns on top deck?"

"Probably thirty heavy guns, the eighteen-pounders," Captain Gray declared, describing the smoothbore cast-iron cannon and the weight of a single-round shot. "They have great range, up to a mile. Eighteen-pounders can tear a ship apart. They'll have some smaller guns on the forecastle and quarterdeck, usually six each, for close combat."

"Like your carronade?" The stranger dropped the telescope and looked at one of the stubby cannons on the main deck.

THE SIGNERS

"Very observant. The carronade is great for defending a ship in close combat. As you can see, we have only four. Not exactly a fair contest if they decide to start a fight."

"Our only hope is to outrun her." The concern on the stranger's face grew.

"We can try, but I'm afraid we are outsailed and outgunned," replied the captain. "Don't worry, they don't want to start an incident. They may board and search us, but that's all. If for some reason they board us, your credentials should be intimidation enough."

"What if they aren't easily intimidated?"

"I've been boarded before. They'll never notice the false wall, but just to be sure, go below and stack more sacks of grain against it. No officers are that eager to move heavy objects around."

"Captain, you and I are the only ones who know about our cargo, correct?" The question was more of a threat, the eyes of the last-minute passenger dark and menacing. Even the tough and experienced Captain Jonas Gray felt nervous around the serious stranger.

"Relax, Ambassador. Your secret is safe with me. If we can't outrun 'em, we'll outsmart 'em. Now, go below and fortify the wall."

The stranger hesitated, delivering one more cold-blooded stare, then bounded off to mask the hidden cargo. He couldn't bear to bring himself to consider the possibility of the British finding it.

"There she is, just as Rourke said it would be," the captain said to his first lieutenant. "The *Treasure*, what an appropriate name," he continued.

"She's at full sail. Do you think they will try to outrun us?" the young first lieutenant asked.

"Let 'em try. Order all men on deck. I will address them immediately."

A bell reverberated throughout the ship as British sailors hurried to order, and the well-disciplined crew was waiting for the captain's orders two minutes later.

"Men, we have an important mission from Admiral Howe. The merchant ship we are in pursuit of just left Philadelphia by way of Boston. They are carrying fifteen American officers that served at Bunker Hill." The captain paused to let the British sailors digest the lie. He smiled as the crew began to mumble about revenge.

The veteran captain raised his hands to quiet the murmuring. "You heard me right, fifteen traitors that killed more than 220 of our brethren, not to mention the maiming of another 800." The captain paused again, glancing at his first lieutenant with a knowing smile as the shouts for revenge grew even louder. "Gentlemen, you will get your chance for revenge, but there is more. It seems these officers are traveling to France with a cargo."

"What's the cargo, sir?" shouted out one of the Marines.

"It seems that the Americans are sending their officers to France to seek a treaty. They are carrying the swords, pistols, and uniforms of our fallen men in Boston, as a tribute to the king of France. They believe this will be proof of their commitment to break away from our king and to form an alliance with France." The captain literally shouted the last line as his crew erupted into more cries for revenge.

"Captain!" yelled one of the gunners. "Caution be damned with these arrogant colonials! Can we send 'em to the bottom of the sea?" His comrades shouted and danced their approval.

The captain's smiled indicated he was pleased with himself. "Lieutenant Prescott, beat the quarters."

"Beat the quarters! Beat the quarters!" screamed the lieutenant as the men scrambled to their duties, duties that involved preparing for battle.

"Clean sweep, fore and aft!" the captain yelled as men began to clear everything from the top decks to be stored below. Furniture, tools, and crates were quickly removed to reduce flying debris, which typically caused most damage during a battle at sea. *Not that they will be able to get off any shots, but better to be safe,* the captain thought.

Crews of sailors hastily mopped the decks with water, while others followed behind, tossing buckets of sand, helping the men with their footing and reducing the risk of fire. Gunnery crews began to prepare the big eighteen-pounders, and powder boys, aged eleven to fifteen, were immediately sent belowdecks to bring up the gunpowder cartridges. Buckets of water were placed next to each cannon as expert spongers took long poles with sponges attached and began to clean out the cannon barrels. The sponge was especially important after every shot, to make sure there were no burning embers remaining inside the barrel. Otherwise, the next powder cartridge could explode prematurely, oftentimes killing or maiming the gun crew.

"Prescott, order the crew to use chain shot. Shoot high. We don't want to sink her, we want to recover our boys' treasures." The chain shot was particularly useful for disabling a ship for the purpose of boarding. When fired, two cannonballs connected together by a chain spun like a bola and did great damage to sails and rigging.

"Smasher crews, prepare the grapeshot," the British captain commanded. The grapeshot was particularly deadly to men on deck. Small one-inch-diameter iron balls were wrapped in canvas bags and scattered with deadly efficiency. Smasher was the nickname given to the smaller cannon or carronade. A short smoothbore, cast-iron cannon with limited range, but in close combat, it was extremely deadly. British captains liked to use it when they were in close proximity and spray the enemy decks with deadly debris or to send round shot smashing through a ship's hull at the waterline, finishing them off.

"Gun captains, aim high, aim high, take down their sails!" roared the captain as he walked down to the main deck, encouraging his gun crews. "Aim high, take down their sails!" he kept repeating.

When the boys returned with the powder cartridges, the gun crews went into action. The gun captains controlled each crew and shouted in unison, "Loaders ready!"

The loaders, or rammers, took the gunpowder cartridge and jammed it down into the mouth of the cannon with a long padded pole, also called a rammer. Next came the wadding, strands of old rope or cloth rammed into the powder cartridge for a tight fit. The loader's assistant then put the chain shot into the barrel, followed by more wadding. The extra wadding helped hold the shot in place and make sure it wouldn't roll out if the gun was pointed downward.

The captain ordered both port and starboard cannons loaded, giving him the flexibility to maneuver the ship appropriately. By the time he caught the *Treasure*, the winds could shift and change his tactics. This was too important not to be prepared for every contingency.

"Run out the guns!" the captain shouted.

Each large gun was fitted onto a gun carriage. The wheeled carriage acted as a cradle for the two-ton cannon, making it easier to move around. Every gun had two protruding trunnions, right-angle stubs in the middle of the barrel that sat down into semicircle cutouts in the carriage. These acted as the pivot points for aiming the powerful weapon. The only other part of the cannon that made contact with the carriage was the base. The crew could raise or lower the cannon by sliding or removing wedges from underneath the base.

Thick breeching ropes connected the gun and the gun carriage to the side of the ship. The ropes kept the gun from recoiling too far. If they didn't hold, the two-ton iron cannon could careen clear off the ship, destroying everything in its path. The gun crew manipulated the carriage through an intricate block-and-tackle system, so running out the guns would place the cannon snug against the side of the ship's bulwark and ready to fire.

"Lower the boats!" the captain yelled out as his crew continued to ready for battle.

All British naval vessels carried smaller boats. Some of the bigger ships of the line carried boats belowdecks, but this was not one of them. Two jolly boats sat suspended from davits located at the port and starboard stern. The oar-propelled boat was versatile, ferrying men ashore, boarding another boat, or in case of emergency, acting as a lifeboat. The captain wasn't taking any chances; if the *Treasure* returned fire, he didn't want the jolly boats damaged. He ordered the boats to be lowered into the water, where they would be dragged behind the ship and out of harm's way.

"Lieutenant Prescott, what's our range?" The captain's eye was good, and he would trust it when it came time to fire, but for now he followed procedure.

"Just under two miles, Captain. They will be in range shortly."

THE SIGNERS

The captain could barely hide his excitement. It was risky, but the reward would be worth it. *Damn,* he thought to himself, *thank God for the rabble-rousing colonials and their hatred of taxes!*

"Captain Gray, how much time before they catch us?" the mystery passenger demanded. The twenty-five-man crew was stunned to hear the stranger talk to their captain in such a tone. The rumors aboard the ship about the mysterious passenger's identity ran the gamut from British spy to a secret emissary to the French. One particularly juicy rumor declared him an assassin, sent by the Continental Congress to kill the king of England.

"Half an hour at best, fifteen minutes at worst, we are running as fast as we can. I could buy us another hour or so by taking evasive action, but unless the wind dies completely, she'll be upon us soon." The captain sounded despondent over their options.

"Captain," the stranger said, pulling him aside and speaking softly, "have you considered throwing the first punch?"

"Are you suggesting I fire upon a British warship first? One that outguns us eleven to one? Sir, are you insane?"

"Surprise them, blow a hole through the mainsail, and put a couple of rounds near the waterline. Hit 'em hard before they can react," the stranger said with passion.

"Sir, if that captain has an ounce of experience, his gun crews are preparing to fire as we speak. Privateers and pirate ships have used your very tactic enough to give caution to any British warship about to overtake a merchant vessel. I suggest we heave to and let them board. Don't give them an excuse to fire upon us."

"Captain, you know what is at stake here? If they find the—"

"Yes, yes, I know, but whatever is in your crates will do you no good at the bottom of the sea, will it? Our best chance is to play the part of an aggrieved merchant. They probably know the *Treasure* belongs to Mr. Hancock. They have been targeting his ships since his election to the presidency last year. They'll search, find no illegal contraband, maybe issue a fine, and we'll be on our way. The Royal Navy has been itching to get aggressive with the smugglers, but the king's orders have been more moderate. Let's not give them any reason to start shooting."

"Very well," the stranger responded, conceding to the captain's logic. "You're probably right, but will you at least prepare your carronade, just in case?"

Captain Gray smiled a wicked grin and removed his still unlit cigar. "Why, of course, but with great stealth. We don't want them to get the wrong idea."

"Lieutenant Prescott, any activities near their guns?" the British captain barked.

"Nothing of any consequence, sir," replied the first lieutenant, gazing through the powerful telescope.

"Good. Let me know if that changes. Marines, ready boarding equipment," the captain called out. Fifty British Marines were assigned to the fifth-rate frigate for just that purpose. They would lay down deadly fire upon the top deck and lead the boarding party with musket and bayonet if necessary.

"Sir, look!" a suddenly excited Prescott called out. "They're heaving to."

Sure enough, the merchant vessel was starting to turn into the wind and was beginning to loosen her sails, a sure sign they had given up attempting to run from the British frigate. The *Treasure* was now dead in the water, her bow pointing straight at the approaching British warship. The captain did some quick calculations and began to snap orders. "Thirty degrees to the starboard," he ordered the pilot. Taking advantage of the light wind, the captain chose to approach from the windward side. "Port guns to the ready." The gun captains began to give final orders.

"Lieutenant, remind the gunners, aim high. We don't want to sink her," instructed the captain. *Not yet.* "Prime the port guns!"

Each of the gun captains took out a pricker, a long thin rod with a sharp end. They thrust the pricker into the touchhole on top of the base of each cannon, piercing the powder cartridge. Next, they jammed a priming tube into the touchhole. Similar to a quill pen, the hollow priming tube was filled with gunpowder instead of ink.

"Ten degrees port!" the captain snapped as the British frigate was now on a parallel approach toward its target. Less than one thousand yards separated the two ships.

"Sir, their gun crews seem very active," declared the boatswain, who was watching the approaching British warship through his spyglass.

"Doesn't seem like he is taking a boarding approach either," added the stranger as the British ship continued to bear down on the merchant vessel. Suddenly, it became crystal clear what the British captain had in mind. "Captain, you better get this ship moving, now, before they blow us out of the water."

The astonished Captain Gray hesitated, trying to comprehend what was happening and why a British naval officer would attack a ship dead in the water. Every sailor looking at the seasoned captain saw the terror in his eyes. By the time he gave the order to tighten the sails, it was too late.

The wonderful aroma of grilled venison drifted up into the second-story room. It was springtime, and most of the taverns moved part of their kitchens outside. City Tavern of Philadelphia was no exception. Located at the corner of Second and Walnut, the tavern was fast becoming one of the most popular meeting places for members of the Second Continental Congress. Unfortunately, this was a well-known fact in a city that was still more Tory than Patriot. That was why the Pennsylvania delegate had secured the second-story

Cincinnatus Room for today's meeting. Named after the famous Roman general Lucius Cincinnatus, who turned down an opportunity to be dictator for life, the room offered privacy from the many Tory spies known to frequent the popular tavern.

Robert Morris was the first to arrive, and he was in a foul mood. The powerful Philadelphia banker was unaccustomed to the trepidation that was coursing through his mind. When he accepted the chairmanship to the secret committee, he knew they would have to be creative and aggressive to secure their goal of attaining weapons from the French. But the current operation was well beyond aggressive. *It was insane. Why did I let them talk me into this?* Morris smiled as the pretty waitress handed him a pint of ale.

"Your face betrays your thoughts. Having second doubts, are we?" declared yet another Pennsylvania delegate.

"Benjamin, you startled me," replied Morris. "When did you get here?"

"I was right behind your attractive waitress, admiring the view," replied Benjamin Franklin.

Morris smiled at the sexual reference and, despite being twenty-eight years younger, shook his head like a loving father attempting to deal with his teenage son. "How did you know I was having doubts?"

"Experience," stated the elderly statesman, tapping the side of his head, "and of course, you literally wear your emotions on your face."

Morris blushed in embarrassment; his wife had told him the exact thing on more than one occasion.

"Gentlemen, good evening," noted the third member of the secret meeting as he bounded into the room. It was John Hancock, the president of the Second Continental Congress. "The ship has set sail with no problems. May God bless its voyage!"

"Mr. Morris is having second thoughts," declared Franklin.

Hancock looked at Morris with disbelief. "Robert, relax. We have planned well. The *Treasure* is my newest and fastest ship. Captain Gray is my most experienced and savvy sea captain. He handpicked the crew. They are all excellent Merchant Marines. I personally saw to the construction of the false wall in the storage compartment. Gray will outrun any British ship, and if somehow they are able to board her, they will never discover the secret compartment. And don't forget Major Hall. He is quite resourceful."

Franklin nodded in agreement, then added, "John is right, Robert. My concern is that we overpaid for the military supplies."

"Now, Dr. Franklin, we've had this discussion before. The front company is already in place. The French will be happy to supply us with all the war supplies we need, and no one will ever know their government was involved. The Count de Vergennes has made it perfectly clear that money must be spread throughout the court to gain continued support," Hancock declared.

"Bribery, you mean," Franklin stated with disdain.

"Bribery, seed money, call it what you will. That's how the French operate," Hancock stated.

"I still don't like it." Franklin creased his famous nose but conceded the point.

"Nasty business dealing with the French. I would much rather reconcile with the king," Morris grunted while polishing off his first pint.

"I'm afraid we have crossed the Rubicon, Robert. There will be no turning back," declared Franklin.

"Independence, that's all the talk lately," cautioned Morris. "I think you're all mad."

"Perhaps so, Robert, but I would have to agree with Dr. Franklin. The world has never quite seen a moment like this. We're like an avalanche cascading down the side of a mountain. Once it starts, it's hard to stop," added Hancock.

"That is my main concern. The amount of money we are giving the French is staggering. If the *Mad King* ever gets wind of this, he will crush us with all the military might at his disposal," a clearly worried Morris noted.

"Don't worry, Robert. Major Hall and the *Treasure* will deliver the gold, and the British will never know a thing," declared Hancock with supreme confidence.

"I pray you're right, John," Morris responded while ordering another round. It was going to be a long night.

Thirteen-year-old Andrew Bruce had never known his parents. Growing up in an orphanage just outside Liverpool, he had run away with his only friend, Jason, one year earlier. The two boys survived by begging and stealing in the seaport city until one day they were cornered by a local constable. Jason managed to run away, but Andrew was caught and sent before the magistrate. He was given a choice between prison and enlistment in the Royal Navy. Adventure on the high seas versus a prison cell made the choice an easy one. He quickly learned that being a powder boy on a British warship was more work than adventure. But he was free, and there was something about the salty sea air that was exhilarating.

He had never seen the eighteen-pounders fired. They had practiced bringing the gunpowder from below and distributing powder cartridges to each of the gun stations, but they were never allowed to practice firing live rounds. The admiralty was under strict orders to conserve powder and ammunition. The French and Indian War had emptied the Treasury, and the king had made major cuts to the Royal Navy. Andrew and his fellow powder boys had delivered six cartridges to each of the gun stations. The boys were supposed to return belowdecks, but in addition to being utterly exhausted, they were extremely curious to witness their first naval battle.

"Aim high!" the captain yelled out. "Fire!"

The explosions rocked the ship as each port gun captain lit his priming tube, attempting to time the rolling waves with the proper angle. The deadly guns roared to life with a deafening boom, followed by another, and another. The pungent smell of gunpowder permeated the air, and smoke quickly engulfed the main deck of the *Richmond*. The piercing whistle of the chain shot rocketing through the air shocked Andrew Bruce. His eyes burned from the gathering smoke, but he remained on deck, mesmerized by the ongoing battle scene. The first volleys seemed to fly too high as the colonial ship tried to get back underway after realizing it was a deadly trap.

"Aim high!" shouted the captain. "Time the roll better!" he repeated several times. The sixteen port guns had all fired their first volleys with little effect. The gun crews raced to fire again. The spongers quickly rammed the barrels to extinguish all burning embers. The loader and loader assistant began the sequence of powder, wadding, ball, and wadding again. Andrew marveled at their speed and skill. Within ninety seconds, the gun captains were firing their second rounds, this time from less than two hundred yards away. Their timing was better, as Andrew watched the whirling chain shot smash into the defenseless ship. The mizzenmast was literally sawed in half as it tumbled to the deck, bringing the sails and rigging with it. Andrew could hear screams of agony across the water as the heavy mast crushed several of the enemy sailors. Another chain shot tore through the mainsail, shredding it to pieces. A third and fourth round found the sail and rigging of the foremast. There would be no escape for the merchant vessel, as all three masts had suffered critical damage.

The smoke was now as thick as morning fog, and Andrew felt like he was choking on the acrid remains of the gunpowder. He watched in amazement as one of the youngest powder boys left the relative safety of the mast base and was standing directly behind one of the eighteen-pounders. Before he could react, Andrew watched in horror as the gun roared to life. The two-ton cannon leaped back, straining the thick breech ropes to the maximum, then suddenly the rope shredded into thousands of tiny fibers. The cannon and carriage hurtled across the deck, smashing into the gun captain, crushing him like he was a rag doll. The powder boy never had a chance, as the heavy gun continued to careen across the main deck, striking the small boy and catapulting him ten feet into the air and twenty yards out into the ocean. The cannon next collided with a starboard cannon and two of her crew. Andrew watched horrified as both cannon and men plummeted off the side of the ship and into the churning water below.

Andrew froze in disbelief at what he had just witnessed. The thirteen-year-old began to sob uncontrollably at the death and destruction that had just unfolded in front of him. He didn't move when a more distant roar of a cannon shot exploded from the colonial ship. A white puff of smoke exiting from the mouth of the cannon was the last thing he saw. The iron ball collided onto the deck of the ship, tearing the right arm off one of the crewman. Andrew never saw the cannonball as it skipped off the deck and instantly decapitated the young powder boy. He would not be the last young man to lose his life in the coming storm.

Chaos, confusion, and death gripped the *Treasure*. A sailor wandered aimlessly on the main deck, his face horribly disfigured from flying shrapnel. Wooden splinters pierced both of his eyes, blinding him instantly. Another sailor lay bleeding to death, calling out for his mother; the full force of the mizzen yard had pinned him to the deck, severing his right leg. Yet another sailor screamed in pain, having received severe burns over 90 percent of his body, courtesy of an accidental explosion of a powder cartridge.

Uninjured crewmen attempted to put out small fires and help their injured comrades. The gun crew had managed to get off one shot. To their delight, it had struck the British frigate's main deck. The second attempt to fire proved disastrous. In the mayhem surrounding them, the gun crew had forgotten to sponge the barrel, and when they attempted to ram a second powder cartridge into the carronade, a burning piece of wadding exploded the cartridge, killing all nearby.

The mysterious stranger had attempted to warn Captain Gray when the British ship maneuvered into a line pattern used to fire on ships. The captain had uncharacteristically frozen, and his delay had sealed their fate.

"Help me get this man below. The ship's doc should be able to close that wound," the stranger said calmly to the boatswain's mate he had earlier disabled.

The boatswain hesitated. The stranger laughed and pointed at the approaching British frigate. "Look, mate, I'm not the enemy, they are. Help me get this sailor below and then we'll find the captain."

"He's below, sir, helping with the injured," he replied cautiously, still not certain of the stranger's motives. Then suddenly, it happened again; without warning, he was thrown roughly onto the deck, his head hitting the hard planking with a thud. "What the—"

The explosion of multiple cannons sounded different this time as the boatswain attempted to get up; he was pulled flat to the deck by the stranger.

"Stay down" was all he said. What happened next seemed to occur in slow motion. A wave of large musket balls passed over the deck of the *Treasure*, mutilating everything in its path. A nearby crewman was ripped to shreds as several of the mini round shots exploded into his body. The deadly grapeshot mowed down at least ten crewmen; there would be no injuries from the blast, only death. The next sound was the distinct echo of musket fire. The Royal Marines were laying down deadly fire, a sure sign they were readying to board the *Treasure*.

"They're going to board us," explained the stranger. "Get below and find the captain."

"What are you going to do, fight them by yourself?" the boatswain asked. "I'll stay here and help you. We may not last long, but at least we'll go down fighting!"

The stranger laughed at the young crewman. "You got guts, kid. I think we got off to a bad start. What's your name?"

"Cushman, George Cushman."

"Cushman?" the mysterious passenger declared, his eyes widening. "Don't tell me you're from Virginia?"

"Yeah. How did you know?" George looked deep into the eyes of the stranger.

"If you got two brothers named Ben and James, I'm gonna have a heart attack right here and now," the astonished stranger replied between the musket balls striking the wooden deck.

George's face instantly revealed the stranger's inquiry as correct. "Just who in the hell are you, and how do you know my brothers?"

"Yeah, I'm not an ambassador. That was necessary, to uphold my cover. Name's Jacob Hall, Major Jacob Hall."

"Jesus Christ, you're Jacob Hall, *the* Jacob Hall, from Fort Duquesne? My brothers have told me that story a million times. No way, you're Jacob Hall?"

Hall nodded as the musket fire continued.

"Where…how…what…?" Cushman stumbled with his words, trying to absorb the stunning revelation. The two men continued to lie flat as the unrelenting musket fire from the Royal Marines sprayed the deck of the colonial merchant ship.

"Formerly, New York militia. Now I'm on an important mission for the Continental Congress. The only reason I'm telling you this is our current lousy circumstances and I may need your help." Hall smiled, allowing himself a second to remember his adventures with the Cushman brothers and George Washington during the harrowing final days of the British assault on Fort Duquesne during the French and Indian War.

"Go on. A few of us had bets as to your real mission," George replied.

The major smiled. He was impressed with Cushman's cool under fire. *Just like his brothers and his father*. Hall decided then and there to reveal his mission. Two minutes later, George Cushman's reaction was predictable.

"How much gold did you say?"

"Let's just say it takes four people to carry one trunk, and there are four trunks," proclaimed the major.

Cushman unleashed a low whistle, trying to imagine so much wealth.

"Do you think you can do it, kid?" the major asked bluntly.

"Yes, I'll do it. Are you sure it's the only way?"

"You got a better idea? I'm willing to listen."

Cushman put his hand through his thick blond hair and shrugged his shoulders.

"Didn't think so. Don't look now, kid, but we are about to be boarded!" exclaimed Major Hall.

THE SIGNERS

Sure enough, the helmsman of the British warship had pulled the larger frigate to within ten yards of their vessel. Royal Marines had already slung several grappling hooks onto the *Treasure's* deck. The hooks dug into the bulwark and gunwale; the Marines pulled the two ships together. Suddenly, the Marines stopped firing.

"What now?" Cushman questioned his newfound friend.

"Stay down. Don't let them see you. You go when I start my act, got it?"

"Yes, sir. And, Major? Please do me a favor."

"What's that, Cushman?"

"Take care of yourself. I don't want to do this alone. Besides, I'd like to hear your side of the story. My brothers tend to brag a little too much."

"I'll do my best, son. Now get ready. They've started to board."

The British Marines placed a portable boarding bridge built for just such purposes over the bulwarks of the two attached ships. Twenty-five Marines stormed the deck and took up ready positions. There was no greeting party, as everyone on the deck was either badly wounded or dead. Major Jacob Hall and George Cushman continued to lie behind a gun carriage opposite the boarding party. Hall slowly worked his way on his belly to another gun carriage, escaping the notice of the Marines. He waited until he saw the first officer appear.

Hall tied a piece of sail to the end of a three-foot splinter of wood and began to wave it back and forth. "Surrender, I surrender!" he called out, remaining behind the gun carriage.

Musket shots rang out as one ball tore the white sail from the stick. Major Hall was happy of his decision to remain in hiding.

"Halt fire!" a stern voice ordered. "You have five seconds to show yourself, or I will order my men to resume firing."

Hall gave Cushman a ready sign and stood to face the British officer. "My name is Marcus Anderson. I am an emissary on my way to the court of King Louis of France. How dare you fire on a merchant ship!" Hall declared, slowly removing a document proving his statement, complete with his false name.

"Emissary? Emissary for whom?" the captain of the British warship wondered out loud.

"For the state of New York."

"Never heard of such a country. I have heard of a British colony named New York. But they have no power to send ambassadors to foreign countries."

"I am duly empowered by the Second Continental Congress," he stated proudly.

"Oh, you mean the traitorous rebels meeting in Philadelphia against the order of the king? That Congress? Well, if indeed you are their representative, you, too, must be a traitor. Do you know the penalty for treason, Mr. Anderson?" The British captain was obviously enjoying himself.

"This was a defenseless merchant ship. It is against British law to fire upon a civilian vessel." Hall was trying to stay on the offensive. He placed a hand behind his back and motioned for Cushman to move.

"You didn't answer my question, Mr. Anderson. Do you know the punishment for treason?"

"I am no traitor, Captain, but you, sir, are a murderer. Look at the deck of this ship. You ordered this slaughter!"

Ten feet away from Major Hall, George Cushman had finished tying the rope to the heavy gun carriage. He managed to slip through a hole in the bulwark and began to lower himself down the side of the ship. Slipping quietly into the water, he began to swim to the bow of the *Treasure*.

"Come, Mr. Anderson, follow me belowdecks and we will examine the remains of the crew and search for any incriminating evidence. In the meantime, my men will prepare a hangman's noose. Maybe now you can guess the answer to my question."

The British captain was accompanied by his second-in-command and four Marines as they made their way below the main deck. The menacing Marines made sure there would be no ambush.

It looked like a hospital ward; the ship's doctor and Captain Gray were tending to injured sailors, as they were the only two men who were unscathed.

Major Hall counted thirteen men still alive, including the captain and the doctor. The British captain demanded his counterpart to step forward.

"I am Captain Gray. How dare you attack a merchant vessel without provocation!" Gray demanded.

"Spare me the indignation, Captain Gray. We both know you're a lying smuggler. Now, why don't you spare us the time and effort and show us where you hid the treasure?"

Captain Gray and Major Hall both looked shocked by the word *treasure*. Major Hall thought to himself, *How did this lunatic know about the gold? Only six men knew about it*. Gray only knew they were transporting something valuable; he didn't know the contents of the four trunks.

"I have heard that smugglers build elaborate-looking false walls." The British captain walked directly to the back of the storage area and knocked on the wall. "Sounds hollow. Let's say we have a look, eh, Mr. Prescott?" He nodded toward his second-in-command.

Without another word, one of the Marines came forward with a sledgehammer and began to assault the wall. The thin structure gave way immediately, revealing four large storage trunks.

"Oh my goodness, it seems someone was trying to hide something from proper authorities. Lieutenant Prescott, you know what to do."

"Yes, sir. You, you, you, and you, come with me," he ordered four of the least-injured Merchant Marines into the hidden room. They were ordered to carry the trunks topside and then across the bridge onto the British ship. No one else was allowed to carry the trunks. It took the sailors four trips.

When they were finished, the men were returned belowdecks with everyone else. "Captain, this is piracy, firing on a merchant ship, stealing her cargo. You will certainly be brought up on charges," Major Hall stated firmly.

"Perhaps, Mr. Anderson, but you will never see that happen. My men are about to witness a traitor hanged from the highest yardarm." The British officer grinned.

Just then, a junior officer came below and whispered something into the captain's ear. The captain's eyes turned angry, and then suddenly he let out an evil cackle. "Irony of all ironies, it turns out there are no yardarms left on this ship of traitors. Seems our gun crews were more than accurate. Very well, then, I have an even better plan. Lieutenant Prescott, take the captain and place him under arrest."

"This is an outrage! You can't do that. We are a legally licensed ship—"

Gray was interrupted midsentence by a vicious backhand from the British captain. "Shut up, Captain! Get him out of here, Prescott."

Captain Jonas Gray was dragged topside as the British captain focused on the remaining crewmen. "As for the rest of you, we will be on our way. If you work hard, you may be able to fix one of your masts and make sail home to your backward country. If not, I am sure another ship will come to your aid. We will leave you with all your provisions."

"Very generous of you." The sarcastic snarl came from Major Hall.

"Mr. Anderson, if that is even your real name, I look forward to seeing you again."

"That makes two of us, only next time the circumstances will be reversed," he sneered, glaring at the British captain.

"Perhaps, perhaps, but I doubt it." He waved the Marines topside.

Once on the deck, the Marines barricaded the only entrance or exit from the storage room belowdecks. Returning to their ship, they began to disengage from the merchant vessel as the captain called out orders to set sail.

"Lieutenant Prescott, you know what to do."

"Yes, sir. Be right back."

"British sailors, Royal Marines, gather around," the captain ordered from his perch on the highest deck on the ship. The men gathered on the quarterdeck and the main deck below. The crew of over two hundred men stood with pride. "Gentlemen, I have never been prouder of you than today. You handled your duties with skill and bravery. Lieutenant Prescott, are you ready?"

"Yes, sir!" a call came from below.

"Very well. As you may have witnessed, we removed four trunks from the enemy ship. I told you they contained gifts from the rebel Congress to the French king. Behold!"

Lieutenant Addison Prescott emerged, holding the remains of several British officers' coats. Bullet holes riddled the bloodstained clothing. He waved them high above his head, causing the crew to cheer for their fallen comrades.

"What else was in the trunks, Lieutenant?" asked the captain.

"British muskets, swords, knives, even some British cannonballs were found in each trunk, making them very heavy to carry." The first lieutenant laughed. Most of the men had witnessed the American sailors struggling with the weight of the trunks. "Bloodstained uniforms of our brave Army were found in each chest with a note to the French king."

"Bring me the note," commanded the captain.

Prescott quickly obeyed.

"'Gracious King Louis,'" the captain began, attempting to imitate a bureaucrat, "'please accept this tribute from the Massachusetts militia. We hope these British war souvenirs will prove to you our commitment to defeat the British and create a new country. We hope you will assist our efforts.' It is signed by members of the rebel Congress."

A cry came up from the crew that rivaled the noise of a cannon shot. The captain leaned over to Prescott and said quietly, "Have the carronade crews stand ready."

"But why, sir?" a stunned Prescott replied, unwilling to believe what was to come.

"There can be no witnesses," he replied angrily. "Don't be a poltroon, Addison."

Prescott bristled at being called a coward. "But, sir, we have the gold. We can't just sink a defenseless ship."

"Very well. Pretend she's firing on us. Do whatever you have to do to ease your conscience. Just remember, you and I will be richer than most kings, as long as we don't panic. Now, order the guns to the ready." The captain glared at his second-in-command.

"Yes, sir," Prescott replied meekly.

The captain continued to address his crew. "Earlier today, one of you suggested getting tough with these colonials and sending one of their ships to the bottom of the sea."

The sailors roared their approval in anxious anticipation.

The captain raised his hands for the crew to settle down. "Gentlemen, today we do just that. What is left of their crew is nothing but traitorous officers from Boston. Shall we leave them to drift, or shall we exact our revenge?"

"Revenge! Revenge!" the crew screamed at the top of their lungs.

"Very well, revenge it will be!" yelled the captain at the top of his lungs. "Carronade gun crews, ready the special *spike shot*."

A spike shot cannonball was like a round shot, only with spikes at each end. They were designed to stick into an enemy's hull. The special spike ball was wrapped in pine tar and burlap sacking. When fired, the ball would ignite into flames and was particularly effective at short range. Sailors faced many dangers navigating the open seas, but none as frightening as fire.

Major Jacob Hall took stock of his situation. The British captain had obviously known about the gold. He cursed himself for not demanding even more secrecy, but the banker Morris had insisted it would be impossible to pull off without the cooperation of the bank president and his assistant. Hall cursed himself again for wasting time rethinking the security for the mission. It had been blown, and now he had to deal with his current circumstance. He recognized the British captain. No, he had never met him personally. He recognized the eyes, selfish and uncaring, evil eyes. He had seen similar eyes while fighting in the French and Indian War, especially the Indian known as *Yellow Snake*, who delighted in the suffering of others. Clearly, his goal had been to steal the gold and nothing else. No attempt to see if the American ship was smuggling taxable goods, only a good old-fashioned robbery, perpetrated by a captain of the Royal Navy. The realization hit Hall hard. The captain was not going to risk discovery, which could mean only one thing. He had precious little time to figure a way off the ship. Hall started for the stairs topside.

"It's no use. They must have placed one of the cannons on top of the hatch. They weigh over a ton." It was the ship's doctor, sitting on the stairs. "We already tried," he added, pointing to two wounded men. "This is all about your secret cargo, isn't it?" the doctor said accusingly.

"I'm afraid so," replied Hall.

"Then we have you to thank for all this?"

"Guilty as charged," responded Hall, sensing the tension of the surviving men.

"So we wouldn't have been attacked if it weren't for you," responded yet another injured sailor.

"Look, gentlemen, stoning me to death isn't going to solve our current problem. That captain isn't going to take the chance of us being rescued. We need to find a way to abandon ship."

"What do you mean? He's going to sink a defenseless ship? No British captain would ever do that," responded a different sailor.

"This is no ordinary cap—"

The sickening sound of cannon shot erupted from nearby, quickly followed by another. Within a second, the ship rocked with a double impact of the dreaded round shot.

"They bounced off!" yelled an incredulous sailor.

"No," Hall responded quietly. "Spike shot. They're embedded in the hull. He's going to burn us alive."

Veteran sailors shouted their agreement as panic set in. Two more violent impacts into the hull of the *Treasure*, followed by the terrifying smell of burning tar and wood, confirmed the intent of the British captain. The greatest fear of sailors from ancient times to the present was to be trapped within the bowels of a sinking ship. Being on deck at least gave hope of swimming to safety or locating buoyant debris.

Hall knew, if they were to survive, they had to act fast. Quickly scanning the large storage area, he found what he was looking for as the cabin began to fill with deadly smoke and flames.

"Do you need help, sir?" It was the ship's doctor.

"Yes," Hall answered. "Stack three sacks of grain on top of this barrel." He pointed to a large barrel of rum opposite the now-flaming hull. "It's got to be high enough, above the waterline, if it is going to work!" Hall shouted.

Finding an ax, Hall walked quickly to the well-marked storage locker, and in one swift stroke, he removed the lock.

"What are you going to do, kill us sooner?" asked the doctor as Hall removed two powder cartridges used to fire the ship's carronades.

Hall smiled and placed the two cartridges atop the sacks of grain. "No, just going to punch a hole above the waterline so we can get the hell out of here," he replied. The port hull of the ship was now in full flame as water began to enter the weakened hull. Major Hall calmly wrapped a rag around a cannon rammer, holding the rammer into the burning hull, which quickly ignited. "Get behind something sturdy!" he yelled and, without delay, laid the burning rag on top of the powder cartridges.

Hall dived to safety as the powder exploded into a fiery blast. The explosion rocked the weakened ship. Hall had underestimated the power of the blast; water began to flow rapidly through the punctured hull.

"Hurry, we don't have much time!" he yelled. Hall and the doctor literally threw men into the waiting sea.

"He's the last," called out the doctor as the ship slowly slid below the waterline. Major Jacob Hall took a deep breath and plunged into the cool, salty waters off the coast of New Jersey.

Cheers erupted from the British warship as the merchant ship *Treasure*, on fire and listing badly, struggled to stay afloat. First Lieutenant Addison Prescott looked on in horror as the ship gradually disappeared into the foaming waters. The burning spiked cannonballs had delivered as promised, lodging into the hull and setting her ablaze. *Must have caught the powder locker on fire,* he thought to himself. *That would account for the explosion.* Prescott hadn't signed on for murder and theft. He cursed himself for falling under the captain's convincing influence. He was in too deep and could see no way out but to go along and not panic. Prescott continued to stare at the sinking ship, now over a half-mile away, completely engulfed by flame, and thought of the men entombed belowdecks and the terrible death they would endure.

"Lieutenant." Prescott's contemplations were interrupted by one of the first mates. "Look," he said, pointing off the ship's stern. "One of the jolly boats has broken loose."

The two men ran aft. Sure enough, only one of the jolly boats remained trailing the British frigate, while the other was floating close to the burning American vessel. Prescott quickly pulled out his telescope to look at the jolly boat. He thought he saw movement inside the small boat but quickly dismissed it to the distance and the gathering smoke from the burning ship.

"Where's the captain?" he asked the first mate.

"He's already celebrating with the other officers in his cabin," he replied. "The whole ship has been given permission to break out the rum."

Prescott thought of turning the ship around to retrieve the jolly boat.

"What should we do, sir?"

"Let her go," he replied. "We'll get another next time we are in port." *What the hell,* he thought to himself. *We can certainly afford it now.* "Let's go join the others." Prescott shrugged, looking forward to a drunken celebration.

Captain Jonas Gray looked at his British counterpart with a hurt look on his face. "You didn't have to hit me so hard," he stated while rubbing his face.

"You must admit that no one will suspect we are in this together," replied the British captain, removing his topcoat.

Gray forced a smile. "I guess I can take a hit for all that gold. But there will be no survivors, so it really wasn't necessary." It was obvious that Gray's feelings were hurt more than his face.

"Relax, Gray. You are now officially richer than God."

Captain Jonas Gray had never committed a crime in his life, but his take of one-half of the gold was just too much to turn down. Still a religious man, he was somewhat taken aback by the words. "Rich as God…I wonder what he would think of all this."

"Why don't you go ask him?" the British captain replied as he raised his pistol and fired, ending the life of Captain Jonas Gray.

Chapter 2

All war is deception.

—Sun Tzu

May 29, 1776
Delaware Bay

The sun was creeping slowly above the dark-blue water, creating a spectrum of bright colors that could only be truly enjoyed at sea. Cool morning air left thin layers of moisture covering the entire exterior of the majestic wooden vessel. Captain George Medford smiled as he gazed at the beautiful orange ball from the quarterdeck of the British war frigate HMS *Richmond*. The 127-foot *Richmond* cut smoothly through the slight chop of the Delaware Bay, heading east out into the Atlantic Ocean. As Medford skillfully guided the nineteen-year-old warship, he reflected upon his current run of good fortune.

His assignment in the colonies had been a godsend, reversing years of bad luck and probably saving his life. Eleven months ago, he was on the verge of bankruptcy and ruin; now he was on the precipice of fame and fortune. It indeed had been a tumultuous few years. Thank God for the dim-witted, pathetic rabble occupying the British colonies of North America. Without their impertinence, he would surely be in jail or dead.

Luck sure was a lady—sometimes good, sometimes bad, but always exciting. Captain Medford thought back to the beginning of his whirlwind of a year.

Medford had lost his commission in the Royal Navy when he ran the *Richmond* aground, in Kinsale harbor, in southern Ireland. It was not the first time he had exhibited poor seamanship. His ensuing erratic behaviors slowly bled his family's small fortune. Between the heavy drinking, a steady stable of prostitutes, and gambling losses, Medford found himself borrowing money from the most dangerous elements of the London underworld. As his debt grew, he feared the moneylenders more than debtors' prison.

Lady luck intervened in the nick of time when Prime Minister North, irritated by continued colonial insolence, sent fifteen British warships to patrol the major American ports and finally put a stop to colonial smuggling. HMS *Richmond*, recently repaired, needed a commander, and due to a shortage of officers, Medford was reinstated to his command. He left England promising to repay the moneylenders, the threat of death hanging over his head, if he returned without payment.

A fifth-rate frigate with thirty-two heavy guns and a crew of 220 sailors, the *Richmond* and the HMS *Jason* were ordered to patrol the coastline off New Jersey. HMS *Richmond* was to specifically target the Delaware Bay region, which led into the Delaware River and the port of Philadelphia. It was part of a British Navy that was woefully unprepared for such an imposing task.

King George III and Parliament had let the British Navy fall off greatly after the French and Indian War. The American coastline was too long, with too many harbors, bays, and inlets. With too few ships to patrol the vast coastline, Admiral Howe had ordered the ships to concentrate on the main ports of Boston, New York, Philadelphia, Baltimore, and Charleston. Captain Medford proved to be quite successful in chasing down the elusive smugglers. He was particularly proud of capturing fifteen of the famous John Hancock's ships; the most recent *capture* had proved *very* profitable. However, Medford knew that for every ship caught smuggling, twenty evaded the blockade. If it were up to him, he would blow every ship out of the water not flying the Union Jack. Soon after Lexington and Concord, the British blockade became more forceful. But after the Virginia planter, Washington, and the peasant army had surrounded General Howe and forced him to evacuate Boston, the patrol ships were given even greater latitude in dealing with colonial ships. While Medford began treating all colonial merchant ships as the enemy, his superiors preferred to look the other way at some of his more aggressive tactics. His encounter with John Hancock's newest ship, the *Treasure*, had gone unreported, the gold stored safely belowdecks. Since then, his last three encounters with smugglers, Medford had forced all the crew into small skiffs and set the ships ablaze, to the enjoyment of his crew. As the *Richmond* sailed away from the burning ships, he had his five-man gun teams practice by targeting the crew's small boats. The captain and the crew cheered loudly whenever they scored a hit. Of course, the British sea captain conveniently left out these encounters when sending his reports to his superiors.

But it was the port of Philadelphia that had given Medford his next great opportunity, and it was that opportunity that caused him to smile. Having resupplied in Philadelphia, the ship was now moving out of the Delaware Bay, where it would prowl up and down the Jersey coast for the next two weeks. Off the port bow, Medford gazed out at Cape May, the northern edge of the bay and the southernmost part of New Jersey. Cape May was fast becoming a summer retreat for affluent Philadelphians; many a fine summer home could be seen from Captain Medford's vantage point. When the colonial rebellion was crushed, perhaps he would build a home at Cape May. He certainly could afford it, especially if he didn't return to England. His smile grew even larger.

The deal had been finalized three days ago. It happened while they were docked in port, taking on supplies and acquiring a new jolly boat. Medford had met with the Irishman at a seedy tavern near the docks. They had been conducting business since before the Breed's Hill disaster, and it had already proved to be a lucrative relationship. The Irishman gave him two hundred pounds every time he made port in Philadelphia, which was once a month. In return, any ship flying the Irishman's specially designed flag was allowed to pass by without inspection. As a bonus, the Irishman would offer valuable information about competing ships' schedules and routes, allowing Medford to be the most successful of all the blockade ships. The Irishman's tentacles ran deep into Philadelphia's elite, and it was his information that had led Medford to the secret gold carried by Hancock's merchant ship aptly name the *Treasure*.

His success in chasing down so many smugglers came to the attention of admiral Sir Richard Howe, who had approached Medford with a delicate mission.

Admiral Howe and his brother, General William Howe, had ordered Medford to meet one of their agents to discuss the coming invasion of New York. The meeting proved to be very fruitful. The agent was given fifteen thousand pounds to gather information in and around Philadelphia, the next major target after the British secured New York City. The money was to be used for gathering information, securing Tory support for operations behind enemy lines, and one major operation that might help shorten the war. It was the third option that enticed Medford to seek the aid of his Philadelphia benefactor.

The English sea captain and the crazy Irishman agreed upon the ambitious and deadly plan. After an exchange of money, expensive cognac was poured, followed quickly by scantily clad prostitutes that would rival anything Paris had to offer. Between the seductive silk and lace negligees, the sweet scent of expensive perfume, and sensual body language, Medford easily fell back into his old habits. The girls the Irishman provided at his own expense were vastly superior to the London prostitutes he was used to. *If everything goes as intended, this skirmish with the colonies could end within a couple of months and I can settle here in luxury,* Medford thought to himself.

"Good morning, Captain." The greeting startled Medford.

Looking up, the captain saw First Lieutenant Addison Prescott.

"A fine morning, Lieutenant Prescott. Can you believe we pulled it off?"

"You were magnificent, sir, a grand plan. But aren't you worried that the colonel might find out about the payment?"

"How would he find out? I doubt if he travels in the same circles as our friend in Philadelphia." Prescott was becoming particularly irksome, ever since they had deceived the entire crew and secured the gold from the *Treasure*. Medford was keenly aware of his disapproving eyes when he had given the order to sink the ship with all aboard. The murder of Captain Gray hadn't helped.

THE SIGNERS

"I wouldn't know, sir. Haven't we made enough money with the bribes and the..." He hesitated and looked around, softly whispering, "Gold? We have made over two thousand pounds just from the Irishman alone. It seems too risky to deceive the colonel. If we get caught, it will mean a hanging," Prescott replied warily. Medford glanced around the ship. Most of the sailors were in crew's quarters, readying for the day, or in the galley, finishing off their breakfast. The captain motioned for the helmsman to take over the ship's wheel. He noticed only a few sailors were working the ropes along the foremast of the HMS *Richmond*.

Perhaps this is the opportunity I've been waiting for, Medford thought to himself as he led Prescott aft toward the poop deck. Prescott's incessant whining was becoming increasingly shrill, not a welcome attitude for a partner who shared such a deep secret.

"Prescott, the money the colonel provided for our mission is a secret. He doesn't want a farthing traced back to him. Once the mission is complete, the Howe brothers will reward him, and they will all be the toast of England, subduing the rebels with minimum cost to the king. I hardly think he will demand an accounting for every pound. Besides, you and I are the only ones to know of the plot, and I will never talk of this to anyone." Medford's tone clearly implied that Lieutenant Prescott had better follow suit.

"What about the Irishman? He could be a problem."

"He may be a good Tory, but he has a greater love for money. Don't worry about him, Lieutenant. He will be taken care of, one way or another. Besides, his share of the gold has made him very satisfied," the captain stated while his mind continued to formulate a plan.

"But the colonel, he is not one to forgive." The lieutenant's whining had pushed Medford toward a final solution.

"Don't worry, Lieutenant Prescott, we will deny everything if something goes wrong. I am quite sure the results will be satisfactory to the colonel and the Howe brothers. No one will find out the British command was involved." Medford asserted this with complete confidence.

"When will the action take place, sir?"

"Soon, my friend, very soon." Medford had made up his mind; the time was right. One more furtive glance around the vacant decks below encouraged his decision to act.

Medford led Prescott to the port rail. "Can you see the beautiful homes?" Medford pointed to several large summer homes on Cape May while slowly reaching into his side pocket. "You and I have enough money to build five homes each, as long as we keep our composure. Between your share of the bribes, the gold, and the colonel's payment, you have become very rich."

Prescott's mind was indeed troubled. He had always dreamed of captaining his own ship. He had never dreamed of obtaining riches, especially ill-gotten wealth. But he had to admit, the deeper Medford had drawn him into his corrupt world, the more he had rationalized his participation. The wealth and power it would bring was an intoxicating siren, calling him closer and closer. But at night, he would read his Bible and the guilt would immediately return. It was no wonder his behavior of late was unpredictable at best.

Medford continued his sales job. "Look closer. There are splendid locations to build a vacation home…"

Lieutenant Prescott unwisely leaned out over the rail to get a closer look; his eyes caught a glimpse of movement, but it was too late. The heavy wooden club came crashing down on the back of his skull, and in that brief instant, he realized that Captain Medford had betrayed him. Darkness washed over him as the intense pain gave way to the illusion of flying. Crashing into the cold blue water below, the body of Lieutenant Addison Prescott began to sink slowly into the waters off the coast of Southern New Jersey.

Captain George Medford tossed his heavy club into the sea and called softly to the disappearing body. "Did you really think I was going to share with you or Gray? Not very smart, Lieutenant, not very smart."

Medford admired his handiwork for a few more moments, noting the helmsman had not heard the splash. He continued to look about, making sure no one had noticed his actions. Medford waited a few more moments, then yelled, "Turn this ship around! Man overboard! All hands on deck! Man overboard!"

Chapter 3

Bella, horrida bella. (Wars, horrid wars.)
—Virgil

May 30, 1776
Halifax, Nova Scotia

The solitary figure paced along the deserted wharf with a worried look. Unseasonably warm weather welcomed him to Halifax, yet he still dressed in full uniform, including the wool waistcoat and matching officer's coat. His dress was prim and proper. He could have been returning from posing for a portrait. He was tall and lean but was just beginning to develop a rich man's paunch. Age lines were starting to appear in the still-handsome face. Curly short dark hair was ceding ground to gray at the temples. His dark-brown eyes darted wearily around the dock. He had recently celebrated his forty-seventh birthday, but a celebration had not been in order. Although journalists in London continued to praise him for his courage and leadership for the victory at Bunker Hill, he knew they were wrong on two counts. Number one, it was Breed's Hill, not Bunker Hill, where the main battle had taken place, and number two, if Breed's Hill was a victory for the British, he would prefer a *loss* similar to that of the Boston Patriots.

The British had lost over one thousand men during the three attempts to storm the Patriot stronghold atop Breed's Hill. If it weren't for the British soldiers' bravery, combined with the Boston defenders running out of ammunition, Breed's Hill would have been a total disaster. General William Howe had personally led the last charge up the hill despite protestations from his junior officers. The British infantry stormed the hill with great resolve, inspired by Howe's disregard for his own safety, and angry beyond belief that the rabble had taken such a heavy toll on their brethren. To Howe's disbelief, his men butchered surrendering minutemen with their bayonets before he could stop the massacre. Fearing his soldiers' fragile state of mind after seeing so many of their compatriots dead on the ground, Howe issued a mild reprimand to his soldiers and reminded them of the rules of engagement and surrender. No one would be court-martialed or punished that day. They had suffered enough. He came away from the battle with a healthy respect for the Boston minutemen. They might be a bunch of farmers and shopkeepers, but they could all shoot a rifle with great accuracy, and they showed creativity in their tactics. The next time General Howe faced the Patriots, he would not underestimate their proficiency with firearms.

The general's reverie was interrupted by the rhythmic pattern of feet striking the wooden dock. Howe glanced up to see the familiar face strolling toward him. William Howe's worried look was replaced by a smile as he greeted his older brother. "Richard, you're late. I was beginning to worry."

"I apologize, Willie. Organizing this many ships"—Richard Howe waved his arm at the hundreds of ships docked and anchored in Halifax Harbor—"is a chore I do not wish upon my most hated enemy."

Admiral Richard Howe was three years older than his brother. Their eldest brother, George, was also a military man, a brigadier general during the French and Indian War. The great British general James Wolf had called George Howe the *best officer in the whole British Army*. George Howe died at the Battle of Ticonderoga, where his unit killed and captured over four hundred French soldiers with minimal casualties of their own. Unfortunately, one of the few casualties was their esteemed brother George, who died in the arms of his friend Major Israel Putnam. Latest word from New York Tories was that the farmer Washington had named as his third-in-command the same Israel Putnam. The Howe brothers had great reservations about the coming war and hoped for a peaceful settlement before hostilities became truly horrific. Friends like Israel Putnam would soon be enemies.

There was no doubting that Richard was indeed brother to William. Although they were not twins, there was no mistaking they were siblings. Tall and handsome, with the same broad nose, Richard wore his hair slightly longer and, although older, did not show any signs of graying. Like his brother, he was dressed in full military uniform. The popular tricorne hat was worn slightly off center, and his sword hung loosely from his waist. Both men looked of royal bearing and actually were distant cousins to King George III, the present king of England.

"Come," Richard said, waving him over, "let's go aboard the *Eagle*. We will have comfort and privacy in my quarters."

The Howe brothers walked past two Marines and up the gangplank of the HMS *Eagle*. The imposing guards saluted their superior officers as they boarded the flagship of the British armada, preparing for the invasion of New York City. HMS *Eagle*, launched two years prior, was the pride of the new Intrepid-class British warships. A third-rate ship of the line, it weighed over 1,300 tons, with a length of 160 feet, and a forty-four-foot beam; the *Eagle* carried sixty-four cannons on her two gun decks, making her one of the most feared weapons of war. The men walked onto the quarterdeck and entered the admiral's quarters. A large stateroom was divided into a comfortable meeting area and the captain's bedroom. An oval oak table sat in the center of the room surrounded by six high-backed chairs.

"I received our orders from the king this morning. I thought it better we go over the details in private. We must close ranks on this. I don't want any dissension among the other officers," Richard informed his younger brother.

"Has he agreed to our plan to cut the colonies in half?"

"Yes. We are to proceed, beginning with New York, but Lord North has overruled your New York plan. He demands we use a two-prong attack. I am afraid you must split your Army in half and proceed from Canada also."

"Damn meddling politicians!" William Howe pounded his fist onto the table. "Richard, you know splitting our ground forces is foolish. The terrain in Upstate New York can be treacherous. Going north from New York up the Hudson is the smart strategy. Your ships can supply us deep into the interior and protect our rear guard. Once we control the middle of New York, we can cut any aid to New England and take our time getting to Canada."

"Willie, you know the Americans have already tried to take Quebec. Lord North insists that Johnny Burgoyne rescue Quebec to secure our northern flank. Controlling the Hudson is the key to victory."

"I agree, but splitting our forces is a bad idea. We can control the Hudson from New York City."

"Brother, I'm afraid the decision has been made for us. Now we must proceed with the two-pronged plan. I have a map on the table. Show me how you will cut the colonies in two."

The brothers pored over the map for close to three hours.

William Howe reviewed what British generals had been discussing for years. Divide the North by controlling the Hudson River, slowly squeezing the New England colonies from the land and the sea. The Southern colonies, made up mostly of Loyalist, would surely support the British efforts. "Gentleman John and I both think this can be done in six months to one year," the general summarized.

"Be careful to modify any of Burgoyne's predictions. He tends to be overly optimistic. If he finds any pretty women in Quebec, he may be several months late getting started." The admiral chuckled, referring to the *ladies' man* reputation of Gentleman Johnny Burgoyne.

Richard Howe reiterated to his brother the poor state of the British Royal Navy and predicted either a quick victory or a protracted war involving the French or the Spanish. In addition, Howe worried about the American merchant fleet, consisting of thousands of ships. They would undoubtedly be granted letters of marquis and reprisal from the outlaw Congress. The private ships could become very bothersome to a British Navy already stretched thin. The younger Howe was somewhat taken aback. He knew the Navy had been neglected, but not to the extent his brother just warned about. "Are you confident of our success around New York?"

"Yes. Once we have secured the harbor, we will have more than enough cannon and plenty of ships to transport troops. It is a perfect situation. We will be able to move your troops from island to island or up the Hudson at will. Washington will have no such luxury. If he holds New York, he would surely be titled Saint George I."

"I agree. Taking New York shouldn't be difficult."

The brothers continued to debate the route of the second prong to come from Canada and eventually settled on two forces coming from the North. A *three*-pronged attack would meet in the city of Albany. From there the British would begin to squeeze the life out of the rebellion.

"Albany, indeed, is the key to victory. The plan is brilliant." The admiral praised his younger brother.

General Howe smiled and accepted the compliment. He had great respect for his brother's opinion. Even into adulthood, the younger brother enjoyed the approval of his older sibling.

"Well, then, before we bring in the rest of the staff, let's go over New York City again," the admiral remarked, knowing full well his expertise would be crucial.

The general nodded. "As you know, the defense of New York will be impossible without a Navy. New York harbor, the Hudson River, and the East River are all wide enough and deep enough for your ships to move freely. We have many Tory spies sending us constant information on the planter Washington's movements in and around the city. We know he is building fortifications on Long Island, near Brooklyn, and on the southern tip of Manhattan. We may just outflank him with your ships and end this war quickly. If we defeat Washington's Army, the whole resistance could crumble quickly."

"Washington is foolish to try and hold an island without a Navy. We should look at several strategies," the admiral suggested.

"I agree wholeheartedly. I will have the staff draw up several different plans. Charles Cornwallis is an excellent strategist. I will put him in charge. Did Lord North give a time frame?"

"Yes, but we have some flexibility. You will arrive in early July. I will follow with the rest of the fleet a week or two later. Willie, do you realize that, despite our neglect of the Navy, when all the ships arrive from England, we will launch a fleet against the colonies larger than the Great Armada?" Howe smiled, basking in the accomplishment of building a larger fleet than the Spanish invasion of England in 1588. "That many ships may cause them to surrender!" The general laughed.

"One can only hope, brother." The admiral hesitated, his face changing instantly from confidence to worry. "We have one more delicate matter to discuss. I received a second letter today. Captain Medford has put into motion *Operation Chaos*. The timetable is soon. This could alter our plans significantly. We should prepare for a successful operation."

"Do you trust Medford?"

"Of course not. He would sell his mother to the devil himself. But he is not so foolish as to betray this opportunity," replied the admiral.

"Then what are you worried about? He seemed competent, sinister perhaps, but competent. The plan has many tentacles, yes?"

"Yes, it does, but this type of thing is below us. We shouldn't have to sink to such depths," Richard Howe pointed out to his brother.

The general replied firmly, "We didn't start this war. They did. If we can save many lives by taking only a few, then it is the right thing to do. *Bella, horrida bella*. Besides, we are well insulated. Even if it fails, it can never be traced back to us. Colonel Parker is the perfect commander for this mission. He is ruthlessly efficient, and his motivation is personal, a fine combination."

"I prefer a direct broadside. These kinds of intrigues are more to the level of the French. We should be above this sort of thing," argued the admiral.

The general nodded. Neither man was comfortable with the underbelly of war, but both were practical enough to realize that in war the winners made the rules.

"Any news from Colonel Parker's other operations?"

"Yes. Everything is going well. He has several spies in and around New York, Philadelphia, Boston, Charleston, and Camden. They should provide us with valuable information. It was very wise of you to anticipate their value," countered the admiral.

"Moving the war from Boston to New York was obvious from the beginning. I knew the king's advisers would figure it out eventually. We have many friends in and around New York. They will aid us immensely. Colonel Parker is the perfect spymaster," concluded General Howe.

"A perfect *maniac* would be more appropriate."

"His methods are indeed barbaric, but unfortunately, these are the types of people that win wars."

"I fear Franklin will be a target. Caroline will never forgive us if she finds out we had a hand in this dirty business," Richard said softly, referring to their sister Caroline, a good friend and chess partner with Benjamin Franklin when he was an American diplomat in London.

"*Bella, horrida bella*, brother. War, horrid war."

Chapter 4

The object of life is not to be on the side of the majority, but to escape finding one's self in the ranks of the insane.

—Marcus Aurelius

June 24, 1776
Philadelphia, Pennsylvania

Dusk was beginning to settle over the largest city in the British colonies of North America. The extremely hot day was transitioning into a muggy evening as the noise and smells continued to drift over the tired young man. The clattering sound of the horse's hooves striking the cobblestone street was an indication he was in a large city. The cobblestones, gathered from the Delaware River, were uneven and jagged but infinitely preferable to the dirt and mud of the roads he had traveled. The city, Philadelphia, had been planned by William Penn to be a spacious green country town. Penn had envisioned a large city, more like an English town, with gardens and small parks in between the homes. Unfortunately, lot owners had sold off their green space to make room for more building. Only small portions of Philadelphia remained as Penn originally intended.

Construction had begun in 1682, but regrettably for Penn, the location was one of the lowest and wettest areas along the Delaware River. Although, one of the most populated cities in the colonies, it remained one of the hottest and dampest municipalities in America.

As he passed a local tavern, the distinct aroma of fried venison drifted through the air and reminded the traveler of how hungry he was. The pleasant odor was soon replaced with the toxic stench of stagnant water and worse. He immediately recognized the disgusting odor of a city sink. Dug throughout most large cities in the American colonies, the *sink* captured water draining from street gutters, but regrettably the wide holes captured more than just the runoff. Dead animals, rotten food, human and animal waste found their way into this noxious soup. The smell was incredibly pungent and common for all large cities. The rider reasoned that sinks were probably a major contributor to the spread of diseases throughout urban areas in America and Europe. Epidemics of smallpox, scarlet fever, influenza, and measles were common to every big city, but not so common in the vast countryside. Locals said that Philadelphia suffered a major epidemic about every two years, a reason many of Philadelphia's wealthier residents would leave the city in the summer and head to second homes along the coastline. *Imagine that,* thought the rider, *having enough money to afford two homes.*

Indeed, the colonies were bursting with unbelievable opportunity, even during the existing turbulent environment. The explosion of wealth had obviously caught the attention of King George and his councilors. The resulting Intolerable Acts had brought the colonies to its current situation.

As he rode past Chestnut Street, he slowed and gazed at the imposing clock tower at the peak of the Pennsylvania statehouse. *What a beautiful building, and what monumental decisions are taking place there!* Decisions that had brought the young country to war.

The Second Continental Congress was currently holding meetings there and thus a target for the British Army, rumored to be arriving at any time. Tories and Patriots generally agreed that when General William Howe and his brother admiral Sir Richard Howe returned, New York would be their likely target. One thing was for sure: sooner or later, the British would be targeting Philadelphia and the traitors who made up the Second Continental Congress. Optimism was not exactly running high for the thirteen rebellious states.

Benjamin Cushman was sure the dispute between the British and her colonial states would end shortly. The quarrel festered soon after the French and Indian War but blossomed into armed revolt fourteen months earlier. He knew that farmers and shopkeepers would be no match for the British regulars. Breed's Hill and Bunker Hill were an aberration. No stranger to warfare, he knew the colonists got lucky in Boston. *The British won't be caught by surprise the next time, and if the rumors were true, the next time the British encountered American troops would be soon. Surely, the politicians on both sides will come to their senses before this thing gets out of hand.*

Cushman was returning East after spending the past fifteen months in remote regions of Ohio. His knowledge of recent affairs consisted mostly of rumors. He was hoping to remedy his lack of current events by visiting his best friend. As he guided his horse onto Walnut Street, he grew anxious with anticipation to meet his old friend. It would be a surprise. He couldn't wait to see the look on his face.

The rider had quizzed a kindly older couple, and after a few questions, he had figured out where his childhood friend would most likely be found. Soon, he located his destination and smiled as he came up with an appropriate greeting.

"City Tavern," the simple sign proclaimed and signaled his destination. Considered one of the finer establishments in the city of Philadelphia, this was where upper-class citizens would gather to eat, drink, and discuss the current affairs of the day. The three-story building had been completed just three years prior and still looked brand-new. The elite of Philadelphia had financed the tavern by selling shares to subscribers, most of whom had made their money as trade merchants. City Tavern had two large kitchens, a fifty-foot-long meeting room on the second floor, and accommodating lodging for overnight travelers on the third floor. But it was the first floor that dominated each evening's entertainment, consisting of a spacious dining room, a bar, and a coffee room, in addition to one of the kitchens. As a matter of fact, so much coffee was served that many locals called it the Merchants Coffee House instead of City Tavern. Merchants from all over the colonies conducted all manners of business, from money exchanges to options trading and everything in between.

The Scottish philosopher Adam Smith had just months earlier published a treatise called *An Inquiry into the Nature and Causes of the Wealth of Nations* in which he championed free market capitalism. City Tavern of Philadelphia was a microcosm of the theory. The

American Revolution was more than a war between Great Britain and her wayward colonies. It was a conflict that had at its core the clash of two competing economic philosophies, the centuries-old mercantile system versus Smith's free market capitalism. Places like City Tavern were making the transition rapidly.

Cushman eased his tired horse to a stop and quickly dismounted. The tavern's hitching post was conveniently located near the front entrance.

A well-dressed gentleman greeted him at the door. "Good evening, sir. How may I help you?" the manager asked him in a friendly but slightly arrogant tone. *Must be my appearance after the eight-day ride,* thought Cushman.

"Well, sir, I am afraid I have come to your fine establishment with bad intentions. You see, one of your fine patrons here tonight is anything but a gentleman, and I am here to get satisfaction." Cushman tried to sound angry and refined but wasn't sure he was pulling it off.

"I assure you, sir, all our patrons are men of honor. You must have the wrong establishment," the manager huffed in his most haughty voice. "Now please leave, or I shall have you thrown out."

"I will not leave," Cushman opened his coat, revealing a pistol. "Now, go get the man that has been sleeping with my wife."

The manager began to waver a bit, so Cushman went in for the kill. "Please tell"—Cushman leaned into the man's ear and whispered a name—"that if he doesn't come out here immediately, I will shoot my way into the tavern, beginning with you. Now go!"

The manager, now completely flustered, ran into the back dining room and headed directly toward a large table of men. Cushman followed cautiously, barely able to stifle a laugh.

The manager abruptly interrupted the seven men sitting at the table. "I am so sorry to interrupt, gentlemen, but, Mr. Jefferson, you must come with me immediately. There is a madman outside, threatening to do you harm. We must get you out of here!"

"Now, now, John, calm down. What exactly did he say?"

"I am sorry, sir, but he said you have been sleeping with his wife and that he seeks retribution."

Twelve eyes immediately focused onto the face of Thomas Jefferson, eager to witness his reaction to such disturbing news. The response was one of extreme embarrassment; his face turned as red as his hair. The tension around the table was as thick as a spring fog on the Delaware.

The oldest man at the table grinned and said, "Thomas, my friend, I didn't expect this from you. Does she have a sister?"

Jefferson's mouth opened to protest both the charge and the humor, but nothing came out. He slowly turned his head away from the gathered men and noticed a shabbily dressed newcomer ten feet from their table. The other men suddenly noticed the stranger; one slowly made a move for his pistol, but no one took their eyes off Jefferson. Normally calm, the young Virginian looked irritated. The glaze of anger in his eyes slowly turned to recognition, and then to everyone's surprise, Jefferson broke into a large smile.

"Oh my god, Ben!"

Cushman's feigned angry stare turned into a huge grin as both men walked quickly into a huge embrace. Six men looked on in astonishment at the sudden turn of events.

Again, the oldest man broke the silence. "Thomas, please tell me this isn't the woman you have been whoring around with. She is as ugly as my horse."

Jefferson grabbed his friend tightly by the shoulders and pressed his face closer. "Your mission, did you find the bastard?"

Cushman's smile told him everything he needed to know.

"Perhaps later you'll indulge me the gory details," Jefferson whispered.

"Absolutely, but when we are alone."

Jefferson slowly turned and faced the table of men, the wide grin still on his face. "Gentlemen, I would like to introduce you to my *former* best friend from Albemarle County, Virginia, Benjamin Cushman."

Cushman grabbed his double-folded felt hat and, in a sweeping motion, brought it down into a slight bow. He immediately recognized some of the men and wondered if he had gone too far with his little prank. Recovering from his brief doubt, Cushman looked at the men and grinned. "Gentlemen, it is a pleasure, but may I ask one question? What the hell have you gotten us all into? Starting a war with Great Britain, are you all insane?"

Every one of the men smiled and realized that the studious and serious Thomas Jefferson had a prankster, and a good one at that, for a best friend.

"Ben, if you can keep quiet for a short time, I would like to introduce you to my colleagues." Cushman nodded and concentrated on the eyes of each man as Jefferson began the introductions. "Mr. Roger Sherman of Connecticut." Cushman studied *Mr. Roger Sherman of Connecticut*, a sober-looking man; there was a warmth and intelligence in his dark, unyielding eyes. Cushman thought he looked like a stern schoolmaster who took enjoyment in torturing his students with boring drills and ridiculing their lame attempts at academia. In fact, Sherman had been a cobbler, was a surveyor, and finally, like many of his fellow delegates, had graduated from Yale and become a lawyer.

"Mr. John Adams of Massachusetts." Cushman was immediately struck by Adams's intensity. This was a man who would get his way come hell or high water. Cushman laughed to himself comparing the stout Adams to a large thirty-gallon keg of rum. The stoic-looking New Englander, cousin of the famous Samuel Adams, had one very distinguishing characteristic that Cushman found both interesting and likable: Adams had a certain twinkle in his eyes that hinted at both a sharp tongue and keen sense of humor. He would later find out he was right on both counts.

"Mr. Robert Livingston of New York." Livingston stood to shake Cushman's hand. His jet-black hair was pulled back, revealing a high forehead and smooth, clear skin, unusual for colonial America in that it was free of any pockmarks. He looked to be the youngest of the bunch, and in fact, he was just twenty-nine.

"Mr. Abraham Clark of New Jersey." Clark looked to be about fifty, but what stood out was his unusually square head. *Don't think I've ever seen a square head.* Cushman chuckled to himself. Clark was good-looking, with a pleasant smile. Cushman observed his stocky build, iron handshake, and large forearms. He thought Clark could probably hold his own in a barroom brawl, a common occurrence in Ben Cushman's world.

"Mr. John Hart, also from New Jersey." Hart's shoulder-length brown hair was streaked with aging signs of gray. He seemed jovial and full of life even though he looked older than all, but the most obvious.

"And last but certainly not least, Dr. Benjamin Franklin of Pennsylvania, by way of Massachusetts." As Cushman studied the eyes of the world-famous Benjamin Franklin, he was immediately struck with a wicked thought. *So this is what I'll be like when I get older.* No mistake about it, Franklin had the most mischievous eyes he had seen since looking into a mirror. The seventy-year-old had a childlike grin on his wrinkled face as Cushman shook the venerable Franklin's hand. The old man's grip was surprisingly strong.

Cushman noted the famous high forehead highlighted by the receding hairline. His shoulder-length hair was still more brown than gray, but there was clearly a battle going on for dominance. Large rounded ears protruded from his thinning hair, looking like two half-moons hanging from the side of Franklin's head. His body resembled the shape of a large bell. Franklin's caring and confident demeanor immediately put Cushman at ease. He felt an instantaneous connection to the grizzled statesman.

Cushman's first impression of Jefferson's colleagues was positive. *Leadership would be important if the war continued,* he thought. *Let's hope they can broker a peaceful settlement before the carnage really begins.* It was the seventy-year-old Franklin who began what would be a long, drunken, and interesting night. "No offense, Mr. Cushman, but you smell awful." Franklin smiled, waving his right hand in front of his nose. "Where in the hell have you been, shoveling manure?"

"No offense taken, sir." Cushman smiled. "I am just returning home from Ohio, where I served in the Virginia militia and, most recently, a hunting trip."

"What were you hunting?" Franklin inquired.

"Injuns," Ben responded intensely.

"Ben fought alongside General Washington at Duquesne," Jefferson added, hoping to change the subject. The others nodded their approval. Franklin made a note to dig further regarding the *hunting* trip.

"I made it a point to pass through Philadelphia to see my old friend *Red*." Ben noted his friend's desire to change the subject. Jefferson blushed at the childhood nickname given to him by Ben Cushman. "Imagine my surprise that while I'm away, you gentlemen start a war."

"I assume, then, Mr. Cushman, that you don't find our little revolution to your liking," John Adams proclaimed, his eyes penetrating Cushman for a clue to his answer.

Before he could respond, a young woman appeared with a tray full of City Tavern's finest ale.

"Ms. Deborah, my darling, where have you been? I am dying of thirst," chimed the playful Franklin. "And I'm not talking about the beer." Franklin smiled and raised his eyebrows in a suggestive manner at the very attractive waitress.

"Dr. Franklin, you know I would marry you tomorrow, but my father would kill me. He loathes your politics," teased Deborah, the twenty-two-year-old daughter of one of the stockholders of City Tavern. Her father was a strong Tory and did indeed hate Franklin, his colleagues, and their politics. Although a major shareholder in City Tavern, he was in the minority regarding the Second Continental Congress, as they were frequent and cash-paying customers. Their fame attracted many of Philadelphia's finest, and business had never been better since the Congress convened on May 10 of 1775. Many Philadelphians declared that the future of the colonies would be decided not in the Pennsylvania statehouse but in the bowels of City Tavern.

"Well, my dear, I shall continue to thrust myself upon you until you agree to enter into marital bliss with me, but in the meantime, please bring another pint for our new friend here," the incorrigible Franklin declared with a sly grin.

Deborah Johnson, confident and outgoing, two traits not exactly common in colonial women, looked away from Benjamin Franklin into the eyes of Benjamin Cushman and was startled at the disheveled stranger. It wasn't the dirty old clothes, unkempt hair, or unshaven face that stunned her. His rugged good looks almost took her breath away. She was embarrassed immediately by what must have been the obvious attraction she felt as she gazed into his eyes. The sharpest emerald eyes she had ever seen, the shade of green so clear and bright she had to summon all her will just to turn away.

Cushman eased her embarrassment by smiling and stating cheerfully, "I would love a pint, but no need to hurry. I have a feeling we will be here a while." He then turned to answer John Adams. "Well, sir, I am no Tory and certainly don't understand all the politics involved. However, I do know the British Army. Better still, I know what they are capable of doing. I fought with them in Ohio and Pennsylvania. I served with General Forbes and Colonel Washington at Fort Duquesne. I have seen how cruel and brutal they can be. I just don't think farmers, shopkeepers, and merchants will stand up against a professional Army, an experienced British Army at that, and the Royal Navy is without peer. I fear a slaughter is in order, and I would urge some type of reconciliation."

"I am sure you have heard of David and Goliath." John Hart smiled.

"True, we may be a heavy underdog," declared the serious-looking Roger Sherman, "but that will work greatly to our advantage. We dispatched them from Boston. We will do it again."

"You have no standing army, no military training, no officer corps, and only a handful of men that served with the British during the last war," Cushman countered immediately. "Even if you could raise a respectable army, where are we going to get our munitions? Do we even have one ironworks to cast cannon? It seems to me more than half of the colonists favor the British, not exactly a formula for success."

"Ben, I for one have to agree with you on everything you have said. However, you are missing one key factor," Thomas Jefferson's softly spoken words had everyone's attention. "A flaming heart," he said as he pointed gently to his chest. "A flaming heart lies in every American who loves liberty. That will be the difference. The Sons of Liberty have inspired more than enough of our fellow citizens to fight, and fight not for wealth or lands or religion but to fight for something more precious than life itself, liberty. Sweet liberty will win the day!"

"British artillery versus a flaming heart. I'll take the iron," argued Cushman.

The pretty Ms. Deborah returned with another pint of ale, placing it in front of Cushman. As she leaned over, all eyes noticed her shapely form despite her unflattering clothes. City Tavern was many things, but it was not a brothel, and their few female employees dressed conservatively.

"To be young again," Franklin called out softly. "I think our Ms. Deborah may be smitten with your friend, Thomas." Everyone ignored Franklin's observation, and multiple conversations broke out around the table.

"Mr. Cushman, I certainly share your concerns, and that is why we are spending fourteen hours each day attempting to solve those problems," said Abraham Clark, for the first time. "We do have a large amount of iron ore and a number of ironworks near the Hudson Valley, and several manufacturers in New Jersey and near West Point. In fact, General Washington is preparing a plan to guard these facilities if the British land an army."

"Not *if*, my friend, but *when* the British land an army. King George and Lord North will not let our actions in Boston go unpunished," declared the young-looking Robert Livingston of New York as he pulled away from the table to join a group across the hall in the tavern room.

"Gunpowder," blurted out John Adams, "our biggest concern is gunpowder. If we don't retain a steady supply, I'm afraid Mr. Cushman will be right. It will be over quickly. Our domestic gunpowder is quite inferior to British, Swiss, or even French powder." He looked directly at Cushman.

"Indeed, Mr. Adams, I know full well." Cushman's mind instantly reflected to the dense forest surrounding Fort Duquesne. He knew firsthand that domestic gunpowder was filled with impurities and not of the highest quality, and that had nearly cost him and his brother James their lives. It had been just outside Pittsburgh, near Fort Duquesne, when his musket had failed to fire on an Indian savage bearing down on him, gleaming knife about to slash. He had pulled the trigger only to come face-to-face with a warrior's worst nightmare, the dreaded *flash in the pan*. The powder in the frizzen pan had ignited but failed to travel down the narrow hole into the barrel in order to ignite the barrel powder.

If not for his brother James, Cushman surely would have been killed. James was nearby and an expert marksman with his Brown Bess flintlock. His shot was accurate. Ben thought back to that terrible day when, later in the skirmish, his brother was captured by Indians and he was wounded and left for dead.

"I have heard that Lord Chatham has persuaded Parliament to take over the Faversham Powder Mill in Kent. They produce over half of the powder for the military. With the government running a private industry, I have no doubt the quality and quantity of their powder supply will suffer greatly," Jefferson proclaimed with a twinkle in his eye.

"Government bureaucracy suffocates private industry every time, hopefully very quickly," added Abraham Clark.

"Death to bureaucrats," Jefferson joked. "British bureaucrats, that is."

Benjamin Franklin fought hard not to enter the conversation. He didn't want to compromise the secret deal worked out between himself and the foreign minister of France, the Count de Vergennes. Shiploads of French gunpowder should be arriving in the next several months, but the secret mission could not be made public or the French would back out. He said a quick prayer that Major Hall's mission was going smoothly. "One must be optimistic regarding powder." Franklin immediately regretted making the comment.

"How so?" Adams's question was more a demand as he glared directly at the seasoned diplomat. He and Jefferson had discussed a rumor regarding Franklin and the French earlier that morning.

"Yes, Dr. Franklin, might you have information that is unknown to the rest of us?" suggested Jefferson, leaning forward, elbows on the table, chin in hands.

Cushman instantly felt the warm conversation turn chilly, and for some reason, his instincts were to rescue the old man. "Don't reveal military secrets on my account," he whispered to Franklin. "Never know who might be a British spy."

"My good friends, we can talk tactics, logistics, supplies, and weapons, and well, we should. However, Thomas is correct: this war can be won, God willing. Our greatest challenge is to rally the good citizens of these colonies against the tyranny of the British crown. George and his ministers have miscalculated our love of freedom. They think we are but wayward children in need of parental discipline. Well, perhaps our fathers and grandfathers were just children of liberty, but we have grown. We are now the Sons of Liberty. The seeds they planted have born a sturdy crop, and this is one crop the British will not harvest." This came from the eloquent yet nervous Franklin. "Of course, if we fail, we will all be hanged," he added.

They all laughed and continued to drink the first-rate ale. Adams stole a look from Jefferson that indicated they would pursue their suspicions at a later date.

Heavy cigar smoke drifted around the room, dishes and silverware reverberated throughout the tavern as multiple conversations broke out around the table. Philadelphians approached the group without hesitation and engaged the delegates in current affairs. Clark and Sherman walked across the hall into the tavern room, where several Tories were loudly debating John Hart and some others.

"Well put, Mr. Franklin, but just how do you convince nearly one-third of Americans who remain loyal to the British Crown and another one-third who sit squarely on the fence?" quizzed Cushman, his arm motioning toward the debate heating up nearby.

Jefferson interjected before Franklin could reply, "Good question. I am sure a number of years ago there were very few Americans who wanted to pick up arms against their British brothers."

"Only my cousin Sam." John Adams chuckled, referring to his first cousin Samuel Adams, who for over a decade was one of but a handful of rabble-rousing rebels who openly talked about armed rebellion. As the leader of the Massachusetts delegation in Philadelphia, Sam Adams was working nonstop behind the scenes, not only to continue the war, but also to work for independence from Britain.

"So true," continued Franklin. "Samuel Adams and his colleagues were a small minority of men who believed in the rights and liberties of mankind held precedent over any absolute rule of the monarchy. Their unwavering belief slowly spread from a few to many in a very short time."

"But that is just one town in one colony," countered Cushman, fully anticipating the history lesson about to come.

"My transformation took time," stated Adams firmly. "When I first saw the Boston Town House at twenty-five years of age, I was impressed with the splendor of the courtroom and its surroundings. The paintings of the British kings above the marble fireplace, James II and Charles II, the judges in the flowing scarlet robes and shimmering white wigs is a memory I will never forget. I was there to watch what I now realize as the beginning of this dangerous road we travel. King George III had ascended to the throne, and the Superior Court was renewing a routine law concerning the writs of assistance."

A collective look of disdain appeared upon every face familiar regarding the universal hatred concerning the common British order granted by the kings' judges for sheriffs and magistrates, a blank-check search warrant allowing authorities to search anywhere, anytime for anything without any sort of oversight.

"I will be the first to admit that the merchants and traders of Boston have gained a great deal of their prosperity by smuggling everything from tea to rum. Customs agents throughout the colonies would accept all kinds of bribes from sea captains to trading houses. But to allow the British to enter our homes and businesses without cause was an abomination," Adams continued to deliver his personal history.

"The writs were greatly abused in Richmond and Baltimore," added Jefferson.

"As well as New York," interrupted Robert Livingston, returning to the table, only to seize his beer mug and return to the raucous debate across the hallway.

Adams continued, "Since 1765, George and Parliament have wanted to raise revenues from the colonies to pay for the French and Indian War. The resulting taxes included the Sugar Act, the Quartering Act, and the Stamp Act. All three either raised taxes or, in the case of the Quartering Act, forced colonists to house and feed

British soldiers. They continue to underestimate our hatred of taxes and interference." Adams pounded his fist for emphasis.

"The Riots of 1765 can be directly attributed to the Sugar Act and the Stamp Act," declared Franklin. The Sugar Act required the colonists to pay a tax on all types of sugar products, including rum, molasses, even nonsugar items like lumber, and foreign wines. The Stamp Act mandated colonists to buy a stamp for every legal document, American newspapers, any pamphlet, almanacs, and even playing cards and dice.

"These unfair taxes were universally despised throughout the colonies. The Boston riots against the stamp master were really the first action opposing the king's ministers," Adams finished. The Sons of Liberty had ransacked the home of the stamp master of Massachusetts Bay, Andrew Oliver, who was forced to flee for his life.

Ms. Deborah interrupted with another round of ale. She lingered near Cushman, who immediately recognized expensive perfume, unusual for a tavern girl.

The unkempt Virginian had not been much of a student in his youth but had a natural curiosity and interest in all things. Despite his lack of formal education, Cushman never felt intimidated by intellectuals. He felt common sense and experience trumped theory and books. His best friend from his youth, Thomas Jefferson, had always marveled at Ben's ability to remember his lessons from Parson Maury, while it took him hours of study. The two boys had both boarded with the Maury family in Fredericksville Parish, Virginia, where James Maury ran a private school. Jefferson was sure Cushman could have been a lawyer or doctor had the parson not expelled him for all his roguish deeds. Jefferson smiled at the memory of some of Cushman's finer pranks.

John Adams slid his chair closer and continued his narrative on the path toward revolution. "The occupation of the different colonies, and especially Boston, was the last straw. The Tories were unabashed in their glee. Even General Gage was unimpressed with what he saw and taunted us by saying, 'A people who have ever been very bold in council but never remarkable for their feats of action.'"

"Never a truer word spoken." The harsh baritone voice interrupted the table conversion. Standing directly behind John Adams, the barrel-chested man staggered with an unfriendly sneer. His companion eyed the four remaining men with suspicion.

"Dr. Andrews, what brings you out of your viper's nest tonight?" Franklin glared at the unwelcome intruder.

"My friend and I were about to enjoy a hot toddy. Seems we stumbled into a meeting of traitors," slurred the Philadelphia doctor with a New England accent.

"Seems you've had one drink too many," added John Adams, his words dripping with disgust at the newcomer.

Dr. Andrews ignored the insult and looked directly at Ben Cushman. "I've never seen you before. Are they enlightening you with their traitorous propaganda?"

Cushman was about to rise in defense of his newfound friends when Jefferson interjected, "Dr. Andrews, this is my friend from Virginia, Major Benjamin Cushman."

Andrews made no attempt to shake hands as Cushman remained seated and nodded.

"A major, huh? In which army?"

"Virginia militia, fought in the French and Indian War," Cushman responded tersely.

"A British soldier if you fought in that war. Whose side you on now, boy?" Dr. Andrews responded, chewing hard on his half-lit cigar.

Jefferson gave Cushman a cautionary look as Ben replied, "I guess that is yet to be decided."

"Andrews, you were with the British Army in Boston. We were just telling Ben about your army's occupation of my city," snarled Adams. "Tell him about your vaunted British soldiers beating small boys. Tell him about the brutal rape of our young women."

"Rape! Hardly necessary. Your *young women*, as you refer to them, pursued our soldiers. Your women were so easy and willing rape was a wasted effort." The heavyset Dr. Andrews smiled.

Adams bolted from his seat, fire in his eyes. Andrews's friend immediately stepped between the two. Cushman moved quickly; in an instant, his hands were firmly grasping the man's waistcoat. Men emptied out of the tavern room, hoping to see a brawl.

"Gentlemen," Andrews said, laughing deeply, "my esteemed friend Mr. Adams is just letting off a little steam. After all, taking part in treason all day long must be exhausting."

Andrews's muscular friend and Cushman continued to stare daggers at each other. Cushman was about to act when Jefferson stood and gently separated the two men. "Mr. Andrews, I think it's time for you and your friend to get your hot toddy."

"Mr. Jefferson, you are an intelligent member of the gentry's class. You should caution your fellow delegates against this continued treason," the doctor said, slurring his words.

Adams refused to relent. "What about Ms. Donally? Remember her, John?"

Dr. Andrews slowly turned toward John Adams, his expression changing as his eyes bore into his fellow New Englander. "An unfortunate situation indeed."

The Philadelphia doctor thought back to the dreadful night in December of 1769. The thirteen-year-old girl had fought hard, and the soldiers had battered her from head to toe. There were three of them, and they all took turns violating the innocent daughter of a local baker. She bled to death in her father's arms as Adams and a neighboring doctor had attempted to bandage her wounds. That neighboring doctor was Dr. John Andrews. "The soldiers wouldn't have been there had it not been for your cousin promoting lawlessness throughout the city."

"You saw what they did firsthand, John. They were never punished! How could you condone such barbarism?"

"You know I don't condone such acts. Every army has its discipline problems," countered the doctor, unconvincingly.

"That's the problem, a standing army. The quartering of troops has caused great alarm throughout the colonies. People rightfully complain that this amounts to an unfair tax to house and feed British troops. It's obvious that British commanders either can't control their troops or..." Jefferson hesitated, then added, "Don't want to control them."

An exasperated Andrews waved his arms skyward and stalked away. His friend slowly followed, all the while staring down Cushman.

"Pleasant chaps," remarked Cushman.

"He was once a friend, but the conflict in Boston drove us apart," Adams muttered softly. "He arrived in Philadelphia last year and has remained a strong Tory."

Cushman saw the hurt in John Adams's eyes; the two must have been good friends. The conflict had already pitted friend against friend, family against family.

The men remained quiet; the arrival of Dr. John Andrews had put a damper on their lively evening. Adams's mind continued to relive the road to war. King George disbanding the New York assembly after it refused to fund the quartering of troops. Colonists protested in all thirteen states for fear that their own assemblies would be disbanded. George and his ministers continued to take a hard line, causing the colonies to begin to push back. The breaking point came on May 5, 1770, what people would eventually refer to as the Boston Massacre. On that date British soldiers would kill five young men during a confrontation between the Boston mob and the Twenty-Ninth Regiment of the British Army. Tension between the citizens of Boston and the occupying army had been substantial. Profanity, fistfights, taunts, and rock-throwing were daily occurrences. Soldiers would swing their cutlasses and swords, tearing clothing, slicing shoulders and forearms. British commanders encouraged this behavior as a form of intimidation. British soldiers particularly liked to use the blunt end of the bayonet. Many a Boston dentist profited from the broken teeth that resulted from such tactics.

"Boston seems to have been quite a powder keg." Cushman awkwardly broke the silence.

"A powder keg indeed. The massacre occurred next, putting us on our current course." Adams snapped out of his reverie. "My law clerk, Jonathan Austin, was on King Street when it happened. A group of boys had been beaten earlier in the day by British soldiers and identified one of their attackers as Private Hugh White, who they found sitting in the sentry box guarding the customs house. They began throwing snowballs and chunks of ice at him. A crowd quickly formed. Private White threatened to shoot them and began to load his musket. This act infuriated the crowd. By the time Captain Thomas Preston brought out six of his men to save Private White, the mob had reached several hundred people."

"Eighteen months of heated occupation were coming to the boiling point," interjected Franklin.

"Exactly, Mr. Franklin. Captain Preston retrieved Private White from the sentry box, but the mob now blocked their retreat. Austin says the people were screaming not to shoot. Tories countered their chants, urging the British soldiers to shoot. Private Hugh Montgomery fired first and put a hole the size of my fist through Samuel Gray's head. More shots soon followed, and five brave Patriots were dead. Samuel Gray, Crispus Attucks, Patrick Carr, James Caldwell, and seventeen-year-old Samuel Maverick all perished that day."

"A dark day indeed," stated Jefferson.

"I don't mean any disrespect, Mr. Adams, but how did you justify defending these soldiers at trial?" Cushman asked; being tactful was not one of his strengths.

Adams and two other attorneys had been sought out by the governor to represent Captain Preston and the other soldiers. John Adams's cousin Samuel actually encouraged John to take the case.

"Not an easy task, I am sure," noted Ben Franklin. "Mr. Adams and I don't always see eye to eye politically, but I have always thought it an example of great courage to stand by your legal principles and deliver these men a just trial."

"Thank you, Benjamin, and yet I must admit, I was very conflicted in this case. I was confident from witness testimony that Captain Preston did not give the order to shoot. On the contrary, he did everything in his power to stop the shooting. As to the soldiers, I must admit, I was less enthusiastic in their defense. However, I still believe the provocations of the crowd were considerable. Two of the soldiers were found guilty of manslaughter, and the rest were found not guilty."

"Verdicts to the contrary, the Boston Massacre turned more fence-sitters into Patriots and continue to this day to rally the colonies against British occupation. For Samuel, the Boston Massacre was heaven sent and the equivalent to Caesar crossing the Rubicon.

There would be no turning back now," noted the politically astute Franklin.

"From my prospective in Virginia," added Thomas Jefferson, "the massacre changed many of my friends and neighbors. Loyalist to the core, they were at least willingly to consider the arguments being put forth by Patriot leaders, especially Samuel. Prior to the massacre, most in my circle of friends considered Samuel to be a raving lunatic."

"Some members of my own family would have agreed with you, Thomas," acknowledged Adams.

Jefferson turned to Cushman and spoke. "Ben, it's important that future generations of Americans know the patient sufferings we've endured before we took up arms, and how the king's actions have led us to our current state of affairs. This Congress is not a gathering of hot-tempered radicals, as painted by our Tory brethren. They are a measured group of Patriots standing on valued principles. These are not hopeless and desperate men. Most are men of wealth and standing. Most have large families to support. They have much to lose."

"Mr. Hart, I believe, has thirteen children," Franklin stated.

"Thirteen children!" Cushman whistled. "Very impressive." The men all laughed at the ribald look in Cushman's eyes.

The tavern was starting to thin out, but there was still plenty of activity in all four first-floor rooms. A beer stein crashed to the floor in the tavern room as two men squared off, ready to settle their differences with fists. Cooler heads stepped between the two combatants.

Cushman nodded toward John Adams. "Gentlemen, I have no doubt concerning the Congress's commitment, but wars are won on the battlefield, not in assembly rooms. If this revolution is to be won, farmers, clerks, shopkeepers, and common, everyday citizens will win it. As much as I admire Colonel Washington, I doubt that even he can turn his ragged volunteers into a fighting force capable of defeating a professional army. I think they got lucky in Boston. I have great reservations, and I am still not convinced that the majority of the people will fight, especially after the realities of battle have been experienced."

"Perhaps, young Benjamin, but I believe we *have* a majority," said the slightly tipsy Franklin. "John, please continue. You are doing a fine job."

Turning toward Cushman, Adams responded, "Lawyers, what can I say? We love to talk. So shoot me."

"Don't think I haven't given it some thought," the witty Franklin snapped back.

Before Adams could continue, Jefferson interjected, "I think two important consequences came from the trial. One, colonists throughout America saw the brutality of the British soldiers, and two, they saw the Boston jury, even under great duress, could administer a just and lenient verdict. The British came off as murderous and brutish, and we came off as merciful. But perhaps the most important consequence was the king's commissioning of Thomas Hutchinson as governor of Massachusetts."

"How so?" Cushman asked.

"The king ended the practice of paying the governor's salary from whims of the Massachusetts legislature. Instead, his salary would be paid by London with money raised by a new tax, the tea tax."

"Exactly!" Adams hammered his fist into the table, rattling every beer stein. "Since Hutchinson's salary was tied to the new tea tax, he was heavily motivated to see to its collection." Adams stood and yelled across to the tavern room, "Mr. Sherman!" He waved for the Connecticut delegate to return to their table. "Tell Mr. Cushman about the *Gaspee*."

Sherman smiled as John Adams left the table to relieve himself in the outhouse, situated out back of City Tavern. "Ever heard of the *Gaspee*?" Sherman asked Cushman, who shook his head in the negative. "The British Navy became very aggressive enforcing smuggling and proper taxes to be paid, especially on tea. Their warship, the *Gaspee*, had been harassing sea captains for months in Narragansett Bay. One day in June of 1772, the captain of the *Gaspee*, William Dudingston, ran aground pursuing a suspected smuggler. Dudingston's brutal treatment of crews of the ships that he boarded was legendary. Word spread like wildfire throughout the local taverns of the *Gaspee's* predicament, and soon a plan was hatched to take care of Captain Dudingston and his ship."

"Liquid courage." Franklin laughed, raising his stein of ale.

Cushman and Jefferson laughed as Sherman continued, "The tavern patrons, using muffled oars and long rowboats, set out with great stealth to board the *Gaspee*. Captain Dudingston was shot and almost died. A Patriot medical student named Mawney saved his life. The British crew was taken from the ship, and the *Gaspee* was set aflame. A large throng cheered from the shoreline. Dudingston survived and even tried to reward Mawney, but all the raiding party had agreed to remain anonymous and he would not step forward to receive his reward. The British reaction was, of course, to tighten the screws and thus turn more people to the side of the Sons of Liberty."

Adams returned and immediately added, "This, of course, was followed by the Hutchinson letters and the Boston Tea Party."

"How in the world did so many Indians get into the middle of Boston?" Jefferson joked, in obvious reference to the Sons of Liberty, not so subtle an attempt to disguise their little tea party.

"Well, you know Indians. They are very resourceful," stated Adams. "Things had quieted down after the massacre. Samuel was quite sure the rebellion would never happen. We had missed our opportunity. Now, Governor Hutchinson was as pompous as ever, and Tories were very confident the Sons of Liberty had been defeated. We had all suspected that Hutchinson was sending biased information to the king."

Adams glanced at Franklin, who stood and bowed. Franklin, ever the showman, walked about as he continued Cushman's education. "It was the spring of 1773. I was still hopeful of reconciliation when I was almost arrested by the king for treason."

"For what reason?" Cushman questioned the grizzled statesman.

"A number of letters had fallen into my possession. These letters showed that American Tories, especially Hutchinson, had urged the king to send troops to halt the disobedience. I mistakenly believed these letters would ease hostilities between the two sides, by showing it was American Tories, not the British Crown, that was fostering these ill feelings. I persuaded my friend to allow me to send some of the letters to Thomas Cushing, the speaker of the Massachusetts House. He agreed, as long the letters would not be published."

Franklin paused to take a swig and then continued, "Of course, someone had the letters published," throwing an accusatory glance toward Adams. "The resulting uproar was predictable. The backlash in London was so severe that I was almost arrested. It wasn't long after that people were whispering about treason and prison for the distinguished gentleman Franklin." As Franklin addressed himself. "I have always said that prison was dangerous to one's health. Returning to America began to look better and better."

"Did you stay on?" asked Cushman.

"Yes. I was convinced I could still help reconcile our differences, but to be honest, I think I was very close to being thrown in prison. Not long after I returned home, a friend from London wrote me that the king and his ministers were angry with themselves for not arresting me. Soon after, I was elected to this fine body."

John Adams was about to continue his tale of tea when two drunken Tories spotted the table of distinguished Patriots and called out tauntingly, "The Howe brothers will be here soon. You dandies better run and hide, or they'll be measuring you all for a pine box."

Ben Cushman began to stand, but Jefferson gently placed his hand on top of his shoulder. "Easy, Ben, they're drunk, and besides, they are not the enemy," reasoned Jefferson. Every conversion stopped at the table as they stared at the two Tories. Weighing the odds, the two decided to beat a hasty retreat, and soon the delegates burst back into conversation.

Adams continued the story of the Boston Tea Party. "I suppose we should go back to 1768, when John Hancock's ship the *Liberty* was intercepted by the British Navy. I defended Mr. Hancock in court, and although we won, this was just the beginning of the harassment of his ships. John was indicted over two hundred times for smuggling. He started the boycott of English goods, mostly tea. His fellow merchants followed suit."

Adams paused, taking a long swig of beer. Merchants throughout the colonies followed Hancock's boycott of the East India Tea Company and continued to smuggle tea in from Holland. Tea smuggled from Holland was cheaper than East India Tea because they paid no tariffs. East India sales plummeted in America, and they almost went bankrupt. Company lobbyists to Parliament earned their pay when they persuaded the British legislature to pass the Tea Act. Instead of the East India Company paying an import tax, the tax was leveled on the American merchants, such as Hancock. East India Tea Company was now a virtual monopoly in the colonies.

The combination of the loss of revenue to Hancock and other American merchants, the inequality of the monopoly, the fact that the tax revenues would go to Hutchinson's salary, the Hutchinson letters, and one more tax placed on the American colonies turned out to be a combustible set of circumstances.

"The perfect storm for Samuel and the Sons of Liberty," chimed in Jefferson.

"We didn't receive much news in Ohio. An occasional rumor here and there. Would you mind giving me some details?" Cushman suggested while enjoying another pull on his drink.

"To say the Boston Tea Party was a well-orchestrated protest concerning the Tea Act would be a classic understatement," added Benjamin Franklin.

"Absolutely correct, gentlemen," continued Adams. "On the day of December 16, there were three British merchant ships being held at Griffin's Wharf." Adams told about the *Dartmouth*, the *Eleanor*, and the *Beaver* and how they had entered Boston Harbor loaded with tea from the East India Tea Company. Patriots had intimidated the East India agents to resign and ordered the crew not to unload any tea. The crew had happily agreed not to do so.

One of the owners of the *Dartmouth*, a young Quaker by the name of Francis Rotch, had come from his home in Nantucket in an attempt to negotiate the release of his tea. In a town meeting, Rotch agreed to send the barrels of tea back to England. However, he had one major problem. Since his ship had been passed through the Customs House, he couldn't get clearance to return it to England until he paid the tea tax. He couldn't pay the tea tax until he unloaded and sold the tea, or he would be ruined financially.

On the morning of December 16, more than five thousand people crowded into and around the Old South Meeting House. Rotch was given one last chance to petition Governor Hutchinson to allow the *Dartmouth* to return to England with her nearly 120 barrels of tea.

Governor Hutchinson had grown weary of the Boston anarchy and had already made plans to draw a line in the sand. Two British warships, the *King Fisher* and the *Active*, would arrive in Boston Harbor within the week. He was feeling confident. Poor Rotch never had a chance when he arrived in Milton to petition the governor of Massachusetts.

Samuel Adams's inner circle had all agreed that Hutchinson would refuse Rotch, and thus a well-orchestrated protest was about to play out. When the meeting resumed at three, the crowd had reached over six thousand.

Adams continued, "Rotch returned to the meeting crestfallen and told the throng that Hutchinson had refused his plea. A cry rang out that could be heard citywide. '*A mob*,' they roared, '*a mob!*' When people calmed down, all eyes turned to Sam, who stood and cried, '*This meeting can do nothing more to save the country!*' Of course, that was the signal, and about fifty Indians broke through the church door. The place exploded! One man was heard screaming, 'To Griffin's Wharf, you Mohawks! It's time to turn the harbor into a teapot!' People stormed out of the church as Hancock roared, 'Let every man do what is right in his own eyes!' I still get goose bumps telling the story." Adams's enthusiasm was very noticeable.

"John, you never told us if you happened to sport a costume that night?" Jefferson asked with a sly smile.

"A gentleman never tells." Adams grinned.

"Is it true that the Patriots—I'm sorry, the *Indians*—did little damage to the ships?" inquired Cushman.

"True, the only damage was to the tea barrels and one broken lock from a storage room. A new lock was delivered to the ship the next day," responded Adams proudly.

"What about the ship's crew?" Cushman asked.

"Because of the large crowd and the raucous mood of the protestors, the crew of all three ships wisely handed over the keys and stood back and watched."

Over 350 barrels of tea were dumped into Boston Harbor that night, about forty-five tons of tea. Damages were estimated at well over ten thousand pounds. It took the *Indians* a little more than three hours to complete their task without any damage to the ships or the wharf. So much tea was spilled that it sat up from the water and began to cover the wharf. The Indians had to shovel it back into the water.

"Paul Revere delivered the news to New York and Philadelphia the following days," added Jefferson. "The reaction in New York was one of jubilation and total support. Even Tories agreed it was a perfect crime."

From London, Ben Franklin had called it *an act of cruel injustice* and urged the city of Boston to reimburse the shipowners. Even William Pitt, one of America's oldest friends, thought the act was criminal and demanded reimbursement.

"I must admit, I was quite embarrassed and demanded retribution. However, upon hearing the full story, I changed my mind and am now ashamed of my actions," Franklin stated softly.

"I believe my cousin had some harsh words for you upon receiving your advice," stated John Adams.

"Yes, I have heard. Something about *'great philosopher, bungling politician.'*" Franklin, who turned to Cushman, laughed. "Remember, young man, if you live to my age, you might make a mistake or two. Trust me, I have made enough for both of us."

Cushman laughed out loud. *The old buzzard is hard not to like.* He estimated the group had been talking and drinking for close to two hours. Although the Congress was in the middle of a hectic schedule, no one seemed to be in a hurry to leave. He was enjoying the conversation immensely. He had always believed Jefferson would be successful, but he was just beginning to grasp the enormity of what they were discussing. These men were conferring about events that could forever change the world, and his best friend was one of their leaders. At the beginning of the night, he thought he might be in the midst of an insane asylum. Slowly he was beginning to think the difference between insanity and genius was minuscule indeed.

As Ms. Deborah brought yet another round, John Hart and Robert Livingston returned to the table, while Adams walked into the front coffee room and began debating two local bankers about the wisdom of attempting to enter into a treaty with France or Spain. "The Port Act of 1774 was appropriately nicknamed the Intolerable Acts. Personally, once I read them, I was convinced there would be rebellion," noted John Hart, deftly picking up where Adams had left off.

"Atrocious indeed, but all we had to do was reimburse the East India Company and the laws would have been repealed," Robert Livingston added. He was one of the few who still held out hope that the spat between father and son could be resolved. Talk of independence would soon come to a halt. Livingston both believed it and advocated it.

"I have to disagree with you, Robert," Hart said in a firm manner. "Giving in to the demands of the British would be construed as weakness. Appeasement has always been an ineffective form of diplomacy. All the previous petitions and protests will have been for naught if we surrender to their demands. We must continue to operate out of a position of strength even if it means more bloodshed. I am the first to admit, the road will be long and fraught with danger. *Audaces fortuna iuvat.*"

Cushman quickly glanced at Jefferson, who smiled and said, "If you hadn't gotten kicked out of Latin class so often, you would know '*Audaces fortuna iuvat*.' Fortune favors the brave."

"I knew that," the grinning Cushman replied quickly.

"The Port Act was an abomination!" snarled Adams, returning to the conversation. "It transferred the Boston customs office to Plymouth and moved the provincial seat from Boston to Salem. Only supply ships would be permitted into Boston Harbor. As a great center for politics and commerce, Boston would be ruined forever."

"Cutting off the head of the snake," added Franklin.

"The British surely had to know that the city would not take this lying down," stated Cushman.

"Lord North told Parliament that if military force was necessary, then so be it. He would enforce the law with military might without hesitation," Jefferson responded. "Supposedly, the king told Lord North, 'The die is now cast. The colonies must either submit or triumph.' King George III had crossed his own version of the Rubicon. There was no turning back."

"Parliament," added Benjamin Franklin, "gave the king the power to name the governor's council rather than our House of Representatives. Towns could only have one meeting per year. The governor would appoint sheriffs and judges, and there would be no jury trials regarding government officials. There would be absolutely no checks on the powers of any branch of government. *Corruptisima re publica plurimae leges.*" Franklin glanced at Cushman. "In the most corrupt state are the most laws."

Cushman smiled a *thank-you-for-the-translation* and then added, "It really seems like tyranny in small bites."

"Like the old adage 'How do you boil a frog?'" inquired the scientist Ben Franklin. "You place it in a pan of cool water and slowly increase the heat. By the time the frog realizes it's in danger, it's too late."

"Well, the British have certainly turned up the heat, and we are most certainly in danger," declared John Hart as he stole a glance toward Livingston, the holdout.

"But unlike the frog, we are responding to that danger," declared Jefferson.

"But are we too late?" inquired Franklin.

"Pray we are not, pray we are not," repeated Jefferson.

Adams continued about the formation of the Committees of Correspondence, set up in each colony to keep everyone informed of the king's tyranny. Ultimately, these committees would call for a national assembly. Each colony elected delegates to attend the First Continental Congress.

"Mr. Cushman, I wish you could have seen the good wishes our Massachusetts delegates received at every town and city on our way to Philadelphia," Adams declared proudly. "Women and children crowded our carriages and screamed support. Fireworks and cannons were fired off in every town. It was as if we were a popular king and his court. This is why I believe we have the support of most Americans. While in New York, we were wined and dined like royalty."

"Careful, John. Tyranny is tyranny, whether perpetrated by a king or by a democrat," warned Jefferson to the sometimes-pompous Adams.

Adams ignored Jefferson's gentle caveat and continued, "We arrived in Philadelphia in late August and immediately came here to City Tavern, which had just opened several months earlier. The enthusiasm of the delegates was never higher. I had never seen such a diverse assembly of gentlemen so focused on the subject at hand. Most of the delegates were lawyers, and as you all know, our profession is filled with quibbling, egotistical know-it-alls."

Jefferson, a lawyer who had very little respect for his profession, nodded in agreement.

"How many here were delegates in the First Congress?" quizzed Cushman.

"Just Roger and I," answered John Adams, pointing to Sherman across the hall, "and as I said, the mood of the delegates was one of great euphoria with grand expectations."

Most agreed that the First Congress had fallen into two camps, Patriots and half-Patriots. The Patriots wanted a more aggressive protest against the king. The half-Patriots wanted to strike a more flexible stance. Fifty-two men of passion had debated for two months, and at times, chaos had reigned. But in the end, they all agreed that the greatest thing to come out of the Congress was the relationships developed. Most had never even met. The current meetings being held by the Second Continental Congress had been more productive because of the relationships forged during the First Congress.

Adams continued, "I kept a journal, and early on I noted a shortage of leadership. However, as the Congress progressed, my mind slowly changed. George Washington's speech about how he would personally lead one thousand men to relieve Boston inspired all who heard it. Patrick Henry of Virginia showed great promise as a motivational speaker. I thought that Mr. Jefferson's cousin Peyton

Randolph did an outstanding job keeping us on task as the president. Of course, Samuel working hard behind the scenes was more effective than all of us combined."

"Hard man to say no to," noted Jefferson.

Cushman nodded to Franklin and asked, "How did the British perceive the First Congress?"

"Well, as you might imagine, the vast majority spoke out belligerently against the *insolent mob*. Only William Pitt and Edmund Burke spoke forcefully for a peaceful resolution. But they were in a minority. Most sided with the king, who believed Americans were cowardly and backward and would retreat on all fronts when confronted with British troops, or be easily conquered if they resisted with force."

Jefferson added, "Soon after, the Virginia delegates returned home and called for a Revolutionary Council. The council was to meet in Richmond, at St. John's Church, to approve decisions made in Philadelphia. We were all confident the British would yield to our demands. After three days of patting ourselves on our backs, we were all jolted from our self-assurance by the finest and scariest speech I have ever heard."

"Would that be Mr. Henry's speech?" quizzed Cushman. "As I said earlier, we didn't get much news out West, but there was a great buzz about a speech given by Patrick Henry."

"You should have been there, Ben. Everyone was mesmerized. The most amazing thing was that Patrick could even speak that day. Earlier in the week, his wife had to be placed in a straitjacket so that she wouldn't take her own life. She had many demons running through her. Somehow he summoned great strength to speak that day," related Jefferson. "I was sitting in a pew with George Washington and a couple of the Lee brothers. My cousin Peyton Randolph was leading the meeting from the pulpit when he recognized Patrick Henry to speak. Henry spoke without notes, but the secretary copied down the speech, and I have obtained a copy. If I may…"

At this time, Jefferson pulled out a one-page parchment and began to read Henry's speech. All secondary conversations came to a halt as the thinning crowds turned to listen to the shy Virginian mimic the words of Patrick Henry.

"'This is no time for ceremony.... Should I keep back my opinions at such a time, through fear of giving offense, I should consider myself as guilty of treason toward my country and of an act of disloyalty toward the majesty of heaven, which I revere above all earthly kings.'"

The din of tavern noise slowly abated as more patrons wandered into the back coffee room.

"'Ask yourselves how this gracious reception of our petition comports with these warlike preparations, which cover our waters and darken our land. Are fleets and armies necessary to a work of love and reconciliation? Have we shown ourselves so unwilling to be reconciled that force must be called in to win back our love? Let us not deceive ourselves, sir. These are the implements of war and subjugation—the last arguments to which kings resort. I ask, gentlemen, sir, what means this martial array, if its purpose were not to force us to submission? Can gentlemen assign any other possible motives for it? Has Great Britain any enemy, in this quarter of the world, to call for all this accumulation of navies and armies?

"'No, sir, she has none. They are meant for us. They can be meant for no other. They are sent over to bind and rivet upon us those chains, which the British ministries have been so long forging. And what have we to oppose to them? Shall we try argument? Sir, we have been trying that for the last ten years. Have we anything new to offer on the subject? Nothing.'"

Ben Cushman looked up as Jefferson continued reading. The entire first floor of City Tavern had now encircled their table and stood politely, listening to Patrick Henry's words. Cushman had never witnessed anything like it in any tavern. Even the waitresses and waiters had stopped their duties and stood captivated.

"'If we wish to be free...we must fight! I repeat it, sir, we must fight! An appeal to arms and to the God of Hosts is all that is left us!'"

Jefferson paused; he was taken by the moment and did not even notice the crowd surrounding the table. "Gentlemen, you could hear a pin drop. The church was filled with over one hundred delegates. The windows were open, and throngs of people surrounded them to hear his elegant oration. On one side of me, Mr. Washington grabbed my elbow and gave me a look of admiration. On the other side, Richard Henry Lee, a brilliant orator in his own right, stood spellbound. Henry's voice grew louder with each sentence."

Jefferson continued, *"'They tell us, sir, that we are weak—unable to cope with so formidable an adversary. But when shall we be stronger? Will it be the next week, or the next year? Will it be when we are totally disarmed and when a British guard shall be stationed in every house? Shall we gather strength by irresolution and inaction? Shall we acquire the means of effectual resistance by lying supinely on our backs and hugging the delusive phantom of hope until our enemies shall have bound us hand and foot?*

"'Sir, we are not weak if we make a proper use of the means which the God of nature hath placed in our power. Three millions of people, armed in the holy cause of liberty, and in such a country as that which we possess, are invincible by any force which our enemy can send against us. Besides, sir, we shall not fight our battles alone. There is a just God who presides over the destinies of nations and who will raise up friends to fight our battles for us.'"

Jefferson's voice grew louder, emulating Patrick Henry's strong finish.

"'The battle, sir, is not to the strong alone. It is to the vigilant, the active, the brave.... There is no retreat but in submission and slavery! Our chains are forged! Their clanking may be heard on the plains of Boston! The war is inevitable—and let it come! I repeat it, sir, let it come!

"'It is in vain, sir, to extenuate the matter. Gentlemen may cry, 'Peace! Peace!' But there is no peace. The war is actually begun! The next gale that sweeps from the north will bring to our ears the clash of resounding arms! Our brethren are already in the field! Why stand we here idle? What is it that gentlemen wish? What would they have? Is life so dear, or peace so sweet, as to be purchased at the price of chains and slavery? Forbid it, Almighty God! I know not what course others may take.'"

Jefferson was now roaring Henry's words. He paused and mimicked Henry with his hands held high, dropping his left hand to his side and balling his right fist high in the air as if holding a dagger. With clenched teeth, he finished Patrick Henry's famous oratory. *"'But as for me, give me liberty.'"* Jefferson paused, then plunged his right hand into his chest and called out, *"'Or give me death!'"*

THE SIGNERS

The distinguished table of American Patriots sat in silence in what seemed like an eternity. The surrounding patrons stood stunned; even Tories could not muster any retorts. Henry's speech had had the same effect on the Virginia delegates ten months prior.

Cushman's strong belief in British superiority and inevitable victory was slowly beginning to fade. Jefferson's imitation of Patrick Henry's speech at St. John's Church had struck him like a lightning bolt. He had thought of himself as a playful rogue, always ready with a clever quip, but the mischievous Cushman couldn't think of a thing to say.

Chapter 5

When beggars die, there are no comets seen; the heavens themselves blaze forth the death of princes.
—William Shakespeare

June 24, 1776
Philadelphia

He sat alone in his luxurious library, sipping an expensive bourbon, a smug smile of self-satisfaction creasing his handsome face. The plan was set, and tonight he would change the world. His thoughts turned to John Hancock. *Hancock,* he mused to himself. *Oh, to be there when it happened.* He knew it was too dangerous. *Maybe I will take the chance. It certainly would be worth seeing the look on his arrogant face.* He took another sip. His thoughts reviewed the turn of events that had led him to this current path, a path he took with great enthusiasm. *I supposed it all started with the wretched old man.*

Patrick Rourke was born in the colony of Maryland. His father, Michael O'Rourke, was orphaned at age twelve and literally survived on his own until he turned fifteen, at which point he made a life-changing decision. Stowing away on the merchant ship *Rebecca*, Michael left Ireland with two pounds in his pocket and the clothes on his back. He sneaked aboard the vessel at the port city of Galway, having no idea of the ship's destination. Eighty-nine days later, Michael arrived in Baltimore and found a job loading and unloading ships in the busy port.

Catholics in colonial America were a small minority and faced a great deal of prejudice and worse. Lord Baltimore had founded Maryland as a safe haven for Catholics in the New World. Michael

O'Rourke's *safe haven* in Maryland was a myth. He was constantly harassed for his religious beliefs, even though he practiced it rarely. After working late one night, O'Rourke was walking home to his tiny one-room apartment. Three young men staggered outside a local tavern and immediately began to harass the young Irish Catholic. In the fight that ensued, Michael had used a board and struck one of his attackers square on the side of his head. The cracking of the skull indicated instant death. The other two quickly ran away, calling for the local sheriff. Michael left Baltimore that night, not wanting to face a trial, even though self-defense was a distinct possibility. He traveled north to the largest city in America, hoping to get lost in Philadelphia. In what would become common practice for many Irish Americans, he dropped the *O* and became Michael Rourke.

He again found work on the wharfs. He labored long hours and, unlike his coworkers, never drank away his earnings. Scrimping and saving, he managed to buy a dilapidated warehouse in Mulberry Ward, near Race Street. He painstakingly repaired the structure, and within two years, he went from dockworker to managing his own warehouse. As it turned out, he was blessed with great management skill, and within ten years, his one property had grown to twelve.

By the early 1740s, Michael Rourke was one of Philadelphia's wealthiest citizens, but his Catholic faith ensured it would only be a second-class citizen at that. Deeply resentful of this prejudice, Rourke remained a bitter and resentful man. Everything changed when he married the daughter of a local Quaker minister. The marriage was somewhat scandalous; Quaker-Catholic marriages were quite uncommon, but the Quaker's famous tolerance for religion would gradually soften Michael. The fact that his wife's first name was Rebecca, the same name as the ship he stowed away on, permitted Rourke to believe theirs was a marriage made in heaven, and indeed it was. He deeply loved his wife, and in the beginning, their marriage made up for a lifetime of heartache. Michael Rourke's heaven on earth lasted for three years and was shattered with the birth of his son, Patrick. In what was a rather-common occurrence in colonial America—the bittersweet birth of the healthy baby boy she named Patrick also led to the death of Michael's beloved Rebecca soon after childbirth. The irrational father, ravaged by anguish, placed the blame squarely on the son. Had it not been for Rebecca's father, Michael surely would have done harm to his newborn.

Michael's resentment of his son continued throughout his childhood years. Although Patrick grew up in luxury and splendor, there was never much of a bond between father and son. He was quiet and shy throughout most of his young life, and no one could foresee the demons developing in the young man. He had formed a morbid fascination about murder, torture, and assassination and studied those subjects with great fervor. Patrick absorbed his father's thriving trade business and, by his eighteenth birthday, showed more guile and understanding of colonial markets than even his father. It was his eighteenth birthday when the demons burst forth. Ironically, it was on that same morning that Michael Rourke had finally come to the realization that he had been a fool for these many years and hoped to change his relationship with his son. Patrick smiled to himself as he remembered his father's awkward attempt at reconciliation. The smile broadened upon his recollection regarding his fine performance that ill-fated day. "Why, Father, you have given me the greatest birthday gift a parent could bestow upon a son. Shall we drink a toast for a wonderful and fulfilling relationship for years to come?"

Rourke remembered how giddy he was as they toasted to a new life together. The new life together, however, would be short-lived. Patrick remembered his father's panicked eyes when he finally realized what was happening to his body. Michael Rourke had attempted to speak but was paralyzed and could say or do nothing. The son had poisoned the father, and he was about to die. Rourke's breathing had soon become labored, but he remained very much awake and aware of his pending doom. The son had laced the wine with enough poison to kill five human beings.

Dendrobates auratus, the poison dart frog found in Central America, was the poison of choice. The deadly toxin actually came from the poisonous ants and tree bark that made up the frog's diet. Native Indians would use the poison to lace their arrows. Patrick Rourke hadn't been sure if the poison would lose its toxicity; therefore, he gave his father a very large dose. Judging by Michael Rourke's reaction, the dosage had indeed been sufficient. With so many ships trading back and forth to the West Indies, it hadn't been hard for Patrick Rourke to find one of the Merchant Marines willing to gather a large number of poisonous frogs and collect the excretions into a specimen jar. The doctor attributed the death to heart failure, which was reinforced by the younger Rourke's statement to the sheriff that his father had experienced severe chest pains. Being the only son and only heir, Patrick received Michael Rourke's massive wealth. The younger Rourke had watched his father with the curiosity of a scientist as he struggled with his last gasps for air. Michael Rourke had tried to speak, but nothing came out. He tried to gesture but could not move a muscle. His breathing had become more and more labored, as if he were slowly drowning. Michael's mind had been clear as he absorbed what was happening to him. Gazing into his son's eyes revealed something he had never seen before. His pending death and the betrayal of his only son were bad enough, but there was something else, something sinister that pierced his still crystal clear mind. As Michael Rourke struggled with his last breath, he came to a horrifying realization: there was no remorse in the eyes of his son, only joy, only amusement. How could he have missed something so painfully obvious? His son was pure evil!

Patrick had properly mourned his father's untimely and early passing without any gossip or scandal. Despite his young age, his business acumen soon became legendary throughout the entire city. Patrick Rourke was soon becoming one of Philadelphia's movers and shakers.

He built a three-story Georgian redbrick house on Front Street, near Elfreth's Alley, not far from his father's first warehouse, a trendy, affluent neighborhood close to the docks and only a few blocks from City Tavern. He joined several elite organizations and was one of the stockholders in several large buildings, including City Tavern. In addition to being one of Philadelphia's wealthiest residents, Rourke inherited the best of his parents' physical qualities. He was over six feet tall, with a lean, powerfully built frame. His face was more like his mother's, with a smooth complexion and small facial features.

Thick curly dark hair added to his allure. Young, rich, and handsome, he was one of the most eligible bachelors in Philadelphia.

There were, however, whispers of Rourke's *peculiar habits*, his vicious temper, unscrupulous business dealings, and late-night adventures. All of which added to his growing reputation. To some, it added mystery to the mix, but to a small group of others, it offered signs of danger.

Smuggling in America's most popular ports like Boston, New York, Charleston, and Philadelphia was as common as the bribes paid to customs officials hired to stop the practice. Patrick Rourke was an expert in both. Like many trade merchants throughout the colonies, Rourke manipulated ship captains, ship's crew, dockworkers, and customs bureaucrats with bribes, threats, and blackmail. One very big difference between Rourke and smugglers like John Hancock was the small army of enforcers employed by Rourke. Workers on the docks of Philadelphia quietly referred to them as *Rourke's Ruffians*. Anyone who challenged Rourke would ofttime end up badly beaten. Others would just plain disappear, and still others were found later, their bodies tortured and mutilated. No one could ever pin these crimes on Rourke, as they were carried out with ruthless efficiency and secrecy.

After George Grenville, the minister of the Treasury and later prime minister, stationed British warships off the American coast, most merchants were slowed greatly. John Hancock had over two hundred ships caught by the Navy and later indicted. Not one of Patrick Rourke's ships had ever gotten stopped. It was obvious to all concerned that Rourke's tentacles reached high into the admiralty of the British Navy.

Rourke's reminiscence returned to the present when he recalled the first time he was introduced to John Hancock. It was in New York, at Job Eaton's lavish summer party. New Yorkers had never seen such an extravagant affair; it was as if the king of England were being honored. More an indication of the changing times, as individual entrepreneurs were making history as capitalism in the colonies had begun to reward private ownership with vast wealth that only kings and their families had ever enjoyed. Job Eaton owned many ships and had created enormous wealth through trade. Like Hancock and Rourke, he chose to broaden his trade beyond the British Isles; his ships traveled throughout the world, but the most lucrative trading was in the West Indies and France, which on occasion required the art of smuggling. Over two hundred guests from six different colonies attended the weekend affair. It was the colonial answer to a weekend at the Versailles Palace, except the elite were merchants, traders, bankers, doctors, and lawyers instead of the royal family.

The party was held in early July of 1771. The previous fall had seen the court case of Captain Preston and the British soldiers, on trial for the Boston Massacre. Rourke frowned as he recalled his introduction to John Hancock. He had been talking privately with Job Eaton when Eaton waved Hancock over to join them.

"Mr. Rourke, I would like to introduce you to Mr. John Hancock," the haughty Eaton announced as if introducing Rourke to the bloody king of England. They shook hands, and Rourke took an immediate dislike to Hancock. Hancock's eyes were confident and alert; his manner was one of superiority, but with a common touch.

"Mr. Rourke is the John Hancock of Philadelphia." Eaton smiled in a vain attempt to flatter both men; he only enraged Rourke, as if placing Hancock on a pedestal.

"Mr. Rourke, it is a pleasure to finally meet you. I have heard many fine things about your organization," lied Hancock, who actually knew a great deal about his competitor from Philadelphia, and most of what he knew troubled him.

"It is an honor to finally meet the great John Hancock," replied Rourke, the sarcasm in his voice hard to miss. "Tell me, Mr. Hancock, as a delegate to the Massachusetts Assembly, when are you and your fellow legislators going to get control over the Boston mob? The more they bellyache, the tighter the British noose gets around our neck. This is not good for any of our businesses." Rourke smiled, hoping to irritate Hancock.

"Well, Mr. Rourke, we"—Hancock made a circular motion with his hand to include all three of the men in conversation—"may not have any businesses left if the king continues to take away our freedoms. His taxes and illegal searches of our ships and warehouses have cut greatly into our profits."

"His Navy protects our ships at sea, and his Army protects our warehouses on land. It seems to me a perfect arrangement for continued prosperity, unless of course you New Englanders continue to complain about the most trivial matters," Rourke said, continuing to goad Hancock.

"I hardly think that writs of assistance, taxation without representation, the quartering of troops, or the murder of five innocent pedestrians to be trivial," Hancock shot back with a confident smile.

Rourke continued to press the arrogant New Englander. "Seems to me the Army should have started shooting Boston hooligans years earlier. The five got what they deserved. They were in a mob, threatening the king's soldiers. They should have killed the whole bunch. As for the Parliament, they have been exceedingly patient with your protests. They even rescinded the sugar tax. You are lucky they don't shut down the Port of Boston. Where will your business be if they blockade the harbor?"

"The Parliament and George continue to treat us as less than second-class citizens and look to the colonies only to fill their coffers. They will continue to gradually reestablish absolute tyranny until they have total control," offered Hancock, who refused to take the bait and remained calm.

Rourke recalled how Job Eaton fumbled uncomfortably with his drink as the two men continued to take measure of each other.

"My god, you sound like that madman Samuel Adams. They should have strung him up years ago. Your speech sounds much like treason, Mr. Hancock. Be careful, you are not in Boston. You never know who might hear you speak of such matters and have you arrested." Rourke's voice continued to get louder, and the more Hancock remained unruffled, the more irritated Rourke had become.

"Now, Patrick, let's not talk politics. We have much wine to drink and beautiful women to dance with," interjected the stunned Eaton.

"Perhaps our guest would prefer to pursue something other than women." Hancock grinned, the insinuation being obvious to both men. Hancock knew immediately that he had struck gold. Rourke's face went red with rage.

The enraged Irishman took one step toward Hancock but slowly defused his temper and laughed too loudly. "*Touché*, Mr. Hancock, but I assure you my tastes run only to the feminine side. Indeed, Mr. Eaton, I think I shall try to persuade one of the young ladies to try out your spacious dance floor. As for you, Mr. Hancock, I would hope you would keep your traitorous talk to yourself, as you are certainly pursuing a path toward ruin. I just pray you won't bring the wrath of the king down on all of us. Good day, gentlemen."

As Rourke stormed away, he could hear John Hancock remark glibly to Job Eaton, "Pleasant fellow, he is. I would like to meet him in a dark alley someday."

Rourke's thoughts returned to the present. "Be careful what you wish for, Mr. Hancock, be careful what you wish for."

The Irish American's reverie was interrupted by the clattering of multiple footsteps descending a spiral staircase on the edge of the massive library. Rourke stood and welcomed in five young women. All were lavishly dressed in evening gowns made of white silk and lace. Their expensive clothing was far from modest, a mix of elite wealthy and tempting seductress. The low necklines, revealing more than just shoulders, were a welcome distraction to any man. Rourke smiled broadly as the most glamorous of the women came to his side and gently placed her arm through his.

"Well, my dear"—Rourke caressed her hand as he spoke—"how did our plan go?"

Lydia Ames pressed her ample breasts into Rourke's arm, knowing full well the effect she had on him. She was one of the most exotic-looking women in Philadelphia, also one of the most scandalous. Born to an English sea captain who had worked for both Patrick and Michael Rourke, Lydia had inherited her father's substantial estate upon his death several years earlier. Philadelphia gossips called her the first courtesan; others referred to her as a benefactor to the arts and to charity. She was all those things and much more.

Lydia's mother was part Jamaican and part Spanish. The combination of English, Spanish, and Jamaican was a sight to behold.

Her olive skin shimmered and offered a striking contrast to the lacy white dress. Her sensual dark-brown eyes sparkled and revealed both intelligence and intensity. Thick jet-black hair cascaded well past her shoulders and rested seductively on her full breasts. A long thin neck led perfectly to her beautiful face, highlighted by rounded deep lips and long sleek eyelashes. Unlike most women of the age, Lydia Ames did not try to hide her attractiveness. She was intelligent and beautiful, but mostly she had an insatiable appetite for money and power. She was a woman playing in a man's game, and she refused to play by societal rules. She knew her greatest weapon was her good looks, and she was not afraid to utilize her assets.

"Just as you expected. Men are so predictable," she teased. "The girls preformed perfectly, and the drugs worked as advertised."

Rourke had always been fascinated in the acquisition and maintenance of power. Certain Roman emperors, mostly the *insane* ones, especially captivated him. He got his idea for the *Rourke's Ruffians* from Augustus Caesar, who used ex-legionaries to dispatch *justice* along certain trade routes in and around Rome. Their tactics were brutal *and* effective. As effective as his *secret police* had become, his lovely ladies had demonstrated an even greater value, at much less expense.

The Roman emperor Caligula had employed courtesans to spy for him, exploiting their charms to extract information. In some cases, the courtesans were used to assassinate rivals, real and imaginary, using exotic poisons imported from around the empire.

Lydia Ames was Cleopatra, and Rourke was her Mark Antony. Passionate and flirtatious, risky and dangerous, it was a skeptical partnership that had worked out well for five long years. Both of them knew it was a volatile relationship that could implode at any time, but the partnership had been lucrative, and they were both hoping for a huge payday involving their current venture.

Lydia motioned for the other girls to leave. "What kind of drug did you put into the wine?"

"Why, my dear, haven't I told you the story of Marco Polo?"

"No. I am unaware of that particular story." She pouted as she brushed the back of her hand seductively across his cheek. As Rourke turned to kiss her, she placed her forefinger on his lips and firmly stated, "Work before play, my darling."

Her sexual jousting always enthralled him. "Very well, my dear, as long as the other girls join in with us later."

"If I like your story, maybe." She tormented him with her most playful smile.

"Very well, then, legend has it that Marco Polo, upon returning from the Far East, told the story of a religious sect, called the Ismailis, who lived in an impregnable fortress somewhere in the mountainous region of Persia. The head of the sect was referred to as the old man of the mountain. When the old man wanted a religious rival or another enemy killed, he called for volunteers. The volunteers were given wine laced with hashish. When they fell into a drug-induced sleep, they were taken to a lush valley and given wine, women, and more drugs." Rourke paused, pulling the beautiful woman closer to him. "After a few days, they were returned to the fortress to carry out the murder. This was their brief glimpse into eternal paradise, which awaited them if they were successful in their mission. The word *assassin* comes from the Persian word *Hashishim*, which means 'the taker of hashish.' The hashish we used tonight was imported from the West Indies, I believe your homeland of Jamaica. I used just enough of the drug to get them motivated, but not so much as to make them useless."

"Oh, don't worry, my darling, my girls got them plenty motivated. They will not fail. They will be well rewarded when they return, no extra charge to you."

"I'm afraid they must seek their reward in paradise. They won't be returning after the job is done. This is much too big. We must make sure no one can trace this back to either of us. Not if we want to remain here in Philadelphia."

"My, my, aren't you the clever one," she purred. "Who will you get to eliminate your assassins?"

"I have been organizing a group, similar to our *Ruffians*," claimed Rourke, who had taken to referring to his enforcers in the same manner as those who whispered of their existence. "They are from Camden and have no clue as to what is happening. They just think it's a standard murder-for-hire."

"Clever and paranoid, a very good way to stay alive. I hope you don't view me and my girls in the same manner," she stated softly, her eyes both questioning Rourke and also warning him.

"Lydia, you are my most valued partner, in more ways than one. I could never hurt you or the girls." He grabbed her by the hand and began to lead her upstairs. "Besides, you know how much I love a crowd in bed. Let's get the girls and celebrate our good fortune."

Lydia Ames sighed gently as she made a mental note to begin to carry a weapon whenever she went out.

Chapter 6

*The secret of happiness is freedom.
The secret of freedom is courage.*
—Thucydides

June 24, 1776
Philadelphia

Benjamin Cushman leaned back in his chair and took a long swig from his exquisitely designed tankard of ale. From the tables and silverware to the doorjambs and crown moldings, the accessories at City Tavern were unsurpassed. The shareholders had spared no expense in surrounding their customers with the finest of everything.

Cushman was enjoying his reunion with his best friend, the brilliant young Virginian Thomas Jefferson. His colleagues in the Second Continental Congress were an added bonus. Their lifelong friendship had been forged at a very early age.

Cushman thought back to their first meeting. Ben was six years old and heading to his favorite fishing hole along the Rivanna River, his five-year-old brother, James, in tow, only to find a boy and two girls sitting on *his* protruding rock. Ben, stubborn and competitive, ordered the three away from *his* rock. The redheaded boy stood his ground, and soon the two were throwing punches and wrestling in the mud. Jane and Mary Jefferson, Thomas's two older sisters, attempted to intervene, despite protestations from James to *"continue to the death."* The girls eventually separated the two, but not before both boys had bloodied each other. Retelling the story throughout their adulthood, both men claimed victory, and from that day forward, the two boys, whose families lived three miles apart for most of their childhood, became inseparable friends.

Both boys loved the outdoors and spent much of their childhood hunting, fishing, riding horses, and rafting on the cool waters of the tranquil river. Ben was the superior hunter; shooting a rifle or a pistol came as naturally to him as breathing air. Almost everyone around Albemarle County could shoot well, but people were amazed at Ben's ability. Even veteran militiamen were astonished that a boy that young had such remarkable marksmanship. But to Ben's chagrin, no matter how much he practiced, his best friend was the better horseman, one of the best he had ever been around. Even in adulthood, Jefferson maintained his superiority. Climbing an old maple tree near the river was undoubtedly their most favorite adventure. Tree branches extending far out into the river made a perfect platform for jumping and diving into the meandering waterway. Eventually, a rope was introduced, allowing the boys to swing out farther into the river, tumbling and flipping before landing at all angles into the cool water of the Rivanna. Jefferson's older sisters, Jane and Mary, and younger sisters, Elizabeth and Martha, often accompanied Thomas. Ben's younger brothers, James, George, and Thomas, would also join in the many adventures in the back woods of Virginia. It was not uncommon for the nine children to be seen running around like a pack of wolves, getting in and out of trouble. Ben was the most daring and mischievous; nearly setting a neighbor's barn on fire was one of their many fond memories. Jefferson was the most inventive, and engineering a bridge across Henderson Creek at the age of ten might have been his most impressive feat as a youngster. Of course, Ben would always claim it was his idea and therefore he deserved equal credit.

Ben was very protective of Thomas's sisters, which endeared him to Jefferson's parents, Peter and Jane Jefferson. Mrs. Jefferson would eventually give birth to ten children, six girls and four boys, but one died stillborn, and another, Peter, died before he reached his first month in 1748. Thomas was twelve years old when Jane gave birth to her last child, Randolph. So in Thomas Jefferson's formative years, he was surrounded by his sisters and the Cushman boys. Peter and Jane Jefferson treated them more like Thomas's brothers than neighbors. Whereas Benjamin pushed Thomas to the extremes of childhood outdoor play, it was Thomas who spurred Ben to work at his studies. Both boys' parents appreciated the positive influence they had on each other. Although Ben tended to get into a great deal of trouble, Peter Jefferson thought he was a perfect friend to his eldest son. Thomas was a sponge to all types of study, from the Greek and Latin languages to the study of philosophy, music, and history. Many believed he could have made a living playing the violin. He encouraged Ben to take his studies seriously with mixed results. Ben was actually a very good student, but when the urge to play struck him, his focus to study ended quickly. It was time to play.

Ben followed Thomas to the learned minister James Maury's boarding school near Gordonsville. Jefferson flourished; however, Ben's mischievous nature was just too much for the stern schoolmaster. His final prank involved Parson Maury reaching for a copy of Caesar's book *Commentary on the Gallic Wars*. Maury had a habit of snatching books quickly from the bookshelf, and as he did so, the rest of the volumes tumbled out, having been glued together. The eight students had attempted to stifle their laughter but were unsuccessful. The next day, Benjamin Cushman was sent home, much to the chagrin of Jefferson, who had to admit he had more time to study after his best friend left. Jefferson's father, Peter, had died just prior to the boys attending Maury's school. It amazed Cushman that a man as strong and healthy as Peter Jefferson had died so young. Father and son had been very close, and his death had a profound effect on the twelve-year-old. Cushman's father, Benjamin Sr., often worried that after Peter Jefferson died, Thomas would get caught up in the gambling, drinking, and other sporting activities that were so common in rural Virginia at that time. Jefferson certainly flirted with all those things, often with the help of young Ben, but Jefferson's love of books eventually won the day over the other distractions.

On weekends, Thomas would return home to help his mother and sisters with the upkeep of the Shadwell estate. Ben, who had returned home to help at the Cushman family farm, always looked forward to the weekends. He would spend most of his time at the Jefferson estate, helping Thomas and the girls. Of course, James would usually tag along. By age thirteen, Ben had developed quite a crush on Jane Jefferson, three years his elder. Revealing his affection for Jane to her brother was one of the worst mistakes Ben had ever committed. Thomas would constantly tease his friend when Jane was near, which was usually quite often. If Jane knew of Ben's secret love for her, she never let on. Being the oldest of the group of nine, she was more motherly than girlfriend. Jefferson would forever tease Ben that he would rather march off to war with George Washington's First Virginia Regiment than acknowledge his crush on Jane. Despite Ben's protestations, there was probably a grain of truth to Ben's decision to join Washington on Forbes Campaign to take Fort Duquesne.

Cushman felt a sudden wave of sadness as he thought of the charming Jane Jefferson, his first real love, one-sided as it was. Her death at such a young age had devastated both the Jefferson and Cushman families. She was gentle, kind, and beautiful; her enthusiasm for life was contagious to all around her. After her funeral, the two best friends tried to console each other. They both broke down and cried. It was the first and only time Cushman had ever cried, and it was just one more thing that strengthened the already-inseparable bond between the two young men.

A flying peanut broke Ben's reverie. Jefferson smiled at his marksmanship. "Awful quiet over there. Can't handle a few pints anymore?"

"Just reminiscing. I miss Jane." He nodded sadly.

Jefferson gestured understanding. "She was quite fond of you also."

Cushman took a sip from his tankard, his mood suddenly melancholy.

"You know, you're not getting any younger. Any prospects, other than the ones you pay for?" Jefferson smiled.

Cushman got the hint and laughed out loud. "Don't run into a lot of refined ladies out West."

"What about Indian women? I've heard they can be quite exotic." Jefferson leered.

Cushman grimaced but said nothing.

"I'm sorry, Ben, the look on your face suggests I've hit a nerve."

THE SIGNERS

Her smiling face flashed into his mind as if she were sitting next to him, and the sudden and painful realization that the two women he had loved both died too young hit him. "Perhaps later, with the other story. You are right, tonight's about celebrating our reunion. Let's get another round."

As if by magic, Ms. Deborah delivered yet another round of ale as laughter again drifted in from the tavern room. The conversion continued among the seven members of the Second Continental Congress and their surprise guest, Benjamin Cushman. Their mission quickly resumed, for tonight their goal was to convince Ben, and perhaps themselves, that the road they were traveling was indeed the proper path for the English colonies of North America. Jefferson's reciting of Patrick Henry's speech to the Virginia Assembly had touched the entire gathering profoundly, none more so than Cushman. He still felt that a war with Britain was not only foolish but would also result in the wholesale slaughter of all American resistance, but he was slowly beginning to believe the Patriots sitting around him were not as crazy as he first thought. As the conversion began anew, it was as lively as before. Cushman, Jefferson, and Adams were debating the effect that Henry's speech had on the entire country, while Franklin and Sherman argued over French aid to the colonies. Hart, Clark, and Livingston were passionately debating the Lee Resolution. A weary traveler was being led upstairs toward the third floor, where beds were rented for one farthing. The reek of his filthy clothes penetrated the back coffee room, causing the men to turn and locate the cause of the stench.

Cushman glanced to his right to see two gentlemen exiting the tavern room from across the hallway. Although he didn't recognize either man, they both seemed vaguely familiar. Both men smiled and approached the gathering, the older of the two glancing around the rectangular table and then settling his eyes on John Adams. "Cousin, it is good to see the committee meeting so late. How is our special project progressing?" the newcomer asked with a smile.

Cushman immediately put a name to the face. *So this is the man that threatened the British Empire to its core.* Samuel Adams looked more like the old uncle every family hoped to hide during the holidays for fear of embarrassment; his receding hairline showed the early stages of baldness. Gray was overtaking his dark hair. His bushy eyebrows contained streaks of gray, and his rugged face showed signs of aging beyond his years. Adam's simple dress was more fitting of a low-paid clerk than that of a leader of a revolutionary movement that promised to shape history. Despite his shoddy appearance, it was clearly evident that the Massachusetts tax collector was a man to be reckoned with. His eyes were observant and sharp; one could sense his intelligence and commitment.

"We have been pleasantly distracted by Mr. Jefferson's childhood friend," replied John Adams. "Thomas." Adams gestured to Jefferson for an introduction.

"Gentlemen, this is my best friend from childhood, Major Ben Cushman." Cushman stood and extended his hand. "Ben, Mr. Samuel Adams and Mr. John Hancock."

"Gentlemen, it is truly a pleasure to meet both of you."

"If it's a pleasure, then I assume you're neither a spy nor a Tory." Hancock smiled.

"Our young friend here remains a skeptic. He believes the British firepower is too much and too few Americans are eager for independence," added Ben Franklin.

"Granted, we face astonishing odds, but don't forget about the Spartans at Thermopylae," said Samuel Adams, referring to the legendary King Leonidas and his three hundred Spartans holding back over 150,000 Persians at the Thermopylae pass in Greece, perhaps the greatest example of courage and overcoming insurmountable odds in history.

"Yes, but how did that work out for them?" the sarcastic Cushman questioned.

"Yes, Mr. Cushman, King Leonidas and his brave band met their demise, but history is a chain of related events, not single isolated events. The Greeks didn't have to conquer Persia, and we don't have to conquer England. Only resist with extreme consequences to the king," responded Sam Adams.

"Breed's Hill," Hancock offered, referring to the huge lose the British took compared to the minutemen before *winning* the battle.

"Exactly," continued Adams.

"I realize the Greeks would eventually thwart the Persian invasion, but as I recall, they had a strong Navy," replied Cushman.

Everybody at the table nodded. British naval superiority was a constant worry for every member of the Congress.

"And…" Cushman hesitated. "I still wonder about the support of the commoners."

"Well, perhaps our little committee here will provide the proverbial straw that breaks the camel's back," stated Adams coyly as he and Hancock surveyed the table of men knowingly.

"Won't you join us? We are having a wonderful time persuading Mr. Cushman the righteousness of our cause." Abraham Clark invited the two men that the king of England considered the most dangerous of all the colonials and thus attached the highest bounty to.

"We would love to join you, but we have an important meeting with a Mr. Tucker at his home. He has indicated a willingness to help finance the war effort. We all know how persuasive Sam can be, so I must insist he come along," Hancock replied.

What a contrast, Cushman thought, the elegantly dressed John Hancock, president of the Second Continental Congress, and the disheveled Samuel Adams. *The coming storm has produced some strange bedfellows.*

"Mr. Cushman, pleasant meeting you. I hope we can count you as one of us," Sam Adams declared with a touch of both hope and command.

"Mr. Cushman"—Hancock grabbed Ben's hand firmly—"I have no doubt that a friend of Thomas Jefferson will be an ally to our course of action."

Turning to the others, Hancock smiled and said, "I think our committee should inform Mr. Cushman of the Lee Resolution." With that, the two Massachusetts Patriots swiftly walked to the door and departed into the cooling night air.

Ben turned to his friend Red Jefferson and asked, "The Lee Resolution! What in the dickens is the Lee Resolution? Which Lee?"

"Richard Henry Lee. You have met most of his brothers," Jefferson noted. "Richard Henry is a close confidant with my cousin, and as you know, both have pushed for independence from Britain, even before Lexington and Concord. They were in a distinct minority for quite some time. I suppose the pendulum began to swing toward a majority with the printing of Paine's pamphlet. We have Dr. Franklin to thank for this."

"Ben, have you read Thomas Paine's pamphlet *Common Sense*?" Franklin quizzed Cushman.

"No, sir. In Ohio the only thing to read is the moss on the trees."

Franklin smiled. He was growing quite fond of Ben Cushman. "I was introduced to Mr. Paine while in London, fall of 1774. He was recently divorced and unemployed. He came to me one evening very discouraged and sought my counsel regarding America. I convinced him that America was a land of opportunity, and at age thirty-seven, he left England to start over in the colonies. My son-in-law hired him as a managing editor for his newspaper."

Franklin paused. A ruckus had broken out in the hallway, but it was over quickly, and he continued his story. "I ran into Thomas last fall when I returned from England, and encouraged him to write a history of the colonial struggles with the motherland. He surprised me with the pamphlet this past New Year's Eve. His words are lofty, passionate, and inspiring, yet appealing to the most common among us. He has truly tapped into the conscience of the American people and has stirred their love of freedom. He denounces the tyranny of the king of England, refers to him as the *Royal Brute of Britain*, and charts out the only course for America: independence from the mother country."

Sherman jumped into the description of Thomas Paine's popular pamphlet *Common Sense*. "He clearly strikes a proper truth when he asked the question, And *will America prosper more with Britain or without?* He presents a powerful argument that all Americans would thrive with independence and that acting in our own self-interest is the natural order of things."

"Yes, gentlemen, Paine presents a number of brilliant practical arguments, but I still think he touches the hearts of the American people with his emotional appeals. If I may." Franklin removed a copy from his coat pocket and began to read. *"'O ye that love mankind! Ye that dare oppose, not only the tyranny, but the tyrant, stand forth! Every spot of the old world is overrun with oppression. Freedom hath been hunted round the globe. Asia and Africa have long expelled her—Europe regards her like a stranger, and England hath given her warning to depart. O! Receive the fugitive, and prepare in time an asylum for mankind.'"*

"I agree, his pamphlet has had an intoxicating effect on the masses, but I shudder at some of his democratic ideas. They are simplistic and dangerous. The masses would destroy themselves without some firm controls of government," stated John Adams, who, unlike his cousin Sam, had little trust in the judgment of the common man.

Jefferson, who had watched his father treat all men, rich, poor, and slave, with equal respect and dignity, bristled at Adams's words. "Better power be dispersed among the many than the few, for if the many are wrong, they will only have themselves to blame and will learn more readily how the correct it. Power in the hands of the few only breeds arrogance, corruption, and loss of liberty."

"Paine's pamphlet will serve its purpose. It will do more to tear down than to build up. I pray we will have the opportunity to rebuild our nation, and men like you and I will argue over the proper path," Adams offered, extending an olive branch to Jefferson and realizing that if they survived the rebellion, they would probably wrangle a great deal over that one fundamental issue of government.

"Paine's words have already born fruit. In April, North Carolina declared independence. Other colonies are meeting as we speak to consider similar action. But I still believe we must give England one more chance to reconcile," stated Livingston, one of the several delegates to hold out hope for a last-minute settlement between Great Britain and her American colonies.

"Robert, I detect a wavering in your voice. Perhaps Paine's words are having the desired effect upon you: *'The blood of the slain, the weeping voice of nature cries, 'tis time to part,'*" Adams replied with one final quote from Thomas Paine.

"I have been torn by guilt in two directions, my family and my nation. There is no convenient time to wage war. I am afraid greater sacrifice is in all our futures. But I truly believe that our God has chosen this time, this place, and these men to be the instrument that will change the world forever. This Congress must act, and act we shall," Jefferson declared emphatically.

Cushman smiled at his friend. Usually shy and reserved, he was enjoying the growing confidence Jefferson was exhibiting. The table erupted into multiple conversations again as they continued to debate the motivational value of Thomas Paine's brilliant pamphlet.

"Speaking of family, how is yours?" Cushman asked innocently.

Jefferson's eyes saddened, similar to those of a man who has suffered immense loss. He looked toward his friend and spoke quietly. "Ben, I just returned to Philadelphia last month. Martha lost another child in birth and has been very sickly. In late March my mother passed away. It has been a challenging year," Jefferson confided in his friend.

"I am so sorry, Red. I hadn't heard any news from home." Cushman was fond of both Jane Randolph Jefferson and Thomas's wife, Martha. He always believed his friend would be a terrific father; he was so kind and patient with children.

"Thank you, Ben," Jefferson added softly.

Benjamin Franklin had overheard Jefferson and offered his sincere condolences but was not surprised that the shy and private Virginian had failed to mention the tragedies to anyone.

John Adams, unaware of the sudden admission by Jefferson, turned back toward Cushman and continued to inform him about the Lee Resolution while Abraham Clark and Robert Livingston also slid their chairs closer. "On the night of June 6, Samuel informed me that on the following day, Richard Henry Lee would make a proposal to the rest of Congress that would surely decide the fate of the nation," continued Adams.

"It was no secret what he would propose. I know Robert and his allies were dreading it," added Abraham Clark.

Livingston nodded and frowned.

"Lee's resolution called for three bold steps to be taken: one, that Congress should begin consultation with foreign countries to form alliances against Britain; two, to begin to draw up a plan of confederation for the Thirteen Colonies; and three, a formal Declaration of Independence." Adams's voice cracked with pride.

Clark spoke next. "I thought this sentence striking." He began to quote Richard Henry Lee's final resolution. *"That these United Colonies are, and of right ought to be, free and independent states, and that they are absolved from all allegiance to the British Crown, and that all political connection between them and the State of Great Britain is, and ought to be totally dissolved."*

Everyone nodded in enthusiastic agreement, except for Livingston. "Three committees were formed to begin to prepare rough drafts for debate to begin next week, on July the first," continued Clark.

"Ben," joked Jefferson, his arms spread wide, "you have interrupted an official meeting of the five members of the committee to draft a Declaration of Independence. Roger, John, Benjamin, Robert, and I were elected to this duty, and Mr. Hart and Mr. Clark were invited to give us counsel tonight. The fate of the country has been delayed by Ben Cushman."

"A Declaration of Independence would surely mean a continuation of the war," Cushman declared emphatically.

"Actually, Ben, before you arrived, we all agreed to allow your friend Thomas to write the declaration. We are here just for the beer and, of course, Ms. Deborah," added the witty Franklin.

"I tried to defer to Mr. Adams, but he insisted I do it. Lucky me!" Jefferson, who indeed had argued with John Adams earlier that it should be Adams, not Jefferson, to create the first draft, laughed. Adams finally had convinced Jefferson with a splash of humor. He had told Jefferson he must do it for three reasons: one, a Virginian should be the leader of independence; two, Adams was too obnoxious and unpopular among the delegates; and three, Jefferson was ten times the writer. The rest of the committee had readily agreed, especially about the obnoxious part.

Indeed, Jefferson would have preferred to return to Virginia and help the state legislatures write a new Constitution rather than write up a bunch of grievances against the king of England, but Adams prevailed.

Ben looked at his friend with admiration, raised his mug, and replied with a wry smile, "A noble task. Don't muddle it up."

Chapter 7

*A lie gets halfway around the world before
the truth has a chance to get its pants on.*
—Winston Churchill

June 24, 1776
Philadelphia

Deborah Johnson enjoyed working at City Tavern. Her natural beauty, combined with her vivacious attitude, was a perfect combination for her daily interaction with Philadelphia elites. Male customers loved her for obvious reasons, and since the vast majority of the tavern's patrons were men, it proved to be profitable relationship for all involved. Her manager immediately recognized her unique personality and physical gifts. On nights she worked, customers stayed longer and spent more money. All in all, Deborah Johnson and the coming war were proving to be a winning combination for the three-year-old business.

Deborah was only two years old when her mother died from the flu. Any memories of her mother were locked deep inside her brain. An only child, she was raised by her father, David Johnson, and their mulatto servant, Sarah. Sarah was only four years older than Deborah and was more like a big sister than nanny.

David Johnson was a member of the burgeoning Philadelphia's affluent class. He ruled over the largest ship supply store in the city. He sold food supplies, ropes, anchors, storage barrels, and even fine china. Sea captains and shipowners could always rely on his steady supply of goods and quality service. Philadelphia's thriving wharfs produced plenty of clientele. His business had always done well, but the last nine years had seen spectacular growth. Because the business demanded most of his time, Sarah practically raised Deborah by herself. Like many men in Johnson's powerful position, he spoiled his only child in an attempt to assuage his guilt.

Like all big cities around the world and despite the heavy Quaker influence, Philadelphia had an immoral underbelly. Rich, spoiled, beautiful, and with very little proper influence, Deborah Johnson had fallen easy prey to its decadent nightlife. She enjoyed fancy parties; her quick wit and easy smile always ensured her a throng of young suitors. But the party scene soon grew old, and she wanted new adventures. Working at City Tavern, where her father was a shareholder, seemed very appealing.

Getting her father's permission to work at the popular inn wasn't easy, but the combination of tears and tantrum produced the desired result, and the next day she was serving the city's elite. When the Second Continental Congress returned to Philadelphia, she began serving some of the richest and most powerful men in the colonies. Her favorite customer was Benjamin Franklin, whose playful remarks were always humorous. It was indeed an exciting time.

The last four months had been particularly exhilarating. Her father, always a strong supporter of the king, was outraged at the behavior of the rabble-rousers. He had a special dislike for the Massachusetts rebels. It was his idea to have her listen closely to the conversations of the members of the Congress as they wined and dined each night at City Tavern.

At first, it was stimulating work, spying for her father. Most of the information she gathered seemed trivial, but her father cautioned her that even the most inconsequential reference could be valuable. So she humored him, wrote everything down and let him sort it out. Although not formally educated, Deborah was clever and observant. She knew the information she brought to her father was insignificant at best. The game soon began to bore her. She was beginning to rethink her treachery until one night, when her father brought home the most beautiful and exotic woman Deborah had ever laid eyes on, Lydia Ames. Deborah likened her to an ancient queen; her bearing, confidence, and intelligence were evident immediately.

Ms. Lydia soon began to tutor Deborah in the fine art of spying. She taught her how to dress more provocatively, to wear delicate perfume, and to bathe daily. She instructed her in the art of conversation: be flirtatious, ask questions, seem interested, but not too interested. Lydia emphasized the importance of listening rather than talking, to observe those who were leaders as opposed to followers, the radicals versus the moderates. To be aware of those delegates that got drunk the easiest and those that seemed the loneliest. Nothing was trivial. Lydia even talked about using the third-story bedrooms to lure unsuspecting delegates to pry information. They talked about using sex to bribe or blackmail. Deborah had yet to use such tactics, but the thrill of prying secrets by using sex had intrigued her. Part of her training included the art of mixing potions into the drink of unsuspecting victims. Deborah's boredom was quickly broken; she couldn't wait to get to work each evening.

The renewed enthusiasm mostly centered on the desire to gain the approval of Ms. Lydia. Lydia would challenge her to bring back specific bits of information from targeted delegates. Each night Deborah would bring home more and more information, and each night her father and Ms. Lydia would praise her efforts. To Deborah, this was an exciting game being played out at City Tavern. Little did she know the game was soon to turn deadly.

Chapter 8

※◊※

Cry, "Havoc!" and let slip the dogs of war.
—William Shakespeare

June 24, 1776
Philadelphia

Deborah Johnson glanced anxiously at the expensive French pendulum clock centered on the entrance hallway. *Fifteen minutes,* she thought to herself as she walked slowly through the back coffee room into the kitchen. She nervously greeted one of the assistant cooks. "Looks wonderful, Gerard. Been busy tonight?" She flashed a flirtatious smile at the recently freed slave.

"Yes, ma'am, we been very busy earlier. Now not so much," he replied, nodding at the shapely waitress.

Deborah glanced around, noticing only two others in the cramped kitchen.

"How 'bout you, Ms. Debby? Been busy out front?" Gerard asked.

"The same. Starting to slow down quite a bit," she answered, anxiously glancing around, her eyes coming to rest on the back door.

"Was that Missa Franklin I saws earlier?"

"Yes, he is with Mr. Jefferson, Mr. Adams, and some others." She immediately thought of the handsome stranger when she said *others. What stunning emerald eyes.* "You look busy. Let me throw these scraps away for you. I have some spare time," she lied and scooped up the scrap bucket and walked toward the back door.

"Why, much thanks, ma'am. Make sure to toss it away from da building. Don't like them critters so close." Sanitary conditions being what they were, many animals, including wild pigs and goats, still roamed major Western cities, looking for food. "Oh, don't forget to locks da door. We been gettin' beggars. They been comin' right through da door, beggin' for scraps," Gerard caution her.

"No problem." She grinned and exited into the back alley.

Several decades before, Benjamin Franklin had introduced streetlamps to Philadelphia, thus becoming the first city in colonial America to do so. Lamps were placed at main intersections throughout the city. At dusk, a lamplighter would travel assigned blocks throughout the city, lighting each candle, which was surrounded by four squares of glass. This simple invention did more to prevent crime in the city, with the possible exception of the colonies' first police force. Both were established with Franklin's urging.

In 1751, the Pennsylvania General Assembly established the first paid police department in Philadelphia. The police unit consisted of wardens and constables, including foot patrols through some of the high-crime districts. The police operated out of the Walnut Street Jail, recently constructed in 1773 and situated several blocks west of City Tavern. Most police activity consisted of constables sitting in watch boxes strategically placed around the city. More like a very small one-man shed. Constables would sit and react to any crime or citizen complaint. One such watch box sat behind City Tavern at the corner of Dock and Walnut. It was a stone's throw from the popular tavern.

Constable Cyrus Rice was running northwest on Dock Street. He was late for his night duty near City Tavern. As he approached Walnut, he could see his *office*, as he liked to call it. Rice was in his fourth month on the job as a publicly paid policeman and running hard because he didn't want to be late for the second time this week. He had been helping his wife with their newborn baby girl.

Light from the moon struggled to pierce the clouds overhead as Rice arrived and entered his *office* briefly. The only time Rice actually sat inside was when the weather was too ugly. He liked to stand outside and talk to people as they strolled along one of Philadelphia's busiest streets. Tonight the street was uncharacteristically quiet. Breathing heavily from the long run, Constable Rice noticed something unusual but initially couldn't quite grasp what it was. As he slowed his breathing and focused on his surroundings, it suddenly dawned on him what was wrong. *The streetlamps.* All along Walnut and Second Street, the streetlamps had not been lit yet. Rice's first thought was that the lamplighter must be sick or very late. But then he noticed that streetlamps farther up Walnut were shining brightly. Just the streetlights surrounding City Tavern were out. *Something is wrong,* he thought to himself. *One, maybe two lamps out, but never this many.*

Rice began to take a closer look at one of the lampposts when he saw a young woman approach him from behind City Tavern. The indoor lights of the tavern illuminated the young and pretty face stricken with fear. Upon seeing Rice, she quickly broke into a panicked sprint toward the young policeman.

"Constable, come quickly! My husband, they beat my husband! Help him, please!"

Rice hurriedly caught up to the well-dressed young woman. They ran past the rear of City Tavern, to the back alley running perpendicular to Second Street. The alley that bordered City Tavern's northern property line was known as Logan's Alley, a treacherous narrow street and the scene of many a crime. Reaching the alley, Rice noticed a shadowy form lying in the middle of the darkened lane. He quickly knelt beside the motionless body and began to assess the situation. A purple cape covering the body stirred slightly. Rice gently shook the man, attempting to revive him.

He had moved his face closer to the dazed victim when a sudden movement caught the corner of his eye. *The wife,* he reasoned, *but why is she moving away?* Before he could speak and question her strange behavior, he noticed the sinister grin plastered on her face. It took Constable Rice another second to realize he was in grave danger. That second would cost him his life.

The left hand of the *beaten husband* quickly came up behind Rice's head while the right hand plunged a six-inch-long knife blade deep into his throat. The knife tore through Rice's esophagus, eliminating any chance of a cry for help. The assassin expertly brought the sharp edge of the blade over and up to the ear, severing the artery in two. Death came quickly.

Two men hurried from behind a nearby tree and unceremoniously dragged Constable Rice's dead body off the alley.

The assassin looked up, wiping his knife clean, and gave a smirk to his female accomplice. She left the alley, turning north onto Second Street and into a waiting carriage.

The three men walked about twenty paces deeper into the dark alley and waited. They were quickly joined by a fourth.

"Nice work. No noise." The leader praised the three men. "Shouldn't be long now. Keep alert," he said as they disappeared into the many trees behind City Tavern.

A few moments later, the back door swung open wide. The bright light of the kitchen silhouetted a young woman standing in the doorway, holding a large pot. She hesitated as instructed and entered the alley, walking to within twenty yards of the hidden four. Tossing the contents of the pot onto the nearest tree, she quickly returned to the tavern, purposely leaving the door slightly ajar.

"That's the signal, men. We'll go in two minutes."

The two men crouching at the northwest corner of the alley saw the murder of Constable Rice. They looked at each other with a knowing nod.

"These guys are good. Using the woman was a stroke of genius."

Christopher Tompkins then questioned his partner, "Your position in the front is satisfactory?"

"Yes," replied Andrew O'Leary. "Particularly since they put out all the lights. It's perfect."

"Good. Look sharp. This could be over quickly," observed the leader.

"They'll never know what hit 'em." He grinned as he picked up his two rifles and jogged away.

THE SIGNERS

Tompkins quickly loaded three Brown Bess rifles and leaned each against the side of the tree. He expertly selected one and rested it on a low-lying branch, sighting the back door of City Tavern. *Three loaded rifles and two loaded pistols ought to do the job,* he thought. He would move closer once the four men left. He smiled to himself and thought of the large payday he was about to collect.

Ms. Deborah delivered another round of drinks and smiled at Benjamin Franklin. "Up awful late tonight, aren't we, Mr. Franklin? Didn't you write something about *'early to bed, early to rise…'?*"

"Now, now, Deborah," Franklin interrupted. "I will not be lectured by someone a quarter my age, especially one who is so attractive."

Deborah bent over, tenderly kissing Franklin on the cheek, exposing her ample cleavage to Cushman seated beside the seventy-year-old playboy. She noticed Cushman staring at her and gave him a knowing smile.

"Gentlemen, please forgive me for a moment," Cushman declared as he stood up from his chair. "I must check on my horse. It has been a hard week. Mr. Franklin, I trust you will guard my beer with your life."

"I promise none of these gentlemen shall drink your beer," replied Franklin.

"They are not the ones I'm worried about." Cushman winked at the patriarch of the Thirteen American Colonies.

As Cushman slowly walked toward the front door, he began to reflect on his future and the future of his country. Up until a few hours ago, he never considered what he would do if the flare-up between the king and the colonies grew to a protracted fight. He sincerely thought that by the time he returned home from Ohio, the Patriots would have reconciled with the British or retreated to their homes, terrified by the might of the king's army.

If the men sitting at the table were right, he might have underestimated the Americans' willingness to fight. He still felt that the Patriots would be no match for an organized British Army with full artillery, cavalry, superior tactics, and supported by the Royal Navy. The British Army, he knew, could be as vicious and ruthless as any army on earth. Farmers and shopkeepers would be no match in any long-drawn-out conflict. But the seven men inside City Tavern had begun to chip away at some of the certitude Cushman possessed of a certain British victory.

What if they were right? What was he going to do? Cushman was old enough not to be carried away by the romance of war. While still in his teens, he had served with British general John Forbes and Colonel George Washington in Ohio and Pennsylvania. He had seen the horrors of war firsthand, his father's brutal injury at the hands of the mad Indian, his own head wound received in the forest surrounding Fort Duquesne, the successful rescue of his brother James from the French fort, and the gruesome discovery of the "petticoat warriors" when they finally took Duquesne.

After the successful conquest at the *Forks* of the Ohio, he had returned to his family's Virginia farm to resume a normal life. Unfortunately, that lasted two months before he was pulled back into the depths of hell, seeking revenge for the brutal murder of his parents. For the next sixteen years, Cushman would return to the Ohio country numerous times, running down leads, looking for an opportunity to find the murderous Indian known as *Yellow Snake*. He supplemented his income doing survey work, fur trading, and doing other various "odd jobs." He allowed himself a knowing smile that his quest was finally over. He knew full well the horrors of war and hated everything about it. But there was only one problem—he was very good at it.

The enclosed four-wheel carriage required two horses to lug it around the cobblestone streets of Philadelphia. The part-time teamster, part-time carriage driver, and part-time enforcer waited patiently in front of the lavish three-story redbrick house. It was by far the most expensive home on Front Street.

Inside, Patrick Rourke pulled on his topcoat. He looked over to the beautiful Ms. Lydia Ames and suggested, "Would you like to join me and witness history in the making?"

"Where are you off to, you old fox?"

"I think I will pay Mr. Tucker a visit," Rourke replied with a wicked grin.

"Is Mr. Tucker entertaining guests tonight?"

"He most assuredly will be, but the guest list is only two. We will be there only to observe the party."

"Sounds kind of boring." She pouted.

"Trust me, it will be one of the most memorable gatherings you will ever attend."

"Count me in. You know I love a good party," Lydia cooed as she readied herself for the night air.

Christ Church of Philadelphia, an Anglican house of worship, was founded in 1695 and represented one of William Penn's grandest ideas, that any denomination would be free to worship in the New World. The idea was tested immediately in Pennsylvania, where the majority Quakers, who came to America to escape the interference of the Church of England, were confronted with this American equivalent. Christ Church had one of the biggest Anglican congregations in all the colonies and was a favorite with many non-Quakers. The church had outgrown its eight hundred parishioners by 1726 and began construction of a new and larger building on the same site the following year. John Kearsley, who also designed the Pennsylvania Statehouse, drew up plans for the ambitious project. Financing was aided partly by a lottery system set up by Benjamin Franklin. Upon completion in 1744, the Georgian-style redbrick was one of the largest buildings in America. The high arching windows on both the first and second stories were a testament to the fine craftsmanship available in colonial America. Because of its splendid steeple, it was also the tallest building on the entire continent.

Christ Church had not escaped the storm developing between the Patriots and mother England. Because the Anglican Church was the Church of England, their practice of swearing allegiance to the king was becoming more and more controversial. Most church leaders had remained loyal to the king, but more and more were calling for separation from the Church of England. Several churches in the South had called for this separation and had led to the establishment of the Episcopal Church, similar to the Anglican Church in every way, except without the swearing of allegiance to the king. Episcopal leaders believed in the *middle way*, halfway between Catholicism and Protestantism.

The beggar stood slumped over. A tin cup protruded outward each time a citizen walked by. He didn't speak, but his condition was obvious to all who scurried around the unwanted obstacle positioned directly across Christ Church. His tattered clothing reeked of urine, causing many to cross the street before reaching the wretched figure. He had been there for close to an hour, his eyes never leaving the front entrance of the magnificent structure.

Many of the delegates to the Continental Congress used Christ Church as their primary place of worship. The beggar was only looking for one of them at this time. Earlier, he had learned from a talkative servant that the man he was looking for always attended the Monday-evening prayer session. His patience was rewarded when the man he was looking for exited the house of worship and began to walk to his extravagant carriage. The beggar bounded up and moved quickly across the street, but not so rapidly as to cause alarm. He approached the target from behind, placing his right hand on the delegate's shoulder, and abruptly spun him around so they stood face-to-face.

"Perhaps you could spare some money for a poor beggar?" the filthy stranger asked softly, his eyes penetrating the wealthy banker, while he held up his tin cup.

THE SIGNERS

"Oh my god, you!" was all Robert Morris could mutter. The wealthy banker turned white, as if he were looking at a ghost. "What the hell has happened?"

The flintlock pistol and musket had truly revolutionized the art of warfare. A wonderfully simple machine, it consisted of the lock, the stock, and the barrel. It was literally a smaller version of a cannon.

The flintlock was reliable and simple to use and produce; armies throughout Europe used it as its most terrifying piece of military hardware. Military tactics were ever changing as generals around the world were constantly trying to adapt new strategies to use and defend against the innovative weapon.

Flintlock pistols came in many sizes, the barrel ranging from three to twelve inches. Well-trained soldiers could reload in fifteen seconds. The technique was simple: half-cock the hammer, pour some gunpowder into the barrel, place a lead ball wrapped in cloth or paper into the barrel, place a small amount of powder into the frizzen pan, fully cock the hammer, and pull the trigger. A piece of flint, held in place by the hammer, would strike the steel frizzen, causing a spark to ignite the powder in the pan. The small explosion would travel through a tiny hole drilled into the barrel, igniting the barrel's gunpowder, thus propelling the ball down the long tube. Effective and deadly, it was relentlessly changing the face of war with its many uses, including the ancient art of assassination. The lead assassin approached City Tavern's kitchen, eyes glued to the sliver of light, indicating the door was still ajar. He wore an excessively large sleeveless waistcoat over his long-sleeve white shirt. The waistcoat easily concealed two French-made pistols, the gun barrels only three inches long. Inside his pockets, he carried a third pistol, extra lead balls already wrapped in cloth, and a powder flask. The three men he commanded were similarly armed. He figured twelve loaded pistols should be plenty to finish the job, but if some do-gooder interfered, it was good to know they had backup ammo. His men could reload their pistols in under twenty seconds if need be.

He burst through the door and purposely stumbled into the kitchen, noticing three cooks in front of him.

"I haven't eaten in days. May I beg of you any food?" he slurred and staggered toward the three.

"Sorry, sir, y'all gotta leave now," Gerard Jackson ordered as he walked toward the tall stranger.

The leader smiled, quickly pulled out a pistol, and pointed it directly at Gerard's head. "I think not, my dark friend, and you will do as I say, or you will all die."

The remaining three assassins bolted through the door, pistols drawn, and surrounded the three cooks.

"Anyone makes a sound and my trigger-happy friends will introduce you to your God tonight. Lock them in that storage closet." The leader waved his gun for emphasis.

Gerard Jackson immediately understood the four strangers' mission; it wasn't food, and it wasn't the kitchen staff they were after. Jackson was born into slavery twenty-two years earlier. His owner was an eccentric inventor who lived in Richmond, Virginia. Jackson and his mother were the only two slaves he owned. His mother's only job was to run the household and cook meals. His job, as long as he could remember, was to assist his owner with his many experiments. He became quite handy. His master taught him to read and write, and within time, the young boy became more than an assistant; he became a partner.

On Gerard's twenty-first birthday, his master set both mother and son free. He had been a free man for only one year, but in that one year he had come to appreciate the simple freedoms more than life itself. The men on the other side of the kitchen door were plotting to change history, and freedom was what they aspired for. Somehow he had to warn them.

Samuel Adams and John Hancock had taken Hancock's carriage from City Tavern, east to Front Street, which ran parallel to the Delaware River, one block from the wharfs at Penn's Landing. Unfamiliar with the area, the two Massachusetts delegates had actually passed Mr. Aaron Tucker's home several blocks back. The secretive Mr. Tucker had instructed Hancock and Sam Adams to a meeting to discuss a sizable donation to the war effort. Both men knew that for the colonies to have any chance of winning the war, borrowing and begging for money from wealthy Patriots would be an unsavory but necessary chore, at least until they got a colonial government up and running, with the power to tax. *How ironic,* Adams thought to himself. *We would fight a war to decrease taxes, only to revive taxes to fight the war. What unusual times we live in.*

Fifteen minutes later, realizing their mistake, Hancock ordered his driver to turn around and head back south along Front Street at a slower pace so they could locate the home of Mr. Aaron Tucker.

Gerard Jackson was determined; he had to take a chance. He quickly assessed the situation in the kitchen. His fellow cooks were already bound and gagged. Screaming out a warning might work, but he doubted if Franklin and his colleagues could hear through the thick walls. Besides, they were on the far side of the back coffee room. Studying the four intruders, he began to form a plan. The tallest was the obvious leader. He kept glancing out the door leading into the dining room. His eyes looked cold and calculating. Jackson determined he was very dangerous.

The shortest trespasser was shoving the first cook into the storage room; he seemed nervous and scared.

The third intruder, heavyset and thuggish looking, began tying Jackson's wrists together. His glassy eyes indicated a willingness to follow the leader.

Intruder number 4 wore a full beard and appeared to be guarding the back door, constantly looking into the back alley, as if awaiting more men to arrive.

"Come on, hurry it up!" *Shorty* commanded *Fatty*. "Gag the darkie and get 'em in here already." He was nervously holding the door to the storage room.

Gerard's hands were now tied in front of him, and his mouth gagged. Fatty pushed him toward the storage room. Using the momentum of the push, Gerard hurtled himself shoulder first into the door with all the force he could muster. *Shorty* was caught off-balance and slammed into the wall, striking his head hard, falling to the floor with a thud.

Gerard whirled around and kicked upward as hard as he could, his foot landing right in *Fatty's* groin, disabling him immediately.

The lead assassin whirled around. He saw the Negro land a kick into the groin of his man Gorman, who went down like a shot.

Gerard broke into a full sprint toward the dining room, hoping to warn Mr. Franklin and his group.

In the back of the kitchen, the bearded lookout turned and raised his pistol at the fleeing cook. Before the leader could yell no, a shot rang out that echoed throughout the kitchen. Just as Gerard Jackson hit the door, the lead ball from the assassin's pistol caught him at the base of the skull, causing instant death. Jackson's body broke through the door with a loud crash.

Cushman's trancelike focus on his future was shattered with the loud bang. No stranger to gunfire, he immediately realized a gunshot had just gone off inside City Tavern. Fearing the worst for Thomas Jefferson and his colleagues, he quickly reached inside his saddlebag, pulled out two loaded and primed flintlock pistols. Traveling alone along the trails and roads leading from Ohio to Philadelphia was still a very dangerous proposition. Being a soldier had taught him many things, but perhaps the most important was to always be prepared.

He stuffed one of the pistols into his waistband as he reached for his two knives, made by a Pennsylvanian blacksmith and patterned after the Indian-style throwing knives. The wooden handle supported a teardrop-shaped sharp metal knife about five inches long. Cushman had learned to use the Indian version of the knife from the son of a famous Shawnee Indian chief. Not all the Indians had fought for the French. Cushman dashed to the front stoop of City Tavern; quietly climbing the stairs, he opened the door.

The lead assassin was furious with his colleague, but realizing quickly the other two might be useless, he waved him toward the door as he burst into the dining room. Brandishing two pistols and walking swiftly toward the delegates' table, he calmly addressed the leaders of the Second Continental Congress.

"Gentlemen, please be seated, and no one will get hurt." The lead assassin was improvising. The original plan was for all four to burst from the kitchen, surround the table, and begin shooting. With two of his assassins temporarily out of commission and the third attempting to revive them, he knew he had to stall. A robbery, with hope for survival, could put the delegates at ease, but he knew he had better frighten them first. He didn't expect much resistance from a bunch of lawyers, but he still had to be careful.

The seven stunned delegates remained seated, not sure how to react. Ben Franklin was the first to speak. "Sir, I demand to know what you plan to do with us."

"I plan to take all your possessions. Now shut up, you fat old man!"

Franklin wasn't sure if he was more offended by the *old* or the *fat*, but he decided not to press the subject.

The lead assassin glanced toward the kitchen. Relief settled in; he saw his comrades emerge, slightly battered, but at least upright. He figured he needed only a couple more minutes before his soldiers were capable of completing their mission. He had to convince the delegates this was a robbery, not murder.

"Take off all your jewelry and place all your money on the table, now!" the leader barked sharply, striking John Adams on the head with the butt end of his pistol.

Adams saw stars but remained defiant and held his head high. The rest of the delegates began to empty their pockets.

In the adjacent tavern room that John Hancock and Sam Adams had left one-half hour earlier, Deborah Johnson watched in horror as the scene unfolded; she was alone and shaking uncontrollably after witnessing the murder of her friend Gerard. Ms. Lydia had told her there might be gunfire but that no one would be hurt. She had been told that a robbery had been planned for the purpose of scaring the delegates into submission. Her role had been simple, to allow the four robbers into the kitchen, then to leave. Deborah could only stare at the bloody body. *She promised no one would be hurt.*

"Be alert. Check out the front room." The leader spoke softly to the heavyset Gorman.

Gorman nodded and started scanning the front coffee room. The entrance door had a small alcove. *Better check it out,* he thought to himself and started walking toward the front of City Tavern.

John Trumbull had been the manager of City Tavern since it opened several years earlier. While attempting to finish daily paperwork in his second-floor office, he was startled at the sound of gunfire. Confused

THE SIGNERS

and alarmed, he went to investigate. Descending the stairs swiftly, he turned into the back coffee room. Trumbull froze in his tracks. Sprawled on the floor was the body of his best cook, Gerard Jackson.

"What in the devil happened?" Trumbull yelled, stepping from the hallway into the dining room. Now in full view of the unfolding scene, Trumbull, not fully grasping the gravity of the situation, demanded answers.

The assassin named Gorman stopped short of the alcove and turned to see the voice of protest. Relaxing a bit, he enjoyed what happened next.

The lead assassin raised his pistol and, without warning, pulled the trigger. The lead bullet hit Trumbull squarely in the chest, shattering his collarbone. He fell hard to the ground and began to bleed profusely.

Ben Cushman stood concealed just inside the subscription room, where tavern customers sat to read newspapers and pamphlets as they waited to be seated. Although it was not a perfect angle to see the entire back coffee room, he had quickly assessed the situation; there were four bad guys, two of whom looked a little unsteady. The tallest of the four stood in front of the table of delegates. He was barking orders and, obviously, the leader. Cushman decided he would be his first target.

A black man lay dead or badly wounded to his left, just outside what was probably the kitchen. Directly across from Cushman in the front coffee room, an older couple crouched cowering in the corner, frozen by the terrifying events taking place in the adjacent room. The seven delegates seemed unharmed, but something told Cushman this was no robbery. What happened next confirmed that thought.

The leader, staring away from the delegates, had suddenly called over his associate and whispered something to him. A heavyset man immediately started walking toward Cushman's hiding place. Cushman was about to act when he heard someone shout something out. He glanced around the doorway and saw a man descending the stairway; it was the manager he had pulled the prank on earlier. The leader immediately raised his pistol and pulled the trigger. Cushman cringed at the cold-blooded manner in which the manager of City Tavern had been dispatched. *These are not robbers,* he thought to himself. *They are…assassins!* The realization struck Cushman like a bolt of lightning. He had to act, and act quickly. The heavyset assassin stood within ten feet of Cushman's concealed location, his back turned in order to watch the murder.

Cushman leaped forward, the throwing knife in his right hand. The sudden movement alerted the assassin, who started to whirl. The startled killer raised his right arm, pistol ready, when Cushman jammed the knife into the right side of the assassin's neck, lacerating his main artery.

The remaining assassins turned to see the commotion in the hallway. What they saw shocked them; their colleague lay bleeding on the floor, his neck sliced wide open. Standing astride him was a strange man gripping a bloody knife, his eyes ablaze with fury. Before they could react, all hell broke loose.

Cushman stood tall, cocked his arm, and threw the knife toward the bearded assassin. The knife tumbled through the air toward its target; droplets of blood seemed to hang in the air, leaving a red trail behind. The razor-sharp weapon landed point first into his left shoulder; the assassin fell backward, stunned and bleeding.

The lead assassin pulled out another pistol and fired as Cushman dived to the floor. The lead ball creased his left forearm and shattered the hardwood floor, sending splinters into Cushman's face. He scrambled to his knees, pulled out his pistol, and took aim at the leader, squeezing the trigger firmly. The lead ball leaped from its chamber and flew forward. Cushman's aim was accurate. The ball entered just above the orbit of the assassin's left eye. With no bone to slow the ball down, it entered instantly into the brain to cause massive damage. The leader was dead before his body hit the floor.

Standing motionless, the remaining assassin, *Shorty*, quickly regained his nerve. Pulling out both pistols, he took aim at Franklin and Adams. Cushman reached for his second pistol, only to have it catch on his waistband. He looked on, horrified, struggling to free his second pistol.

Shorty smiled as he began to pull the trigger. He was about to kill Benjamin Franklin.

Thomas Jefferson squeezed the heavy beer tankard hard and swung it in a wide arc with all his might. It came crashing down on the assassin's head the instant he pulled the trigger. The assassin's arm jerked as he fell into unconsciousness. Cushman stared in disbelief as the gun went off. The assassin had dead aim at Franklin's head. Franklin flinched but remained upright, the lead ball only scratching his cheek. Jefferson's well-aimed beer mug had hit home just in time.

While all eyes were riveted to the very near assassination of Benjamin Franklin, the wounded assassin seated on the floor had struggled to his knees. Disregarding the extreme pain caused by Cushman's knife, the bearded killer smoothly pulled out one of his pistols. The closest target he recognized was the arrogant New Englander Adams. Along with Franklin and Jefferson, Adams had been a top target. He took aim and began to squeeze the trigger. A shot rang out, and all went silent. Less than one minute had passed since the shooting began.

Cushman reacted immediately; his second gun was now free as he turned to see yet another stranger standing directly behind him in the middle of the hallway. The shabbily dressed newcomer held two guns, one aimed inward at the congressional delegates, smoke still billowing from the barrel, the other at Cushman. Cushman didn't hesitate; he quickly raised his pistol and had begun to squeeze the trigger when suddenly Benjamin Franklin bolted between the two gunmen and cried at loudly, "No, don't shoot! You're on the same side!" Ben's trigger finger froze just in time as Franklin positioned himself between the two men and heaved a sigh of relief. Neither man had triggered their pistol.

Ben Cushman lowered his gun, realizing for the first time that the ragged stranger had not fired at the delegates but instead had taken out the last assassin. His aim had been true, the ball entering just below the assassin's left ear, and death came quickly to the bearded assassin, who had gunned down Gerard Jackson.

Cushman took a deep breath, thankful he had not killed the Good Samaritan and obvious colleague of Ben Franklin. The stranger looked familiar, and when Cushman finally took time to study the chiseled features of the newcomer, he saw a huge smile spread across his face while commenting to Ben, "Oh my god, how many times do I have to save your ass?"

John Hancock's carriage driver eased the horses to a slow stop in front of the home of Aaron Tucker. The large three-story mansion had two massive chimneys on both sides of the brick structure. It was set back off the street, which probably explained why they had missed the house during the first pass.

Samuel Adams and John Hancock jumped out of the carriage and walked swiftly up the stone pathway. A spacious porch covered the front of the house, and before they could step up onto the wooden structure, the front door opened. A friendly servant appeared and promptly led the two famous revolutionaries into a large library off the main entrance hall.

"Mr. Tucker will join you shortly. Please be seated. May I offer you anything to drink?" The servant gestured toward three large chairs placed in front of a massive fireplace.

"Cider would be fine for me," replied an anxious John Hancock.

"Cider sounds good," agreed Samuel Adams as both men eased into comfortable chairs.

"You two know each other?" an astonished Franklin asked while Thomas Jefferson attempted to tend to Franklin's minor wound.

Franklin waved off Jefferson. "It will be fine, just another conversation starter for all my lady friends," the irrepressible Patriot added.

"Yes, just what you needed. You're so shy with the ladies," responded Roger Sherman as he hurried by to help the injured John Trumbull.

Ben Cushman hugged the Good Samaritan and smiled. "Know each other? Why, I owe this man my life!"

"How do you know Major Hall?" Franklin was astonished to see Hall, who should have been in France and who was equally astonished that he knew Jefferson's friend.

"Dear Dr. Franklin, I believe I told you about the time George Washington and I helped to rescue the last remaining prisoner at Fort Duquesne," Hall said softly.

"Yes, yes, something about two brothers," Franklin recalled.

Hall smiled and nodded toward Cushman.

"This is *that* Major Hall?" Jefferson exclaimed, recalling Ben's tale of the rescue of his brother James at the famous French fort.

"One and the same. I am forever in his debt. Without Colonel Washington and Major Hall, James would no longer be with us," Ben declared with a smile.

"You didn't do too bad in Ohio, even if you were a snot-nosed kid at that time," Hall praised Ben, recalling Cushman was only fifteen at that time.

"Jacob, seems I owe you another huge debt of gratitude. Your timely action saved many lives tonight, including my own." Ben slapped his old friend on the back.

"Oh, I don't know. You seemed to have the situation well in hand, and speaking about your brother, I have some news for you." Hall smiled.

"You've seen James?"

"No, your younger brother, George. Seems I owe your *family* a debt of gratitude, for if not for the bravery of your brother, I would surely not be here tonight," announced Major Jacob Hall.

"How is that so? George is a Merchant Marine. I'm not sure which ship he is currently working on. How would a major in the Army come in contact with my brother?" Ben asked, still shaken from the assassination attempt, the arrival of one of his greatest mentors, and now the information that Hall had met his brother George.

Jacob Hall shot a troubled look at Benjamin Franklin. His face could not hide its deep concern.

Franklin reacted immediately. "Major Hall was traveling to Europe recently. I'm sure that is where he met your brother. Please excuse us a moment, Ben. I need to talk to Jacob. Then he can tell you about your brother." There was an awkward silence as Cushman stared at both men. Neither man could look him directly in the eyes. Instinct and experience told Cushman that both Franklin and Hall were hiding something, and he wasn't in the mood to let them off easily.

Franklin finally broke the uncomfortable moment by grabbing Cushman gently by the arm and whispering into his ear, "Major Hall was involved in a very delicate mission. Even Thomas doesn't know the full details." Franklin glanced toward Jefferson. "I'm sorry, I can't tell you more."

Cushman wasn't happy but understood instantly that Benjamin Franklin had probably revealed more than he should. He knew that Hall had been involved with Franklin since the French and Indian War and that he had loaned Hall to General John Forbes in his march to retake Fort Duquesne. It was during that march that their paths had crossed, forever endearing the young boy and the master spy forever. "But what about my brother?"

"Let me speak with Major Hall, then the two of you can talk, I promise," Franklin replied, his eyes reaffirming his honesty.

"Very well," Cushman added softly, then looked directly at Hall. "Please don't leave. I must hear about your encounter."

Hall smiled and nodded affirmatively. Franklin then hustled the younger man across the hallway into the empty tavern room. The conversation immediately turned serious.

A firm slap on the back broke Cushman's focus on the two. It was Jefferson. "Nice job" was all he said.

Cushman grasped both shoulder of his old friend and smiled. "What about you? Nice swing, just in the nick of time. My gun got stuck in my waist. Sorry."

"Sorry?" Jefferson countered in mock anger. "You almost single-handedly prevented a major assassination plot, took out half of the

THE SIGNERS

assassins, and you apologize. Besides, you were always a glory hound, always wanting to be the hero. You must learn to share in the glory."

"Well, someone had to save the day. Everyone knows you fight like a girl," teased Cushman with a smile and an awkward attempt to further ease the tense situation.

Turning serious, Jefferson looked his lifelong friend in the eyes. "Ben, God placed you here for a reason tonight, to protect us. Thank you so much. The political ramifications, had they been successful, are too much to think of."

Cushman blushed. The uncomfortable look on his face quickly gave way to apprehension. He grabbed his friend's shoulder. "Red, what if you weren't the only targets?"

"What do you mean? You think they may have targeted others?" Jefferson's face showed immediate concern.

"Look, it makes sense. You said British ships have been sighted off New York, that Washington is in New York, making preparations for an invasion. What if right before the invasion takes place, the leadership is taken out? The combination of a large British invasion and the loss of the leaders of the Continental Congress would be a devastating one-two punch. What did Alexander the Great say? *'Bring me the head of Darius and I will conquer Persia.'*"

"I hardly think the death of the seven of us would derail our efforts," Jefferson countered unconvincingly.

John Adams, seated near the two, looked up and interrupted. "I overheard your concern, young Benjamin. Thomas, I have to disagree with you. Like it or not, great movements in human history frequently revolve around the talents of a few inspiring the many. Jesus comes to mind. It indeed would be an excellent strategy by our enemies to remove the leadership of the Congress. It would make more sense to eliminate…" Adams hesitated. He couldn't finish his sentence.

"John, Samuel," Jefferson whispered.

"Killing the president of the Continental Congress and the moral leader of the revolutionary movement would deliver a blow we may never fully recover from," Adams suggested, his face revealing frightful concern to the possibility.

Chapter 9

Democracy is two wolves and a lamb voting on what to have for lunch. Liberty is a well-armed lamb contesting the vote!

—Benjamin Franklin

June 24, 1776
Philadelphia

Aaron Tucker was in his late seventies. His father and mother met on a ship coming to America in 1698. Within one year, the couple married, and Aaron was born in 1700. His father made a good living as a carpenter in both New York and Philadelphia. Aaron inherited the same passion and skill as the father but applied it in a different manner, barrel-making. Aaron Tucker loved making barrels. His father's best friend was a master cooper who eagerly took on young Tucker as an apprentice. Eventually, the father joined the son and created *Tucker Barrels*, Father and Son.

As colonial trade began to expand unlike anything in history, *Tucker Barrels* of Philadelphia would ride a wave of success. Almost everything transported on ship, wagon, or cart, including cotton, rum, sugar, wheat, corn, tea, and spices, was placed in barrels.

Aaron Tucker not only was a talented cooper; he was also a visionary in running a small company. Tucker divided his workforce into individual units. Competitors poked fun at this division of labor, but customers were not only satisfied but were thrilled; they received a better barrel at a lower price.

Aaron Tucker and his father grew very wealthy through their hard work, attention to detail, and commitment to excellence.

Unfortunately for Aaron Tucker, those same qualities were not passed down to his only son, Jacob.

Jacob Tucker smiled as he pushed his father into the library in a wheeled chair. *Tucker Barrels* especially made the chair for their founder.

"Gentlemen, my name is Aaron Tucker," Tucker said in a quiet voice. "This is my son, Jacob."

Both Hancock and Adams rose from their comfortable chairs and approached the wheelchair-bound Mr. Tucker.

"A pleasure to meet you, sir. John Hancock, president of the Continental Congress." Hancock was surprised at the strong handshake he received from the old man, not so surprised by the feeble handshake delivered by the frail and scrawny son. "Indeed a pleasure, sir. Samuel Adams, Massachusetts delegate to the Congress." Adams received similar handshakes and a knowing arch of the eyebrows from Hancock.

"I certainly know who you are. But what do I owe this visit from such distinguished gentlemen?" the older Tucker said genuinely.

The look of sheer surprise registered strongly on the faces of two congressional delegates. The wide smile on the face of Jacob Tucker went unnoticed.

Deborah Johnson took a deep breath and slowly exhaled. She stood on the back patio of City Tavern, still in shock. Her manager was badly wounded; her friend Gerard was most certainly dead. *They tried to kill them. She lied to me.* Deborah took another deep breath and began to consider damage control.

She was certain her role would remain concealed. However, she had no desire to go to prison. Deborah had to be certain. She immediately shifted into survival mode. She quickly tore at her blouse, nearly removing the entire left sleeve. Next, she violently slapped herself on the cheek several times. Finally, she dug her fingernails into her bare shoulder until she brought blood.

Deborah softly stepped off the rear patio. She silently worked her way to the same outside kitchen door the assassins had used to enter City Tavern. Upon entering the kitchen, Deborah heard noises coming from the storage closet. A plan began to take hold in her head as she moved to free her fellow workers.

She found the cooks, bound and gagged, quickly removed their bindings, and motioned them to follow her into the back coffee room. As the door to the dining room flew open, it stopped short on the feet of the slain Gerard Jackson. Deborah gasped loudly at the bloody sight of the former slave.

Ben Cushman spun quickly around, gun in hand. Recognition came quickly as he lowered his pistol and walked toward the frightened staff.

The sight of her dead friend overwhelmed Deborah; she fell into Cushman's arms and began to sob heavily. An awkward moment passed before she looked down at his arm and pulled away. "You're bleeding."

"I'm fine. Just a scratch." He smiled but winced in pain when she grabbed his arm for a closer look.

"Liar." She gently tore away part of his sleeve and wiped clean his wound. Their eyes met briefly. He turned away first, blushing like a teenager. A faint hint of a smile appeared on her face.

"I'll be fine, but you look awful. What happened to you?" He guided her to an empty table and motioned for the two workers to join them.

The younger of the two cooks spoke first. "A man burst into the kitchen from the back door, pretending to want food. He pulled a pistol. Soon three more came in. They tied us up, put us in the storage room. Gerard tried to warn you."

Six delegates gathered around, listening to the story. Franklin and the mysterious Major Hall were still speaking in hushed tones across the hall.

"He knocked down one of the men and kicked the other. Then, he ran for the door....They shot him, shot him like an animal! He was a good man, a good man," declared the fellow cook.

THE SIGNERS

"That's him, that's the guy who shot Gerard." Cook number 2 pointed to the bearded assassin with a large hole in his head.

"Well, Major Hall delivered rapid justice to him," Cushman said, trying to console them.

"We started to run, but he produced another pistol and forced us back into the storage room. He locked the door from the outside. That's all we know. Ms. Deborah just freed us," the first cook finished his story.

All eyes turned to Ms. Deborah to hear her account.

"I can't add too much." She began crying softly; the tears were real, but she was torn by the betrayal from Lydia, and possibly her own father, and her desire to keep her role in the horrible affair a secret. "I was cleaning up Mr. Hancock's table when I heard a gunshot. I ran around back, into the kitchen." Deborah pointed to the rear of the tavern. "The bearded one was helping that one over there." She pointed toward the unconscious assassin, courtesy of Jefferson's heavy tankard.

"I don't know what came over me. I ran at them. They grabbed me and hit me. I fought them, but they were too strong. I must have fallen and passed out. When I came to, I heard noises in the storage room and let them out," she said, nodding to the cooks.

Deborah's mind raced rapidly, trying to think of every variable that could trip up her story. What if the cooks couldn't remember a struggle? What if the assassin woke up and started spilling his guts? Luckily, no more questions came her way. Cushman listened to the beautiful waitress intensely. Even in her condition, she seemed poised and confident. He wanted to continue to speak with her, but he had more important things to worry about. Was this just the beginning? Were they still in danger? Perhaps more assassins were awaiting them outside? He needed answers but had only one lead. Cushman grabbed a full tankard and launched it into the face of the unconscious assassin, getting the reaction he hoped for. The assassin began to stir.

"A perfectly good waste of beer, Mr. Cushman." Benjamin Franklin had returned and placed his hands on top of Cushman's shoulders and grinned. "What are you thinking?"

"I'm thinking this degenerate knows something," replied the Virginia militiaman.

"If he does, I'm sure he won't offer it up freely." Franklin arched his eyebrows and frowned.

"He'll talk. I'll make him talk, one way or another," grunted Cushman.

Directly across from City Tavern, Andrew O'Leary lay in a vacant lot with a direct view of the front entrance. To his left was Constable Rice's empty watch box. He lay prone on a tattered blanket, several old crates on either side of him, a smaller crate directly in front of him. British soldiers referred to this as *sniping*, to shoot from a hidden place. It was in reference to hunting the difficult and elusive game bird the snipe. Future generations would call this a sniper's nest. O'Leary could rest his rifles on the crate for a steady aim. At less than one hundred yards, it would be easy shooting.

Something's wrong, O'Leary thought to himself. *Something is very wrong.* He quickly began reviewing what had just occurred. A man had exited City Tavern to tend to his horse. When a single gunshot was fired a few minutes later, the man did not run or ride away like a normal patron. Instead, he reached into his saddlebag and crept back into the tavern. O'Leary couldn't see what he had retrieved, but he assumed it was a pistol; moments later, there had been more gunshots. At the time the shots were fired, a strange man arrived at the tavern, expertly dismounting his horse, and, with pistol drawn, stealthily entered the front door. Another gunshot soon followed, but since then, nothing but silence. It had been at least five minutes since the last shot, and no one had exited or entered the popular tavern.

His mind raced. If the assassins had retreated through the kitchen, then Tompkins would have taken care of them. He was a crack shot. But there hadn't been any further gunfire. There were no side entrances or exits. What about the strangers? Had they interrupted the attack? But how could they know? And besides, they were but two to their four. O'Leary was tempted to go look into one of the front windows, but Tompkins had given him strict orders to wait. He couldn't run for instructions, for fear of missing the intended victims. *If we do this again,* he thought, *we must bring a third man to act as a messenger.* It had been over eight minutes. *Something has gone wrong!*

Suddenly, the front door sprung open. O'Leary sighted his gun at the new target. Disappointment washed over him as he quickly realized it wasn't one of *Rourke's Ruffians.* He watched as the young male ran straight for the police watch box. Finding no one inside, he continued west down Walnut as fast as his feet could fly.

Something has gone very wrong!

Ben Cushman threw another mug of beer into the face of the assassin now sitting upright in a chair.

"Hey, enough already! Whaddu trying to do, drown me?" The defiant tone in his voice was reassuring to Cushman. Defiance meant confidence, confidence meant hope, and hope meant this criminal wanted to keep on living. Cushman knew then he had a chance.

"Tell me what I want to know and maybe I won't hurt you, you sack of pig guts," Cushman whispered softly in his ear.

"Kiss my arse," he hissed, then spit in Cushman's direction.

Cushman clenched his fist and punched the assassin directly in the chest, knocking him onto the hard wooden floor. He looked toward Jefferson and whispered, "Don't want him knocked out. We need him awake and afraid."

Cushman yanked the assassin back into the chair. "Now, now, there is no need for profanity. I just want you to answer a few questions."

"The hell with you!"

Cushman's punch slammed into his face. He collapsed to the floor, blood streaming down his face, while the colonial delegates looked on squeamishly.

"What happened to 'We need him awake'?" Jefferson queried, a slight smile on his face.

"Ah, more afraid than awake." Cushman shrugged while effortlessly pulling the assassin up and roughly dumping him back into the chair. "I said no profanity. Now, I've grown weary of your insolence, so here is what we are going to do. We are going to play a little game I learned from the Shawnee Indians. I am going to ask you a question and you are going to give me an honest answer. If you refuse to answer, or if I think you told a lie, I will cut off one of your fingers." Cushman emphasized his remark by twisting the assassin's right small finger. "We will continue the game until you have no fingers left. Then I will cut off other, more private extremities, if you know what I mean." Cushman stared into the killer's eyes; they were filled with anger and hate. But more importantly, they were also filled with fear. *There's a chance,* Ben thought. "Ready to play?" Cushman grabbed his hand, putting it flush on the table, his knife firmly placed atop his right small finger.

"Benjamin." Jefferson slid close to his friend and whispered softly in his ear, "We are honorable men here. I don't think what you are about to do is appropriate—"

Cushman shot a look at Jefferson, stopping him in midsentence. It clearly indicated to all present that their talents were more suited for the political arena, whereas this was his area of expertise.

Major Hall nodded his consent, and Jefferson nervously backed away.

Steady and confident, Cushman continued his interrogation. "Who ordered this assassination?" The Virginian applied enough pressure on the knife to begin to pierce the skin. Major Hall held him still.

The assassin's eyes bulged. Fear replaced confidence. "I…I…I… don't know, honestly, I don't know," he stammered.

"Wrong answer," Cushman put all his weight on his knife, and it easily sliced off the killer's finger. The separated finger began to float on an ever-forming pool of blood. A piercing scream reverberated throughout the room as most of the people turned away in disgust. Franklin looked on with curious interest in Cushman's interrogation, but the rest of the delegation appeared shocked at the violent act. Deborah Johnson ran from the room, distressed by what had just happened.

"Let's try again before you pass out."

"No, no, please, I don't know who hired us. All my orders came from Mr. Black." He pointed to his dead boss; Cushman had put a ball into his eye.

Cushman brought the knife firmly down on the assassin's ring finger. "Okay, maybe I believe you, maybe not, so there better be no doubt in your next answer. Were there other targets at other locations?"

The assassin hesitated, and Cushman pushed the knife deeper into his ring finger. "Wait, please, wait!" The assassin was now screaming. "Yes, yes, there was to be more, tonight and later this week!" he cried out, the pain throbbing with each breath.

"Who? Where?" Cushman placed more pressure on the finger.

"I don't know! Please, I don't know! But…but…I overheard the boss talking with one of the others. He said they would all die, all the leaders."

"What else?" Cushman demanded.

"A name, somebody's name, I can't remember," the assassin stammered, his eyes filled with hatred and pain.

Cushman took a handful of hair and placed the knife along the killer's neck. "I'm growing weary of this game, and we are jumping ahead to the finish. Remember that name or I will cut your throat."

Major Hall held the captive firmly; the expression on his face clearly displayed his approval of how Cushman was handling the interrogation. He was the only one. Even Franklin appeared to be getting worried over the violent tactics.

The assassin trembled with fear. "I'm trying, honest…something like Temper…no, Taylor…no…"

Cushman looked at the men surrounding the table. "Where did Hancock say they were going tonight, some financier…?"

Livingston remembered first. "I'm sure they said Tucker, yes, Mr. Tucker."

"That's correct, Robert, it was a Mr. Tucker," Abraham Clark stated confidently.

"Was it Tucker?" Cushman growled at the beaten assassin, pressing the knife firmly into the killer's neck.

"Yes, Tucker, it was Tucker!" An unsure relief settled over the assassin.

"Does anyone know this Tucker?" Cushman glanced around the room. "Anyone?"

Everyone looked at one another and shrugged.

"Afraid not, Ben." A dejected Franklin summarized the mood of the room and the realization that John Hancock and Samuel Adams were in grave danger.

Suddenly, a quiet voice was heard. "I'm not sure, but..." All eyes turned to the back of the room, from whence one of the two surviving cooks began to speak. "But there was a Mr. Tucker who came here frequently when the tavern was first open. A barrel maker, I believe... *Tucker Barrels*. He stopped coming about a year ago because of some illness or injury."

"If he owns a barrel company, he could be wealthy enough to donate money," observed John Adams.

"It's the only lead we've got. Do you have any idea where he lives?" Cushman questioned the young cook.

"They said it wasn't far from here," declared John Hart.

"I believe somewhere down on Front Street, near the wharfs," the cook said proudly.

Cushman grabbed the assassin by the shirt. "Is there anybody else coming here?"

"No, I swear, no. There were only four of us, I swear!"

Jefferson pulled Cushman aside and quietly spoke to his friend. "Ben, I sent the other cook to find some police and a doctor. They should be here soon. What about Hancock and Adams?"

Cushman's mind worked quickly. "Okay, here's what we've got to do. Gentlemen, it is very obvious a major plot was aimed at the leadership of the Continental Congress tonight. It may still be going on. There may still be people outside, waiting for you. Stay put until help arrives. Red has sent for a doctor and the police. I will ride down to Front Street and warn Mr. Hancock and Mr. Adams.

"I'm going with you." This was Jefferson in a commanding voice.

A chorus of "Nos!" rang out from the other delegates.

"It's too dangerous," declared Sherman.

"You're too valuable. You must finish the Declaration of Independence," stated Hart.

"Thomas, no, we need you." This from Adams.

"Stop. We don't have time to argue. Ben, do you know your way around Philadelphia?" He didn't wait for Cushman to answer. "No, you don't. I will not put my friend in such danger. Besides, if something happens to me, Mr. Adams will have to write the declaration, and that will suit me just fine, even though I am ten times the better writer." Jefferson glanced at Adams, throwing his words back at him.

Benjamin Franklin looked over to Major Hall, who nodded enthusiastically. "Gentlemen, perhaps a better solution would be to send Major Hall with our Mr. Cushman. He is, after all, more suited for this type of thing, and he is familiar with Philadelphia."

"I will be happy to help Mr. Cushman." Hall spoke with a confident tone.

All eyes turned to Jefferson, who stubbornly retorted, "Very well, but I'm still going along. I will let these two handle any trouble that may result."

Adams smiled. "Well then, go. Be careful, and please help my fellow Bostonians."

O'Leary was starting to think he should leave. But his greed got the better of him. *No bodies, no pay.* The pay was more than he could make in three years working on the docks. No, he could stay a while longer.

Just then, the front door burst open again as three men ran out and headed for the hitching post. Again, they were not his targets, so he relaxed the gun and tried to recognize the men. *The same horse, he jumped on the same horse with the saddlebag,* he thought to himself. The other man leaped on a horse at the end of the post. *The late arriver.* The third man boarded a horse a block farther down. He was becoming more confused by the minute.

As the three men rode toward the river, O'Leary heard more noise. It was coming from the opposite direction, the unmistakable clip-clopping of horse's hooves striking the cobblestone streets. Four horses carrying five people. *Now what?* The riders eased the horses to a stop in front of City Tavern and hurriedly dismounted. O'Leary recognized the young man who ran from the tavern earlier. *He must have finally found some police. Yep, three uniforms.* He wondered who the final man was, older and well-dressed. They entered the tavern rapidly. *Now what?*

After explaining the situation, Benjamin Franklin ordered two of the three constables to find the Tucker home. Luckily for Franklin, the two constables were both self-proclaimed Patriots. The rebellion was depending on their swiftness and courage, Franklin had impressed upon them. They left quickly. The forth man to arrive with the group was Dr. Abraham Presser.

Dr. Presser tended first to City Tavern's manager, John Trumbull; he repacked the one-inch wound near his shoulder. Sherman and Hart helped move Trumbull into the tavern room, where a cot was found.

Dr. Presser spoke quietly. "I have given Mr. Trumbull a dose of laudanum. It will ease the pain and allow him to sleep."

"Laudanum?" Hart looked puzzled.

"An extract of opium mixed with sweet wine. It is an effective pain reliever. Unfortunately, there is no exit wound. When he recovers, we will need to remove the lead ball. It is dangerous to leave it in," Dr. Presser answered confidently.

The three men returned to the back coffee room. The one remaining constable was getting ready to move the prisoner to the Walnut Street Jail. Dr. Presser noticed the blood oozing from his right hand and quickly noticed the severed finger. He looked at Benjamin Franklin. Franklin responded by shrugging his shoulders with a questioning look on his face. The doctor decided not to pursue the matter.

Halting the constable, Dr. Presser bandaged the assassin's mangled hand and then went to check on Deborah Johnson's injuries.

Franklin pulled the constable aside and quietly instructed, "Be careful, Constable. This man is a trained killer. We need to question him about many things."

"Don't worry, Mr. Franklin. I have a strong personal stake in this one. My best friend, Cyrus Rice, is supposed to be on watch tonight, across the street." He pointed in the direction of the watch box. "He wasn't at the box and hasn't been seen. I fear the worst, and if this guy can lead us to him, I will take very special care of him."

"I am truly sorry about your friend. I'm afraid this crime was carefully planned out. Your fears are warranted. Please let me know when you learn anything. By the way, Constable, what is your name?"

"Thorp, Edward Thorp," the constable replied. He was properly impressed by Mr. Franklin's seemingly genuine concern for his fellow policeman. The rumors about Franklin's having the *common* touch were indeed legitimate. "Thank you, sir, I will do my best." The constable began to escort his prisoner out the front door of City Tavern.

"Good luck, Mr. Thorp, and thank you," hailed Franklin.

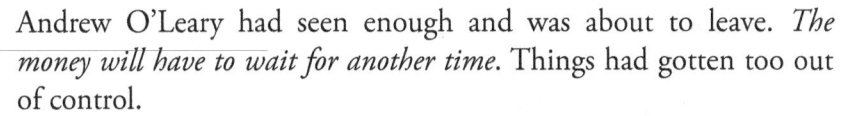

Andrew O'Leary had seen enough and was about to leave. *The money will have to wait for another time.* Things had gotten too out of control.

Before he could stand, the front door opened again. It was another constable, and *yes, yes,* it was one of *Rourke's Ruffians*. That crazy Rourke had made both Tompkins and O'Leary watch the ritual the assassins had gone through, complete with the wine, hashish, and the women. He thought the ritual foolish, but he enjoyed the interaction with the women. There was no doubt the constable was leading one of the killers from the building.

O'Leary didn't hesitate. He sighted his rifle carefully and squeezed the trigger. The hammer drove the flint into the frizzen, lifting it to expose the gunpowder. The spark ignited the powder. The lead ball exploded out of the precision-rifled barrel at approximately four hundred feet per second. An expert marksman he was, the speeding ball striking the assassin just below his right temple. Part of the assassin's head exploded into blood, skull fragments, and brain tissue, showering the constable.

Constable Thorp's instincts kicked in. He dived behind the watering trough. Staying down for what seemed like an eternity, he slowly peered over the trough into the dark, vacant lot. A noise to his right indicated a door rapidly opening.

"Get back inside!" Thorp screamed. "Keep that door closed!"

Benjamin Franklin obeyed, relieved that Constable Thorp was alive.

Thorp pulled out a pistol he carried unbeknownst to his superiors. Scanning the lot from his protective perch, he spied several crates, a possible hiding place.

Thorp's anger over the probable loss of his best friend and the death of his prisoner overtook any caution he might have felt. He sprinted across the street at a forty-five-degree angle, grateful to make it to a lone tree. Taking aim at the crates, Thorp threw caution to the wind and ran toward the hideout, and with pistol drawn, he launched himself feetfirst into the tallest crate, causing it to crash forward. The crate turned over with a thud as Thorp popped up from the ground. No one was behind the crate. A tattered blanket was all that remained.

"It's quite obvious." John Adams was speaking to the remaining delegates and looking at Constable Thorp holding up the tattered blanket. "Whoever planned this wanted to make sure that the assassins would never be able to talk. Actually a brilliant plan."

"*Diabolical* would be more accurate," countered John Hart.

"We are not dealing with rank amateurs here. This plot was well financed and well-thought-out. I fear we were not the only targets," Roger Sherman suggested.

"It had to be local Tories," Adams interjected.

"No, local Tories don't have the guts for something so vicious. It has to be the British," suggested Hart.

"Or both," reasoned Franklin.

"Benjamin, what is it? You look puzzled?" questioned Hart.

"It just doesn't make sense. Don't get me wrong, I understand: kill the assassins and leave no trail. But how come only one to handle four? How did they know they would exit out the front door? Why not the back kitchen door, where they entered?" Franklin contemplated his theory out loud.

"Or the back hallway door," added Hart.

"Maybe they didn't," cautioned Clark.

"Maybe they didn't what?" Livingston countered.

"Maybe they didn't know which door they would leave. There are only three exit doors, one in the front and two in the back," Clark responded.

"So maybe there were two assassins, one outside in front and one in back." Franklin finished Clark's thought for him.

"Were? What about there *are* two assassins." Adams joined into the speculation.

"You mean…" Clark hesitated. "Out back?" he theorized.

Everybody looked toward the rear of City Tavern. "Wait just one moment," Constable Thorp barked in a commanding voice. "If anybody is going to investigate, it will be me."

"Constable, I appreciate your valor, but we are all in this together. Being a citizen legislature does not exempt any of us from being a citizen soldier, with the possible exception of Mr. Franklin, of course," Clark stated, referring to Franklin's age.

"Mr. Clark, I take that as a compliment and promise not to criticize any of you for your youth and inexperience regarding the waging of war," observed the seventy-year-old Franklin.

"*Touché*, Mr. Franklin. Constable Thorp, if you have a plan, please include *all* of us," ordered Clark.

"Very well…look, if there is someone waiting to kill the remaining assassins, they have most likely fled by now. To guarantee success, they would have had to place killers in positions to see both the front and back doors. They would need a clear line of sight to pick them off as they exited the building. If he is still out there, waiting, maybe we can lay a trap."

"Go on. Sounds good," encouraged Clark.

"Sounds dangerous," added Adams.

"I will attempt to surprise the killer by getting behind him," stated Thorp.

"But there are too many hiding places," claimed Livingston.

"True, but I can narrow it down. Assuming these two were a team, they would have used the same weapons and tactics. The ball that killed our assassin had to have been fired from a rifle, not a musket," concluded Constable Thorp.

"How would you know this?" questioned John Hart.

"The crates that were set up across the street were positioned to hide the killer. They were over 250 feet from the entrance. Muskets are only accurate from about 100 feet, and even then, you better be a great marksman. No, this killer had a rifle. So in order to find his lair, I will search for a concealed area about 250 feet from the back of the tavern, someplace that would cover both doors. Shouldn't be a problem at all," a confident Thorp suggested.

"Impressive, Mr. Thorp," praised Franklin. "Now, what do you need of us?"

"A target," replied Thorp.

"I'll do it. I'm the oldest," volunteered Franklin.

"No, no, can't lose all that experience," joked Clark. "I have a better idea."

Ten minutes later, Thorp was positioned in a small grove of trees behind City Tavern. He had exited the building from the front, circled around to the back, and surveyed the area for over five minutes, looking for any movement within the wooded area. He was confident he had located the sniper's nest. *There*, approximately 230 feet from the rear of City Tavern, a small grove of trees sat isolated beside Logan's Alley. It was the perfect spot, well placed for both distance and stealth. *If they're still out there, that has to be the place.*

Crouching low and staying in the shadows, he slowly worked his way toward the target. He could feel his heart racing, sweat pouring from his face. A lone tree stood approximately thirty paces from his position and the suspected assassin. A perfect place to observe. He made his way forward, wiping the sweat from his forehead, trying desperately to block the building fear of the moment.

A noise. Thorp glanced to his left. The kitchen door at City Tavern began to slowly open. He noted a dark form slowly moving out of the doorway toward the alley. The person was tall, with a long coat; a tricorne hat was pulled down low, concealing the face. The figure came to a stop, as if contemplating his options. Thorp took a deep breath and continued moving forward.

There, something moved. Now or never. Thorp broke into a full sprint, eyes never wavering as he neared the grove of trees. *Almost there.* Suddenly, Thorp stumbled, tripping over an unseen barrier, landing flat on his face, his pistol knocked clean out of his hand. He scrambled to his knees, desperately reaching everywhere for his weapon. He was in the open and defenseless.

Abruptly his hands came in contact with something. His mind was racing, and his heart pounded so hard he thought it would leap out of his chest. His hands quickly canvassed the object when it suddenly hit him. It was a body. His eyes gradually focused on the deep gash in the neck and the face that was unmistakable, his best friend. Cyrus Rice was dead. Fear and grief gripped Constable Thorp. His eyes filled with tears as he stared at his best friend.

Fearing the worse, Abraham Clark bolted from the back door, knocking over the coatrack decoy they had cleverly pushed into the alley. Pistol drawn, he came to the kneeling Thorp. He immediately understood but continued to scan the tree line.

Within seconds, the remaining delegates stood surrounding Thorp and the dead body. Clark walked slowly into the trees and returned within a minute, a long rifle in his hand.

"Well, gentlemen, our instincts were correct. Must have left in a hurry. Forgot one of his rifles." Clark held the gun like a trophy as he strode toward the group.

"This must be your friend, Constable Thorp." Ben Franklin placed both hands upon Thorp's shoulders. "Let's come inside, and we can prepare—"

Thorp suddenly bolted up and looked at the faces of the delegates to the Second Continental Congress.

"Gentlemen"—his steely eyes penetrated each of them and then settled on the kindly old Ben Franklin—"promise me, promise me that my friend will not have died in vain. Promise me we will prevail. Promise me we will be a free nation. Promise me you will punish whoever did this to my friend!"

They looked around at one another, each of their eyes showing great resolve. The most unlikely voice rang out with steady firmness.

"Constable Thorp, all I can promise in the days ahead is hardship and suffering. But when the dust settles, I promise you we will prevail, we will unite as a new nation, free from tyranny. I promise…" Robert Livingston's voice trailed off.

Adams smiled and shook Livingston's hand. "Truer words were never spoken. Welcome aboard, Robert."

Patrick Rourke and his exotic companion, Lydia Ames, sat comfortably inside his expensive carriage parked two hundred yards from the home of Aaron Tucker. The carriage was the newest and most recognizable status symbol of the wealthy class of colonial Americans.

It was built by H. J. Mulliner and Co. of Northampton England, and Rourke had personally traveled to the carriage builder's factory in Northampton to oversee the final construction. It was the most expensive carriage the company had ever built because of the accessories Rourke had added. From glass windows to velvet interior, it was as luxurious as a royal coach.

The exterior was purposely plain, painted black without any sign of opulence. Once rare in the colonies, comfortable horse-drawn carriages were becoming more commonplace in many of the larger cities. Rourke worried about taking the carriage so close to the scene of the crime, but his worries were trumped by his desire to watch the demise of the arrogant Hancock.

The Tucker home was set back farther than his neighbors', making it harder to see the front exterior. A line of trees protruded from both sides of the house, midway to the street. However, directly across the street was a streetlamp that gave the couple a decent view of the front yard. Rourke *was* probably too close to the unfolding scene, but he didn't rise to his current circumstances by being cautious. *Besides,* he thought, *watching these two traitors get their comeuppance will be worth the potential danger.*

Lydia Ames moved closer to Rourke, placing her right hand on Rourke's thigh with a gentle squeeze. "How much longer, my love?" she cooed.

"Soon, very soon," he said with excitement in his voice.

"Where are your men positioned?"

"Look closely. They are located near the trees on each side of the house, two to the north and two to the south." Rourke pointed as he spoke.

"You don't like Hancock very much. Why is that?"

"He's a cocky bastard, thinks he's better than everybody else. Besides, my ships compete with his. This will be good for business," Rourke responded, his resentment of Hancock was deep.

"What about the other one, Adams? Which one?"

"Samuel. He is the key. He is one of the smartest of the rebels. A natural leader, he is not pursuing this course for personal gain. He truly believes all the drivel that comes from his mouth. No, these two are the biggest targets. If all else fails and we only get these two, it will have been a successful night. Then we can move to the next wave."

Lydia smiled, recognizing her recent secret meeting in New York with Dr. Smith and Mrs. Gibbons would soon bear fruit.

"I'm sorry, but didn't you invite us here tonight, to discuss aiding the war effort, Mr. Tucker?" An exasperated John Hancock stared at his wheelchair-bound host, Aaron Tucker.

The son, Jacob, stepped from behind the wheelchair and replied, "Gentlemen, please forgive my father. His health has been poor this past year, and it seems to have affected his memory."

"But didn't you send word through Sam? Who set this meeting?" Hancock questioned his colleague.

"Why, Morris, of course," responded an equally frustrated Adams, referring to the Philadelphia banker and fellow delegate.

"Well, of course, my father and Mr. Morris are close friends. I know my father has spoken to Mr. Morris recently and extended invitations for delegates to visit our home. However, they spoke nothing of finance. Gentlemen, I apologize if you thought otherwise," commented the younger Tucker.

Samuel Adams studied the senior Tucker as his son spoke. There was something odd about Aaron Tucker, something wrong, but Adams couldn't put his finger on it. Maybe it was his eyes; they seemed to stare off in the distance. But he had noticed clarity when they were introduced. It was strange. The old man was almost childlike, attentive for one moment, then totally unfocused the next. His handshake had been firm and steady, rare for a man in his seventies. *Something is odd here. Yes, something is definitely wrong. Either old man Tucker is a very good actor or he truly doesn't know about tonight's meeting.* Adams thought of a third possibility. *Perhaps age has indeed taken his memory away.*

"It seems like a terrible misunderstanding, gentlemen. I knew of your arrival tonight, but I assumed it was just a courtesy call. My father knew as well. He tends to forget these types of meetings more and more," Jacob Tucker continued.

Rourke's plan was working to perfection. He had assured Jacob Tucker that a little miscommunication, added to his father's illness and bad memory, would provide for a perfectly harmless misunderstanding. No one would ever think they were part of a complex conspiracy. Combined with the other assassinations, the Tuckers would become sympathetic figures caught in the middle of a terrible plot. No one would ever blame them.

"Please, gentlemen, finish your cider, but as you can see, my father is in no shape to discuss serious matters," Jacob Tucker commanded.

Hancock teetered between anger and pity. Angry for what looked like a perfect waste of time, and pity for old man Tucker's condition and his peculiar son. He had no desire to stay another moment. A reaction Rourke had predicted.

Hancock gave Sam Adams a *let's-get-the-hell-out-of-here* look. Adams shrugged his shoulders in agreement.

"I am also sorry for the misunderstanding, but Sam and I are both very busy and must attend to other business," an annoyed Hancock declared.

The unusual night took yet another turn when Hancock was startled as he took one last glance at the trancelike stare of Aaron Tucker. It was as if a fuse was lit behind his eyes. Suddenly they were clear and alive. "Gentlemen, must you leave so soon? Aren't you going to try to talk me out of my money?"

The two Massachusetts rebels came to an abrupt halt and turned to scrutinize the old man. Both were shocked at the transition that came over Aaron Tucker. It was as if a new person was occupying the wheelchair. His eyes seemed alert, not distant; his demeanor was friendly and inviting.

"After all the trouble of coming out tonight, we might as well discuss the current political situation. Maybe you can convince me your side is in the right." He smiled and gestured for them to return to the comfortable chairs near the fireplace.

No one noticed the amazing transformation of Jacob Tucker. His face was flush with anger. *Damn drugs,* he thought to himself. *Should have used a stronger doze. They are outside, waiting. What now?* Trying hard not to panic, he envisioned several different scenarios. Ultimately his decision was to do nothing; his father couldn't entertain too long into the night, and the end result would still be the same, later rather than sooner. He saw no downside to his decision. Tucker wondered if he should warn Rourke's henchmen of the delay, then thought better of it. *Full deniability.*

The twenty-eight-year-old paced back and forth in front of the luxurious carriage. The New Englander felt lucky to be working for John Hancock. His father was a major partner in Hancock's thriving business empire. A stint as Hancock's coachman and personal assistant would only enhance his position in his father's eyes. The young man was not too worried about his more distant future but was exceedingly anxious about his near future. Hancock had said the meeting should be over quickly, and if that were true, he would have time to meet with her again tonight. He had met her at a dance not long ago, and although she never charged him money, he swore she was a prostitute. She was exciting and vivacious, and he couldn't wait to see her again tonight. *What is taking them so long?*

"Hey, mate, wouldn't 'appen to 'ave a cigarette now, would 'cha?" The stranger had appeared out of nowhere and startled the coachman.

The New Englander's anticipation of his nightly dalliance with the beautiful Ms. Sally had put him into a good mood, and he cheerfully replied, "Why, sure, here you go." He reached into his pocket and pulled out a pouch of tobacco and some papers. The two men began to roll the cigarettes. The anticipation of a good smoke and what was to come later tonight put the young driver into an even better mood. *If only Hancock and Adams would hurry* was his last thought.

"What now?" Ben Cushman shouted as he reined in his horse.

The three men stopped directly in the center of the intersection at Walnut and Front Streets. They searched for a clue as to the whereabouts of the Tucker home.

"This is Front Street, but which direction?" Cushman's head was on a swivel.

"I don't know. Penn Landing is there." Jefferson pointed toward the river. "It could be either direction along Front."

"Or he could live down one of the accessory roads that lead down to the river," suggested Major Hall.

"Red, how do they normally travel, by horse or carriage?" Cushman continued to gaze nervously in all directions, desperately looking for an answer.

"Usually by horse, but Hancock has a brand-new carriage, and I know he has a driver ready to work at all times," replied Jefferson.

"If I went begging for money, I would want to make a good impression," added Jacob Hall.

"Okay, then it's settled. We need to look for a carriage and driver," declared Jefferson.

"Mr. Jefferson, this could get dangerous real quick. I think it best that Mr. Cushman and I take it from here," Major Hall suggested. Cushman nodded in agreement but knew what was coming.

"Major Hall, I appreciate your concern, but we will need to cover a lot of ground in a very short period of time. Since there are three of us, it makes sense that each one of us search a certain direction," Jefferson pointed out logically.

"No use arguing with him when he gets this way," Cushman stated emphatically while grinning at Major Hall. "But no one goes it alone. We meet back here in five minutes, ten tops, and exchange notes. Agreed?" Everyone nodded.

"What if there is more than one carriage?" Jefferson asked.

"Remember the location, and then we'll cross that bridge," responded Major Hall as he rode away.

It was too late and too much to hope for a pedestrian to point out the home of Mr. Aaron Tucker. The carriage was their only hope, and that hope came with a caveat. What if they rode horses tonight?

Cushman headed south on Front Street, spotting no carriages after one block. He passed Spruce Street, two blocks, and still no carriages. As he approached the third intersection at Pine Street, he finally spotted one. Steering the horse toward the coach, he found it empty. He carefully studied the homes nearby and made mental notes, keenly aware of the possible danger. But time was a luxury, and caution was not an option.

Dismounting effortlessly, Cushman grabbed the bridle of the nearest of the team of horses, placing his hand gently on its chest. The heart rate was rapid, indicating the team had recently stopped. Cushman estimated that Hancock and Adams would have been gone from City Tavern for over two hours; the odds of this being Hancock's carriage were not good.

Cushman decided to ride half a block south of Pine with no luck. He had been gone for close to ten minutes. He pivoted on his horse and urged it into a full gallop, heading back to meet Jefferson and Hall, hoping they had better luck.

Jefferson's reputation throughout the colonies was that of a splendid scholar, writer, and inventor. Few realized that Jefferson was also a gifted athlete. Tall and rangy, he was able to outrun most of his friends in his youth, with the exception of Ben Cushman. An excellent shot, he could handle both a pistol and a rifle; he was a talented hunter and fisherman. A fine swimmer, he often would swim across large rivers without a problem. But without question, his greatest skill was his horsemanship. Even the rugged and athletic Ben Cushman could not match his expertise on a horse.

Jefferson rode north easily, scanning both sides of the street for Hancock's carriage. *No luck.* He continued on past Chestnut Street.

Jefferson noted the housing seemed to be getting more lavish as he worked his way toward Market Street. Up ahead, under the soft light of the streetlamp, Jefferson spotted a potential target. He approached cautiously and decided to stay in the middle of the road, casually glancing in and around the carriage as he continued to ride past. *This could be it,* he thought nervously, trying desperately to remain calm. If a trap had been set for Hancock and Adams, he didn't want to wander into the middle of it. Nearby the carriage, he noticed two men talking softly while smoking cigarettes. He decided not to approach the men, fearing their loyalties. The two men briefly acknowledge the passing horseman, then resumed their conversation as if Jefferson were a beggar.

Urging his horse forward, Jefferson took mental pictures of the home directly in front of the carriage, also noting the neighboring homes. Across the street, he spied an empty lot. The home directly in front of the carriage was set back deeper than its neighbors. Lights were shining through several windows, whereas the neighboring homes were dark. Jefferson's instinct's told him Hancock and Adams were here, and he almost turned to head back to meet the others. He decided to continue north, not wishing to alert the two smokers. He nudged his horse forward, increasing to a gallop. Jefferson felt a surge of both fear and excitement. He prayed his friends were unharmed.

When Patrick Rourke first noticed the horseman riding toward the Tucker home, he immediately ordered his driver to dismount.

"Hide over there," Rourke ordered. "Make sure your pistol is ready, but wait for my signal."

"What's wrong? It's just one horseman." Lydia Ames spoke softly.

"Nothing, but I'm not taking any chances. These Patriots are all Good Samaritans," he added, noticing the lone horseman had hesitated in front of the Tucker home but was now continuing directly toward them.

"Close the curtains and sit quietly."

Rourke pulled the interior curtain to his window closed, leaving just enough to glimpse the approaching rider. His mind told him he was being overly vigilant, but then again, these were unusual times.

Jefferson immediately spied the second carriage. It was close to the intersection of Market and Front. It, too, looked new and very expensive. Could this be Hancock's carriage? He was so sure the first carriage was Hancock's, but now doubt began to creep into his mind. "Why don't they just carve their names into the side doors? It would make things easier," Jefferson whispered out loud.

Choosing the same tactic as before, Jefferson slowed as he approached the two horses and the top-of-the-line carriage. His plan was to pass by slowly, assessing the neighboring homes as he rode by.

Approaching within three horse lengths, Jefferson was concentrating on the carriage when he thought he saw a curtain on the side door move slightly. Startled, he nearly came to a stop but managed to keep the horse moving ahead.

Rourke's caution turned to worry as the rider drew closer with obvious interest in the parked carriage. Rourke stared through the slit in the curtain as the rider came within ten paces.

"Jesus, this can't be!" Rourke gasped, pulling back from the curtain. "It's impossible. He's supposed to be dead," Rourke swore under his breath, pounding his thighs with his balled-up fists.

"Who is it?" Lydia knew better to engage Rourke in conversation when he was like this, but her curiosity got the better of her.

"Jefferson, Goddamn Jefferson. I can't believe it. They were my best men! How could they have failed?"

"Maybe they didn't. Maybe he was the only one to escape," Lydia reasoned.

"But why would he come down here, alone? Something went wrong!" Rourke groaned as he pushed aside a small portion of the curtain and noticed Jefferson had ridden passed the carriage and was continuing north toward Arch Street.

"Maybe so, but he is alone. This presents us with another opportunity," Lydia calmly pointed out.

Rourke's tantrum slowly subsided as he thought of the delicious possibilities, but he quickly dismissed the idea.

"No, we mustn't jeopardize the operation involving Hancock and Adams. They are more important. If the opportunity arises afterward, we will act, but not before," he ordered forcefully.

Lydia Ames knew not to press her point. "Very well, but make plans nonetheless. Luck favors the bold."

Noting Jefferson was no longer in sight, Rourke signaled his driver to the carriage and spoke briefly to him. The driver quickly disappeared into the cool night air.

Jefferson continued riding to the intersection of Front and Arch. His mind raced to piece together what had just transpired. *No doubt*, he saw movement and then heard voices. The voices were barely audible, but he definitely heard two distinct voices, and one sounded female. At first he thought the voices were Hancock and Adams, possibly held hostage. But that made no sense.

Maybe it was a late-night tryst, a wealthy married man not wishing to risk exposure in public. Despite the rigorous religious and moral code of Pennsylvania, this was not an uncommon practice. That seemed the most logical explanation, but something continued to worry Jefferson about the second carriage. It was time to head back. Perhaps the three of them could figure it out.

Jefferson firmly placed two heels into the horse's flanks and began to gallop back toward Front and Walnut to exchange notes. Perhaps being overly cautious, he decided to ride quickly by both carriages rather than gather any more information. His instincts told him they were close to Hancock and Adams.

Arriving at the intersection without incident, Jefferson immediately noticed Cushman riding directly at him. Hall was nowhere to be seen.

Jefferson spoke first. "Find anything?"

"One carriage. Horses were still breathing hard. I don't think its Hancock's. What about you, any luck?"

The conversation was immediately interrupted when they heard the rapid approach of horse's hooves beating into the cobbled road. It was Hall, and his face betrayed the fact he had no leads. "Nothing," he announced dejectedly. "Either of you find anything?"

"Yes, I think so. Two carriages, both two blocks up, about two hundred paces apart. The first one is most promising. No one was inside, but two men standing nearby, probably drivers. The house directly in front of the carriage has several candles lit, and the neighbors' homes are completely dark."

"What about the second carriage?" Cushman asked anxiously.

"Odd, as I approached it, I saw a curtain move, then heard two voices. I believe a man and a woman."

"Probably someone is strapping a wench." Hall laughed.

"That's what I thought, but there was something very strange. I could feel it."

"You have good instincts. I trust them. But if you're sure you heard a woman, then I say our best bet is the first carriage and the house with the lights. Let's get started," Cushman declared.

The three unlikely comrades began to ride toward what they hoped would be Mr. Aaron Tucker's home, just two blocks to the north, praying they were in time to stop the assassination of the leaders of the American Revolution.

The two young constables dispatched by Benjamin Franklin to aid the trio of Cushman, Hall, and Jefferson had only gotten out of sight of City Tavern when the lead rider felt his reins go slack. Dismounting, he discovered the bridle had broken where the reins attached to the bit. Having both grown up in Philadelphia and not exposed to horses, neither constable was able to figure a temporary fix. After several attempts to jerry-rig the device, they decided to send one rider back to Walnut Street Jail for a replacement.

Without saying a word, Cushman motioned to Jefferson and Hall to ease their horses to the edge of the road, where the cobblestones ended and dirt began. The noise created from the horse's hooves contacting the cobblestone street was very noticeable, especially late at night, when there was little traffic.

Jefferson pointed, then whispered, "There. See the carriage? About three hundred yards. The house is set back, lots of trees on either side."

"A perfect spot for an ambush," remarked Cushman, recalling his skirmishes with the Shawnee Indians, in particular the famous Indian chief named Cornstalk.

Cushman noticed a small tree with a narrow trunk and signaled to stop. "Let's tie the horses here. We'll walk the rest of the way."

"Good idea. Like back home, out in the woods," Jefferson commented.

"Red, I think it's too dangerous. We need you to stay here and guard the horses," Cushman commanded while reaching into his saddlebag to retrieve weapons. Major Hall did the same.

Jefferson began to protest, but the stern glare he was receiving from the two militiamen caused him to halt immediately.

"Now that you're a famous lawyer, do you remember how to use one of these?" Cushman handed his friend a pistol.

"You know I do," responded Jefferson confidently as he lifted the deadly weapon for weight and feel. "Fully loaded and primed," the Virginia delegate noted. "Did you lose your memory in those cold Ohio winters? I was the one who taught you how to shoot." Jefferson smiled, palming the flintlock pistol.

"That wasn't you. It was Jane."

Major Hall immediately guessed that the resourceful Cushman and the famous Virginian had been boyhood friends, and stifled a silent laugh. "You two finished reminiscing? Mr. Jefferson, please stay back and out of sight."

With that, the two men began to jog toward the carriage, hugging the side of the road. They were concealed fairly well by the dark, moonless night. The next streetlamp was directly in front of what they hoped would be the Tucker home.

Cushman slowed to a stop and began to observe his surroundings. They knelt next to a waist-high wooden fence three houses from their target. The homes were offset from the street about twenty yards. Unlike in some of the neighborhoods toward the center of town, where the residences were connected into row houses, clumps of deciduous trees acted as a barrier between each of the impressive dwellings.

Cushman elbowed Major Hall and pointed to the trees. "Look there, Major. The trees run from the middle of the front yard to the back of the house. I'll bet my last pound there are two or more assassins waiting in those trees."

"If that indeed is the plan, then I would have men on both sides, no place to run," added Hall.

"I agree. The assassination attempt at City Tavern was well financed and well-thought-out. Whoever is responsible didn't spare any expense. What do you think?"

Hall pondered a moment, then spoke. "Well, we can't just walk up to the front door and order everyone to stay inside until help arrives. We either have to warn Adams and Hancock or take out the assassins."

Cushman hesitated. "Why do you think they just don't storm the house? It's pretty isolated for a neighborhood. Burst in, kill everybody in sight, and run to safety. Chances are pretty good they would accomplish their mission and escape. I would have done that as soon as Hancock and Adams had arrived, but no, they are obviously waiting until they leave. Why?"

"Do you think Mr. Tucker is in on the plot?" Hall asked while pondering several scenarios.

"It would make sense. If Hancock and Adams were killed leaving the home of a fellow Patriot, Tucker would be alive and have plausible deniability. He could even attempt to bring them into the house, nurse their injuries, and send for a doctor," concluded Cushman.

"If you're right and it does make sense, then my bet would be a very short meeting. We probably don't have much time," Hall added.

Without another word the two men continued along the fencerow. They were now to the south side of the house next door to what they hoped was the Tucker home.

"Look, a trail. Might have a better vantage point from the back," suggested Hall.

The men tore off down the path and circled behind the house. They could see the target house more clearly now. Being set back farther off the street, Cushman and Hall were now staring at the middle of what they hoped to be the Tucker house. Both men were concentrating at the clump of trees along the edge of the property line, where they suspected the ambush to come from.

"I don't see anybody," Major Hall whispered.

Cushman was about to agree when he saw a slight movement. He tapped Hall on the shoulder and pointed. "There, leaning against the tree."

Sure enough, where the light from the streetlamp filtered through the clump of trees, a human form was leaning against the tree, holding what appeared to be a rifle.

"This must be the house," Hall noted. "Your friend has good instincts."

"You're right. Just don't let him know that. He'll never let me forget it."

"You two are pretty close, aren't you?" Major Hall was scanning the tree line intensely.

"Best friends since I can remember. Families lived nearby. Can't remember a day growing up when we didn't get into some type of mischief."

"Wait, fifth tree in, is that what I think it is?" Hall pointed while he spoke.

"Bloody-noddy, he's smoking a cigarette, not very bright," added Cushman.

"I don't see any others. How about you?"

"No, just the two. If your theory is correct, then at least two more are in the trees to the north, and maybe a teamster or two are in on it."

"Major, wait here. Let me do some reconnaissance. I will be right back," Cushman ordered.

Hall resisted the urge to rebuke Cushman, being that he was his superior in terms of rank. Both men had served in their respective state militia, but this was hardly a normal military operation. *Besides,* Hall thought to himself, *I'm no longer a military man. I'm a spy.* The thought sent shivers through the veteran warrior as he recalled the last month of his life and how it had brought him back here to Philadelphia.

Cushman, using the same tree line as the assassins, moved quickly between the trees, and within a moment he was hidden from the assassins, tucked tightly behind the south chimney, which split the house in half. He slowly peered into the closest window, glancing through the glass panes; he spanned what looked like a library. A black servant was holding a tray of drinks. He could see several chairs, and they looked to be facing the fireplace. *Yes, there are three men sitting in the chairs, in obvious discussion.* Standing nearby was a wheeled chair; he had never seen such a thing.

Cushman concentrated on the men sitting around the fireplace. He could not see their faces. Tonight had been the first time he had ever met John Hancock or Samuel Adams. He couldn't be sure if it was the two leaders of Congress.

Doubt consumed Cushman, his left arm beginning to ache from the earlier wound. He took a deep breath and decided to report back to Hall. A movement in the room caused Cushman to halt and look inside again. A younger man entered the room, elegantly dressed in very obvious expensive clothes. The look on his face was definitely one of great aggravation. He stared closer as the young man approached the three chairs.

Cushman noted the newcomer was young, perhaps in his midthirties. His hair was long, tied neatly into a ponytail. He had regal bearing and strutted toward the chairs rather than walked. His eyes were dark and hollow; his long narrow nose dominated his face. Cushman had an immediate dislike for the newcomer.

Samuel Adams could not have been more shocked if King George had walked through the door and granted the American colonies their freedom. The transformation in Aaron Tucker was unlike anything he had ever seen. His eyes, once glassy and distant, seemed clear and bright, his weak voice steadily growing in strength. But most importantly, he was starting to come around to their way of thinking.

Hancock had just finished making a point when Tucker sat up straight in his chair and replied, "Gentlemen, my father left England in 1698 at the tender age of nineteen. His father, my grandfather, had passed away several years earlier. He left behind his mother, two brothers, three sisters, and all his friends. I asked him one day when

I was young, what would cause a man to leave the comfort of his family and friends for the vast unknown of America? You know what he said?" Not waiting for the others to answer, Tucker continued, "Freedom. One word. That was it, freedom. My father was a man of few words. He was a gifted carpenter, but when I finished my apprenticeship and became a master cooper, my father came to work with me. We started *Tucker Barrels*. Trade in the colonies began to explode with growth. We became the largest barrel maker in the Americas. One night, not long before he died, we were discussing our business success when he said something I will never forget. Now, remember, my father was not a great orator."

Both Adams and Hancock leaned closer, obviously interested in Tucker's tale.

"'Aaron,' he said, 'America is like no other place on earth. America is responsible for our success.' I replied, 'I thought it was our barrels.' Like a good father, he laughed, then got serious again. 'America is freedom. Freedom allows ordinary people, like you and me, to achieve extraordinary success. In America, there is no royalty or privileged class, no king or prince or priest telling you what you must do. There is only freedom, freedom to fail or to succeed, and if you fail today, you wake up with the freedom to succeed tomorrow. Freedom with all its consequences, good and bad, allows a man or a woman the choice to pursue that which they love. From an early age, you had the love and passion to produce quality barrels. The reason I left the carpentry trade was to work *with* you. It was a choice I made and have never regretted. The ability to pursue that which makes us happy, without interference from kings or governments or bureaucrats or the church, is what makes America different from the rest of the world.'"

Hancock looked at Adams, and both men smiled, knowing the night was not a waste after all.

The rejuvenated Aaron Tucker continued, "In my old age, I have grown complacent with wealth and privilege. I'm afraid my son has not learned the great lessons freedom teaches. He is spoiled with material comfort he didn't earn and privileged circumstances throughout his life. The king of England threatens the very freedom which has made America great. I regret that my only thoughts of late have been to the status quo. Rebellion brings uncertainty and change. I was fearful of that change. But I now realize that freedom comes at a cost, and probably always will. I no longer fear the future, for freedom will always be worth the fight. Mr. Hancock, Mr. Adams, your visit tonight has rekindled the spirit and passion I had as a youth. I owe you a great debt of thanks. Gentleman, my fortune is yours. When you succeed, and I have no doubt you will, please put in place a government of limited powers, especially the power of the purse. Nothing retards freedom like a corrupt and bloated government."

John Hancock looked at Samuel Adams. His eyes revealed what Hancock felt, jubilation and astonishment. He also thought he noticed a tear. Sam Adams was as uncompromising and cutthroat a politician as he had ever met. But no one could ever question his loyalty and love for his country. Hancock knew most people thought of Sam Adams as arrogant, aloof, and unemotional. He just wished that those same critics could see the scene unfolding as Adams bolted from his chair and bear-hugged the astonished Tucker, tears streaming down his cheeks, as the two men celebrated a monumental triumph for the financing of the war effort.

Standing behind the three men, Jacob Tucker nearly collapsed when his father finished talking. It took every ounce of willpower not to strike out at the bewildered old man. The spoiled son knew what he had to do, and without a moment to spare, he decided to do it.

Cushman carefully retraced his path back to the edge of the neighbor's tree line.

He questioned Hall, "Anything new?"

"Other than they're both smoking a cigarette now, I'm sure there are only two on this side. How was the spying?"

"There are three men sitting in front of the fireplace. A servant was serving drinks. Unfortunately, their backs were to me. A younger man entered from the hallway. He looked irritated, made me feel ill at ease." Cushman paused as both men pondered the next move. "One more thing, next to the three men was a chair with wheels."

"A wheeled chair, clever idea. Could be helpful for the old or injured. Better mention it to your inventor friend Mr. Jefferson." Hall paused and pondered Cushman's reconnaissance. "So we have three men talking together, which could certainly be Hancock, Adams, and the mysterious Mr. Tucker. The servant indicates wealth. And of course, our friends out front practically assure us we've come to the right party."

"If we could only take out the two smokers without alerting any others. There is just too much open ground between us," Cushman concluded.

"We could shoot them," suggested Hall.

"Yes, but if there are others, which we both believe there are, then we alert them and no longer control the situation."

"What about going in the back, through a door or window, and trying to sneak them out?" Hall offered.

"Possible, but remember, somebody lured those two to this trap, knowingly or not. If we have an enemy within, he could shoot them immediately," countered Cushman.

"I say we try for the two smokers. We'll get them one way or another. If we alert the others, we engage them. At least Hancock and Adams might have a decent chance of escape once they hear the gunshots," suggested Major Hall.

"Not exactly Alexander the Great, but we have to act quickly. I'll lead and try to get them with my throwing knives. You follow. If they discover us, shoot the first smoker. I'll take the second. Be careful." Cushman was already starting to move.

Hall grinned and palmed his pistol. Cushman had come a long way from the frightened teenager he had met on the road to Fort Duquesne. The two men began to slowly creep forward.

The sinister figure had seen enough. He started sprinting at full speed to report his findings. Patrick Rourke would not be pleased. Rourke had sent the coachman to follow Thomas Jefferson. He was ordered to eliminate the Virginia delegate if he stopped at the Tucker house. The coachman had stayed on foot, following from the opposite side of Front Street, and had stopped across the street from the Tucker home, feeling regret when Jefferson had continued on. He watched from a concealed vantage point as Jefferson headed south.

Rourke's orders included watching the scene and to help the four assassins if Jefferson returned with help. He didn't have to wait long.

A few minutes had gone by when the coachman heard the faint clip-clop of horses approaching from the south; he decided to investigate and found three horses tied to a tree several houses from Tucker's. Correctly figuring that Jefferson had found some allies, he returned to his vantage point and keenly watched for the three coming from the south. Again, he didn't have long to wait, spotting a man slinking amid the trees to the rear of the Tucker home.

At this point, the coachman began running at full speed to report his findings to his boss.

Abandoning any attempt at stealth, he came noisily to a stop at the carriage door. Rourke, observing his arrival, quickly threw open the door and greeted him with an astonished look on his face.

"What the hell is going on?" Rourke bellowed.

The coachman, breathing heavily, gasped out, "He returned with two others. One of them slipped to the back of the house, peering in the window. That's when I came back here. What do you want to do?"

Rourke was furious. How did this happen? Who was helping Jefferson? Rourke was famous for his temper—the crazy Irishman frightened even the hard-edged thugs he employed. There were many a story, some true, most not; the most recent rumor had Rourke personally torturing a competitor for information before finally ending his life by forcing wet concrete down his throat.

In fact, Rourke did possess a fierce temper, but as he grew older, he was able to control it and use it to force himself to concentrate even harder. This was one of those moments. He quickly thought out several scenarios and all the resulting consequences.

The coachman was surprised when Rourke's face changed from livid to calm to smirk. Rourke smiled at Lydia and stated simply, "Fortune favors the bold."

In a quiet but determined voice, he hissed, "Hurry, tell them we have a new plan. Send the men in. Kill everyone inside and out."

"But what about young Tucker? He's your friend, your ally," responded the bull of a coachman.

Rourke thought about young Jacob Tucker. A weak, sniveling coward whose sexual preference turned to young boys. Tucker had been a good ally. With his father dead, he would probably inherit the family business, properties, and substantial wealth. Rourke had no doubt he could manipulate young Tucker and his newly found wealth. Rourke made up his mind quickly. *Hell with his wealth and hell with him! He failed me.* "Kill them all, including Jacob Tucker, and make sure you find Jefferson. Kill them all. Now hurry."

The two men were practically crawling from tree to tree in their attempt to remain quiet. Cushman bit down gently on the knife between his teeth, concentrating hard to breathe through his nose. Cornstalk had taught him many things, chief among which were stealth and patience, skills necessary to survive as long as he did in the Ohio Country. *Melt into the forest like the devil cat.* He tried hard to avoid stepping onto dried sticks and alerting the two men twenty yards ahead. Major Jacob Hall followed closely behind, a pistol in each hand.

One more step. Cushman was behind a large tree between himself and the assassins. He motioned for Hall to come closer, indicating they would launch their attack from there. Taking his knife from his teeth, he took out a second knife and whispered softly, "Ready?"

Hall nodded.

Cushman quietly maneuvered beside the tree, cocked his right arm, and took aim at the farthest assassin. Before he could toss his knife, all hell broke loose.

Rourke's coachman came running up the stone slab pathway leading to the Tucker home. "Follow me!" he cried out loudly, abandoning any attempt of stealth. "Storm the house! Follow me, to the house!"

Four men armed with muzzle-loading flintlock muskets scurried from the trees, two from the north and two from the south. They had actually covered such a scenario while planning the operation. The coachman, carrying a pistol in both hands, led the four onto the front porch. He directed one of the assassins toward the rear of the house; the rest took up positions behind him as they waited the signal to enter the home of Aaron Tucker.

Jacob Tucker took the stairs two at a time, reaching the second floor and bolting into his bedroom, pulling a large trunk from under his bed. Extracting his favorite pistol, he pivoted and bounded back down the stairs. His mind was racing, attempting to remember the protocol to implement the contingency plan he and Rourke had agreed on earlier in the week. The emergency plan was a drastic change from the preferred outcome. *As they leave, my boys will take care of them and the driver,* Rourke had promised. *No witnesses, no other casualties.* The contingency called for the assassins to enter the home and kill everyone, including Jacob's father, Aaron, and their only servant, Andrew. Jacob worried as he started to open the door to signal the assassins inside. Not that they would kill his father or his faithful servant. Jacob had to be placed *above suspicion*; therefore, he would have to allow one of the assassins to strike him on the head, rendering him unconscious. *A convincing tale of robbery and murder.*

Rourke had sold him on the idea. He shuddered at the thought of being knocked unconscious, but the resulting control of his father's entire wealth was a strong incentive, and it was necessary to avoid any suspicion.

Throwing open the door, he was startled to find two pistols aimed directly at his head. "What the—"

The coachman, recognizing Jacob, dropped his pistols to his side and brought his trigger finger to his mouth in the universal sign to shut the hell up.

"We've got a problem. Where are they?" Rourke's coachman was an intimidating bull of a man, short and powerfully built, his eyes intense and frightening.

"In the library, two doors down on the right," replied Jacob.

"You know the plan. Turn around, I'll make it quick," he ordered.

The coachman grinned, enjoying thoroughly his next move. Pulling up his pistol and placing the barrel at the base of Jacob Tucker's skull, he pulled the trigger, ending the life of the son of one of Philadelphia's wealthiest men.

Cushman stood motionless, stunned at the turn of events. As the two assassins bolted from their positions to join the man on the front porch, Cushman turned to Hall. "Did you hear that? Something's gone awry!"

"I did. What now?" Hall calmly replied.

"Well, let's try plan B, to the back window," suggested Cushman.

The two men sprinted toward the window Cushman had spied through earlier. They were so focused on quickly warning Hancock and Adams that they didn't notice one of the assassins coming from the front porch. The assassin reacted swiftly to the strange men, dropped to a knee, and sighted his rifle.

Hall roared, "Ben, look out!"

THE SIGNERS

Hall's reaction was swift; he took aim and fired. Two shots roared out, followed quickly by a third. Cushman dived swiftly to the ground, landing hard on his right shoulder, rattling his teeth. *Too late.* Searing, hot pain shot through his left shoulder as the assassin's ball struck the upper half of his arm, ripping flesh near the triceps muscle. Hall's warning had saved his life, but the pain in his shoulder and the gunshot wound were both intense. He slowly rolled over onto his hands and knees. Regaining his senses and ignoring the pain, he jumped up and ran to the window.

Jacob Hall's aim had been true; it was not the first man he had ever killed. The ball hit the assassin directly under his right arm just as he had squeezed the trigger. The lead bullet tore through the pectoralis major muscle, between the fourth and fifth ribs, tearing through his lungs and directly into the heart. The assassin had just seconds to live. Hall felt no remorse for the man who would have killed Benjamin Cushman and the leaders of the rebellion. He immediately scooped up the assassin's musket and followed Cushman to the window.

John Hancock was more of a businessman, trader, scholar, and politician than a soldier. But like all colonial citizens of the time, he had hunted and trapped in his youth. He had even hoped to be placed into the command of the newly formed Continental Army, having many supporters. However, backers of George Washington had carried the day, led by his friend Samuel Adams, the ultimate politician, who believed a Virginian should be put in charge of the Army.

Hancock reacted quickly when two shots rang out from outside the house. As he ran to the library door, he heard a third shot that sounded like it came from down the hallway. Bolting an interior lock, he began to pull a large desk toward the door; Adams hurriedly joined him. Meanwhile, Aaron Tucker had struggled mightily to lift himself from his chair, collapsing while attempting to reach his wheelchair. Hancock and Adams ran to his aid, quickly depositing him into the wheelchair. The old man pointed to a large trunk in the corner. "There should be a pistol and powder in the trunk. Hurry, I fear something dreadful is upon us," he commanded.

Hancock ripped open the trunk, searching for a weapon. Loud voices could be heard from the hallway. "Mr. Tucker, are you all right? Get out—"

Followed by another gunshot, just outside the door.

A dreadful scream had followed the shot as Aaron Tucker yelled out, "Andrew, Andrew, they shot my servant, Andrew!"

The doorknob rattled as someone attempted to open it. The heavy door and a large wooden desk were all that stood between the three men and a group of crazed assassins.

Hancock tore the pistol from the trunk and began pouring powder down the barrel and into the frizzen pan. As he was stuffing a ball into the barrel, he jumped from a loud crash of broken glass. Fearing the worst, he scrambled for the ball as another windowpane shattered. He looked to the windows; the only thing he could see was the end of a rifle butt shattering glass and wooden spines. He groped for the lead ball, unable to tear his eyes away from the threat coming from the window. Relieved, he found the ball and jammed it into the barrel of the pistol and took aim.

Samuel Adams had grabbed a heavy iron fireplace stoker and moved rapidly toward the threat coming from outside the window. With adrenaline flowing rapidly from the brain to the nervous system, both men were getting ready to fight for their lives.

Thomas Jefferson heard three gunshots in rapid succession. Without hesitation, he did what came natural to him throughout his entire life. He ignored conventional wisdom, and instead of running for help, he ran hard in the direction of the gunshots.

"Mr. Hancock, Mr. Adams, are you all right?" a voice, vaguely familiar but not recognized by either man, filtered through the broken window. Hancock relaxed his trigger finger slightly as a bloody arm came through the window, followed quickly by the rest of the torso.

Outside, Hall strained to push Cushman through the opening. A sudden noise caused him to whirl quickly, and Cushman nearly fell back out but managed to stumble in the room with a lurch. Hall raised his pistol, only to be surprised by the sudden presence of Thomas Jefferson.

"What the hell! I told you...," Hall blurted out, unable to finish his sentence.

"Sorry, I don't take orders very well," Jefferson stated calmly, then strode past Hall to the window. "Gentlemen, hurry to the window! You are in grave danger!"

Hancock and Adams exchanged glances; they recognized the man on the floor as Jefferson's friend. Both men immediately recognized the voice of Thomas Jefferson.

Cushman stood, brushing away shards of glass, angered at hearing his friend's voice, putting himself unnecessarily into harm's way. *Not surprising, though.*

Outside, Hall thought the same thing, astonished at either the foolishness or bravery of the man from Virginia.

Dropping his pistol to his waist, Hancock walked quickly toward the man now standing in front of the window. It was Jefferson's boyhood friend. *Ben...Ben something.* His left arm was bleeding badly, and upon closer inspection, his right forearm was also bleeding.

"Cushman!" cried out Adams. "What are you doing here? What has happened?"

Cushman quickly assessed the situation as men were beginning to batter the door with heavy objects from the hallway. *Only a minute or two.* "Just in the neighborhood. Thought I'd drop in. Now, we must hurry. Out the window. Major Hall will help you down," Cushman ordered.

Cushman guided the older Samuel Adams through the window, trying to avoid shards of glass, Jefferson grabbing his legs and easing him to the ground. Cushman shot his friend an angry glance, only to receive a grin in return.

While Adams was being helped out the window, Hancock wheeled Aaron Tucker over to the escape route. "He's next," stated Hancock firmly.

Cushman didn't argue, but Tucker did. "Nonsense! Give me a pistol. I will hold them off while you escape."

Just then, the bolt holding the door broke free, and the heavy desk began to slide slowly back into the room. They only had seconds.

"Enough arguing!" Cushman actually smiled at the two men as he grabbed Hancock and lifted him toward the window. Hancock raised his legs just in time to slide along the window's bottom, Jefferson and Hall steadying him to the ground.

Hancock immediately recognized Major Jacob Hall; the surprise on his face caused the major to smile. "What in the devil are you doing here? Why aren't you in Fran—"

Hall's stern look was enough to cut off the president of the American Congress. "Not now. Let's get you to safety first." His steely eyes persuaded Hancock to obey, but Hancock's mind began to imagine a multitude of explanations as to why the American provocateur was rescuing John Hancock and Sam Adams in Philadelphia when he should have been halfway around the world. And all those explanations ended badly.

The door was now opening faster as voices in the hallway urged more effort. A head peered through the slot to survey the room. The coachman immediately recognized what was happening and ordered two assassins outside to cut off any escape.

A shot rang out, and a ball whizzed by the coachman's ear, so close he could hear it. The ball shattered the wooden doorframe and sent splinters into air. He quickly pulled back, unharmed.

Hall had bought Cushman and Tucker a few seconds with his timely shot. Unfortunately, they only had two remaining loaded pistols.

Cushman lifted Aaron Tucker out of the wheelchair, setting him on the window ledge, with his legs dangling outside. Grasping Tucker by the shoulders, he began to lower him down to the others. Another shot rang out as the door flew wide open, the desk now totally clear. Cushman followed Tucker out the window by placing his left hand on the ledge and jumping into the air, vaulting his legs first through the window, pushing hard with his injured left arm. Cushman barley cleared Jefferson as he landed awkwardly, his multiple injuries reawakened.

Scrambling to his feet, he hoisted Aaron Tucker over his shoulders. Tucker moaned in pain. Cushman's right hand felt something warm and sticky as he adjusted the old man on his shoulder. *Blood*, he thought.

"Leave me. I'm an old man. Help the others," he stuttered weakly.

"No chance, Mr. Tucker. You're going to outlive us all," Cushman lied.

Jefferson had led Hancock and Adams to the neighboring tree line, pausing until Cushman arrived with Mr. Tucker. Major Hall guarded their retreat.

"We've got two loaded pistols, yours and Tuckers…and the knives," stated Hall.

"Red, get Mr. Hancock to help you carry Mr. Tucker. Lead them back to the horses and get out of here. Major Hall and I will stall them."

Jefferson pointed in the direction of the horses as Sam Adams worked his way through the darkened backyard. Hancock, like Cushman, noticed immediately the large amount of blood soaking through Aaron Tucker's shirt.

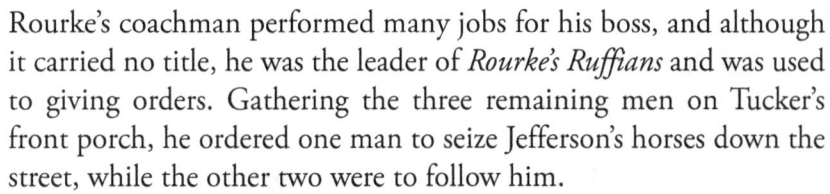

Rourke's coachman performed many jobs for his boss, and although it carried no title, he was the leader of *Rourke's Ruffians* and was used to giving orders. Gathering the three remaining men on Tucker's front porch, he ordered one man to seize Jefferson's horses down the street, while the other two were to follow him.

He correctly analyzed the escape route and maneuvered the men toward the backyard of the neighbor's house. Muskets ready, the two assassins worked from tree to tree while their leader followed closely behind, a pistol in each of his hands.

Cushman scrambled quickly behind a bush running parallel to the neighboring house; he got halfway down its length when the hedge ended. He rapidly dropped to his stomach, ignoring the shooting pain in his left arm.

Major Hall also dropped to his stomach, lying flat between two trees, eyeing the Tucker tree line for movement. A dark shadow was slowly emerging from behind the tree; the streetlamp behind the assassins was a distinct advantage for the two militiamen. Hall took a long breath and squeezed the trigger. The shadowy figure lurched backward and fell with a thud. The American spy scrambled to his feet and ran to the edge of the house.

Cushman waited patiently, scanning right to left slowly, looking for any type of movement. Fifteen degrees to his right, he spotted the long barrel of a musket protruding from beyond the tree. He waited patiently. *No movement.*

Blindly moving his hand along the ground, Cushman found what he was looking for. Grasping the small rock, he hurled it toward the tree. It rattled home, causing the assassin to expose his body while readying his musket toward the noise.

Seizing the opportunity, Cushman steadied himself and triggered his flintlock pistol. The ball tore into the assassin's right shoulder, shattering the humerus bone. Dropping his musket to the ground, the assassin began to charge Cushman's position while grasping at a pistol from his waist belt with his left hand.

Cushman propped up to his hands and knees, reaching into his waistline for his knife. Another shot rang out; Cushman saw the flash, twenty degrees to his left. He heard the ball whizzing by his ear and crashing into the neighbor's home. He cocked his right arm and launched the knife through the air, striking the oncoming assassin in the middle of the throat, stopping him in midstride.

Rourke's coachman quickly pondered his options. Three of his crew were dead or badly injured. After killing Jacob Tucker and his servant, he had reloaded both his pistols while the others attempted to open the study door. He fired a shot once the door was open,

THE SIGNERS

confident he had hit someone escaping out the window. His last and most recent shot must have missed the shadowy target.

His analysis complete, he thought of Falstaff leaving the battlefield in Shakespeare's *Henry IV*. *Discretion is the better part of valor.* Some might have thought Falstaff's discretion more like cowardice, but the coachman thought it appropriate for his circumstance. He began moving quickly in the direction of Rourke's carriage, astonished that their carefully laid-out plans had failed so miserably. His rage continued to build as he executed his escape. *How could a lawyer like Thomas Jefferson defeat them tonight? And whom were the people helping him?* He would surely find out and deal with them in the appropriate fashion. The rage continued, but he smiled as he envisioned the painful tortures he would inflict on Jefferson and his partners.

The remaining assassin had no idea of the outcome back at the Tucker home. He quickly identified the three horses twenty paces from his current position. He was kneeling behind a three-foot-high horse trough, his patience rewarded almost immediately. He grinned broadly as an older man began to emerge from the side of the house and move toward the horses.

Shouldering his musket, he took aim. Before he could pull the trigger, however, he noticed two men emerging from shadows. They were carrying yet another man, who was obviously wounded very badly. There were now four potential targets. He lowered his musket to rethink his strategy. He had the musket, a pistol, and of course a knife.

He quickly formulated his plan. *Musket for one, pistol for another, and finish off the wounded man and the old one with the knife.* In less than one minute, he would score the largest payday of his life. The assassin rose up to a full stance and shouldered his musket and took aim at John Hancock.

Hancock was kneeling to lower Tucker to the ground, while Jefferson went to rein in the horses. Aaron Tucker knew he was dying but was amazed at how clear his mind was. While Hancock was gently lowering Tucker to the ground, the wounded tycoon immediately noticed a man standing twenty paces away, a musket aimed directly at Hancock's back. Tucker's voice was too weak to warn him. Instead, as Hancock began to rise up, Tucker sank his fingers into the shoulders of Hancock's expensive coat and pulled with every ounce of strength.

Caught off-balance, the bewildered Hancock stumbled head over heels, doing a complete somersault and landing on his backside. The gunshot that followed struck the tree directly behind Hancock. Had Tucker not yanked him down, he surely would have been killed. Angered by the missed opportunity, the assassin threw down his musket, pulled out his pistol, and walked quickly toward the unarmed foursome. Raising his arm to shoulder level, he took direct aim at Hancock again.

John Hancock had been in some close calls in his life, but he was now keenly aware the grim reaper was seconds from claiming his soul. Somebody was going to be collecting the five-hundred-pound bounty on his head. He raised his hand and tried to speak, but it was too late.

Not one but two shots rang out. Hancock flinched but quickly realized the assassin had missed. Hancock's mind ferociously attempted to process what had just happened. There were two shots, not one, then his eyes finally focused on the assassin. He was no longer upright but lying in the street, blood oozing from his chest. Hancock shook his head in an attempt to clear his thoughts. Turning slowly, he saw two armed men running at him. Something was different about these two; Hancock felt everything was happening in slow motion, the haze of combat, as soldiers oftentimes referred to it. Then it struck him. *Uniforms.* They were both dressed in uniform, the uniform of the Philadelphia police. Hancock didn't know what God had planned for him in the future, but he was fairly sure of one thing: he would never see a more wonderful sight.

Thomas Jefferson quickly began to administer aid to Aaron Tucker but soon realized nothing could be done. He was dead from the gunshot wound.

The two constables were both shouting, "Mr. Hancock, Mr. Adams, Mr. Jefferson?"

"Yes, thank God you arrived when you did!" exclaimed John Hancock, picking himself off the ground while dusting off his expensive clothing.

The constables looked at each other knowingly; the equipment failure had not produced the disaster they had envisioned. "Mr. Franklin ordered us into this area, searching for you. Mr. Jefferson, are you sure you're all right?" The tall constable was shocked at the blood-soaked clothing of the gentleman from Virginia.

"Yes" was all Jefferson could say. He couldn't remove his eyes from the dead body of Aaron Tucker.

Both constables bolted upright when two men materialized from the shadows. Pistols were raised as they assessed the threat.

"Wait!" Jefferson cried loudly. "They are the men that saved us tonight."

The constables relaxed; neither had ever fired a gun in the line of duty until tonight, and both men were glad the threat was over.

"Sam, John, are you all right?" Jefferson asked, now staring at the body of the dead assassin.

"Yes, yes, we're fine, thanks to all of you. But I'm afraid, as you can see, that Mr. Tucker didn't make it," declared Sam Adams.

Major Jacob Hall had seen many a soldier perish from gunshot wounds and just as many who survived horrid-looking injuries. A quick examination of Aaron Tucker confirmed everyone's instincts; the wealthy barrel maker had died from the gunshot wound. "I'm afraid you're correct," he concluded.

"And just who are you, young man?" Samuel Adams glared at the major.

"Major Jacob Hall, Mr. Adams. Glad to make your acquaintance," replied the composed ex-militiaman.

"Mr. Cushman, you are injured," proclaimed Hancock with a worried look on his face.

"I'll be fine, thank you. Gentlemen, we can never thank you enough." Cushman directed his remarks to the young policemen.

"However, I'm afraid our work is not done. There is at least one more assassin, back there."

"I think he has fled," added Hall.

"Maybe, but let's be sure. We'll reload and have a look," Cushman ordered.

They were gone for less than five minutes. The two young constables were sickened by the carnage they viewed inside and outside the Tucker home. Six more dead bodies. Cushman and Hall, both veterans of the French and Indian War, seemed unaffected, but deep inside Ben Cushman's anger boiled. He knew someone had given the order to launch this major assassination plot, and in the end, many innocent people were dead because of it. Cushman vowed to himself to find the answers and exact revenge.

Unfortunately, when they arrived at the Tucker home, it was empty. Acting on a hunch, Cushman had ordered the constables to search the house and grounds while he and Hall rode north to search out the mysterious carriage Jefferson had reported seeing. Knowing it was a long shot, they returned disappointed, having found no sign of a carriage.

Two more Philadelphia police arrived on horseback, escorting the delegates back to City Tavern. Hall and Hancock slid away, engrossed in conversation.

As Jefferson and Cushman slowly maneuvered their horses up Walnut Street, Jefferson looked over to his boyhood friend and smiled. "Do me a favor. Next time you come to see me, send me a note before you arrive. That will give me time to depart with haste."

Lydia Ames watched from the side of the street as the carriage pulled away from her modest townhouse. The night had been a huge disaster, with still no word on what happened at City Tavern. She was confident nothing could be traced back to her. But she was worried nonetheless.

She had never seen Patrick Rourke as angry as he was tonight. When Rourke's coachman had reappeared with the news, Rourke had pulled his pistol and stuck it under the coachman's left eye. She was surprised when he pulled back the gun. Instead, the volatile Irishman hit him with a punch that sent him sprawling.

The only words spoken after they had gotten away from the crime scene were an order given from Rourke to his shaken employee. "Find out who foiled our plot. I want them dead before the weekend."

The two Virginians rode in silence as they came within sight of their destination, City Tavern. A sudden thought swept over Ben Cushman. His skill as a soldier had been tested tonight, and his training and experience had been critical in producing a positive outcome. In his mind, he had done nothing extraordinary. As much as he hated to admit it, he was an extremely skilled warrior. Major Hall had been a godsend. His skills, both as a warrior and a government secret agent, were legendary. But what struck Cushman as extraordinary was the bravery and courage of the delegates at both City Tavern and the Tucker household. No one ran, no one cowered in fear, and no one panicked. They remained calm in the face of extreme danger, despite the fact that none of the men had any real experience in the military. Some were merchants, some lawyers, and some career politicians, but they all had performed like grizzled veterans. Cushman took an odd satisfaction that these men would be leading the nation in a time of war.

Chapter 10

When the people fear their government, there is tyranny. When the government fears the people, there is liberty!

—Thomas Jefferson

Early morning, June 25, 1776
Philadelphia

John Hancock's state of mind was bordering on insanity. He had just survived an assassination plot that had come within seconds of succeeding, not once, but twice. He had been rescued by a friend of Thomas Jefferson, whom he had met only hours before. To his surprise, the shy and bookish Jefferson had also participated in the daring rescue. The third member of the rescue trio was well-known to Hancock and cause for great concern.

He was Major Jacob Hall, a decorated veteran of the French and Indian War. His exploits and daring had earned Major Hall a well-deserved reputation as one of the fiercest warriors in the Thirteen Colonies. However, his current mission as an undercover agent, representing the Second Continental Congress, was known to only a handful of men, of which Hancock was one. Not that Hancock was unappreciative of Hall's intervention, which surely had saved his life. But Hancock knew Major Hall's current mission should have placed him in France, where he was to procure over twenty tons of gunpowder and other munitions for the coming war. The Willing and Morris shipping-banking firm had financed the mission, and the Continental Congress's Secret Committee had signed off on the three-million-dollar shipment of gold. If Hall was in Philadelphia instead of France, *something had gone very wrong. Indeed, something had gone terribly wrong.*

Adding to the mountain of emotional trauma, Hancock had just learned that his carriage driver had been found under a small grove of trees bordering the Tucker property. In all probability, the team of assassins outside the Tucker home had slit the coachman's throat from ear to ear. The young man had been more than Hancock's personal driver; he was the son of one of Hancock's most trusted partners back in Boston. The close-knit family would be devastated by the loss of their eldest son. The war was beginning to hit very close to home for Hancock, both financially and personally.

John Hancock felt very alone as Major Jacob Hall maneuvered the expensive carriage through the streets of Philadelphia. Hall had graciously volunteered to command the one-ton vehicle as Hancock contemplated the night's events.

In the aftermath of the assassination attempt, Hancock had cornered Hall, peppering him with question after question. Hall calmly cautioned the Boston merchant that they should seek a more private place to conduct their conversation. Hancock agreed to take Hall back to his boardinghouse across from City Tavern. Arriving well past midnight, the two went straight to Hancock's spacious room in Mrs. Sarah Yard's boardinghouse.

The room served as both a bedroom, at the far end of the room, and a small meeting room consisting of a table and four chairs.

"Major Hall, may I offer you a whiskey? It has been a horrifying night, and I doubt sincerely I will be able to sleep anytime soon." Hancock stood beside a makeshift bar and began to pour himself a tumbler full of scotch whiskey.

"Perhaps a small glass is in order."

Hancock removed his topcoat and loosened his shirt. He brought two tumblers and the whole bottle of whiskey to the table. He raised his eyebrows and suggested, "Perhaps we'll need more."

Hall nodded in agreement, and the two men sat down with a thud. A befuddled Hancock asked softly, "What on earth happened?"

"We have a traitor in our midst!" Hall blurted out as he downed the strong whiskey.

"How so?" Hancock remained calm outside, but the tangles of nerves on his insides were straining his capacity to make good decisions.

"They knew, the fuckin' British captain knew it was gold. He knew our departure schedule, that I was not an ambassador, and that we had constructed a fake wall below in the storage deck." Hall's anger was beginning to grow as he thought of the deranged British captain and the death he had reigned upon the merchant ship *Treasure*.

"But how?" An astonished Hancock knew all the men involved and would vouch for every one of them.

"I don't know, but when I find out..." Hall didn't finish the threat, but Hancock shuddered at the thought of Hall carrying it out.

Hancock's mind raced to review what had brought them to this point. The Second Continental Congress formed the Secret Committee on September 18, 1775, for the sole purpose of securing foreign arms and munitions; it was exactly five months after the Battle of Lexington and Concord and during the siege of Boston. From the very start, the committee had acted aggressively, fully believing that war was inevitable. Two members of the committee presented a bold plan to Hancock in a secret meeting in April of 1776. Benjamin Franklin and Robert Morris had pleaded with Hancock in the very same room they were currently occupying. The plan was simple but wrought with danger for all involved. The Willing and Morris shipping-banking firm would loan the Congress three million dollars to purchase the necessary gold that the French had demanded in return for gunpowder and other munitions, including cannons and cannonballs. However, the loan would be an off-the-book transaction. In other words, no one could know the details until after the war. Morris and his business partner, Thomas Willing, were bypassing their other investors, making a loan they didn't have the authority to make, and Hancock and the Secret Committee were accepting the loan without the authority to do so. Even the great lawyer John Adams couldn't save the men involved if the secret mission ever became public.

"Only two members of the Secret Committee had any knowledge of the operation, right?" Hall broke Hancock's train of thought.

THE SIGNERS

"Correct. Only Mr. Franklin and Mr. Morris. The only other members of Congress that knew were Mr. Willing and myself," replied Hancock.

"Add myself." Major Hall added a thumb to his tally of four fingers.

Hancock nodded in agreement.

"The last person was Mr. Willing and Mr. Morris's accountant. I forget his name."

"Yancey, Mr. William Yancey."

Hall held up six digits on both hands. "That's six. Six people knew of the contents of those trunks. One or more of them are traitors," Hall said with conviction.

"I find it hard to belief any of—"

Hancock was cut off in midsentence.

"Trust me, Mr. Hancock, I was there. They knew. The British captain knew everything, and since I didn't tell him, I've narrowed it down to five."

An offended John Hancock nearly leaped from his chair. "Surely, you're not implying that I am a suspect!"

"Relax, Mr. Hancock." Hall grinned. "I've already eliminated you and Mr. Franklin."

Hancock was still offended that he had even been considered, but also relieved that Hall had come to the proper conclusion. "You say you eliminated me as a suspect."

"Yes, for two reasons. Number 1, Mr. Franklin and you are two of the most ardent Patriots in America."

"And number 2?"

"Number 2, you're too good of a businessman."

Hancock looked puzzled at the second reason. "So?"

"So a good businessman would have stolen the gold without sinking a valuable ship with all hands on board." Major Hall let his words sink in to the stunned president of the Continental Congress.

Hancock knew immediately that Hall was telling the truth. Hall's reputation was without peer, but more telling were the depression and disappointment seared into his gray-blue eyes. Hancock was devastated; he dropped his head into his hands. "The *Treasure*, gone? All the men on board dead? What about Captain Gray?"

"Captain Gray was taken away as a prisoner on the British warship that sank the *Treasure*."

"A British captain purposely sank my ship. That is not the actions of an honorable captain of the Royal Navy."

"This captain was the opposite of honorable. He was a madman and a murderer." Hall paused as both men contemplated the monstrous episode. "His ship was fast. I tried to persuade Captain Gray to outrun him or to fire on the British ship first. Gray dismissed me as mad and convinced me they would board and then leave us alone. He was probably correct, except for one thing. They knew about the gold and had planned all along to leave no witnesses to the crime.

"Captain Gray turned into the wind and allowed them to board. By the time we realized they were readying to fire upon us, it was too late. They took down our masts and sails. Their Marines raked the deck with deadly fire, and their cannons fired grapeshot to kill all on deck. When they came on board, I tried to muster my best arrogant, bureaucrat imitation, but to little avail. They went straight for the false wall. He didn't discover it. He knew about it. He locked us belowdecks, then fired spike shot into the hull of the *Treasure*."

"Flaming spike shot?" Hancock asked, still with his head in his hands, growing more depressed as Hall continued his tale.

"Yes." Hall then explained how he orchestrated their escape from the burning ship.

Hancock looked up in admiration. "Quick thinking, Major Hall."

Hall nodded, then continued, "There were eleven of us who swam through the hole in the ship. Three drowned immediately. They were already badly injured from the attack. The rest of us were able to make it to the jolly boat."

"Jolly boat? How on earth were you able to get the jolly boat off the davits so quickly?" Hancock was astonished.

"It wasn't our boat, it was theirs."

"Even more astounding, how?"

"I believe I failed to mention I had some help. Interestingly, the man's name was Cushman, George Cushman."

Hancock absorbed the information and stood up. "It couldn't be, could it?"

Hall shrugged. "As it turns out, yes, he is Ben's younger brother."

Hancock smiled. "I only met Ben Cushman tonight, at City Tavern. Mr. Jefferson said he was his best friend growing up. Seems he and his brother—"

"James," Hall added with a weak smile.

"Yes, James, were out in Ohio, fighting Indians and doing some survey work," Hancock continued.

"Well, that's partially true." Hall's smile widened as he retold the story of how he had met Ben and James Cushman during the Forbes Expedition to take Fort Duquesne. He recounted the remarkable tale of how he, along with Ben and George Washington, were able to rescue James from the executioner's ax at Fort Duquesne.

Hancock let out a low whistle and remarked, "Seems I've heard rumors of Washington participating in such an endeavor. Never heard any other names involved. So you and Cushman have quite a history together?"

Hall nodded. "There is more. The real reason he and James continually returned to the Ohio country, but perhaps another day."

Hancock's interest was piqued, but he realized he would have to wait. "Very well, back to the *Treasure*. What happened next?"

"I had devised a plan while Cushman and I were on deck, dodging all the lead the British were throwing at us. When they boarded and I played my ambassador role, Cushman slid over the side and swam to one of the two jolly boats the Brits were dragging. He succeeded in cutting the line without getting spotted, and the boat began to drift. We swam to the boat. Cushman was able to get us all aboard. We were lucky because he was able to maneuver the boat directly behind the burning *Treasure*. I had everyone lie down flat for over an hour, hoping their spotters wouldn't see us, or if they did, they decided not to retrieve it."

"So there were a total of nine survivors. That was almost two months ago. What happened next?"

"We waited until they sailed away and attempted to return to the *Treasure*. But everyone was either exhausted or badly injured. By the time Cushman and I were able to maneuver the boat close enough, it was nothing more than burned-out ashes."

Hall continued his depressing review, "We lost two more that night. We put them into the sea with some proper words. The next morning, dark clouds began to brew in the north, and by the afternoon we were in the middle of a god-awful tempest. The waves grew to at least fifteen feet. We held on as best as we could. I managed to tie a rope to my leg just before the boat capsized and threw everyone overboard. Eventually, I was able to swim back, and with the help of several others, we were able to right the boat. When the storm relented, we were down to just three men, Cushman, the ship's doctor, and I."

"What did you eat, drink?" Hancock's attention was focused on every word.

"We drifted aimlessly for over a week. We were able to store some of the rainwater from the storm and managed to capture two sea birds. Doc passed away after a week. Just threw him into the sea and waited for our turn to die. That night, another storm hit and we were tossed about like a toy. Didn't remember much after that. Next thing I know, I was in a bed and Cushman was right next to me. Seems we washed ashore onto a barrier island, half-dead. We owe our lives to an old widow and her slave."

"Where exactly did you wash ashore?" Hancock was now fascinated by Hall's tale of survival.

"Didn't know at first. For days I would drift in and out of consciousness. Mrs. De Groot, the old widow, said I was that way for over two weeks. As it turned out, Cushman had suffered similar effects, but not as severe. By the time I fully recovered from the ordeal, Cushman had already been helping around the house. Mrs. De Groot turned out to be a loopy old bird. She was always singing bawdy songs. Her curse words would make a pirate blush. She was kind, but very lonely. Turned out to be an able nurse, though."

"Then what?"

"While I was ill, Cushman had made inquiries at some neighboring farms. Seems Mrs. De Groot was the widow of a famous Dutch sea captain by the name of Deidrick De Groot. He had been lost at sea and presumed dead two years earlier and left his widow with a beach house, one slave, and a rumored fortune in jewelry and precious gems. No one had ever seen the alleged loot, but everyone insisted it existed."

"Buried treasure, maybe?" Hancock poured both men another shot of whiskey.

"The nearest town was called Chincoteague. It's Indian and means *'beautiful land across water.'* The low-lying island is part of the large peninsula that borders the eastern edge of the Chesapeake Bay. Three colonies all claim parts of the peninsula, Delaware, Maryland, and Virginia."

Hancock nodded; he was familiar with the Chesapeake Bay and her surroundings. Many of his ships sailed into Norfolk, at the southwestern edge of the bay and Baltimore, situated on the northwest edge of the bay. The northeastern landmass of the peninsula actually formed the western boundary of the Delaware Bay.

"I ordered Cushman to leave and get to Philadelphia, in order to warn you all. He refused, wouldn't leave without me."

"Refused your order? Must be either very brave or very dense," replied Hancock.

"I think brave, and loyal. We shared *death's doorstep* every day and managed to survive together. It created a strong bond."

"Naturally. How did you get off the island?"

"Every two weeks a ferry boat arrives from the mainland, delivering supplies. The local farmers send their crops back to be sold. Mrs. De Groot secured us passage once I was ready to travel. It was June 21 when the boat arrived, but we were delayed for two days by a violent storm. Cushman and I arrived on the mainland on June 23. We immediately bought two horses and headed north toward Dover. It took a day and a half."

"Wait a minute, how did you get money to buy the horses?"

Major Hall smiled and replied softly, "Mrs. De Groot. She gave us several valuable gemstones to complete our journey."

"So the rumors were true about her husband and the jewels?"

Hall grinned. "I would say so. The amount she wanted to give us at first was unbelievable. Turns out we were very lucky that Lena De Groot was in fact a strong Patriot, and it was her small contribution to the war effort."

"When did you arrive in Philadelphia?" Hancock's mood was strangely getting better as he listened to the incredible tale.

"Early this evening. We had exchanged for fresh horses in Dover and had gotten a few hours of sleep the night before. We rode all day and arrived in Philadelphia at about four o'clock this evening. I went straight to Mr. Morris's house and learned he was at Christ Church. I'm afraid I gave him quite a fright when he exited the church."

"What about Cushman?"

"About three hours into our ride from Chincoteague, we came upon a small tavern. Cushman recognized a patron. Turns out the two had attended the same church for several years. Cushman learned that his brother James was serving as General Washington's aide-de-camp in New York City. George decided that after we arrived safely in Philadelphia, he would ride on to New York and seek out James."

Hancock absorbed the information, then changed the subject. "How did Robert take the news?"

"Not well, as you could imagine. After he calmed down, he strongly suggested I seek out Mr. Franklin. I arrived at his home at about seven o'clock this evening."

"Actually, it is now last evening," Hancock suggested, pointing to his Swiss-made clock, which read three o'clock in the morning.

"I stand corrected," replied the undercover agent. "Mr. Franklin's servant instructed me that he was dining at City Tavern."

"Upon arriving there, I was startled to hear gunfire. I made my way into the tavern, concealing myself along the hallway wall. The back dining room looked like a war zone. I quickly assessed the situation. A wounded man with a knife stuck in his shoulder was rising up and aiming in the direction of Mr. Adams and Mr. Jefferson. Another man was struggling to get a gun from his waistband. I had two pistols and was about to shoot both of them."

"What happened next?" Hancock was on the edge of his chair, no longer in a foul mood.

"I shot the wounded man in the head and was about to kill the other man when Mr. Franklin jumped up and ran between us."

"It was Ben Cushman, wasn't it?" Hancock smiled.

"Correct. Didn't recognize him from behind, and it has been quite a few years since I've seen Ben. Didn't exactly expect to see my old friend. Seems he had almost single-handedly taken out all the assassins."

"Is he as good as you, Major?"

All great warriors were resourceful and brave, and most had great confidence in their abilities. Hall was no exception, so when he smiled and said, "Almost, but he's younger," John Hancock was quite sure that Major Hall had paid him a fine compliment.

"How did you know they would try for Sam and me at the Tucker home?"

"Cushman figured it out, with some gentle prodding of the one surviving killer." After making the statement, Hall thought *that* only a fellow warrior would refer to the cutting of a finger as gentle prodding.

"He is very resourceful and intelligent. He would be a perfect candidate for what I do. When we finally found the Tucker home, we were able to formulate a plan. Except all hell broke loose and we had to improvise. They had at least five assassins waiting for Mr. Adams and you. It's also possible that the son was in on the plot."

"Now that you mentioned it, when the older Tucker regained his energy, the younger Tucker seemed perturbed. Wouldn't be the first time a son conspired against his wealthy father."

"He was shot in the back of the head, close range. There was no damage to the front door. Either the killers conned their way in or they were allowed in," noted Hall. "It's possible he let them in and they eliminated him to cover their tracks. That's exactly what they did at City Tavern. Whoever is behind this was very meticulous and ruthless. Of course, you were part of the rest of the story," Hall concluded.

Both men sat silent, still sipping the warm whiskey, reviewing the night's extraordinary events. Hancock broke the silence. "A few moments ago, you said something odd, something about a crime. You said the British captain had planned to leave no witnesses *to the crime*. What gave you that impression rather than the British Navy stopping a ship smuggling gold?"

"I don't know. I guess my impression of the captain and his crew that this was a robbery and not an interdiction."

"Perhaps your instincts have proved correct once again, Major Hall." Hancock's tone was animated. "I have had hundreds of my ships stopped by the British Navy during the past few years. They have never even so much as fired a warning shot when boarding. They would board, sometimes confiscate certain contraband, and on several occasions forced the ship into port and go through the courts to officially seize it."

"What's your point?"

"My point, Major Hall, is that I have become a politician during this crisis, and I have to think like one. The British admiralty has kept their warships under tight scrutiny. It would be a lot easier for their Navy to stop our smuggling by blowing every American ship out of the water. The smuggling would soon become too expensive and therefore stop. They have not done that because they are still hopeful of reconciliation with their most profitable colonies. They believe that a majority of colonists still support the king. Both sides are waging a public relations war rather than a real war at this time. A British captain who stopped a shipment of gold intended to buy munitions from the king of France would be political godsend for King George. Most Americans still fear the French more than their king. Producing the gold, the ship, and the crew would be a propaganda bonanza for the king and his ministers."

"I'm starting to see your point, Mr. Hancock. At no time did the British captain act in the manner you describe."

"Exactly! This British captain didn't stumble upon the gold and then decide to keep it for himself. No, this captain's intent was to steal the gold all along, keeping if from his supervisors. You were right, Major Hall. We have a traitor in our midst."

"So you think he has no intention of alerting his superiors of the treasure?"

"Exactly," stated Hancock with excitement. He noticed the confused look on Hall's face. "This is good news. The British captain will try to keep this a secret. We may have a chance to reclaim the gold. We are at a crossroads in the war. One-third of the American people don't support our efforts, and another one-third is still on the fence. If word leaked out we were actively courting the French, we may lose that support."

Major Hall nodded in understanding. He was anything but a politician, but he was intelligent enough to realize that no war was ever won without the support of the masses. "What now?" Hall stood and stared into Hancock's eyes.

"Did this British ship have a name?"

"Yes, sir. It was the *HMS Richmond*," responded the proud warrior.

"Then, Major, I think you should start inquiring about the *Richmond* and her commander. Perhaps something good can come of this yet."

"I'll get on it first thing this morning. One more thing, sir."

"What's that, Major?"

"The traitor, he could lead us to the *Richmond* and the captain."

Hancock cringed at the thought. He knew Hall was referring to three people. Both Robert Morris and Thomas Willing were respected members from the Pennsylvania delegation, although suspiciously, both were known to oppose the Declaration of Independence. "Here's to hoping it's the accountant," Hancock stated wearily, referring to the top accountant at Willing and Morris Company, William Yancey.

Hall shrugged and smiled. He began to formulate a plan to catch a traitor.

Chapter 11

If ever time should come when vain and aspiring men shall possess the highest seats in government, our country will stand in need of its experienced patriots to prevent its ruin.

—Samuel Adams

June 25, 1776
City Tavern, Philadelphia

The war zone that had been the main dining room at City Tavern was no longer littered with dead bodies; employees and delegates together had removed them to the back alley. Workers scoured the wooden floors, attempting to remove the dark, bloody stains. The coroner would arrive in the morning to remove the bodies and begin an investigation that might just shock the world. John Trumbull, City Tavern's manager, had been removed to his home at the insistence of his wife, who stated unequivocally she would tend to his wounds, not some "highfalutin doctor." Benjamin Franklin was famous for his numerous daily naps. The seventy-year-old would doze off during general meetings, committee meetings, and just about any other gathering, always awakening at the proper time to make lucid and valid arguments. Delegates learned quickly never to underestimate his uncanny ability to awaken at the most proper time. Despite the late hour, Franklin was moving around, shouting out orders, consoling workers, and even helping to carry one of the dead assassins.

Finally taking a seat beside John Adams, he whispered a concern to his colleague. "John, tomorrow the coroner will arrive and open an investigation. Jurisdiction for this crime is not entirely clear. I fear the coroner will attempt to overtake any investigation. I know this particular coroner, Joseph Giersch, a Tory if there ever was one. I am afraid a partisan investigation could prove uncomfortable for all of us."

At the onset of the war, a curious mix of government continued to operate, some effectively and others not so effectively. Depending upon the size of the local government and the proximity of the British Army, a hodgepodge of conflicting jurisdiction littered the Thirteen Colonies. Preferring order over anarchy, the city of Philadelphia continued to function under local government operated by British-paid bureaucrats, such as fire and police departments, sheriffs, judges, and coroners. Many were unabashed Tories whose situations were tenuous, but they held on, for no one could read the future. They went about their business and, in most cases, kept their loyalties to themselves. Smaller towns and villages had long since ousted any British authority and practiced vigilante justice or waited for the Continental Congress to replace bureaucrats with Patriots.

"I'm not sure I follow, Ben. It seems pretty straightforward. Assassination attempts were made on key delegates at two different sites. In addition, they tried to cover their tracks by killing the assassins. If not for the heroics of Mr. Cushman and Mr. Hall, they surely would have succeeded. How could a Tory coroner misinterpret that?" Adams was concerned; Franklin was not one to fabricate problems. On the contrary, he was usually too optimistic and cheerful, unlike Adams's Puritan values of stoicism and tolerant suffering. Adams, in particular, had a most deserved reputation of a top-notch complainer.

"Please bear with an old man, John. I know this may sound implausible, but I have seen how English bureaucrats work and think. As a lawyer, I'm sure you know about the history of the coroner's office. I won't bore you with details, but what if Mr. Giersch indicts us all for failing to raise the *hue and cry*. He could drag everyone here tonight into court, with the possibility of fines or even prison. The resulting delays and scandal could be disastrous, even if we were cleared of everything. You know how lawyers can twist facts. He may even try to turn the events of this evening into a plot against the Crown. We may end up having to defend ourselves against treason.

With an invasion imminent and the vote on independence coming soon, I fear a disruption of our assembly."

"Failing to raise the *hue and cry*. Interesting, Dr. Franklin, interesting. You know that dates back to the twelfth century?" Adams remained silent, his furrowed brow indicating he was in deep thought. "You are right, this could be a problem. Loyalist could gain political points with moderates. The delays could be as damaging as an indictment, especially with the vote on independence growing near. But you sent the constables to the aid of Ben and Thomas. That could be construed as a pursuit," added Adams.

"True. But common law demands a first finder alert at least four households. I have no doubt that we would prevail eventually, but we can't afford to be bogged down in this mess," reasoned Franklin. "We could simply ignore the coroner, paint him as a political hack. After all, I hardly think the king will hang us twice!"

"True, but I think Philadelphia is a microcosm of the entire country. Part Patriot, part Loyalist, and part fence-sitting. Getting a Tory like Giersch to proclaim the truth would be a great victory for us and perhaps would help bring some of the fence-sitters to our side," responded Franklin. "Of course, failing that, it will add one more crime for King George to complain about, failure to comply with the king's coroner." Both men sat back, tilted their heads skyward, and began to contemplate this potential predicament.

Battered, bruised, and bloodied, Thomas Jefferson and Ben Cushman walked into City Tavern with all the energy of two eighty-year-old men. It was way past midnight as they approached the assembled delegates; all had remained to hear news of their colleagues John Hancock and Samuel Adams.

Cushman and Jefferson were set upon immediately. John Hart fussed over Cushman's wounds, dressing them with a clean cloth napkin, since Dr. Presser was no longer around. Abraham Clark was astounded by the exploits of the shy and bookish Jefferson; he didn't hide his admiration for the bravery and ingenuity he had shown in such dire circumstances. As for Cushman and the mysterious Major Hall, Clark thought their heroics were Herculean in stature. Roger Sherman fired question after question, his analytical mind attempting to piece together the chaos that had disrupted their perfect evening.

Robert Livingston mostly remained quiet as Jefferson and Cushman recounted their harrowing escapades, although he noted that Hall and Hancock had not returned to City Tavern. Livingston observed that both Jefferson and Cushman were extremely humble in recounting their story. An incredibly heroic tale and yet not one boastful word, no bragging, no embellishment of any kind; these Southerners were truly dissimilar from his friends in New Jersey and New York. Where he hailed from, braggadocio was as common as stars in the sky.

Cushman soon tired of the interrogation and waited patiently for a lull in the conversation. As if by sheer will or just plain luck, the lull he had hoped for came soon after. Without hesitation, Cushman excused himself and started wandering toward Adams and Franklin, hoping to quell something gnawing at his brain since he had returned to City Tavern.

Cushman had been anxiously searching for the attractive waitress Ms. Deborah. She was nowhere to be found. He felt uncomfortable inquiring about her, fearful his intentions would be misread. He wasn't even sure of his real intensions, but one thing was certain: she had somehow breached his female defenses. Recalling her gentle touch while she had examined his injured arm had sent a sudden shiver throughout his body. He tried to think of something different, but the only thing he could conjure up was her leap into his arms as she emerged from the kitchen. Her warm embrace, satin-like skin, and the gentle scent of exotic perfume had sent a bolt of lightning through his entire body. Her piercing ocean-blue eyes had commanded him to rescue her from all danger and whisk her away to safety. The embrace had lasted less than ten seconds but seemed like hours. *No doubt about it,* Cushman thought to himself, *you've been bitten-bitten very hard, indeed.*

Cushman sheepishly asked Franklin, "Have you seen Ms. Deborah?" Before he had finished his sentence, he regretted asking the playful Philadelphian.

"Don't worry, Ben, I had one of the constables escort Ms. Deborah home a while ago. She was greatly upset. Why do you ask?" Franklin's tone and the sparkle in his eyes indicated he was aware of Cushman's interest in the attractive waitress.

"No reason. I was just concerned about her well-being," Cushman's rapid response and defensive tone told Franklin his instincts had once again been dead-on. "But I'm glad she escaped unharmed." The normally poised Cushman blushed like a child caught in a lie. He felt like he was twelve years old again.

Franklin smiled knowingly. "Don't worry, you will see her again, I'm sure." Turning toward the others, Franklin called out, "Gentlemen, I think it is time to get some rest. Tomorrow will be very important, so remember the plan. Mr. Adams and I will return here early and try to head off Mr. Giersch. The rest of you will attend to congressional duties, and remember, be as vague as possible when discussing tonight's events." Turning toward Cushman, Franklin continued, "Mr. Cushman, have you arranged for lodgings?"

Jefferson spoke before Cushman could answer. "He will stay with me. I have room in the parlor and enough blankets to make an acceptable bed. Besides, my humble quarters will remind him of his common upbringing." The twinkle in Jefferson's eye spoke volumes for the friendship these two shared.

"If you're lucky, I may even help you finish your project for the committee," added Cushman, referring to the Declaration of Independence.

They all laughed and headed toward the front door, Jefferson firmly patting his friend Ben Cushman squarely on the back. "It's always something with you."

Chapter 12

When the white man discovered this country, Indians were running it. No taxes, no debt, women did all the work. White man thought he could improve on a system like this?

—old Cherokee saying

June 25, 1776
The Graff House, Philadelphia

They laughed like children as they outran the white foam churning forward, threatening to overtake their sprint. Hand in hand they stopped, taunting the rushing water as it slowed and reversed itself. Tiptoeing back quickly toward the shore, they approached the large body of water and dared another wave to try to catch them. The warm sun beat down on them as they watched their footprints disappear in the cool, wet sand as each wave came roaring in off the massive freshwater lake. Whitecapped waves appeared to be four to six feet high as the northeast wind whipped the lake into a powerful wall of water, attacking the shoreline with a rhythmic repetition every few seconds. They followed the retreating water to the very edge of the lake, then spun quickly and ran to avoid the next giant wall of water. Their bare feet penetrated several inches into the wet sand, slowing their retreat and adding to the adventure of being caught up in the pounding surf. Breathing heavily from the short sprints, the two embraced, pulling each other close and gazing out over the shimmering body of blue water. A bright, cloudless morning sky seemed to melt into the clear blue waters of Lake Erie in Northern Ohio. It was difficult to tell where one ended and the other began.

The brisk wind made her long flaxen hair dance around her perfect face, teasing him to come closer. He slowly turned and gazed into the most stunning sapphire eyes he had ever seen. Her mouth parted knowingly as he slowly lowered his lips onto hers, electricity thumping throughout his entire body. Satiny, soft hair gently whipped his face, the clean fragrance igniting his sense of smell. The crash of the waves grew louder and louder, over and over, again and again. Crashing waves were soon replaced by a different sound. *What was it? Bang! There it was again. Bang! Bang!*

Ben Cushman stirred; the sound grew louder as a sharp pain radiated from his arm. He shook his head quickly, only to be rewarded with a sharp ache emulating from deep inside his brain. Reality rapidly set in as Cushman awoke from the best dream of his young life. The pain in his arm reminded him of the life-and-death battle the night before. The pain in his head was courtesy of the multiple rounds he had consumed with his newfound friends. The loud noise sounded again, and Cushman, now half-awake, recognized the clamor. Someone was splitting logs outside. Cushman sat up on the bedroll his friend Thomas Jefferson had laid out. He took in his surroundings as the sun broke through all four windows, despite the thin curtains. A small fireplace dominated the interior wall. A very thin mantel held two candlesticks and a cigar box. In the center of the twenty-by-twenty-foot room sat a round table with four chairs. A smaller circular table sat in the corner. Large stacks of books were piled near a small desk in the corner of the room. An odd-shaped box sat on the desk, next to some papers, several quills, and a large bottle of ink.

Cushman repositioned himself. Prone on the floor, he gazed up at the ceiling and clasped his hands behind his head. Eyes closed, he tried to visualize the dream again. He wasn't surprised that he had dreamed of Deborah and a romantic romp on the sands of Lake Erie. *Sakes alive!* He didn't even know her last name. Having such a dream about a girl he had just met and didn't even know the last name of. He was becoming a poodle-faker. British soldiers used the slang term to describe a man who spent too much time with women at dances and tea parties. *Ben Cushman, the poodle-faker.* He was surprised at the intensity of the dream, how they both seemed so madly in love. Cushman had never truly known love, with two possible exceptions.

His first was his one-sided infatuation for Jane Jefferson, Thomas's older sister. She had never known, or at least had never let on that she had known anything of Benjamin's crush. Her death at the young age of twenty-five had been very hard on Ben. The second possible relationship that might have blossomed into love was his brief encounter with a beautiful Indian squaw while he was taking care of business in Ohio, *Falling Star.* Her untimely death had added to the many heartaches Cushman experienced during early adulthood. Ben rationalized that the dream with the tavern waitress was somewhat understandable; after all, his encounter with Ms. Deborah was indeed a memorable experience, one he would not soon forget. For the dream to take place on the shores of Lake Erie was also logical, as he had just returned from a fifteen-month mission for vengeance in the lush, forested region known as Ohio.

Cushman's lust for revenge had taken him deep into Ohio Country in search of the murderess Indian called *Yellow Snake*. The dangerous mission had actually led Cushman to experience many a fine adventure while seeking to track down his deadly prey. He thought of his brother James and Elinipsico, the son of Cornstalk, chief of the Shawnee tribe. They had helped him throughout his search for *Yellow Snake*, only to miss out on the final chapter due to illness. He thought again of *Fallen Star* and what might have been. A satisfied smile slowly appeared on Cushman's face as he remembered *Yellow Snake's* eyes, the realization that a Cushman would be the last thing he would see before they were shut forever. His last journey into the Ohio Territory had finally borne the sweet fruit of revenge. A chance conversation at a tavern outside Fort Pitt had changed Cushman's plan from returning to his home in Virginia and instead to take Forbes Road to Philadelphia and spend some quiet and relaxing time with his best friend. *Wow, that sure backfired. What was the saying? From the frying pan into the fire.* It was now official. Like it or not, he was caught up in the revolutionary fever that was spreading throughout the Thirteen Colonies.

Chapter 13

If a nation expects to be ignorant and free, in a state of civilization, it expects what never was and never will be.

—Thomas Jefferson

June 25, 1776
Philadelphia

Cushman stood, gazing through the open window at the street below. Having arrived well after midnight and dead tired, he hadn't noticed much of Jefferson's boardinghouse or its surroundings. He was surprised when he realized they were outside the city, even though they traveled only a few blocks. Directly across the street was a stable, the smell of fresh manure differed only slightly from the strong stench of the city sinks. Next to the stable, a stack of firewood lay neatly piled against a rail fence, the axman having disappeared. In both directions, farmland stretched for hundreds of yards. Cushman moved to the front window; he could see the homes and buildings that made up the city of Philadelphia. The morning breeze cooled the room but brought with it the aggressive horseflies, forcing Cushman to swat away at the pesky insects.

The sudden footsteps bounding up the stairways startled Cushman; he reflexively walked toward his pistol lying next to his boots. Bursting through the door, the redheaded Thomas Jefferson smiled and greeted his weary friend. "Good, I'm glad you survived last night. The sounds coming from your room were downright morbid." The tall Virginian tossed his trifold hat on his bed. Jefferson folded his arms and glared at Cushman, eyeing him from head to toe. "Looks like everything is still intact. How does your arm feel?"

"I suppose I'll survive, but I think I'll head back to Ohio. It's a lot less dangerous. There, I only had to worry about bloodthirsty Indians, wildcats, and the extreme weather. A much safer place than Philadelphia."

"If you think it's dangerous now, it will soon be much more so. While you were sleeping the day away, I took a ride into town and received some interesting news. Scores of British ships have been spotted off Staten Island in New York. It seems the Howe brothers have finally decided to act. If Washington can't hold them in New York, Philadelphia will surely be their next target."

"You doubt the general's skill as commander?" Cushman questioned while examining bullet wounds in both arms. "Alexander the Great couldn't defend New York from the British. Our fellow Virginian has been dealt a very bad hand."

"How so?"

"Well, first of all, despite the optimism at our table last night, you may be right. Our citizen soldiers may not be as enthusiastic for battle as we thought. Word comes from General Washington to the Congress that many in the Army are returning home after their enlistment ends. Many just leave in the middle of the night. That's the Continental Army. The state militias are far worse. The general has enacted harsh penalties for those caught deserting, but even the lash of the whip has not slowed the departures. Camp illness is even worse. Washington estimates that at least half of the Army has taken with camp fever."

"Disease has been the dread of every army from Alexander to Washington. The men get lazy and do their necessities too close to camp. General Forbes made us dig latrines five hundred paces from our encampment. Anyone caught not using them would be given the lash," Ben replied.

"His correspondence was depressing in other ways. The principal difficulty, according to the general, is the geography of New York. Are you familiar with the city?"

"Never been there," admitted Cushman.

"New York City is basically made up of three islands, Staten Island, Manhattan Island, and Long Island. The Hudson River runs along the west side of Manhattan and divides it from New Jersey and Staten Island. The East River runs along the east side of Manhattan, dividing it from Long Island. The Harlem River connects the East and Hudson to make Manhattan an island.

"The East and Hudson Rivers meet at the southern tip of Manhattan, forming the Upper New York Bay, which leads out into the Atlantic Ocean. It is common knowledge that the British strategy to defeat the rebellion is to divide the Northern States by way of the Hudson River, then constricting them like a large snake. They figure they can pacify the South with so many Tories living there. New York is the key to controlling the Hudson, and to control New York is to control the waterways around it. If General Washington fortifies Manhattan or even Long Island, Admiral Howe can land troops farther up the Hudson or East Rivers and trap Washington between the British bayonets and the Navy's heavy guns. The citizens of New York and our Congress have demanded that General Washington defend the city at all costs. I'm no military man, but common sense tells me that to defend New York without a navy or heavy guns to halt British ships from entering the harbor will end badly," Jefferson declared without emotion.

Jefferson pulled out a map of New York City. Laying it out across the desktop, he began pointing out the geography of the second largest city in the colonies.

"What about putting heavy guns here?" Cushman pointed at the narrow channel between Long and Staten Islands.

"A distinct possibility. I believe Washington is placing cannons here in Brooklyn." Jefferson jabbed at the map and the borough of Brooklyn, located at the southwestern tip of Long Island. "Two problems: it's not that narrow, close to a mile wide, and we don't have enough guns. Howe's navy is said to be the largest armada ever seen in history. According to one source, we only have a single battery of nine-pounders situated in Brooklyn and none on Staten Island," Jefferson conveyed the report Congress had received earlier that day.

Cushman contemplated his friend's words and replied, "Perhaps General Washington will force the British to attack a heavily guarded high ground, like Bunker Hill."

"That is a possibility, Ben, but if truth be known, I am sure Washington would prefer to take on the British in more favorable circumstances and outside the range of Admiral Howe's guns," Jefferson added.

"I agree. The best chance to defeat a superior British force would be to lure them inland and away from the support of their navy. Can't we somehow disrupt Howe's ships?" Cushman questioned his friend.

"The Congress is close to granting letters of *marque and reprisal* to American merchant ships, which might help harass Howe's navy. However, the best scenario would have us enter into a treaty with France. They are the only nation in the world that could counter the British Navy," Jefferson stated without emotion.

"France? Are you serious, Red? I fought against the French. I have a better opinion of the American Indians," Cushman countered with astonishment, his eyebrows arched skyward.

"I understand, Ben, but this war is unlike any war in history. Aid from France or Spain will be needed, and needed soon. The resulting independence of these United States will in itself change the world. This revolution will not stop here. It will spread to all freedom-loving people throughout the world. Old rivalries will be replaced by new friendships, and old friends will become new enemies. This war will truly turn the world upside down."

"We better win, then, or I think your vision will be just that, a vision, not a reality," replied Cushman.

"I just wish we could get the entire Congress to see the vision. We still have too many moderates who wish to negotiate with the British or to find common ground with the king," Jefferson declared.

"What about this Declaration of Independence you talk about? I thought all were on board with it."

"Not all. Dickinson of Pennsylvania and Rutledge of South Carolina are vehemently against independence. Both want reconciliation. They hold sway over the others, like Mr. Livingston."

Ben recalled Livingston's transformation the previous night and wondered if it was all an act. "After last night, I think Mr. Livingston has been won over."

"I would have to agree, but he certainly wouldn't be the first politician to change his mind again," noted Jefferson.

A wicked look came over Ben. "Who do you suppose is worse, a politician or a lawyer?" Cushman asked of his friend, who happened to be both.

Jefferson laughed loudly. "Maybe I should stick to farming." The Virginia delegate slowly shook his head from side to side. "Sam Adams thinks it's going to be difficult to convince the moderates, the appeasers. I just hope my declaration can change some minds."

"'Thus Belial, with words clothed in reason's garb, counseled ignoble ease, and peaceful sloth, not peace,'" Cushman quoted.

An astonished Jefferson clapped his hands together, recognizing the famous John Milton line from *Paradise Lost*. "Parson Murray would be very proud of you, remembering one of his lessons."

"Well, I didn't get kicked out the first day. I occasionally read an assignment."

"The people must realize that our mother country has abandoned us. After Bunker Hill, there will be no reconciliation. Any attempt at appeasement will only mean defeat and loss of freedom. How many times must history repeat itself?" Jefferson's mood grew somber.

"Perhaps your declaration will inspire the doubters. Even I have to admit that at times you can be pretty persuasive," Cushman declared, starting to dress for the day.

"I have one other piece of news I think you will find interesting," a coy Jefferson stated. "The messenger delivering Washington's correspondence had an interesting conversation about last night's events with Abraham Clark. Clark casually mentioned your heroics. The messenger seemed quite excited, for he also was serving with a Cushman, your brother James. James has been assigned to General Washington as one of his aid-de-camp."

"James is serving with Washington! Hall mentioned that last night. Did he mention George?"

"Nothing about George. According to the messenger, James joined the general soon after he took command in Boston," noted Jefferson.

"I sent James home from Ohio in late January. He had the flu so bad he was slowing me down. I had Eliniscipo escort him to Fort Pitt, where a group of Virginia militia was heading home. I haven't heard from my other brothers for close to a year. I knew George was working as a Merchant Marine. Major Hall revealed their little adventure together last night, although with scant detail. Last I heard about Thomas was that he was working somewhere in New York City. James always did admire General Washington. It comes as no surprise that he would seek him out."

"Well, if I know James, he will soon be giving orders to the general." Jefferson laughed.

"Very true. I pray the general won't grow tired of his incorrigibility and have him in front of a firing squad."

"Speaking of Ohio, when are you going to tell me about *Yellow Snake*?"

"That, my friend, is a very long story that will take all day at your favorite tavern. Suffice it to say that the cowardly bastard is now rotting in hell."

The grin on the face of Edward Van Dyke increased the pain around his swollen eye, but it didn't stop him; he was a happy man. His walk quickened with the confidence of a man who had accomplished an important mission. Passing a nearby hardware store, he slowed and gazed at his reflection in the storefront window. His hand gently grazed over the swollen right eye. A dark bruise formed beneath the eye socket, immediately changing his mood from gleeful to angry.

Angry at his crazy boss, who delivered the blow to his eye, angry at the Virginian Thomas Jefferson, but most of all angry, at Jefferson's companions, who had halted the attack at the home of Aaron Tucker. The anger grew when he remembered the recently obtained knowledge that they had been instrumental in thwarting the assassinations launched at City Tavern as well.

But vengeance would be his. He had a name, only one, but it was a start. *Ben Cushman!* Van Dyke had just left the home of Alexander Lisberger, a first-year Philadelphia police officer who enjoyed exchanging police-related information for money. Van Dyke had managed to help Lisberger escape a particularly embarrassing situation involving a married woman and her irate husband. Grateful for the intervention, the rookie policeman had given Van Dyke several nuggets of information. The bribe money had been small at first but had recently grown with the Continental Congress in town.

That morning, Van Dyke had set out early to Lisberger's run-down apartment, hoping for information regarding the previous night's activities at City Tavern. As luck would have it, Lisberger had been on duty at the new Walnut Street Jail when two of the officers had returned from the double crime scenes. Even the prisoners were fascinated by the tale the officers retold, and Lisberger had remembered the name of Ben Cushman. The second Good Samaritan remained a mystery, but this did not dampen Van Dyke's mood. He had a name. *Ben Cushman, Ben Cushman,* Van Dyke repeated to himself. A sinister smile crossed his face as he envisioned the misery he would bring to Mr. Ben Cushman.

At the same time Edward Van Dyke was contemplating his revenge, Deborah Johnson walked hesitantly toward the three-story redbrick mansion. The message delivered by one of Rourke's goons was short and concise. *Get to Rourke's house immediately.* Deborah walked the two and a half blocks quickly, growing anxious as she climbed the last step to the front door. Although her father and Patrick Rourke had had a friendly relationship for years, this would be her first time visiting the home of one of Philadelphia's richest men. She had only met Rourke a few times, the most recent at a party several months earlier, and only remembered him because he later appeared to be in deep conversation with a most beautiful woman. That woman Deborah identified as her new tutor, the exotic and charming Ms. Lydia. The exchange between the two appeared to be more than just small talk. More like a physical cat-and-mouse game between the two as they brushed up against each other in a seductive manner, suggesting they were more than casual acquaintances. Deborah wondered as she lightly banged on the door who controlled who in the relationship between Patrick Rourke and the intriguing Ms. Lydia.

A large black servant opened the door immediately. His size and demeanor intimidated Deborah. *Run,* she thought to herself, but her legs felt like rubber. He led her to the back of the house and into one of the most magnificent private libraries she had ever seen. The servant smiled and left without saying a word, leaving Deborah alone to soak in the entirety of the room. Soft dark wood dominated the library. From the shimmering mahogany floor to the rectangular Persian rug, everything seemed perfectly coordinated. The two side walls were covered with books, from the floor to just below the ceiling; the mahogany bookshelves matched the floor. Deborah had never seen so many books in one place.

But it was the back outside wall that dominated the room. The long structure consisted of four large vertical windows, easily ten feet high, each with matching mahogany panes every two feet. Floor-length dark-violet curtains divided each window, tied halfway to allow the morning light into the glorious room. The windows were capped by matching valances with white-fringed tassels hanging from the bottom. Directly in the middle of the four windows was a massive fireplace; the hearth could easily fit several people inside. The top corners of the fireplace mantel had the ornately carved heads of two lions. Mounted on the wall, above the mantel stood an array of ancient and modern weapons, some of which Deborah had never seen before. Suspended directly over the fireplace was a large bow with a quiver full of arrows. To the right appeared a two-foot wooden pole with an attached chain approximately three feet long, connected to a large metal ball with sharp spikes. Slightly higher on the wall was a similar weapon, a two-foot wooden shaft with a metal ball attached, and again the protruding spikes. To the left of the centered bow and arrows was a long spear-like object. The bottom half of the spear appeared to be made of wood, and the narrower upper half was made of some type of metal with a sharp point at the end. In addition, there were several different styles of muskets and handguns. A number of odd-shaped devices sat on top of the fireplace mantel. Taking a closer look, Deborah suddenly felt a shiver of fear crawl up her spine.

"Admiring my collection, my dear?" The deep voice so startled Deborah that she jumped, only to turn and come face-to-face with Mr. Patrick Rourke.

She was taken aback by the realization that he was only an arm's length away and she had never heard him enter the room. His dark curly black hair framed a rather-feminine face, with its smooth complexion and smallish features. The lean, powerfully built body stood a head taller than Deborah and was anything but ladylike. His long-sleeve shirt was made of the finest silk she had ever seen. A beige linen cravat covered his neck; it was tied in a fashionable bow. He was as handsome as anyone she had ever met. For some odd reason, Deborah's thoughts turned to the other handsome gentleman she had encountered the night before, Benjamin Cushman. She compared the two men, and there was one unmistakable difference. Cushman's deep emerald eyes were pleasant and kind. Rourke's dark-brown eyes were different. At first, she couldn't quite come up with a comparison, but then it struck her like a bolt of lightning. His eyes penetrated into her like a sharp beam of light. They were wild and soulless. They were evil eyes, and all of a sudden, Deborah Johnson felt very frightened.

Chapter 14

It is the trade of lawyers to question everything, yield nothing, and talk by the hour.
—Thomas Jefferson

June 25, 1776
Philadelphia

At City Tavern, they interviewed the two surviving cooks, examined the dead bodies, and surveyed the back coffee room, where the attack had occurred. The two men had been there for over an hour. Previously, they had made stops at the home of Mr. John Trumbull, the manager of City Tavern, and then to the Walnut Street Jail, where they interviewed the three young constables who performed so heroically the previous night.

The men were elected officials of Philadelphia County; one was the county coroner, and the other was the county sheriff.

"So," Coroner Joseph Giersch proclaimed to his companion, "we have identified the constable as Mr. Cyrus Rice."

"His young wife just left, very distraught. They've got a little one, can't be more than three months old. Yeah, she identified him. Pretty little thing. Shouldn't have trouble finding another husband," responded Sheriff Silas Otto.

Giersch glanced up at his fellow bureaucrat, who stood at least six inches taller, and smiled, always amused at the sheriff's morbid gallows humor and his disdain for proper deployment regarding death.

"Nothing on the other four?"

"No names, no wives coming forward, no family. Seems like they came out of thin air," replied Otto as he removed a small hand knife and began to pick at his teeth.

"What about the waitress? What's her name?" Giersch barked.

The sheriff checked his notes and announced, "Johnson, Deborah Johnson. According to the cooks, Mr. Franklin had her escorted home last night, and she's not scheduled to work today."

"Well, we need to talk to her. She could have some useful information," Giersch demanded.

"Mr. Trumbull said her father is a shareholder here. He also gave us their address," countered Otto.

"Good. We will go visit Ms. Johnson when we finish here. Where are those damn delegates? I thought we agreed to meet here at noon. It's fifteen minutes past!" Giersch barked at his colleague.

"Maybe the news of British sails off New York forced the cowards to flee," opined Sheriff Otto.

"If we could only be so lucky. Damn traitors. Mr. Otto, if it pleases you, perhaps you should seek out Ms. Johnson while I wait to speak with our distinguished delegates."

"Good idea. According to the cooks, she is very beautiful," noted the sheriff.

Giersch just shook his head. Silas Otto wasn't very smart, but his down-home attitude was attractive to voters. The power-hungry Giersch didn't mind sharing *some* power with Otto. He was easily manipulated, and despite their positions being considered equal, Giersch could always convince him of the superiority of his opinion. The sheriff was a useful idiot, and the coroner knew how to control him.

County Coroner was just a stepping stone to higher positions, and Giersch's loyalty to the king would certainly pave the way for future promotions. The den of traitors known as the Second Continental Congress would hang soon enough, hopefully, right here in Philadelphia. Giersch could think of nothing more satisfying than to oversee the execution of the Philadelphia delegates. The vision of their bodies dancing at the end of a rope brought a smile to his face.

In the meantime, he saw an opportunity in last night's carnage. If played properly, he could undermine any progress the delegates might have made. There were rumors of a declaration of independency that could be imminent, and Giersch had to admit that more and more of his Tory friends were worried that the popularity of the revolution was slowly increasing. Giersch knew that once General Howe landed in New York, the rebel army would fall quickly. But Howe certainly was taking his time, and the longer he waited, the more persuasive the rebel leaders were becoming. Philadelphians were becoming enamored with the famous delegates, particularly those from Massachusetts and Virginia. Even some of Giersch's closest Loyalist friends had begun to waver. He would clearly have to execute a delicate dance to pull off what he was contemplating. The local mob was nothing like Boston's, but he had to be mindful of their contradictory behavior. He reflected back to a recent correspondence with his brother and an interesting trial regarding the *first finders* of a body, who failed to raise the *hue and cry*. Giersch's brother Robert, also a coroner in London, had dug up the old law and applied it twice to towns responsible for failure to raise the *hue and cry*. The resulting victories in court and large fines made Robert Giersch a rising star in the king's circle.

Could it be done here? No one had alerted the nearest four households at either of the crime scenes last night, and in each case the *first finders* were all delegates to the Second Continental Congress. *Similar scenario here with perhaps even greater results.* He envisioned a trial in Philadelphia, where he would parade the leaders of the revolution into a public courtroom. If he was clever enough, he could expose them for the dishonorable traitors they were.

The potential propaganda bonanza could be vital in winning over the fence-sitters and maybe some of the more moderate revolutionaries. Giersch realized he was on shaky legal ground, but none more so than his brother, and he had won, not once, but twice. He knew the jurisdictional judge was a strong Loyalist who would allow him great latitude in the prosecution of the case. As a bonus, he would be prosecuting some of the most extreme leaders of the revolt, Franklin, Adams, Jefferson, and John Hancock. Even if he lost the case, the reputations of those leaders would be sullied. With Howe taking New York soon, Philadelphia would not be far behind. The king would surely recognize his contribution. His reward would be colossal, perhaps a governorship. Giersch smiled. If he was careful, he could see no downside, none at all.

She stepped back and took a deep breath. Her instincts told her to run, but she was frozen in place by his wild dancing eyes.

"I'm sorry, my dear. Did I startle you?" Rourke's smooth delivery was messianic.

"Yes. I...I...didn't hear you enter, Mr. Rourke," she stammered, trying to hide her fear.

Rourke smiled and gently motioned toward two large chairs facing the massive fireplace. "My servant will bring in some wine. Come sit down. We must talk. I saw you admiring my collection. I have always been fascinated by weapons of war, and I have been collecting these for many years." He waved to the weapons mounted above the fireplace.

"An interesting collection," Deborah stated, slowly regaining her composure.

"The English longbow, over six feet, six inches," Rourke declared gleefully, "can shoot an arrow over three hundred yards. Not very accurate, but when you launch thousands at the same time, the results can be devastating. The English longbowmen helped defeat the French cavalry during the One Hundred Years War at the Battle of Crecy in 1346, the Battle of Poitiers in 1356, and the Battle of Agincourt in 1415. It was the most efficient weapon of its day, especially if the soldiers or horses were not wearing armor."

"Horses wore armor?" Deborah asked. "Never heard of such a thing."

"Most certainly. No better way to defeat a cavalry charge than by taking out the horses," Rourke claimed gleefully.

"What about the spiked ball on the chain?" Deborah feigned interest in hopes of winning over Rourke.

Rourke smiled, seemingly pleased that she showed an interest in his passion. "Ah, the flail, one of my favorites, a popular weapon for armored knights on horseback. They preferred this weapon as they rode into battle. When the ball would make contact, it wouldn't transfer vibrations from impact like a sword or an ax, because of the hinged chain. Also, it was hard for opponents to parry a blow since it would curve around a sword or shield. This was of critical importance because you didn't want to get knocked off-balance and fall off the horse. Immobile, horseless, armored knights were easy pickings for opposing forces."

Rourke effortlessly slid to the opposite side of the fireplace, pointed to the spear, and continued, "The long spear is called a Roman pilum. It's a throwing spear, used by Roman legions. Oftentimes, legionnaires would carry two pilums into battle. They would throw the first and use the second in close-quarter combat." Rourke continued to relate the historical significance of each of the mounted weapons. Deborah quickly grew bored but continued to feint interest for fear of provoking Rourke.

Fortunately for Deborah, Rourke ran out of weapons to lecture about, but then she did something she would later regret. She looked at the wicked-looking devices on the fireplace mantel and casually commented, "And what about these? They don't look like weapons."

"*Au contraire*, these are the secret weapons of war. Information can be far more valuable than soldiers or weapons, and these devices can guarantee information from anyone, and I mean anyone!" Rourke had seemed enthused when discussing the weapons but became downright giddy when talking about the torture devices. His eyes danced with delight as he described the ancient torture implements and the resulting effect.

"This is the cat's-paw." He picked up a metal claw with four fingers about the size of a large man's hand. The four-inch-long fingers were curved downward into sharp points and attached to a three-inch wooden handle. Rourke slowly moved the claw toward Deborah's cheek; her eyes betrayed her fear, which only encouraged Rourke to continue. "The torturer could rip the flesh from any part of your body. They would usually start on the back or your chest, then work to the face, and finally more private areas."

The unusual whip, or cat-o'-nine-tails, was next as Rourke talked about the Spanish Inquisition and the effectiveness of such torture devices. Rourke's cat-o'-nine-tails was a short whip with nineteen tails, not nine; each tail had a sharp metal barb attached to the end, ensuring the recipient a bloody and painful experience.

"Very efficient. Had to be careful, though. Didn't want the victim to die before you got the proper information out of him or her." Deborah thought he put particular emphasis on the word *her*, sending chills up her spine. She began to seriously question the sanity of Mr. Patrick Rourke.

Rourke reached for the next torture device, handing it to Deborah. "What do you think this was used for?"

Cautiously turning it over in her now-trembling hands, she examined two six-inch metal bands, roughly one inch wide, one-quarter inch thick, with multiple sharp spikes on the interior of each band. Two long thick screws at each end connected the two bands. The one screw had an L-shaped cap that obviously was used to open and close the device. Deborah imagined all sorts of body parts that could be placed into the screwing mechanism and finally asked softly, "Your fingers?"

"Close!" Rourke yelled in delight, obviously enjoying the conversation. "Very good, my dear, very good. Actually, it is a thumbscrew. See, you place a person's thumbs here." Rourke placed Deborah's thumbs into the torture device and slowly began to turn the screw.

Exhaling a nervous laugh, she pulled her thumbs away, joking she had no secrets to hide from him.

"We shall see." He didn't finish the sentence, but Deborah thought there was a hint of a threat, and her fear continued to mount.

Her eyes moved to an odd pear-shaped device at the end of the mantel, Rourke saw the eye movement and smiled. "Ah, yes, my favorite, *poire d'angoisse*, the pear of anguish." It was a pear-shaped mechanism about four inches long; at the skinny end of the pear, a ring was attached. The device was sectioned into quarters, and when Rourke began to twist the ring, it expanded, revealing the interior.

The ring was in fact a four-inch-long screw attached to a spring that when turned expanded the four sections outward; each section appeared to have sharp edges and a pointed tip.

"The pear of anguish is becoming very popular in Europe again. Many police agencies like its effectiveness, since there is no visible damage. *Confessions* appear to be given freely, without any coercion." His glee was easily evident in discussing such matters.

"I'm not sure I understand." Deborah had not comprehended the procedural use of the pear of anguish.

Rourke's smile got larger as he continued, "The pear is meant to damage a person's sensitive insides. After being inserted, the pear would be expanded to do great harm to the soft-tissue areas. For instance, people accused of committing homosexual acts would have the pear inserted anally; a whore or a wife refusing her duties, vaginally; and a wicked tongued gossip, orally." Rourke paused to allow his description to fully sink into Deborah's psyche. Rourke received the reaction he expected when she finally comprehended the damage the *pear of anguish* could deliver. The shocked look on her face gave great pleasure to Rourke. So much so that he was getting aroused and began to think of taking the young Ms. Johnson. The thought quickly passed; he needed to get information. *Maybe later.*

Deborah struggled to maintain her composure and, for the second time, considered running. Before she could make a decision, Rourke's demeanor changed drastically. "Enough of this." He managed a sinister smile. "Sit and tell me all about last night."

She told Rourke everything, how the cook Gerard was killed, John Trumbull's injury, the heroic intervention of Jefferson's friend, and a mysterious stranger. In addition, she told Rourke of her final deception to keep from being suspected. Deborah failed to mention her attraction to the mysterious man from Virginia. Her account lasted over fifteen minutes, and at no time did Rourke interrupt her to ask questions; he just listened with great intensity.

Rourke was impressed with Deborah's ingenuity and ability to lie under pressure.

"Do you think you convinced them of your story?"

"Without a doubt, no one questioned it at all," she promised, not mentioning the look that *green eyes* had given her, perhaps seeing through her ruse.

"This meddling friend of Jefferson's, did he have a name?"

The conflict within Deborah had been percolating all day. Cushman had caused their mission to fail, and despite the deception and violence, she still believed in the Tory cause. However, the attraction she felt for him was undeniable. Her hesitation in answering Rourke's question did not go unnoticed.

"Cushman," she stated softly, "Benjamin Cushman was his name, boyhood friend of Jefferson. I overheard one of the delegates say he was a veteran of the French and Indian War, served with Colonel Washington."

The mention of Washington caused a curl of a smile on Rourke's face. He stood and took Deborah by the hand and led her to the library door. Grasping both hands firmly, he gazed into her eyes. "You did a very good job last night, and I know your father is very proud of you. I want you to continue to listen and record everything you hear and see. Lydia will be in touch with you periodically. Mark my word, the traitors will pay for their treachery, and you will be rewarded handsomely for your efforts. One last thing, the mysterious stranger, did you get his name?"

Deborah didn't hesitate. "No, sir, no one seemed to know his name. It was very chaotic."

Rourke seemed satisfied and didn't press the nervous waitress. He would deal first with Jefferson's friend. His torture devices would get Cushman to reveal the mysterious interloper.

Seemingly out of nowhere, the black servant was at her side. "George will show you out." He leaned over and kissed her cheek. Rourke stood in the doorway, watching her shapely form glide down the hallway.

While Deborah made her departure, the secret door built into the bookcase slowly slid open and a newcomer walked gracefully forward, reached up, and firmly grabbed Rourke by the shoulders. Peering around his arm, she watched as Deborah Johnson left the

THE SIGNERS

mansion. Pressing close to Rourke, the extraordinary beauty spoke softly. "What do you think? Was she telling the truth?"

"She was lying about something. I think we should kill her tonight," Rourke stated tersely.

Lydia Ames was learning how to control Rourke, so she remained quiet and continued to press her well-shaped body into his back. "She could still be useful. Her performance last night may have endeared her to some of the least-talkative delegates."

"She's definitely hiding something. I don't think we can take a chance. She knows too much."

"This Cushman, do you think she lied about him?" Lydia asked gently.

"I'm not sure. Could she be that ignorant? Van Dyke should be back soon, and then we will know," Rourke declared more calmly as Lydia continued to squeeze him.

As if on cue from a stage play, the door knocker rang out, and sure enough, George was soon escorting Edward Van Dyke into the house.

"Well?" Rourke's one-word question was more of a demand.

Van Dyke smiled and stated loudly, "Ben Cushman is his name."

The Irishman looked back to Lydia and said quietly, "She lives, *for now*."

Rourke turned to Van Dyke. "What are you still doing here? You know what to do. Go!" Rourke waved his arm, dismissing his top henchman.

Van Dyke turned and headed toward the door, thinking how much he hated his boss, and yet there was an important part of him that wanted to please Rourke and make up for last night's failure.

"There had better not be another failure, Van Dyke," Rourke called out as he was leaving.

Van Dyke turned and called back, "There won't be a repeat of last night, and I will personally see to that." He stormed out the door, more determined than ever before.

Rourke turned to face Lydia. Her seductive touching was succeeding.

"Are Dr. Smith and Ms. Gibbons in place?"

"Yes, all is ready. Do not worry, all this intrigue has made me hungry for you, my darling," she teased.

"You don't have to ask me twice."

Ben Franklin and John Adams arrived at City Tavern at the same time. They had been involved in early-morning committee meetings and had both read the letter sent by George Washington. Like Jefferson, they were disappointed in the contents, but both were eager to engage the British. Adams felt confident that Washington would give the British a thrashing similar to Breed's and Bunker Hill. Franklin, like Jefferson, was concerned with the terrain and morale of the troops. Adams was adamant that Washington was the right man at the right time. Others were not so sure; in fact, a small faction was pushing hard for Washington to be replaced by his second-in-command, General Charles Lee, also from Virginia.

Adams's thoughts drifted toward the haughty Lee, considered by many the brightest military mind in the Continental Army—even Washington conceded it was true. For any further evidence of Lee's military brilliance, *one* only had to ask Lee. Cocky, highly opinionated, and profane as a street thief, Lee seemed to be a character right out of a Fielding novel. He was tall and very thin, with a hooked nose, sunken eyes, and a dark, bony complexion. Perpetually disheveled, even in uniform, he had served in the British Army, with tours in Spain and with General Braddock and Colonel Washington in the French and Indian War. In addition, he acted as an adviser to the king of Poland and even married the daughter of a Seneca Indian chief. He never traveled anywhere without his numerous dogs, two of which were said to be as large as small horses, and his prize Pomeranian he called Spado. Lee had advised Washington that New York could not be defended without a navy. Washington's bosses felt otherwise, and the battle for New York was rapidly approaching. Adams concluded that with all of Washington's problems preparing to defend New York, perhaps the greatest threat came from within.

Adams quickly dismissed the negative predictions coming from the North and began to concentrate on their present problem, *Giersch*. They had agreed to arrive an hour late, a strategy developed by Franklin to ensure a more subservient attitude by Coroner Giersch. Neither man expected Giersch to be cooperative, but both were soon taken aback by his discourteous and arrogant manner.

"Gentlemen, I realize I am but a humble servant of the king and you are both famous." Giersch paused for a dramatic effect and produced a condescending smirk. "*Rebels.*" He pronounced the word like it was an incurable disease. "But I must remind you both that as coroner of Philadelphia, I have both investigative and prosecutorial powers. I do not appreciate your lack of respect for the law with your blatant tardiness. In addition, I thought we agreed to meet with all involved. Where are the others?"

John Adams, the confrontational lawyer from Boston, was ready to launch into a counterdiatribe when Franklin gently grabbed his elbow.

"My dear Mr. Giersch, we both apologize for our lack of punctuality. Important matters before Congress delayed our arrival this morning. As to the others, those important matters continue to demand their attention. Mr. Adams and I were able to break away, but alas, for only a short time. I am sure the two of us will be able to answer all your questions. After all, it was a pretty straightforward attempt at assassination."

"Mr. Franklin, I presume no such thing. In fact, after questioning the police and the staff of City Tavern, I am more suspicious than ever into the murderous events of last night." Giersch stomped his foot to the floor to emphasize the last few words. "Tread very carefully, gentlemen, for this is very much an open investigation."

Adams was about to explode but instead took a deep breath and hissed slowly, "Mr. Giersch, are you threatening us?"

Giersch, unmoved by Adam's growing fury, shot back with equal forcefulness, "Mr. Adams, you're a lawyer of some repute. Perhaps you're familiar with penalties for first finders failing to raise the *hue and cry*. Did you or any of your colleagues think to alert any nearby households to search for the killers?"

"We were too busy defending ourselves against their attack," countered Adams, his frustration mounting. He had to admit that Franklin had correctly predicted Giersch's response, but he was still astonished the coroner could take such an obviously bias tactic.

Most European visitors to the American colonies expected to find an untamed wilderness combined with unmatched lawlessness. To Europeans, America was no different from Africa or India, vast untapped resources with little or no civilized culture. Those who visited were surprised to find a system of laws, traditions, and even government bureaucracies not unlike those of their homeland. One of those government bureaucracies imported from England was the Office of the Coroner.

The Office of the Coroner had been evolving since the 1100s. It was founded under the reign of King Richard the Lionhearted. While Richard was off fighting in the Crusades, the archbishop of Canterbury, Hubert Walter, was left to try to rule over England and endeavored to fill the empty coffers to pay for Richard's costly wars.

To wring even more money from the people, Walter established the Office of the Coroner. The goal was to bring more tax revenue to the Crown and undermine the local sheriffs, who were legendary in their ability to extort and embezzle money from the peasants, at great expense to the king. Sheriffs were common throughout the Thirteen Colonies, another import from the motherland even older than coroners. Like all his counterparts in Europe, the English king owned all the land, and these lands were divided into smaller regions, called shires. The king would reward nobility and ensure loyalty by allowing lords to manage the shire and all serfs that lived on the land. The serfs would farm the land and pay a certain percentage of their crops to the lord, usually 25 to 50 percent. The king, in turn, would receive payment from the lord. A very dangerous dance between serf, lord, and king regarding the size of the percentage or tax became a common practice; thus enter the sheriff.

The attempt to balance these payments fell to the annual practice of the serfs electing among themselves a reeve to help supervise the lands for the lord. The reeve had many duties, making sure that serfs began work on time, investigating crimes, arresting criminals, and most importantly, ensuring that no one was cheating the lord out of his fair share of the money. Eventually, the reeve of the shire became its most powerful administrator. Ultimately, the official title was shortened to shire-reeve, and finally melting together to become *sheriff*. As the sheriff's powers grew, so did the deserved reputation for bribery, blackmail, and all types of corruption.

It was into this cauldron of corruption that Archbishop Walter placed the Office of the Coroner, officially called the keeper of the pleas of the Crown, or *custos placitorum coronas*. As time wore on, the position was referred to as *the crowner*, and later *the coroner*.

The major duty of the coroner was to service the royal courts of law or the general eyre. The general eyre was, in fact, the original circuit court, traveling throughout England, administering justice. With great fanfare, the court traveled in a circuit that covered the entire country. It was not uncommon for the court to arrive to administer justice every seven years or so. One town waited nearly forty years for the return of the traveling court.

Therefore, it was essential that every detail of every major event since the last court appearance be recorded. Every crime, death, murder, suicide, and marriage was to be examined by the next visiting court. All details were scrutinized, and because the kings had made the legal process so complex and tortuous, it was nearly impossible for the town or borough to comply completely. Failure to properly comply meant large fines incurred by individuals, different groups of people, or whole towns. It was imperative to the king's revenue stream that detailed records of all major proceedings be kept. The keeper of these records fell to the Office of the Coroner.

In time, the American colonies adopted many British customs, including the Office of the Coroner. The evolution of the position continued in the New World, and while many of the Middle Age duties remained, the main function of the colonial coroner involved death—the investigation of, the determiner of, the cause of, and most importantly, that death indeed had occurred.

The unsanitary conditions of the Middle Ages produced some of the most virulent ailments known to mankind: smallpox, dysentery, measles, leprosy, typhus, pneumonia, flu, and the bubonic plague were just some of the deadly diseases to ravage Europe. With the onset of exploration, trade, and wars, the deadly mix was spread worldwide. Medieval cures for such diseases oftentimes did more harm than good. When family members were beset with such disease, the only real hope was for their body's immune system to be stronger than the invading illness. Lapsing into a coma became a common occurrence when battling these horrific diseases. Without proper medical knowledge or tools, family members would often bury their loved ones when they refused to wake up. Many thousands around the world would face the horrifying realization of emerging from a coma, only to be locked in a casket, buried alive.

One town in England, running out of wood to bury the dead, hired a local carpenter to dig up older graves, to reuse the wooden caskets. His gruesome discovery would lead to additional duties for the Office of the Coroner. Of the one hundred caskets that were pulled from the ground, twenty-five contained casket covers with scratch marks on the inside. Some of the skeletons even had bony hands in the proper position, attempting to claw through the top of the coffin. Others had splinters of wood embedded into the distal phalanges, the top bone of each finger.

Ever so gradually, the coroner's role shifted away from record keeping and tax collection to examiners of death. Many famous legends arose from this infamous time in European history, some absurd, but most exceedingly authentic.

Coming upon a "dead body," family and friends would place the body on the kitchen table for three days. They would eat and drink around the body, waiting for the individual to wake from their sleep. Thus, the celebration of eating and drinking in honor of the recently departed became known as a *wake*.

Colonial coroners, careful not to duplicate the horrors of burying victims alive, would tie a string around the finger or wrist of the corpse. The string would be led through a hollow bamboo shoot to above the ground and attached to a small bell. Coroners would hire young boys to sit in the graveyard at night, listening for a bell, thus serving a *graveyard shift*. Upon hearing a bell, the boy would run to the coroner or owner of the graveyard to organize a rescue; thus, they were *saved by the bell* or were sounding an alarm for a *dead ringer*.

Amid all the folklore, the Office of the Coroner was cemented into colonial bureaucracies through tradition and common law. Franklin's concern in referencing the *hue and cry* dated back well into the 1200s and, although rare, was occasionally still used in both England and her colonies. English common law demanded that anybody coming upon a dead body would be deemed the first finder. The first finder would have to raise the *hue and cry*, to initiate a manhunt for the killer and rouse the four nearest households to join in the search. The penalties for the first finder and the nearby households for not raising the *hue and cry* and beginning a manhunt were severe. Therefore, it was common practice to bypass a dead body, hide it, or even transport it to the nearest town, for the court was known to punish an entire town for dereliction of their duties.

Benjamin Franklin had read about two such incidents while serving in London. In both cases, the judges upheld the coroner's condemnation of the failure of the first finders to raise the *hue and cry*, and fines were issued to over twenty individuals in one case, and in another case, an entire town was fined. Much was made of the two episodes because it had been many decades since coroners and judges had used the ancient custom. What troubled Franklin even deeper was that the coroner who successfully prosecuted both cases was named Giersch, Robert Giersch. His younger brother, Joseph, was the coroner in Philadelphia. Giersch was to Philadelphia what Thomas Hutchinson was to Boston. Franklin knew Giersch as a capable and intelligent bureaucrat and fiercely loyal to King George. In addition, Giersch's reputation as being ruthless, ambitious, and cunning was exceedingly accurate. Giersch despised the Patriots and their cause. He would definitely cause problems.

"Let me be perfectly clear, gentlemen, I take my responsibilities as the king's coroner with great seriousness. It is my job to follow the laws of Pennsylvania and the king of England. I will apply each incident to the letter of the law. There will be no exceptions. Under no circumstances will I be intimidated by your illegal band of representatives you call the Continental Congress."

"I am certainly happy to see our distinguished coroner will show no prejudice concerning his investigation into last night's assassination attempt," replied John Adams, the sarcasm dripping off his tongue.

Giersch smiled, unaffected by Adams's words, and looked directly at Franklin while continuing to talk as if John Adams weren't in the room. "Mr. Adams has much to learn about Pennsylvania courtrooms, doesn't he, Mr. Franklin? This is not Massachusetts. There will be no dim-witted rabble sitting in the jury box, easily persuaded by the rebellious oratory of some New England lawyer. No! The jury will be made up of Pennsylvania Quakers, commonsense folks who look unkindly upon propaganda and smooth-talking city lawyers."

Benjamin Franklin shot Adams a look that clearly indicated he had been correct in his predication about Giersch. "Surely, Mr. Giersch, you are not implying that this was anything but a group of delegates defending themselves against a murder plot," Franklin stated calmly.

"As well as I can determine, Mr. Franklin, there will be many aspects to this case. Perhaps you and your friends will be exonerated of any murders, but it still does not excuse your duty as English citizens to raise the *hue and cry* to find the criminals responsible. I will not look the other way when a law is broken, even if it involves prominent citizens."

Adams stepped closer to Giersch and hissed his reply. "I am sure if we were all good little Tories, your *hue-and-cry* ruse would not even be mentioned, so spare us the lecture about duty." Adams's eyes were ablaze with contempt for the king's bureaucrat.

Giersch, momentarily taken aback, regained his pomposity and replied firmly, "Mr. Adams, make no mistake that I will pursue this case with more vigor than any case I have ever tried. I am sure Mr. Franklin can attest to my tenacity in both the investigation and inside the courtroom. It will be a very pleasurable day when a judge rules you gentlemen guilty." Retrieving his hat from a nearby table, Giersch started to leave, then swung around to take one more parting shot. "I sure hope the looming trial doesn't forestall your little rebellion. After all, the penalty for failure regarding the first finder is just a fine, and maybe a few years in jail. Correct me if I am wrong, but isn't the penalty for treason death by hanging? Gentlemen, have a good day." With that, Giersch walked out the door, smiling from ear to ear. It wasn't often anyone got the last word on Dr. Franklin and John Adams.

John Adams was known for a fierce temper. This was one of those times, his face turning redder with each word Giersch had spoken. As Giersch walked away, Adams began to follow, ready to unleash a verbal assault, and possibly a physical one as well. Anticipating Adams's reaction, the older Ben Franklin used two hands to hold back the Massachusetts delegate. "John, now is not the time. We must think this out."

"Ben, we are at war, and men like Giersch are the enemy. If we lose this war, it will be because of Tories like him." Adams could have easily pulled away from Franklin but chose to stop and listen to his esteemed colleague.

"Of course you're right, John, but let us use a different tact. Perhaps if we expose Giersch's Tory leanings to the proper crowd." The sly Franklin's head tilted upward as a plan began to formulate in his fertile mind. "And who better to incite the proper crowd?"

Adams smiled, instantly realizing Franklin's plan. "My cousin?"

"Your cousin." Franklin's grin widened.

Adams wasn't sure how the rebellion would turn, but he sure was glad Benjamin Franklin was on their side.

Chapter 15

We hold these truths to be self-evident, that all men are created equal, that they are endowed by their Creator with certain unalienable rights, that among these are life, liberty, and the pursuit of happiness.
—Thomas Jefferson,
Declaration of Independence

June 25, 1776
Philadelphia

"Ughhhhhh!" Ben Cushman clenched his teeth, trying not to scare the two-year-old tottering at his knee. The little boy let out a deep, guttural laugh, apparently enjoying Cushman's discomfort.

"Now, Mr. Cushman, what kind of example are you setting for Frederick? Sit still. I am almost finished," she stated firmly. "My family has always treated wounds this way. My grandmother was a midwife and swore by the medicinal properties of good whiskey. But it has to be Irish whiskey, not Scottish whiskey. Irish whiskey is blessed by the monks."

Little Frederick continued his belly laugh, watching Cushman's face contort with each application to his multiple wounds. The two men in the corner did little better than Frederick, failing in their attempt to hold back laughter. Thomas Jefferson and his landlord, Jacob Graff, continued to bask in Cushman's misery as Graff's wife, Catherine, administered to the friend of Jefferson.

A large city by any definition, Philadelphia still had many attributes of a small town. Like all small towns, news of unusual

THE SIGNERS

events traveled with the speed of lightning. Aaron Tucker had been a well-known businessman, and Jacob Graff had done several jobs for the Tucker family. His murder, along with the attempts on the most famous of the congressional delegates, was the talk of the town. Jacob and Catherine Graff had grilled both men for details, but with little success so far. Jacob Graff, a Philadelphia bricklayer, had rented the two second-story rooms to Thomas Jefferson for the past several months. He had personally built the three-story home and had finished just a year earlier. His wife, Catherine, an ardent supporter for independence, was quite fond of the younger Jefferson and watched over him as if he were her son. When Jefferson and Cushman had started downstairs, the husband, wife, and grandchild were waiting with breakfast and a healthy curiosity concerning last night's events.

Before Jefferson could complete the introduction of his best friend, Catherine had sprung into action and had begun the current process of treating Cushman's wounds, to the delight of the two men and the small child.

"Catherine, I think the left arm could use another dose, don't you?" Jefferson tried to stifle another laugh.

"Perhaps the right arm too." Jacob Graff smiled.

"Pay no attention to them, Mr. Cushman. My grandson is more mature than those two. Grandmother said whiskey promotes healing faster. She also believed in changing the dressing every day. Will you be staying with Mr. Jefferson very long? I will be happy to change the dressing." Her motherly instincts were kicking into high gear.

Cushman knew he had better speak quickly; he was beginning to understand a conversation with Mrs. Graff could be very one-sided. "Mrs. Graff," he started.

"Please call me Catherine," she interrupted.

"Catherine, your skill and kindness are exceptional. But I was always under the impression that the whiskey should be taken internally." Cushman winked at the two men.

"Well, as you might guess, Grandmother was Irish, and she believed very strongly in the healing properties of whiskey, both *internally and* externally." Catherine managed a slight laugh and handed Cushman a shot of the *medicine*.

Cushman raised both hands. "With all due respect to Grandmother, I think I had enough *medicine* last night."

They broke the fast with sausage, bread, and eggs. Cushman enjoyed hearing about Jacob Graff's family and his thriving business. Being pampered by Catherine Graff was not unpleasant and caused Cushman to think about Deborah and his lack of female companionship for the last year or so. Settling down and raising a family hadn't been a high priority. Jefferson had married Martha four years earlier and had two daughters, although tragically, their second daughter, Jane, named after Jefferson's oldest sister, had died when only one year old. Most of Cushman's other friends were also married, and even his younger brother, Thomas, was to be married later that year. But with the rebellion brewing, it probably wasn't the best time to court a young lady, let alone to settle down and start raising a family. After almost a full year of military inactivity, the standoff seemed to be coming to a tipping point. Washington's army was in New York, preparing for the Howe brothers' armada. The Congress was contemplating a Declaration of Independence. An assassination plot had been orchestrated against members of the Continental Congress. A chance of reconciliation between king and colonies was growing dimmer and dimmer. The future was anything but clear, but one thing was becoming painfully obvious: the future would not be peaceful. The gnawing uncertainty troubled Ben.

Breaking away from the good food and pleasant conversation was not an easy task, but eventually the two Virginians excused themselves and returned to the second-story sitting room, where Jefferson sat at his desk and motioned Ben to bring up a chair.

"Ben, I am nearly finished with the declaration. I was wondering if you would read through this rough draft. I would value your opinion."

"Since when would you value the opinion of someone expelled from one of the finest schools in all of Virginia?" Cushman smiled.

"Up until your expulsion, rumor had it you were a rising young Aristotle. Just misunderstood and a tad bit mischievous," teased Jefferson.

"Surely, you should seek out Dr. Franklin or John Adams for their advice," replied Ben, suddenly realizing the enormity of the task Jefferson was asking of him.

"Unfortunately, their counsel will come soon enough. I fear they may decimate my work," a clearly worried Jefferson added.

"It's not like you to be so unsure of yourself, especially regarding your writings. I could understand if you had to deliver a speech to the assembled members," Cushman stated, referring to his friends' reluctance to speak out publicly. Cushman was one of the few people who knew that Jefferson was very shy regarding public speaking. Ben believed his friend was embarrassed by a slight lisp and much preferred the pen to do his talking.

Cushman continued, "There are very few men in this world who have your passion, commitment, and knowledge regarding the natural rights of man. You are the perfect vessel to communicate this to the American people and the people of the world. Trust me, Red, Mr. Adams and the rest knew what they were doing when they chose you to author this declaration."

"I still would value your opinion. It isn't very long, only four pages. I just have to tinker with the last paragraph."

"Very well. I never could say no to you. Remember the time you persuaded me to test the bridge over Henderson Creek? You know, I almost drowned."

"We were ten years old, and the stream was only three-feet deep," responded Jefferson.

"Still, it was a raging torrent that day," countered Cushman.

Jefferson rolled his eyes back, shook his head, and thought about his past. He had spent almost every day of his childhood with Ben and his brothers. In the passing years, he had seen less and less of Ben. In college, Jefferson preferred the company of older, more serious men. His marriage to Martha, the never-ending management of Monticello, and the political turmoil of the day consumed all his time and energy. Being with his friend again was like going back in time. Jefferson knew that responsibilities of adulthood weigh heavily on all men, but Ben's youthful attitude and demeanor seemed to lift those burdens away, at least for the time being. He made a promise to himself to never be separated from his best friend for such an extended period.

"Don't make me ask you twice!" Jefferson laughed.

Cushman glanced at the four-page document, noticing multiple corrections, crossed-out words, smudge marks, and of course, the familiar handwriting of his childhood friend. He noticed some words were printed with all letters capitalized for obvious bold pronouncements. Cushman took the first page into both hands, leaned back, and began to read Thomas Jefferson's Declaration of Independence. The very first sentence boldly proclaimed, *"A Declaration by the Representatives of the United States Of America, in General Congress assembled."* Jefferson had written the *United States Of America* in print form with all capital letters; the rest of the sentence was written in the standard English cursive, or what many referred to as joined-up writing. This struck Cushman as bold and decisive, a direct challenge to the king and Parliament, and, for some reason, caused him to feel proud and attached to the other colonies.

He was about to say something when Jefferson noticed his quizzical look. "Read through it all first, jot down notes if you like, but wait until you are finished to ask questions or give comment," he instructed while settling into his desk and jotting down some notes of his own.

Cushman nodded and dived into the political treatise.

Jefferson sat at his desk while attempting to cultivate new ideas, but his mind was focused elsewhere. He watched as Benjamin Cushman continued to read the four-page declaration. Fiddling nervously, he jotted down several ideas on a separate sheet of paper. He was actually anxious concerning his friend's opinion. For much of his adult life, Jefferson had been associated with some of the most brilliant men of the time. Despite his many achievements throughout his young life, at this particular point in time, Jefferson prayed for a positive review from a man who had been expelled from prep school.

Cushman finished the last page and noted Jefferson's anxiety. Enjoying the moment, he wagged his index finger back and forth, smiled, and began to re-read the four-page document. Jefferson's shoulders sank, to the enjoyment of his fellow Virginian.

Cushman finally spoke after what seemed like hours. "Locke, Rousseau, social contract, natural rights," Cushman stated, as if vocalizing a list of items needed from the general store.

A smiling Jefferson responded, "Well, yes, I suppose you could add Hobbes and Plato." The two began to compare notes regarding the philosophy of the men noted.

Plato, the famous Greek philosopher, who, along with his teacher Socrates and his student Aristotle, helped develop much of what was considered modern Western thought, including the relationship between different classes of people and the government. It was the English philosopher Thomas Hobbes who, in the last century, theorized at length the social contract and the natural rights of man. According to Hobbes, man was born into a state of nature. This state of nature allowed every human being to be totally free. Free from any rules or laws, each individual was a state onto themselves. But because everyone practiced total freedom, each person was free to do as they pleased. A person was only truly free as their physical prowess would allow them to practice their freedom. Thus, a person in possession of a herd of goats would lose the herd if a stronger person came along and simply threatened to kill the goat herder and stole the valuable animals.

Hobbes summarized that in this state of nature, which was basically anarchy, life was *nasty, brutish, and short*. Accordingly, humans entered into a *social contract*. The social contract was an agreement between the citizens to set up a government that would guarantee most of the natural freedoms yet impose a set of agreed-upon rules and laws. Thus, government would gain its limited powers from the consent of the people, creating the idea of popular sovereignty, an idea made popular as far back as Plato and the Greek philosophers.

Fellow Englishman John Locke extended Hobbes's natural rights theory to include private property ownership and the separation of powers to further limit the power of the government. Most recently, in 1762, the Swiss philosopher Jean-Jacques Rousseau published *The Social Contract*. Rousseau argued that as a society grew, men would find themselves in increasing competition with his fellow man for property and possessions, while at the same time developing increased dependence with the same men. This conflict between competition and dependence would threaten both his survival and his freedom. To save both themselves and society, they would enter into a *social contract* to give up some of their natural rights and, for the good of the whole, create rules of conduct, thus preserving the most basic freedoms within an orderly society. Since the rules would be agreed upon by the will of the people, natural freedoms would remain, since no freedom-loving man would give up their freedom for more safety or rules.

"Of course, to promote such theories of natural rights, freedom, private property, popular sovereignty, and limited government would get a person imprisoned or worse back in Europe. I doubt King George is a proponent of these theories," noted Cushman.

"Divine right is dying right before their very eyes, and yet they don't see it," responded Jefferson. "The idea that God magically bestows the divine right to rule on certain European royal families, granting absolute power, is abhorrent to enlightened men."

"The coming conflict seems to be a clash of ideas," intoned Cushman.

"A historical crossroads of epic proportions." Jefferson grinned.

"Seems like you did a lot of research."

"Not really. I recently sent my version of a Virginia Constitution to the Virginia State delegates for consideration. In doing so, I had highlighted the crimes of the king and Parliament. Many of us have been making these arguments for years now. It wasn't that difficult to put it all into words," declared an unassuming Jefferson.

"Did the Virginia delegates accept your version for their Constitution?"

"Latest word from Williamsburg is that they would meet to consider some of my proposals," replied Jefferson.

"What were you hoping for?"

"I stressed very limited powers for the state government and protections for our civil liberties," Jefferson stated proudly.

"What type of civil liberties?" Cushman asked while continuing to shuffle the four-page Declaration of Independence.

Jefferson replied without hesitation, "No capital punishment, total religious freedom, civilian control of the militia, extending the right to vote to all adults, allowing farmers to develop lands in the West, and guaranteed decent treatment of Indians."

"Pretty radical coming from a lawyer," Cushman observed slyly.

"I'm a real revolutionary." Jefferson smiled.

"You will be if the Congress approves this." Cushman waved the four pages in front of Jefferson, his face turning serious and worrisome. "The king will not look upon this as an exercise in the freedom of speech. This is treason, and they will hunt you down, hunt down your wife and children. Anybody that signs this document will be committing treason. They will come not only for you but all the representatives and their families as well. There will be no need for a jury trial. Your signature guarantees your guilt. Red, they will hang you, Dr. Franklin, the Adamses, Hancock, and the rest. They will make an example out of you all."

Jefferson smiled, took a deep breath, and replied. "I think it may have already started after last night. Well, then, we had better win this war, hadn't we?"

Cushman smiled back at his friend, admiring his courage in what was clearly a very dangerous situation. "Am I right in assuming King George has his back to the wall? He can't afford to lose his most prosperous colonies. He is in debt from the French and Indian War. Kings around Europe, especially France, would look upon George as a weak appeaser if he let the colonies go peacefully. Even his enemies in Parliament would be emboldened to continue their opposition to the king's positions."

"All you say is true. What point are you driving at?"

"My point is that the king has truly been backed into a corner, which makes him very dangerous. He will lash out. For all we know, he or his associates were behind last night's assassination attempt. He will wage all-out war, without regard to human life or property. It seems to me that rebellions against governments have always been organized by people with little or nothing to lose. The leaders of this revolt are mostly wealthy men with much to lose. Your friends are family men, god-fearing Christians, intelligent, and thoughtful men who have seen years of diplomatic efforts ridiculed by career politicians and a young, confused, and desperate king. Their comfortable and pleasant lifestyle is about to be torn to shreds, and yet they continue to provoke the king and Parliament. All for what? More land, more money. No, they have all that. You don't keep poking a bear with a stick without bad results." Cushman had rolled the declaration into a tube and pointed at Jefferson. "You and your friends are fighting for an idea. A damn good idea contained in this document." Cushman pointed at the tubular document emphatically. "This document is like throwing rocks at a wolf backed into a canyon," Ben continued with yet another analogy. "The result will be the same. The frightened wolf will attack with all its might."

"Surely, the British will recognize certain rules of war, avoiding civilians and private homes at the very least," responded a somewhat-naive Jefferson.

"I don't think so," countered Cushman. "I think the situation runs parallel to the frontier Indians. I had many interesting conversations with the chief of the Shawnee Indians, a very intelligent man by the name of Cornstalk. As you know, I have a very low opinion of American Indians. Their ways of war are as you described here." Again, he waved the declaration with his hand held high.

"Indiscriminate, attacking women and children, brutal torture, taking scalps, and beheading their captives. I have little regard for their species. However, when James and I sought out Chief Cornstalk to sign a peace treaty with Lord Dunmore, I was shocked by his intelligence and insight. He spoke perfect English, you know."

"How so?"

"Missionary, stayed with the tribe. Cornstalk and his son Elinipsico were gifted with great language skills, and both speak English fluently," Ben continued. "Cornstalk believes the Indians should have rallied together years ago to defeat the white man, and since they didn't, the white man will continue to expand westward. He believes all tribes are doomed. I tend to agree and believe this is one reason they fight the way they do. They are desperate to preserve their way of life, and to do so, they will do anything without regard to any form of civilized conduct. I have witnessed the British adopting a similar strategy to defeat the Indians and the French. I have no doubt that the king and Parliament will be unable to rein in their commanders from abusing their powers on our fair land from three thousand miles away."

"It has been reported that British soldiers massacred surrendering colonials at the last engagement at Breed's Hill," a somber Jefferson noted.

"After the beating they took, I'm sure their officers looked the other way," Cushman remarked, not knowing the accuracy of his assessment.

"I'm sure your Indian friend is probably right," the ever-thoughtful Thomas Jefferson replied. "A cornered bear shows his claws."

Cushman smiled. "More like thousands of bears." The gallows humor made them both laugh nervously. The two Virginians sat silently and pondered the grim realities awaiting their country in the not-so-distant future.

"Let's continue with your appraisal," Jefferson suggested.

Unrolling the four-page document, Cushman pointed to the opening paragraph and read aloud. *"When in the course of human events it becomes necessary for a people to advance from that subordination in which they have hitherto remained, and to assume among the powers of the earth the equal and independent station to which the laws of nature and of nature's god entitle them, a decent respect to the opinions of mankind requires that they should declare the causes which impel them to the change.'"* Cushman repeated the final thought silently. "A perfect introduction. The rest of the document flows from that line, but *'Advancing from that subordination,'* maybe something stronger!"

Like most accomplished men, Jefferson resented criticism. However, because of his lifelong friendship with Ben, his keen mind was ever alert for the challenges Cushman might throw before him. Sitting back in his chair, he mulled a few ideas, then a slight smile came over his face. "How about 'For one people to dissolve the political bands which have connected them with another…'?" he trailed off into further thought.

Cushman repeated the new line in his head several times, then shouted, "Perfect!"

Jefferson grabbed his ink pen and slowly crossed out the *subordination* line. He then wrote above the crossed-out line *"Dissolve the political bands…"* When finished, Jefferson ruffled Ben's hair. "See, I knew I could count on you."

"Onward," Cushman stated, running his finger across the next line. "This line truly speaks to me, and I love it. *'We hold these truths to be sacred and undeniable, that all men are created equal and independent, that from that equal creation they derive rights inherent and inalienable, among which are the preservation of life, and liberty, and the pursuit of happiness."*

Cushman hesitated, then continued. "This will speak to the people."

Jefferson smiled, then produced some notes he had jotted down. "While you were reading, I wrote down a few ideas concerning that very sentence. What do you think? *'We hold these truths to be self-evident, that all men are created equal, that they are endowed by their creator with certain inalienable rights, that among these are life, liberty, and the pursuit of happiness."*

Cushman silently repeated Jefferson's revision. Over and over he repeated the new line in his head, finally grinning. "I hate to admit it, but there was a reason Adams dumped this assignment on you. You're good, very good, indeed."

"You really think it's better?" Jefferson quizzed his friend.

"Absolutely! I think you summed up the social contract in one line," Ben added.

"I have juggled a thousand different words in my head for this particular sentence," Jefferson responded.

"It is language worthy of the high regard the committee placed in you," Ben continued. "*'All men are created equal'* is appealing to the common man."

"My intention is both theoretical and practical. Rights and freedoms are not handed out by governments but by God. If governments parcel out our rights, then any right they grant can be taken away at a later date. The proof of this is in the listed grievances against the king. God gives us equal freedom at birth, and it is our duty as citizens to never let any government take away those natural freedoms."

"Government of the people, not the other way around," summarized Cushman.

"Exactly. The God that gave us life gave us liberty at the same time. A government's main purpose is to secure those God-given rights, and very little else."

"Why the *'Pursuit of happiness'*? Isn't the phrase usually *'Life, liberty, and property'*?"

"Keen of you to notice." Jefferson grinned. "The *pursuit of happiness* is the essence of freedom. Freedom to pursue that which makes one happy, whether it be medicine, manufacturing, farming—"

"Even being a lawyer?" interrupted Cushman, always ready to mock Jefferson's chosen profession.

Jefferson laughed, ignoring Ben's jab, and continued, "If governments would stop abusing their power, then the average man could practice happiness. A happy man is a contented and prosperous citizen. The most successful people work at jobs they love, free to pursue that which they are good at, thus ensuring excellence. This freedom will unleash the creativity, industriousness, and entrepreneurial spirit within each individual."

"How do we keep future governments from abusing power?" Cushman asked his friend.

"Give them very little power to abuse. Create a constitution granting very limited powers and that guarantees the protection of life, liberty, happiness, and of course, property, private property. Property that belongs to individuals, not kings or nobles. Property that government can never take away, property that can be passed down from generation to generation," responded Jefferson quickly. "Each future generation must sharpen these limitations, for it is my belief the natural progress of things is for liberty to yield and government to gain ground. We must elect men of courage, selfless men who will put country before self, or group. Timid men prefer the calm of despotism to the tempestuous sea of liberty. As long as liberty trumps safety, we will survive. The generation that puts safety ahead of liberty, I'm afraid, will have neither."

"What if they succumb to safety's chains?"

"I suppose another revolution. Future rulers must fear the common man's spirit of resistance, his love of liberty. That is why liberty must live in the hearts and minds of every American. For every ruler, whether despot or democratic, will desire more power. Beware the ruler who will help you. Fear any government that promises to make your life more comfortable. People cannot always be well informed, so they must always reserve the liberty to rise up and overthrow burdensome government. I have often said that the tree of liberty must be refreshed from time to time with the blood of patriots and tyrants. It is its natural manure."

"What about the slaves?" Ben questioned regarding the *equal* clause.

"You know my feelings about the issue. I would hope to outlaw the practice sooner than later, starting with the slave trade, and eventually slavery itself."

"Perhaps this passage will turn people's attitude," countered Cushman, who like his friend was uncomfortable in attempting to defend the institution of slavery.

Jefferson, using his pen like a sword, crossed out words and wrote the new line onto the rough draft.

Cushman waited patiently, then continued to read from the young document. "*'That to secure these ends, governments are instituted among men, deriving their just powers from the consent of the governed; that whenever any form of government shall become destructive of these ends, it is the right of the people to alter or abolish it, and to institute new government, laying its foundation on such principles and organizing its powers in such form, as to them shall seem most likely to effect their safety and happiness.'* Powerful, very powerful!" Cushman stated emphatically.

"I'm sure the king will find offense," countered Jefferson.

"A suggestion, because your emphasis on the inalienable rights, life, liberty, and happiness. Why not repeat it again, 'That to secure these rights,' instead of 'These ends'?"

Jefferson's response was an immediate "Yes, yes, I like it." Jefferson's pen came alive to scratch out the word *end* and above wrote the word *rights*.

"*Deriving their just powers from the consent of the governed,*" Cushman read aloud. "So all powers given to the government will come from the people? You see the formation of some type of democracy?" Cushman's face contorted as he framed the question.

"I envision a republic, a representative democracy, maybe some type of confederation of the Thirteen Colonies, but most assuredly a society where government powers are only granted from the will of the people, not reversed," replied Jefferson, comfortable in his advocacy for more power to individuals.

Cushman's knowledge of the philosophy of a democracy was limited to his schooling regarding the Greeks. Before he had left for Ohio with his brother James, he had read several of the recent musings of Locke, Hobbes, and Rousseau. His instincts responded favorably to the idea, yet his experience with the *common man* led to an entirely different conclusion. He could envision some future charlatan convincing a majority of the people with high rhetoric and enticing promises, only to abuse power like a king. *Monarchial or democratic corruption—what's the difference*? Cushman thought. His friend seemed to have more confidence in the *common man* than just about anybody Ben knew, including the *common man* himself. Fearing a long sermon on the merits of democracy, Ben decided to keep his thoughts to himself and continue the task of dissecting Jefferson's Declaration of Independence.

"The list of charges, a couple dozen at least, seem to be vented only at King George and not Parliament. The colonies have been railing against the Parliament for decades. Most Americans still feel an allegiance to the king. Isn't it a mistake to only blame the king?" Cushman inquired, looking at Jefferson's list of grievance that made up two-thirds of the document.

"I had to consider several ideas in singling out King George. First of all, I considered Paine's pamphlet *Common Sense*, a very popular document, perhaps because he attacked the monarchy. Second, by personalizing the grievances toward George, I hope to give no alarm to any other crowned heads in Europe, especially in France or Spain, potential allies to our cause. A third reason, and maybe most important of all, is the idea that this document will help sway a significant number of fence-sitters to our cause. It is easier to convince people of the corruption of one man as opposed to an entire body of them."

Seemingly satisfied of Jefferson's explanation, Cushman again questioned his friend, "So many *injuries and usurpations*, do you think you need that many?"

"A first-year schoolchild could easily list the grievances that have circulated throughout the colonies. It wasn't very difficult. I tried to have several examples from each section of the country. For instance, both South Carolina and Massachusetts have had their *legislative bodies moved*, thus *exhausting their representatives*. Massachusetts, Virginia, and South Carolina all had their *legislatures dissolved* at one time or another. He has *obstructed naturalization laws* in more than four colonies, and he has *quartered troops* in both Massachusetts and New York. Most of these are not trivial. These encroachments cut to the very fabric of our liberty. I guess the lawyer in me figured overwhelming evidence is preferable to underwhelming evidence."

Cushman laughed at Jefferson's attempt of self-deprecating humor, then added, "The last grievance against the king, the *execrable commerce*, the evil of slave trade, you are certainly opening up yourself to charges of hypocrisy. Will Southern States go along with that?"

Peter Jefferson had bequeathed over 60 slaves to his son, Thomas. Jefferson later inherited over 135 slaves from his father-in-law, John Wayles. As a Southern landowner, Jefferson had profited from his ownership of slaves, but the conflict between the philosopher and the farmer was very real. Jefferson never mistreated his slaves and, as a lawyer, had argued before a judge for the freedom of a slave who claimed to have a white grandmother, using the idea that *all men are created equal by God*. The judge predictably ruled against Jefferson.

"Without a doubt, nothing vexes me more than the slave conundrum. On one hand, it is an offense against God and a violation of man's inherent liberty. On the other hand, it has existed around the world since the beginning of civilization. I doubt we can unite to defeat the British and end slavery at the same time. Southern economies are too dependent on the slave system. I will continue to push to end the evil trade system, and thus, Southern slavery will wither on the vine and die a proper death. It is a hypocrisy I am forced to live with, I am sure, for the rest of my life." The introspective Jefferson sighed.

"The last paragraph is good, very good. I especially like the last line," continued Cushman. "*And for the support of this declaration we mutually pledge to each other our lives, our fortunes, and our sacred honor.*' Do you think the signers will abide by this pledge?"

"If they adopt this resolution, I am confident that history will look back with great pride at the bravery and commitment of the signers," stated a self-assured Thomas Jefferson.

Cushman looked up to his friend with great pride and stated, "I have no doubt you will be right."

Chapter 16

Government, even in its best state, is but a necessary evil; in its worst state, an intolerable one.
—Thomas Paine

June 26, 1776
Philadelphia

"Damn it!" he proclaimed loudly, struggling to pry open the second-story window. The profanity seemed to help as the window slowly began to rise. The overweight bureaucrat was sweating profusely. Joseph Giersch stood panting, hoping the morning air would infiltrate his office and bring relief from the heat and humidity. Instead of a cool breeze, he was greeted with the foul stench of the unsanitary jail on the floor below. Giersch cursed his bad luck and decided to keep the window open, preferring the stench to the oppressive heat. His foul mood was getting fouler by the minute.

"Mr. Giersch, any more news on the Tucker killings." Silas Otto poked his head into Giersch's office.

Giersch bit his lip, trying to keep from tearing Otto's head off. He took deep breaths to help control his anger. He would need the sheriff in the coming weeks. Instead of ripping into the lanky Otto, Giersch issued a mild rebuke. "When in tarnation are you going to clean up the jail downstairs? It stinks worse than a stable!"

The two county employees worked out of the Philadelphia City Hall, located near the Delaware River on Second Street. The bottom floor of the two-story building had been the county jail for years. The upper floor held offices for the mayor, the mayor's court, the coroner, the sheriff, and some other public officials. With the completion of the Walnut Street Jail, most of the inmates had been moved to the new facility, but not all, to the great consternation of the second-floor residents. Construction for a new city hall, located next to the Pennsylvania statehouse, had begun, but promised money had dried up. Giersch's anticipated move into a new and larger building had run headlong into a dawdling bureaucracy and the damn rebellion.

"Soon, them criminals should be moving to Walnut Street by next week."

"It's about time," Giersch replied tersely.

"So anything new on Tucker or at City Tavern?" Otto persisted, ignoring Giersch's grumpiness.

Giersch indeed had nothing new, and in fact the stories told by the *traitors* had held up with all he had interviewed. He still believed he could pull off the *hue-and-cry* prosecution and had a very productive meeting with the jurisdictional judge Erik Karlsen. Giersch and Karlsen were friends; both had attended the University of Pennsylvania. The two men had much in common, not the least of which was their unwavering support for King George III and a lust for power.

"No, nothing new. I may not be able to get a murder conviction, but I sure as hell will raise the issue of the *hue and cry*. Have you been able to interview the Johnson girl yet?"

"Yes, early this morning. The rumors were true." The sheriff smiled.

"What rumors?" Giersch was anticipating new and damaging evidence.

"She is a most beautiful woman," replied Otto, remembering his morning interview with Deborah Johnson.

Giersch's eyes rolled back in disgust. "Enough of your lusting! Did she have anything worthwhile to add?"

"Nothing, really, but there was one thing, though." The sheriff hesitated.

"Well?" Giersch's demeanor bared his impatience.

"Nothing she said. It was in her eyes," replied Otto.

"Yeah, yeah, I know, they were beautiful, right?"

"Well, yes, but something else. There was fear. I clearly saw fear in her eyes."

The rugged-looking fifty-three-year-old man walked quickly up the brick-paved path toward the Pennsylvania statehouse. His alert eyes immediately located the man he was looking for. Veering toward the wooden bench, he greeted the famous older gentleman.

"All is set. I think our little problem should disappear," he stated optimistically.

"Very good. I worry we don't overstep and turn people away. It is a very bold plan," replied the elder statesman.

"Have no fear. I have thought of everything. We will get rid of that little maggot without any repercussions," he stated happily. "Are you going in today?" He pointed toward the beautiful brick building, the epicenter of world-changing events.

"Yes, but later, I have a meeting with Mr. Jefferson in a few minutes. He has finished with the declaration. Your cousin and I are reviewing the document today."

"I'm sure it will be first-rate. I look forward to seeing it soon."

The meeting had lasted less than three minutes; the two men hopped up from the bench and walked their separate ways. To the average observer, they looked like a couple of grandfathers out for a leisurely stroll, but to the king of the most powerful nation on earth, these were two of the most dangerous men in America.

Once a week the evening waitresses at City Tavern worked the lunch crowd. Wednesday was her turn. Deborah Johnson's day had already been difficult. Another interrogation, this time conducted by *that creepy sheriff*, had gotten the day off to a bad start. Returning to City Tavern for the first time since the assassination attempt brought back too vividly the madness and mayhem that she had helped orchestrate. Guilt was a powerful emotion, but so was fear. Her meeting with Rourke was still fresh in her mind, and on top of everything else, the place was swarming with customers. Word had spread quickly about the shoot-out at City Tavern two nights ago. The rumors ranged from George III attempting to assassinate members of Congress to a colonial plot to make it look like a failed British plan, in order to gain sympathy for the move toward independence. Only the *Pennsylvania Evening Gazette* had made mention of a murder-assassination, a small article with scant details. The remaining newspapers wouldn't even go to print until Saturday, since all but the *Gazette* published once a week.

Amid all this chaos, her mind continued to think about him. The conflict continued to grow within her. Was he the enemy that Ms. Lydia insisted he was, or was he the kind, gentle, and heroic white knight that had ridden in and saved her from destroying her life? Deborah still believed in her father and his cause, but she felt betrayed. *They were supposed to frighten them, not kill them.* The night of the assassination attempt had affected her more than she could ever imagine, especially her encounter with Benjamin Cushman. Either way, a new fear had begun to develop. A fear she might never see him again.

That fear evaporated twenty seconds later when the door opened and Cushman walked into City Tavern with two other men. She breathed a heavy sigh of relief. Johnson recognized the other men immediately and walked over to greet the threesome. She couldn't hide her smile as the men approached her. To her great joy, she was rewarded with a grin from all three.

Thomas Jefferson was the first to speak. "Ms. Deborah, how nice to see you. How are you recovering from the other night?"

"I'll be all right, sir," she answered, but not very convincingly.

John Adams was the next to comfort her. "Well, my dear, having witnessed such a dreadful event at your young age would be very discomforting. It will take some time to recover."

"Thank you, Mr. Adams. I appreciate your concern," she stated genuinely.

Cushman had been studying Deborah Johnson while she chatted with Jefferson and Adams. He, too, was conflicted. He was intoxicated by her smile and felt the shivers running up and down his body again, but were they shivers of attraction or shivers of danger? He shrugged it off. *After all,* he thought, *aren't all women dangerous?*

"Ms. Johnson, so nice to see you again. I pray there won't be a repeat of the other night." Cushman grinned in an awkward attempt to make light of the recent occurrence.

"Well, Mr. Cushman, I promise not to start anything if you do the same." She smiled.

John Adams gave Jefferson a knowing glance. The attraction Cushman and Johnson shared was hard to hide.

Deborah motioned the men toward a large table in the front coffee room; she stepped aside, allowing Jefferson to go first, noticing he was carrying a long tube used to hold valuable papers. Next came Adams, and finally Cushman came alongside the pretty waitress. She playfully grabbed Ben by the elbow and whispered, "How's the arm? Getting any better?"

Her touch was gentle but firm enough to force Cushman to stop and stare into her blue eyes. *Big mistake,* he thought. *I could drown in those eyes.* Finally, he stammered out, "Doing better. Thomas's landlady is a fine nurse, although it seems all her remedies begin and end with whiskey."

"Well, then, I'll see if I can rustle up a bottle," she teased the blushing Cushman as she walked away to tend to another table, her mood greatly improved.

Cushman stared at her shapely form; he had never been around a woman who flirted so brazenly that didn't expect to get paid at the end of the night. She certainly was different. *No Falling Star, that's for sure. Perhaps the rebellious American spirit has caught on to the young women of Philadelphia.*

Jefferson and Adams felt like teenage boys poking fun at their love-struck colleague. First, it was Adams. "Ben, it seems like you've made quite an impression on our Ms. Debby. After all that time in Ohio, do you remember how to court a woman?"

Jefferson added quickly, "I hope you do better with Deborah than you did with Becky Sterling. He chased her with a king snake all the way through old man Renner's back field!"

"I was nine years old at that time," countered Cushman.

"Is it still your favorite method of courtship?" Jefferson mocked.

Cushman took the good-natured ribbing in stride; he even managed to toss a few jabs back at Jefferson.

Deborah walked briskly back to their table and placed a bottle of whiskey in front of Cushman. "I'll be right back to take your order. Here's a little medicine for all that ails you."

They all had a good laugh, and later when, Deborah brought them coffee, each man added a shot of the whiskey.

As they slowly sipped their drinks, Adams finally got around to the reason they had come to City Tavern. "Well, Thomas, I assume by your invitation to lunch and the way you've been protecting that paper tube you have finished the declaration."

"Very observant of you, John. Yes, I have finished with a little help from my friend," conceded Jefferson.

Adams shot a quick glance at Cushman with arched eyebrows and a slight grin of surprise.

Cushman took another sip of coffee and shrugged his shoulders. "What can I say? Everyone always said I was the smartest one in Albemarle County. But I must leave you to the task of editing Thomas's wonderful work. Your cousin has given me a most delicate mission, and I mustn't be late."

"Are you sure of the directions?" Jefferson asked his friend.

"I'm starting to think of Philadelphia as a second home. I won't get lost."

"Be very clear with him," added Adams. "There must be no confusion."

"Don't worry. As long as he's not French, we'll get along."

Jefferson retrieved the four pages of the rough draft and laid them out on the table between the whiskey and their coffee. He gave Adams the same instructions he had given Cushman the night before. "Read it in its entirety first. Comments come later." He then added one more thing, "I've become quite fond of her, John. Please be gentle."

Adams smiled and began to read for the first time the Declaration of Independence.

Ben Cushman rode his horse slowly through the cobbled streets of Philadelphia. He was becoming more familiar with William Penn's well-laid-out green city. Although he preferred the countryside, the unofficial capital of the rebellious states of America was beginning to grow on him. He turned north onto Fourth Street, his destination now just a block away.

His mind was not focused on his pending meeting. Ben had left City Tavern even more confused than ever. He thought about what had just happened and shook his head.

After leaving Jefferson and Adams poring over the Declaration of Independence, he had sought out Deborah. His clandestine meeting was set for 5:00 p.m., and he had over an hour to waste. Having never gotten to talk alone with the attractive waitress, he decided to take a chance.

"Looking for me?" She giggled from behind, so startling him he nearly fell over, causing her to laugh even more.

Regaining his composure, Cushman replied, "Yes. Can you talk now?"

"We've slowed down quite a bit. Follow me." She grabbed him by the hand and led him through the same kitchen that two nights before had been the scene of the crime. Outside, she stopped underneath a large maple tree. "How's this? A little quieter?"

"Much better," Cushman stated, still not sure what path he was headed down. One thing he did know was that he was very comfortable in her presence.

She broke the ice. "I don't think I have properly thanked you for saving so many lives, including mine." She reached up and kissed him on his cheek. Cushman blushed. Deborah, on the other hand, felt guilty, first for being part of the plot, and second for telling Rourke about Ben Cushman.

"You were the brave one, standing up to the assassins, risking your life. Not many women could have done what you did," he replied.

She felt guiltier yet somewhat relieved that he had bought the lie. "Well, thank you, Mr. Cushman. I guess we could go on and on about how brave we both are. Is there something else you wish to talk about?"

Cushman had rarely been in the presence of such a strong woman. He had heard John Adams speak of his wife, Abigail, as a strong force in his life but had never witnessed such a creature in person. *Falling Star* was gentle, strong in her own way, but not aggressive or confident, like Deborah. Somewhat taken aback, he regained his composure and replied, "I was wondering if it would be okay with you if I could..." He hesitated slightly, only to be interrupted.

"Call on me. Why, Mr. Cushman, are you asking for permission to call on me, to court me?" Deborah's smile was captivating and comforting, but Cushman was still knocked off guard by her aggressive attitude. He was glad Jefferson wasn't nearby; he would never let him live it down.

"Well, yes...er, no...I mean, shouldn't I ask your father first?" stammered Cushman.

"I am twenty-two years old, and although I love my father very much, I will choose who may or may not court me," Deborah stated emphatically.

Cushman nodded, slowly working up his courage. He finally replied, "Ms. Johnson..." He hesitated again, then continued, "You know, you sure are an exasperating woman—"

"I'll take that as a compliment," she interrupted again, staring up into his emerald eyes; she wasn't going to make it easy on him.

Cushman was actually beginning to enjoy the cat-and-mouse and stated slyly, "You know, I think I've changed my mind..."

Her reaction was immediate and playful; she slapped his left arm with her right hand, forgetting Cushman's injury from two nights before. Unable to block the blow, Cushman winced in pain as her hand landed smack-dab on the bullet wound; the pain on his face was real.

Deborah's face turned to horror. "I am so sorry! Are you all right?" She held on to his arm, examining it closely.

Ben grabbed both of her shoulders and said softly, "I think I'm going to need more whiskey."

Her vivacious laugh echoed in the nearby alley. She looked up to Cushman with a large grin on her beautiful face. "Mr. Cushman, I would love for you to call on me."

They stayed under the tree for another ten minutes, talking like two teenagers. Everything seemed too perfect, until they went back into City Tavern.

Upon returning, Cushman had looked over to wave goodbye to Jefferson and Adams when he noted that Dr. Franklin had joined them. He motioned for Deborah to wait and walked over to the table.

"Hello, Dr. Franklin, have you and Mr. Adams rewritten Thomas's work yet?" He was half-kidding but wary of his friend's sensitivity toward any type of alteration to the document.

Jefferson looked relieved; his declaration must have survived editing from the two brilliant Patriots.

"A tweak here, a tweak there," responded the ever-energetic Franklin. "*Inalienable* to *unalienable*, a few other small changes."

Jefferson intoned, "Surviving the editing pen of these two is bad enough. I fear the entire Congress may not be so agreeable."

"Fear not, Mr. Jefferson. I will fight for every word. It is truly magnificent. It will change the world," a confident John Adams proclaimed.

"Don't be so certain, John," cautioned Franklin. "The slavery paragraph, for one, will not sit well with our Southern brethren."

"It is the greatest of all the injuries Thomas listed against the king," Adams countered quickly.

"Maybe so, but we will not win this war without the Southern states. We must be pragmatic. If we win, we can work to end the foul practice. If we lose, it will be the least of our problems," Franklin countered.

"As usual, you're probably right, but I will still fight for its inclusion," stated John Adams.

"Thank you, John," responded Jefferson.

"Enough already. There will be plenty of debate in the coming days," Franklin pointed out. "I understand from my colleagues, Mr. Cushman, that you are trying to steal my girl, right from under my nose. Is there any truth to this gossip?"

Cushman's sheepish grin signaled that indeed he had made some progress with Deborah Johnson. "Dr. Franklin, your harem is rumored to be very large. Surely, you can spare one of them for a backwoods Virginian."

"Very well, if I can't do the conquering, I suppose the next best thing is to play the matchmaker. I will give ground to you, Mr. Cushman, but let me warn you, if you muddle this up, I will be there to pounce."

Cushman smiled, believing the seventy-year-old to be joking, but not entirely sure. "I owe you one, Dr. Franklin."

"Be wary, Ben. He will collect," added Jefferson.

Cushman's back was away from Deborah Johnson as he spoke to the three revolutionaries. It was fitting that Benjamin Franklin noticed the stunning newcomer first. Cushman noticed all three men's eyes moved to a spot beyond him.

"Who do we have here?" The old romantic beamed a wicked grin. Even the stoic and faithful husband John Adams took sharp notice at the newly arrived beauty.

"Well, well, the plot thickens," suggested a grinning Thomas Jefferson. "Your new girlfriend runs in interesting circles."

Cushman slowly turned to see Deborah in deep conversation with another woman. Not just any woman, one of the most exotic women he had ever seen.

Cushman wasn't sure what was most striking about the well-dressed lady. Was it the long straight black hair, the smooth, well-tanned skin, the shapely body filling out the immodest dress, or the beautiful, striking face highlighted by deep, full lips?

Perhaps they were all equally enthralling, Cushman decided, and then it hit him. It was her eyes, her deep-brown eyes, outlined by long sleek eyelashes. Her eyes were full of life, dazzling, sparking eyes that penetrated into one's soul. They were playful yet mysterious, flirtatious, and dangerous all at the same time.

Cushman turned to the three members of the Second Continental Congress, all still mesmerized by the stunning beauty, and bravely announced, "Gentlemen, I think this calls for rapid reconnaissance, and since I have scouted for both the Virginia militia and the British Army, I will volunteer for this dangerous mission."

"Don't be afraid to call for backup!" shouted Franklin as Cushman made his way toward the two beauties. "Dangerous mission, indeed," he stated softly. "If only I were twenty-five again."

Approaching the two in conversion, Cushman noticed Deborah's mood had changed dramatically; her confident, aggressive demeanor seemed gone. He was instantly alert for trouble. Deborah stepped toward him nervously. "Ben, I would like you to meet a friend of mine. Ben Cushman, this is Lydia. Lydia, this is Ben."

Lydia Ames slowly lifted her chin. Her smile was warm, inviting, and her eyes looked Cushman up and down. As in polite society, she lifted her gloved hand for him to kiss. Cushman hesitated; not traveling in elite circles for years had left him rusty. He gently took her hand. The scent of perfume was fragrant and alluring. Her body language was like a mountain lion, muscular and poised, ready to strike at the slightest provocation.

Lydia Ames gently brought her hand toward her body, forcing Cushman to move closer, and thought to herself. *So you are the son of a bitch who thwarted our plan.* "So you're the young man who saved our Debby. Please accept my heartfelt congratulation." The words rolled smoothly off her tongue as she continued to gently hold on to his hand. "Debby's father and I are good friends and business partners. He wanted her to stop working here. I told him he was being foolish."

"Just what is your business?" Cushman replied, pulling his hand away slowly, feeling all of a sudden like a fly about to be ensnared in her exotic spider's web. His eyes drifted below her face; the tight, low-cut dress revealed naked shoulders and cleavage. Her lack of modesty was only equaled by her stunning beauty. Ben looked quickly at Deborah. Her face suggested worry or something even worse.

"Trade, Mr. Cushman. I am involved in trading numerous items. Perhaps if you are looking for a job, I could help. We are always looking for bright young men who can think on their feet." She spoke with a slight accent, Cushman guessed somewhere in the Caribbean.

"Thank you for the offer, Ms. Lydia. I'm afraid I'm rather busy at the present. Perhaps sometime in the future," he offered without much conviction.

"One never knows about the future. These are tumultuous times we live in, Mr. Cushman. The best way to guarantee the future is to always be on the winning side." Lydia smiled and glanced knowingly toward her young protégé, the message crystal clear to Deborah.

"Ben is a good friend of Mr. Jefferson. He is just visiting, right?" Deborah looked at him, her eyes revealing concern for his answer.

"Yes, I will probably spend a few more days getting reacquainted, then head home to Virginia," he announced even though he had not given his future plans much thought.

"A lovely place, Virginia, from what I hear. I have never been there. Perhaps Deborah and I could visit you. Would you open your home to a couple of adventurous young women, Mr. Cushman, or would that be too scandalous?" Lydia questioned him with her brightest smile.

Two forceful women in one day, thought Cushman. *The country sure has changed since I went to Ohio.* "I'm sure my brothers would be thrilled to have you both as guests," he suggested.

"Well, if they are all as handsome as their brother, we will have to make sure we visit." Lydia glanced at Deborah with a clever grin.

"A wonderful adventure it would be," Deborah announced, as if on cue.

"Ladies, I would love to continue to talk to the two most beautiful women in Philadelphia, but unfortunately, I have an afternoon meeting I cannot be late for." Turning toward Deborah, Cushman added, "Be back around eight o'clock. Perhaps we can continue our previous conversation?"

Deborah Johnson nodded while grabbing his hands and squeezing. "I finish around nine. Do be careful. Philadelphia can be dangerous at night."

"Hopefully, no more dangerous than the other night." Cushman laughed. "Ms. Lydia, it has been a pleasure making your acquaintance. I hope I will see more of you."

"Have no fear, Mr. Cushman. You have not seen the last of me." Her words seemed innocent enough, but combined with the steely look she gave Cushman, it seemed to imply a threat. Cushman was not comforted as he walked out the door. He looked back. Lydia appeared to be scolding Deborah as if she were a child. He left conflicted.

The conversation Cushman couldn't hear had left Deborah stunned. Lydia's words cut like a knife. "Make sure, my dear, you remember whose side you are on. Mr. Rourke deals harshly with any type of disloyalty. Whether it is your father or you that gets hurt will be irrelevant. One way or another, he will accomplish his goals, and anyone who gets in his way will be dispatched. Am I making myself clear?"

Deborah Johnson shook her head. The exhilaration she had felt just minutes before while flirting with Ben Cushman had been replaced by a deep dread of future events spinning out of control.

Cushman's reverie came to an abrupt halt as his horse reared to avoid a streaking object. It was a rat the size of a large house cat, scurrying across the road. Tightening the reins, Ben quickly regained control. The sign he was looking for loomed straight ahead: *Indian Queen Tavern*. Arriving ten minutes early, Cushman decided to stake out a table where he could have his back to a wall and be able to see all entry locations. There was no such thing as being too careful.

Thomas Jefferson had suggested the tavern to Sam Adams as an ideal meeting place. Jefferson had lived above the tavern on the second floor before moving to the Graff house. The *Indian Queen* was sympathetic to the Patriot cause—no Tories were allowed in the door. That and the fact it was in the target neighborhood provided a perfect place to base the operation from. The tricky part was putting the final touches on the plan. Cushman, by volunteering to be the go-between, had solved their biggest problem. No one from the Congress could be remotely involved if things went wrong. The potential propaganda fallout would be disastrous.

Cushman ordered a coffee and retreated to his chosen table. He didn't have long to wait; the would-be collaborator waltzed through the front door at exactly five o'clock. Samuel Adams had described him perfectly. A mountain of a man, he had to turn sideways to enter the front entrance. His long blond hair cascaded past his shoulders. A pair of suspenders held up his cheap wool pants. The short-sleeve white cotton shirt had multiple stain marks from either food or blood or a little of both. He looked as if he had just arrived from the fields after tending to crops all day.

Walking directly toward Cushman, and with little or no regard for concealment, he blurted out in a booming voice, "Ya Cushman?"

The tall Virginian stood to offer his hand, and looking up a good five inches, he answered, "Yes, sir."

"Good," the walking mountain took one giant step up to the bar. "Barkeep, give me four pints and a bottle of yar finest whiskey." Looking back to Cushman, he smiled, revealing several missing teeth. "If we're talkin', we're drinkin'."

Cushman lowered his head and muttered to himself, "Oh no, here we go again."

Chapter 17

They that can give up essential liberty to purchase a little temporary safety deserve neither liberty nor safety!

—Benjamin Franklin

June 26, 1776
Philadelphia

Dusk was beginning to defeat the warm, sunny day, reminding Philadelphians that the sweltering-hot and humid summer days of July and August were just around the corner. Wealthy citizens were making plans to spend the next two months along the Jersey shore, in places like Cape May. Of course, not all the Philadelphia elite would head to the ocean this particular summer. After all, who would be around to advise and entertain the members of the Continental Congress. It was indeed an exciting and dangerous time in the American colonies, much of which centered on her largest city. Potential opportunities proliferated throughout the city, opportunities that would be well worth the risk of the annual summer diseases.

The man stumbling down Second Street was searching for one of those opportunities. His right hand squeezed the neck of the old clay jug and quickly brought it to his lips, guzzling the sweet Jamaican rum, the light-colored alcohol dripping across the four-day-old stubble on his chin.

It was early Wednesday evening, and many Philadelphians were heading to one of the 120 different taverns located within the city limits. Despite being in the heart of Quaker country, the city had a thriving nightlife. It was often called the Paris of America. Sidewalks, streetlamps, and a police presence provided for a safer environment than most big cities in America or Europe, but there was still an element of hazard. The diverse tavern scene ranged from the most elegant, such as City Tavern, to literal holes-in-the-wall. A five-block area on Second Street, between Pine and Arch, contained over twenty taverns competing for various patrons. The worst section, called *Hell-Town*, consisted of tippling houses, which were unlicensed bars, and other unsavory establishments. *Hell-Town* taverns competed for prostitutes, pirates, thieves, gamblers, and transients passing through the city.

Closer to the Delaware River, many of the taverns along Second Street attracted dockworkers, sailors, artisans, and merchants from around the world. Sundry clientele made for stimulating and exciting evenings near the riverfront, albeit ofttimes stimulating and exciting turned into dangerous and deadly. An obnoxious Patriot walking into a Tory tavern might be found floating facedown in the Delaware the next morning.

Philadelphia taverns offered more than libations; they sold coffee and food, and many second floors would act as boardinghouses for weary travelers. Not the greatest accommodations. Oftentimes men slept four to a bed. The beds were rarely washed and were loaded with lice, ticks, and other bedbugs.

Colorful names were common, such as the *Indian King*, the *Crooked Billet Inn*, the *Half-Moon Tavern*, *Conestoga Inn*, the *Three Jolly Irishmen Inn*, and the *Black Bear Inn*.

Heinrich Boninghausen knew full well the risks associated with each individual tavern along Second Street. Each tavern could be labeled as a Patriot bar or a Tory bar. He made it a practice to frequent both, listening closely for commentary about the coming war.

As he continued walking, he took out a bottle of rum and took a long swig. Soon he spotted his destination; it was one block away. Hanging over the main entrance door was the familiar but unusual sign. The top of the sign proclaimed, "Est. 1759." Beneath was a picture of a well-dressed elderly gentleman wearing a trifold hat along with his Sunday best clothes. Walking arm in arm was his wife, dressed conservatively in a long reddish dress. In her free hand, she carried what looked like a picnic basket with a cat on top. What made the sign perfectly ridiculous was a monkey perched precariously upon the man's left shoulder, staring down toward a parrot clinging to the man's outstretched right hand. The defiant-looking parrot stared right back at the monkey. Below the feet of the odd couple announced the name of the tavern, "*A Man Full of Trouble.*" Boninghausen smiled to himself as he glared at the sign. *Of all the taverns in Philly,* he thought. *How appropriate.* For Heinrich Boninghausen had a secret, and tonight that secret could be exposed if he was not careful.

Unfortunately for Joseph Giersch, his day had not gotten any better. If possible, his mood had gotten much worse after his morning encounter with Sheriff Otto. The more he examined the witness testimony and the evidence, the more he was inclined to think that indeed there had been a well-organized plot to take down the leadership of the Second Continental Congress. Had they succeeded and taken down the leaders of the rebellion, it would have ended the war before it had a chance to restart.

Giersch thought it was an ingenious plan and envied the conspirators. All that was missing was a plot to kill the Virginia farmer Washington. He wondered if the idea had come from the king and his advisers or some desperate Tories attempting to gain favor with the king. What bothered Giersch more than anything was the fact that the assassination plot had failed so miserably. All those guns, all those assassins, and not one of the intended victims had been eliminated. It was a miracle that none of the targets had been killed. Not so much a miracle, more like Jefferson's friend Benjamin Cushman and a mysterious unnamed man. Not only had they thwarted the assassins at City Tavern, but they then also jumped on their horses, found the Tucker home, and with some help from Jefferson, managed to save the traitors John Hancock and Sam Adams.

All told, the carnage was formidable. At City Tavern, four unknown dead, presumably the hired guns, a dead police officer, and a dead cook. The tavern's manager, John Trumbull, had been shot, but he would survive, and the waitress had been roughed up. The Tucker home was even worse. Aaron Tucker, a well-known barrel maker; his son, Jacob; their freeman servant, Andrew; and John Hancock's driver had all been murdered. Cushman, the mysterious stranger, and a Philly policeman had killed four more unnamed assassins.

The six known dead seemed to be innocent bystanders caught up in the conspiracy. Perhaps they were not so innocent, thought Giersch. There were witnesses to explain the deaths of Gerard Jackson, Aaron Tucker, and his servant, Andrew, but there were no witnesses to the deaths of the police officer Cyrus Rice; to the younger Tucker, Jacob; or Hancock's driver.

The police officer's death seemed easy to explain. The assassins wanted to remove the only threat to their operation. Same with Hancock's driver. Both men were stabbed in the throat, probably lured to their death through subterfuge. But the death of Jacob Tucker was puzzling. He was found at the front entrance hall by the door. He had been shot in the back of the head. There had been no forced entry into the home; the home had a bolt system to lock the door. The killers either conned their way into the home or they were allowed in. *Why would Jacob Tucker allow the killers into his home? What could the younger Tucker gain by the death of Hancock and Adams?* Perhaps both Tuckers had lured them to their home, only to have everything go wrong. Perhaps Jacob Tucker was a Loyalist who happened to want his inheritance sooner than later, which would explain a great deal. Kill off the traitors and Daddy—two birds with one stone. Giersch made a mental note to look further into Jacob Tucker's money situation and his associations.

And what about the surviving assassin that Cushman had surely tortured? As he was being led outside City Tavern, someone shot him from across the street. *Was the police officer the real target? Bad marksmanship? Were assassins sent to kill assassins?* It was certainly a perplexing case.

Most of Giersch's cases were dull and routine, fishing drunks out of the river, barroom brawls gone badly, and the occasional jealous husband revenging his wife's honor. This case offered many twists and turns that stimulated Giersch's brilliant mind. But the opportunity to help bring down the revolutionary leadership was just too great. He didn't care if he had to lie or produce faulty evidence. Opportunities like this didn't come along very often. He could ruin their cause, which would greatly enhance both his reputation and his pocketbook.

The *hue-and-cry* prosecution would be saved as a last resort. Giersch was still hoping to pin them with murder, but he would have to get someone to change their testimony or possibly plant some phony evidence. Giersch's mood improved as he left Philadelphia City Hall and thought of ways to make members of the Second Continental Congress culpable for murder. He could even enlist the aid of Silas Otto.

The county coroner stuffed some papers into his saddlebag, mounted his horse for the brief ride home from city hall. Straight down Market Street for two blocks, then north on Fourth Street, halfway down the block was his modest two-story brick home. Giersch envisioned a new home and mingling with Philadelphia elite; perhaps the king would honor him with knighthood. Giersch's mood had done a three-sixty. Thank God for the revolution. Tomorrow was going to be a great day.

The largest man in the world, or at least that was what Cushman thought, had just taken a seat, two pints of ale in each hand. The bartender brought over a bottle of Irish whiskey. "Lad, my name is Tressach, Thaddeus Tressach. If ya haven't figured it out by now, I've got a wee little Irish blood in me." The friendly giant had a thick Irish brogue.

"Ben Cushman, Mr. Tressach. You could have fooled me. I would have sworn you were Cherokee Indian," Ben replied impishly.

"Ha!" responded Tressach, laughing loudly while giving Cushman a slap on the back that might have killed a lesser man. "Ya're a funny one, I can tell. Mr. Adams said I'd like ya. Now drink, lad. Let's see if your English blood can stay up with the Irish," Thaddeus Tressach grabbed the bottle of whiskey, placed it to his lips, and took a long chug. Handing the bottle to Cushman, he gloated, "Come on, my little Englishman. Let's see what ya're made of."

Cushman, not one to pass up a challenge, took the bottle. "The things I do for God and country," he said and proceeded to match the Irishmen's pull on the bottle.

Tressach smiled. "Which country, lad?"

Ben took a deep gasp, the whiskey lighting a fire from his throat into his belly. "Well now, that's a good question. Until a couple days ago, I thought we were all good Englishmen quarreling over some contentious issues that got out of hand up in Boston. I was sure cooler heads would eventually prevail. After all, it has been more than one year since a battle has been fought. Since arriving here, however, I have seen a revolutionary fervor in men of prosperity, an assassination plot foiled, and most importantly, an amazing document that summarizes thirty years of British abuse of Americans, and outlines an enticing future. So to answer your question, I guess the country I support has yet to win its freedom. Perhaps in a few years we will pledge an allegiance to a new country, an American nation free from British tyranny."

Tressach again gave Cushman the piano smile, took another long drink, and replied, "A simple Patriot or Tory would've sufficed."

Cushman laughed and grabbed the bottle from Tressach, thinking it was going to be another long night.

Tressach remained silent for a long moment. "Cushman? That is English, right? How long has your family been in America?"

"Descendent of the *Mayflower*. My great-grandmother was Mary Allerton. She was only four when the *Mayflower* landed at Plymouth. She married my great-grandfather Thomas Cushman. He arrived with his father in Plymouth the year after, in 1621, aboard the ship *Fortune*. He was thirteen years old. They married around 1636 and had eight children. Lived into their eighties, had over fifty grandkids, my dad being one of them," Cushman calmly informed the Irish giant. "When she died in 1699, she was the last surviving *Mayflower* passenger."

"Lived into their eighties, did they? You come from some good stock, lad. You should live a long and prosperous life," the Irishman proclaimed.

"Not if I keep hanging around the likes of you." Cushman grinned.

"Aye, it's not me ya've to worry about. It's that damn Sam Adams. He's a very persuasive man. He will surely lead us into a war with the British. Not that I'm against killin' British. Don't particularly like 'em, present company excluded, of course."

"Of course," mimicked the Virginian.

"My uncle brought me here when I was eight. Both my parents were killed by British soldiers. They had been searchin' for five men. All they found in our house was me futter, mutter, and me."

"What happened?" Cushman knew where this was going but had to ask.

"They lined us up outside our house and shot me mutter and futter dead. They put a gun to my head and pulled the trigger. The chamber was empty. The soldiers got a good laugh out of it. The British officer said to me, 'We were lookin' for someone else, but they seemed to have gotten away. We can't go to bed without killin' some fukin' Irish. Make sure ya tell all your friends and relatives this is what awaits them if your god-forsaken people continue to give the king trouble.' Even at eight, I understood the hatred. My uncle had us on a boat to America within the month. We settled in Philadelphia, lived here ever since." The gregarious Tressach had gotten sullen retelling the painful tale.

"What happened to your uncle?" Cushman inquired.

"Oh, he's still alive. Like your bloody ancestors, he'll never die."

Cushman decided he'd change the subject. "Tressach? Interesting name."

"I believe me mutter had a twisted sense of humor," he responded.

"Don't they all."

Thaddeus Tressach wagged his index finger at Cushman. "Adams was right. He sure was right about ya. Ya probably know, almost every Irish name, first name and surname, has meanin' behind it. Well, *Tressach* translates into 'warlike' or 'fierce warrior.'"

"And Thaddeus?"

"Thaddeus is a poet, a bloody poet! See what I mean? Me mum had a strange sense of humor," he concluded.

"A poet-warrior," Ben commented. "Thaddeus Tressach, the poet-warrior. I think your mom was a genius. I also think you'll have plenty of opportunity to practice both in the coming months."

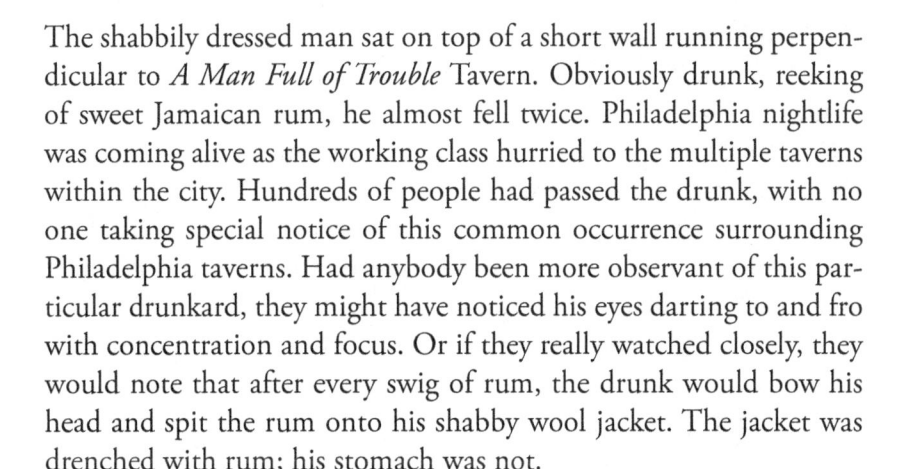

The shabbily dressed man sat on top of a short wall running perpendicular to *A Man Full of Trouble* Tavern. Obviously drunk, reeking of sweet Jamaican rum, he almost fell twice. Philadelphia nightlife was coming alive as the working class hurried to the multiple taverns within the city. Hundreds of people had passed the drunk, with no one taking special notice of this common occurrence surrounding Philadelphia taverns. Had anybody been more observant of this particular drunkard, they might have noticed his eyes darting to and fro with concentration and focus. Or if they really watched closely, they would note that after every swig of rum, the drunk would bow his head and spit the rum onto his shabby wool jacket. The jacket was drenched with rum; his stomach was not.

The three men he had been waiting for had entered five minutes earlier. Continuing to scan in all directions, he was finally satisfied the men had not been tailed or had any accomplices stationed nearby. Heinrich Boninghausen knew that in his line of work, the people he dealt with were about as trustworthy as a politician. He fingered his pistol, holstered inside his oversize coat, and made the decision to keep the meeting. His source had a checkered history but had become a very valuable asset, and after all, his main job since being stationed in the New World was to establish valuable assets. In his line of work, most of the assets were men of questionable character. Taking one more cautionary look around, he staggered to the front door of *A Man Full of Trouble*.

Several miles away, across town at another tavern, the evening patrons had pushed the tavern to full capacity. Ben Cushman and Thaddeus Tressach were finally getting down to business.

"So Mr. Adams desires a favor from us tonight. Before we get into details, please tell me how he knew about our little activity tonight?" Tressach quizzed his newfound friend.

"I've only met Mr. Adams the one time, but he seems to be a very resourceful individual. I'm sure he has sources throughout the city," Cushman added.

"A simple *'I don't know'* would've been sufficient," declared the blunt Irishman.

"Very funny. Now tell me, how did tonight's episode come about, and can you accommodate a second *victim*?"

"Our target tonight is a local loan shark. Not just any loan shark, this guy is connected to powerful people. His name is André Chevalier," Tressach literally spit out the name.

"Frenchman, that will make it easier to stomach," commented Cushman.

"Rumor has it he was bankrolled by a powerful merchant in town who owns a small bank," whispered Tressach.

"Why would a merchant-banker back a loan shark?"

"Actually, it makes perfect sense," the giant Irishman suggested. "Banks make legitimate loans to honorable people. The loan sharks make illegitimate loans to desperate people. This way, the bankers've an interest in all loans. The only difference is their method of collectin' delinquent loans. One is somewhat civilized, the other far from it."

"I assume, then, tonight is payback for a collection gone badly?"

"He was a good friend of mine, even t'ough he was English. His name was Andrew, Andrew Bowen. He borrowed ten pounds sterling from Chevalier. He demanded t'irty by week's end. Andrew came up

THE SIGNERS

with twenty. T'ere would be no leniency. While his associates held him down, Chevalier took a blacksmith hammer and proceeded to pound his left leg to a pulp. His leg was so mangled the local doctor had to amputate it. Gangrene set in. The doctor applied maggots to the wound. The fever set in, and in two days he was dead. All because he couldn't come up with the extra money." Cushman looked away as the giant Irishman wiped tears from his eyes.

"What about the sheriff? Didn't he arrest Chevalier?" Cushman was astounded.

"Well, t'at is what brings us here tonight and why Mr. Adams is so clever," responded Tressach. "You see, my friend Andrew was a well-known supporter of the Patriot cause. Sheriff Otto, on the ot'er hand, is a fervent Loyalist. Alt'ough I can't prove it, I believe Otto received money from t'is merchant to look the other way. T'ere are other rumors that Otto is on his payroll and does more t'an just look the other way."

"Who is this Machiavellian merchant?" Cushman inquired, sipping on his beer.

"Several names've been tossed about, but so far the lead is cold," Tressach responded sadly. "The coroner was even more blatant in his bias and suggested that Andrew got what he deserved," Tressach continued.

"Am I to assume the coroner's name is Joseph Giersch?" Cushman smiled as he had connected all the dots.

"Ya assume correctly, my friend. Ya can be assured that my people will act accordingly. Mr. Adams and Mr. Franklin have t'rown us a little bonus," Tressach noted with a wry grin.

"Well, this was the easiest negotiation I've been involved in. What about Chevalier?"

"He is awaitin' his fate in the stable across the street," answered the Irishman.

"And Giersch?"

JIM BOLLENBACHER

The massive Irishman smiled with a twinkle in his eye. "He should be along anytime soon."

Boninghausen recognized the man in the middle immediately. The British captain George Medford's description was dead-on. He was totally out of place, dressed in expensive clothing, a dead giveaway in a bar like the *Trouble*. His face was handsome, almost feminine. Thick dark hair was covered with an expensive trifold hat. The two men on his flanks were most assuredly his henchmen. They stood in stark contrast; henchman number 1 was a bull of a man, short and stocky, sporting a black eye that looked rather new. Henchman number 2 was tall and lanky. Boninghausen categorized them as armed and dangerous.

Approaching their table, *Short and Stocky* stood and glared at the newcomer.

"Now, now, Mr. Van Dyke, I am sure if our friend meant any harm, he wouldn't have come alone. My name, as I'm sure you already know, is Patrick Rourke. I'm afraid you have the advantage on me. I have no idea who you are," Rourke said in measured tones, inquisitive and restrained, holding aloft a small piece of paper.

"Forgive me for my clandestine behavior, Mr. Rourke, you were recommended by a mutual acquaintance," replied the tall stranger.

"I have many acquaintances," an irritated Rourke said firmly, "and your note implies threatening behavior if I didn't attend this secretive meeting."

"Again, Mr. Rourke, please forgive my caution. After I have explained everything, I am sure you will understand my vigilance."

"Very well, allow me to introduce *my* vigilance, Mr. Edward Van Dyke and Mr. Christopher Tompkins." Rourke smiled as neither man offered a hand or even an acknowledgment toward Boninghausen. "Trust me when I tell you that both men are very proficient at what they do, and in most cases, what they do is not pleasant." The threat was not subtle in the least.

THE SIGNERS

Boninghausen smiled, looking each bodyguard up and down. "Very impressive, Mr. Rourke. Now lose these two goons or the meeting is over before it starts."

Both Van Dyke and Tompkins glared and stepped forward, ready to inflict punishment on the arrogant newcomer. Rourke laughed and raised his hand. "Very well, my friend. For now you have the upper hand. I will hear what you have to say. But I can assure you, if you are wasting my time, I will not hold back my associates."

Both Van Dyke and Tompkins looked annoyed that they would not get the chance to inflict punishment. The two men retreated to a nearby table, never taking their eyes off the stranger.

"My name is Heinrich Boninghausen, Mr. Rourke. A mutual friend gave me your name. George Medford of the *HMS Richmond* said you were a loyal subject to our king, as long as the money was good." Boninghausen offered his hand.

He noted that Rourke's laugh was somewhat fanatical as he responded, refusing to shake his hand. "Captain Medford, how is the old sea dog doing? Still chasing down all those smugglers?"

"Captain Medford's accomplishments have been quite astounding, I understand, with some help from you."

"Your note said that you are willing to pay a large sum of money. How large?" Rourke glared directly into the newcomer's eyes, uncomfortable in the stranger's knowledge of his relationship with the British captain.

"Captain Medford thought you would accept my offer, and if you don't, then all I demand from you is your silence. The money will be significant."

Rourke pondered the stranger's words, and finally his curiosity got the better of him. Staring straight into Boninghausen's eyes, he responded, "Continue, sir. I will hear your proposal."

"Please forgive me, Mr. Rourke, but I know a great deal more than you think. For instance, I know of your illegal relationship with Captain Medford, your smuggling operation that never seems to draw the attention of the British Navy. How odd that almost every other smuggler in America, including Mr. Hancock, has had ships detained, but not one of yours? I also know about another operation that took place a couple of nights ago. Exactly how did that turn out?" Boninghausen was testing the American Tory, a dangerous but necessary gambit.

Rourke's face turned bright red; he managed to control his rising temper and hissed, "I am sure I have no idea what you are talking about." Rourke was already visualizing the torture-murder of Captain George Medford.

Boninghausen studied Rourke's reaction. So much of what he did was based on instinct, and so far, his instincts had kept him alive in some very dire circumstances. Rourke was dangerous and unpredictable, but in his line of work, every so often you had to dance with the devil. He decided then and there to do business with Rourke but, like dealing with any dangerous animal, to use extreme caution. "Don't worry, Medford is not the enemy. I have many sources, some even higher than the good captain. You and I both know your recent action turned into a huge failure. Before I offer you another opportunity, I would like to ask you a few questions about that fateful night." The tone in Boninghausen's voice offered a hint of reconciliation.

Rourke had survived in most of his illicit businesses by being ruthless and relentless. He used Lydia Ames for subtlety; her expertise was in the persuasive arts. His first instinct was to put a hole into the head of the insolent Mr. Boninghausen, if indeed that was his real name. But the desire for power and wealth was what drove Patrick Rourke, and since the relationship with Captain Medford had been very lucrative, he decided to listen a bit further. "I really have no idea what you're talking about, but ask me questions if you like," ordered Rourke.

Boninghausen smiled; he knew he was about to snag a big fish. *Just have to reel 'em in slowly.* He thought back to the recent covert meeting with the British captain. Medford had sailed his ship *HMS Richmond* from Philadelphia, where the captain had made the final arrangements with Patrick Rourke, to New York for the express purpose of updating the mastermind of the entire operation. The operation, code-named *Chaos*, was a bold attempt to cut off the head of the snake, in this case many heads. The targets were the key members of the Second Continental Congress and certain others, to render the rebels leaderless.

The idea was the brainchild of Lord North. A reluctant General Howe was placed in charge of implementing the plan. No one knew if Lord North had informed the king or if, in fact, the king had planted the seed to North. Howe realized immediately that if the plan was successful, naysayers in the Parliament would not make much fuss. However, if the plan backfired, members like William Pitt, Lord Chatham would create enough trouble to end the general's career in disgrace. Like all good politicians, Howe created a complex web of lies in order to cover his trail. Howe met only with Colonel Parker; he would be the tip of the spear for *Operation Chaos*.

Colonel Nathan Parker was the most decorated officer in the British Army. A veteran of the French and Indian War, he had served with General Edward Braddock and was beside the general on that fateful day in June of 1755, when he was killed. One of the youngest officers in the British Army, Parker had idolized General Braddock and was serving next to him when he was shot during the first day of fighting at the Battle of the Monongahela. The general would die four days later. Parker's rage over losing the great general was aimed at the French, the Indians, the colonial militia, and George Washington.

Parker believed the French had targeted British officers with their guerrilla war tactics. Indeed, of the eighty-six British officers, twenty-six were killed and thirty-seven were injured.

He was incensed by the Indian tactic of firing their weapons from behind trees and rocks, a ploy Parker thought as cowardice and yet proved successful. When the battle was finished, the British had lost 456 dead and 422 wounded. Of the fifty women traveling with Braddock's army, all but four were killed, including Parker's fiancée. The French lost only eight men, with four wounded, while the Indians had fifteen killed and twelve wounded.

As much as Parker hated the French and Indians, he had even greater loathing for the colonial militia and their volunteer aid-de-camp, George Washington. When the battle had commenced, Braddock and his officers continued to try to regroup their disillusioned troops along the open roadway, making tempting targets for the enemy. The colonial militia, including future frontier legends like Daniel Boone and Daniel Morgan, more in tuned to Indian-style warfare, left the open road for cover in the woods. According to Parker, this led to greater confusion and limited the actions of the general. Parker viewed the colonial militia as more cowardly than the French and Indians and the ultimate cause of the great general's death.

In the aftermath of the famous battle, George Washington was praised for his bravery under fire and in coordinating an orderly retreat by establishing an efficient rear guard. Washington's disregard for his personal safety endeared all who witnessed his bravery and created a stark contrast with many of the British leaders. Parker and several other officers believed that the British still held the upper hand and could still win the day. But in fact, most of the British officers were disorganized and confused and held out hope that their seriously wounded leader would miraculously recover and lead them out of their predicament. Almost every British officer under Braddock resented Washington's heroics, because it most assuredly revealed their lack of leadership after their boss had been seriously wounded. Parker's hatred of Washington and the criticism of British officers became legendary.

In British Army circles, it was no secret that Colonel Parker's loathing of Washington and all colonial militia was without peer. While most British officers looked forward to reconciliation between Parliament and the colonies or a quick and decisive war, Colonel Parker wished only to unleash death and destruction down upon them and the total destruction of Washington's army and his reputation.

Heinrich Boninghausen, whose real name was Major Hadden Campbell, had been with Colonel Parker throughout his service in America. Second-in-command to the colonel, he was his boyhood friend, and they had joined the Army together at age seventeen. They were both relatively young, twenty years old at the Battle of Monongahela, and shared more than just friendship. Both had fallen in love with Virginia girls who traveled with General Braddock's army as nurses. Both women were killed during the cowardly attack, and both British officers chose to blame the colonial militia and Colonel Washington.

The secretive meeting between Captain Medford, Colonel Parker, and Major Campbell had taken place at a small Loyalist farmhouse on Staten Island. Colonel Parker had been quite pleased with Medford's arrangement with Rourke. Major Campbell, who had been assigned to recruit Loyalist in and around Philadelphia, had been deemed too valuable to be involved in the actual assassinations. The ambitious two-part plan involved Rourke's assassins taking care of the rebel leadership. Part 2 would occur once Howe's army landed. Colonel Parker's cavalry, along with Major Campbell, had a special job to accomplish. All three men were satisfied with the plan; Campbell knew an approximate date for Rourke's operation. One of his spies, who worked in the Philadelphia Police Department, alerted him the day after the failed plot. It was the failed attempt that had produced the current meeting, as Major Campbell gambled he would have a compliant ally.

"Okay, have it your way. I suppose you heard about a shoot-out at City Tavern and, later that same night, at a private home of a wealthy barrel maker named Tucker," offered the British spy.

"I am aware of the tragic occurrence. A real shame it wasn't successful," countered the still-suspicious Rourke.

"As am I," replied Boninghausen. "What went wrong, Mr. Rourke?" Ending all pretenses, Boninghausen fired the question at the Irishman.

Rourke studied his adversary-ally and immediately decided to throw caution to the wind. "One man," snarled Rourke, raising his right index finger for effect, "well, one man and a mysterious Good Samaritan. The man is a friend of the Virginian Jefferson. The stranger seems to have come and gone. These men saved every one of those thieving lawyers. According to my sources, Jefferson's friend had just arrived in town and then, almost single-handedly, stopped the whole operation. Supposedly, he was a member of the Virginia militia. As for the other man, we know nothing, but that will change soon."

Boninghausen's face flashed angry at the mention of the Virginia militia. "Does this one-man army have a name?"

"Yes," replied Rourke. "His name is Ben Cushman."

Boninghausen did a quick memory search, but Cushman's name did not sound familiar. "Did they capture any of your assassins?"

"Yes, but one of my men saw to it that he paid for his incompetence with his life."

"I'm impressed, Mr. Rourke, but are you sure he didn't reveal anything to connect you?" Boninghausen's eyes demanded an honest answer.

"I have a source on the inside at City Tavern. The assassin gave away Tucker's name, but nothing else." Rourke was embarrassed to admit that piece of information.

"This Cushman, is he still in town?"

"Yes, he is, and I have plans for his demise." The smile on Rourke's face and the tone of his voice reminded the British officer of an uncle back in England who had to be put into an insane asylum.

"Perhaps I can be of some assistance," suggested Boninghausen.

"No thanks. My people will handle it just fine," Rourke bragged.

"Like they handled City Tavern?" the British spy mocked the Irishman.

"How, sir, might you help me, and what do you want in return?" Rourke fought hard to keep his temper in check.

"If you have the right state of mind, failure can ofttimes produce opportunity. I will help you kill Cushman because I hate that he spoiled your well-designed plan, and honestly, I hate all Virginia militiamen. As for what I want in return, nothing. I simply want to hire you to do a rather-simple job, for which you will be handsomely rewarded." The spy grinned with confidence.

Rourke quickly calculated his options. He appreciated the compliment regarding his *well-designed plan*. He was always willing to be *handsomely rewarded* for his services. Another potential reward would come when the British finally landed in New York and marched on Philadelphia. He would be in a position of great influence with the conquering British Army. "Just how handsome of a payment?"

"How does ten thousand pounds sterling sound?"

THE SIGNERS

Rourke whistled. He was rarely shocked, but the fee was significant. He leaned across the table while extending his hand. "Mr. Boninghausen, I think Captain Medford was right. How can I help you?"

The British major smiled brightly, handing Rourke a small piece of paper.

Rourke read the short note, glanced up, and spoke in amazement. "This is all you want?"

"That is all I want."

"This will be the easiest money I've ever made," an almost-giddy Rourke stated.

"Trust me, Mr. Rourke, you deliver that and it will eventually win us the war," he bragged.

Standing diagonally across the street from the *Indian Queen Tavern* was an old blacksmith forge. A dilapidated one-story barn stood at the rear of the property. An open pushcart and a firepit were the only other distinguishable items on the property that straddled the northwest corner of Market and Fourth Streets. A beehive of activity surrounded the forge as Ben Cushman and Thaddeus Tressach exited the *Indian Queen*. Approximately thirty-five people were milling around the property. Some were busy doing various chores, but most were passing around jugs of whiskey and rum. The two conspirators quickly negotiated the short walk and headed straight for the firepit. Flames were beginning to shoot skyward, engulfing a large iron kettle suspended above the pit.

"Kerry, how's yar witches' brew comin' along?" Tressach's Irish brogue was lyrical; Cushman was growing fond of the giant Irishman.

"Just fine, Uncle. It'll be ready soon." The younger Irishman didn't have the heavy accent of his uncle. *Already Americanized,* thought Cushman.

"Very good, lad. Shouldn't be long now," he informed the younger man. "Not really my nephew. He just likes callin' me Uncle.

Son of an Irish friend of mine. He works at the ship repair yard. His expertise will come in handy tonight."

"Is there anything you need me to do tonight?" Cushman asked.

"No, lad, ya've done plenty."

Cushman's arched eyebrows revealed his surprise.

"Mr. Adams may'ave told me some of yar recent exploits. Without yar skill and bravery, the cause may've been lost," suggested Tressach.

"I wasn't sure a few nights ago, but now I believe this cause is greater than any one man," replied Cushman.

"Ah, but with any great cause comes great leadership. Make no mistake, the British will target t'at leadership. T'at's what t'ey did in Ireland, t'at's what t'ey will do here." The giant Irishman led Cushman inside the small barn.

The small structure was dark. Cushman squinted, trying to focus on the occupant.

"Are ya ready for justice?" snarled Tressach at a man standing in the corner. He was tied to a post, hands behind his back. Each leg of his trousers had been cut off above the knee. It was the only clothes he had on. His muscular body was layered with sweat.

"Please, how much money? You name the price, I will pay it. How much to get me out of here!" the loan-shark-enforcer had been reduced to pleading like a small boy about to be punished by a strict father.

"How about ten pounds? T'e ten pounds ya killed me friend over," Tressach reminded Chevalier. "Was t'at all Andrew Bowen's life was wort', ten pounds?"

"It was an accident. He wasn't supposed to die. We had to make an example of him," countered the terrified André Chevalier.

"Just as we will make an example out of ya tonight," snorted Tressach.

Cushman watched the exchange with cool detachment. He had no sympathy for people like Chevalier. Hard-nosed bullies when they had power over you, they turned to spineless cowards when the tables were turned. *The British Army and the militia are filled with men like Chevalier,* Cushman thought. *Loudmouth braggarts, they surrounded themselves with willing followers and strutted around like peacocks. But when a battle started, they were always the first to run.* Contempt was all Cushman felt for the man standing in front of him. He would get what he deserved tonight.

"Come," Tressach announced loudly, "let's go retrieve our second victim for tonight."

Joseph Giersch always enjoyed his ride home at night. The rhythmic prancing of his horse along the cobbled Philadelphia streets seemed to melt his problems away. Still single at his age, he was too busy forging his career to pursue a proper woman; he would retire alone to his modest home on Fourth Street. With his salary he could afford a servant, but he would rather prepare his own meals and save the money. He had big plans, and being frugal at this time in his life was part of that plan. Revolution in the colonies was about to bring down the heavy hand of the king. The aftermath would surely be a boon to his career.

Giersch first noticed the looming crowd from one block away. *What now?* He thought to himself. *That damn tavern again.* Barroom brawls typically spilled out onto the street, cheering spectators enthusiastically encouraging the combatants rather than doing their civic duty to break up such nonsense. Usually, these occurrences happened later in the evening and on Friday or Saturday night. Still, Giersch felt no sense of danger. Drunk or not, the peasants would never bother someone as important as the county coroner. He knew the patrons of the *Indian Queen* were anything but Tories, and yet no one had ever bothered him, not even a profane shout.

Giersch's first sign of worry came as he drew within a hundred feet of the throng. Some seemed drunk, as expected, but others appeared calm, as if waiting for something to happen. A short time later, a second warning sent the hairs on the back of his neck on end; everybody was watching his approach, as if he were the guest of honor. Despite the instinctive warnings to flee, Giersch maneuvered his horse to make the right-hand turn onto Fourth Street. His home was just a half-block away. He was now directly in front of the stable. Arrogance dulled his instincts, and as soon as he slowed to make the turn, he knew he had made a huge mistake.

The crowd immediately surrounded Giersch; his horse came to an abrupt stop. Undaunted, the haughty bureaucrat bellowed, "How dare you! Move aside, you dirty rabble. Do you know who I am? Move aside!" Giersch began to reach inside his saddlebag, frantically feeling around his pistol.

"Now, now, Mr. Giersch, ya don't want to draw a weapon on t'is crowd." Giersch froze; his eyes located the speaker, a giant of a man emerging from the crowd. Next to him stood a man with a Pennsylvania rifle aimed directly at his head. Fear swept over Giersch like he had never felt before. A warm sensation began to run down his pants; the embarrassed Giersch had wet himself.

As if on cue, Giersch was pulled unceremoniously off his horse. The frightened bureaucrat managed one final arrogant bluster. "Take your hands off me! What do you think you're doing? I am the coroner to Philadelphia. I answer only to the king!" Giersch unsuccessfully struggled with the men as they led him toward the pull cart.

"Don't worry, darling, we're going to gift-wrap you for the king!" a middle-aged woman yelled out, to the delight of the growing throng.

"But if he dies, who will pronounce him dead?" joked another woman, causing the crowd to laugh in delight.

Giersch was thrown onto the cart and held down while two men cut away his pants, just above the knee. Another man ripped off his shirt. Giersch began to cry in agony as someone tightly tied his hands behind his back. Adding to his fear and embarrassment, one of the men held up a torn pant leg and yelled out, "My god, it's all wet—the man pissed himself!" The crowd roared its approval.

Cushman stood beside Tressach, the crowd spilling into the street as everyone jockeyed for position near the pull cart. Another roar of approval. André Chevalier was being led from the small barn and hoisted onto the cart with Giersch. The two men created quite a contrast, the heavyset, doughy bureaucrat and the muscular loan shark. One thing they did share was the look of absolute terror in their eyes.

Giersch took little comfort knowing he wasn't the only victim and turned to the stranger. "Why are they doing this? Who is doing this? Do you know?" His eyes searched for any hope the newcomer might have to offer.

Chevalier took comfort that someone was actually more fearful than he was. "What is your name?"

"Giersch, Joseph Giersch. I am the coroner for Philadelphia." His voice trembled with fear.

Chevalier was familiar with most law enforcement officials, and although they had never met, he knew about Giersch and was beginning to see a connection. He was smart enough to realize that his occupation had inherent risks, including vigilante justice. He was also aware that his boss had corrupted several members of the police department, his prize being Sheriff Otto. They were paid well to look the other way or to give valuable information. His boss had tried to pay off Giersch once but was rebuked, not because of honor or honesty, but because the bribe was not large enough. No, Chevalier knew why he was here, knew that someday something like this was bound to occur. *But going after the coroner? This is crazy! Maybe in Boston, but not here in Philly.* "You have no idea why you are here?" Chevalier asked the frightened bureaucrat.

"No, do you?"

Chevalier carefully crafted his reply. *After all,* he thought, *having the coroner as an ally might be helpful.* "I work for a bank. I loan money. They say I'm responsible for the death of one of their friends. I am innocent. The boy hurt his leg and got sick, and he later died. They are trying to blame me."

Giersch's memory was excellent; he remembered a case not too long ago. "Bowen," he said out loud. "Andrew Bowen, died from the fever, complications from the leg being amputated, as I recall. They said he had been beaten."

"It's a lie, Mr. Giersch. They are trying to frame me," the loan shark lied convincingly.

"People that borrow money should expect those types of things. That's why we have debtor's prison," Giersch stated, his belief system unchanged, even under the current duress.

Chevalier's confidence grew. Giersch could be a powerful ally, even if the mob followed through with tonight's punishment. "You have no idea what awaits you tonight, do you?"

"No. Do you?" Giersch asked for a second time. His eyes again revealed the fear was building.

"Don't worry, Mr. Giersch, to my knowledge, no one has ever died from being tarred and feathered." The words came out of Chevalier's mouth soothingly, yet his eyes betrayed him. He, too, was fearful of what was about to transpire.

"Tar and feather, oh my god!" Giersch shuddered in terror.

Tressach's *nephew* applied concentrated oxygen into the firepit by pumping the accordion bellows through a narrow opening in the brick pit. This helped heat the fire to 160 degrees, necessary to liquefy the pine tar contained in the iron pot. The flames danced higher and higher as the crowd continued to pass around the jugs of alcohol. Tar was plentiful in the colonies and used in many industries, like barrel making, shipbuilding, and roofing on homes and businesses. For tonight's purpose, the tar would be used to punish the two men; the feathers, applied immediately after, would be more for increasing the embarrassment factor.

Like tar, feathers were plentiful throughout the colonies. Almost every town had a hog butcher, and most butchered more than just hogs. Goose, chicken, and turkey were common edible fowls, and while every colonial farmer was handy at plucking and dressing birds, many bigger cities had specialists. The leftover feathers had many uses, from lining in blankets to padding for pillows, and on special occasions, the vigilante led tarring and feathering.

Giersch's mind raced for solutions to avoid his seemingly inevitable fate. Escape seemed impossible, as did reasoning with his captors. He looked at his fellow victim; he seemed to be resigned to the final outcome. Joseph Giersch had always been in charge, had always been the one giving orders. In his panicked state, it occurred to him that his best chance of surviving might be to ally with the total stranger.

"What is your name?" Giersch whispered.

"Chevalier, André Chevalier."

"Mr. Chevalier, do you think the Bowen case is why I am here tonight?" Giersch still could not hide the fear in his quivering voice.

"Yes," assured Chevalier. "Perhaps they feel your investigation didn't produce an indictment."

"But even if what they say about you is true, your actions did not directly cause his death." Giersch looked at the Bowen case through the prism of the legal system and how it could enhance his power, not the cause-and-effect consequences that the beating had produced.

Remaining in the background, Cushman observed Tressach work the crowd into a frenzy. The giant Irish immigrant appeared to be a natural leader. Cushman envisioned him fitting right in with the Boston mob. No wonder Samuel Adams had recruited Tressach to the cause of liberty. Of course, his recruitment was made easier knowing he had witnessed British soldiers' murder his mother and father.

The Irishman effortlessly leaped to the back of the cart and landed with a thud. His wingspan was huge as he held up his arms, signaling to the emotion-laced crowd that tonight's festivities were about to begin. The crowd pushed closer to the pull cart.

"Lads, lasses, we'ave before us tonight two men, one responsible for the death of our good friend Andrew Bowen, and t'e other man responsible for denyin' any justice to his family and friends," Tressach said softly, gradually raising his voice. "I'm sure both t'ese men would love to try and convince us t'ey did nothin' of the sort. Should we give t'em a chance to talk?"

"No!" a loud chorus of shouts reverberated through the streets as the crowd, now nearing a hundred, continued to lust for justice.

"Did Mr. Chevalier ever t'ink to give Andrew more time to repay his usurious debt?" Tressach's voice grew louder.

"No!" the crowd roared in unison.

"Is t'is the first time Mr. Chevalier has resorted to gruesome violence to collect a debt?"

"No!" Cushman couldn't believe the crowd could get even louder, but it did.

"What about our county coroner, Mr. Giersch. Did he initiate a proper investigation?"

"No!" Giersch shuddered at hearing his name and the crowd's scathing reaction to it. The slight hope of teaming with his fellow victim vanished into the building crescendo of noise generating from the mob.

"Do ya know what I t'ink? I t'ink Mr. Chevalier bribed Mr. Giersch into lookin' the other way." The louder Tressach's Irish brogue bellowed, the more disturbing the mob's reaction. Giersch's protests were drowned out by the chanting rabble.

Benjamin Cushman had gradually maneuvered back to the barn and opened the door, only to be greeted by a welcome sight. He gently closed the door and returned to listen to Tressach's closing remarks.

"What should we do to t'ese two?" he roared.

"Tar and feather, tar and feather, tar and feather!" The mob repeated the rhythmic chant over and over as they began to circle the cart, clapping and shouting, over and over.

Kerry, the ship repairman, carried a large cupped ladle of hot tar and handed it up to Thaddeus Tressach, being careful not to spill the burning-hot substance. Chevalier struggled to break free of the two men pushing him closer to the edge of the cart.

"If ya continue to struggle, I'll 'ave the men hold ya down and we'll pour it down yar t'roat. I'm sure ya know what t'at will do. Now stop strugglin' and take yar punishment like a man," Tressach declared, raising the ladle of steaming-hot tar over Chevalier's head.

Scorching-hot tar struck his head, searing off large chunks of hair. Chevalier shrieked in pain as the syrupy tar rolled down his face onto his neck, shoulders, and back. His skin turned bright red from the burning tar, then black as more and more ladles of the burning tar were poured over his entire body. The tar was so blistering hot

THE SIGNERS

Chevalier thought he was on fire; he closed his eyes as tightly as possible to keep the vile substance from blinding him.

A tough man for most of his life, Chevalier whimpered in pain as nerve endings throughout his body sounded alarm bells to his brain. Never much for religion, he silently prayed to God for someone to shoot him, to deliver him from such pain. No such luck would save him tonight. Without any warning, a shovel handle was placed squarely in his back; he was pushed off the end of the cart, landing awkwardly amid the rabid crowd. A new pain shot through his left shoulder, which took the brunt of the fall.

Several women rushed forward with pillows full of feathers, emptying the contents on the disoriented Chevalier. The feathers adhered to the hot tar, creating an amusing caricature of the formerly haughty loan shark. Pulled to his feet, he staggered in the midst of the crowd like a wounded animal surrounded by a large pack of hunters. The multitude of people poked rifle barrels and large sticks into his ribs to keep him from getting them dirty.

The tar began to cool and harden slightly, making it difficult for Chevalier to move. Two pairs of strong hands steadied the Frenchman as a large fence rail was placed between his legs. Again, without any warning, the rail was lifted roughly between Chevalier's legs, propelling him airborne. Two men placed the rail on their shoulders while others steadied the victim. He was unable to balance himself without the use of his hands, and the full brunt of his weight bore down on the rail, cutting and tearing at his crotch. The combination of second-degree burns and the new pain became unbearable as Chevalier began to black out. His final sensation was the ringing sound in his ears; he could hear the feverish throng chanting over and over, "Tar and feather, tar and feather, tar and feather!"

The large mob parted as a smaller portion of the crowd began to march the loan shark up Fourth Street, where he would be ridden out of town on the rail. The majority of the mob would wait for round 2 to begin.

Although the nightmare had lasted only five minutes, to Joseph Giersch it seemed like an eternity. He had anticipated some type of anarchy before the king's troops could deliver Philadelphia from the clutches of the traitorous rebels. But surely, nothing like this, especially to someone in his high position. Watching Chevalier suffer the horrible punishment was agonizing enough; he realized his turn was coming. Chevalier was younger and more fit than Giersch. He had seemed confident and steady, someone who could endure any torment. Giersch began to entertain thoughts he might not survive the ordeal. For the first time in his entire life, the arrogant coroner had lost all hope and began to resign himself to the terrible torture ahead.

The same two sturdy men who had pushed Chevalier to the front of the cart did the same to Giersch. This time, however, they lowered him to the ground. Instead of the ladle, Tressach produced a brush full of tar and proceeded to paint Giersch's right shoulder and his upper back. The pain was worse than he could imagine. His skin was on fire as he screamed in pain, begging for mercy. Tressach's eyes revealed no sympathy, only disdain. Giersch braced himself for the next batch of tar.

Ben Cushman caught Tressach's eye, and both men nodded. "Here comes the tricky part," Cushman noted softly to himself as he strode quickly to the barn. He poked his head inside and spoke softly. "You're on. I hope to hell you know what you're doing. If not, we might get torn to shreds."

"O ye of little faith" came the reply as the two men came strolling out onto the stable yard.

The chanting was not as vigorous as it had been with Chevalier but was still intimidating. At first, no one took notice of the three men approaching Tressach, who was about to apply a second coat of tar to the county coroner. A slight grin came over the giant Irishman. "Well, well, Dr. Franklin, Mr. Jefferson, what brings ya to our little party."

The mob slowly fell silent, pointing in the direction of the famous Philadelphian. If William Penn was the father of Philadelphia, Benjamin Franklin was surely her first son. Born and raised in Boston, Franklin had a similar Puritanical childhood as John and Sam Adams. Puritan values of self-reliance, individual freedom, hard work, a vigorous resentment to excessive power, and equality were paramount to the current group of revolutionaries. Franklin never surrendered his childhood values, even when he had run away at age seventeen to Philadelphia, looking for a fresh start. He had thrived in his adopted hometown, and the lists of his achievements were already legendary. His return as one of the most influential members of the Continental Congress was just icing on the cake. Despite his celebrity, he had trespassed into an emotionally charged atmosphere. The crowd eyed him suspiciously, and even more so the Virginian Jefferson.

"Well, sir, I'm afraid I am at a disadvantage, as you know my name, but I not yours," said the elderly Philadelphian.

"Thaddeus Tressach, lad. A pleasure to meet ya." The Irishman shook both Franklin's and Jefferson's hands. Cushman had slid behind the two and closer to Giersch, chuckling to himself after hearing Tressach refer to the seventy-year-old as a *lad*.

The crowd began to grow antsy. An obviously drunken woman shouted out, "We love you, Dr. Franklin, but you're interrupting our entertainment!" A simultaneous cheer erupted from the crowd.

Jefferson elbowed Franklin, offering a concerned look.

"People, people!" Franklin raised both hands in an attempt to quiet the crowd. "My friend Thomas and I have just finished working and decided to come to the *Indian Queen* for a few pints. As many of you know, Mr. Jefferson used to live above the bar. Imagine my surprise that when we arrived, we walked straight into a good old-fashioned tarring and feathering."

While Franklin continued to try to defuse the raucous crowd, Giersch attempted to figure out the stunning turn of events. His frantic mind bounced around endless scenarios in an attempt to fathom what was happening. Just then, a hard voice whispered into his ear, "I bet you're wondering why two of the men you're attempting to destroy would come to your rescue."

"What, what are you talking about?" Giersch stammered, still shaking in fear.

"What I'm talking about is your attempt to prosecute innocent men, whose only crime was to defend themselves from assassination."

Giersch turned his head to see the stranger. "Who the hell are you?" he demanded to know.

"I'll leave that for you to guess." He pointed to Franklin and Jefferson. "Those are two of the finest men I have ever had the privilege of knowing. They are kind and decent. On the other hand, I am none of those things. You don't want to know what I am capable of doing to protect those two." The voice hesitated, letting the threat sink in.

Giersch stared into the sharp green eyes and recognized the steely determination of a warrior.

"I have an offer for you to ponder. How would you like to get out of this mess with no further pain or embarrassment?"

Despite the burning pain, Giersch, for the first time, began to regain hope that this nightmare might end. "What do you want?" a suspicious, but hopeful Giersch replied.

"Very simple. You get on your horse tonight and ride to New York. Never return to Philadelphia," the hardened man demanded.

"What would I do there?"

"For all I care, you can sit in New York and wait for your beloved British Army to land."

"And if I refuse?" Giersch mustered what little dignity he still had in an attempt to negotiate better terms.

"Perhaps I misled you, Mr. Giersch. This is not a negotiation. You do as I say or I will halt Mr. Jefferson and Mr. Franklin from intervening on your behalf. Then the pain will start again, and you will join Mr. Chevalier. If you survive that…" The man hesitated, allowing his words to penetrate into Giersch's confused mind. "I will then hunt you down and kill you. You shouldn't be too hard to find. The one with all the feathers, right?"

Giersch looked into the hard green eyes and blurted out, "Cushman, you're Cushman."

Ben smiled and continued, "Mr. Giersch, you have five seconds to decide."

Giersch's shoulders sank in recognition that he had no choice; he dropped his head and softly remarked, "I will leave for New York tonight."

"Very good. There is just one more thing."

"What is it?" Giersch suddenly felt betrayed.

"You'd better hope Dr. Franklin can persuade this mob to back down."

"What if he can't?"

"All bets are off."

Ben Franklin had always thought of himself as a man of the people, but in reality, his later years had been spent with English and French royalty. Even in America, his relationships were among the affluent. He had grown accustomed to the finer things in life. Midway through his address to the rancorous crowd, he figured his chances of success where about sixty-forty, 60 percent chance the mob would continue the tarring and feathering and perhaps make him the third victim, and 40 percent chance they'd back down. At that instant, Franklin decided to throw away his preplanned speech and rely on his wits.

"Ladies and gentlemen, if I could only have a few more moments of your valuable time," lamented the elder statesman.

A young voice rang out from the back. "This better be good, or we may have a third victim tonight."

"Very well. That's fair." Franklin moved away from Jefferson and Tressach, walking slowly into the mass of people. "Our deliberations are secretive, and I may get in trouble revealing what I'm about to say. Today, I sat down with my esteemed colleague Mr. Jefferson for the expressed purpose of editing a most remarkable document. To be honest, there wasn't much to edit. I'm sure most of you have heard that we have a committee working on a declaration of independency. In truth, Mr. Jefferson is a committee of one. As most of you know, I am getting on in years."

"You're still very handsome!" a pretty middle-aged woman interrupted the venerable Franklin as everyone laughed.

"God bless you, young lady." Franklin gently stroked her chin and gazed into her eyes, removing his spectacles. "But I think you need these more than I do." The people laughed at the distinguished Franklin as she modeled his eyewear.

"I have seen great change in my lifetime, things that no one could have predicted. But I will make a bold prediction. The document Mr. Jefferson will put before the Congress, his Declaration of Independence, will bring about change like no one has ever seen. His words will wipe away centuries of tyranny. His words will unify a divided America and set her upon a destiny for greatness. His words will strike fear into the hearts of the kings and queens around the world that abuse and corrupt the powers they are given. The Declaration of Independence will wipe away the old world and usher in a bright, new world!"

Franklin hesitated, letting his words sink in. "Where equality is the rule, not the exception. Where justice is sought, not to enhance the power of the government, but to reduce the government's powers. That our rights come from God, not the king. That they are unalienable, they can't be taken away. Among those cherished rights are life, liberty, and the pursuit of happiness."

"Dr. Franklin, this Declaration of Independence sounds wonderful, but what does it have to do with him?" a middle-aged shopkeeper wondered out loud, pointing toward Giersch.

"Well, my friend, I think it has everything to do with him," countered the eloquent Franklin.

Cushman stood in amazement; the unruly crowd now hung on every word Franklin uttered. Rather than shout, Franklin had lowered his voice, forcing everyone to move closer and be more attentive. The mob grew closer and closer, entranced by his soothing words.

"Mr. Jefferson's document summarizes the abuses King George has piled upon us. The king's arbitrary misuse of power is chief among the many abuses. If we indeed throw off these shackles, will they be replaced with new but only different types of shackles, or will we produce a society whose paramount job is to protect us from the misuse of government power? Tyranny is tyranny, whether practiced by a king, a democrat, or…" Franklin paused for effect. "A mob."

The large crowd was silent. Finally, an older woman spoke. "But, Mr. Franklin, what about Andrew Bowen?"

"I am sure Mr. Bowen would prefer a just world practiced by imperfect people over a tyrannical state pursuing their idea of a perfection, only to create one plagued by injustice and inevitable corruption. We should never forget Andrew Bowen or Patrick Carr or Samuel Maverick or Crispus Attucks or Samuel Gray or James

Caldwell or any other of the thousands of people who have suffered from the arrogant abuse of power." Franklin quietly connected Bowen's death to the victims of the Boston Massacre. "But in honoring their passing, we should make a pledge to protect the liberties of all men and women, not just those that are popular or in the majority. Mr. Giersch may indeed be guilty of biased views, of being a Tory. But after all, weren't we all Tories at one time or another? Whether we are called Patriots or rebels depends upon your current loyalties. We should not sink to the desperate actions of an unworthy tyrant. Rather, we should rise above those corrupt acts. We should convince all our fellow Americans, Tories and fence-sitters alike, with words and actions that we can look back upon and be proud of what was said and what was done. Let us convince them with our good words and our good works. I say to you one more time, tyranny, whether practiced by a king or a democrat, is still tyranny."

Franklin's words hung in the air like a humid summer day in South Carolina. No one spoke. Finally, it was Thaddeus Tressach who broke the silence. "Perhaps Mr. Franklin is right. We should all go home now."

"Or back to the *Queen*," a middle-aged man suggested loudly, followed by an approving roar of the crowd.

And with that it was over. Cushman stood beside Giersch, amazed at how Franklin had controlled the hysterical mob. The Virginian knew that no human experience could match the intensity and fear of battle. But tonight's events were a close second. How literally one man had brought the crowd to a dangerous frenzy of emotional chaos and yet another man had slowly depressurized the situation back to normal.

Ben Cushman whispered to Giersch, "You're a lucky man, Mr. Giersch, a damn lucky man. Come, let us get your horse. I will ride with you to the edge of town."

Giersch began to protest; he wanted to be able to arrange for his belongings to be sent to New York, but looking into Cushman's eyes, he decided it would fall on deaf ears. He was resigned to the fact that he would not see Philadelphia again until the British Army arrived to put down the rebellion. Giersch's depression was slowly lifted as he thought of the sweet revenge he would receive with the aid of General Howe and the British Army. Giersch had a new motivation to live, to exact revenge upon the people responsible for tonight's nightmarish episode. A sinister smile pursed his lips as Cushman led him to his horse.

Jefferson, Franklin, and Tressach walked into the rickety old barn. A single lamp cast a dim light throughout the small interior. Samuel Adams emerged from the shadows, a giant grin upon his round face. "Gentlemen," he called out, shaking their hands one by one. "Well played" was all he said. "Well played."

Chapter 18

The spirit of resistance to government is so valuable on certain occasions that I wish it to be always kept alive.

—Thomas Jefferson

June 27, 1776
Philadelphia

Benjamin Cushman hopped down from his horse. An unfamiliar steed was tied to a nearby hitching post. After City Tavern, he was taking no chances; his senses went on high alert.

"Benjamin, I missed you at breakfast this morning. Would you like some lunch." Catherine Graff smiled as she rose up from her knees.

"The flowers look beautiful," commented Cushman, interrupting her gardening at the base of the three-story brick home. "Do you need any help?"

"Nonsense. You're a guest here. Now, how about that lunch?"

"No, thank you, Catherine."

"Mr. Jefferson told me that you've been struck by Cupid's arrow." She did enjoy some good gossip.

"Mr. Jefferson has a big mouth."

"Not at all. He's just looking out for you. Mr. Adams is upstairs, visiting. Been here over two hours." Her face showed a motherly concern for her famous renter.

Cushman relaxed upon learning Adams was the visitor. "You really look after Red, don't you?"

"Someone has to. His wife is too sickly to come and visit, even for a short stay," she stated. "As smart as Mr. Jefferson is, he still needs someone to look after his daily needs."

"I've always said he was pretty helpless," joked Cushman as he entered the Graff home.

He took the stairs two at a time and almost collided with John Adams at the top of the landing.

"Whoa, Ben, where you going in such a hurry?" The Boston lawyer adroitly slid out of Cushman's path.

"Sorry, Mr. Adams. Old habit, running upstairs."

"Usually, he is falling down them." Jefferson laughed, sticking his head from inside the sitting room.

"I hear from my cousin and Thomas here that last night's events proved to be very successful," commented Adams.

"Your cousin has a devious mind. I'm glad he's on our side," Cushman responded. "But the night belonged to Thaddeus Tressach and Dr. Franklin. They were both magnificent."

"So I've been told. How was your ride with the good coroner?"

"Pretty quiet at first, but as we departed, he regained his arrogance and threatened all of us to eternal damnation."

"The only way he'll come back to Philadelphia is on the back of Howe's army," declared Adams.

"Unfortunately, that could be sooner than later," commented Jefferson regarding the news of the massive British fleet approaching New York.

"Washington will treat them to another Breed's Hill." Adams thought very highly of America's first general.

"Let's pray you're right," responded Jefferson.

Jefferson caught Cushman's worried gaze and informed Adams, "Ben's younger brother James is serving as an aide-de-camp for General Washington."

"Perhaps George too," stated Cushman, remembering his conversation with Major Hall.

"Under normal circumstances, they would be safe, serving with a general on the back lines. However, Washington is not your typical general," Adams commented.

THE SIGNERS

"You're right, Mr. Adams. The general will be directing the battle from the front lines. He will expect his lieutenants to be beside him." Cushman's face revealed his love for his younger brothers.

"Well, if I know James, he'll probably shoot General Howe right between the eyes," offered Jefferson.

"What have you got there?" Cushman quizzed Adams, attempting to change the subject. Adams held a cylinder tube similar to the one Jefferson used to carry around the Declaration of Independence.

"Thomas was kind enough to allow me to copy his declaration in my own hand."

"We have both been recopying my rough draft. I can't really hand in the original, with all the alternations," Jefferson added.

"Oh, I don't know. Future generations should know what a true slob you really are."

Adams smiled. "I wanted to make a copy of Thomas's original document, as we both fear that Congress will make changes."

"Come!" Jefferson waved his friend from the hallway into Cushman's new bedroom, pointing to the small table Jefferson had especially built for his writings. "There is the finished copy we will present to Congress tomorrow."

Cushman walked to the desk and glanced through the document he had actually helped revise two days earlier. Indeed, Franklin and Adams had persuaded Jefferson to make many small changes, but the great body of the document remained as Cushman remembered.

"So tomorrow's the big day. How long will Congress debate the issue?" inquired Ben.

"Pennsylvania, New York, and South Carolina seem to be wavering. They could stall the matter indefinitely," replied John Adams.

"Dickinson remains a real problem, and Delaware isn't a given either," added Jefferson.

"I have never been surer of the need for separation, and this is the perfect instrument to convince all doubters. I will do everything in my power to make sure this gets passed," Adams declared, holding up his copy of the Declaration of Independence.

"After watching Dr. Franklin charm last night's rabble, it's hard for me to believe he couldn't convince Dickinson and the others within the Pennsylvania delegation," opined Cushman.

"Make no mistake, John Dickinson is a Patriot. He wants what we want. But he is overly cautious. He still believes there can be reconciliation," Jefferson reflected out loud.

"You're being too kind, Thomas. He is an appeaser. His time has passed. It is time for men of action to take control and lead this country through the difficulties that lay ahead," grunted Adams.

"If his principles are too conflicted, he should just remove himself from the vote," Cushman, the nonpolitician, offered to the others.

"Benjamin, that's a wonderful idea. I must file that," Adams promised, tapping his forefinger to his head.

"John and I are riding to the statehouse. What adventures are you up to today?" Jefferson asked his friend as he made for the stairs.

Cushman hesitated; his eyes fell toward the ground. Jefferson relished in his discomfort. Finally, Cushman blurted out, "Deborah doesn't work until evening, and we are going for a picnic down by the riverbank."

The two happily married Patriots smiled at each other, perhaps remembering the awkward courtships that they had gone through in earlier years.

"Well, well." Adams sighed. "Might our Ms. Debby snare the frontier warrior?"

Jefferson stood still, nodding, his grin measured from ear to ear. "You old dog, you're twenty years her elder," he exaggerated.

"Only ten," countered Cushman.

"I find attitude and attraction more important than age," responded the philosopher Adams.

"Still a handsome *young* woman," Jefferson stated with a heavy emphasis on the word *young*.

THE SIGNERS

"I hope you two are done having fun," implored Cushman. "I have to go put on some courting clothes," he stated, leaving the two rebels laughing all the way down the stairs.

It was difficult to hide the excitement in her voice as she repeated over and over, "Five thousand pounds sterling!"

"That's correct, five thousand pounds," Patrick Rourke lied to his part-time partner and lover, Lydia Ames.

"And this is all he wants," she announced, waving the small note that Heinrich Boninghausen had given to Rourke the past evening. "What do you suppose he will do with the information?"

"He didn't say. I have my theories, but in reality, I couldn't care a whit, as long as he forks over the money," declared Rourke. "I want you to instruct all those gathering information to specifically look for those two things." Rourke pointed to Boninghausen's short note.

"Should be no problem." Lydia smiled. "How long do we have?"

"He wants it all by the end of July. That should give us plenty of time, don't you agree?"

"Yes, perhaps much sooner. Most all the delegates frequent City Tavern. We can gather the rest at parties and gatherings. My girls will be perfect for this job," Lydia declared. Her love of money was equal only to her love of power. "Our usual fifty-fifty split?"

"Of course," Rourke answered with a smile. "That's 2,500 pounds simply to engage them in normal conversation. Not bad... not bad. But what about Deborah? Can we still trust her?" Rourke's obvious glare revealed what he thought the answer should be.

Lydia Ames thought carefully before answering, "She has established trusting relationships with almost all the delegates. Replacing her now would create more problems than it would solve. My only concern about her is that she seems to be smitten with Mr. Jefferson's friend."

"Don't worry about him. He won't be around much longer," promised Rourke.

"I do hope you'll include me in your diabolical scheme," purred the scandalous beauty.

"Perhaps, my dear, but we mustn't underestimate him. He is resourceful. I don't know what would happen to me if I lost you." Rourke's charming smile revealed a soft spot for Lydia Ames.

Lydia relished the idea to seek out revenge against Ben Cushman. She took the failed mission personally. Unlike Rourke, whose temper oftentimes interfered with his judgment, she possessed the most important virtue when seeking revenge, patience.

The general was seated alone in the captain's quarters, poring over maps of New York City. His concentration was disrupted with a loud rap on the cabin door.

"Enter," he called loudly. His eyes never stopped studying the maps.

Sunlight filtered into the room as the door flew open. General William Howe looked up to see who had the audacity to interrupt his preparation. Readying a verbal reprimand, he stopped before he started.

Standing in front of the general was Colonel Nathan Parker, an imposing figure—even General Howe was slightly intimidated by his presence. Unlike most British officers, the six-foot-tall Parker had no visual paunch. With his lean and muscular build, his physical prowess was well documented among the soldiers and officers alike. Fast and strong, he could outrun, outjump, outthrow, and outlift them all. He was extremely handsome, so women flocked to his side at popular parties back home.

His long black hair was tied into a ponytail; he was dressed immaculately in the uniform of the First King's Dragoon Guards. The bright-red jacket was outlined in blue velvet facings, highlighted by the gold epaulettes on both shoulders. A bright-yellow stripe ran up both sides of his blue breeches, and ankle-high black boots were shined to perfection.

"Colonel Parker, thank you for coming on such short notice," the general greeted his fellow officer.

"I must admit, it is a welcome break. I greatly prefer the stable earth to the rolling sea," the cavalry officer intoned.

"Getting a little seasick, are you?"

"Not yet, but I will be grateful when we land, sir. How long until we make New York?" Parker steadied himself as another large wave rocked the British war frigate.

"Shouldn't be long. In a few more days we will anchor off Staten Island and finalize our plans."

"How long before we can begin our operation?"

"Please sit down. That is what I wanted to see you about." Pointing to a large map of New York City, Howe continued, "As you can see, New York is basically three separate islands, Staten Island, Long Island, and Manhattan Island. Our spies indicate to us that Washington is fortifying Long Island here in Brooklyn." Howe pointed to the southwest corner of Long Island.

"He has left Staten Island without any significant defenses. My plan will be to occupy the island and use it as a staging ground for our conquest of New York City. My brother's ships should have no problem moving our troops anywhere they might be needed," gloated the confident general.

"It would seem to present a tremendous advantage, being able to ferry troops up and down the Hudson and East Rivers." Parker moved his fingers along the map, illustrating his point.

"It will be Washington's downfall," General Howe concluded.

"What about us?"

"Ah, yes, the point of the spear." An excited Howe grinned. "Look here. While we occupy Staten Island, you have ample room and supplies to train your men for your mission. When we attack Washington in Brooklyn, you will make your way here, across this narrow channel, into New Jersey. From there, you have a two—or three-day ride to Philadelphia. According to Major Campbell, New Jersey and New York are mostly Loyalists. You should have no problem through the New Jersey countryside."

"No country rabble shall delay our mission," boasted Colonel Parker.

Howe's experience with the *rabble* in Boston had lessened his bravado, but so much of being a military commander was to convince your troops of their superiority over the enemy. Not wishing to dampen Parker's enthusiasm, Howe could only reply, "Colonel, be careful. This promises to be a war like no other."

"Don't forget, General, I fought here with General Braddock. The Virginia militias are a bunch of cowards. I expect little resistance in New Jersey."

"How will you proceed?"

"I will descend upon Philadelphia, sending several men ahead disguised as farmers. They will meet with Major Campbell. By then he should have the information we need to execute our mission. We will concentrate on those living in and around Philadelphia. I will separate my men into ten-, twenty-man squads to pursue multiple targets."

"You know, in all probability, I will not be able to support your mission until New York is secure." Howe repeated the weak link in the aggressive plan. "There will be no supply line."

"We will live off the land if we must. However, Major Campbell has assured me that Loyalist farmers will provide more food than we will need. If they don't, we will take what we need at the point of a gun."

"It may come to that," replied the general.

Parker hesitated. "Sir, may I speak freely?"

"Of course, Colonel." Howe knew what was coming, but he did not let on. "Your reputation as a fearless soldier has earned you that right."

"General, I believe you know my utter contempt for the rebels. In truth, I have very little respect for Tories either. The colonials have bastardized the English race. They have mingled their blood with Indians, French, Spanish, and even Africans. They are but distant relatives to true Englishmen. In order to win this war, we will have to crush their resistance with little regard for civilians. We must assume anyone not wearing a British uniform is the enemy. They must have no hope, none whatsoever," Colonel Parker demanded, his intense eyes boring into the general.

"Colonel." Howe had prepared his response with much thought. "War is unpredictable and oftentimes very messy. I expect you to use good judgment in carrying out your assignment, and I expect your reports to me will bear out nothing but good character of you and your men. We will talk later. Good day, Colonel."

Parker saluted the general and turned to leave, a large smile spread across his face. *So,* Parker thought to himself, *the general is willing to look the other way as long as my written report reveals all actions to be above board.* It was obvious to Parker that General Howe would pursue a career in politics after they banished the rebel scum. But more importantly, Parker knew he could wage all-out war upon the colonials without regard to the consequences. He couldn't wait to begin to spill some blood.

They looked out over the grassy bluff onto the Delaware River. Several merchant ships drifted lazily toward the city, sailors scurrying to lower more sails as they prepared the docking process.

"How did you find this spot?" Cushman said while launching a coin-size stone toward the nearest merchant ship.

"Not even close." She laughed, attempting to match Cushman's throw, only to fall short of the river.

"At least I hit water." He watched his second attempt sailing far out into the river.

"My father used to take me out here for Sunday picnics after my mother died. It became our weekly ritual when I was a little girl. He would pack a lunch, Sarah and I would ride up front, my dad would let us hold the reins." Deborah's voice turned melancholy as she remembered her youthful excursion to the south bluff overlooking the Delaware River.

"When did your mother die?"

"I was only two years old. I really don't have any memories of my mother."

"Well, she must have been very beautiful." Cushman smiled, tossing another rock.

"Why, Ben Cushman, did you just pay me a compliment?" She teased him and grabbed him by the hand, leading him toward a winding path sloping gently toward the river's edge.

"Where are you taking me?" Cushman asked. Her gentle touch caused his heart to race.

"This path leads down to the river." They snaked their way lower. The path was bordered on both sides by six-foot-high grasses, and the slightly worn trail was their only map. Cushman thought back to his Greek mythology lessons from Parson Maury. He enjoyed the story of the labyrinth constructed for King Minos of Crete by the great architect Daedalus. The elaborate maze was built to house the Minotaur, half-man and half-bull. Cushman imagined he was Theseus, the Greek hero who eventually slew the Minotaur.

The two emerged hand in hand to a small sandbar at the edge of the Delaware River.

"Before we had the picnic, my father would bring Sarah and I down here to swim. He would watch over us until we were exhausted, then we'd climb back up to finally eat. Those are some of my fondest memories." She sighed.

"They are beautiful memories. Never forget them."

"It was so much simpler back then. Things are so confusing now." She gazed up into his sharp green eyes, clutching both of Cushman's hands. "What will you do, Ben? Will you fight for the rebels?"

Cushman returned her stare, admiring her ocean-blue eyes, dancing with merriment and a touch of sadness. "I think I already have, but so have you. Standing up to the assassins like you did, you were amazing."

Suddenly her eyes changed. Sadness replaced merriment, and she immediately buried her head into Ben's chest, squeezing him with all her might. Ben was somewhat startled, but he returned her embrace, patting her gently on the back and whispering softly, "It will be all right. Don't worry, it'll be all right."

Cushman held Deborah close. His mind remained conflicted. Their loving embrace stirred his entire body, but something had caused her to break into tears. Cushman had heard all the stories of the complexities of women, and he was now in the midst of one of them. His attempt to understand the sudden breakdown was short-lived, as her exotic, fragrant perfume and her gently heaving body were making it very hard for him to concentrate. The rhythmic clapping of waves onto the isolated sandbar added to the romantic setting. Deborah slowly relaxed her arms around Cushman's shoulders, her sobbing now under control. "I'm so sorry, I just…"

Ben gently tilted her chin upward. Her eyes were moist with worry but still the most beautiful eyes he had ever seen. She tilted her head sideways, gazing upward as he lowered his head. Their lips met for the first time. He kept his eyes open, soaking her up with all his senses. Jefferson was right again. Cupid's arrow had struck Cushman hard.

Samuel Adams exited the Pennsylvania statehouse into the back courtyard. He couldn't believe it was now over one year that he had served in Philadelphia as a representative to his beloved Massachusetts. He missed his family but understood that the ultimate goal of freedom and independence demanded the tremendous sacrifice. Adams was motivated more than ever. He knew there was much to do but actually believed the hardest part was almost over. Adams believed that motivating the average American to pick up arms against King George would indeed be the most difficult task. Once the war began in earnest, there would be no turning back. Adams thought the colonials would eventually wear down their British oppressors. Much blood would have to be spilled, but in the long run America would emerge as an independent state. Jefferson's declaration would be the catalyst for this world-changing event. Adams knew he would need all his political acumen to help steer it through Congress.

Men like Jefferson, Franklin, Hancock, and even his cousin John saw the ultimate destination far better than he did. They needed to lead from the front. Adams preferred the backroom deal making, forging alliances, and destroying opposition. He had worked tirelessly to achieve the necessary coalitions to lay the path toward independence. From the moment Adams had arrived in Philadelphia, in May of 1775, he had worked hard to create a support system similar to Boston. From local city, county, and state officials, to movers and shakers within the city, Adams created a support network that was quite impressive. Next, he began to forge friendships and alliance among his fellow delegates. Not everyone succumbed to his charm, but no one wanted to be on his bad side. Unlike most politicians, Adams couldn't care less about fame or fortune. His love of country made him virtually incorruptible. His talents to persuade were perhaps his greatest gift, but also a burdensome curse. Everyone sought his council; he rarely had time to himself. But Adams accepted his destiny and believed the Christian adage "To those who are given much, much is expected in return."

This was one of those times when Adams felt compelled to meet with the local farmer. His mind raced over the million things he should be doing, preparing for the Lee Resolution the most vital. Tomorrow would begin the most important few days in his life, and he was meeting with someone he didn't know, at the request of someone he really didn't like. Several times during the day, he had decided to cancel the meeting, only to change his mind. His curiosity won out over his caution. According to the king and Parliament, the Second Continental Congress was meeting illegally in Philadelphia. Because of this, the windows to the statehouse had been ordered shut while the delegates met. During the hot summer months, the statehouse became a hothouse. It was common for many of the delegates to hold small meetings outside, in the spacious courtyard, under the comfort of shade trees. The green space spanned the entire city block, all the way to Walnut Street. Surrounded by a seven-foot-high redbrick wall, it was the perfect spot for delegates to talk privately and away from the oppressive heat of indoors. As a constant reminder of

THE SIGNERS

why they were there, rows of gunpowder and cannon were currently stored inside the large courtyard.

Adams walked toward the two men. He immediately recognized the low-level bureaucrat who worked for the governor of Pennsylvania. Adams didn't care for the man, but he had been useful and trustworthy.

"Mr. Post, your message sounded urgent. Is everything all right?" Adams stated, hoping to sound annoyed so that the meeting would be a short one. Adams thought Lucas Post looked nervous, but then again, *didn't he always look nervous?*

"Thank you for meeting us, Mr. Adams. I wouldn't have bothered you if I didn't think it was important," answered the short public official.

"This is Mr. Norman Bindernagel. His farm is just south of town. Every Wednesday he brings his produce into the city. I can assure you of his loyalties. He is a true Patriot."

"Mr. Post is a good friend to our cause. He says you have important information for me." Adams was already regretting this meeting; his mind was starting to drift toward today's duties.

Bindernagel's dress clearly indicated he was a farmer. He looked uncomfortable but spoke clearly. "Since my wife died last year, I usually spend Wednesday nights in the taverns. I only go into Whig taverns. It's become too dangerous to do otherwise."

"Tell Mr. Adams about last night," Post stated nervously, sweat dripping from his brow.

Mr. Bindernagel cleared his throat. "I was drinking with a man I have known for several years. He is a quiet supporter of the rebellion. He presents a neutral face because of his job. He deals with many Tories and doesn't want to lose the business. He has a wife and five children and is afraid to get involved."

"Involved in what?" Adams asked.

"As I said, many of his associates are Tories. He will even go to taverns with some of them. Early last night, one of these Tory associates began to brag about a big job he just completed. He was quite drunk, but something about his tone indicated to my friend he was being sincere."

Adams's interest started to get piqued. "What type of job?"

"An assassination!" Bindernagel's eyes got big as he pronounced the word.

An astonished Adams mouthed the words "An assassination?"

"He said he was supposed to shoot anybody who came out the kitchen door at City Tavern. He was ordered to kill the assassins." Bindernagel was clearly nervous as he spoke.

"What happened?" Adam's mind was trying to process all that he knew about what had happened at City Tavern.

"Nothing" was the simple reply.

"What do you mean nothing?"

"He said no one came out the door. He heard gunshots, waited for about half an hour, and then left. He said something had gone wrong. He went back to a designated rendezvous. His partner also made it back and bragged about killing one of the assassins. They didn't realize fully what had happened until the next day."

"Did he say who hired him?" Adams couldn't believe his good luck; he had honestly thought they would never solve the mystery.

"Yes. He told my friend, but my friend wouldn't tell me," Bindernagel declared uncomfortably. He was clearly intimidated by Adams.

Post interrupted again, "Tell Mr. Adams the deal."

Adams furrowed his brow. His instincts were sending mixed signals, the opportunity to apprehend the mastermind behind the assassination plot appealing. But his experience accepting secondhand and thirdhand information was mixed at best. Bindernagel appeared concerned but spoke calmly. "As I've said, this man does much business with Tories. He doesn't want to be exposed. But he wants to help the cause. He said the man in question is a powerful man. If he found out, my friend was scared, he could be killed. He told me if I could talk to you, I could broker a deal."

"Why me?" Adams asked.

"Everyone says you're a man who can be trusted, an incorruptible politician," replied Bindernagel.

Adams blushed at the complement, then asked, "What kind of deal is he proposing?"

"Simple. He will only deal with you, Thomas Jefferson, or an associate designated by both of you. I will take that person to a designated spot somewhere in the city."

"Why Jefferson?"

"Same reason as before," Bindernagel proclaimed.

A skeptical Adams remarked, "Then what?"

"Then he will tell you the man responsible for the massacre on Monday night."

"What does he want in return?" Adams thought the deal breaker was on the way.

"Anonymity. As I said, he is a good Patriot. He is scared word will get out that he revealed the organizer. He is afraid for his family. All he wants is a promise you won't reveal where you got the information."

"This could be nothing more than a trap to kill off Mr. Jefferson or myself." Adams's mind was racing, trying to consider all the angles.

"I said the same thing to him. That's why he would agree to a representative of your choosing, someone both of you would trust," Bindernagel replied.

"Why wouldn't he just have you tell me now? His anonymity would be guaranteed," Adams's mind continued to race. "I guess he doesn't trust me with the name. He is afraid whoever this man is, he has him spooked. He wants to deliver the name to one of you. He knew of my friendship with Mr. Post." Bindernagel patted Post on the shoulder. "And that he could set up today's meeting."

Sam Adams felt conflicted, but not because he was frightened by making a tough decision—he had made enough of those for two lifetimes. No, he was conflicted because he felt rushed. His instincts urged caution; he needed to calculate all angles, but that would require more time, and time was a luxury he didn't have. Tomorrow, Jefferson's declaration would be introduced to the Congress. It would have to be steered through all the delegations with care; there were still too many factions to worry about. Any delay could cause irreparable damage. He had already stopped one potential delay with the delicate removal of Giersch. Delegations were receiving instructions from their colonial legislatures every day. It was doubtful that the

New York delegation would receive permission to even vote on the declaration. If Howe's army landed soon, and rumors were rampant he would, producing a strong British presence could win the day for the appeasers. No, they had days, not weeks, to declare independence. Patriotism had never been higher, thanks to Breed's Hill, Paine's *Common Sense*, and Patrick Henry's speech to the Virginia legislature. If Howe landed his army and scored a quick defeat of Washington's ragtag rebels, the revolution would be over. Moderate voices would petition Howe for a ceasefire, and the British would then negotiate from a position of strength.

Adams had made his decision. As tempting as it was to capture the man or men responsible for the assassination plot, he could not be absent from Congress for the next few days. Even more important was that Jefferson be present during the deliberations. Although Thomas was reluctant to speak out, he would let others do it for him. His presence would be necessary to defend the declaration from doubters. Everyone respected his intellect, his passion, and his character. It would make it harder to criticize his work if he was present.

"I am sorry, Mr. Bindernagel. Tell your friend I cannot meet with him for at least one week, and maybe more. There is just too much important activity transpiring in the next few days. Mr. Jefferson has a more demanding calendar than I do."

A distressed Bindernagel immediately pleaded his case again. "Don't forget, Mr. Adams, my friend knows you are both busy. That is why he would talk to a representative of your choosing."

Adams's sharp political instincts kicked into gear. *Perhaps there is still a way to investigate this further.* He immediately thought of Jefferson's friend Ben Cushman. He certainly was resourceful and could take care of himself if there was any trouble. "Perhaps I can work something out, but I will need to consult with someone."

"Who might that be?" Bindernagel seemed eager to discover the name.

Suddenly, Adams felt better; he was now controlling the negotiations, something he was infinitely more comfortable with. "If Mr. Post could meet me here early tomorrow, say, seven o'clock, I will either refuse the meeting or have a representative. We will then set up the meeting according to his timetable. If that is agreeable to you, gentleman, we will have a deal."

Post looked anxiously at Bindernagel, almost fearful, but Bindernagel nodded, placed both hands up to assure Post. "Mr. Adams, your terms are acceptable, except I know Mr. Post has to travel tomorrow. Would it be agreeable to you if I replaced him? My friend wants this to happen as soon as possible."

Adams knew time was critical regarding both the coming debate for independence and tracking down the killers. Both situations held great risk; bold action would have to replace caution. *Besides,* he thought to himself, *Cushman could always say no to the meeting.* "Agreed" was his only comment.

They shook hands, and Adams and Bindernagel agreed to meet the following morning. As Adams shook hands with Lucas Post, he noticed that the bureaucrat still seemed agitated, but his mind soon began to concentrate on his next meeting involving key members of the New Jersey delegation still sitting on the fence. Samuel Adams smiled as he walked toward the Pennsylvania statehouse, ready to do what he was born to do, wage battle in the arena of ideas.

Lucas Post's face reflected the fear he felt. "You said it would be over today. I did my part. You must…"

Norman Bindernagel leaned in closely, his mouth inches from Lucas Post's ear. "You did just fine, Mr. Post. Everything will be fine. You lived up to your part of the bargain."

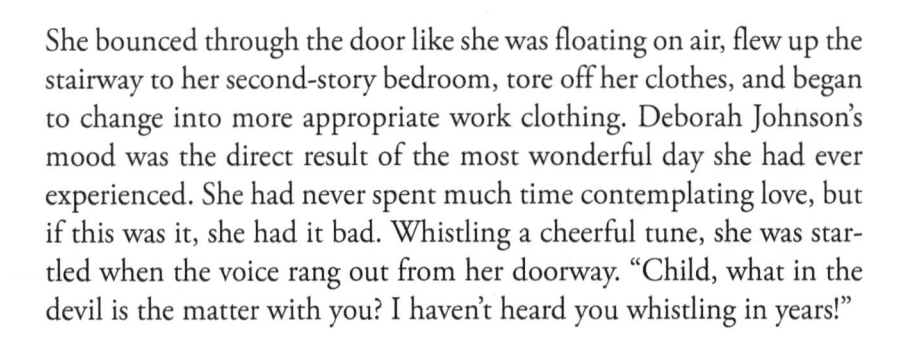

She bounced through the door like she was floating on air, flew up the stairway to her second-story bedroom, tore off her clothes, and began to change into more appropriate work clothing. Deborah Johnson's mood was the direct result of the most wonderful day she had ever experienced. She had never spent much time contemplating love, but if this was it, she had it bad. Whistling a cheerful tune, she was startled when the voice rang out from her doorway. "Child, what in the devil is the matter with you? I haven't heard you whistling in years!"

"Sarah!" She ran to her house servant, embracing her in a tight hug.

The pretty servant had lived with the Johnsons her whole life. Her mother had managed the large house, which included a servants' quarters. Sarah, born out of wedlock, grew up in the house as if it were hers. She was only four years older than Deborah, and so they played together like sisters. In fact, the wagging tongues, which made up the Philadelphia upper crust, insisted the two shared the same father. The attractive and intelligent young woman did indeed share similar facial features with Deborah. If it weren't for Sarah's coffee-colored skin, the two could have easily passed the sister test. Neither girl ever mentioned their similarities, preferring instead to be satisfied with their never-ending friendship. David Johnson had treated her like family, but his wife was not nearly as kind, adding to the speculation of an illicit affair. After the death of Deborah's mother, Sarah took on more household chores but still spent the majority of the time watching after Deborah. At age sixteen, Sarah became the woman of the house when her mother fell victim to the influenza outbreak that hit Philadelphia in 1766. As David Johnson's business grew to greater heights, he spent less and less time at home. Sarah Johnson—she had adopted the family name—had become sister and mother to Deborah, a difficult job, to say the least. As wonderful as Deborah had been as a child, her adolescent years had been a disaster. The more successful David Johnson became, the more headstrong she became. Her scandalous behavior was well-known throughout Philadelphia's elite circles, but her father's wealth at least kept her in the circle. Sarah was never able to properly balance being a friend and a surrogate mother. Deborah's attitude and behavior gradually improved when she started working at City Tavern. The job demands had begun to change the spoiled young woman into a more responsible adult. But that was nothing compared to what she was witnessing at that moment—the transformation was truly remarkable.

"Tell me, dear, why so delirious?" Sarah smiled, acting more like the big sister.

"Sarah, do you think you have ever been in love?" Deborah broke her embrace and did a tiny pirouette. "Because I think I may be."

Sarah Johnson knew what love was, because she had loved Deborah like a mother loves her daughter. As far as the other kind, she had to admit, she hadn't been so lucky. Tears of joy began to well up in her eyes; she hadn't seen Deborah this happy since childhood. "What is his name? When did you meet this young man?"

"Ben Cushman is his name!" Deborah replied enthusiastically.

"Cushman, Cushman...why does that name sound familiar?"

They quickly embraced again, both young women giddy with excitement. Sarah racked her memory for the name, and then it came to her. David had mentioned the name when talking in hushed tones to the dragon lady. It had been earlier in the afternoon; her haughtiness had demanded to see David at once storming past Sarah like she was invisible. The two had ducked into the library but left the door open. Normally, Sarah would never think to eavesdrop, but she had come to loathe his newest female acquaintance. Her position outside the library did not allow her to hear the entire animated conversation, but when the name Cushman came up, it was anything but a friendly reference. In fact, she had gotten the impression that somehow they wanted him dead.

Although not formally titled, she carried out the responsibilities as the matriarch of the Johnson family, and like a lioness, she was very protective of her brood. The dragon lady, who went by the name of Lydia Ames, had entered their lives a little over one year ago, not long after the Second Continental Congress began to meet in Philadelphia. David and Lydia shared the same politics and would sit up late debating the king's strategy and colonial response. They didn't always agree on everything. Some of the arguments got quite passionate. In the end, they always agreed that rebel leaders, like Adams, Jefferson, and Franklin, were marching Pennsylvania and the rest of the American colonies toward ruin. Sarah hated her from the beginning. At first, she tried to convince herself she was just jealous of Lydia's ravaging beauty, expensive wardrobe, and European sophistication. But the warning bells went off in full force when Lydia began to befriend Deborah. Sarah tried to warn Deborah, but the impulsive youngster dismissed her objections as outlandish. To Deborah, Lydia Ames was everything she wanted to be, independent, provocative, and powerful. Sarah was smart enough to realize this was an argument she couldn't win. She would bide her time and try to reason with Deborah at some point in the future. But in the meantime, she would keep a sharp eye on the dragon lady.

"Well, tell me all about Mr. Ben Cushman." Sarah's smile left no doubt of her deep affection for the twenty-two-year-old waitress-heiress.

While Deborah dressed for work, she enlightened her servant-confidant about everything. Everything, that is, except her complicity in the City Tavern affair, her meeting with Patrick Rourke, and her continued alliance with Ms. Lydia. Deborah attempted to rationalize the conflict racing through her mind. *I'm not really lying to Sarah, just isn't telling all.* Ben Cushman had changed everything; he was turning her world upside down. Getting involved with Rourke and Lydia had given meaning to her meaningless life. It was exciting, adventuresome, and even a tad romantic. Seeing her friend Gerard Jackson lying dead on the floor of City Tavern had jolted her back to reality. Lydia had warned her there would be casualties in war, but she wasn't prepared to see the carnage that had taken place that night. And yet it could have been worse, much worse, had it not been for Cushman. The horror of what had almost transpired struck her hard the next day, after the mad Irishman had threatened her and her father. Ms. Lydia had reinforced that threat later that day at City Tavern. She thought of Thomas Jefferson, John Adams, and of course, Benjamin Franklin; they had been so kind and helpful, especially after the attack. They were men of great character, and she had almost been an accessory to their murder. What if Cushman hadn't acted when he did? What if the assassins had killed him first? Thank God that Cushman was resourceful. She felt so naive. They had convinced her it was just to scare the delegates, nothing else. Instead, she would have been an accessory to murder. It had all been part of an exciting game until blood was spilled. She realized now that her spoiled and selfish ways had allowed them to lure her into their web of deceit. They were playing for keeps, and she was starting to realize she was on the wrong side.

Staring hard into Sarah's eyes, Deborah realized that they had driven a wedge between the two of them. *Something else to repair*, she thought. Giving Sarah a big hug, she stated in a serious tone, "I owe you a big apology. We need to have a long talk. But not now. I can't be late for work."

Sarah waved goodbye as Deborah ran down the stairs, almost calling her back. The meeting between David Johnson and Lydia Ames had been disturbing; she wanted her to warn Ben Cushman. *Well*, she thought to herself, *I guess it could wait until tomorrow*. She looked forward to her talk with Deborah; there was much to catch up on.

City Tavern was bursting with customers, and as usual, there were many delegates from the Second Continental Congress milling about. Intense discussions regarding tomorrow's landmark conference could be overheard throughout the tavern. The mood was festive. Rumors of the declaration had been circulating for months, but here at the epicenter of the revolution, people were starting to believe it would happen, and happen soon. Only a year ago, Tories had outnumbered Whigs three to one at City Tavern, but tonight the chance of finding a Tory in the tavern was about as good as King George appointing John Hancock as his foreign minister. The air was thick with anticipation and excitement, and that meant it would be a long and profitable night for the shareholders of City Tavern. Her mood hadn't changed. Darting from table to table, she had a smile that practically lit up the entire tavern. Deborah hadn't been working ten minutes when she saw Lydia Ames strutting through the hallway. Conservations in each room came to a screeching halt as all eyes followed the striking beauty to the back coffee room.

"The hell with her," Deborah mumbled softly under her breath. "She's not going to ruin my night." She decided to waste no time in confronting her. Somehow, she had to end the relationship with Lydia and Rourke. They had threatened both her father and Ben, and she was certain they would make good on those threats. She had to figure a way to break free and protect them both.

Lydia Ames saw determination in Deborah's face and instantly decided to use a different strategy. "Deborah, you look wonderful tonight. Do you have time for a short word?" The tactic seemed to work; the young waitress was caught off guard at the compliment.

"Uh, yes" was all she managed to get out.

"I know Patrick and I have asked much of you lately, perhaps too much. I apologize if we have put you into circumstances beyond your abilities."

Pride defeated logic as Deborah blurted out, "It wasn't too difficult. I handled my end." She immediately regretted saying it.

Lydia congratulated herself on changing methods at the last second; her instincts were sharp as ever. "I am not criticizing you. You did as well as can be expected. But it turned into a violent operation, and you ended up right in the middle of the mayhem."

This time Deborah controlled her emotions and decided to test the waters. "Perhaps you're right. The bloodshed was horrifying."

"Yes, but you weren't supposed to be involved with that part of it. The idiots we hired went too far. They disobeyed our orders. Things don't always go as we planned. Of course, your new friend Cushman's interference didn't help."

Deborah knew immediately she was being manipulated, and wasn't fooled. She knew it was an assassination attempt and felt contempt for Lydia. *Treating me like I'm an imbecile.* Rourke would seek revenge. Deborah had tried to bury the truth, but it kept bubbling to the surface. Unfortunately, it felt like she was caught in the middle of a Shakespearean play, and what little she remembered from her limited schooling was that in most of his plays, the main characters died.

The truth was that Rourke would kill Ben Cushman unless Deborah stopped him. But how? If she warned Ben, he would learn of her role in the assassination plot. It was official; Lydia had indeed ruined her night.

There was no way out of this mess, unless…She stared at Lydia. Lydia could intervene for her. Deborah had seen her manipulate Rourke many times with a look or a touch. It was a long shot. *What other choice do I have?* If she went against them, they would hurt her father. If she continued to help them, then they would surely come after Ben. Lydia was her only hope. She decided to roll the dice. "Lydia, you and I both know I'm not cut out for spying. It was exciting at first, but after seeing Gerard killed…" She hesitated, summoning tears, part real and part fake. "It's…it's just been so hard to get over all the killing." More tears rolled down her cheek.

Lydia studied Deborah Johnson with a keen eye, dissecting every word. She realized immediately that acting was not in the Johnson genes; she was terrible. Most importantly, she realized that Deborah was desperate, and desperate people were the easiest people to manipulate. "Now, now, dear, just relax. We can work this out."

The words were like magic. *There might be hope with Lydia.* "I just don't think I can do it anymore." Deborah took a long breath and laid out the rest of her cards. "Lydia, I have grown fond of Cushman. I know Rourke wants revenge. Please, you have to help. Please help!"

Lydia smiled, not because she felt sympathy for the young waitress, but because her instincts had been correct. Rourke didn't think they could trust her. He was right, but as usual, his solution to kill her was wrong. She could still be useful. Lydia could still extort what she needed from Deborah by threatening Cushman and David Johnson. A new strategy began to present itself as she pondered her next move.

"You are right about Rourke. He wants revenge for Cushman's interference. I can't ask him to forgive Cushman just because you have fallen for him. You need a bargaining chip. Something Rourke wants more than the death of your boyfriend," Lydia stated, probing Deborah's psyche for an opening.

"Bargaining chip? I don't have a bargaining chip! Any information I've gotten from here, I've turned over to you."

"What if I told you there was a way out of this jam? What if I told you that if you perform one more job for me, I can persuade Rourke to leave all of you alone, forever?"

Deborah was skeptical, and it showed in her reply. "What kind of job?"

"I think you'll be pleasantly surprised at how easy it will be," Lydia lied.

Deborah's skepticism hadn't abated. "How easy?"

"As you know, Rourke is a Tory, but he did not get rich being stupid. First and foremost, he is a businessman. He wants to be able to cover himself in case the rebels actually succeed. All I need you to do is gather the addresses of the delegates. Here in Philadelphia and back home."

"That's it? What's the catch? It's hardly a secret where most of the delegates are boarding." Deborah was immediately suspicious, but the possibility to solve her problem soon overwhelmed all common sense.

"I'll need you to compile a list of all the delegates. Some of the delegates live on farms and don't have street addresses, so I will need directions to their homes."

"Why does Rourke want this information?"

"As I said, he is a cautious man. If by some miracle the revolution succeeds, these men will populate the new government. Mr. Rourke will want to send them certain gifts to congratulate them on their successful overthrow of King George."

"Sounds like bribery!"

"Call it what you will. It doesn't matter. If it's the king or some new form of government, money will always be needed to influence the new rulers."

"But that's the type of corruption this war is fighting to end." Deborah realized she sounded like John Adams or Thomas Jefferson.

"Don't be so idealistic, Deborah. People invented governments in order to protect themselves from themselves. The rulers have the power but need money to consolidate that power. Men like Rourke have the money but need power. It's a cozy corruption that has existed since civilizations began. Men like Jefferson and Adams are fools. They think they can create the perfect society, but it will never happen."

"If I do this, how can I be sure Rourke will not come after my father or Ben?"

"I suppose my word isn't good enough for you?"

"Sorry, but no." She wanted badly to trust Lydia Ames.

"Look, you do this for me and I will make sure Rourke doesn't hurt your father or Cushman. At the very worst, I promise to warn you if he even thinks of seeking revenge. You must understand, he doesn't do anything without consulting me first." Her eyes were genuine, and her voice oozed sincerity.

Deborah looked into her dark eyes, hoping upon hope that she could trust Rourke's top lieutenant. A wave of dread washed over her, a final realization that she had no other choice; she had to trust Lydia Ames. It was her only hope.

"Okay, I'll do it, Lydia. Promise me you'll control Rourke!"

"Don't worry, I promise nothing bad will happen."

Half an hour had passed since Lydia Ames left City Tavern. Her open-carriage trip down Front Street had drawn the usual astonished looks from Philadelphians. Half were outraged that a woman would be riding in the carriage without a proper escort, and the other half captivated by her remarkable beauty. Rourke's servant, George, showed Lydia into the massive library without a word. Rourke arrived several moments later. He looked like a European prince dressed in the most expensive clothing of the day.

"Well, was I right or not? Ms. Johnson can't be trusted, can she?" His brash smile suggested the confidence of a king.

"Perhaps you were right, but she can still be useful."

"Ha, right again! Why you would ever doubt me is beyond me." Most people were turned off by Rourke's arrogance. Lydia found his confidence seductive. It was the key to controlling him.

"Indeed, she has fallen for Cushman. However, we can use this to our advantage. I can motivate her to carry out the current mission by threatening Cushman *and* her father."

"Her father? But David can still be useful."

"You know that and I know that, but she doesn't know that."

"Look, you can play all these head games with her, but by tomorrow night I will be torturing that son of a bitch Cushman." Rourke's eyes were wild with excitement.

Lydia Ames anticipated his remarks. "But I promised her I would stop you from harming him."

"Did she believe you?" Rourke's voice was incredulous.

"Of course! She's not very bright. I only ask you delay his death for a few days," Lydia begged.

"That's not a problem. I have several new toys I will test out on Cushman, and it could take a few days to realize their full effectiveness." Rourke's fascination with torture and death was well-known to Lydia. She found it amusing that a man of such wealth and personality would be so absorbed by the macabre. "So you have made up your mind?"

"Tomorrow's the day. The plan is set. Are you on board?"

"Yes. Go ahead and kill Cushman. Just don't do it right away." Lydia smiled as she already had thought of the perfect lie to tell Deborah in order to keep her on task.

Cushman was excited to receive the message. Catherine Graff was just as excited to give it to him. "A rider delivered it just about an hour ago, said it was important you get this note." Having Jefferson as a boarder, and now Cushman, had enlivened the Graff household immensely. The comings and goings of some of the most famous delegates had made Catherine Graff the star of her weekly sewing circle. She had grown very fond of the two Virginians and was equally enthusiastic about their cause.

Cushman re-read the short note. "'Meet for dinner at City Tavern, six o'clock, my treat. TJ.'" Cushman was happy for two reasons. One, Jefferson had offered to buy dinner, a definite rarity, and two, he would see Deborah again. He thought back to the wonderful day they had spent together and how eerily similar it was to the dream he had about Deborah a few nights before.

"You'd better get going if you want to get there by six."

Cushman smiled, admonishing the older woman, "Catherine, you read the message? Shame on you."

"Well, if they didn't want me to read it, then they shouldn't have made it so easy to open."

"Spoken like a true spy. Very well, Catherine, I'm off." Cushman laughed as he turned his horse and headed back into town.

"Be careful! There are many criminals out at night!" she yelled as Cushman rode away.

"Yes, Mother!" Cushman hollered back, now in a full gallop toward his destination.

Ten minutes later, Cushman was sitting in the tavern room with Thomas Jefferson and Samuel Adams. A huge smile spread across his face as Deborah placed three tankards of ale in front of them and took their food order. Deborah and Ben traded knowing smiles. Adams glanced toward Jefferson; his arched eyebrows signaled his keen perception regarding the two. Jefferson's grin confirmed his observation. The body language that followed indicated his approval. Adams raised his drink, and the others soon followed. "To tomorrow and a new dawn for America!"

"Hear! Hear!" both Jefferson and Cushman nodded.

"Thomas, I hope you're not mad, but John stopped by today and showed me your declaration."

"Not at all, Sam. I would value your thoughts prior to tomorrow's baptism under fire." Jefferson was sincere; he respected many of his fellow delegates, none more so than Samuel Adams.

Adams's face turned red. "I am not afraid to say it, I cried. I cried out loud for the first time since I was seven. I wouldn't change a single word. I love it! I love it! Thank you, Thomas, for all your time and effort. It is a magnificent statement to the world, but mostly to the American people."

"I had help, Sam. It was a committee of five. Even Ben here gave me a couple good ideas."

"Don't be modest, Thomas. I know for a fact you did yeomen's work on it."

Cushman attempted to manufacture a wisecrack, but nothing came to him; he was proud of his best friend. "Thank you both, Sam, for the nice compliment, and, Ben, for withholding any flippant comment." Jefferson laughed at his friend.

Adams turned serious, looking at Jefferson. "You know, Thomas, there will be changes, especially from your Southern brethren."

"You're referring to the slavery clause?"

"Yes. I doubt very seriously they will wish to take up that issue at this time."

"Mr. Franklin and your cousin agree with you," responded Jefferson.

"We also agreed that we would fight as hard as we can to keep the declaration as is." Adams hesitated as he ended his sentence.

"But…" Cushman beat his fellow Virginian to the word needed to end Adams's sentence.

"But," Adams said, acknowledging Cushman, "we are a delegation of politicians. Politicians need to feel relevant. No matter what happens the next couple of days, I want you to know that a few words cut here and a few words added there will not reduce the powerful effect of your wonderful document."

"I wish I shared your optimism. I fear they will shred the soul of my work."

"Have no fear, my friend. The document will remain strong," Samuel Adams declared.

Adams's words offered Jefferson some hope; perhaps it wouldn't be as bad as he originally thought. He began to cheer up when Deborah brought them three new pints.

"Deborah, from the grin on your face and the matching grin on this dullard here"—Jefferson grasped Ben's left shoulder—"I must assume your picnic was a triumph."

THE SIGNERS

Deborah smiled and blushed slightly. "A lady never gossips, Mr. Jefferson, but I would like to assure you that your friend was quite the gentleman."

"You overestimate Red's ability to identify a gentleman." Cushman chuckled. "He wouldn't know a gentleman if he bit him in the—"

"Benjamin," she admonished Cushman before he could use the common vulgarity. They all had a good laugh as she took away three empty tankards.

Adams, the older statesman, looked Cushman's way and remarked, "Ben, wartime is hardly a perfect time to start a courtship, but then again, when is a perfect time? Sometimes I find women more frightening than a regiment of British soldiers."

"What are you all laughing at?" The booming voice of John Hancock echoed in the tavern room as he approached the table along with two other delegates.

Sam Adams was the first to stand. "Gentlemen, please join us."

They all stood, greeting one another enthusiastically.

"Ben, how are your wounds healing?" It was Abraham Clark, the delegate from New Jersey.

"Just fine, sir, thank you for inquiring."

"You look remarkable, considering you were shot three days ago." It was another New Jersey delegate, the jovial John Hart.

"That's because he's in love." Jefferson smiled.

"Our Ms. Debby?" Clark asked.

All the men nodded in approval as Cushman shook his head, staring daggers at Jefferson. "Thomas, we will introduce your declaration first thing tomorrow morning. Mr. Adams informed me everything is complete," Hancock, the president of the Continental Congress, relayed to Jefferson. He received a big *thank-you-for-changing-the-subject* look from Cushman.

"You can count on New Jersey. Everybody is onboard," reported John Hart.

"New York hasn't received permission to vote yet," added Clark. "I am also fearful that South Carolina and Pennsylvania will be hard to win over."

"Don't forget Delaware. They are not guaranteed either," Hancock grumbled. Although only a select few had read Jefferson's work, all the men standing at the table were heartily in favor of independence. There was no doubt in their minds that Jefferson's Declaration of Independence would be a work of art. If only Jefferson could get over the nagging feeling that the Congress was going to decimate his baby.

As the threesome turned to leave, Hancock eyed his fellow Massachusetts delegate and declared, "Sam, we've come a long way in five years. Tomorrow begins what could be the greatest episode in human history. We need everyone at their best, especially you."

"Have no fear, John. Mr. Jefferson's document will convince the naysayers. I am confident," replied the heart and soul of the American Revolution.

Cushman nodded at the three Patriots as they left City Tavern. It was odd that even though he had known them for only several days, he felt as if they were lifetime friends. *I suppose that happens to people who share near-death experiences,* thought Cushman. Deborah returned to the table, and the two made plans to spend the following day together while Adams and Jefferson continued to strategize. She left quickly to continue her duties. City Tavern was quickly filling to capacity.

Four blocks south of City Tavern, a lone man hurried past a recently lit streetlamp. His heart was racing like never before. He turned the corner and immediately noticed a light in the front window. *That has to be a good sign,* he thought to himself. Without pausing to think of the consequences, he broke into a full sprint. As he ran toward the smallish one-story home, his mind raced through hundreds of scenarios, all of which ended badly. He had never been so frightened in his entire life.

Deborah Johnson delivered the third round of ale, flirted with Adams and Jefferson, but ignored Cushman. As she left, she looked back at Cushman and gave him a seductive wink and smile. "Benjamin." Adams had to speak loudly to carry his voice above the din of the crowd. "I had an interesting meeting today. Late last night, I received an urgent message from a Pennsylvania bureaucrat. His name is Lucas Post. He works for Governor Penn. He claimed he had information from a local farmer that was very important. Against my better judgment, I decided to meet with him earlier today."

"Why? Are you suspicious of Post?" Cushman asked.

"No. He is a bellyacher, but he has always been trustworthy. I guess it was my instinct. With so much going on, I didn't want to take time out of my busy schedule."

"Did you sense a trap?" Jefferson had a concerned look on his face.

"I don't know, but I agreed to meet behind the statehouse. Post brought a local farmer along. The farmer claims his friend was involved in the interesting conversation. Says he was in a Tory tavern and a customer began bragging about the assassination plot at City Tavern. Supposedly, he was hired to shoot the assassins as they exited the back of the building. His partner was positioned in the front to do the exact same thing."

Both Jefferson and Cushman sat in stunned silence. Finally, Cushman asked, "Why didn't the friend come to the meeting?"

"Said he was too frightened, didn't trust anyone with the information. Said he would only talk to Thomas or me. Or he would talk to an associate of both of ours. He is willing to reveal the mastermind behind the plot."

Cushman absorbed the information, trying to assess every angle. "One thing is for sure: whoever this guy is, he is not just spinning tales. Not many people know about the two men covering the only entrances and exits to the tavern."

"True. Tory newspapers have ignored the story completely, probably because it would paint our side in a good light. Whig papers covered the murders, but with little or no analysis. For some reason, Mr. Franklin doesn't want them digging into the story, and he carries great weight with the editorial staffs," Adams commented.

"This farmer, what was your impression?" Jefferson quizzed Adams.

"Post vouched for him, said he was a good Patriot. His name was Norman Bindernagel. He seemed like the genuine article. I told them that Thomas or I could not meet tomorrow, but Bindernagel agreed to take a representative to meet with his friend."

"Sam, I agree with your instincts. Something seems amiss," suggested Jefferson.

"I would agree if one of you two were to go, but why not send me as your representative? The benefits seem to outweigh the risks," Cushman offered with his ever-present smile. "Besides, the only trouble I'll be in is if I'm late for dinner with Deborah tomorrow evening."

A worried look came over Jefferson. "It just seems so rushed. I think we should take more time to investigate this."

Sam Adams nodded in agreement.

"Nonsense! It is too important of a lead not to follow. Whoever masterminded the assassination plot is sure to try again. Besides, gentleman, I can take care of myself," Cushman promised.

Norman Bindernagel watched from across the street as the panicked man ran into the small one-story home. His eyes scanned the neighborhood, looking for the telltale sign of betrayal. He waited a few more moments, and still nothing. He smiled, acknowledging to himself, *It is going better than I had imagined. Just one more item to clean up and call it a night. Yes, things are going smoothly.* He began to walk across the street.

Bursting through the door, Lucas Post quickly swiveled his head from side to side. The hope he had experienced a moment ago was extinguished when he didn't see her. He was overcome with anguish. A muffled sound emerging from the bedroom renewed both hope and terror. Without regard to his own safety, he exploded into the room and was met with twin emotions. Post was exuberant to see that his wife was alive and unharmed, but alarmed by the look of fear in her beautiful eyes.

It was only one year ago that Post, a thirty-four-year-old government bureaucrat, had resigned himself that he would never be married, destined to spend the rest of his life as a spinster. Colleagues had introduced him to Gloria. She was eight years younger than Post and recently widowed. She was pretty and vivacious, and Post fell in love with her that day. They were married six months later. He adored her with every fiber of his being.

Seeing Gloria tied to the bedpost, her eyes trembling with fear, filled Post with unimaginable horror. He quickly moved to her side, beginning to unravel the knotted rope.

"That won't be necessary, Mr. Post. Have a seat next to your pretty wife." The voice came from the darkened corner of the room, the image slowly emerging from the shadows. A long pistol was prominent in his hand. Post knew immediately who it was. He had entered their home the previous evening, masquerading as a policeman. He was a bull of a man, and the masquerade was soon unmasked when Bindernagel had arrived and forced him to write a note to Samuel Adams. Post's compliance with Bindernagel earlier that morning was directly related to the fact that his wife was being held at gunpoint in their home by this monster. His wild eyes gave the impression he was capable of all sorts of violence.

"I did my part. Bindernagel promised to free my wife. I did my part." He was pleading with the lone gunman.

"Don't worry, you will both be free. You must be patient," replied the wild-eyed kidnapper.

"But I did exactly as you said. The meeting is set for tomorrow. You don't need me anymore," Post frantically continued his pleading.

"Mr. Van Dyke." A new voice materialized at the bedroom door; it was Norman Bindernagel. "I guess he is right, we don't need them anymore."

"Bindernagel, tell him, I did my part. You promised to let us go!" Post's voice was laced with hope now that Bindernagel had arrived. Bindernagel had forced Post to go to work after their morning meeting with Samuel Adams, convincing him that his wife would be shot if anyone even approached his home during the day. Bindernagel had staked out Post's office building, making sure no police were summoned to help the bureaucrat. He had followed Post home and was now satisfied that Post had not contacted anybody about his kidnapped wife. "Relax, Mr. Post. Everything will be fine. Now, tell me, did you talk to anybody about your wife being held hostage? Be careful with your answer. I will know if you have lied." Bindernagel's voice reassured Lucas Post.

"No one! I have talked to no one about what has happened. I love my wife. I would never risk her life. I did what you said. Please, let me release her!" His eyes begged the more reasonable of the two, Norman Bindernagel.

Bindernagel nodded as Post began to untie his frightened wife.

"Did they buy it? Are they sending Cushman?" Edward Van Dyke lowered his pistol and quietly spoke to his partner.

"They will send a representative. It will be Cushman. I guarantee it."

"How can you be so sure? They must have many duel acquaintances?" Van Dyke looked nervous; he wanted Cushman so badly, and he didn't trust Bindernagel.

"All their mutual friends are part of the Congress, and according to my sources, the Congress will be very busy the next few weeks. Besides, I know how they think. They'll be suspicious. Who better to send than an ex-militiaman? No, I have no doubt they will send your friend. Besides, if they send someone else, I will take him to a rendezvous point and no one will show up. I will plead ignorance and leave.

We can then start over with a new plan. Now, there is just one more thing to do." Bindernagel glanced toward Lucas and Gloria Post.

Lucas had finished untying his wife; they embraced tightly as he attempted to reassure the terrified love of his life. He mustered up enough courage to speak softly. "Mr. Bindernagel, I have done everything you have asked of me. Now please, leave us alone."

"Yes, you have, Mr. Post, but I am afraid I must ask you both to do one more thing for us," Bindernagel calmly stated.

An exasperated Post blurted out, "Now what must we do?"

"Die," he whispered as two shots rang out, ending the blissful marriage of Mr. and Mrs. Lucas Post.

Chapter 19

If ye love wealth greater than liberty, the tranquility of servitude greater than the animating contest for freedom, go home from us in peace. We seek not your counsel, nor your arms. Crouch down and lick the hand that feeds you; and may posterity forget that ye were our countrymen.

—Samuel Adams

June 28, 1776
Philadelphia

Edward Van Dyke couldn't remember the last time he had witnessed *the boss* in such high spirits. Arriving as ordered at seven o'clock in the morning, Patrick Rourke usually left him waiting for a half an hour or more. "*Punctuality* is for the poor," he was fond of saying whenever he showed up late, which was all the time. *Not today*. Today, he had met Van Dyke as he approached the door and even offered him coffee and a pastry. At first, Van Dyke declined, but Rourke had insisted, and the two sat in the main dining room of the luxurious home, discussing the plan to kidnap Benjamin Cushman.

"What makes him so confident that Adams will send Cushman?"

"The Brit said that all of Adams's and Jefferson's mutual friends are members of the Continental Congress. According to his spies, the next few days Congress will be discussing important matters. The rumor around town is that the Congress will declare independence from the king."

Rourke knew it was more than just a rumor. He had been receiving weekly reports from one of the lesser-known delegates from

Pennsylvania for nearly two months now. One of Lydia's girls had seduced the married politician, and the steamy affair was producing a wealth of information. The man loved to boast, and his pillow talk had confirmed that the Lee Resolution would be acted upon today. Rourke was confident that the rebellion would crumble with the arrival of Howe's army. But he was intelligent enough to realize that a Declaration of Independence would make it more difficult to achieve that end.

"And if they send someone else?"

"He'll make up some excuse as to why his friend didn't show, and we will employ the plan involving Ms. Johnson." Van Dyke had lobbied for Deborah Johnson luring Cushman outside the city, where they would ambush the couple. Rourke had decided against it because Lydia still thought Deborah was a valuable asset at City Tavern.

"We need to buy some time for Lydia. She only needs a few more days, and Deborah will have all the information we need. We don't want her getting suspicious, or she will turn into a liability." Rourke summarized their thinking.

"Understood, boss." Although he didn't really understand. Van Dyke would just as soon walk into City Tavern, put a bullet into Cushman's head, and take his chances of escaping. As much as Van Dyke disliked his boss, he knew Rourke was always thorough and had never gotten caught in any of his illegal activities. He paid generously for services rendered, and that offset Van Dyke's disdain for him. "If Cushman shows, Bindernagel said he would make up a story and buy us a few days."

"Bindernagel? He's going by the name Bindernagel now?" the boss asked with an astonished look on his face.

"It took some getting used to. I thought it odd that he used an alias," Van Dyke replied.

"Who knows? Now that I think of it, I'm doubtful his real name is Heinrich Boninghausen," Rourke suggested.

"Why would he use so many false names?"

"Protection."

"Protection from whom?"

"Protection from his enemies. He may be playing both sides. If so, it's a dangerous game he's playing. We will need to keep a close eye on Mr. Boninghausen-Bindernagel, whatever his name is."

"No problem, boss. Anything else?"

"Any problem with the Posts?"

"No. They were very cooperative, right up to the very end." Van Dyke had a twinkle in his eye.

"What did you do with the bodies?"

Van Dyke smiled. "Put them into their bed, as if they were sleeping."

Rourke's mood turned sour instantly. "What? A relative or neighbor could stumble onto the bodies. If Sam Adams finds out about the murders, his suspicions would turn into a full-blown alarm. Are you crazy? Why did you let him do something so ignorant?" Rourke's face was red with anger.

Van Dyke smiled and replied, "We boarded up the windows and locked the doors. Then we placed a *Quarantine* sign on the front door. The sign said, *'Quarantine, two adults with the pox.'* No one will go sneaking around there for weeks. By then it will be too late to do anything."

Rourke's anger was quickly replaced by a pleasured grin. He gave a nod of appreciation to Boninghausen's ingenuity. "Well done, Van Dyke, well done," Rourke repeated himself. "Is everything set at the warehouse?"

"Yes, sir, everything is in place."

"Very well, and one more thing, Mr. Van Dyke." Rourke stood, which meant that their meeting was over. "You had better not fail me again. I want Cushman, and I want him today."

"I am confident in the Brit's plan, sir. I will make sure it proceeds without a hitch." Without another word, Edward Van Dyke was moving toward the door, eager to start the wheels in motion.

THE SIGNERS

Thomas Jefferson was up at dawn. He had tossed and turned all night, his mind bouncing back and forth between twin worries. Today, he would present his Declaration of Independence to the full Congress for debate, discussion, and the dreaded editing. Equally troubling for Jefferson was the clandestine meeting his best friend, Ben Cushman, would attend in his stead. Ben had assured him that it was the right move. Finding the mastermind behind the assassination plot was worth the risk. *He is probably right. As long as the men responsible are still at large, there is a real danger that they will strike again.* Still, Jefferson's suspicions were extremely aroused. Meeting with complete strangers was dangerous enough, but to do it alone was just plain suicide. Jefferson had pleaded with his friend during the night, but to no avail. Cushman had many fine traits, but his unyielding stubbornness was not one of them. He was able to elicit one small concession from his fellow Virginian, and that was why Jefferson was dressed and ready to go at the crack of dawn.

Jefferson poked his head into the parlor room, where he had written the declaration and which was now serving as Cushman's bedroom. "You're still here. Aren't you ever going to leave?"

"Actually, Mrs. Graff wanted me to stay and asked if I could get you to leave instead," responded Cushman as he finished cleaning his pistol.

Jefferson laughed. "I'm ready as soon as you are."

"Red, you have probably the most important day in your life ahead of you. You don't need to watch over me. I've told you, I can take care of myself."

"Ben, we settled this last night. I will attend this morning's meeting. After all, you are representing both Samuel *and me*."

Cushman shrugged. "Very well, I hope the Congress changes every word in your declaration."

Both men laughed and descended to the first floor, where Catherine Graff had prepared a hearty breakfast of eggs, bacon, and hot biscuits. To Catherine's dismay, they wolfed down the delicious food within minutes, begged her forgiveness, and bolted out the door, where they mounted their horses for the short ride to the Pennsylvania statehouse.

Two important meetings would take place today. One, the representative body known as the Second Continental Congress would debate the merits of dissolving the Thirteen Colonies from the British Empire, and the other would perhaps solve the mystery surrounding the attempted assassination of the leadership of that very same body. Little did they know the two would be connected.

The Pennsylvania statehouse was bustling with anticipation as Jefferson and Cushman walked into the courtyard behind the stately brick structure. Even though deliberations weren't scheduled until 10:00 a.m., many of the representatives had already arrived and were clustered into small groups, attempting to read the mood of each of the thirteen delegations. Adams and Bindernagel had agreed to meet under the same tree at nine o'clock. Adams was waiting when the two Virginians arrived ten minutes early. Jefferson carried the declaration in a long tube to protect the important paper. All eyes drifted toward the tall intellectual and at the document he carried. Today would take them one step closer to committing treason against the Crown, and they all knew the penalty. A somber mood echoed throughout the courtyard; the serious nature of their business was never more apparent.

"Thomas, there was no need for you to attend," Adams cautiously warned Jefferson.

"If you're worried that Mr. Bindernagel will be upset by my presence, I would remind both of you that the mysterious Patriot demanded to see one of us." Jefferson pointed toward Adams, then back to himself.

"As usual, you are right Thomas, forgive me, I am still worried about Mr. Cushman and, of course, today's events."

"If I promise to be careful, will you two stop worrying about my welfare?" Cushman grinned, his eyes casually scanning the courtyard, recognizing many of the delegates.

"Mr. Bindernagel has arrived." Adams nodded toward the walkway.

Major Hadden Campbell, of the British First King's Dragoon Guards, approached the three men. He immediately recognized Samuel Adams and took only a few seconds to identify the famous redhead, Thomas Jefferson. The third man must be his target, Benjamin Cushman. Lydia Ames had provided a physical description of Cushman, and the closer he got to the three men, the more he was convinced it was him. His plan was working to perfection.

Campbell's pulse was racing as he approached the three revolutionaries. A crazy thought raced into his mind. *Why not take out Adams and Jefferson right here and right now?* His pistol was primed and ready to fire. He could easily shoot Jefferson and then slit the older Adams's throat before anybody could react. Maybe he could even take out few more delegates before attempting an escape. That would surely deliver a major blow to the rebellion. He thought of Rourke's warning not to underestimate Cushman. Campbell quickly decided against the impromptu act. Determining his odds of escaping to be slim to none, he decided to stick to the original plan, and committing suicide was definitely not part of that plan. *Besides*, he thought to himself, smiling, *Colonel Parker will be here in several weeks, and I don't want to miss out on all the fun.*

The British major turned his attention toward Cushman. So this was the Virginia militiaman who thwarted Rourke's assassination plot. Typical backwoods scum. His clothes looked like they had never been laundered. His disheveled hair and unshaven face reminded Campbell of the vulgar Virginians he had fought with during Braddock's retreat. How the colony of Virginia could produce such crude men and such beautiful women was beyond the major's comprehension. Cushman might be dangerous, but he was no match for his skills and intellect. Campbell was confident that Cushman was too young to have served during Braddock's retreat, but just in case, he rehearsed a convincing lie in his mind.

Campbell viewed Jefferson as a rare exception to the Virginia rabble. Fashionably dressed and distinguished-looking, the tall redhead had a bearing that was more English than American. He had read several of Jefferson's essays and found him to be a strong writer. If Samuel Adams was the heart and soul of the American rebellion, then Thomas Jefferson was clearly the brain. He had outlined with intellect and clarity the colonial causes, and his arguments had proved very persuasive to the common American. Campbell thought

Jefferson's arguments somewhat simplistic and naive, but he had to admit, he was an effective writer. He promptly decided not to make an issue of Jefferson's unscheduled appearance.

Approaching Samuel Adams, Campbell slipped into his Norman Bindernagel character. "Mr. Adams, I am so glad you decided to hear out my friend." Turning to Thomas Jefferson, he said, "Mr. Jefferson, I am sorry to be so presumptuous, but I think everyone in Philadelphia could recognize you. My name is Norman Bindernagel."

Jefferson extended his hand. "Mr. Bindernagel, we meet under very unusual circumstances. Mr. Adams has told me of your friend's situation. I am confused as to why your friend wouldn't just accompany you here today, reveal his secret, and be done with it."

Ignoring Cushman, the British spy shrugged his shoulders and continued, "I'm afraid he is very fearful, and unfortunately, his mistrust has grown even greater."

"What are you talking about?" Adams questioned the go-between.

"I'm afraid my friend has grown quite paranoid. He sees a spy behind every tree."

"Does this mean he will not talk to us?" Adams's voice sounded incredulous.

"No, no. He is eager to be done with this mess. But yesterday, after our meeting, he fled to his brother's farm south of Philadelphia. He took his whole family. I am sorry, but it is a day's ride to the farm."

"Where is this farm?" Jefferson's voice couldn't hide his suspicion.

Bindernagel shrugged his shoulders, a frown covering his face. "As I said, my friend has become quite paranoid. If you agree to his terms and leave today, we will stop at a tavern on the edge of town. The bartender will give us directions to the farm. I know what you're thinking. I tried to talk him out of all this, but he wouldn't listen. I'm afraid he may change his mind if we don't act soon."

Cushman had been listening intently and had noticed something odd. "Bindernagel, sounds German. You from around here?"

Bindernagel turned toward Cushman slowly, his eyes focusing on the source of the irritating interruption.

"Terribly sorry, Mr. Bindernagel. This is Benjamin Cushman, a friend of both Thomas and I." Adams purposely neglected to tell Bindernagel of Jefferson's close relationship with Cushman.

Bindernagel's irritation soon gave way to a warm smile. "Mr. Cushman, will you be traveling with me as their representative?"

Cushman nodded and said nothing, staring directly into the stranger's eyes.

"Yes, to answer your question, it is German. I was born in London. My parents had immigrated to England several years earlier. When I was fifteen, my uncle, a Moravian preacher in Philadelphia, offered me a job. Six months later, I landed here."

"That explains the slight British accent," declared Cushman.

Bindernagel tried mightily to hide his shock. His talent for language was legendary in the British officer corps. Although he found mastering the Middle Colony dialect difficult, no one had questioned his accent since arriving in the New World and being assigned to the Philadelphia area. He was good with all languages and was especially talented in nuances and inflections, but obviously most people were not as observant as Mr. Cushman. Luckily, the story he had fabricated would take into account his less-than-perfect dialect. Rourke's warning sounded in his head. He would *be sure not to underestimate Cushman*. "Is it that obvious?"

Cushman shrugged.

"Mr. Bindernagel, please give us a moment alone. We would like to discuss the new terms," Adams suggested.

Bindernagel bowed slightly and backed away as the three men huddled closer to discuss the new developments.

Jefferson was first to speak. "I don't like it, not one bit. We don't know anything about this Bindernagel. For all we know, he could be making this all up."

"But, Red, what would motivate him to deceive us? I could understand if his demands involved leading both of you to some strange farmhouse. There are people, Tories and British alike, who would love to see you both dead. No one, except maybe my brothers, would care if I met my Maker." Cushman laughed.

"Well, perhaps you're right, Ben, but you must return as soon as you know the person responsible. I don't want you running off trying to be a hero. Whoever is behind the assassination attempts probably has many friends in high places," Adams cautioned.

"I still don't like it, but your logic is sound," responded Jefferson.

Cushman appreciated both men's concern and replied in typical fashion. "Well, then, that's settled. I think I'll go catch a killer."

They returned to face Bindernagel. "Your terms are acceptable. Mr. Cushman will accompany you on your journey," Adams stated dryly.

Bindernagel tried to hide his excitement of a well-executed plan coming off perfectly and knew he shouldn't press his luck but decided to take one last chance. "According to my friend, his brother's farmhouse is rather large. If you and Mr. Jefferson would like to come along, you're more than welcome. We would be back in Philadelphia before Monday's session." Bindernagel waved his arm to emphasize the gathered representatives. *Snaring Jefferson and Adams in the net cast for Cushman would be a perfect day indeed,* Major Campbell thought to himself.

"I'm afraid Ben will have to do our bidding," Jefferson responded. Adams nodded in agreement.

"Very well." Bindernagel knew not to push it and looked to Cushman. "Are you prepared to leave now?"

"No time like the present," Cushman responded without hesitation.

"Good, I will meet you in front of the statehouse in ten minutes. Mr. Adams, thank you very much for your time. Mr. Jefferson, it was a pleasure meeting you. I do hope we meet again in the future." Bindernagel shook their hands and left.

"Maybe I should go with Ben. Sam, you could present the declaration to the Congress as a whole. I don't have to be here today." Jefferson looked at Adams for confirmation but found none.

"Thomas, I'm afraid your presence will be crucial today," Adams stated softly, looking at Cushman for reaffirmation.

"Have no fear, Red. I could use a break from your company. This is the most time I've spent with you in years. Besides, Deborah will probably kill you for telling her I won't be able to make our date this evening."

Jefferson smiled. Cushman's arrival several days earlier had proved to be a godsend to the weary and worn-out Jefferson. Prior to his arrival, Jefferson had been suffering bouts of depression, which in turn caused him painful headaches, headaches that had rendered him bedridden for days on end. The combination of the ill health of his wife, Martha; his mother's recent death; and the pressure-filled duties in Philadelphia had brought Jefferson to the brink of breaking down. With Ben's arrival, it felt like he had been dipped into the fountain of youth, so many pleasant boyhood memories springing forth because of Cushman's reappearance into his life. Maybe it was just that Cushman made him laugh, but Jefferson was feeling better than he had in a long time.

Suddenly, a chill crept down his spine as he watched Ben walking away toward a potentially dangerous mission. Only Adams heard Jefferson whisper, "Be careful, my dear friend. God be with you."

At exactly 9:55 a.m., Thomas Jefferson and Samuel Adams approached the only door facing Chestnut Street and entered the long rectangular lobby separating the two large meeting rooms that made up the first floor of the Pennsylvania statehouse. Both men practically threw their tricorne hats on the hooks alongside either interior wall. They were the last to arrive.

Walking swiftly to the double doors that led into the assembly room, Jefferson hesitated and took in the picture before him. At the back of the room, centered between two fireplaces and elevated two steps, sat John Hancock, the president of the Second Continental Congress. He was talking to Robert Morris, the wealthy banker from Philadelphia, a proud member of the Pennsylvania delegation and the Secret Committee.

Jefferson smiled. He thought *the fireplaces would certainly not be needed today*; it was a typically hot summer day in the nation's largest city. The tall rectangle windows on both the north and south walls were open to allow for a cooling breeze, but that would soon change. A decorative three-foot-high rail separated the main floor about six feet into the room. Its double gates were swung open to allow the latecomers into the room. Thirteen tables were aligned three deep in a semicircle facing Hancock, with a small aisleway dividing the tables. The tables were aligned geographically, north to south. Seated on the left side of the middle aisle were the six northernmost states, starting with New Hampshire. The seven tables to the right side of the room included the middle and southernmost colonies, ending with Georgia.

Each table had an appropriate number of comfortable chairs. The largest delegations present were Pennsylvania and Virginia with seven each. The smallest delegation was Rhode Island with two; both Stephen Hopkins and William Ellery were in attendance. Each table was covered with a green velvet cloth that hung to the floor. Quill pens, inkwells, paper, and record books were centered on all thirteen tables. The several candles adorning each table were functional, not decorative, as many sessions advanced deep into the night. To Hancock's right, at floor level, in front of one of the fireplaces was a smaller desk for the secretary of the Congress. A magnificent chandelier hung in the center of the room, holding ten candles to help illuminate nighttime procedures. The walls were painted a bright white, and two impressive Doric columns framed each fireplace. Although the room appeared cozy, the high ceilings gave it a feel of grandeur. Along the front wall, opposite Hancock, was an impressive panoply, which included drums, guns, swords, and banners seized the previous year by the forces of Ethan Allen and Benedict Arnold at Fort Ticonderoga. All in all, the assembly room of the Pennsylvania statehouse was a magnificent room to plot a revolution.

The tension within the room was thick. Nervous men made small talk and fidgeted at their tables. At any given time during the past year, an average of about fifty members attended the sessions. Some members had been recalled by their home state and may or may not have been replaced. Others had to attend important duties at home. Unlike most days, today it seemed like everyone was in attendance. If that was the case, a total of fifty-six delegates would participate in today's historic event.

All eyes slowly turned to Jefferson and the long cylinder tube he was carrying gently under his arm. Every delegate knew that the next few days would be unlike anything they had been through since the Congress was called into session some thirteen months ago. Vigorous and passionate debate would attempt to persuade the undecided. What they were attempting was monumental. And dangerous. Jefferson continued to size up the group; they were serious men, each one sent to Philadelphia because of their high standing back home, and interestingly, only a few were career politicians. Mostly younger men. Eighteen were under forty years old, and three were in their twenties. At seventy, Benjamin Franklin was the only, truly old man. All but two had families, and most had large families. They were men of means; most had economic security that very few had ever possessed. In some cases, their wealth rivaled that of the princes of Europe. Twenty-four of the delegates were either lawyers or judges. Eleven had made fortunes as trade merchants, nine were farmers and large landowners, and the remaining twelve were ministers, politicians, and doctors. The president of the Congress, John Hancock, was one of the richest men in America, but Charles Carroll, the delegate from Maryland, made Hancock's wealth seem small.

Jefferson gazed back at the men he had come to know and respect. He knew every single one of them had more to lose from a revolution than they had to gain. Jefferson thought of the historic context. The men before him were well-educated and thoughtful men. They were not desperate men, wild-eyed fanatics with nothing to lose, typical of most revolts in history. *Not these men.* There was no doubt—history had never seen such an occurrence, and Jefferson knew he was walking with giants. He prayed his declaration would live up to their high standards.

Hancock banged his gavel, and all eight of the large windows were closed to keep both a noisy public and Tory spies from overhearing the debate. In addition, all doors were closed and locked. The heat was about to rise in more ways than one.

They rode in silence as they traveled east on Pine Street. The Delaware River was now in sight when Bindernagel pointed. "There." Just ahead, a small one-story ramshackle building sat at the corner of Pine and Front.

Cushman noticed a small sign. It was broken in half, but he could still read the *Dead Dog* on the upper half and *Tavern* on the lower half. The tavern looked more like a house. A house that *should have been torn down years ago*, Cushman thought to himself. "Looks friendly enough." He dismounted with ease and tied his horse to a nearby hitching post. Bindernagel followed suit, and the two men walked into the *Dead Dog Tavern*.

The contrast was startling. While the outside of the *Dead Dog* looked like it was about to collapse, the inside was remarkably clean and functional. A long L-shaped bar extended across three-quarters of the back wall. A door leading into a storage room completed the back. The mahogany bar and eight matching stools sparkled from obvious tender maintenance. Two regulars had gotten an early jump on a Friday celebration and were the only people in the tavern. There were five tables strategically placed in the remaining space. As Bindernagel and Cushman sat down at one of the tables, the storage room door opened. A young woman emerged; she had four decorative beer steins, two in each hand. She backed through the opening in the bar, setting down the beer steins, and began to walk toward the two regulars.

"Hey, where did Fred go?" slurred one of the locals, shocked to see a pretty, well-dressed woman behind the bar at the *Dead Dog*.

"He had to run an errand. Said he'd be back in an hour. What's wrong? Haven't you ever seen a woman work a tavern before?" She stood hands on hips, glaring at the two young drunks.

"Not as pretty as you." Local number 2 also slurred his words.

"Easy, sonny, I'm only here to serve whiskey and ale, nothing else, got it?" She stood defiantly. Cushman thought she could probably handle the drunkards without any help.

Bindernagel smiled and informed Cushman, "That's her. She's the one who will give us the final directions to the farm. Her name is Rebecca."

"She's the bartender? She looks like a princess." Indeed, her curly blond hair hung down past her shoulders. Her short-sleeve white blouse was buttoned to the neck but was tight enough to reveal a fine figure. A colorful blue scarf was wrapped around her shoulders, matching a navy skirt, secure around a narrow waistline. Her face was tan and smooth, without a single pockmark. Before coming to Philadelphia, Cushman had never seen a woman working in a tavern; now he knew two, and both were beautiful. If this was the new trend in the tavern industry, he was all for it.

"Now, then, when did you two sneak in here?" Rebecca appeared genuinely startled as she spotted the two newcomers. Walking quickly from behind the bar, she approached with a smile. "I can see why those two started early." She lifted her right arm, pointing her thumb at the two locals. "But you two look halfway respectable."

"I don't know about *respectable*, but your suspicions are right. We're here on business," Cushman stated with his usual impish grin.

"We are here to get information from you regarding the location of a certain farm," added Bindernagel, getting right to *business*.

"Oh, you're here about Adam," she replied, unwittingly revealing the first name of the farmer.

Bindernagel stiffened at the mention of the name Adam. He had only referred to his informant as his *friend*.

Cushman immediately noticed the reaction. He had been guarded the minute they had left the Pennsylvania statehouse and had come prepared, as if Jefferson's instincts were correct and this was an ambush. Both pistols were locked and loaded in his saddlebag, in addition to the Indian knife he carried on his person.

There was little reason to kill or capture him other than revenge for his role in thwarting the plot. But if that was the case, how did they know him, and why would they waste valuable time and energy seeking revenge on Cushman? *No,* Cushman thought, *only a madman would attempt to seek out vengeance. The real targets were the members of the Continental Congress. Powerful Tories, or perhaps even British spies, were behind the killings. If Bindernagel could lead me to the source of the plot, then it is unquestionably worth the risk.* He felt strongly that whoever they were, they would try again. Bindernagel's reaction to the name *Adam* actually put Cushman more at ease. It made sense to guard his name until they had actually met. His reaction to Rebecca's gaffe caused Cushman to let down his guard.

Rebecca had also caught Bindernagel's reaction and became somewhat flustered. "I'm sorry, I'm not very good with all this secretive stuff. Adam…" She threw her hands up in frustration. "Our mutual friend," she emphasized, "drew a map to his brother's farm. I'm familiar with the area. You should get there before sundown. The map is in the storage room. Can I get you a drink while you wait? We've got coffee, whiskey, and beer."

Bindernagel shrugged his shoulders and gave Cushman a "Why not?" look.

"I suppose we have time, but better make mine coffee. If I have whiskey, I might not leave here," joked Cushman.

Bindernagel laughed and agreed. "Make that two. I have a hard-enough time riding my horse sober."

"Let me get your coffee, then I will get the map." Rebecca smiled as she walked behind the long bar.

Relaxing a bit, Cushman began to engage Bindernagel in small talk. He wasn't watching closely as Rebecca poured the coffee, but even if he was, it was doubtful he would have seen her covertly place the powdered substance into his coffee. So expertly done even the two regulars hadn't noticed anything unseemly. Returning quickly with the hot coffee, Rebecca placed down the two cups. "Be right back. I'll get the map." Both men watched the shapely waitress walk away. Cushman caught himself thinking immediately of Deborah and felt guilty. He considered it a good sign.

Rebecca returned quickly, placing the crude map in the center of the table as they slowly drank their coffee and plotted out their next move. Cushman concentrated on the map. The coffee was passable; he had tasted better and briefly considered an odd smell he couldn't place. He quickly attributed it to the run-down conditions of the *Dead Dog Tavern*.

Cushman was halfway done when it started. A sudden sharp pain in his stomach caused him to double over. As the pain receded, he sat up straight, only to be overcome by dizziness and drowsiness. A wave swept over him, as if he were no longer in control of his body. He tried to speak, but nothing came out. He looked across the table at Bindernagel, attempting to warn him not to drink the coffee. All he saw was a smiling face. The pain returned, causing him to double over again. He heard voices, new voices, something about the storage room. Strong hands seized his arms, dragging him across the floor. The room was spinning quickly, and darkness started to drift over Cushman. The strong hands released their pressure. His arms, shoulders, and head thudded against the wooden floor. His eyes focused, for the last time, on a face lying next to his. There was something odd about the clean-shaven face. Cushman struggled to grasp at one last conscious thought when it struck him. The neck of the man staring back at Cushman had been slashed from ear to ear. Cushman had one final thought as the blackness came over him. *So that's what happened to Fred.*

Thomas Jefferson began to make his way to the Virginia table. In order to do so, he had to walk in front of the Pennsylvania delegation. Before he could make the right-hand turn toward his fellow Virginians, Benjamin Franklin grabbed him by his coat arm and motioned for the tall Virginian to bend over.

"Mr. Hancock will not allow us to act on the declaration today. He will only allow a formal presentation of your document so that everyone will have a chance to read it over the weekend. We will officially act on Mr. Lee's resolution on Monday."

Jefferson's face showed his disappointment.

"You needn't worry, young Thomas. This is a good thing. Give Samuel and some of the others more time to extol the virtues of your work. Not all are yet in favor." Franklin's eyes moved quickly to his right.

Jefferson understood instantly that the man seated next to Franklin would be the most difficult to convince, the honorable John Dickinson.

Dickinson had become quite popular in the Thirteen Colonies with his now-famous *Letters from a Farmer in Pennsylvania*. In a series of twelve letters signed simply *The Farmer*, he helped unite the colonies against the Townshend Acts. His contention that Parliament had acted without authority and had interfered into our internal affairs was considered popular throughout America and had earned him instant fame.

Dickinson was a strong follower of the Pennsylvania Quakers. He was trying to follow their pacifist beliefs and still held out hope for reconciliation with the king. A gifted orator, he still held sway over the majority of the Pennsylvania delegates. One of the wealthiest men in America, he would be a major stumbling block toward independence.

Before Jefferson had reached his seat, President Hancock stood to address his fellow delegates. "Gentleman, I have had many requests to table Mr. Lee's resolution until Monday, to allow everyone to look over the committee's Declaration of Independence. It seems a very reasonable request, and we have many other items on today's agenda. Is everyone in agreement?"

All heads nodded as the venerable Franklin rose from his chair. "Gentlemen, there is one correction I must remedy. As much as this old man, Mr. Adams, Mr. Livingston, or Mr. Sherman would love to take credit for this incredible document, we must yield to the gentleman from Virginia. They are his words and his only. Please keep that in mind as you read over the document and arrive here on Monday ready to mangle those words."

"Mr. Jefferson's Declaration of Independence shall be entered into today's proceeding. If there are no objections, then the Lee Resolution will be taken up first thing on Monday, July 1. Mr. Jefferson, please bring your document forward. The secretary will accept it for Congress," responded John Hancock. "How many pages, Mr. Jefferson?"

"Four pages, sir," Jefferson replied as he handed over his proud words to the secretary of the Congress.

"Very good. Gentlemen, please be sure to read the declaration before Monday and come prepared," replied the president of the Congress.

A seated Franklin added loudly, "Yes, gentlemen, for after Monday we must surely hang together or most assuredly we will hang separately."

A gentle rumble of thunder rippled through the old warehouse as the rain continued to pelt the second-floor office windows. Thunderstorms blew through Philadelphia somewhat regularly during the summer months, temporarily cooling down the city. Once the storms cleared the area, however, the hot sun mixed with the moist air to create a hothouse of humidity. The cooling breezes of the Atlantic Ocean were over sixty miles away and couldn't help the beleaguered city. The rain began to subside as the three men unceremoniously dumped the body unto the wooden floor. The austere room consisted of two chairs and a small rectangular table. It hadn't been cleaned in years; dust and dirt covered the floor and furniture. Two large grimy windows overlooked the Delaware River. Norman Bindernagel picked up an old rag and wiped one of the windows relatively clean. "Wonderful view, waterfront property. What more could a prisoner desire?" *Ah, the life of a spy,* Campbell thought to himself. He enjoyed the intrigue and even the danger. But best of all, he enjoyed playing the role of another person. He took great pride preparing for the role, from the appropriate clothes he picked out to mastering a certain dialect. Often, he would spend hours practicing certain facial expressions, from a warm smile to a menacing grin. Campbell had often joked with his friends that he could always find work as an actor after his military career was finished.

"Mr. Boninghausen, I must hand it to you. Your plan worked perfectly." Van Dyke extended his right hand to congratulate his accomplice.

"Aye, me too, Mr. Boninghausen. I had me doubts, but it worked out just like you said it would," Christopher Tompkins added.

"Gentlemen, I am hurt by your doubts, but we must give credit to your wonderful bartender, Rebecca. She played her part beautifully," Boninghausen replied. "And whatever concoction she gave him worked to perfection."

"Ms. Lydia is rather talented when it comes to mixing potions. Her girls are very good at what they do. She has trained them well," Van Dyke stated with a sense of pride. Rebecca was one of Lydia's most competent ladies. Orphaned at age fifteen, she had been taken by Lydia under her wing. Rebecca had blossomed into a beautiful young woman, and her loyalty to Lydia Ames was unquestionable.

Campbell had familiarized himself to various poisonous cocktails and certain types of *knockout* drugs. Examining Cushman's coffee afterward, he thought he smelled traces of opium and the root of the valerian plant. He would have to get the formula from Lydia. It certainly could come in handy in his line of work.

"Mr. Tompkins, you did a fine job of taking care of the bartender," Boninghausen added without a touch of remorse. *Just one less potential rebel,* he thought to himself.

Tompkins smiled his appreciation for the compliment, then added, "Should we tie him up yet?"

"Yeah, we better," answered Van Dyke. "Lydia said it should start to wear off anytime soon."

The three men lifted Cushman's lifeless body onto one of the chairs, tying his hands behind the chair back. There was no indication he was about to wake anytime soon.

"What now?" Tompkins asked. He had not been privy to what Rourke had in store for Cushman.

Van Dyke was first to answer. "You and I will take watch for the night. He can scream his lungs out. No one will hear him." They had chosen one of Rourke's many warehouses along the Delaware. Only one and a half blocks from the *Dead Dog Tavern*, it was located between Lombard and South Streets at the edge of the river. After Cushman had passed out, the men had wrapped him in the blanket and tossed him on the back of a waiting cart. Van Dyke had tossed several bales of hay on top of Cushman, completing the camouflage. Rebecca remained as the *substitute* bartender until the cart had pulled away. At the last minute, Boninghausen decided not to kill the two customers. Rather, Rebecca left them in charge of the *Dead Dog* while running a pretended errand. Praising their good fortune, they were well on their way toward a night of splendid drunkenness. Rourke's two henchmen had wanted to kill the pair but laughed aloud when Boninghausen had shared his idea that they would probably be blamed for the murder of the tavern owner.

"What about him?" Tompkins asked, pointing to Boninghausen.

"Gentlemen, I'm afraid I have completed my mission for Mr. Rourke. As much as I'd like to participate in the torture of Mr. Cushman, I have to be moving on to a more important assignment. I trust you'll be able to handle it from here?" the British spy answered smoothly.

Tompkins looked at Van Dyke for reassurance as Van Dyke continued, "Mr. Rourke will be here in the morning, and he wants Cushman awake and alert for what he has in store for him."

Rourke's servant poured the imported French wine into the two glasses and quietly backed out of the elegant library. "Boninghausen said he wanted the list by the end of July. We would still be three weeks early. All I need is four or five more days for the list to be completed." Lydia Ames was pleading her case to Patrick Rourke.

"They will expect Cushman to be back by Sunday, Monday at the latest. Their fears will be full blown when he doesn't show," Rourke replied, sipping his wine slowly.

Lydia knew it would be counterproductive to remind Rourke that she had suggested he wait a few more days before kidnapping Cushman. "Isn't there something you can do to stall their suspicions?"

Rourke stroked his chin slowly, concentrating on a way to slow down any investigation into the disappearance of Cushman. Boninghausen had promised Samuel Adams that Cushman would return by Monday at the latest. If they could alleviate their fears for a few more days, then it wouldn't matter when they found out that Cushman was gone forever. A smile slowly spread across his face. "I just might have a way. Yes, it just might work!"

Lydia knew not to interrupt. He would reveal his plan when he was ready. She raised her glass of wine, acknowledging his brilliance. Rourke responded with a similar salute. Tomorrow was going to be a very productive day.

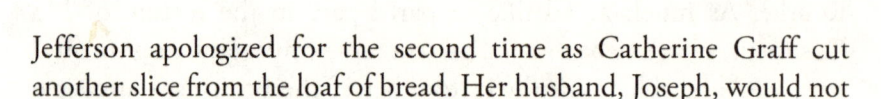

Jefferson apologized for the second time as Catherine Graff cut another slice from the loaf of bread. Her husband, Joseph, would not be home until later, so the two were eating alone.

"I'm so sorry, Catherine. It completely slipped my mind about Ben. He probably won't be back until Sunday or Monday."

"But where did he go in such a hurry? He didn't even say goodbye."

Jefferson was about to fashion a tall tale when he decided she deserved the truth. "Catherine, Ben was sent on an important mission."

"By whom?"

"Well, I suppose by Samuel Adams and myself. But in fact, a mission that would benefit the entire Congress," Jefferson replied truthfully.

"Is this mission dangerous?" Her eyes penetrated into Jefferson like a protective mother's.

Jefferson hesitated, all but ensuring the answer to her question. "I have my suspicions, and yes, it could very well turn out to be dangerous. He is investigating a situation that could very well uncover the man or men behind Tuesday's assassination attempt."

"He's going after the men who tried to kill you? All by himself?"

"No. He is following a lead." Jefferson related the entire story, actually hoping Catherine would approve of the decision to allow Cushman to go at it alone.

"Sounds kind of fishy to me" was her only reply.

Jefferson smiled, having made the same comment. "Yes, I agree, but Ben felt the reward was greater than the risk. He left early this morning."

"Where are they meeting this mysterious farmer?"

"On his brother's farm, about a day's ride from here. Seems our farmer got spooked and left town."

"Mr. Jefferson, you know Jacob and I are behind the Congress and think the world of you. Please keep Benjamin safe from harm. I have grown quite fond of him."

"You're not the only one, Catherine." Jefferson's worried look did not reassure her.

She immediately went to the front room, took out the family Bible, and began to say some prayers for Benjamin Cushman.

The voices were faint at first, mumbled jargon, meaningless noise. The inside of his mouth tasted odd, nothing he had ever experienced or would prefer to ever experience again. His head pounded as if he were hungover. He attempted to move, but all four of his limbs were tied down. *Tied to a chair.* His normally sharp senses were foggy at best. He tried to concentrate on the voices. *One sense at a time.*

The conversation taking place involved two men, but their words were still indistinguishable. Cushman slowly opened his eyes, his brain gradually regaining some cognitive skill. He wasn't dreaming; he was about to call out to the two men, then stopped. *Let's gather some more information,* he thought as the realization of his predicament came back to him slowly. He thought back to the *Dead Dog Tavern. They must have drugged me. The waitress, Rebecca, was she part of the plot? She must have been. The coffee tasted odd. The dead man, throat sliced from ear to ear.* It all came flooding back. *Bindernagel, not affected by the coffee—he was the mastermind.*

The pounding in his head was gradually subsiding, his mind slowly regaining normal function; the only major side effect of the drug appeared to be the odd taste in his mouth. The voices continued from across the room. Cushman let his eyes slowly adjust to a dim light. An old lantern sat atop a small table, surrounded by two men conversing as if he weren't there.

It was definitely a kidnapping. A direct result of his heroics at City Tavern and the Tucker house. *Bindernagel, a plant, obviously working for whoever ordered the assassinations. Which means two things: they are very well organized and they would strike again.*

Movement! Cushman closed his eyes and listened closely.

"She said he would be awake by now." A set of footsteps began moving toward him.

"Relax, Tompkins. The longer he is out, the easier it is for us," the other voice snorted.

Cushman felt a cold hand grab his cheeks and squeeze hard. "Nope, still out," the voice called Tompkins noted. As the footsteps retreated, Cushman opened one eye, trying to gather information, clothing, body type, posture, and *smell. Whoa!* The smell hit him, delayed by fractions of a second. He fought a gag reflex from the foul smell of the one called Tompkins.

"She said he would be awake by now." The barmaid, Rebecca, was in on the plot. Cushman focused on the two men silhouetted across the room. Tompkins was tall and thin, with long dark hair and a scraggly beard. The other man was short, built like a barrel. Cushman knew immediately, a man one would rather not meet in a dark alley.

"When you comin' back, Van Dyke?" Tompkins muttered softly.

"Just gonna check the grounds one more time. The boss will have extra security here in the morning."

"Take your time. He ain't gonna cause no trouble," Tall and Thin replied.

"Remember what I told you, be careful with him. He's dangerous," Barrel snorted.

Tompkins and Van Dyke, Cushman thought to himself. *Van Dyke is clearly the leader on-site. Is his boss the man responsible for the assassination plot against the leaders of Congress?*

A door slammed shut, followed by the echo of steps descending an open stairway. *At least the second floor, two guards, more to come in the morning.*

Cushman thought about engaging with the underling Tompkins but quickly decided he wasn't physically or mentally up to the task. Instead, he attempted to take stock of his situation. *Why didn't they kill me at the Dead Dog? They must need me alive, but why? Bindernagel tried hard to get Red and Adams to accompany them. Will I be the bait for a second attempt? The frightened farmer willing to identify the mastermind behind the plot, most assuredly a fabrication. Lured into a trap by a phony story. Red was right to be worried all along. Thank God the two men stayed behind.*

Cushman spent the next hour reviewing everything he knew, concocting multiple scenarios, most of which ended badly. He was angry with himself for letting his guard down. His survival skills had been sharpened after years in the wilderness. Daily and constant vigilance were necessary to survive in the Ohio Country. His return to civilization caused him to relax his guard, a potentially deadly mistake. He knew now that his opponents, whoever they might be, were just as vicious as the mountain lion, just as cunning as the Indians, and just as deadly as the diamondback rattler.

Cushman concluded, the only positive to emerge was that Adams or Jefferson had not accepted the offer to ride along. In addition, whoever was responsible for the attempted assassinations had somehow found out that it was Cushman who had stopped the murders. That was reason enough not to engage Tompkins. Whoever, was behind all this was sure to make himself known to him. It was a golden opportunity to learn their identity. On the other hand, Cushman was not so naive to think that they would let him live long enough to reveal their identities. Whatever they had in store for him, he knew he would have to survive.

Chapter 20

The jaws of power are always open to devour, and her arm is always stretched out, if possible, to destroy the freedom of thinking, speaking, and writing.
—John Adams

June 29, 1776
Philadelphia

The violent storms had passed through Philadelphia by morning; high white clouds feathered the morning sky, the bright sun was warm, but surprisingly, the humidity was low. Rourke led the threesome, taking two steps at a time, as he ascended the stairs to the warehouse office. He was like a child at Christmastime, but this present would be better than any toy.

He burst through the threshold, and it was just like he had pictured it. Before him sat Cushman, blindfolded and securely tied to one of the two chairs. Rourke thought the blindfold was hardly necessary. Cushman would never leave here alive. Lydia insisted, as she had met Cushman at City Tavern. Rourke had teased Lydia when she made the request. *What's he going to do, come back and haunt you?* Christopher Tompkins stood to Cushman's right side, his face revealing he had just woken up.

"Tompkins," Rourke roared loudly, "how did our prisoner behave last night?"

"No problems, sir. Didn't say a word."

"Very good. We'll take over now. Did Van Dyke go over your schedule?"

"Yes, sir. I'll be back tonight at six o'clock."

"Good. When you return, you might not recognize our prisoner." Rourke laughed and moved closer to Cushman.

Thomas Jefferson awoke early and took his customary ride into the countryside. It was his time to get away and think. Heading west, Jefferson rode to the Schuylkill River and was now returning to the Graff house for breakfast. After the fourteen-mile roundtrip journey, Jefferson was refreshed and ready to take on his rigorous schedule. Today was different, though; Cushman's mission weighed heavily on his mind. He even considered riding south, in hopes of picking up Cushman's trail, but quickly dismissed the idea as foolish. He was certainly no tracker. He made a quick decision and rode past the Graff house; instead, he headed into the city.

Jefferson stopped at a general store and purchased some items for his wife, Martha, picking out several pairs of gloves and stockings. Many Philadelphians recognized the famous Virginian and stopped to ask him questions. Not much of a talker, he still enjoyed the give-and-take with the average citizen. These were the people he needed to reach with his declaration. The common man must be able to understand the consequences of nonaction. These hardworking people made the country work. They planted, tended, and harvested the food. They built the roads, the docks, and the wagons that transported everything from food to supplies. They were the backbone of the nation, not the lawyers or politicians. Lawyers did nothing to add to the country. In most cases, all they did was take. Politicians mostly created only hot air, and unfortunately, that hot air could not be harnessed to serve a useful purpose. No, Jefferson and his fellow congressmen had a role to play, but it would be the farmers, shopkeepers, tradesmen, and teachers who would win the coming conflict. Their sacrifice, their heroism would be needed if the British were to be defeated. Before Jefferson knew it, a crowd had gathered around him as he talked to a couple of teenage boys.

"Mr. Jefferson, what will happen to these young boys if we declare independence? Will it mean war?" an older woman asked.

"I'm afraid so, ma'am. But I remind you, we are already at war. Hundreds of our brethren in Boston have already lost their lives fighting back at the British." Jefferson was stuffing his recent purchases into his saddlebag; he turned to face the still-growing crowd.

"But we're no match for the British Army. They'll tear apart our boys," called out an older gentleman.

Jefferson tousled the hair of the two teenage boys and replied, "I don't know. I think these two ruffians will hold up well against the Brits. As a matter of fact, I feel sorry for anybody that has to tackle these young men." Both boys beamed with pride at the compliment.

"But George is our king. How can we go against the king? Who will rule over us?" a young woman cradling her infant child called out to Jefferson.

"A king whose character is marked by every act which may define a tyrant is not fit to be the ruler of a free people," responded Jefferson, borrowing a line from his Declaration of Independence. "Who will rule over us? you ask. We will. Written laws produced from free debate and not the whims of men or political parties." Jefferson walked deeper into the crowd and continued, "Our natural rights that come from God shall be protected by a Constitution set up to restrain the power of government. Many of our state governments are in the process of adopting one as we speak. King George has given us certain rights, but he has just as easily taken those rights away. Only God can take away our natural rights. Governments shall be instituted among men, deriving their just powers from the consent of the governed. Our king has become nothing more than a tyrant. He has taken away our God-given rights, and I am quite sure he will not give them back."

Several in the crowd were taken aback by the blunt talk from the soft-spoken Virginian. Although they were not Tories, the tradition of supporting the king was passed down from generation to generation. Indeed, up until now, most criticism had been directed toward Parliament, the prime minister, Lord North, or the British Army. King George III had been spared for the most part. Thomas Paine, in his pamphlet *Common Sense*, and an occasional editorial cartoonist in one of the American papers, had attacked George; however, the king was still respected by much of colonial America. Jefferson knew it was a risk to attack the king, as he did in the declaration. Franklin had warned him to be careful. But Jefferson instinctively knew that to keep the focus on King George III would be necessary to win a protracted war. Having a common enemy had turned out to be a motivating force throughout history.

"Ah, young Jefferson, you would have made a fine teacher. Just like Socrates, students of all ages surrounding their master, peppering him with question after question." The crowd parted as two men approached the tall Virginian. The contrast was astonishing, as if David and Goliath had come to visit. The man who had spoken was tall and heavyset. His companion was just the opposite, under five feet, six inches, and probably weighing 125 pounds. Both men had been strolling and had noticed the crowd.

Many in the crowd immediately recognized the fifty-year-old delegate from Virginia, Benjamin Harrison. No one recognized Elbridge Gerry, who was overshadowed by his fellow Massachusetts delegates in both size and fame. Gerry didn't mind being in the shadow of his more famous brethren, John Hancock and the Adams cousins. He was much more sensitive to his diminutive stature. Like all small children, he had to scrap to be taken seriously. His combative spirit and intellect had won him many admirers in the Second Continental Congress.

Jefferson smiled as the two men settled next to him. He had always admired Harrison, seventeen years his elder. A man with a keen sense of humor and a hearty laugh, Harrison kept the Virginia delegation loose with his witty stories and ribald comments. Gerry fit the perfect stereotype of a Massachusetts Puritan, a work ethic that would put most men to shame. "Ladies and gentlemen, I'm sure most of you know the famous delegate from Virginia, Mr. Benjamin Harrison, and his colleague from Massachusetts, Mr. Elbridge Gerry."

Both men received an enthusiastic applause as the crowd continued to grow.

"Mr. Harrison, do you agree with Mr. Jefferson that we must overthrow the king?" a young boy shouted; he couldn't be more than thirteen.

Harrison looked at Jefferson with a knowing smile and responded, "I have found it most embarrassing to be on the opposite side of anything Mr. Jefferson thinks."

The crowd roared their approval.

"What about you, Mr. Gerry, you ever disagree with Mr. Jefferson?" a middle-aged woman asked; her lack of teeth magnified a lisp in her speech pattern.

"Bear with me as I tell a short story. When I arrived in Philadelphia, a little more than a year ago, I thought it would be impossible to work with my fellow delegates from the South. As many of you might know, I abhor the practice of slavery and expected to run into a stone wall when discussing this objectionable practice. On the contrary, I have found that many of my fellow delegates, Mr. Jefferson included, are quite willing to debate the issue and seek eventual abolition of the evil practice. As much as I would love to end slavery today, I realize it will take some time. It has been practiced on every continent for thousands of years, but I have never been so encouraged that in the near future, we can bring an end to it."

"But, Mr. Harrison, Mr. Jefferson is talking about overthrowing the king, and you know the punishment for treason," a middle-aged man with a Scottish accent proclaimed.

"I do, indeed." Harrison's grin covered his entire face. "But it will be over quickly for me, maybe in a minute, but my friend here"—he pointed to the tiny Gerry—"he will be dancing on air an hour after I am gone."

The crowd laughed loudly at Harrison's gallows humor. Jefferson laughed as well. The three delegates continued for another half an hour, answering the questions of the troubled Philadelphians. For everyone had heard the consistent rumors of a large British fleet heading for New York, and everyone knew that if Washington couldn't hold New York, the next British target would surely be Philadelphia. It was only ninety miles away. They answered serious, intelligent questions and even silly, gossipy questions.

And at the end, it was a gentle old woman, dressed in rags, nearing the end of her life, who summed it all up. "Gentlemen, when do you think the last time the king of England spent an hour with the likes of us?" She waved her hands over the crowd. She continued, "If we are to win our independence, I hope you will remember to keep in touch with us commoners."

Jefferson, obviously touched by the old woman's words, embraced her gently and gave her a kiss on the cheek. "You have my word, young lady."

Cushman knew his situation was grave. His only hope was, since they had not yet killed him, they must want something from him. Or they were going to kill him slowly. Neither thought was comforting.

Cushman's mind was clear now, and he continued analyzing information he had gathered. He knew he was on the second floor. The echo from the creaky stairs indicated a large open building, probably a warehouse. At some point in the night, they had slipped a blindfold over his eyes, and yet not so tight as he could see shafts of light, suggesting windows.

One thing was for sure: he was near the river. Ship bells, sailors' shouts, and the flapping of large sails were the first sounds Cushman heard when he awoke from a fitful sleep. *A warehouse on the Delaware River.* Since the *Dead Dog Tavern* was only about a block from the river, he figured they hadn't traveled far. There was straw inside his shirt. He figured, they had tossed him onto a wagon and thrown straw over top of him. Carts of straw were quite common throughout the city. Cushman was sure he was still in the city.

Tompkins had called the new arrival *sir*. During Cushman's time in the Virginia militia, he had seen the interaction between officers and soldiers. Discipline among the colonial militia was a joke compared to the British Army. Attempting to copy the British manual, colonial officers demanded soldiers to address them as *sir*, with widely varying results. In Cushman's experience, only one officer he had served with received the greeting with respect, and that was George Washington. Some received it through fear of the whip, but most received it with sarcasm or disdain. Tompkins's *sir* had definitely been delivered with fear. Cushman was sure he was about to meet the man who had organized the assassination of the leaders of the Second Continental Congress.

"Well, well, if it isn't Mr. Benjamin Cushman. I finally get a chance to meet the friend of the famous Mr. Jefferson." Rourke now stood directly in front of Cushman.

"If you'd untie my hands, I'd be happy to give you a proper greeting," Cushman calmly suggested, speaking for the first time.

"Ah, I see you have a sense of humor. We will see how long that lasts," responded an equally calm Rourke.

"Just who might you be, good sir?" Cushman continued to push. *If this guy is as crazy as I think, maybe I can press the right button.*

Van Dyke moved closer, hoping Rourke would allow him to start. Lydia Ames softly glided behind Cushman, analyzing him with cool detachment.

"I'm sure you're wondering why I have brought you here." There was a sinister tone to his question.

"My guess is you have some real estate you want to sell me. But these sales tactics are a little too strong for my taste," responded Cushman.

Lydia Ames smiled and worked hard to stifle a laugh. Rourke had never been spoken to in this manner. She was amused and wondered when Rourke's fuse would light.

"You're very funny, Mr. Cushman. Too bad I have no need of a court jester." Rourke's temper was starting to boil. He nodded to Van Dyke.

Van Dyke had been waiting all day. He wound up and delivered a vicious blow across Cushman's jaw, lifting the chair off the ground. Cushman crashed to the floor, his face scraping across the rough wooden planks. Van Dyke effortlessly righted the chair. The next punch landed in Cushman's stomach. Being unprepared for the blow, he struggled to regain his breath. Another blow to the jaw followed quickly. A second blow to the stomach caused Cushman to gasp for air. His lungs were now on fire for lack of oxygen, and his jaw felt like it was broken. Rourke held up his hand for Van Dyke to stop. Cushman slowly regained his ability to breathe.

"Now, my good sir, have you anything else to say?" Rourke asked with mock politeness.

"I told you these sales tactics are much too strong. You have to learn to be more subtle." Cushman spit out the words while gasping for his breath.

Rourke nodded, and Van Dyke began again, this time a total of eight blows. Cushman's face was now covered with blood; he was sure his nose was broken, and possibly his jaw. Lydia Ames continued to watch; she felt no pity for Cushman but grudgingly admired his courage.

"Very good, Mr. Van Dyke. Let's take a short break. We don't want Mr. Cushman to die too soon." Rourke had regained his composure and was enjoying every moment.

Cushman knew he should probably shut up, but he was mad. "You're a pretty tough guy, having your goon pummel a defenseless man. What say you untie me and you and I will go at it? What do you think, big talker? Let's go!"

"Oh, don't worry, Mr. Cushman. I will introduce you to some of the latest torture devices known to man. Before I'm through with you, you will be begging me to kill you. And who knows, maybe I will, maybe I won't." Rourke nodded to Van Dyke, and the beatings continued for another five minutes. Van Dyke finally stopped when Cushman passed out. His hands were cut and bleeding, but the smile on his face indicated he couldn't wait until Cushman woke up for another round.

The flow of blood actually helped moisten his parched lips, but the salty taste, he could do without. Cushman had withstood the first round, but he realized surviving several more like this morning's beatings would be highly improbable. He had to admit that the son of a bitch could throw a punch. He was strong and powerful. Cushman had never been hit that hard, and he had been in more than a few scrapes. Although his body had taken a beating, Cushman's mind continued to function. Before Van Dyke had started using him as a human punching bag, he had noticed a distinct scent of perfume. The scent came from behind him and seemed familiar, but he couldn't place it. So a woman had entered with the two men to witness the thrashing of Cushman. Whereas most women would abhor such behavior and either cry out or leave, the mystery woman did neither.

Cushman's respite was short-lived; Van Dyke returned with an evil chuckle, and the beatings resumed, albeit with a new tactic, this time Van Dyke concentrated his blows on Cushman's arms and legs. Cushman would pass out a second time, after Van Dyke punched him between his legs, sending pain to every corner of his body.

The cold water felt good. Cushman did his best to catch any drips on his tongue as he hadn't had anything to drink in close to a day. Van Dyke threw a second bucket of water to make sure he was awaken.

"Mr. Cushman, would you like me to call off Mr. Van Dyke? Would you like that?" Rourke whispered softly.

Cushman struggled to answer, knowing what he wanted to hear, but it wasn't in him. "My offer still stands. Me and you, one-on-one. You might stand a chance in my current condition." Cushman scolded himself for taunting *the boss*, but he just couldn't help himself.

He braced himself for another beating, yet nothing came. "What's wrong, Van Dick? Did I wear you out? Van Dick, do you like your new name?" Lydia Ames had remained in the room and was sitting on the far wall. She knew Rourke's temper was about to explode. She stood quickly to get Rourke's attention and pointed to her fingernail. Rourke understood and smiled.

"Mr. Cushman, I do so appreciate your gallant actions so far. But you have no idea how far I'm willing to go to cause you pain. In a few days, you'll look back on this day as your fondest." Rourke motioned to Van Dyke.

THE SIGNERS

Cushman felt two strong hands collapse around his left wrist. His hands were still tied behind his back, so he was puzzled as to why Van Dyke would try to immobilize him further.

"Mr. Cushman, you were right, Mr. Van Dyke's tactics were much too barbaric. See how you like my more subtle approach." Cushman could feel the hot breath of his torturer. Suddenly, his entire body went rigid; excruciating pain coursed throughout every nerve ending. The ring finger of his left hand felt like it had been sawed in half. He began to spasm in pain. Rourke drove the sharp needle deeper under the fingernail as Cushman clenched his teeth, refusing to let out a scream. His muscles tightened so hard he thought they were about to break in half. Rourke changed to Cushman's little finger. Cushman writhed in pain but couldn't escape from Van Dyke's iron grip. Soaked in sweat, Cushman fought the pain but finally called out, "Stop, please stop!"

Rourke drove the needle deeper, just to prove a point, and then removed it suddenly. "Had enough, Mr. Cushman?"

A slumped-over Cushman grunted softly, "Yes."

"You see, Mr. Van Dyke, eventually they all come around. Mr. Cushman caved quickly. I rather thought he would be a little tougher, but I was wrong." Rourke was enjoying the mental torture, but not quite as much as the physical torture.

"Mr. Cushman, if you want the punishment to stop, then you will write a short note to your friend Mr. Jefferson. If you cooperate, the torture will end for the time being. If not, I will begin again."

"How long?"

"Oh, perhaps until tomorrow," Rourke answered, nodding toward Lydia to wait outside.

Cushman heard the third person walking across the floor; the door creaked open, then closed. He was now positive the third person was a woman. "No, how long, the letter?"

Rourke laughed. "Not long. Just write what I tell you."

Van Dyke removed the blindfold. The bright sunlight filtered into the room as Cushman gradually exposed his eyes to his surroundings. Van Dyke turned the chair around in one motion. Cushman was now facing a four-foot-long rectangular table. Situated in the center of the table were a piece of blank parchment, a quill pen, and a small bottle of ink.

Van Dyke kneeled down and loosened the rope holding Cushman's wrists together. Cushman briefly thought of making a move, but he was in such a weakened state, and the fact that his legs were tied to the chair made the decision easy. He would bide his time, and now was not the moment.

Cushman flexed his right hand, looking over his shoulder as he did so. There he was, his mysterious captor. Cushman first noticed the fine clothing and expensive leather shoes. His face was handsome, very feminine, with small facial features. Obviously a man of wealth. His thick dark hair was relatively short. He was not as tall as Jefferson, but he was close. Cushman glanced to his left; Van Dyke hadn't changed, ugly as ever, his scowl indicating he was hoping Cushman did something stupid. Short and powerfully built, he was a bull. The mysterious boss and Van Dyke were polar opposites except for one thing, their eyes. If Shakespeare had wanted to portray evil eyes to his audience, then these two would have been perfect examples.

"Comfortable, Mr. Cushman? Now, do as I say and I promise some time to heal. If not, Mr. Van Dyke will continue."

"I can go till sundown, mister—boss." Van Dyke caught himself. Rourke gave him a scathing look.

"Sundown is not for another seven hours," Rourke informed the wounded Virginian.

Cushman's eyes were now adjusted to the light, and he glared at his captor. Cushman's mouth said he would cooperate, but his eyes said the exact opposite. They sent shivers down Rourke's back. Rourke had a fleeting thought to put a bullet into the traitor's head and end it now. However, he had promised Lydia, and he had to admit that torturing someone like Cushman was as good as it got. He made a mental note to increase security around the warehouse.

Regaining his air of superiority, Rourke explained to Cushman exactly what the letter should say. Ordering Cushman to write quickly, he left to join Lydia on the first floor.

Beaming with pride, Rourke embraced her and gave her a deep kiss.

"My, my, I should let you torture people more often."

"It's going better than I had hoped."

"Is he writing my letter?" she asked.

"As we speak. Have you thought about how you plan to deliver it?" Rourke had left it to her to find a persuasive way to deliver the letter to Jefferson.

She had given it careful thought and proudly proclaimed, "Deborah Johnson!"

Rourke looked puzzled, but before he could reply, she continued.

"I will have a boy deliver the note to City Tavern with instructions for Deborah to deliver the letter to Jefferson. The boy will be a *neighbor* to the farm Cushman is staying at. He is running an errand into town, and yes, *he could deliver a message for Cushman*. Cushman would figure that the boy would have trouble finding Jefferson, so he sends him to City Tavern, knowing Debby would deliver the message."

"Not bad. I like it. But what about the boy? If they are suspicious, they will seek him out to question him," Rourke cautioned.

"I will send him away, or..." She didn't finish her thought.

"You know there is an old saying that dead men tell no tales. It applies to boys too." Rourke's eyes bore into Lydia.

"Very well. That will tie up any loose ends." Lydia's conscience had rarely been bothered by any of her dealings with Rourke. But killing an innocent boy seemed excessive. She quickly shrugged off the rare moment of compassion and rationalized that scores of Philadelphia youngsters died every day. *What's one more?*

Van Dyke emerged carrying a single parchment in his right hand. Quickly descending the stairs, he handed the letter to Rourke. "No problem, boss. He wrote exactly what you told him."

"Van Dyke, you've done a good job today. When Tompkins returns, I want you to get three of our men to guard the ground floor."

Van Dyke beamed; it was probably the first compliment he had ever received from Rourke. "Do you really think it's necessary? He's hardly in any condition to escape," Van Dyke reasoned, a new sense of confidence beginning to show.

"Perhaps you're right, but I don't want to take any chances. Cushman is cunning. I can see it in his eyes. We will resume his punishment tomorrow. I will bring some of my favorite devices."

"Very well, boss. Consider it done." Van Dyke smiled and thought, *What a great day!*

Rourke held up the letter:

> *Thomas, the man is scared and uncooperative. Bindernagel and I will stay one or two days longer. I think he will eventually reveal the name, but we need more time. I should be back on Tuesday or Wednesday. Everything is fine, just like the first time we met. Thomas, I told you there was nothing to worry about.*

"Perfect! I told you I would gain you more time." Rourke smiled at Lydia.

This time she embraced Rourke and initiated a long, deep kiss. "You are right once again, my darling. Now let's get out of here." She gave Rourke her most seductive look while grazing his cheek with her fingernail. "I have plans for you."

His heart was pounding harder as his stride length grew longer. He had run at least two blocks, and *the damn shopkeeper* was still behind him. *Whoever he was, he was not a normal clerk.* Most gave up as soon as he broke into a sprint, but not this one; he was actually gaining ground. It had been a long time since he had gone into the alley, but that was now his strategy. If he could hold him off until he reached the alley, he was sure he could get away. His bare feet were used to the cobblestone streets, but at this speed the cuts and bruise were going to be significant. Slowing to make the ninety-degree turn, he could hear his pursuer closing in. Accelerating out of the turn, he made his decision; it was all or nothing. The pursuing clerk immediately recognized the boy's predicament and slowed to a walk. The alley had no exit. A ten-foot-high wooden fence divided the alley in half. He smiled to himself as he closed in for the kill.

The young boy continued to run as fast as his battered feet could take him, heading straight for the wooden barrel centered at the base of the fence. Waiting to the very last minute, he leaped forward, his feet landing on top of the barrel. Redirecting his momentum vertically, he exploded skyward. Placing both hands atop the fence, he pushed upward, extending his elbows as his lower body smoothly cleared the hurdle. Landing softly like a cat, he didn't look back but smiled, knowing that his pursuer could not duplicate his athletic move.

The clerk's mood changed immediately, from certain capture to a complete getaway. His only conciliation was that he had gotten a good look at him. He would definitely remember that face.

Billy Smith cut through one more alley to make certain of his escape. Satisfied, he paused to catch his breath, lifting his makeshift satchel over his head. He emptied the contents onto the ground, admiring his handiwork. Two sterling silver candleholders, three diamond-studded brooches, and one gold braided necklace. No wonder the clerk had pursued him with such vigor. The old man would pay a fortune for this haul. Placing the stolen items back into his satchel, the fifteen-year-old whistled happily as he headed home. His luck had finally turned. Nothing could stop him now.

Jefferson's day had been very productive. Saturdays were typically set aside for reading, writing, and entertaining the occasional visitor. After the shopping and the impromptu town meeting with Benjamin Harrison and Elbridge Gerry, Jefferson had visited several key delegates, preparing for Monday's debate on the declaration.

Stopping first at the lodging house of James Wilson, Jefferson found the Scottish-born immigrant struggling with his vote concerning independence. A strong advocate for independence for several years now, Wilson had two concerns. First, he was indebted to his friend and fellow Pennsylvanian John Dickinson. Dickinson had hired the struggling young lawyer, and Wilson had flourished under Dickinson's tutelage. Wilson eventually opened his own office in Carlisle, where in the past couple of years he had earned a small fortune. Of course, Dickinson was leading the opposition. Wilson also felt his constituents were not in favor of independence.

Jefferson listened to Wilson's concerns and countered them by emphasizing Paine's pamphlet *Common Sense* had changed many American minds in a very short period of time. Jefferson was encouraged when Wilson referred several times to specific references he admired in the declaration, a good sign that he had taken the time to read the document. After a good hour of give-and-take, Jefferson left Wilson's lodging hopeful. Although he despised gambling, if a wager was to be made on Wilson's vote, he would bet on an affirmative one.

Next, Jefferson visited Edward Rutledge at a small coffeehouse on the corner of Chestnut and Fourth. Although he was only twenty-six, Rutledge's success as a Charleston lawyer had put him in the powerful position of leading the South Carolina delegation. Like Dickinson, Rutledge was in favor of reconciling with the king. His greatest fear was that a revolution would upset the current economic state of the colonies. A slave owner like Jefferson, he did not share Jefferson's desire to eventually end the practice. Like Wilson, Rutledge had read the Declaration of Independence and made note of his dislike of Jefferson's paragraph condemning slavery and the slave trade. Originally against the Lee Resolution, Rutledge was deeply moved by Jefferson's argument for independence. Like Robert Livingston of New York, Jefferson thought he detected in Rutledge a gradual warming to the idea of liberty.

Jefferson's final stop was to his close friend John Hart. The New Jersey delegate had been present during the assassination attempt at City Tavern. He reassured Jefferson that the New Jersey delegation was totally in favor of independence and that he and fellow New Jersey delegate Abraham Clark were lobbying hard with their Pennsylvania and Delaware neighbors. A large majority had come out in favor of the Lee Resolution, but a unanimous front was needed, according to

Sam and John Adams. Anything less could lead to disaster. A united front concerning such a unique and historic opportunity was needed to bolster the fledgling country.

Jefferson felt better after speaking to the different delegates in an informal setting. He understood politics, but unlike Samuel Adams and Dr. Franklin, he preferred not to partake in the blood sport. Jefferson's vision of a republic with extreme limitations placed on the central government's power and a citizenry left free to pursue their life's dream was unyielding in his conception. Politics always created gray areas and certain exceptions. This was the hideous ploy practiced in past democracies and always led to their downfall. Jefferson was wise enough to realize that compromise would always be a necessary component to a democratic republic, but he would never compromise on his belief of placing individual freedom over government power.

The sun was beginning to set, and Jefferson had one more task to complete. A task he was not looking forward to. He had vowed to Ben that he would go to City Tavern and personally deliver the message to Deborah. Cushman had promised to escort Deborah home after work, to meet her father and servant-friend, Sarah, a very big step in their budding relationship. Jefferson dreaded being the bearer of bad news, especially since he had sanctioned Cushman's potentially dangerous mission.

It was close to eight o'clock when he rode in front of City Tavern. A frequent customer, Jefferson had never been there on a Saturday night. He had never seen it so busy; the place was crawling with customers. Benjamin Franklin was holding court in the front coffee room with several delegates and two lovely ladies. Franklin motioned to Jefferson above the din of the crowd to join them at his table. Jefferson extended one finger in a universal sign indicating *one moment* and headed toward the tavern room, looking for Deborah.

She finally appeared, emerging from the kitchen carrying several plates of food. Her smile beamed from ear to ear; it was quite obvious to Jefferson the person most responsible for her happiness. Unlike Ben Franklin, Jefferson had always been somewhat awkward around beautiful women. Most women found it rather charming, but Jefferson knew the history books would never write about his prowess with the ladies. He dreaded telling Deborah because he knew he couldn't hide his own worry for Ben's safety. Like any good men facing a similar problem, he did what came naturally. Jefferson ordered a beer.

Billy Smith threw open the door, hoping to surprise his mother. No such luck. She had already left for her second job, cleaning the old widow's fancy home down on Front Street. During the day, the twenty-nine-year-old Lisa Smith worked in a small bookstore several blocks from their run-down apartment complex on Locust Street. During the evening, she spent four hours cleaning the huge mansion of Mrs. Marion.

Billy rarely saw his mother, because on weekends she would spend most of her time bouncing from tavern to tavern. Not exactly an idyllic homelife. As a result, he had turned to petty crime, mostly stealing small items and selling them to the old man down near the wharfs.

"Billy, Billy, come here." Standing in the open doorway, Billy turned and smiled. He knew her voice instantly and ran quickly across the street. Her small one-story home was neat and clean, with flowerpots arranged in perfect order along the front of her house. Billy felt his breathing get heavier and the chills run up and down his arms as he drew closer to her. She had moved in three months ago, and Billy had helped her with some of the heavy furniture. At twenty-three, Honor Simmons was the most beautiful woman he had ever seen. They had become friends; she would send him on small errands or have him do chores around her home. He would fantasize about marrying her, and of course, his lust-filled dreams kept him awake at night.

Billy envied her exotic lifestyle. Elegant horse-drawn carriages were constantly picking her up and dropping her off. Billy's mother said she was just a high-priced whore; he would scold her for being jealous. Honor said she was invited to many fancy parties around town. The arrival of the Second Continental Congress prompted Philadelphia elites to throw numerous lavish parties to entertain the famous body. Even at a young age, Billy understood the attraction of beauty and power. Again, today an elegant carriage was parked in front of her quaint home.

"Billy." She smiled. "Are you doing anything of importance tonight?" Honor asked him while she brushed her hair. She was dressed in just a petticoat and a thin undergarment, and Billy tried not to stare at the stunning young woman, but he failed miserably.

"No, Honor, is there something you want to do?" His tone was more hopeful than questioning.

"How would you like to make a lot of money?"

Disappointed temporarily, Billy quickly cheered up with the mention of *a lot of money*. "Sure, whad'ja have in mind?"

Billy was so enthralled by Honor's beauty he never even noticed the other woman. "Billy, this is my boss, Ms. Lydia."

His eyes nearly popped out of their sockets. He had never seen anyone like Ms. Lydia. Even Honor looked plain compared to the woman standing before him now.

"Nice to meet ya," he stammered and stuck out his hand like he was greeting a man.

Lydia laughed gently and shook hands with the starstruck teenager. "How would you like to make ten pounds tonight, young man?"

"Ten pounds, are you kidding? I don't have to kill no one, do I?"

"No, no, nothing so dramatic." Lydia and Honor laughed lightly, Honor slipping on her dress while the conversation continued. "I have an acquaintance that wants to surprise his girlfriend with a big party later on tonight. However, he wants her to think he has been held up on business and won't be back home for a few days. After an hour or so of disappointment, he will burst through the door for a huge surprise."

"Sounds like fun, but why do ya need me?"

"We need someone convincing to deliver the message, someone she doesn't know. Honor said she had the cutest neighbor boy who would be perfect for the job," Lydia purred, flaunting her advantage.

Billy glanced at Honor and blushed. *She has called me cute,* he thought, *so maybe there is hope after all for the two of us.* She smiled back. "Sure, I'll do it. When do I get paid?"

Lydia pulled out a sealed envelope and handed it to Billy. "Take this envelope to City Tavern and ask for a waitress named Deborah. They probably won't let you in, so make sure they bring her to you. Don't give the letter to anybody but Deborah Johnson."

"That's it, all I gotta do is run this over to City Tavern and I get ten pounds?" he asked, not believing his good fortune.

"That's it. Here is five now." Lydia handed him five British one-pound notes. "I will need you to return with confirmation she got the letter. Then I will give you an additional five."

"So I come back here to get the rest of the money?"

"No, Honor' and I are going to the party, so meet my carriage at the corner of Dock and Second Street. We will wait there for you. Can you remember what my carriage looks like?"

"Yes, ma'am. I sure do. Do you want me to deliver it now? I can get there in ten minutes if I run," Billy bragged, hoping to impress both women.

"I bet you can. No, you don't have to leave yet, in about an hour. Why don't you sit down? I'll get you a glass of wine, and we can go over some additional instructions."

Whoa, Billy thought to himself. *What a day! First, the jewelry, and now this, being with two beautiful women and getting ten pounds just to deliver a letter. What a great day!*

Deborah Johnson had not seen Thomas Jefferson standing in the corner of the tavern room. She was talking to a member of the Congress, William Floyd.

"So your family estate is on Long Island. My aunt Elizabeth lives there. Where exactly is this country estate? Perhaps I will call on you next time I visit my aunt?" Deborah asked casually.

Floyd happily went into details concerning the location of his estate on Long Island.

Jefferson watched curiously as Deborah moved back toward the kitchen, stopped, and began to write something down. Jefferson thought it odd but quickly forgot about it. He had decided to wait until she was finished working before breaking the news concerning Ben. *Speaking in front of Congress* was preferable to confronting an irrational woman.

Deborah finally spotted him in the crowded tavern. She smiled and ran to the redheaded Virginian.

"Mr. Jefferson, how long have you been spying on me?" She laughed and gave him a big smile.

Jefferson's face gave away his concern, and she read it immediately.

"My god, is something wrong? Did something happen to Ben?"

"No, no, everything is fine..." Jefferson hesitated, then revealed the entire story. He left out nothing, from Samuel Adams to Norman Bindernagel and Lucas Post. When finished, he paused and waited for the storm.

It came quickly. "What!" Deborah screamed out.

Jefferson braced himself for the full brunt of her fury.

"How could you, his best friend, let him go on such dangerous mission? What were you thinking? These people are murderers, and they will stop at nothing to achieve their goals!" Deborah stopped; it suddenly dawned on her that she was mostly responsible for Cushman's situation. Her first thought was that it was a trap, and she was equally sure that Rourke was behind it. *I gave his name to Rourke. How could I be so stupid?* Millions of questions raced through her head. Did Lydia know? If so, how much? She had promised she would stop Rourke. Had Lydia lied to her, or was she overreacting?

Jefferson had expected the verbal assault. What he didn't expect was the sudden change in her reaction. Her attack on Jefferson was short-lived, replaced by an introspective and sullen mood change.

Jefferson was about to speak when she began to sob and fell into his arms and kept repeating, "It's all my fault."

Incredibly, Jefferson was able to find a small private booth away from prying eyes. They sat facing each other, her beautiful eyes filled with tears. She looked like she was about to unburden herself when suddenly he noticed a young man rapidly approaching.

"Ah, there you are. I've been looking for you." Deborah looked up. It was the acting manager, who had temporarily replaced John Trumbull. Like Deborah, he was the child of a shareholder in City Tavern.

"A ragged young man is demanding to deliver you a message. He refuses to give it to me. He insists he must give it to you in person. What do you want me to do?"

Deborah almost told him to dismiss the lad, but curiosity won out. "Thank you, Alistair. I will take care of it."

Feeling protective, Jefferson followed Deborah outside.

"You Deborah Johnson?" a shabbily dressed boy called out as the two moved toward the hitching post, the same hitching post where, five nights earlier, the only surviving assassin had been gunned down.

"Yes. Just who are you, young man?" Deborah asked while trying to withhold her sobbing.

"My name is Billy. I live about a day's ride south of town. My neighbor, Mr. Black, had two visitors yesterday. When they found out I was riding into Philly, one of them asked me to deliver this letter to Deborah Johnson at City Tavern. Told me to tell her it was from Ben Cushman. He said you would know what to do with the letter."

"Where's your horse?" Jefferson quizzed the boy.

"I, ah…" Billy hesitated. *Ms. Lydia never said anything about any man.* Billy didn't want to spoil the surprise. "Ah, I left it at the general store, a block from here. Figured I'd give her a rest." Billy was proud of himself for thinking so quickly.

"What kind of supplies were you getting?" Jefferson continued pressing.

"Ah, you know, the usual stuff," Billy stammered; he was clearly unnerved by the appearance of the strange man with so many questions.

"Now, now"—Deborah put her hand on Jefferson's shoulder—"no use grilling the boy. He's only a messenger. Look, good news." While Jefferson was questioning the boy, Deborah had ripped open the letter and read it twice. Perhaps she was wrong; perhaps

THE SIGNERS

Cushman's mission was indeed legit. Maybe she had overestimated Rourke's lust for revenge, or perhaps Lydia had persuaded Rourke not to seek his vengeance. Either way, she was happy. "You know his writing, Mr. Jefferson. Is that his hand?"

"Yes, yes, it is" was all Jefferson could mutter as he read the note over and over.

> *Thomas, the man is scared and uncooperative. Bindernagel and I will stay one or two days longer. I think he will eventually reveal the name, but we need more time. I should be back on Tuesday or Wednesday. Everything is fine, just like the first time we met. Thomas, I told you there was nothing to worry about.*

Billy began to walk away when Jefferson called out, "So you met Cushman, did you?"

Billy was uncomfortable answering all these questions but figured he was almost done. "Yes, nice fellow."

Jefferson smiled and relaxed. Walking toward the boy, he handed him two one-pound notes. "Thank you for your effort, young Billy."

"And thank you, sir." Billy couldn't believe his good fortune, twelve pounds for doing nothing. *What a great night!*

Jefferson took a step back toward City Tavern, then stopped. Turning back at the boy, he said, "Cushman, did you notice the nasty scar on his left cheek? He got that during the French and Indian War."

"Indeed I did, sir. Very misshapen." Billy smiled and rapidly walked away. With all this money, he might even impress Honor. *What a great night!*

And just like that, every horrible scenario flew back into Deborah's head, and she almost collapsed back into Jefferson's arms.

"Stop him, Mr. Jefferson, or follow him. How did you know?" Deborah's voice was full of panic.

"No, let him go. If these are the same people who planned out Tuesday night, then they won't be so careless to allow the boy to lead us to them."

"You knew all along. How did you know?" Deborah repeated herself as her shoulders sank in despair.

"I didn't know all along, but I was very suspicious. This mission was fraught with misgivings from the very beginning."

"But what makes you so sure now?" Deborah was now crying uncontrollably.

"The letter," Jefferson replied confidently.

"The letter? But the letter is the only thing that gives us hope. You said it was his writing," she sobbed.

"Oh, it's his writing, all right. There is no doubt, it's his writing."

Deborah's confusion mounted. "Well, if it's his writing, then he's got to be safe."

"I'm afraid not, but at least he's alive. Whoever is holding him went to great lengths to assure us of his safety. For whatever reason, they want us to think he is fine and completing his mission. Ben was supposed to return Sunday, Monday at the latest. The note wants us to believe he won't return until Tuesday or Wednesday. It seems like they want to keep us from mounting a search for at least three or four days. If it were simple revenge, Ben would be dead and no elaborate rouse would be needed to calm our worries. They don't want to arouse suspicions. But why?"

"You still haven't answered my question. What is in the letter that makes you sure Ben is in trouble?"

"Why, quite simple, my dear. It's Thomas," the tall Virginian replied calmly.

"Thomas, what are you talking about? Your name is Thomas." Deborah's voice trembled with fear.

"To everybody but Ben Cushman. Ben has called me *Red* since as long as I can remember. Even in the rare letter, he would always call me *Red*. He never calls me Thomas, ever. In this letter, he called me Thomas, not once, but twice. It's a signal, and it's a signal that all is not well."

"What do we do now?"

"Mr. Post brought this Bindernagel character to Sam Adams. I am going to pay a visit to Mr. Post," Jefferson promised firmly.

It took the two fifteen minutes to find someone who knew Lucas Post. "Of course I know Lucas," he stated, stumbling over his words. "And his very pretty wife…can't remember her name."

It took a few minutes, but he eventually came up with an address. Jefferson quickly made for his horse.

"Mr. Jefferson, please let me go with you." Deborah's eyes pleaded with Jefferson.

Jefferson hesitated for a moment. If Post was part of a conspiracy to abduct Cushman, then the situation could get dangerous. The last thing he wanted to do was put someone else in danger; he felt guilty enough about Ben. Perhaps it was the chivalrous thing to do. Perhaps it was the guilt and anger he felt having allowed Ben to be abducted, but ultimately, it was her eyes, sad and determined, that convinced Jefferson he had no choice but to bring her along.

A few moments later, they were riding south along Second Street. She insisted on sitting behind Jefferson, her arms wrapped tightly around his waist.

"Are you sure you're comfortable, Deborah?" Jefferson was somewhat alarmed that she would not ride sidesaddle and insisted upon riding like a man. "Good thing it is nighttime. This would cause quite the scandal among the Philadelphia gossip circuit," Jefferson commented as the horse approached South Street and the address they had been given.

"Wouldn't be right for Mr. Jefferson to be seen with some tavern girl?" Deborah slapped his shoulder and laughed nervously.

"I think we've known each other long enough for you to call me Thomas, and I was referring to your unladylike riding style."

"Very well, but may I call you Red instead?" Her attempt at a joke just added more to her nervous state of mind. "And I'll have you know my father taught me to ride when I was very young. I guess he had always wanted a boy, so he treated me like one."

"There it is, straight ahead." He pointed excitedly.

Jefferson quickly secured his horse and began to assess the neighborhood, trying to notice anything out of place. Deborah stood beside him and waited patiently while he continued his surveillance. Finally, satisfied that everything seemed normal, Jefferson motioned to Deborah, and the two approached the house gingerly.

As they stepped onto the modest yard, Jefferson sensed something was wrong immediately. The windows were boarded up, and there was a sign tacked to the front door. He gently grabbed Deborah's elbow and signaled her to stay put. He pulled out his favorite pistol, fully loaded and primed. Walking slowly to the front door, he read the sloppy handwriting, "Quarantine, Two Adults with the Pox." He attempted to open the door, but it was locked with a deadbolt.

He felt a hand grab his shoulder, causing him to jump slightly. "Nervous." Deborah grinned. She then read the notice. "The pox, maybe we should go."

"Something's not right. Post brought Bindernagel to meet Sam Adams two days ago. He made no mention that he or his wife had the pox."

"Maybe he didn't know at that time," Deborah mused out loud.

"No," Jefferson stated firmly. "Something is very wrong here." He ran to his horse and reached into his saddlebag, returning with an iron rod.

Deborah looked at him curiously.

"Protection" was all he said.

Prying off several of the boards used to cover the window, Jefferson peered through the glass into the darkness.

"See anything?" she whispered. Jefferson looked around. The street was empty. Raising his left elbow, he smashed it into the front window. The cascade of broken glass made noise, but no one came to investigate. Jefferson used the rod to break out all the smaller pieces.

"Why, Mr. Jefferson—excuse me, why, Thomas, is breaking and entering one of your hidden talents?"

"You hang around Ben long enough and some things just rub off. Come on, let's take a closer look."

Jefferson went first, followed by Deborah. A nearby streetlamp provided enough light for Jefferson to find what he was looking for. Taking a candle from a nearby table, he told Deborah, "Hold this," as he reached into his coat pocket. Unfolding a wad of paper, Jefferson removed a thin piece of wood that looked like a toothpick. He gently pushed the head of the wood into the paper, then quickly jerked it through. The paper burst into flame. Jefferson managed to light the candle before the flame engulfed his hand.

Deborah stood amazed, as if Jefferson were some sort of sorcerer. "How in God's name did you do that?"

"Rather simple, actually. A little over one hundred years ago, an alchemist by the name of Brandt discovered that you could produce a pasty white substance called phosphorus."

"Alchemist, aren't they lunatics trying to turn everything into gold?" She stood in awe as Jefferson quickly swept the living room of the small house.

Jefferson held the candle to his face and smiled. "Lunatics maybe, but their experiments have produced some wonderful things. Phosphorus, for example. You see, the paper was laced with phosphorus, as was the piece of wood. By passing the wood through the paper, the friction caused the paper to burst into flames, allowing me to light the candle. I always carry several of these around. Never know when you'll need to start a fire."

"But where did you get this phosphorus?" She struggled pronouncing the word.

"Very simple. I made it myself." Jefferson began to move slowly toward what looked like a bedroom door.

"How do you make it?"

"I take a beaker of my urine, let it set for a week, and then boil it. Voilà, phosphorus."

"Urine, did you say *urine*? Yuck!" Despite the gravity of the situation, Deborah was beginning to enjoy her adventure with Thomas Jefferson.

Jefferson took two steps into the bedroom and stopped in his tracks. He attempted to halt Deborah, but it was too late. She took in the sight of a man and a woman propped up in their bed. Obviously, both were dead. Hundreds of flies hovered around the two just as the smell struck them both. Deborah ran from the room but didn't make it far before she knelt over and vomited all over the Posts' dinner table. Jefferson remained and examined the bodies for clues.

Finishing quickly, he took a spare blanket and covered the couple. "Come on, let's get out of here," he said, gently leading Deborah through the window out into the fresh air.

One block south of City Tavern, Billy Smith walked swiftly through the intersection of Dock and Second Streets. *There it is, just like she said.* The carriage was sitting unattended, the two horses resting quietly. Overhead, clouds blocked out the moon and the stars. The night was dark and foreboding. Billy's giddy mood was briefly replaced by caution as he approached what looked like an abandoned carriage. Sure enough, when he opened the door, it was indeed empty. Confused, Billy stood there, contemplating his next move. It never crossed his mind that they might not pay him the remaining five pounds. After all, Honor lived right across the street. She would never let Ms. Lydia double-cross him. Billy began to worry that maybe something bad had happened to the two beautiful women.

"Hey, kid, over here." The voice came from a small alleyway. "Yeah, kid, over here, if you want your money."

"Who are you?" He approached the man in the shadows cautiously. Making a living on Philadelphia's tough streets had made Billy careful when dealing with an unknown. No one had ever run him down, so as long as he could stay a couple of arm's length away, he felt confident he could escape unharmed.

"I'm Lydia's coachman. She and Honor are visiting a friend down the street," he pointed south down Second Street. "I got the rest of your money."

Billy relaxed once he saw the money, but was disappointed he wouldn't see Honor and Lydia. The man appeared from the shadows, holding the money out in front of him. Billy was somewhat startled; the man was as wide as he was tall. He looked like an alpha bull, one that none of the other bulls would go near.

THE SIGNERS

"Here's the money." He handed Billy the rest of his payment. "How did it go? Did she act disappointed?" He quickly took the money and backed away.

Billy absentmindedly counted his reward, still disappointed that Honor and Lydia were not here to greet the conquering hero. "Everything went as Ms. Lydia said, except—"

"Except what?" The bull's tone caused Billy to look up and note his piercing eyes.

"A man. A man came outside with the waitress. He seemed very protective of her. He kept asking me stupid questions."

"Like what?"

"I don't know, like where my horse was or what supplies I was getting. Don't worry, though, he didn't suspect a thing. He even gave me a tip." Billy regretted telling the stranger about the tip.

"What did he look like?"

"I don't know. He was tall, had red hair."

The bull looked concerned. "Did this man with red hair have a name?"

Billy thought for a second, and then it came to him. "She called him Mr. Jefferson. Yeah, it was definitely Mr. Jefferson. You think the girls will be coming along anytime soon?" Billy hoped he would be able to see them tonight.

"So this Mr. Jefferson read the letter? You saw him read the letter?"

"Yeah, he read it. I saw him read it," Billy said enthusiastically, telling the man what he wanted to hear.

The man smiled and spoke in a soft voice. "Perfect. Billy, you did an excellent job. So well, in fact, here is an additional ten pounds." He stuck out his hand; it was filled with a wad of bills.

"Whoa, you're not fooling around with me, are you?" Billy couldn't believe his great fortune. The sting of the girls not being present disappeared as he reached out for what would be the biggest payday of his young life. Even in his best day of thieving, the old man had never paid him what he made tonight. His thoughts turned to his neighbor Honor Simmons. Maybe now, with all this money, she would look at him as more than the neighbor kid.

"Congratulations, kid, you did a great job. Shake hands like a man." The bull extended his right hand.

Billy hesitated. *What the hell! He gave me an extra ten pounds.* As soon as they shook hands, Billy Smith realized he had made a critical mistake; his hand felt like it was caught in a vise. He looked up, expecting to see evidence of a practical joke. Instead, he saw a cold and calculating smile as the bull tightened his grip. Billy panicked and attempted to run. It was futile; the man was as strong as he looked. He kicked with both feet and clawed with his free arm, but he knew he could never get away. Billy felt the other hand seize his neck, and just like that, both hands lifted him off the ground as he fought to draw a breath. He couldn't believe how careless he had been. Kicking as hard and as fast as he could, Billy knew he was running out of time. With all the energy he could muster, he sent a vicious kick toward the man's groin, just missing his target and glancing off his thigh.

A wicked grin spread across the man's face, as if he knew that was Billy's last chance. Blackness washed over Billy as he struggled to take another breath. It never came. Edward Van Dyke looked up at his handiwork with the satisfaction of a farmer harvesting a perfect crop. He tossed the lifeless teenager into the darkest shadows of the alleyway. Just one more Philadelphia street urchin found dead in the morning. It happened all the time, and no one would even suspect foul play.

They had ridden quietly across town, neither of them speaking a word until Jefferson pulled alongside her father's home.

"This is it," Deborah said softly.

Jefferson gently guided her down from the back of his horse.

"You have a beautiful home," Jefferson commented as they walked up the path bordered on both sides by colorful flowers in full bloom.

"My father loves this home. It was built during my mother's pregnancy with me. He says that she was always chiding the builders about their craftsmanship. Seems my father had to ban her from the site or the tradesmen were all going to quit."

"Your father seems like a very patient man," Jefferson stated kindly.

"I'm afraid he wouldn't like you standing on his porch. He is very much a Loyalist and a strong supporter of King George."

Jefferson smiled, then added, "It is a difficult time for everybody, Deborah. I'm sure your father has his reasons. I feel men like your father will eventually see the wisdom of our cause."

"You don't know my father." She smiled.

"Ben says your mother died when you were very young. That had to be very difficult for you."

"I was two. My father tried, but he was always gone. His ship supply store is the largest in the country. I suppose he spoiled me. Luckily, our servant, Sarah, has been like an older sister to me. She probably kept me from going totally crazy."

Jefferson looked into Deborah's eyes; he saw sadness, but also confusion. He felt like she wanted to tell him something and couldn't find the words.

A unique feature of the Johnson home was a four-foot-wide front porch that ran the length of the front of the house. Deborah sat on a bench and motioned Jefferson to join her. With her elbows on her knees and her hands covering her face, Deborah asked Jefferson in a voice he could barely hear. "Are they going to kill Ben?"

"I'm not sure. Whoever is holding Ben may want to use him for some form of ransom or an exchange of some kind," Jefferson said, trying to reassure her.

"So you are hopeful?" Her tone was more pleading than question.

"Yes and no. Ben's kidnapping was no random act. It was well planned and carried out. I think I have a pretty clear picture of how they did it. Bindernagel used Lucas Post to introduce him to Sam Adams."

"How do you know Post wasn't in on it?" Her head shot up in surprise.

"I believe they blackmailed Post," Jefferson stated firmly.

"How do you know that?" she asked with a look of astonishment.

"When I examined the bodies, I noticed Mrs. Post had rope burns on both her wrists. They must have held her hostage, probably threatening to kill her if Post didn't cooperate with Bindernagel. I'm sure Post was told that if he cooperated, they would both be safe."

"Then why kill them?" Deborah asked in disbelief.

"Whoever is behind all this is ruthlessly efficient, and the best way to leave no trail is to kill the accessories. Remember, there were two assassins waiting outside City Tavern. By killing the assassins, it effectively ends the investigation as to who is responsible."

Deborah shuddered; she immediately thought of Rourke and his promise to kill her father. She was tempted to tell Jefferson everything, but her fear of Rourke delivering on his promise was paralyzing. She no longer had any lingering doubt that Lydia Ames had lied to her. She was sure that the letter was aimed as much to ease her doubts as it was Jefferson's.

Jefferson continued, "Ben was prepared for a double-cross, so they must have caught him off guard or overwhelmed him with force. I don't know what they've done with him, but he was still quick-witted enough to send me a warning and a clue."

"A clue? What clue?"

Jefferson pulled out the note delivered by Billy Smith. "You see, he used *Thomas* twice. That was a warning. But look at this line." Jefferson held up the letter so Deborah could see. "Look here, *'Everything is fine,' just like the first time we met.'* I think that's a clue."

"How so?"

"Well, the first time we met, we were both six years old. I was fishing with my older sisters at our favorite fishing hole. Along came Ben and his younger brother James. We argued about just whose fishing hole it was."

"Then what happened?"

"We fought, lasted for a good half-hour. My sisters finally stopped us, although I must say by then we were both exhausted."

Jefferson smiled. "I know you're dying to ask who won. I always tell people I did, and Ben always tells people he did. In truth, it was probably a draw. Been best friends ever since."

"Boys, do you ever really grow into men?" Deborah lightly punched Jefferson in the shoulder as she laughed softly.

"I certainly hope not. Every man should carry his carefree childhood with him till he dies."

"Very philosophical, Thomas, but I still don't see the clue in that sentence," Deborah suggested.

"I'm not exactly sure yet, but remember, he is under duress. They probably dictated to him what he had to write. He couldn't exactly come out with an *'I'm here, come and rescue me.'* " Suddenly, Jefferson bolted upright. "Just like the first time we met…that's it, that's it! Just like the first time we met. The first time we met was at the fishing hole, on the river. He's being held somewhere along the river."

"It's hardly a clue. Where along the river? For that matter, what river?" Deborah seemed skeptical of Jefferson's sudden epiphany.

"I know it's a stretch, but remember, the letter itself tells volumes. Why force him to write the letter? Because they wanted to make sure you and I weren't worried."

Deborah could easily verify Jefferson's assumption as 100 percent correct but again chose not to. "They delivered it to you, guaranteeing you would read it, but it was addressed to me, making sure you would show it to me. They need to buy some time. Otherwise, they would have just killed Ben once they had him. I don't think Ben would have written the letter without some type of coercion."

Deborah knew Jefferson meant some type of force or even torture. She thought back to Rourke's library and all the torture items displayed over his fireplace. "Oh my god," she blurted out, "it's all my fault!"

Jefferson noted that it was the second time Deborah had used that phrase. The first time, he dismissed it as a general catchall, people assigning themselves irrational blame for harm done to a loved one. But now, he wondered if he was missing something. "Is there something you wish to tell me, Deborah?"

She looked at him, her face filled with guilt. "I..." Suddenly, she caught herself. Her face went blank. "I...I am just afraid of what they might do to him."

Jefferson gazed into her face, convinced she was lying. *Why would she lie to me?* he thought. *She couldn't hide her affection for Cushman?* Their fondness for each other was definitely genuine. He proceeded cautiously, hating himself for doing so but finding it necessary to protect his best friend. "They didn't have much time to kidnap him, transport him to a safe place in broad daylight, and force him to write the letter. I would bet my horse they are holding him somewhere on the Delaware River, not far from Philadelphia."

Deborah's face still showed worry. "But there are hundreds of places along the river."

"True, but where could you hide a prisoner? Taverns and stores can be eliminated. They have too many customers. Private homes are possible, but the most likely place is a warehouse, especially one where they don't load and unload goods every day."

"But there are so many, at least twenty, maybe more." Deborah's voice was filled with worry. Jefferson thought she was either a great actress or was truly conflicted.

"Yes, but at least it's a start," he stated with confidence.

Jefferson left soon afterward. His ride home was filled with a million scenarios, most of which ended poorly. It was going to be a difficult night to sleep.

The quaint two-story home was nestled in a quiet middle-class neighborhood located on Fourth Street. Its owner, an eccentric widow, had left to tour Europe more than a year ago. She was scheduled to return within the current year. When, nobody knew for sure. All that her neighbors knew was that she had left behind her pretty young niece from New York City to watch over the house. Her name was Abigail. In truth, the niece had been sent to visit her aunt, but not to house-sit. Her attorney father had dispatched her to Philadelphia to give birth to her illegitimate baby. She had arrived with a letter of instructions and a great deal of money the day after the aunt had left for Europe. The headstrong daughter used the opportunity to deceive the father and was now living in the home. As fate would have it, the daughter had a miscarriage several days later. Free from the responsibility of motherhood and any adult supervision, she quickly fell into a fast crowd. Within two months of her arrival, she was being mentored by the mysterious and somewhat-scandalous Lydia Ames. As Patrick Rourke called them, *she was one of Lydia's girls.*

Abigail Baker entered the bedroom wearing an evening negligee that would have made a French libertine blush. The white silk garment clung to her curves and accentuated every one of her perfect feminine features. She glided effortlessly toward the bed and slid under the covers to embrace her lover. He had been waiting impatiently while she had prepped herself in the adjoining room.

His mind had been anticipating the pleasure to come, and as usual, she would not disappoint him. He no longer felt the guilt after they were done. She was so young and intoxicating to the older man that he forgot about his wife and only concentrated on his new mistress.

"Will you spend the night?" Abigail purred while running her fingers through his hair.

His libido said yes, but his brain cautioned him about the importance of Sunday brunch at his father-in-law's home. His father-in-law was a powerful Philadelphia lawyer whose best friend was Thomas Willing. The same Thomas Willing who was a member of the Continental Congress and had partnered with Robert Morris to form the Willing and Morris shipping-banking firm, one of Philadelphia's largest commercial banks. The man lying next to Abigail Baker was its top accountant. One word from his father-in-law and it would be *former* accountant. No, William Yancey wasn't so independently wealthy to risk alienating his dullard wife. He could always come up with appropriate lies concerning his late nights, but to remain out the entire evening would set off alarms for even his dense spouse. "Sorry, my beauty, but I will have to get home tonight."

"Now, what does your wife have to offer that I can't give you?" Abigail asked playfully.

William Yancey thought about it before answering carefully. "Not a thing, my love, not a thing. Perhaps I could stay a little—"

The thunderous boom reverberated throughout the room. The bedroom door violently rebounded off the wall and came crashing to the floor, completely torn from its hinges. Both Abigail and William were stunned and frightened. A large man was standing in the doorframe; his eyes immediately indicated that they were in trouble.

As the chief accountant at Willing and Morris, William Yancey answered only to the two partners. He was used to giving orders and bullying his staff. He quickly fell into work mode. "How dare you, sir? What is the meaning of this intrusion? I demand that you leave at once!" he blustered while attempting to stop his hand from shaking.

The stranger continued to stand over them without speaking a word; a sly grin soon replaced the menacing glare.

Abigail screamed out, "Get out of my house immediately!"

"Your house?" The stranger pulled a wicker chair close to the bed with one hand while brandishing a twelve-inch-long pistol in the other. The mistress and her lover recoiled at the sight of the gun. The stranger spun the chair around and sat beside the bed, resting his forearms on the chair back. "Let's talk, shall we?"

Major Jacob Hall smiled as the two squirmed in fright. Yancey was the traitor, or at least an unwitting accomplice seduced by a scheming temptress. He would soon find out which.

All along he had hoped the accountant would be the guilty party. Hall knew it had to be one of three people, Robert Morris, Thomas Willing, or their chief accountant, William Yancey, who had betrayed his mission to France. Both Morris and Willing were delegates to the Continental Congress. It was their company that had loaned the Secret Committee close to three million dollars in gold to buy munitions from the king of France. Hall thought it didn't make much sense to steal their own money. But Hall was a thorough man and had followed both men for three days. It was actually easy since they were together much of the time. Finding nothing out of the ordinary, Hall turned his attention to the most obvious suspect,

William Yancey. It was Friday, after work, that Hall had followed Yancey to this house and discovered the illicit affair. Quiet inquiries among the neighbors helped paint a very interesting picture. Although there were still many blanks to fill in, Hall's instincts told him he was about to crack the case wide open. And his instincts were almost always correct.

Yancey turned to the subject he knew best, money. "If it's money you want, I have none with me. But I can get some. Please don't hurt us."

"Mr. Yancey, I'm hurt that you don't remember me."

Yancey was startled upon hearing his name. *This is no run-of-the-mill criminal,* he thought. "I'm sorry, do I know you?"

"We had a brief meeting concerning the delivery of a very large and rather-heavy loan," responded Hall.

Yancey's brain went into overdrive attempting to piece together what he meant by a *heavy loan*. As he concentrated on the stranger's face, it finally struck the accountant. "You're Hall? But aren't you supposed to be in France?" Yancey's voice trembled as he recalled their brief meeting and Thomas Willing's description of the man who would deliver the gold to the king of France. A sudden chill raced down Yancey's spine as he remembered Major Jacob Hall's special attributes.

Hall studied Yancey closely. This was the moment that was so important. The sudden realization that his treachery had been exposed revealed almost everything. Even the best of actors or liars struggled to continue their deception at this particular moment. Hall was genuinely surprised at Yancey's reaction. It was not one of discovery but one of sheer surprise. He studied the accountant a while longer, but nothing changed.

Major Hall immediately turned to the young girl and smiled. "So it was you all along?" Hall's eyes bore into the girl, and her expression revealed he had found his traitor.

Chapter 21

I know no safe depository of the ultimate powers of the society but the people themselves, and if we think them not enlightened enough to exercise their control with a wholesome discretion, the remedy is not to take it from them but to inform their discretion by education. This is the true corrective of abuses of constitutional power.

—Thomas Jefferson

Sunday, June 30, 1776
Philadelphia

Church bells echoed throughout the town. The summer storms had lifted; it was a glorious Sunday morning in Philadelphia, Pennsylvania. The streets were lined with citizens dressed in their Sunday best. Little boys broke from their families and hurdled puddles of water left from the summer rains. Parents yelled at the boys as pretty girls giggled at their athletic displays. One young boy misjudged the distance of a particularly long puddle and landed on his backside, completely ruining his best set of clothing. Everyone laughed except his parents.

Even Thomas Jefferson laughed at the young boy's misfortune. It reminded him of his childhood and all the mischief he helped create with Ben.

Cushman was the reason Jefferson had risen at daybreak and was currently in the middle of searching for his friend. He had spent most of the night poring over city maps of Philadelphia and plotting his morning's strategy. He had considered going to the police but decided against it. With little or no evidence to back up his kidnap theory, he would probably be lucky that they didn't throw him into an insane asylum. Besides, it was patently obvious that certain Tories were behind the plot. Even more sinister, *what if the British were the architects behind everything?* Many bureaucrats, including police, were still loyal to the king.

Jefferson had focused all his deductive powers into Ben's kidnapping and came to several conclusions. Bindernagel had mentioned they would receive a map at a tavern. The more Jefferson thought about it, the more he believed Cushman was overpowered while in the tavern. If Bindernagel had drawn a gun on Ben while on horseback, it wouldn't have been a fair fight. Ben was an expert with both the gun and the horse. Ben would be alert to anything fishy. No, it made sense to make their move while in or near a tavern. Associates, probably in place, could have helped Bindernagel overpower Cushman. Cushman wouldn't be compliant, so they would have to transport him without causing suspicion. A carriage or a cart would be the most suitable, someplace near the river. Considering the roads running parallel to the Delaware River and the approximate speed of a horse-drawn carriage, he calculated time and distance. The maximum distance Jefferson figured would be fifteen miles north or south of the central city. However, riverfront buildings stretched only about three miles to the north and to the south about four miles. There were still many caves along the riverbank being used for various enterprises, but Jefferson ruled them out because of their openness. According to his calculations, Cushman was being held somewhere within a seven-mile range along the river. Of course, all that would be irrelevant if he had misread Cushman's clue about the river.

Jefferson rode north as the sun peeked over the Atlantic. His plan was to ride north, then start back south. *Needle in a haystack,* he thought as he approached the first warehouse about three miles from Penn's Landing. It was abandoned, and Jefferson thought he might get lucky early. It was a perfect place to hold a captive. A quick search of the one-story building proved useless. The only things occupying the building were dog-size rats.

The next potential structure was a half-mile south. Jefferson's curiosity was piqued. *Men working on a Sunday?* He quickly rejected it as a possibility. At least twenty-five longshoremen were unloading cargo from a three-mast schooner. *Too much activity.* Jefferson noticed the name of the merchant ship, *Independence*, and remembered that tomorrow's historic debate would begin in earnest.

Approaching the central city, where the riverfront buildings stood side by side, Jefferson cursed himself. *An impossible mission.* He knew he couldn't be as efficient as necessary; each time he eliminated a structure, for whatever reason—too busy, private home, or plain old instinct—he might be condemning his best friend. Time and lack of resources were his enemy, and he was slowly succumbing to a reality, a reality he was terrified to accept.

It was noon when he reached Penn's Landing, his estimated midpoint. The temperature was rising, and Jefferson decided to find some water for his horse and some tea for himself. He stopped at a small tavern at the corner of Dock and Front Streets.

After the brief respite, Jefferson walked slowly to his horse. He recognized the beginning of one of his headaches; the tension was causing his muscles to tighten and his head to ache. Tomorrow would be perhaps the most important day in his life, and he was on a wild-goose chase. What if he was wrong about the supposed *clue* Ben had slipped into the note? What if they had already killed him? He knew he had to continue, but he felt totally alone and helpless. The headache began to pound unmercifully. He noticed a crowd milling about farther up Dock Street as two young boys came running past him.

"Come on, if you want to see a dead body, you have to hurry!" the older boy cried out to his younger comrade.

"You better not be lying this time," replied the younger boy, trying to keep up with his friend.

A sudden dread crept over Jefferson. Instinctively he followed the boys toward the assembled crowd. Jefferson's body contracted in pain. He stumbled forward, his eyes glued to a cart. A motionless body lay inside, covered by a soiled and tattered blanket. Two Philadelphia police officers stood nearby, unmoved by the common occurrence. An older woman was explaining for the second time how she had found the body.

Jefferson walked past both officers, staring at the covered body. He was frozen with fear and could not lift the tattered blanket.

"Here now, what ya think yar doin', mister? Yar interferin' with police business," the officer scolded in a slight Scottish accent.

Jefferson continued to stare at the body, his mind racing in a thousand directions. "Sorry, Officer. My name is Thomas Jefferson." His eyes never left the body.

"It's a pleasure to meet ya, Mr. Jefferson. Me friend Sean was one of the officers that came to yar aid at the Tucker house last Tuesday. He told me all about ya and yar friends' heroics."

Jefferson shook his aching head, slowly recovering from the shock of the body before him. "Was your friend the officer who saved Mr. Hancock?" Jefferson asked, attempting to refocus, his eyes still transfixed on the motionless form.

"Aye. First time he ever shot at a real person. He was awfully nervous," replied the young officer.

"He is to be commended for his heroic action."

The officer's face beamed with pride from Jefferson's compliment. "I will tell 'em tonight."

"What's the story here, Officer...?"

"Duncan McCabe," he introduced himself to Jefferson. "Young boy, no older than sixteen, I would say."

Jefferson's eyes finally turned toward the officer. A sense of relief began to creep into his mind. "Did you say a young boy?"

"Yes, sir. Unfortunately, we find 'em all the time. The woman talkin' to me partner says she found him about an hour ago, behind several boxes in that alley." Officer McCabe pointed to the end of the narrow alley.

A shudder of relief exploded through his body, quickly replaced with a new, gnawing pain, as he was unable to assuage building guilt for feeling such exuberance. The body was not Ben's, and yet another young life in Philadelphia had been snuffed out at such a young age.

"Mind if I take a look, Officer McCabe?" Jefferson's heart raced at the thought of what he might find.

"Not at all, sir." McCabe led Jefferson to the cart and removed the blanket covering the body.

"Billy!" Jefferson exclaimed softly, recognizing the face immediately.

"Did ya know the boy, Mr. Jefferson?"

"Met him last night. He delivered a message to a friend of mine at City Tavern. Whoever sent him to deliver the message must have murdered him."

"Murder? Why do ya think it was murder?" Philadelphia police were used to finding dead bodies, but in most cases, they were attributed to illness, starvation, or exposure to the elements. Murders were uncommon.

"You see the bruising around the neck?" Jefferson placed his hands over the bruises. "Whoever did this had very big hands and was extremely strong."

McCabe mimicked Jefferson's actions and cursed himself for not noticing it first. "I think ya're right, Mr. Jefferson. I don't know why I didn't see that before. It's been a tough day around here. Now we'ave two murders."

"Two murders?"

"Yeah, couple blocks from here, bartender at the *Dead Dog Tavern* was found in the storage room, neck sliced from ear to ear. There was blood everywhere. Two drunks just sat there all night and drank for free. Told some crazy story. Nobody believed."

Jefferson's mind was spinning. His head continued to ache. Could he be that lucky? "What kind of crazy story?"

"Somethin' about a beautiful woman replacin' the regular bartender and some customer collapsin' and bein' hauled out of the tavern. They believe those men and the woman somehow murdered the bartender. I've heard some whoppers, but those two might hold the record."

Jefferson's body was literally shaking as he interrupted Officer McCabe. "They said a man passed out and was dragged from the tavern. Do you think they could identify the man?"

"I don't think so, Mr. Jefferson. They were mighty drunk, them two."

"I'm sorry, continue your story." Jefferson's mind was entertaining numerous scenarios.

"Soon thereafter, the beautiful bartender leaves, puttin' the two drunks in charge of the tavern. Later that night, probably about two in the mornin', a couple of regulars got suspicious and discovered Fred, the bartender, in the back room. As I said, his throat was slit from ear to ear. If somebody hadn't warned one of our watch officers, the crowd would have torn those two apart. Apparently, everybody liked Fred."

"Where are these two drunks now?"

"Walnut Street Jail. The coroner has gone missing. I understand Sheriff Otto will be handlin' everythin'."

Jefferson's mind briefly pictured the coroner, a broken Joseph Giersch, being ridden out of town, but quickly returned to the present. "Officer McCabe, I must speak with those men immediately!"

"Mr. Jefferson, ya seem awfully agitated. Is somethin' wrong?" McCabe's eyes indicated a willingness to help.

Jefferson felt he could use an ally about now and decided to tell McCabe everything he knew about Ben's kidnapping.

Rather than doubt Jefferson's deductions, McCabe reacted immediately, yelling to his partner, "Oliver, finish up here! I have to go with Mr. Jefferson right now."

Oliver's cries of protest fell on deaf ears as both men quickly mounted their horses and sped toward the Walnut Street Jail.

Thomas Jefferson was not the only early riser. Deborah Johnson was awake at dawn, although technically she might have never fallen asleep. All doubts had been removed concerning her feelings for Ben Cushman. She loved him. It felt good to finally admit it. She knew her father and Sarah would dismiss it as just another crush; there had been many since she had reached her teen years. *No one could fall in love that soon,* her father would rationalize. Perhaps it was the extreme circumstances as to their meeting or the uncertainty of the times, a revolution about to entangle an entire country. Whatever the reason, it was no longer possible to deny the fact that she had fallen hard for the rugged Virginian. Deborah was devastated over the thought that she could lose him forever and that she was responsible.

The guilt was beginning to overwhelm her. She had almost told Thomas Jefferson everything, but she couldn't bear to see the disappointment or anger in his eyes once she communicated her treachery. Besides, Deborah had no doubt in her mind that if Rourke found out, David Johnson would be the next murder victim. Knowing that Lydia Ames had lied to her only reinforced her decision. The letter was meant as much for her as it was Jefferson. Sarah had been right all along: Lydia Ames had used her.

Convincing herself there was no other way out, she began to ponder the improbable rescue of Ben Cushman.

The pleasant fragrance of the expensive French perfume permeated the bed. Her warm, soft body pressed lightly against his back. Listening closely to the rhythmic sound of her gentle breathing, he decided to lie still and not wake her. As if reading his mind, Lydia Ames took a deep breath and began to stir. She wrapped her long lithe arms around his body and squeezed him playfully. "Good morning, darling. Are you recovered from last night?" she whispered softly into his ear.

Rourke laughed and turned quickly so they embraced each other face-to-face. "You were amazing, as usual, my dear, but we mustn't sleep the day away. I have packed my favorite instruments and can't wait to start on Cushman." Giving her a quick peck on the cheek, Rourke rolled out of bed.

"Come back here. I'm not through with you yet," she purred seductively, throwing back the comforter, revealing a scandalous negligee that could only be purchased in Paris.

Rourke balked, looking at the most perfectly formed body he had ever seen. Lydia Ames defined the word *temptress*. She was Helen of Troy and Cleopatra all rolled into one. But like her ancient counterparts, her ambition trumped her beauty and, therefore, made her untrustworthy. Rourke knew he was playing with fire, but he loved the heat. Besides, no one had ever gotten the better of him, and he wasn't about to let this siren be the first.

"Sorry, my love, but pleasure before pleasure." Rourke chuckled lightly at his clever play on words. "Cushman will lose any remaining arrogance after I'm through with him today."

"If he lives through it," Lydia commented as she resigned herself to the fact that there would be no more lovemaking and gracefully climbed out of bed.

"Oh, he'll live through it. I'll see to that. I want him to suffer at least till the end of the week."

"Then go slow. You don't have to use all your torture devices today," she stated with emphasis on the word *today*. Lydia watched Rourke finish dressing. She marveled at his complexities. On one hand, he was Philadelphia's richest and most eligible bachelor. He could have any woman he wanted, and that included most of the married ones. Yet on the other hand, he got great pleasure in conducting ancient tortures.

Lydia thought she understood his idiosyncrasies; after all, she was no saint and, like Rourke, believed strongly in the Machiavellian ideal that the end justified the means. However, that was where Rourke and Lydia were different. Oh, Rourke believed in the same Machiavellian philosophy, but what gave him the greatest joy was completely destroying any opposition as he clawed his way to the top. More than anything, he loved to watch those people suffer, both mentally and physically. He would rather torture Cushman than make love to her. Very few people knew of this dark side, but those that did thought him quite mad. Lydia preferred the Roman philosopher Seneca's explanation: *There is no great genius without some touch of madness.*

While Rourke dressed, he explained in detail what he had in store for Cushman today. The giddy, graphic descriptions of the various torture devices continued into breakfast, causing Lydia to poke at her eggs. Undeterred, Rourke wolfed down his breakfast of bacon, eggs, and cheese.

The sudden pounding of footsteps interrupted their conversation. Edward Van Dyke burst through the door.

"Van Dyke, what the hell are you doing?" Rourke's penetrating glare halted Van Dyke midstride.

"Boss, we got a problem," he blurted out, gasping for air.

Rourke immediately grew angry. "Not Cushman?"

"No, boss, no! It's the Camden warehouse. It's on fire, and you can see it from Front Street!" Camden, New Jersey, sat directly across from Philadelphia. Although it was not nearly the size of Philadelphia, it was linked economically. Vigorous trade between the two had existed for close to a hundred years. Hundreds of ferries operated between the two cities, and Rourke owned close to fifty of them. His one warehouse on the New Jersey side of the river was the largest and busiest.

Rourke wasted no time, immediately shouting orders to Van Dyke. "Get to the dock. Have one of the ferries ready to go. I'll be there in three minutes." Rourke looked at Lydia; she wasn't sure if the disappointed look on his face was because of the fire or the fact he couldn't torture Cushman.

"Don't worry, go save your warehouse. I'm going to follow up with several of the girls. We only need fifteen more addresses."

"Very well. Get word to Tompkins. Use my carriage if you have to. Tell him that he probably won't be relieved until tonight," Rourke finished his command as he bolted from the room, furious that his Sunday torture of Benjamin Cushman would have to be delayed.

Cushman's night had been uneventful. They had kept him blindfolded and tied to the chair, making it difficult to sleep. He debated whether his lack of sleep was from his uncomfortable condition or Tompkins's snoring. Although battered and bruised, he managed to sleep in short periods and felt better than expected. He believed his injuries were mostly bruises, maybe a broken nose. His will to survive was still strong as his mind continued to plot an escape.

The creaking stairway alerted Cushman that Tompkins was probably returning or, worse, his boss was back with Van Dyke to begin round 2. He was pleasantly surprise when he caught the sweet aroma of hot coffee.

"Listen to me, Cushman. The boss doesn't want you dying just yet. Me, I'd just as soon shoot you right now. But I got my orders, so this is what we're gonna do." Tompkins removed the blindfold as he talked to Cushman.

Ben saw the tray on the small table; it had a mug of coffee, an apple, and a large piece of bread on it. "I'm gonna untie your wrists. If you try anything funny, I will slit your throat. I don't care what R—I don't care what the boss says. You hear me?"

Cushman caught the slipup. Van Dyke had almost made the same mistake. For whatever reason, their boss didn't want them using his name. Cushman was quite sure that when they were done with him, he would be killed. He found it hard to understand why his captor wanted to remain anonymous. "You seem like a pretty smart guy Tompkins. Why are you taking orders from that lunatic you call boss?"

"How'd you know my name?" Tompkins sounded genuinely surprised.

"You blindfolded me, you didn't stuff my ears with cotton. I heard you talking to Van Dick," Cushman casually explained while taking long sips of coffee.

Tompkins chuckled at Cushman's nickname for Edward Van Dyke. "Just eat. The boss wants you well-fed and alert. He is eager to test out some of his new gadgets."

"You mean torture devices. Just say it. Look, your boss is nuts. Who goes around torturing people for pleasure? This isn't the Spanish Inquisition."

"Spanish what?"

Not well-read, are you? Cushman thought. *I suppose most assassins aren't well educated.* "Inquisition, the Spanish Inquisition. The Spanish king Ferdinand and queen Isabella began the Inquisition in 1478. The goal was to make sure everyone in Spain was practicing Catholic orthodoxy. So any Jews, Muslims, or Protestants were forced to convert or else."

"Or else what?" Tompkins actually sounded interested.

"Or else they were tortured until they converted, and if they didn't convert, they were usually burned at the stake."

"Far as I'm concerned, they can do what they want with them Jews. Nothing but trouble," Tompkins noted while sipping his coffee.

"You seem more like a real soldier. How come you're not in the militia?" Cushman probed.

"Got kicked out of the New Jersey militia. Guess I wasn't too good at takin' orders. I was the best shot in my unit, and no one could outride me," Tompkins bragged, pulling up the other chair and sitting across from Cushman.

"So how'd you end up here?" Cushman tore into the bread.

"A friend of mine introduced me to Van Dyke, said he could get me steady work and good pay. We do jobs for him in New Jersey. This is the first time we've worked in Philly," Tompkins grunted.

"So you were involved in the assassination plot at City Tavern?" Cushman arched his eyebrows.

Tompkins hesitated, remembering Rourke's promise that Cushman would be dead in a couple of days. "Yeah, I was there. Our job was to kill the assassins after they finished. Pretty smart, eh? No leads to the boss. Only problem is, they never came out. Guess that was you that stopped 'em?" Tompkins was feeling pretty proud of his involvement. "Wouldn't suppose you'd give me the name of the fellow that helped you at City Tavern?"

Cushman's foggy mind was shocked. *How did Tompkins know about Major Hall? Someone inside or maybe the police?* "No. It was pretty much me, but now that you know everything, I'd watch my back if I were you, Tompkins," Cushman continued to press the henchman.

Tompkins's face revealed that Cushman was right. "Don't worry about me, Cushman. I wasn't born yesterday."

"Maybe so, Tompkins, but I've seen a lot of lunatics in my day, and your boss takes the cake." Cushman finished his meal and downed the last drop of coffee. "When you're done here, I'd be very, very careful."

Without saying a word, Tompkins removed the tray and carefully retied Cushman's hands. Replacing the blindfold from behind, he couldn't see that Ben Cushman was smiling.

The traditional Sunday breakfast at the Johnson home was started soon after Deborah's mother had died. Deborah's father, David Johnson, wasn't much of a churchgoing man, so he tried to make up for his absence during the week by spending every Sunday with his daughter.

They would start with a huge breakfast consisting of thin slices of ham, eggs, smoked fish, and a variety of sweet pastries.

Because of the unusual circumstances of the family, each member was responsible for preparing a portion of the Sunday-morning tradition. David Johnson would fry the ham and eggs, Sarah would prepare the fish and coffee, and Deborah would travel one block to purchase the pastries at a small German bakery.

"Father, everything looks delicious." Deborah announced her return from the bakery.

"The pastries smell heavenly. Just out of the oven?" David Johnson smiled and leaned in to give his daughter a kiss on the cheek.

"Everything's ready. Let's eat!" Sarah chimed in as she delicately placed a fillet of fish on each of the three plates. "Cider, coffee, or both?" she added, adroitly handling a pot of coffee in one hand and a pitcher of cider in the other.

The three sat down to the morning feast. Conversation, as usual, began with politics. Soon David Johnson was railing against the rumored Declaration of Independence, probably the worst-kept secret in all of Philadelphia.

Deborah decided now was a perfect time to change the subject. "Father, just how close are you to Patrick Rourke?" Sarah's head perked up immediately. Rourke or Lydia Ames had never been discussed at Sunday breakfast.

David Johnson appeared somewhat uncomfortable but answered anyway. "Well, as you know, he is one of my best customers. Our pleasant circumstances are the result of customers like Patrick Rourke."

"And you're comfortable with his politics, correct?"

"Well, yes. As you know, we are both strong supporters of King George. Patrick has commented many times of how valuable the information you gather has been to our cause. Is something bothering you, Deborah?"

"No, but there are rumors that Mr. Rourke is not above using violence to get his way," Deborah stated cautiously.

Johnson hesitated; he, too, had heard the rumors. He had seen Rourke's temper firsthand yet had never witnessed any displays of violence. But Johnson had always thought that Patrick Rourke's eyes told a different story, that he was capable of almost anything. Had it not been for Lydia Ames, Johnson would have stopped seeing Rourke, except to do business. "I have never heard of anything unseemly concerning Patrick," he stated unconvincingly.

"What about the harpy?" Sarah entered the conversation, eager to expose Lydia Ames as the witch she felt she was.

"Now, Sarah, if you're referring to Ms. Lydia, I think you have her all wrong."

"I don't think so, Mr. Johnson. She's got evil eyes. I don't trust her at all," Sarah declared without hesitation.

"Father, I'm afraid I'd have to agree with Sarah," Deborah added.

"But, Deborah, you and Lydia have gotten along wonderfully. I have never even seen you two disagree."

Deborah had to tread carefully. Although her father knew of the relationship between his daughter and Rourke, he was unaware of its depth. "As you know, Father, I have passed on information to both of them. I suppose if this were a real war, I would be a spy. Most of the information I have passed along is fairly harmless. However, recently I have come across certain evidence that proves that Lydia and Rourke have been lying to me and that they are involved in more than just a little harmless spying."

"What type of evidence?"

"I think they were behind the murders at City Tavern." Deborah still couldn't bring herself to tell the whole truth. She awaited her father's reply, which she anticipated to be along the lines of "How could you make such outrageous accusations without proof?"

Instead, David Johnson's only remark was, "Is that so?" After Tuesday night's deadly rampage at City Tavern, he had forbidden Deborah to return to work. As usual, she had disobeyed him and he did nothing. Once he realized his stubborn daughter would not listen to him, he did the next best thing. He persuaded his fellow shareholders to increase security at the popular tavern. Two full-time, gun-carrying guards were hired without any fanfare. Undercover at all times, they had the job of protecting the employees first, and customers second. In addition, Johnson began making shadowy inquiries into the events of Tuesday, and one name kept popping up, Patrick Rourke.

"Is that all you can say? Your daughter was almost killed, and two of your associates may have been responsible." Sarah had never spoken in such a forceful manner, but her protective instincts were in full gear.

Deborah smiled at her unlikely ally and added, "Father, I don't trust them. I am sure they are capable of doing very bad things. I just want you to be careful. I don't want anything to happen to you."

"Listen, you two, I appreciate your concern, but I'm sure you're both overreacting to Patrick and Lydia. But if it makes you feel better, I will promise to be extra careful."

Deborah reached over and grasped her father's hand, squeezing it gently. "Thank you, Father. I know I am right about them."

"Deborah, now, I have to ask you a favor. Sarah, you as well. Lydia is stopping by today. Can I count on you two being on your best behavior?" David arched his eyebrows high, signaling his desired response.

Both girls nodded and continued to eat their Sunday breakfast.

Although he had ridden by it hundreds of times, Thomas Jefferson had never visited the relatively new Walnut Street Jail. Designed by Philadelphia's most famous architect, Robert Smith, it was open for business early in 1774. Ben Franklin had always bragged that Smith was the best architect in the colonies. Of course, Smith had designed and built Franklin's home. The U-shaped jail was considered a model of efficiency. Inmates from the overcrowded and run-down old city jail soon had the Walnut Street Jail bursting at the seams. The fastest-growing city in America also had the fastest-growing prison population.

Constable Duncan McCabe led Jefferson into the bowels of the large prison. They stopped at the desk of a lone prison guard outside the cafeteria. Jefferson heard a commotion that sounded remarkably like an all-out barroom brawl. The guard seemed unmoved by the interior racket. "Matthew, this is Mr. Jefferson. He needs to speak to the two drunks from the *Dead Dog Tavern*."

"Nice to meet you, Mr. Jefferson. I like your politics. You tell old George to leave us alone." The rail-thin guard stood while speaking clearly, a large plug of tobacco resting firmly between cheek and gum.

"Nice to meet you, Matthew. Aren't you concerned with what's going on inside?" The noise level was increasing.

"Nah, just blowing off steam. Happens at least twice a week," Matthew stated calmly while unlocking the door. As the door swung open, it introduced a scene right out of Dante's *Inferno*—at least fifty inmates, fists flailing, with bodies flying everywhere. Men were screaming in pain, others just screaming profanity-laced invectives at the top of their lungs. The scientist in Jefferson wondered about the animalistic impulses displayed by men in a prison setting. The reformer wondered about an appropriate penal system of rehabilitation versus pure punishment.

THE SIGNERS

The explosion pierced his ears and caused the riot to halt immediately. Matthew, the prison guard, had fired a pistol into the roof. A startled Jefferson looked on in amazement as every inmate stopped fighting. "The two men from the *Dead Dog*, I need to see you, *now*!"

From different corners of the room, two men began to work their way through the mass of prisoners. From the left side of the room, a young man who looked to be in his twenties limped forward. His lip was bleeding and had already swollen to double its size. The other young man approach from the opposite side of the room, his shirt torn half off his back, but otherwise he appeared to be unscathed. The door was quickly locked behind the two prisoners, and to Jefferson's amazement, the brawl did not resume. Matthew, the jailer, noticed Jefferson's surprised look. "Told you, Mr. Jefferson, just blowing off some steam."

McCabe escorted the two prisoners to a small table. "You two in here for what happened at the *Dead Dog Tavern* on Friday night?"

"We didn't kill Fred, if that's what you're asking!" Bloody Lip stated emphatically.

"He's tellin' the truth. We didn't kill nobody," Torn Shirt added. Jefferson resisted his instinct to correct the man's use of a double negative.

"Maybe you did, maybe you didn't. This is Mr. Thomas Jefferson. He has some questions to ask the both of you."

Before Jefferson could talk, Bloody Lip injected, "We know who Mr. Jefferson is. Mr. Jefferson, please believe us, we didn't kill Fred."

"Well, first of all, gentlemen, please introduce yourselves, and second of all, I just may believe you."

Bloody Lip turned out to be Duane, and Torn Shirt was Adam.

"Tell me about Friday, when Fred disappeared."

Duane started, "Neither one of us was working on Friday. We went to the *Dead Dog* early, about ten or eleven in the morning."

"Closer to ten," interrupted Adam.

Duane shot his friend a nasty look and continued, "We were just drinking beer, no whiskey."

"Yet." Adam did it again.

Another nasty look. "The point I'm trying to make is that we got drunk, but that was later on, after everyone had left."

This time Adam just nodded, confirming what Duane said.

"Fred had served us about three beers when two men walked in. They stood down near the storage room. Fred went down to wait on 'em, and after a few minutes, they all went back into the storage area."

"Can either of you describe the two men?" Jefferson asked.

Adam responded first. "Well, sir, the one man was sort of normal. Normal height, about like me, not really heavy, but not skinny like the guard over there." Adam pointed toward Matthew. "But the other one, he was different. Not real tall, but he was thick, big back, big arms, and big head. Looked like he could break a man in half."

Duane nodded in agreement, then continued his story. "Fred was gone about five to ten minutes."

"Weren't you worried something had happened to him?" Jefferson questioned the two.

"No. Sometimes Fred will go into the back room to throw dice," Duane answered. "The girl arrived a few minutes later, acting like she had worked there forever."

"Had you ever seen her before?" Jefferson was sure he was on to something important.

"No, but I have to say, I ain't seen a girl so pretty in all my days," Adam offered.

"That's true. She was as beautiful as a painting," countered Duane. "She said she was fillin' in for Fred, that he had to run an errand for the two men. Not long afterward, two new men came in. They sat at a table across the room."

"Were you able to get a good look at them?" Jefferson began to shake as both Duane and Adam went on to describe Ben Cushman and Norman Bindernagel from the clothes they were wearing to the color of their eyes.

"The man that collapsed had the greenest eyes I have ever seen. Could see them clear across the bar," Adam stated without hesitation.

THE SIGNERS

Jefferson had no doubt that the two were telling the truth, yet he had to be thorough. "What happened next?" Jefferson asked dejectedly, knowing what was coming.

"The waitress served them coffee. I remember 'cause I figured 'em for businessmen. You know, not drinking that early in the morning," responded Adam.

"A few minutes later, old Green Eyes passed out right at the table," added Duane.

"Did both men drink coffee? Did you see the waitress put anything into the coffee?"

Both men agreed that she poured two coffees, but neither saw anything unusual.

"After he collapsed, the other man yelled something, and the two men who had come in earlier appeared and carried him into the back. The waitress came back and bought us a beer, apologizing for all the commotion."

"And a whiskey," added Adam.

"Yes, that was when we started drinking whiskey. She said the man's partner took him outside to get some air. That he passes out all the time and there is nothing to worry about. After a while, she left the bottle of whiskey in front of us and said we can have it for free if we'd just watch the place while she ran home to check on her mother. She never came back."

"Ain't real proud of what happened next. Anybody that came in, we acted like we owned the place and poured everything for free," Adam conceded. "We got stone-cold drunk ourselves. Mr. Jefferson, we ain't no killers. Neither one of us is perfect, but we couldn't do what happened to Fred."

"That's the God's honest truth, Mr. Jefferson. You gotta believe us," added Duane.

Jefferson felt sorry for the two; he had no doubt Bindernagel manipulated them. Their story had filled in several blanks, especially using a knockout drug to subdue Cushman. It was a well-thought-out plan and carried out without a hitch. As a bonus, they were able to cast suspicions away from themselves and place it on the two innocent drunks. "Gentlemen, I believe you. I'm going to present some additional information to Constable McCabe here. I think after he has conferred with his superiors, you should be able to walk out of here as free men. If not, I will be happy to represent you both, free of charge, in your coming trial."

Duane shook Jefferson's hand, but Adam embraced the tall Virginian with tears in his eyes. "Thank you, Mr. Jefferson, thank you."

"She's been down there, flirting away like a schoolgirl, for near an hour," Sarah commented as she paced back and forth across Deborah's well-furnished bedroom. "You seem way too calm. I thought you said you don't trust her. Why are you so calm?"

Deborah smiled at Sarah, finally ratcheting up enough courage to tell someone the truth about her involvement with Patrick Rourke and Lydia Ames. She told Sarah everything, including her role in the assassination attempt at City Tavern and Cushman's kidnapping. Sarah listened in stunned silence as Deborah recounted her fall into the abyss. When she was finished, they were both crying, embracing like the sisters they were.

"Can I count on your help?" Deborah asked between the sobs.

"You know you can," Sarah responded, gently stroking Deborah's hair.

"Deborah," the voice of her father echoed from downstairs and interrupted the girls.

"Yes, Father?" she answered, dabbing softly at her tear-soaked eyes.

"Could you come down for a minute? Lydia wants to say hello."

"Be right there." Deborah gave Sarah a reassuring wink and quickly walked downstairs.

She found them sitting in the parlor room, a private and cozy meeting place, just off the front foyer.

Lydia was dressed casually for a Sunday; a multicolored shawl covered a white silk blouse, and her ankle-length black skirt looked

THE SIGNERS

brand-new. She wore her jet-black hair pinned up, revealing her long thin neck. "Deborah, darling, it is good to see you."

David Johnson kissed his daughter on the cheek and whispered, "Be nice," and walked away. "I'll prepare a lunchtime snack. Why don't you two talk awhile?"

Lydia's smile seemed contrived. Deborah had always looked up to her as the perfect woman. Now it was like they had never met before. Deborah's acceptance of Lydia's treachery was liberating; she saw through her deception with amazing clarity.

"Lydia, you look beautiful. How on earth do you ever manage to look so young?"

Lydia was somewhat taken aback. She didn't know whether to take Deborah's words as a compliment or some kind of mocking condescension. She was always used to being in control, even with Rourke. It was an uncomfortable feeling. She gave Deborah a serious look and asked, "Do you have the rest of the addresses?"

Deborah stared at Lydia with contempt as she thought of Ben being tortured by Rourke. "I'm sorry, Lydia," she said softly, "the last couple of nights has not been very productive."

"What do you mean?" Lydia looked agitated. "I thought you only had ten or so to gather."

"Yes, but some of the men haven't come into City Tavern, or they were not very talkative if they did. You told me not to push, that we had plenty of time."

Lydia reined in her anger; she had instructed Deborah accordingly. "Yes, that may be true, but the last time we talked, you indicated you could get all the assigned addresses."

"Has your deadline changed? Should I try to get the remaining addresses as soon as possible?" Deborah asked innocently.

"Yes, yes, of course, as soon as possible." Lydia took a deep breath; she didn't want to alarm Deborah.

"Very well. I work tomorrow, Tuesday, and Wednesday. I should have them all by then," Deborah suggested confidently.

Lydia did some calculating. She doubted she could keep Rourke from killing Cushman, but it wouldn't be till Wednesday or Thursday before Cushman would be missed. "Very well, Deborah, but I must have all of them by Thursday. If you can't do that, I will have to get someone else."

"No, Thursday shouldn't be a problem." Deborah forced a smile.

"Well, then, on to a more joyful subject. How is your friend Mr. Cushman." Lydia's tone indicated she thought their relationship was growing.

"He had to run an errand out of town. He was supposed to be back today." Deborah's frown showed worry.

Now it was Lydia's turn to worry. Van Dyke had specifically stated that Billy had seen both Deborah and Jefferson read the letter. *Did he lie to Van Dyke? If he did, then he most certainly got what he deserved.* "He hasn't shown up yet. I've heard of some flooding…" Lydia hoped to plant some seeds, if indeed the boy had lied.

"I was worried last night, but thank God, Ben was able to deliver a message to me. He has been delayed. However, he is safe. Actually, the message was meant for Mr. Jefferson, but he had a boy deliver it to me." Deborah beamed as she emphasized *me*.

Lydia smiled proudly; her plan had succeeded without a hitch. She couldn't wait to tease Rourke about what a genius she had become. "I hope you were able to get the message to Mr. Jefferson and ease his worries."

"Yes. He was at City Tavern at that time. He, too, is relieved that Ben is safe and will return soon," Deborah suggested, hoping Lydia didn't see through her forced smile.

Lydia relaxed. Perhaps she read too much into Deborah's greeting. Everything was going smoothly; her part in the plan had come off perfectly.

Deborah also relaxed. Her plan was to buy as much time as possible to find Cushman. The next part was a big gamble, but it was the only thing she could think of. It had to work.

Chapter 22

In general, the art of government consists of taking as much money as possible from one party of the citizens to give to the other.

—Voltaire

Sunday, June 30, 1776
Philadelphia

The Pennsylvania statehouse stood empty, majestically watching out over the entire neighborhood. Under its sturdy roof, the Second Continental Congress had managed to keep a struggling nation together during the past tumultuous year. Tomorrow, Monday, July 1, 1776, the Congress would determine the most significant resolution, perhaps in the history of time, but most certainly in the short history of British North America. It came down to a simple idea: independence or no independence.

Possibly the most important individual to the coming debate, Thomas Jefferson rode quickly by the regal redbrick structure. Had it not been for the clock tower striking four o'clock at that very moment, Jefferson might not have lifted his head to gaze at the monumental building. He had been busy since leaving the Walnut Street Jail. Returning to the Graff house for certain supplies, he had hired two local boys to deliver urgent messages to several of his colleagues. Jefferson was riding east on Chestnut to meet with these men. He only prayed that the boys were able to locate all of them. The clock tower reminded him that he would be a few minutes late. Grabbing firmly to the reins, he urged his steed to go faster.

Jefferson arrived at the boardinghouse three minutes later. Situated directly across from City Tavern, the boardinghouse was run by Mrs. Sarah Yard. She played housemother to the entire Massachusetts congressional delegation. Jefferson had been a guest many times. A comfortable parlor room was used to entertain guests, and tonight the men filling the room were impatiently waiting as the quiet Virginian burst through the door.

"Thomas, we got your message. What is this emergency, and why so secretive?" John Adams wasted little time getting to the point.

"Gentlemen, thank you for coming under such bizarre circumstances." Jefferson looked around the room. They were all here. He had chosen the men carefully. He wanted men with some military background or at least men who could handle a gun. In addition, he chose men who owed Ben Cushman their lives. Abraham Clark and John Hart, both from nearby New Jersey, had been at City Tavern, targets of the assassins, as was John Adams. Jefferson didn't want to ask John Hancock because of his important position as the president of the Congress. But Cushman had saved Hancock's life, and his military background was essential. What he had planned was very dangerous. "I apologize for the secrecy and urgency, but I'm afraid time is our enemy."

Jefferson rapidly reviewed the situation involving Ben Cushman, leaving out no details. The mood in the room went from impatience to anger as Jefferson went on to map out his plan to save his best friend. Men who moments before were preparing for the most important debate in their lifetimes were now focused on one thing: the rescue of Benjamin Cushman. "I know it's a long shot, and I am positive it will be dangerous. I don't know whom else to turn to. The police would think I'm crazy, and we all know there are many Tories among their ranks. I will make one promise: I hold everyone here in extreme high regard, and I promise I will continue to if you choose not to help. What I'm asking you all to do is irresponsible, but I know Ben would do the same for me."

"Thomas, you ask us all to take a leap of faith to help your friend. Yes, there will be danger, and perhaps sacrifice. How is that any different from what we will do tomorrow as we will ask a nation to take a leap of faith, which will also produce danger and demand sacrifice? Have no fear, my friend. We will do whatever it takes," John Adams said as each man nodded in agreement.

"Gentlemen, as much as I agree with Mr. Adams, I think I can recruit someone with the proper background to lead our little rescue army," Hancock stated.

All eyes focused on Hancock, and it was Jefferson who quietly asked, "Major Hall?"

"Yes, if I can locate him."

Lydia Ames waved goodbye to Deborah from the step of her carriage. She pressed her body close to David Johnson, purposely lingering longer than proper society would allow, and gave him a kiss on the lips. With a smile and a seductive wink, she slipped gracefully into the carriage. Her hand continued to grip his as the carriage began to roll away. Lydia congratulated herself; she was controlling David Johnson like a puppet master. Deborah, on the other hand, was becoming something of a problem. She sensed her attitude had changed, probably because of her involvement with Cushman. *Well, that would all change soon.* When Cushman was gone, Deborah would either come back into the fold or Rourke would deal with her the way he dealt with all disloyal employees. She felt sorry for Deborah. *Such great potential, but she has made her choice.* Rourke had wanted to deal with Deborah for some time now, but Lydia had defended her as someone she could work with. At that moment, Lydia decided to defend her no more and to let Rourke make the decision.

She immediately felt better. With the pressure of the decision lifted, she stuck her head out the window and yelled to the carriage driver. "We have to make a short stop at the warehouse. You know which one." The driver nodded and urged the two-horse team into action.

No one looked twice as the dark-skinned boy emerged from the stable across the street. His baggy cotton shirt was tucked loosely into even baggier wool pants. His long dark hair was pulled up under a broad straw hat. The hat was pulled down to his eyebrows, covering most of his delicate face. He looked like a hundred other servants running errands in the large city. Except this servant was riding a horse, and if anyone was to look close enough, they would discover that this servant was not a boy. It wasn't a perfect disguise, but they didn't have much time to come up with anything better. The hope was that Lydia would lead her to Rourke, and Rourke would lead her to Cushman. Despite the risk, Sarah Johnson was willing to help her half-sister.

As much as Patrick Rourke hated Benjamin Franklin, he had to admit that without his influence, it would have been much worse. By the time Rourke had crossed the river, the Camden volunteer fire brigade had been at work for over an hour. It was modeled after Franklin's Philadelphia Fire Department design, and the Camden volunteers met once a month to discuss fire safety and firefighting techniques. Like any other city that had firefighting volunteers, the method was the same. Leather, fire buckets were used to carry water to the fire. A brigade line was formed as each firefighter passed the bucket of water to the next man in line. Another line would use the same method to return the empty bucket to the water source. To keep the men fresh, they would change lines every ten minutes. Since Rourke's warehouse was right on the Delaware River, the water source was not far, and more than one line was formed. The warehouse suffered damage, but the structure was saved, and most of the contents were unharmed. Rourke and Van Dyke walked through the building, assessing the damage. It appeared to be minimal, but they still had half the warehouse to examine.

"Hire more guards for the next few days," Rourke ordered Van Dyke. "Dirty scavengers will think they can come in here and take what they want. Make sure the men patrol with rifles. That will keep the vermin out."

"We owe those volunteers a great debt. Without them, everything would have been lost," Van Dyke suggested.

"Yeah, yeah, that's what they volunteer for. They're just doing their jobs. Make sure none of the fire brigade hangs around and tries to steal anything." Rourke's mood was still sour. "Make sure you keep a ferry here also. I may still want to go to the warehouse and visit Cushman!" Rourke growled.

His thoughts turned to Ben Cushman. His mood quickly brightened. There might still be time to have some fun. If not, then it would be tomorrow, a full day of breaking Cushman. Rourke's mood continued to brighten.

The two strong horses managed to negotiate the slight decline effortlessly as the carriage made its way onto the warehouse property. Rourke had indeed increased the security around the vacant property. Three armed guards were in view, patrolling around the warehouse. One of the men ran up to greet Rourke's carriage.

"Good afternoon, ma'am. We were expecting Mr. Rourke. Has there been a problem?" The guard looked like a stereotypical criminal element that frequented the worst riverfront taverns in Philadelphia. A mouthful of rotten teeth might have been his best feature. His pockmarked face was littered with scars of all shapes and sizes. The top half of his left ear looked like it had been bitten off. His tattered clothing reeked of a foul odor that Lydia found as repugnant as anything she had ever smelled.

She quickly brushed him aside, ignoring his question, and headed for the main door. Her original intent was to summon Tompkins to the main floor and deliver the order from Rourke. But upon her entering the warehouse, a strange desire to see Cushman overcame her. It was as if the stairs were daring her to visit the bound captive. Three more of Rourke's Ruffians were stationed inside as one of the men came to greet her.

Before he could speak, Lydia demanded, "Take me upstairs. I assume Tompkins is still with the prisoner?"

"Yes, ma'am," replied the thoroughly intimidated guard.

Cushman heard the multiple footsteps approaching. A chill went up his spine, and he began to anticipate the worst. Listening intently, he heard a soft knock on the door, followed by Tompkins's footsteps. He heard whispering but couldn't make out any voices. Soon there was only silence, an occasional creak of a loose board; it was as if someone was stalking him. Then it hit him, perfume. The visitor was the same woman who had witnessed his first beating. If she was here, could Van Dick and his lunatic boss be far behind?

"That perfume, I've smelled it before. I just can't place it. How about you come over here and untie me? We can catch up on old times." Cushman decided he had nothing to lose.

Unfortunately, he couldn't see the astonished look on Lydia's face. She quickly recovered and contemplated playing cat-and-mouse with Cushman.

"You obviously enjoy watching me suffer. Is it something I did to you, something I said? How can we be friends if you won't talk to me?" Cushman continued to probe.

"Shut up, Cushman, before I knock out all your teeth!" Tompkins yelled at Cushman, walking quickly toward him.

Lydia raised her hand to stop Tompkins and motioned for him to wait outside the door. He started to protest, but her second gesture was less friendly, so he meekly shuffled out the door.

"I'm sorry, did I get old Tompkins worked up? He really needs to work on controlling his temper."

Lydia so loved a challenge and decided to play with Cushman, but she would play only by her rules. And even though Rourke would eventually have Cushman killed, her instincts told her it was best to keep her identity secret.

"Don't be shy on my account. There's not much I can do in my current situation, unless of course you want to untie me."

Positioned directly behind Cushman, Lydia suddenly seized the rope securing his wrists and gave it a hard tug.

"That's it, just remove the ropes. We can talk like civilized adults," he suggested.

Lydia began to walk her fingers up Cushman's bruised arms. Her long fingernails dug in lightly. She placed her chin on his shoulder; her warm breath softly caressed his ear. Running her fingers slowly through his hair, Lydia slid effortlessly in front of Cushman, hiked up her skirt, and sat on his lap, straddling her legs seductively around his body. She pulled herself close, pressing her ample breasts into Cushman like two long-lost lovers. Stroking his face with both hands, she began kissing him with passion and purpose. Achieving the desired reaction from Cushman, Lydia slowly retreated and smiled. Attempting to disguise her voice with a Southern accent, she softly cooed, "It's unfortunate we had to meet under such circumstances. We could have made sweet love together."

Cushman wasn't sure what he expected from attempting to draw the mysterious woman into conversation, but that certainly wasn't it. Temporarily stunned, he quickly regained his composure. "Sorry, you're just not my type. Too much perfume makes you smell like a prostitute."

Lydia was stunned at first; she had never had a man refuse her advances. She quickly regained her composure and whispered into Cushman's ear. "Too bad, I may have been your only chance of survival. Now that will never happen. Goodbye, Mr. Cushman."

She walked slowly toward the stairs, her anger building. Perhaps Rourke was right; *Cushman was too dangerous.* He had to be dealt with immediately. Smiling to herself, she plotted the perfect means to bringing about his demise. *Might as well have a little fun,* she thought. And test her influence over Rourke.

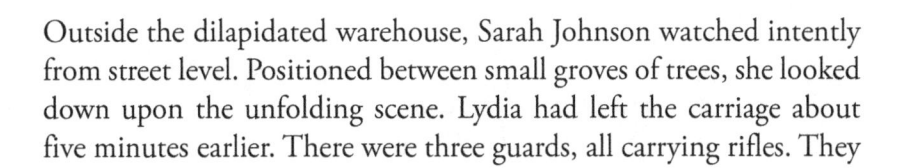

Outside the dilapidated warehouse, Sarah Johnson watched intently from street level. Positioned between small groves of trees, she looked down upon the unfolding scene. Lydia had left the carriage about five minutes earlier. There were three guards, all carrying rifles. They were clearly hired to keep anybody from entering the warehouse. It struck Sarah as odd that the men were dressed like longshoremen, no militia or police uniforms. Why would Lydia Ames visit a run-down warehouse that had obviously been abandoned some time ago? Why would three armed men be patrolling that same warehouse? Could it be that simple? Could this be where Rourke was holding Ben Cushman?

Her pulse racing and sweat beading on her forehead, Sarah made up her mind; she had to learn more. Leaving the relative safety of her concealed position, Sarah walked quickly down the incline dirt road leading to the warehouse complex. *Rotten Teeth* saw her first and approached rapidly, gun leveled directly at her.

"What the hell you doin', boy? Get on out of here now!" *Rotten Teeth* scolded.

Sarah breathed a sigh of relief that her disguise had at least fooled the first guard.

"Sorry, sir, my masta' gave me strict orders to meet him at this here warehouse. He said I got to help unload one of his ships."

"This warehouse hasn't been used to unload ships in years."

"Well, if it ain't used no more, how come y'all are guarding it? Something must be in there." Sarah's confidence grew as she engaged the hired thug.

Rotten Teeth looked at his two colleagues, who had just arrived. Both men quickly noted his look of confusion.

"None of your business what's inside, boy. Now get outta here before I shoot you," Guard 2 hollered. His eye patch made him look like a pirate.

Sarah's first instinct was to run, but she had gone this far and ginned up enough courage to continue the showdown. She looked directly at the *pirate*. "Look here, my masta' is a mean son of a bitch. He will whup me good if I don't show up to unload that ship. He told me it was this warehouse."

All three guards looked at one another, their confusion obviously growing. Van Dyke's orders had been to keep anyone from entering, but most importantly, he didn't want any unwanted attention drawn to them. Killing the slave boy might do just that. "Look, boy, you seem to be a smart kid, but this ain't your warehouse. Our boss has important goods inside that he doesn't want the tax collectors to know about. You understand?" The *pirate* received well-done looks from his coworkers.

"I understand. Your boss is a smuggler. Well, my boss is no Tory, and I sure don't like the British, so your secret's safe with me. But I still need to make sure. Can't I go inside to look around?"

Both guards looked at the *pirate* for directions, Van Dyke's warning about drawing unwanted attention forefront in his mind.

It happened while he was still pondering his next move. The warehouse door burst open with a loud bang. The woman stormed through the door. The look of anger on her face was recognizable from fifty yards away. She marched toward the carriage, situated halfway between their position and the warehouse. All three guards looked her way in terror. They knew her relationship with Rourke, and they knew Rourke's reputation.

Lydia saw the guards surrounding what looked like a young slave boy. "What in God's name are you doing? You are being paid to guard the warehouse, not haggle with some slave boy!" Lydia's face was red with anger as she passed the carriage and continued toward the four-some.

Sarah had recognized her precarious situation immediately yet was frozen. If Lydia recognized her, all would be lost. *Why had she been so bold? Better yet, why had she been so stupid?* Lydia was closing fast, within twenty yards, and Sarah knew her disguise would be worthless if she got any closer. She looked at the three guards with a knowing smile. "Gentleman, I think your masta' is meaner than mine. I'll be goin' now." And with that she began to run up the dirt road and the safety of her horse. Half-expecting to hear the roar of rifle shot, she kept running, only to hear Lydia continue to abuse the three guards.

After delivering the vicious tirade, Lydia paused to listen to the guard's story. Something wasn't right, and now she regretted not having the guards run after the slave boy. The boy was out of sight. She pondered telling Rourke her concern and quickly decided against it, since she had allowed his escape.

"Come, we must hurry," Lydia commanded her driver. "Back to Rourke's." Her thoughts quickly returned to Cushman's rebuke; she would enjoy her revenge, and she knew just how to gain it.

He stood outside the *Dead Dog Tavern*. An examination of the run-down tavern had revealed nothing new. Jefferson looked to the west and calculated at least another hour of daylight. Darkness would be an enemy to their plan, so the next hour or so would be critical. It really was a simple strategy. Army scouts had been using it for centuries, and it was especially simple because they were looking for a fixed position along a narrow corridor. The fixed position would be anywhere they could hide a person, both day and night. The narrow corridor was somewhere along the Delaware River not too far from the *Dead Dog Tavern*. It was Hancock's idea. He had served in a Boston militia known as the Boston Cadets. He had held the rank of colonel, and although he saw no real military action, he had taken to reading as much as possible on the subject. If not a real military man, at least he had read up on modern tactics and strategies. Hancock had used Jefferson's assumptions. Drawing a straight line from the *Dead Dog Tavern* to the Delaware River, they established a center point. From there, they went two miles north and two miles south along the river. Abraham Clark and John Hart would start at the northern point and ride south even though they would be covering territory examined earlier by Jefferson. Meanwhile, John Adams and John Hancock would ride south to north.

Hancock had hired three boys to search for Major Hall; each was given written instructions describing in general their location and a brief description of the rescue plan. Hall was to come immediately. The boys were given different areas to search, and a promised bonus would hopefully ensure their enthusiastic hunt for the secret agent.

Thomas Jefferson, after investigating the *Dead Dog*, would meet them in the middle. There, they would discuss any potential targets. Hopefully they would have a good lead. Of course, everything was hinged upon one main assumption, that Cushman had left a clue in his letter to his friend. Jefferson said a short prayer as he mounted his horse to head for the designated rendezvous point.

Despite almost falling from her horse twice as she sped through the city streets, Sarah Johnson returned home unharmed. Deborah had seen her coming from the upstairs window and was now helping her secure the horse in the stable. Deborah's mood had run the gamut from mortified to hopeful and everywhere in between. As much as she wanted to ask her hundreds of questions, she knew it would have to wait a little longer as Sarah attempted to regain normal breathing.

Entering their luxurious two-story home, they sat in the same parlor room that David Johnson and Lydia Ames had met in earlier in the day. Sarah began to speak between her heaving breaths. "I…I…think I found where they are keeping him," she blurted out.

"Slow down, Sarah. You did wonderful. I'm so proud of you."

"She saw me."

"Who? Lydia? How? Where?" Deborah gently grasped Sarah's shoulders.

"I followed the dragon woman about a mile, just south of Lombard. Her carriage went down into what looked like an abandoned warehouse. But I'm sure it wasn't abandoned."

"Why not?"

"Well, you don't have three men carrying muskets, walking outside, patrolling the grounds of abandoned warehouses, do you?"

"I would think not. It must have had something of value inside."

"Exactly. I just had to find out more." Sarah's head glanced down; she couldn't look Deborah in the eyes.

"Sarah, what did you do? I told you to take no chances."

"I know, I know, but I couldn't pass up the opportunity. I went down and approached the guards. Of course they threatened to shoot me."

"Sarah!" Deborah's eyes revealed her worry. *If anything had happened to Sarah because of her stupidity...*

"It's all right, I'm fine. But I could see it in their faces they were hiding something. The one-eyed pirate told me they were guarding smuggled goods being hidden from the tax collector. I didn't believe him and tried to get inside, but that was when the dragon woman came outside and almost caught me."

"Did she see through your disguise?"

"I don't think so. I didn't let her get very close, and I made a quick excuse and ran like hell." Her breathing was slowly returning to normal.

"So you think they may be hiding Ben in there?" Deborah's voice was hopeful.

"She stayed inside for a good fifteen minutes. I doubt if she was taking inventory," Sarah stated emphatically.

Deborah looked away, pondering her next move.

"Now what? I doubt if the police would be much help. Besides, people like Rourke usually own half the police department. We can't just waltz in there and bring him home."

"Why not?" Deborah smiled and looked at Sarah.

"Quit joking around. We have to go to your father. He'll know what to do."

"No, no, we can't do that," Deborah responded quickly. "Rourke promised he would kill him. You don't know Rourke like I do. He is sick, he is crazy. We can't let Father anywhere near that place."

"So your plan is to go in there by yourself. Now who's crazy?"

"Well, you'll be nearby with the getaway horses," Deborah suggested coyly.

"Me! You're even crazier than I thought. I'm not going back there unless George Washington's army is with me," Sarah declared firmly.

"Oh, I hardly think we'll need General Washington tonight." Deborah smiled confidently.

Deborah's smile disappeared instantly when she looked up and saw her father, hands on hips, standing in the middle of the threshold. The look on his face told her he had heard everything.

"Is this true? Patrick has threatened you with your life?"

The question surprised her greatly. There was anger in his eyes yet also a determination that she had never seen before. Deborah didn't hesitate; she broke down and told him everything, her involvement in the assassination attempt, how she suspected Rourke was torturing Cushman, and how he had threatened to kill her father if she didn't cooperate. Knowing his politics, Deborah was surprised again with his response.

"I don't know this Cushman, but no one has the right to torture an innocent man, let alone threaten my family. Patrick has gone too far. I will deal with this immediately."

"But, Daddy, Rourke is a monster. He will kill you!" Deborah started sobbing.

"Darling, I can take care of myself. Patrick will listen to me, one way or another."

"Let us go with you. We can help," Deborah begged as Sarah nodded in agreement.

"No! I must do this alone. I put you into this dangerous situation at City Tavern, and it has come to this. This is my fault, and I will fix it. Sarah, tell me exactly where I can find this warehouse."

Rourke was waiting in the library when she returned. He stood as Lydia entered and, without asking, poured her a drink. "Let's celebrate, my dear. The fire was controlled. The finest cognac money can buy. Comes from the Saintonge vineyards in France. Rumor has it that the emperor Diocletian planted the vines. No doubt he got the seedlings from the Roman gods themselves."

Lydia took the drink and chugged it down like it was apple cider.

Rourke laughed. "Lydia, my love, you don't gulp down cognac that has been centuries in the making. You enjoy it, sip by sip." Rourke went to pour her another drink but stopped immediately, catching the sadness in her eyes. "What is wrong, my dear? Are you all right?"

Tears welled in her eyes as she unexpectedly embraced Rourke, burying her head into his shoulder. "It was my fault. I'm sorry, it was all my fault."

"What are you talking about, Lydia? Are you all right?"

"I shouldn't have gone upstairs." Her tears turned to sobs as Rourke led her gently toward the large couch.

"Now, take a deep breath and tell me what happened." The concern on Rourke's face was real.

"All I had to do was tell one of the guards to notify Tompkins he had to stay because of the fire, but for some reason, I went upstairs to tell him myself." Her sobbing was slowing, but the tears were streaking her beautiful face.

"Was Tompkins inappropriate to you? I'll kill that bastard!"

"No, not Tompkins." Lydia sobbed and added no more.

"Well, if it wasn't Tompkins, who…" It suddenly hit Rourke. "Cushman? Was it Cushman?"

She didn't have to answer; it was written all over her gorgeous face. "Tompkins had removed his gag, but he was still blindfolded. I shouldn't have said anything to him, but he said he liked my perfume. At first he was nice, complimenting the perfume, asking for me to intercede on his behalf. But when I told him I couldn't do that, he became angry and started to yell threats at me. He was profane and threatened he would do horrible things to me if he ever escaped."

Rourke's temper had always been a problem, but in recent years, he had begun to tame it. The episodes were fewer, and the magnitudes of the explosions were smaller, but today he was going to revisit the past. "Van Dyke, get in here now!" Rourke growled. Striding quickly to the fireplace, Rourke snatched a large bag he had packed the night before.

Van Dyke came running into the room as if someone had been shot. "Are you all right? What happened?"

Rourke literally ran toward Van Dyke, tossing the canvass bag to his henchman. "Get the carriage ready. We are going to make Cushman wish he were never born."

THE SIGNERS

Van Dyke hurried from the room, beaming from ear to ear. He couldn't wait to inflict some real damage unto Cushman.

While Van Dyke and Rourke readied themselves for the journey, Lydia Ames smiled and walked to the table. She fingered the expensive bottle of French cognac and filled her glass to the rim. Slowly sipping the smooth drink, she congratulated herself for one of the finest performances of her life and looked forward to witnessing the complete destruction of Benjamin Cushman.

The first stages of dusk began settling over the city. Most Philadelphians were sitting down to their traditional Sunday dinner, the biggest meal of the week, and both children and adults looked forward to the weekly feast. There would be no feast for Ben Cushman, only a piece of bread and a small glass of wine. At least Tompkins had left his gag and blindfold off. The two had been talking for about half an hour. Cushman was making progress.

"Look, Tompkins, I got nothing against you. Actually, you and I have a lot in common. On occasion, you have been hired to kill people, correct?"

"Mostly threaten 'em, sometimes beat 'em, and yeah, on occasion I have killed people," he bragged while gulping down another glass of wine.

"Well, when I was with the Virginia militia, on occasion we had to kill people too. Indians mostly, but I killed my share of Frenchmen too. Your crazy boss paid you, and the Commonwealth of Virginia paid me."

Tompkins smiled at the comparison. "Never thought of it quite like that. I guess I am like a soldier, but better, 'cause I don't have to follow any rules."

"Don't be so sure about that, Tompkins. You've been guarding me over twenty-four hours. Wouldn't you rather be doing something other than this? You don't have a choice, do you? Might not be rules, but you sure aren't doing what you want to do, are you? At least in the Army you got relieved from duty after a while."

"Maybe so, but I'm gettin' paid pretty good money," Tompkins grunted, pouring his third glass of wine.

"If money's all you're after, why didn't you say so? How much money to let me go?" Cushman stated, half-joking.

Tompkins laughed. "You're pretty funny, Cushman. Too bad we hadn't met sometime earlier. I might have taken you up on that."

Cushman's mind was racing quickly. Tompkins's guard was down, and this might be his last chance.

"Very true, Tompkins. I can see us walking into a tavern and taking on all comers. I bet you were pretty good in a tavern brawl."

"Very perceptive of you. I don't think I've ever been on the losing side of one. Most of the scuffles came after I took everybody's money," Tompkins boasted.

"You some kind of thief, Tompkins? I don't have much respect for thieves."

"No, no, arm wrestling. No one could beat me. Some nights I'd win twenty pounds. Lots of irate people after you took that kind of money. Had to fight my way outta many a tavern."

Cushman's excitement over Tompkins's revelation was hard to suppress. "Arm wrestling, you say? Let me tell you something, Tompkins. There's not a man in Virginia who can say he ever bested Ben Cushman in an arm-wrestling contest. I'm sure you're good, but there's no way you could ever beat me." Cushman was being truthful, only because he had never arm-wrestled.

Tompkins stood; his tall lean body had surely been tested. "Cushman, you think I'm stupid?"

Well, yes. That's why we're having this conversation, you idiot. "Afraid you might lose to someone in my condition? Be pretty tough to live down."

"Cushman, on your best day you could never beat me." Tompkins started to get agitated.

"You talk a good game, Tompkins. Believe me, even in my current condition, it wouldn't take me sixty seconds to put you down." *Come on, you moron, take the bait.*

THE SIGNERS

Tompkins clearly was struggling; his competitive instincts were starting to defeat his common sense, and the wine was helping.

"You're afraid I might try to escape, aren't you? Even if I did, where would I go? I've heard the guards downstairs. I just think someone's afraid he's going to lose. Look, all you have to do is untie my right arm. You can even tie my legs to the chair if you want."

Clearly debating the warrants of disobeying Rourke's orders or fulfilling a juicy challenge, Tompkins's slightly drunken mind was racing. The look on Cushman's cocky face tipped the scales. "That's a good idea, Cushman." Tompkins walked to the corner of the room, gathered some rope, and began to tie each of Cushman's ankles to the front legs of the wooden chair. Cushman flattened both feet firmly into the floor as Tompkins finished his work. Untying his right arm, Tompkins made sure Cushman's left arm was tied securely to the back of the chair. He looked down at his handiwork and smiled. "Okay, Big Mouth, let's see what you got."

David Johnson urged his horse gently down the descending dirt road. The warehouse was in sight, but there were no guards as Sarah had described. He continued cautiously toward the old structure, determined to make right a terrible situation. Although he still believed strongly in supporting the king, he could not condone an *ends-justify-the-means* strategy. Rourke had crossed the line, and he was going to make it right. He was confident he could reason with Rourke, but just in case, he was packing two revolvers in his saddlebag.

The building looked empty as David Johnson rode to the open side door. As he dismounted and before he could set his second foot upon the ground, he was suddenly surrounded by three armed men. They had sprung from the warehouse and quickly hustled him inside without a word.

Deborah and Sarah looked on in terror as they watched their father dragged into the warehouse. They were watching from the same grove of trees where hours earlier Sarah had observed Lydia

Ames. After their father had left, Deborah had summoned his personal carriage driver, and the girls had arrived at the warehouse soon after the father did.

"What are we going to do?" Sarah demanded. The fear in her voice was palpable. Two guards exited the warehouse and began to walk toward their position.

Deborah reacted without hesitation. "Arthur!" she called, pulling Sarah into the carriage. "Take us down that road toward the warehouse."

"Yes, ma'am," Arthur responded, and in seconds he was negotiating the heavy carriage onto the property of Patrick Rourke.

The two guards immediately raised their weapons and ran toward the oncoming carriage. It was the second one today and the third *visitor*; this was becoming more than the hired muscle had signed up for. Sarah froze. It was *Pirate and Rotten Teeth*, and she had spoken to both just hours before. Deborah squeezed her knee, reassuring her. Sarah's bright-red dress was cut relatively low, revealing cleavage that was covered only by a see-through silk shawl wrapped around her shoulder. Her curly dark hair was loose and hanging down to her shoulders. She looked like she was heading to a party that only Philadelphia elites could attend. In fact, she was wearing one of Deborah's most expensive dresses, bought for those exact occasions. Deborah's dress was not as lavish but still looked magnificent on her.

"I'm sorry, sir, this is private property. You'll have to leave at once." *Pirate* motioned to David Johnson's personal driver to turn around. Before the driver could answer, the carriage door opened and Deborah hopped out. "Take me to the prisoner. I'm in a hurry," Deborah demanded, trying to sound like Lydia.

"Not so fast, lady. Who in the hell are you?" The *pirate* couldn't believe he had to deal with two pushy women in one day.

"My name's Deborah. This is Samantha. We both work for Lydia Ames."

Rotten Teeth looked into the carriage and smiled. Deborah was right; he hardly looked at her face.

"We are on our way to Mr. Rourke's party, but first, I have to deliver a message from Ms. Lydia."

Not her again. *Pirate* was confused, and he certainly didn't want another tongue-lashing. "What's the message?"

Victory! Deborah thought. She struggled to hide her emotions. "Well, sir, if it were for you, I would have given it already. However, it's for the prisoner. I believe his name is Cushman. Now please, we're in a hurry."

Guard 3 had seen the carriage arrive and remained at the far end of the warehouse. He had witnessed the abuse dispensed by Rourke's woman and chose discretion over valor. His partner continued to question the man who had just arrived. He claimed to be a friend of Rourke's, but they were taking no chances and kept a gun leveled at him at all times.

Pirate hesitated and assessed his options. His partner was busy flirting with the mulatto woman.

The woman obviously knew Rourke and Lydia Ames. She even knew the name of the prisoner. *Why risk further abuse?* Since Van Dyke wasn't here, Christopher Tompkins was in charge. *Let him deal with these pushy women.* With a sigh of relief, *Pirate* made his decision. "What did you say your name was?"

"Deborah. I work for Lydia Ames, at City Tavern." Deborah's heart was pounding as she began to realize the first part of her plan might work.

"Yeah, yeah, I got it. Follow me."

"Just one moment." She held up one finger and walked to the carriage window. "Be ready to move quickly."

"Are you sure you know what you're doing?" Sarah's hands were trembling.

"I'm quite sure I don't, but we have to do something. Daddy could be in trouble, and I don't want to think about what they have done to Ben." Deborah followed *Pirate* toward the warehouse, afraid what she might find but hoping upon hope that the threat of Rourke's temper and a little bit of blustering would be enough to pull off her bold plan.

Tompkins smiled as he looked at the grimacing face of Ben Cushman. Without much effort, Tompkins had managed to put the back of Cushman's hand within inches of the tabletop. One last burst of effort finished the job. Cushman's hand hit hard as Tompkins jumped up from his chair in celebration. "You never stood much chance, Cushman. No one's beaten me in years!" Tompkins laughed. He had actually expected a better match from the brash Virginian.

Cushman's head hung low in defeat. He gasped for air, as if he had just run ten miles. While Tompkins reveled in his glory, Cushman casually dropped his free right arm to the floor, slumped over in defeat. While planting his soles firmly into the floor, he managed to loosen the ropes securing his legs higher.

Tompkins continued his verbal assault. "Didn't even break a sweat, Cushman. Thought you said nobody ever beat you before?"

Cushman looked up with a wry smile. "Tompkins, I'll give you credit, you caught me off guard with your strength. One more chance? I guarantee the results will be entirely different."

Without any hesitation, Tompkins agreed. Rourke's warning not to underestimate Cushman now had an empty sound to it. *Why even bother to restrain him?* He had no doubt he would defeat Cushman in close-quarter combat. Perhaps the Virginia militiaman was good with a rifle, but that was it. He would surely cower if confronted by the likes of Van Dyke or Tompkins. "I'll try not to break your arm," responded Tompkins as he steadied himself for round 2.

"Go!" barked Tompkins as both men fought the initial contraction of muscle movement. This time, Cushman surged to an early advantage, bending his opponent's forearm toward the table. The astonished look on Tompkins's face was music to Cushman's ears. Redoubling his efforts, Tompkins slowly began to regain control.

Patience, Cushman thought to himself, *patience.* He quickly regained the edge, only to feel the resistance he had hoped for. *Now!* Cushman totally relaxed his right arm, allowing Tompkins to drive his arm to the table but causing him to lose his balance. Cushman used the force of the momentum to cock his arm and twist his body like an archer. Cushman dug his feet into the floor and unleashed a powerful punch. Aiming for the middle of Tompkins face. Cushman had to settle for the point of his chin. Tompkins's head snapped back as the vicious blow landed, and he tumbled off his chair, hitting the floor with a loud thud. Without waiting to see the results, Cushman scooted himself closer to the sturdy table. His focus was steady. He knew he had only time enough for one attempt; he had better do it right the first time.

The three guards patrolling inside the warehouse were not nearly as paranoid as their colleagues outside. All three were armed to the teeth and were experienced warriors. A wealthy store owner and a young woman were no cause for alarm. Seated in a chair against an inside wall, David Johnson let out an audible gasp as his daughter was led through the door by the one-eyed guard. Their eyes met as she attempted to appear casual.

"Men, they all react the same way when a pretty girl enters a room, like heathens. Now, who is in charge here?"

David Johnson's instincts to protect his daughter were battling with her eyes, which were telling him to go along with her charade. Her eyes won out as he nodded slightly, signaling her to play out her game.

Pirate pointed to the guard still aiming a rifle at the heart of David Johnson. "Mr. McIntyre, this lady says she works for Ms. Lydia and needs to leave a message for the prisoner." McIntyre leered at the attractive stranger and instantly decided to let Tompkins make the decision on this one. "Leave her here." He signaled *Pirate* to return to his duties outside. McIntyre huddled with the remaining two guards. "Take him outside. We'll wait until Rourke arrives to see if he's telling the truth. But keep a gun on him." As they led David Johnson out the door, he looked back at Deborah. Her eyes reassured him that she had a plan, and for the first time in his life, he realized that his little girl had turned into a woman.

McIntyre was leading Deborah up the stairs when a muffled thud startled them both. "Stay here," McIntyre ordered as he cautiously began to pour gunpowder into his Pennsylvania rifle.

The punch had caught Tompkins completely by surprise. Rourke's warning raced through his head. Lying flat on his back, Tompkins was more embarrassed than worried. The punch had hurt, yet he had never lost consciousness. He knew Cushman was tied securely to the chair and no danger to him. He took an assessment of his body as he slowly staggered to his feet.

At the same time, Cushman readied himself, his peripheral vision telling him Tompkins was beginning to stir. Placing his free right hand on the table, he hunched his head and shoulders forward, rolling up on his toes. When Tompkins had tied his legs to the chair, Cushman had pushed both heels into the floor, creating some space between the chair legs and his feet. Losing the first competition on purpose, Cushman had moved the rope higher up his legs, giving even more separation, while feigning depression from the loss. Coordinating his movements, Cushman bent his knees, lifting the back legs of the chair off the floor. Knees bent, he began to rock back and forth from heel to toe, attempting to gain momentum. Finally, with a mighty push from his right arm, he extended his knees and pushed off his toes. The right side of his body landed hard onto the table complete with the spindled chair. Without pausing, Cushman extended his right arm, launching himself off the table, twisting hard in midair. He landed with a crash, the wooden chair hitting the floor first. Just as he had hoped, the chair splintered under his weight. Stunned and bruised from the impact, Cushman found his left arm free. He quickly began to untie his legs.

THE SIGNERS

Tompkins was now standing and had watched in amazement at Cushman's maneuver. Slow to react, Tompkins composed himself, pulled out his knife, and ran toward Cushman.

"Faster, Van Dyke, faster!" Rourke roared out his carriage window as Van Dyke guided the carriage south on Front Street. "Damn it, Van Dyke, I said faster!" Rourke yelled seconds later at the top of his lungs.

Lydia Ames gripped the handrail, trying to maintain her balance. The slight discomfort of the bumpy ride was worth it. She jokingly measured Rourke's explosions of temper after famous volcanic eruptions. This was Vesuvius. Her face beamed with a look of smug satisfaction. Her performance pretending to be outraged by Ben Cushman's nonexistent tirade was what had set off *Mount Rourke*. Her only concern was that Rourke would go too far and too fast. Lydia wanted Cushman to suffer for days, not hours.

Van Dyke took the corner descending into the warehouse property so fast that the carriage rode up on two-wheels. Van Dyke expertly shifted his weight, quickly bringing all four wheels to the ground and to a sudden stop.

Sarah Johnson shuddered upon hearing the distinct sound of a horse-drawn carriage. *Rotten Teeth* was still trying to strike up an intelligent conversation. Sarah peered out a small opening in the back of David Johnson's carriage. Spasms of fear rippled up and down her body as she immediately recognized Rourke's lavish carriage. Leaving no doubt it was Rourke, Sarah gasped at the sight of his massive henchman, Edward Van Dyke.

Van Dyke leaped to the ground as Rourke exited the coach. He was carrying a large bag; Sarah had no desire to learn its contents. She recognized Rourke's foul mood immediately as fear continued to grip her entire body. She tried to remember Deborah's explanation to the *pirate*. A small ray of hope pushed aside her fears as she prepared to tell the same story that Deborah had delivered. Then it happened.

She saw the other door to Rourke's carriage open. Out walked Lydia Ames in all her splendor. The terror quickly returned. Her mind raced to create a viable reason for their presence at the warehouse. Panic set in as Rourke approached her position. Her only instinct remaining intact was that she should run. Grabbing the handle to open the door, she suddenly stopped. There, standing in front of her, was David Johnson's driver.

His name was Arthur Kopp. He had been a blacksmith and ran a thriving business not far from David Johnson's ship supply store. Several years ago, a horrific accident had caused Kopp to lose his left arm just below the elbow. There wasn't much use for one-armed blacksmiths, and he soon lost all his customers. David Johnson had just purchased his new carriage. He immediately offered Kopp a full-time position as carriage driver. Kopp accepted and soon was managing Johnson's stables and all maintenance outside their Third Street home. A proud and private man, Kopp had an enormous appreciation toward David Johnson's gesture. He was a loyal and hardworking employee.

"What in the hell is going on here?" Rourke roared to no one in particular. *Rotten Teeth* stood at attention, as if Rourke was a general in the British Army.

He attempted to talk first. "Sir, we are—"

"Shut up, you imbecile!" He was now standing within an arm's length of the carriage driver. "I know you. You're Johnson's driver." Rourke normally would never have recognized common help but remembered David Johnson had a one-armed driver. "What in the hell are you doing here?"

"Mr. Rourke, please forgive me, but Ms. Debby needed to get an urgent message to her father," the fast-thinking Kopp stated calmly.

"David's here? Why?" Rourke's anger continued to mount; he hated surprises.

"Mr. Johnson came looking for you. He tried your home, but you weren't there. I happened to mention to him that I passed by here yesterday and saw your carriage." Kopp pointed to the warehouse.

"That's not what the girl told me," *Pirate* stated suddenly. "She said she was delivering a message to the prisoner from her." He pointed toward Lydia.

Rourke pondered the information for only a few seconds. "What is your name?"

"Kopp, sir, Mr. Arthur Kopp," replied the ex-blacksmith with unusual composure.

"Well, Mr. Kopp, somebody is lying." With one smooth motion, Rourke swiftly removed his Catalonian flintlock pistol. A decorative gold-patterned handle highlighted the seventeen-inch-long firearm. Rourke pointed it directly at the heart of Kopp, who remained calm. Quickly redirecting his arm, the gun was now pointed directly at *Pirate*. Sarah Johnson sat stunned, hoping perhaps Rourke had bought the servant's story. Unfortunately, it was not to be.

Rourke suddenly retrained his pistol onto Arthur Kopp and fired. A loud explosion echoed through the warehouse complex. The lead ball ripped into Kopp's chest, producing a large wound. Kopp crumpled into the carriage door, blood spurting everywhere. Sarah Johnson screamed in horror as she was suddenly drenched in Arthur Kopp's blood.

"Guess what, Mr. Kopp? I believe you are the liar." Rourke spoke to the dead body without a single ounce of emotion.

Sarah Johnson looked into the evil eyes of a madman and felt a wave overcome her. Within seconds, she had passed out.

David Johnson recognized Rourke's carriage immediately. "Here he is now. You will see that we are friends." The two thugs exchanged glances; perhaps they were being overly paranoid.

"Wait here," one said, still brandishing the rifle. "Rourke will come to you."

Deborah's arrival had complicated David's planned confrontation of Rourke. He began to rethink his approach. He suddenly became alarmed when he saw Rourke pull a revolver on his loyal driver, Arthur. David reacted immediately. "Gentlemen, I am going to talk to Patrick. Shoot me if you must, but I am going." David had begun to run hard toward the unfolding scene when the unthinkable happened—the sickening sound of Rourke's revolver echoed throughout the shipyard.

Cushman, still somewhat stunned from his fall from the table, dived to his left to avoid being speared by the tip of Tompkins's eight-inch-long knife. "Not very sporting, Tompkins. Why don't you throw your knife away and fight fair?"

Furious, Tompkins lunged again at Cushman, who easily avoided the sharp weapon. "I don't care what Rourke thinks! I'm going to kill you, Cushman!"

"So your boss is named Rourke. Probably the shipping magnate I've heard about?" Cushman smiled; the look on Tompkins's face was worth the beatings he had taken.

"It don't matter now!" Tompkins growled. "Dead men tell no tales." Tompkins continued to circle the unarmed Cushman, patiently stalking, waiting for the right moment to strike.

Cushman quickly analyzed his situation; it wasn't good. Weakened from the beatings, lack of sleep, and lack of food, he realized his opponent could easily wear him down if he was patient, and of course, he had the only weapon. In addition, there were additional guards on the first floor. Cushman knew his only chance was to act quickly and force Tompkins into a mistake.

"Tompkins, you know Rourke will kill you for letting me escape?"

"Sorry, Cushman, you ain't escapin'. You're going to die, and I'm usin' the same knife I used on that bartender." Cushman continued to dodge Tompkins's thrusts, which were becoming more and more undisciplined.

Cushman flashed back to Fred, the bartender at the *Dead Dog Tavern*, his throat sliced open from ear to ear. "So you always kill defenseless men. You're the very definition of a *coward*." Tompkins's face turned bright red.

"Time to die, Cushman." Tompkins charged straight ahead, overlooking all tactics. He raised the knife above his head and struck. Cushman fell to his knees, rolled sideways, taking his enraged opponent's legs from under him. Tompkins fell with a hard thud. As he struggled to regain his footing, Cushman accelerated forward, launching himself feetfirst into the air. Tompkins saw the move coming and reacted rapidly to avoid the attack. Too late—Cushman's coiled legs extended, catching Tompkins square in the face. The blow caused his head to snap backward as he crashed roughly into the wall. Cushman pounced up like a cat and disarmed Tompkins before he could recover.

The explosion echoed through the empty warehouse like clap of thunder. Cushman knew immediately it was a musket shot, followed quickly by the distinct whistle of a bullet whizzing past his ear, penetrating the left shoulder of Christopher Tompkins. Tompkins yelped in pain. Cushman rolled quickly away from the wall, expecting another shot to follow. His eyes saw a man kneeling in the doorway, priming his gun for a second shot. Cushman was scrambling for Tompkins's knife. The rifleman was steadying for his second shot. Suddenly, he was catapulted sideways, crashing through the flimsy guardrail. A loud scream and a sudden crash verified what Cushman thought he saw. Someone had pushed the gunman off the staircase while he was focusing on putting a bullet into Cushman's head. It took a few seconds for his mind to comprehend it, but sure enough, standing in the doorway was a woman dressed in an evening gown. It was Deborah Johnson. She ran straight into Cushman's arms, squeezing him with every fiber of her being. Tears streamed down her cheeks as she wrapped herself around Cushman like a boa constrictor. Ben held her tight, wiping the tears from her face and looking down into her beautiful blue eyes, eyes he never thought he would see again. They stood together, hugging each other, like there was no tomorrow. No words spoken; their eyes said it all.

It was Cushman who finally broke the spell. "I don't know what you're up to, but I'm sure glad to see you. But how did you find me?"

Before Deborah could answer, the sound of stomping feet could be heard below. "We're not out of the woods yet. How many guards are downstairs?"

"Five more. I have a carriage waiting, and my father is downstairs." Deborah relaxed her grip on Cushman, but not totally.

"Your father?"

"It's a long story. He came here to confront Rourke. Sarah and I followed him. They have him downstairs, under guard. Come, we can still bluff our way out."

"Not after that gunshot. We'll have to come up with a new plan," Cushman stated while he peered down into the shadows of the warehouse. He heard excited voices coming from the door entrance. Quickly closing the door, Cushman pulled the heavy oak table and wedged it under the doorknob, trying to buy some time while he pondered their escape.

The two guards had decided not to shoot at David Johnson. *Perhaps he was a friend of Rourke*, they decided. They did run after him and were about to seize him when Rourke's gun roared to life. The wealthy merchant had killed the carriage driver without hesitation. The smile on his face revealed great satisfaction, even glee at the cold-blooded murder. *Pirate* was terrified; he immediately thought of Deborah Johnson visiting the prisoner. The execution of the driver must mean her arrival at the warehouse was unauthorized, and worst of all, he had given her permission to enter.

Rourke looked up and saw David Johnson approaching; the horrified look on his face amused the wealthy merchant. The remaining guards stood frozen in their tracks. Van Dyke was at his side, while the beautiful witch trailed the twosome.

"Patrick, are you crazy? What have you done?" David Johnson yelled as he stared at the body of Arthur Kopp. "How dare you threaten my family! I will—"

David never saw the punch coming. Van Dyke's massive fist got him square on the jaw. Blackness washed over him instantly as Rourke gave his top henchman an approving nod. Rourke was about to speak when another gunshot rang out. The distinctive sound of musket fire reverberated within the warehouse.

Some in Philadelphia called it Delaware Avenue; old-timers referred to it as Columbus Street. Running parallel between Front Street and the Delaware River, the unpaved dirt road acted as an access to the many warehouses and docks. Seedy taverns and brothels littered the dirt road. It was one of the heaviest crime neighborhoods in Philadelphia.

Jefferson was the first to arrive. John Hart and Abraham Clark arrived from the north soon after. Jefferson immediately saw their faces were filled with disappointment.

"Thomas, I'm sorry, but neither of us saw anything that would cause us to believe that Ben was being held there. Almost every warehouse had evidence of heavy use. Hopefully, John and John had better luck." Abraham Clark couldn't hide his disappointment.

Jefferson nodded, and they silently waited for John Hancock and John Adams to arrive from the south.

They had almost missed it. A thick grove of trees surrounding the property made it difficult to see. Hancock noticed something and quietly alerted his partner.

"John, look down there," Hancock whispered to his fellow Massachusetts delegate.

Adams repositioned his horse to get a clear view through the trees. There, along the river, was a small warehouse in obvious disrepair. There were none of the trappings of recent activity. No boxes piled near the warehouse, no heavy equipment needed to unload large commercial ships. Yet just outside the warehouse, a lone carriage attached to two sturdy horses sat stationary. A driver sat atop the carriage, while a man leaned up against the carriage window, in obvious conversation with the occupant. The two revolutionaries decided to take a closer look as they dismounted, leading their horses deeper into the grove of trees, off the dirt road. Just as they left the road, they were alerted to the familiar pattern of horses' hooves and rackety wheels. A speeding carriage appeared over a slight hill at breakneck speed. Hancock thought the carriage would topple over as he watched the driver expertly maneuver the left turn onto the property, down the incline, and quickly approached the stationary carriage.

Adams looked intently at his partner, his eyebrows arched high. "John, something tells me this is it. What do you think?"

Hancock nodded in agreement. "According to my calculations, our meeting point with the others is just under a mile. Why don't you ride ahead and tell them what we've found? Bring them here as fast as you can. I will stay here and continue to scout."

Adams didn't like leaving Hancock by himself but chose not to argue the point; he quickly mounted his horse. "I'll be back in a few minutes. Don't try to be a hero. Wait till reinforcements arrive."

"Don't worry, John, I won't get myself killed the day before the independence vote, I promise. Now hurry. I fear for Cushman's life."

Adams urged his steed forward and bolted from the trees. Pushing his horse hard, Adams had ridden about two hundred yards when he heard the recognizable blast of a firearm. Resisting the urge to go back and investigate further, Adams dug in and rode as fast as he could.

Jefferson heard the pounding hooves first. Looking up, he saw John Adams riding hard as he bore down on the threesome. Adams brought his horse to a skilled stop. Gasping for air, the forty-year-old lawyer spoke excitedly to his fellow delegates. "We have a possible location on Ben. John stayed behind to investigate further. As I was riding away, I heard a gunshot. Hurry, we think this is it."

THE SIGNERS

Without any debate, the men started to follow John Adams. Jefferson was soon side by side with his fellow delegate. The determined look on both men's faces was overshadowed by the worry that they might be too late. As they concentrated guiding their horses forward, none of the men noticed the lone rider approaching hard from their rear.

Benjamin Cushman had been in some tight spots. Fighting with his brother James in the French and Indian War as a teenager, later in the Frontier Indian Wars, and of course, his pursuit of *Yellow Snake*. He had been a participant to enough adrenaline-filled situations for any lifetime. One of the main reasons he had chosen to ride through Philadelphia on his way home was to spend a few quiet days catching up with his boyhood friend, Thomas Jefferson. *Some quiet days,* he thought to himself. He looked over at Deborah Johnson and smiled. "You know, you saved my life just a minute ago. I forgot to thank you."

Deborah's eyes sparkled when she smiled. "It will be my mission in life to never let you forget it."

"Great, I suppose I have to return the favor." He laughed. The merriment ended immediately when they heard the footsteps charging up the stairs.

Cushman quickly grabbed a chair and launched it through the window. Fragments of sharp glass covered the bleeding Christopher Tompkins. Within seconds they were balancing on a small ledge outside the warehouse. Inside, men were shouting orders and beginning to batter down the door.

A two-foot ledge separated the first and second floors of the old warehouse. Cushman took Deborah's hand and started to edge away from the window. Scanning the scene below discouraged him. He had hoped to be able to jump into the river. Unfortunately, the old dock extended well out into the Delaware. They continued to work their way toward the corner of the building. They were about thirty feet from the window when he saw the head. The head had an eye patch and screamed, "They're outside on the ledge!"

"Damn!" Cushman cried out.

"Ben, what's wrong?"

"We're out of room." The ledge ended at the corner of the building; there was nowhere to go.

The deafening explosion of the gunshot resounded in their ears. Wood fragments showered the two as the lead ball made contact with the wooden building inches above Cushman's head. Deborah lost her balance and was beginning to topple off the ledge when Cushman pulled her smoothly back to safety.

"Can't sit here all day. I'm sure not all of them are that bad of a shot." Cushman bent down and grabbed the ledge, slowly lowering himself so he was hanging above the dock that ran the length of the warehouse. He dropped ten feet onto the wooden planks, stumbling to remain on his feet. "Your turn!" he called up to Deborah.

"Are you crazy?" Deborah responded, clinging to the side of the building.

"Better than being shot." Cushman saw another gun emerging through the broken window; they were about to fire again. "Better yet, jump!" Cushman urged, pointing to the person taking aim at Deborah.

Without thinking, Deborah Johnson jumped. Cushman steadied himself and reached high to help break her fall. She landed awkwardly in his arms. His strong upper body cushioned the blow, but he was knocked off-balance as the two crashed onto the dock surface. Deborah lay sprawled across Cushman, their faces inches apart.

"You'll do anything to try to kiss me?" Cushman grinned.

Deborah laughed nervously and gave him a playful slap across the face.

Another shot rang out; this one wasn't close but reinforced to them that they weren't out of trouble yet.

"My carriage is around to the front. We have to make a run for it." She grabbed his hand but met resistance.

"No, it's too dangerous. You can swim, right?" Cushman questioned while eyeing the Delaware River.

THE SIGNERS

"I can swim to New Jersey if I have to," Deborah said proudly.

"Don't do that. Swim south, along the shore. The current should help. Don't come ashore for at least a mile. Make your way home. I will find your father and Sarah, and I will meet you there."

"I'm not going to leave you!" Her eyes pleaded with Cushman not to separate.

"Nonsense! I will lead them away. No arguing. You must go now." Without another word, Cushman produced the knife he had taken from Tompkins and quickly cut Deborah's dress just below her waist.

"Hey, that's an expensive dress," she mildly protested and realized immediately she wouldn't be able to swim without his alteration.

They had worked their way to the end of the dock. Cushman could hear voices; they were no longer on the second story of the warehouse. He held Deborah by her shoulders, pulling her close. Their lips came together in a passionate kiss.

"Remember, stay close to the shore."

"Ben..." She hesitated before diving in the Delaware River.

"Yes." Cushman gazed into her sparkling blue eyes.

"I love you." And with that she turned and dived into the murky water.

Patrick Rourke was furious. He couldn't believe what had just happened. Upon entering the warehouse, they had found McIntyre; his neck was twisted into a grotesque shape. Rourke had ordered his men to the second-story office, only to find the door had been barricaded. It took several minutes to break through, only to reveal his worst nightmare. Cushman was gone. Tompkins lay bleeding against the back wall. Severely injured, he was able to point to the window, indicating Cushman's escape route.

"How could you let this happen?"

"Boss, should we get him to a doctor?" Edward Van Dyke mustered up enough courage to question Rourke.

"No. He won't be needing a doctor." And with that Rourke produced a six-inch-long knife and cut Tompkins's throat from ear to ear.

Next, he had ordered his guards to shoot the two while on the ledge. Furious that the one-eyed guard had missed, Rourke then fired at the two while they were sprawled on the dock. Missing by a wide margin only further enraged the millionaire shipping magnate.

"Spread out. They can't go far!" Rourke screamed as they scrambled down the stairs and began to search the grounds for the two traitors.

Lydia Ames approached Rourke with a worried look on her face. "Patrick, perhaps you should let the men find them. It could get dangerous."

Rourke looked at her with disgust. "He's unarmed and in a weakened state. If your protégé hadn't helped him, he wouldn't have gotten away."

Lydia, too, was disappointed in Deborah Johnson, but not surprised. *Love can do strange things to people.* "That's true, but even you have admitted that Cushman is resourceful. Let the others do the hunting."

Normally, Lydia would have been able to calm Rourke down and get him to take the intelligent course. But this was not one of those days. Rourke took a deep breath and answered, "Lydia, go back to the carriage and wait. I'm going to find those two and kill them." With that, Rourke headed behind the warehouse, determined more than ever to hunt down and kill Benjamin Cushman.

Cushman felt a great sense of relief as he watched Deborah swim away. Her strokes were graceful, and it reminded him of Jane Jefferson swimming in the Rivanna River. He said a short prayer that it would not be the last time he saw her and sprinted to the northern edge of the property.

While running, he took stock of his situation. He had to stall them long enough to save Deborah. This meant he couldn't go into the river, not yet. Tompkins's knife was his only weapon. Unfortunately, they all had guns. The twilight was turning into darkness, and that would be Cushman's only advantage. There was only one way to get out of this mess, divide and conquer.

The warehouse was easily thirty years old. Cushman noticed several boards had been used to cover up rotting planks at the northeast corner of the building. A strong tug separated the planks from the decomposed wood. Cushman silently crawled through the hole, back into the warehouse. It was empty. A lone candle lantern gave a dim view of the warehouse floor. Cushman saw the body of the man Deborah had pushed. *One less thug to worry about.* Working slowly, he made his way to the main entrance. He could hear multiple footsteps on the dock he had just left, and then he heard words that sent shivers of fear throughout his body.

"Look, down there. Someone's in the water." Reacting quickly, Cushman grabbed the lantern and burst outside, running toward a small group of trees just to the north. "Hey, you bunch of lunatics, I'm right here! Come and get me." Tossing the lantern straight into the air, Cushman darted into a grove of trees. They provided adequate cover as he moved away from the warehouse. He hadn't traveled long when his heart suddenly sank. An eight-foot-high plank fence blocked his retreat. It ran the length of the property, from river to road. He thought about returning to the dock, but two men had taken up a position, effectively blocking him from the river. He was cornered.

Still others began to rally to the front of a carriage. Cushman could barely make out the shadowy bodies, but they didn't look like friendlies. The situation quickly got worse. Each man began lighting a lantern, illuminating a small circle of dangerous men. It was clear they would slowly surround Cushman and flush him from his hiding place.

Working his way to the northernmost trees, Ben decided to climb onto a low-hanging branch and study the whereabouts of the enemy. Behind him and farther south, he could still hear the two men staking out the dock. He had to assume one or two of Rourke's men were sent to investigate what they had seen in the water. Cushman's hope was that Deborah had gotten a large-enough lead and the darkness would make her difficult to spot. He was certain that most of the guards were now surrounding his position. Although the candle lanterns enabled Rourke's thugs to see, it was also a big advantage for Ben to track their whereabouts.

Cushman breathed a sigh of relief when he saw the tactics that would be employed. Rourke's men began to fan out and slowly make their way forward into the tree line. They were about thirty yards apart and moving in a straight line. Cushman zeroed in on the man closest to him. At his present pace, he would be directly below the tree in ten paces. Cushman thought of his friend the Indian chief Cornstalk. They had spent many nights talking warfare and tactics, especially tactics versus a superior foe. Chief Cornstalk talked at length about the need for stealth and hit-and-run tactics. He always concluded each session with his two key objectives, to keep the enemy off-balance and to always stay on the offensive. Ben figured no time like the present to test the chief's theories.

The lantern grew closer. The light it produced was dim, but it was enough to illuminate the face of the man approaching. He was looking straight ahead, not up into the tree. Waiting until the assassin was directly underneath, he gripped the branch firmly and swung from behind, scissoring the man's head between his thighs. Squeezing with every ounce of strength, Cushman twisted violently, snapping the man's neck and causing instant death. He lowered the man slowly with his legs and fell softly to the ground, crouching low.

Luck was with Cushman; the lantern had remained lit, causing no reaction from the others. Searching the body produced more good luck, a fully primed rifle and pistol. Sweeping up the newly acquired arsenal, Ben continued to walk parallel with the other killers, intentionally moving closer to the man on his right.

"Psst, over here. I think I found something," Cushman whispered in his best imitation of a low-life killer.

"Quiet. Don't alert the others."

Cushman knelt down, attempting to look as if he had found a clue. "What have you found?" the killer asked, much too loud for Cushman's comfort.

THE SIGNERS

"Look." As the man bent over to examine the clue, Cushman's right hand shot up, plunging his knife into the unsuspecting victim. Driving the knife deep into his throat, Cushman hoped this maneuver would sever the man's vocal cords while causing instant death. Unfortunately, Cushman's luck ran out; the assassin screamed out in horrible pain. Death came quickly, but not soon enough. In addition to the noise, the assassin's lantern was instantly extinguished, giving a visual point to locate Cushman.

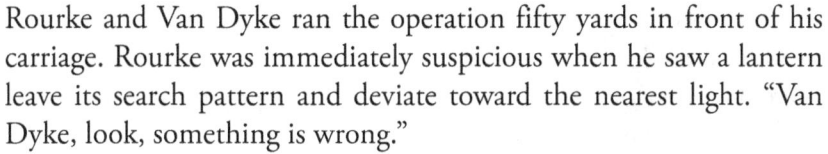

Rourke and Van Dyke ran the operation fifty yards in front of his carriage. Rourke was immediately suspicious when he saw a lantern leave its search pattern and deviate toward the nearest light. "Van Dyke, look, something is wrong."

"Maybe they found something," Van Dyke reasoned.

"No, they are supposed to call out if they find him," Rourke stated firmly. "Get ready to shoot."

"But which one? They could both be our guys."

"It doesn't matter. I can hire twenty more tomorrow, but if I'm right, one of those lanterns is being held by Cushman. Wait for my signal. You shoot right, I'll shoot left."

Van Dyke actually admired Rourke for his ruthlessness, just so long as it wasn't aimed at him. He took aim and waited for Rourke's signal.

Suddenly, the lantern on the right shook violently and was no longer visible as a scream broke the silent night.

"Now!" Rourke yelled. "Now!"

Two shots rang out as the flintlock rifles spit their deadly lead balls toward the targets. Darkness now dominated the events taking place, but a second scream indicated that at least one of the balls had found its mark. Seconds later, the other lantern was also extinguished.

Sarah Johnson shook her head, trying to awaken from a most horrific nightmare. Night had replaced dusk as she continued to function midway between sleep and full consciousness. Her senses slowly returning, the horrible memory of the murder of Arthur Kopp rekindled instant sadness and panic. She ran her hands over Deborah's favorite dress, recognizing immediately the sticky warmth of Arthur's blood. Sarah felt the acid climb in her throat as she fought off the first signs of vomiting. Fully awake, she now puzzled over why she was even alive. They must have known that Deborah had betrayed them. Rourke had to murder Arthur Kopp for that very reason. *Where was her father?* Sarah cautiously peered out the carriage window at the sight unfolding before her eyes. She immediately recognized Rourke and his main henchman, Van Dyke. Their position was illuminated by two candle lanterns. Suddenly both men raised their muskets and fired. The roar of the guns was followed by a ghastly scream. Sarah had seen enough.

Without any hesitation, she snapped open the opposite door and started running toward the dirt road she had traveled earlier in the day. Sarah hiked her dress and ran as fast as possible, never looking back. The grove of trees was now in sight. She struggled to keep momentum as she ascended the gradual incline. Sarah could feel the ground leveling as she reached the top of the hill, only five more yards to safety. Suddenly, a tall man blocked her path. Before she could react, he grabbed her, placing his hand over her mouth. Struggling to break free, Sarah realized immediately he was too strong. Her adrenaline rush to freedom was now replaced with the sheer terror of failure. Her failure to protect Deborah, Arthur Kopp, David Johnson, and even herself came crashing down like a waterfall. The fear she felt earlier was replaced by a deep despair.

"Now, now, just who might you be?" her tall captor asked gently, reducing his grip slightly but still maintaining control over Sarah. "Do you have a name? And what is your purpose here? Keep your voice low or I will be forced to gag you."

Sarah was now confused. *His voice is gentle, soothing.* She looked up for the first time. Indeed, he was tall, over six feet. His long red hair was fastened into a ponytail, and his tricorne hat was tilted

THE SIGNERS

slightly to the side. Sarah looked deep into his eyes and, for the first time, began to feel safe; they were sympathetic and caring.

"My name is Sarah, Sarah Johnson. I work for David Johnson and his daughter, Deborah," Sarah whispered. She couldn't take her eyes off the chiseled and handsome face. She had seen him before, but where?

Upon hearing the name Deborah, the man released her and gave out a soft whistle. Suddenly, four men appeared as if out of nowhere.

"Sarah, we are here to find Ben Cushman. Have you seen him?"

Out of the blue, it hit Sarah. "You're Mr. Jefferson, aren't you?"

"Yes, but please, Sarah, we don't have much time. Is Ben Cushman down there?"

"Yes, he is being held prisoner by Patrick Rourke. My—Deborah's father came here to confront Rourke. He had threatened our family. Mr. Johnson was taken prisoner, so Deborah and I tried to bluff our way in."

"Deborah is here?" Jefferson asked in disbelief.

"Yes. Everything was going well until Rourke showed up. He murdered our driver while Deborah and her father were inside the warehouse, trying to rescue Ben. He shot him for no reason, Mr. Jefferson." She began to cry at the memory. Between the sobs, she continued, "I must have passed out. When I awoke, I saw Rourke shoot at someone. Then I heard a scream."

"Sarah, tell me, how did you know how to find this place?" Jefferson asked suspiciously.

"Rourke is a friend of Deborah's father" was all Sarah would say.

Jefferson knew she was holding something back, but before he could reply, he was interrupted.

"Rourke is a shipping tycoon. I've met him. He's a Tory and quite mad, if you ask me, a very unlikable man. There is a rumor that he is in tight with the British admiralty. None of his ships ever get boarded for inspection," the newcomer announced as he appeared at Jefferson's side. He was not as tall as Jefferson; he was thinner, with dark hair. His rugged face was well tanned, and like Jefferson, he had the look of a man of character. Sarah recognized John Hancock, president of the Continental Congress, by the time he had finished his sentence.

"Someone is coming," whispered John Adams. The clip-clop of horse's hooves could be heard nearing their hiding place. Abraham Clark leveled a rifle at the incoming rider.

"Mr. Hancock, is that you?" the voice called out in a loud whisper as he descended from his horse, gun in hand.

"Hall? Over here," Hancock replied in a hushed tone.

Major Jacob Hall sauntered into the gathering; his presence immediately lifted hopes that perhaps their mission might succeed. "I picked you up about a half-mile back. I got your note. What's the situation?"

"This is Sarah Johnson. She is Deborah's servant. Tell Major Hall what you told us," Jefferson ordered the frightened girl.

Sarah quickly recapped her story.

"Rourke!" Hall literally spit the name out.

"Are you familiar with him?" Hancock asked, surprised at Hall's reaction.

"Yes. He is the man responsible for the *Treasure*'s demise."

Hancock absorbed the information; he couldn't hide his building anger. The others looked on in confusion, and it was Jefferson who asked. "The treasure? What treasure?"

Hancock recovered and simply stated, "I owe you all an explanation, but not now. We must hurry if we are to save Cushman. Rourke is a madman. He will not hesitate to kill your friend."

All eyes turned to Hall as he began to bark orders to the delegates of the Continental Congress. When he was finished, the men readied themselves and waited for his signal.

Jefferson turned to Sarah Johnson and spoke softly. "Sarah, I want you to take my horse and ride to City Tavern. Across the street is a boardinghouse. Tie up my horse, go inside, and ask for Mrs. Sarah Yard. Tell her your story and ask her to take you in tonight. Tell her Mr. Hancock and Mr. Adams want you protected. It is too dangerous to go home tonight. Do you understand?"

"Yes," Sarah replied as Jefferson easily lifted her onto his horse. "Please, Mr. Jefferson, save my—Mr. Johnson and my Deborah. She loves Cushman and risked her life tonight to save him."

THE SIGNERS

"Sarah, we'll do our best. Now go."

Cushman tensed when he had heard the shots ring out. One of the lead balls found its mark into the man he had just killed. Another bullet struck his lantern, tearing it from his hands. Thinking fast, Cushman let out a piercing scream and dropped to the ground. Crawling quickly and silently, he fell behind another tree and paused to catch his breath. *Relax,* Ben thought. *Breathe through your nose, slowly, deeply.* The trick, taught to him by his grandfather, seemed to always work.

Cushman analyzed his situation. It was not good. He had hoped to be able to retreat to the river if all else failed. But he could still hear the men on the docks; he was surrounded. The good news was that four bad guys had been eliminated. Unfortunately, there were at least four men remaining. The snap of a twig caught him by surprise. Reacting like a snake, he sprung to his feet and assumed a crouching position. It was too late. The rifle stock came down on him from above. Only Cushman's quick reaction deflected the impact and saved his skull from being crushed. The hard wooden stock did its damage as Cushman was knocked to the ground. He was dazed, and his ears rang from the blow.

The shadowy figure standing over him raised the rifle and hammered the butt toward Ben's face. Cushman spun quickly to his right, barely avoiding the deadly blow.

Scrambling to his feet, Cushman stood facing his favorite torturer.

"Van Dick, so nice to see you—"

Before Ben could finish his sentence, the crack of a bullwhip permeated the air, followed by a burning sensation tearing through Cushman's right forearm.

Cushman turned to face his new attacker. "Ah, you again. I assume you are Rourke?" Ben snarled. He began to back away from the two, only to be surrounded by the other guards. It was an odd sight; the five men, three of whom still carried the candle lanterns, surrounded Cushman. The guards had their rifles leveled at the prisoner, but it seemed they had something else in store for him.

"It seems I am always one step ahead of you, Mr. Cushman. Only this time there will be no escape." Rourke held a whip in one hand and a gold-embossed pistol in the other. He motioned to the one-eyed guard, who came in and removed Cushman's pistol and his knife.

"Mr. Van Dyke has earned the honor of finishing you off. Farewell, Mr. Cushman." Rourke began to walk back toward his carriage.

"What's wrong, Rourke? Afraid to get your hands dirty, or worse yet, afraid of what I might do to you?" Ben taunted the hot-tempered Irishman.

Rourke stopped and slowly turned to face Cushman. "Mr. Cushman, your attempt at psychology is pathetic. I thought you might be a worthy adversary, but you turned out to be nothing more than a brainless, backwoods Virginia farmer. You didn't even know that your girlfriend set you up this whole time." Rourke watched with satisfaction the pained expression on Cushman's face. "That's right. She was working for me the entire time, and you were just a pawn in the game. A very weak pawn at that. Van Dyke, kill him quickly. I grow bored of this whole mess. Oh, one more thing, Mr. Cushman. Please don't whine about an unfair fight. Winners get to set the rules." With that, Rourke walked toward his carriage.

Ben felt like he had just been kicked in the stomach. He was about to reply to Rourke's accusations when he realized there were many unanswered questions concerning Deborah. Unfortunately, those would have to be answered at another time. Van Dyke was bearing down on Cushman, an eight-inch-long knife poised to strike; the other guards began to cheer Van Dyke on.

No more talking. The look in Van Dyke's eyes said everything. This would be a fight to the death, and there was no doubt that Cushman would be doing the dying.

Ben circled Van Dyke, looking for weaknesses. Unlike Tompkins, Van Dyke waited patiently, closing in while faking thrusts with his knife hand. The short bull of a man kept a perfectly balanced stance as he danced around Cushman, waiting for an opening. The guards hooted and hollered, sensing a quick kill. Van Dyke's smile grew wider as he, too, sensed the thrill of a quick victory.

Ben concentrated on his opponent's knife hand and his right leg. Every time Van Dyke took a short jab at him, he did so with a short step forward, followed by the thrust of the knife. It was a classic fencing move, but with a knife. Van Dyke obviously had some training, but Cushman thought he could use that in his favor.

Allowing Van Dyke to get closer with each thrust, Ben waited patiently to make his move. The guards had lowered their rifles and were continuing to cheer loudly for Van Dyke to fillet the Virginian.

Ben fought his instincts, knowing he might have only one chance. He knew he had to avoid close contact with his powerful adversary. *Now!* Cushman reacted to the next thrust, stepping smoothly to his right. Both his hands shot out, wrapping his fingers tightly around Van Dyke's wrist. Pivoting on his left foot, Cushman raised his right foot and drove his heel into the side of Van Dyke's exposed right knee. A crunching sound came from the knee as he let out a painful scream. With the same motion, Cushman's left heel followed, again landing on the wounded right knee. Van Dyke buckled to the ground, and Ben flipped over his fallen foe, twisting his wrist with the full force of his body. The knife fell harmlessly to the ground as Ben scrambled to retrieve it.

The three remaining guards were stunned to see their boss writhing on the ground in such pain. They had never seen anyone even try to get the better of Van Dyke, let alone actually do it. Cushman struggled to his feet. One of the guards lurched forward toward him, and Cushman easily sidestepped him and was shocked when the guard crashed awkwardly to the ground in a heap. A nine-inch knife was still quivering from side to side, planted firmly between his shoulders. *What the...?* Cushman tried to process what had just happened, while the two remaining killers recovered quickly from seeing their boss disabled. They raised their rifles as Ben dived for cover. Multiple shots exploded above him. Cushman hugged the ground, confused. Generals, from Julius Caesar to the great British general James Wolf, often described a battle scene as mass chaos. Cushman's confusion might have been explained by the chaos of battle, but he could have sworn that the musket fire came from the opposite direction. He slowly lifted his head and saw that he was right; the three guards were all lying prone on the ground, dead or wounded.

"You know, I've been bailing you out of trouble since I was five years old." The familiar voice chuckled, its owner standing over Ben Cushman.

Cushman lay stunned on the ground, a big smile slowly spreading across his pale face. "Damn, Red, did you have to cut it so close?" Cushman waved off efforts to help him up, the adrenaline-laced escape beginning to wear off. It was replaced by an unusual weariness he had never experienced before. He struggled mightily just to stand.

The five members of the Second Continental Congress gathered around Ben to inquire about his fitness. He thanked each man with a handshake and a hug, a simple task that proved difficult. It was then he recognized another man standing in the background, a familiar and welcome face. "Jacob, I should have known."

Major Jacob Hall stood motionless, a smoking pistol hanging from each hand. He had the knowing smile of a warrior who had completed his mission. Cushman looked around and did a quick inventory of the death toll. One guard lay dead, with a knife protruding from his back; the other two had died quickly, both having taken bullets to the head. Van Dyke remained sprawled on the ground, writhing in pain from the knee injury inflicted by the weakened Cushman.

"Thank God Major Hall arrived when he did. He is a one-man army," Jefferson whispered to his friend while placing an arm around his shoulder.

"Mr. Cushman, you sure have brought some excitement to the lives of a bunch of stuffy politicians," commented John Adams as the men checked on the condition of Rourke's killers.

"I think the war has spread to Pennsylvania, and you gentlemen have fought in the first couple of skirmishes. Handled yourselves pretty well for a bunch of lawyers," Cushman smiled but, in doing so, grimaced at the sharp pain stabbing his brain.

"All dead," Abraham Clark declared. "Except the big one over there. He won't be walking right for a long time."

"Van Dyke," Cushman noted. His head was spinning. He felt confused. *What is happening?*

"The big fellow is Van Dyke?" John Hancock queried. "We came charging down the hill when we saw you were surrounded. The guards were so enthralled with your fight they never saw us coming. They both got off one shot. They didn't even aim properly. Major Hall did the rest. We didn't even need to fire a shot."

Cushman looked around and saw that the group Jefferson had recruited was each carrying a firearm.

"How did you find me?" Cushman looked up at Thomas Jefferson.

"Long story, but I was able to narrow the search because of your clue," Jefferson replied proudly.

"What about Rourke?" Cushman asked anxiously, trying to fight the dizziness and nausea building in him.

"Sorry, didn't see him. Must have hidden under the carriage when we were coming down the hill. After the firefight, we heard one of the carriages pulling away. It must have been Rourke," recalled Jefferson.

"Deborah, have you seen Deborah? What about her father?"

"Haven't seen Deborah, but Sarah is safe, and David Johnson is over there, being tended to by Mr. Clark."

Cushman looked up to see a man, probably David Johnson, walking unsteadily toward him.

"Mr. Cushman? Thank God you are alive. I am Deborah's father. Where is she?"

"She swam away…to the south.…Red, something's wrong. I don't—"

That was all Cushman said before collapsing to the ground.

Chapter 23

The time is near at hand which must determine whether Americans are to be free men or slaves.
—George Washington

Sunday, June 30, 1776
Philadelphia

Patrick Rourke maneuvered the carriage through the streets of Philadelphia with little regard for anyone's safety, including his own. A fine horseman, he was a little rusty manipulating the two-horse carriage through the narrow streets. He concentrated as hard as he could, but the night's events continued to distract him. Without question, the night had been a disaster. *Fucking Cushman!*

Inside the carriage, a disheveled Lydia Ames held on for dear life. Just now, she was beginning to normalize her breathing. It was Lydia who first noticed the men running down the hill and was able to warn Rourke. They dived beneath the carriage just as the men passed by. During the ensuing confrontation, the two had quickly recovered and were able to make their escape.

Her supreme confidence had been shaken during the episode at the warehouse. She had always known the cat-and-mouse game that had played out between her and Rourke was dangerous. An ability to eventually influence him toward her view was always a constant. But their connection with the British spy was turning into a disaster. If Cushman survived tonight, their involvement in Tuesday night's assassination plot and the subsequent kidnapping of Cushman would be common knowledge throughout the city. Even Tory sympathizers would be hard-pressed to rescue Rourke's reputation and influence, let alone keeping him from being arrested. Lydia's connection to Rourke would not be hard to prove. Nothing short of an immediate invasion by General Howe could save them. Lydia Ames began to plot her escape route in her mind.

Suddenly, the carriage came to an abrupt halt. Rourke quickly hopped down and opened the door. "Come, we have one more item to take care of."

Lydia looked around; she was confused. They were nowhere near her home. Looking around, she tried to find a familiar landmark. Due west she recognized the *Indian Queen Tavern*. They were on Market Street. "Patrick, why are we here? You know, if Cushman survives he will be able to lead them to us."

Rourke, not so gently, snatched her hand and began walking to the corner of Market and Third. "We're parking here so they won't see us."

"Who won't see us?" Her confidence in controlling the situation was rapidly spinning out of control. As they rounded the corner and headed south on Third Street, Lydia looked up and was immediately stunned. She stopped trying to free herself from Rourke. "Patrick, no, we can't go here. You're crazy! We can't do it."

Rourke gripped her hand like a vise, causing her to wince in pain. "We will go there, and you will help me. Nobody gets the better of Patrick Rourke, nobody." His eyes were ablaze with hatred. Lydia shook with fear, realizing she could no longer control the mad Irishman. "As for me being crazy, perhaps just a tad, my dear, just a tad."

Deborah Johnson shivered uncontrollably; her teeth were literally banging together. "Would you like another blanket, ma'am? I have another in my saddlebag."

"Yes, please" was all she was able to mutter between the shivers.

The summer storm had brought cooling northern winds to the city. Although still relatively warm for late June, the contrast between the water and the cool night air was significant. She had been in the water for close to an hour. They had spotted her from afar, and fearing they would catch her, she redoubled her efforts, not stopping for a good ten minutes. Nearing total exhaustion, she began to drift with the current, listening for any potential signs of danger. Panic set in when Deborah realized she had drifted into the middle of the Delaware River a good three hundred yards from shore. It took all her energy to maneuver back to the western shore, where she crawled onto a muddy flat and lay panting for air.

Fearing for her father, Sarah, and Ben, Deborah willed herself to climb the steep riverbank. She imagined that if *Rourke's Ruffians* were searching for her, they would be looking along Columbus Avenue, the nearest road parallel to the river. To be safe, she ran all the way to Third Street before she headed north and to the safety of her home. She dreamed of the wonderful reunion when Cushman would appear at her doorstep.

It being a Sunday night, the streets were nearly empty. He had surprised her from behind; there had been nowhere to hide. *What a sight he came upon.* Her expensive evening dress was torn at the hip, and the water soaked-material clung to Deborah, highlighting her feminine curves. Soaking-wet hair that resembled a wet mop completed the look of a drunken prostitute or a homeless street dweller. Luckily for Deborah, the gentleman from New Jersey was in town to visit his uncle, a local minister in one of Philadelphia's many Presbyterian churches. The young man was studying to follow in his uncle's footsteps at the College of New Jersey. Princeton College, as it was oftentimes called, was the foremost college for producing ministers in the colonies. The ferryboat he had boarded in New Jersey had run aground on a sandbar. The boat wasn't freed until late in the evening, and it wasn't ten minutes later he had come across the troubled girl. Deborah thanked God that such a man had rescued her.

David Abernathy produced the second blanket and turned to cover her. She had insisted upon riding on the back of his horse like a man. Of course, the young divinity student was shocked by such brazenness, but considering her circumstances, he decided not to make an issue of it. After all, he thought, she certainly qualified as a damsel in distress, and she was quite beautiful, despite her appearance.

The second blanket helped. For the first time since seeing Ben alive, Deborah felt like everything was going to work out. "I don't know how I could ever repay your kindness. I'm sorry, what's your name again?" she managed to say without stuttering her words.

"David, David Abernathy. Don't worry, Ms. Debby. It has been my pleasure to make your acquaintance, despite the unusual circumstances. I'm sure the good Lord made that ferryboat run aground so that I was delayed. May I ask you a question?"

"Why, certainly," she said softly, still shivering under the blankets.

"Exactly what happened to you?"

"David, let's just say I got caught smack-dab in the middle of this revolution that Mr. Paine talks so eloquently about." She beamed.

David Abernathy smiled a big toothy grin. "You know what they say, if you're in the middle of the road, pretty soon you'll get run over by a big old wagon."

Deborah sighed and returned his smile. "Never truer words to be spoken."

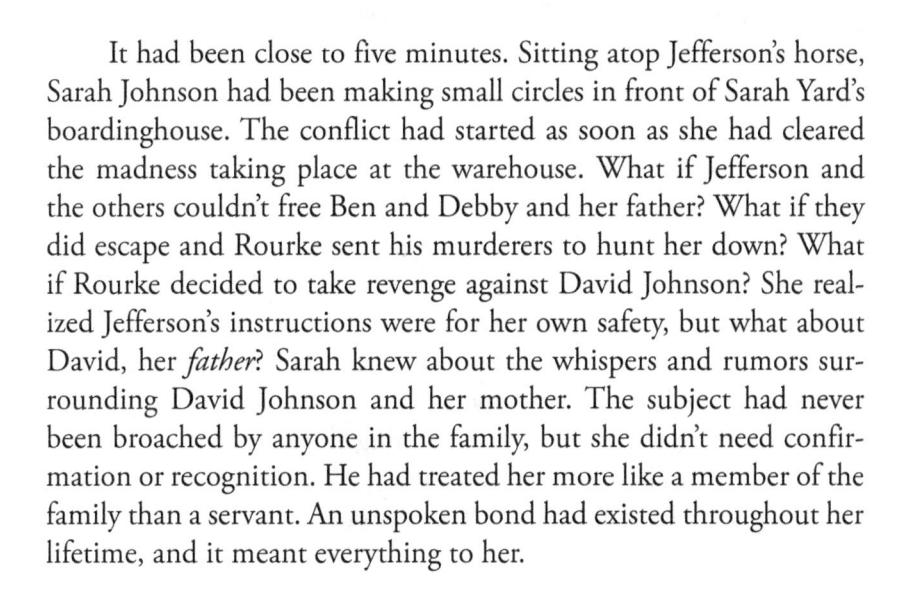

It had been close to five minutes. Sitting atop Jefferson's horse, Sarah Johnson had been making small circles in front of Sarah Yard's boardinghouse. The conflict had started as soon as she had cleared the madness taking place at the warehouse. What if Jefferson and the others couldn't free Ben and Debby and her father? What if they did escape and Rourke sent his murderers to hunt her down? What if Rourke decided to take revenge against David Johnson? She realized Jefferson's instructions were for her own safety, but what about David, her *father*? Sarah knew about the whispers and rumors surrounding David Johnson and her mother. The subject had never been broached by anyone in the family, but she didn't need confirmation or recognition. He had treated her more like a member of the family than a servant. An unspoken bond had existed throughout her lifetime, and it meant everything to her.

Her mind made up, Sarah urged the horse forward. She had to see if David Johnson had survived. He would certainly return to his house. It was the least she could do. She had to be sure he was safe. It would only take a few minutes. The Johnson home was only two blocks away. In and out, then she would return to Sarah Yard's boardinghouse, as Mr. Jefferson had ordered.

His nervous pacing was starting to wear into the ten-foot-long Persian carpet. One of the many perks of dealing with Merchant Marine captains. The front room was filled with treasures from around the world. The Swiss clock that graced the fireplace mantel was the highlight of the glorious room. A golden statue of a striking French baroness playing her harpsichord sat atop the framed handmade Swiss clock, also decorated with pearl inserts. Furniture from Denmark, fine cherry tables and chairs from Germany, and several Italian paintings adorned the lavish room.

David Johnson had returned home after searching along Columbus Avenue for any sign of Deborah. Abraham Clark had joined him in the search. It was Clark who suggested David return home to wait for Deborah, while he continued to search along the west side of the river.

Guilt attacked his mind as seconds turned to minutes, and minutes to hours. Why hadn't he spent more time with Deborah? Why had he gotten involved with Rourke? Was Lydia really interested in a lonely man, or was it all a charade to use him and his daughter? He wanted to go back out and search, but he had no idea where to start. So he waited and paced back and forth, imagining the unimaginable.

The loud knock on the front door startled David from his reverie. He sprinted to open the door.

"David, you look upset. Is everything all right?" Patrick Rourke spoke evenly, but his eyes had a wild look about them. Lydia stood by him; they were hand in hand, the look on her face disturbing.

THE SIGNERS

David was stunned to inaction. He knew Rourke had escaped, but none of the delegates believed he would be so brash to come to Johnson's home. Even the warrior Major Hall suggested he return home after the river search, to await Deborah's arrival. His abrupt words still haunted David. "If she survives the swim, she will certainly make her way home."

Rourke didn't wait for an invitation to enter; he barged past his host with Lydia in tow. "You know why we're here, David! It's about your traitorous daughter, Deborah. And your other daughter the mulatto no one ever talks about. Come on, David, do you really not see the resemblance? Everyone in Philadelphia knows it's your bastard daughter."

"How dare you speak to me that way—"

The blow struck David Johnson's face like a hammer. Rourke's punch landed right on the tip his the nose, breaking it immediately. Johnson fell into the German coffee table, shattering it into pieces. Staggering to his feet to continue his protest, David Johnson stood motionless, staring down the barrel of Rourke's gold-plated pistol.

"Sit down, David. I don't want to kill you. I just want your cooperation. Oh, make no mistake, I will kill you if you don't give me what I want."

Johnson sat, holding his nose with both hands, a large puddle of blood pooling at his feet. "Patrick, why are you doing this? Have you gone completely mad?"

"You're the second one tonight who has questioned my sanity." Rourke shot an evil look toward Lydia.

"Did you know your daughters betrayed me? That's right, both of them. After all I did for your precious Debby, she betrayed me. You helped them, didn't you? Your carriage was there. You led them to Cushman and to me!"

David Johnson glanced up. His eyes were starting to swell, but he could clearly see that Rourke was a raving lunatic. There would be no reasoning with this madman, Johnson thought to himself. *What a fool I've been!* Not only had these two duped him, but also his stupidity had placed his daughters' lives in danger. It was the first time in twenty years that he had thought of Sarah as his daughter. Of course, he had known all along; he had just chosen to ignore it. Knowing immediately what Rourke wanted, David Johnson decided then and there that he had to do everything in his power to stop this madman.

"Patrick, I have no idea what you are talking about. Ask Lydia. She was here today. Tell him, Lydia. Debby and you talked for a long while. She would not harm either of you. I came to the warehouse to speak to you. The girls must have followed me—"

"Enough of your lies!" Rourke roared, exploding the back of his hand into David's face. The blow staggered him, but he remained seated and glared at Rourke. "You'd like to kill me, David, wouldn't you? Well, here's your chance." Rourke set his pistol on a nearby table and walked directly in front of him. "Well, what are you waiting for? We are both unarmed."

David glimpsed at Lydia standing over Rourke's right shoulder. Her eyes warned him of the danger, but she said nothing. David no longer hesitated; he knew the girls would die if he didn't stop Rourke. He reached for the pistol, but Rourke's left hook sent David sprawling to the floor.

"You're such a fool, David. Tonight I will kill your entire family, and there is nothing you can do to stop me."

"Are you sure?"

"Yes, Mr. Jefferson, I am sure. Nobody has been here all night. Mr. Paine and Mr. Gerry both went to bed over an hour ago, and Mr. Sam…well, you know Mr. Sam. He said he would be home late. I imagine he is out politicking."

"Very well, Sarah. Thank you again for your hospitality," replied Thomas Jefferson.

"Your friend, will he be all right? Is there anything more I can do?" Sarah Yard asked as she continued to apply a wet cloth to the forehead of Benjamin Cushman.

"We have sent for Dr. Rush. He should be here shortly," Jefferson responded just as the sound of horses' hooves came to a halt in front of her home.

Jefferson was half-disappointed when Dr. Benjamin Rush bolted through the front door, a black satchel in his hands. He had hoped to see Sarah Johnson. She should have been here long before they had returned. Rush said nothing and went straight for Cushman. Immediately after Cushman had passed out, they had commandeered the Johnson carriage. With Major Hall driving, Jefferson and John Adams steadied Cushman in the back coach. Abraham Clark had accompanied David Johnson to search for Deborah. John Hancock had escorted all the horses back to the Yard residence, while John Hart had ridden off to find Benjamin Rush. Luckily, Rush had been at his home and came as soon as he was summoned.

"Thomas, your friend is breathing easily. That is a good sign. From what Mr. Hart has told me about his capture, and after examining his wounds and bruises, my best guess is that his body has been so stressed it just shut down. Normally, I would recommend bloodletting, but gauging from his wounds, he has probably lost enough blood. I cleaned and bandaged a couple of bullet wounds." Rush hesitated, then continued, "While I was studying medicine in Scotland, a friend of mine advanced a theory concerning dehydration, the lack of water in the body. Considering Cushman's treatment the past few days, he could simply be suffering from the lack of fluids."

"Will he awaken, Dr. Rush?" A distraught Jefferson asked the question softly.

"I believe he will, Thomas. We just have to give it time, and when he does, make sure he gets plenty of tea, water, or beer to replenish his fluids." The doctor grabbed Jefferson by the shoulders, attempting to reassure him. "Do you feel satisfactory, Thomas? You look rather pale. Get some rest, young man. Tomorrow is a big day for all of us, especially you," the delegate from Pennsylvania commented.

Jefferson hadn't thought about tomorrow's continued debate concerning his Declaration of Independence. Perhaps it was a good thing; he was occupied with the rescue of Ben. As important as tomorrow was, Jefferson continued to pray for his friend and wonder what happened to Sarah Johnson.

Sarah Johnson dismounted awkwardly. Several of Franklin's streetlamps illuminated the road well enough to notice if anything was out of place. Their neighbor directly across the street had a new carriage, which they kept parked in front of their house. Other than that, everything looked normal. Sarah's attention moved to the Johnson house. There was a light in the main living room in the front of the house. After tonight's intrigues, Sarah was taking no chances. Approaching the wraparound porch cautiously, she peered into the front window. What she saw made her freeze in horror; she began to scream, but nothing came out. Sitting on a chair, soaked in blood, David Johnson had the look of a defeated man. There was the witch holding a gun to his head. They seemed to be having a heated argument.

Sarah couldn't believe the nightmare was continuing. Her mind raced for a solution, but nothing came. She stood stunned, frozen in place. Suddenly, her feet were in the air. A muscular arm clamped around her neck. She was airborne, gasping for breath. She could feel his warm breath on the back of her neck; the smell of red wine clipped her nostrils. The strong arms constricted her breathing. She gasped for air that wouldn't come. Bright stars filled her vision as the air was rapidly leaving her lungs. Just as she was about to pass out, her body crashed to the floor. She heard voices arguing. Hitting the floor had jolted her hard, and life-giving air began to enter her lungs again. She felt his embrace and comforting words. Holding her gently, David Johnson said softly, "Sarah, are you all right? Sarah, everything will be fine." All while he was stroking her hair and cradling her gently.

"Where is she? Where is your mistress, your *sister*?" Rourke cackled while kicking Sarah in her side.

"Stop, Rourke, stop! Can't you see she is frightened to death?" David Johnson stated as he pulled her away from Rourke's violent kicking.

"She has every reason to be frightened, and you too, David. If your daughter doesn't return soon, I will have no choice but to kill you both. And don't worry, I will find Deborah and send her to visit you in hell."

David continued to comfort Sarah as Rourke paced back and forth; his eyes resembled those of a wolf pack stalking their target. David and Lydia's eyes met, holding for a few brief seconds. He didn't see the same confident eyes from before. There was confusion and, more importantly, fear in her eyes. Perhaps she could be useful, after all.

"That's it, up ahead." She pointed toward the Johnson house.

"Looks like someone is up waiting. There is a light on downstairs," David Abernathy pointed out.

"I'm sure my father is worried sick."

"Like all fathers," responded the divinity student.

"Oh, I get it." Deborah, not much of a churchgoer, grinned. "I bet more people would attend church if they had handsome ministers like you, David."

Abernathy blushed over the compliment. "Thank you, Ms. Debby, but God's message is far more powerful than a pretty face."

"Maybe so, but until God comes and delivers his message personally, it doesn't hurt that his spokesmen are handsome like you."

Abernathy laughed as he helped Deborah down from his horse.

"Seriously, David, how can I ever repay you? Please come in. After my father finishes yelling at me, he will give you a nice reward. I promise."

David smiled. "Delivering you home safely is reward enough, but if you really want to reward me, there is something you can do," he declared with a sly look on his face.

"Really, what is that?" Deborah replied coyly.

"If…when, I get my own church, would you do me the honor of attending my first sermon? It would really mean a lot."

Deborah smiled; the young divinity student had indeed been a godsend. He had delivered her safely through the valley of death. She stood on her toes and kissed his cheek. "I promise you, I'll be there. Thank you so much."

Abernathy blushed for a second time. "Would you like me to wait, to make sure everything is fine?"

"No need. Let me know when you get your own church. Bye." With that, Deborah ran happily to her front door and disappeared inside.

John Adams walked into the front parlor room. "He's resting comfortably, Thomas. There is nothing more you can do for him tonight. Why don't you head home? Tomorrow is going to be the most important day of your young life! No need for you to appear haggard or, worse yet, sleeping through the debate."

"You know me, John. I've done my work. I'm not much of a talker. Tomorrow will be up to you and some of the other gifted speakers. But mostly you, John. You speak most passionately from the heart, better than the others."

"I am humbled by your praise, but I fear I have not the words for such a monumental task."

"Keep in mind the events since Ben has arrived. Tyranny surrounds us even on a smaller scale. Someone has tried to enforce his tyranny through murder, torture, and intimidation. Is this our future, bowing to the king and his followers, who have no shame in using such tactics? John, keep in mind recent events. They are a microcosm of what the British government has done to us the past ten years. Speak from your heart, John. The words will come. I promise you, the words will come."

"I will certainly try, my friend. But you still need your rest. Shall I have Sarah make up one of the couches rather than you going all

THE SIGNERS

the way to the Graff house?" John Adams yawned. The day's events had caught up to the forty-year-old delegate.

"Thank you, John, that's a good idea, but before I retire, I must check something out," Jefferson responded while putting on his signature tricorne hat.

"You're worried about Sarah, aren't you? She should have been here by now," replied Adams.

"Yes. Something must have happened. May I borrow your horse? I know where the Johnsons live, and it is only a few blocks from here. I shouldn't be long."

"Of course, Thomas. Would you like me to come along?"

"No, John, you have a big day tomorrow." Jefferson threw Adam's words back at him. "I'm sure all is well, but I will sleep better knowing for sure."

"What about Major Hall? He can accompany you."

"Mr. Hancock sent him on another errand, I believe."

"Very well, then, make sure you're armed," ordered Adams.

Jefferson patted his holstered pistol. "Always."

"Here, take mine too. Just in case. It's primed and ready to go."

Jefferson smiled and walked out the door. An exhausted Adams headed for his bedroom, feeling guilty about sending Jefferson off alone. *Oh well,* Adams thought to himself. *This Rourke character isn't so crazy to go after one of his own partners.*

Deborah didn't think twice about the door being open and not locked. Her father was probably waiting in the living room, ready to read her the riot act. She really didn't know what to expect as she turned the corner and entered the living room. Deborah was about to jump for joy. There, sitting in the middle of the room, was Sarah. Deborah immediately recognized her father sitting beside Sarah with his back to her. Running toward Sarah, she saw the terror in her eyes. Her father slowly turned, revealing a swollen and bloody face. His eyes were more sad than terrified as Deborah embraced them both without speaking.

"How very touching! What a wonderful family portrait!" The familiar voice emerged from behind the fireplace mantel.

Deborah looked slowly at Rourke, her anger building. "What have you done to my father? How dare you—"

Rourke's open palm caught Deborah square in the cheek, sending her sprawling to the floor. David Johnson sprung from the chair, only to have the barrel of Rourke's pistol shoved under his eye. "Careful, Daddy. Don't want to make your darling daughters orphans at such a young age."

Lydia Ames emerged from the adjoining anteroom, pistol in hand.

David Johnson reached down to help his daughter. They embraced. "I'm sorry, Deborah, I'm so sorry."

"Shut up!" Rourke bellowed. "Move over here!" He pointed to a five-foot-long love seat. The three were squeezed together as Rourke looked them over. "We're going to play a little game. I'm going to ask a question, and if I don't like the answer, someone is going to be shot."

Rourke handed Lydia Ames a pouch; it was filled with paper and gunpowder, along with eight lead balls. Placing it on a nearby table, Rourke continued, "If I don't like your answer, I will put a ball into an arm or leg. While I ask more questions, Lydia will be reloading each gun. We can play my game for a long time." He pointed to the multiple lead balls.

"Let's get started. I don't know about you, but this is going to be fun!" Rourke cackled, his fanatical eyes dominating the room.

"Rourke, you're crazy. You can't do this," David Johnson blurted out.

Rourke lifted his pistol and fired. The ball hit David in the left arm, just above the elbow, blood splattering everywhere as the girls screamed and Lydia Ames winced at the brutal behavior. Grabbing

THE SIGNERS

the other gun from her, Rourke barked, "I forgot to tell you that if you speak out of turn, you get shot. Now, to the first question."

Thomas Jefferson was startled to see another rider so late at night. He was coming from the direction of the Johnson home. His instincts kicked in, and he reached for his pistol. The well-dressed rider appeared young, perhaps college age. Jefferson hailed him. "Good evening, sir. What has you out so late at night?"

The rider replied calmly, "No need to draw your weapon, sir. I am just a humble man of God, a Princeton student visiting his uncle here in Philadelphia."

Jefferson relaxed his grip but still rested it upon his pistol. "Even men of God rarely travel at this time of night, sir. What is your name?"

"Abernathy, David Abernathy, sir." He doffed his hat. "And whom do I have the pleasure of conversing with?"

"Thomas Jefferson."

"Well, I'll be! The famous Mr. Jefferson of Virginia?" David Abernathy looked quizzically into the eyes of the Virginia delegate.

"One and the same, Mr. Abernathy, but you still haven't answered my question," insisted Jefferson.

"A mission of mercy, Mr. Jefferson. Seems a young lady had some misfortune tonight. She was quite distraught and soaked like a rat. As if she sprung from the river," David Abernathy stated thoughtfully.

Jefferson's body immediately stiffened, his mind racing back to the events of the day. "Did this young woman have a name?"

"Why, yes, she did. It was Debby, Debby Johnson."

Before Jefferson could reply, a gunshot rang out; it came from the direction of the Johnson house. "Mr. Abernathy, do you know how to use one of these?" Jefferson asked as he whipped out the pistol given to him by John Adams.

"Never fired one in my lifetime, Mr. Jefferson. Is there trouble at Ms. Debby's house?"

"Yes, there is," Jefferson replied quickly, thrusting the pistol into the reluctant divinity student's hand. "Just aim and pull the trigger, but wait for my instructions. Come on."

Abernathy didn't hesitate as the two men rode toward the Johnson house. Jefferson immediately recognized his horse. *Sarah is here.* Dismounting quickly, Jefferson climbed onto the wraparound porch at the far end of the home. Abernathy followed, the two men creeping toward the middle window. Peering through the modern glass, Jefferson saw two women and a man seated with their backs to him. A well-dressed woman was facing him; she was busy reloading a pistol. She looked familiar to Jefferson, and then it hit him. The woman from City Tavern who had been talking to Deborah. Cushman had spoken with her while Jefferson, Adams, and Franklin had admired her from afar. Another man was waving a pistol in front of the threesome.

Jefferson refocused on the couch, recognizing Debby and Sarah immediately. The wounded man seated with them was Debby's father. Suddenly, the wild-eyed tormentor turned toward the window. *Rourke, it had to be Rourke,* Jefferson thought to himself. Hancock had said the man was a lunatic. Gazing into this man's eyes confirmed Hancock's opinion.

Jefferson heard the man scream, "Okay, first question, remember what happens if I don't like the answer!"

Inside the Johnson home, Deborah Johnson could not believe what was happening. Her father was writhing in pain while Sarah cried uncontrollably. Lydia Ames looked pained; however, she continued to help Rourke. Deborah knew she had to do something, and quickly.

"Enough of this game, Patrick. You came here to kill me, so go ahead, but leave these two alone," Deborah ordered, her eyes flashing determination and courage.

An evil grin spread across the Irishman's face as he slowly repeated his words. "Ah, oh, you didn't follow the rules." He slowly raised his pistol, ready to fire.

The unexpected loud crash startled Rourke, causing him to flinch. His gun roared to life, landing with a loud plunk into the back of the love seat, just missing Deborah. Out of the corner of his eye, Rourke spotted what looked like at large flowerpot propelling through the window. The flowerpot crashed to the floor, and shattered glass resonated throughout the room.

Rourke kept his eyes on the window while reaching back. "Lydia, another pistol, now!" he roared. No pistol materialized. He turned only to find no sign of Lydia. *At least she left the pistol on the table,* a furious Rourke thought as he leaped to grab the weapon. Deborah reacted swiftly, sticking her leg out, successfully tripping the madman. An enraged Rourke recovered. Reaching the gun, he turned quickly to face the new threat.

Rourke's instincts told him to flee, but he decided to finish what he came to do. Taking aim at Deborah Johnson, he pulled the trigger. Another shot rang out, disintegrating Rourke's pistol and severing his trigger finger. Rourke screamed in pain and had begun to run for the rear of the house when a second shot was fired. The ball splintered the wood doorway frame, missing Rourke's head by an inch.

Thomas Jefferson burst through the window, following Rourke to the rear of the house. "Take care of them, David. I'll be right back."

Jefferson paused, listening for any sign of Rourke. It was too dark to reload his pistol; he shuffled slowly into what must have been the kitchen. The back door was wide open. He heard footsteps retreating from the house. He quickly weighed his options and decided to stay with the family, hurrying back to the living room, only to be dismayed by what he found.

Deborah Johnson lay flat on the carpeted floor, while a shirtless David Abernathy applied the white cotton garment to her head. It was soaked in blood. David Johnson, in obvious pain, knelt over his daughter, begging her to wake up. Sarah Johnson sat curled into a ball, staring off into space, as if in a trance. Jefferson knelt beside David Abernathy.

"Head wound. Grazed her temple, lots of blood. She's breathing, but unconscious. We're going to need a doctor." The young student spoke nervously while maintaining control of his emotions.

"Continue to apply pressure." Jefferson walked to the window and tore down a set of curtains, ripping them in half. "Here, use this. Keep changing the dressing and let me know if the bleeding slows."

"Mr. Johnson, let me look at that arm," Jefferson urged softly while forcing the distraught father to his feet.

"Is my Debby going to make it?" he asked over and over as Jefferson examined his wounded arm.

"It looks like the bullet grazed her head, enough to render her unconscious. Her bleeding seems to be slowing. That's a good sign. Honestly, it's too early to tell. There is some good news on your arm. The ball exited out the back." Jefferson wrapped the arm in the remaining curtain material. Finished with the crude bandage, Jefferson pointed to Sarah. "Go to her and see if you can bring her back to us."

Abernathy stood; his hands were shaking as he approached Jefferson. "Mr. Jefferson, what just happened? Was this some kind of robbery?"

Jefferson stared at the young student. *So young, so innocent. These will be the boys we will send off to war.* The author of the Declaration of Independence shuddered at the thought of so many young men just like David Abernathy going off to war to maim or be maimed. He cursed the king and the Parliament for forcing it to come to this, war and all the death and destruction that would come. *Why do people in power always demand more? More power, more taxes, more control over all aspects of an individual's life? Why can't they understand that power always leads to corruption? The greater the power, the greater the corruption.* "I don't know your politics, Mr. Abernathy, but I'm afraid you landed smack-dab in the middle of the war. And like all wars, innocent bystanders just got hurt."

Chapter 24

The first maxim of a man who loves liberty should be never to grant to rulers an atom of power that is not most clearly and indispensably necessary for the safety and well-being of society.
—Richard Henry Lee

July 1, 1776
Philadelphia, Trenton, and New York City

John Adams finished dressing and was already sweating from the hot and sticky morning air. The humidity had returned with a vengeance, and the sun had not yet peaked through the eastern horizon. Dark clouds promised a stormy day in more ways than one. Adams fanned his face with several sheets of paper; he sat down to write a letter to his friend Archibald Bulloch. Bulloch was a former delegate from Georgia who was currently serving as the first president and commander in chief of the key Southern state.

"Good morning, John." Thomas Jefferson stood next to Adams; he, too, was dressed and ready to begin this important first day of July.

"Goodness, Thomas, you startled me! How did you sleep?"

Jefferson sat to put on his boots. "Not well, I'm afraid."

Adams suddenly remembered Jefferson's late-night excursion. "When did you return? What happened at the Johnson house? Did you find Sarah?"

Jefferson recounted the events of late last night. Adams dropped his quilt pen and stared at his friend in amazement. "Is Deborah going to survive?"

"David Johnson's neighbor is a doctor. Mr. Abernathy was able to rouse him. He was able to halt the bleeding, but she hadn't regained consciousness before I left. He seemed more worried about Sarah. She just sat, curled in a ball, staring off into space. It was very unsettling. One day this man had a happy, prosperous family, and the next day it lay in tatters."

"I'm afraid many American families are in for a similar fate in the coming months, Thomas. The British will not back down," Adams predicted.

"I have no doubt that you are right. It would not surprise me one bit if the British had something to do with Rourke's exploits."

Adams agreed. "Any change in Ben?"

"I just checked on him. Although he seems to be breathing without much exertion, I was unable to wake him," a discouraged Jefferson responded.

"Sarah will take good care of him," reported Adams.

"Yes, I'm sure she will. I am going to ride to the Graff house for a change of clothing."

"You were able to recover your horse?"

"Yes. Yours is tied up out front, and here is your gun." Jefferson handed John Adams his expensive pistol. "Mr. Abernathy was not a great shot, but he managed to scare off Rourke after I struck him in the hand."

Adams expertly handled his gun and replied, "I'm glad it was useful. Any further word on Rourke?"

"Mr. Abernathy was going to report everything to the sheriff early this morning. I'm sure they will find Mr. Rourke quickly," Jefferson suggested without much conviction.

"Take care, Thomas. I will see you at the statehouse soon."

Checking in on Cushman one more time, Thomas Jefferson said a short prayer and headed out to begin the most important day of his young life.

THE SIGNERS

Dark rain clouds continued to gather in the west. Thomas Jefferson stood alone in the courtyard. Fellow delegates filtered by slowly as the deadline quickly approached for the morning session to begin. Jefferson watched as traces of lightning flickered in the distance. *Looks like the good Lord has decided to add some of nature's fireworks to today's proceedings,* Jefferson thought to himself as he made his way into the monumental meeting.

"Thomas." It was Benjamin Franklin, clutching to Jefferson's elbow and whispering into his ear. "I fear Pennsylvania is in disarray, and maybe several others, but I am hopeful of an eventual positive outcome," the venerable Franklin stated with a cheery smile and a wink.

"You always stay so positive, Dr. Franklin. Why is that so?" Jefferson quizzed the patriarch of the Second Continental Congress.

"Ah, Thomas, an old family secret. You see, the opposite sex will have nothing to do with grumpy old men. Therefore, if I am to continue to attract the lovely ladies that I desire, I must present a cheerful front. Quite simple, you see."

"So it's always about attracting women!" The shy Virginian laughed.

"From the time you notice they are different until the time you die, yes, Thomas, it is all about the women." The old Lothario chuckled.

Jefferson gave Franklin a friendly slap on the back and headed toward the Virginia delegation, seated in the back right. He stood beside the window and continued to monitor the coming storm.

"Mr. Jefferson, how do you see today's proceedings going?" The questioner was Benjamin Harrison, one of the senior Virginia delegates, who, along with Elbridge Gerry, had helped Jefferson carry off an impromptu town hall meeting just two days earlier.

"It seems like everything that has been said about the issue has already been said," replied Jefferson to his fellow Virginian.

"Which of course means that it will be said yet again, but probably in triplicate." The heavyset Harrison laughed.

Jefferson laughed, nodding in agreement. John Hancock brought down his gavel, opening the meeting. Several clerks began to close all the windows and the doors. Jefferson glanced at the clock. It was exactly ten o'clock. With the windows now closed, it didn't take long for the heat to build within the room as many delegates began to remove their coats and ready themselves for the coming storm.

"Mr. Secretary, please begin with Mr. Lee's resolution," John Hancock stated firmly and without any introduction.

The secretary of the Congress, Charles Thomson, rose to read the Lee Resolution. Thomson had emigrated from Ireland to the colonies when he was ten years old, along with his father and three brothers, soon after their mother had passed away. The penniless boys had arrived as orphans after their father died at sea. The boys were separated, and they never again saw one another. His fellow delegates knew of this remarkable story and had great respect for his ability to overcome such adversity. Jefferson listened intently as the forty-five-year-old began to speak with a lyrical Irish brogue still apparent. "Resolved, T'at t'ese United Colonies are, and of right ought to be, free and independent States, t'at t'ey are absolved from all allegiance to the British Crown, and t'at all political connection between t'em and the state of Great Britain is, and ought to be, totally dissolved."

"Let it be noted, Mr. Thomson, that the Congress will resume consideration as a committee of the whole to further discuss the resolution and the Declaration of Independence introduced last Friday by Mr. Jefferson and the rest of the committee," Hancock declared.

Jefferson noted only seconds had passed when John Dickinson rose to speak first. Benjamin Franklin, seated next to the independence holdout, shook his head ever so slightly as the eloquent Dickinson began his arguments against separation. Jefferson thought that the elderly Pennsylvanian looked exhausted. His normally pale skin looked ghastly white, the wrinkles throughout his face seemed to have doubled, and his lean body appeared emaciated.

"I know how unpopular I have become taking the stand I now prepare to defend. My conduct this day, I expect, will give the finishing blow to my once-great and now-too-diminished popularity. But thinking as I do on the subject of debate, silence would be guilt," the Pennsylvania delegate continued to address his fellow members.

Jefferson marveled at his persuasiveness. If *he* were on the fence, Dickinson's words might have persuaded him that day. But he was not on the fence, and as Dickinson continued his methodical assault against independence, Jefferson looked around to see the faces of the other delegates. *Not good,* he thought to himself. The others looked sympathetic to his words. Even some of the staunchest supporters of independence seemed entranced by Dickinson's logical argument.

"To proceed now with a Declaration of Independence would be to brave the storm in a skiff made of paper." Dickinson's finishing remark caused an extraordinary silence to overcome the assembled body. No one spoke. The frail Pennsylvanian sat, and the rest of the assembly reflected on a remarkable performance denouncing the drive for independence. The only noise came from the rain, which began to pelt the windows as the summer storm raged into the city and offered a fitting end to the brilliant speech.

Thomas Jefferson, so sure of the passage of the Declaration of Independence just minutes before, now looked around the room, which remained in stunned silence. Everyone sat in his seat. No one moved. *Would Dickinson's words turn the other delegates away from the path of independence? Would the frail Pennsylvania lawyer crush the revolution?* Jefferson, the shy and reluctant public speaker, was about to rise when movement came from the Massachusetts table. It was John Adams, and Jefferson took a deep sigh of relief.

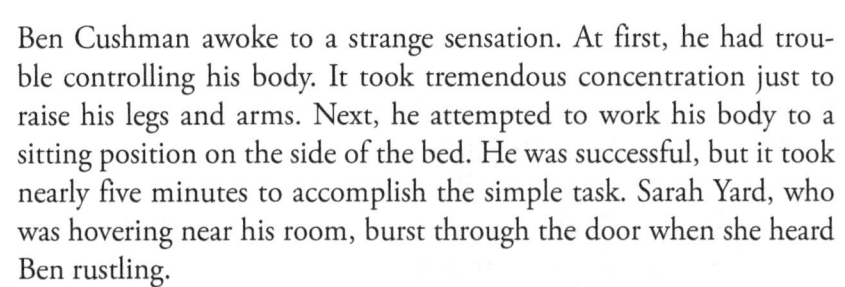

Ben Cushman awoke to a strange sensation. At first, he had trouble controlling his body. It took tremendous concentration just to raise his legs and arms. Next, he attempted to work his body to a sitting position on the side of the bed. He was successful, but it took nearly five minutes to accomplish the simple task. Sarah Yard, who was hovering near his room, burst through the door when she heard Ben rustling.

"Whoa, slow down, young man," Sarah ordered, sidling up close to her new patient.

Cushman looked stunned as his eyes circled the room, finally settling on the strange woman. "Pardon my language, ma'am, but who the hell are you, and where the hell am I?"

Sarah Yard blushed but stood her ground. "Dr. Rush predicated you'd be disoriented when you awakened. My name is Sarah Yard. I run a boardinghouse. Mr. Jefferson, Mr. Adams, and the others brought you here last night, hoping you would recover." She spoke softly while pouring Cushman a cup of tea. "Here, Dr. Rush believes you're dilated or hydrolated—oh, I forget what he called it. He said I had to get you to drink a lot."

"Good. How about a beer?" Cushman remarked with a slight smile; he was starting to regain some muscle function.

"Let's start with the tea, Mr. Cushman," scolded the elderly caretaker.

Cushman attempted to stand, only to topple back into the bed.

"Easy. Go slow, Mr. Cushman."

Undaunted, Ben tried again, and although wobbly, he remained standing. "Mrs. Yard, I appreciate all you've done for me, but I really must get going."

"Not before you finish that tea and have something to eat. Go ahead and get dressed. I will finish preparing your breakfast," Sarah demanded.

"Yes, Mother," Cushman whispered under his breath as she marched out of the small bedroom.

The storm continued to grow as thunder clapped loudly, and brilliant streaks of lightning lit up the darkened room. The rain was blowing sideways, assaulting the windows, as if demanding to enter the debate.

John Adams began slowly, methodically making the case for independence as he had done hundreds of times before. He spoke without notes, but from his heart, producing word upon word, sentence upon sentence, weaved together from conviction and passion.

THE SIGNERS

"I see a new nation, a nation where people from every corner of the globe will look with admiration and envy. Objects of the most stupendous magnitude, measures in which the lives and liberties of millions, born and unborn, are most essentially interested are now before us. We are in the very midst of revolution, the most complete, unexpected, and remarkable of any in the history of the world."

As he did when John Dickinson spoke, Jefferson took note of the men soaking in every word spoken by the Boston lawyer. Like with Dickinson, they seemed to be enthralled as Adams continued to make the case for independence.

John Hart and Abraham Clark of New Jersey nodded in passionate agreement as Adams continued. Jefferson noted that the other members of the New Jersey delegation were not in attendance. Benjamin Franklin, who ofttimes would secure a quick nap during long speeches, remained alert and supportive, with the occasional tapping of his cane onto the floor. Even the reluctant Robert Livingston of New York appeared to be moved by Adam's argument. *It's not like they hadn't heard both sides of the issue many times before,* thought Jefferson. *Perhaps it was the fact they were so close to making a decision.* Jefferson was encouraged that even men like Edward Rutledge of South Carolina were giving Adams their full attention.

Adam's fervor for independence continued to match the storm's intensity. As the thunder echoed through the chamber, he continued with the brilliance of an ancient Greek orator extolling the virtues of a new and independent country.

Long since discarding his coat, Adams loosened his kerchief, undid the top button to his silk shirt, and rolled up his sleeves. The violent storm had not cut into the humidity, and the hall seemed at least ten degrees warmer. Everyone, including the president, John Hancock, had removed their coats while fanning themselves in an attempt to fight the heat and humidity.

A brief commotion caused Jefferson to look away, but Adams remained focused, not missing a word. Three men were entering the chamber. Jefferson took note of the missing three delegates, all from New Jersey, the president of Princeton College, John Witherspoon; Francis Hopkins; and Richard Stockton. The men quietly made their way to the New Jersey table, shaking off their rain-soaked clothes as they went. Minutes later, John Adams ended his address to the assembly and sat down. Similar to the Dickinson speech, the men of the Second Continental Congress sat in silence, absorbing the brilliant oration of the man from Braintree.

"Mr. Adams." It was Richard Stockton speaking sheepishly. "My friends and I apologize, but we were obviously late and missed the body of your argument. Would you please consider repeating what we missed?"

Adams had been on his feet for over an hour, delivering the speech of his life. "Dear sirs, I think not. I'm hardly an actor here to entertain this wonderful audience," Adams stated with a wide smile.

"Please, Mr. Adams, your command of the facts clearly comes from your principles and conviction. Who better than you to relate what was just said than by you?" Surprisingly, it was Edward Rutledge who urged Adams to grant the request, despite the fact the South Carolinian had earlier argued against independence. Jefferson was encouraged by this new development.

"But it is Mr. Jefferson who so brilliantly pieced together the Declaration of Independence," Adams countered half-heartedly.

All eyes turned to the young Virginian, who had not yet spoken.

Jefferson gave a slight nod toward John Adams. "Thank you, John, for those kind words, but I think all in here are aware that my talent lean more toward the pen than to the tongue. I can think of no man who could lend a proper voice to what I have written than you, Mr. Adams. I urge you to grant the request of the gentlemen from New Jersey."

The confident and brash New Englander rose to his feet and did just that. For the next hour, Adams repeated his steady case for independence. The men hearing it for the second time seemed just as interested as the first. Jefferson noted that many of the men who looked kindly upon the words of John Dickinson appeared to be swayed more fervently with the words of John Adams. Jefferson was hopeful but still wary of the moderates in the room. Adams hadn't really said anything new, and while neither polished nor elegant, his words had stirred the assembly like never before.

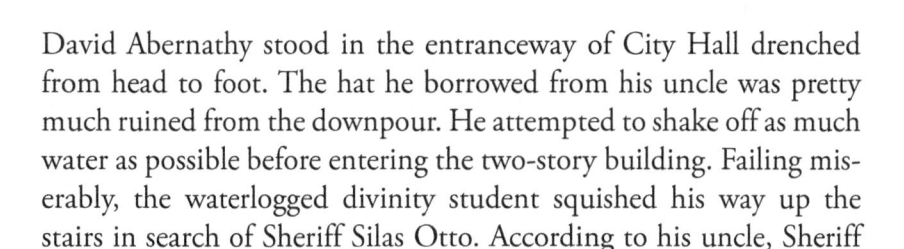

David Abernathy stood in the entranceway of City Hall drenched from head to foot. The hat he borrowed from his uncle was pretty much ruined from the downpour. He attempted to shake off as much water as possible before entering the two-story building. Failing miserably, the waterlogged divinity student squished his way up the stairs in search of Sheriff Silas Otto. According to his uncle, Sheriff Otto was a bit of a dullard but a competent lawman.

Abernathy began to recall the most adventure-filled night of his young life. Once the doctor had arrived and things had calmed down somewhat, Thomas Jefferson had pulled him aside and asked him if he wouldn't mind reporting this incident to the proper authorities the following day. The famous Virginian relayed that he would be unable. *Something important happening in the Congress.* He had agreed to Jefferson's request, and that had brought him to City Hall, in search of the sheriff.

"Excuse me, where can I find Sheriff Otto?" Abernathy questioned a young man as he entered the second-floor hallway. The young clerk threw his arm back and pointed to the next door on the left.

The door was open, but David decided to knock anyway. Sitting behind a massive wooden desk, a tall thin man looked up and motioned Abernathy into the room, pointing to a chair in front of his desk. *Doesn't anybody speak in this building?* David thought to himself as he sat down.

"I'm a very busy man. State your business," ordered the sheriff without looking up from his paperwork.

"Sheriff Otto, I presume?" David stood to properly introduce himself.

Otto finally looked up from his paperwork and stared at the intruder. "No, I'm King George III. Now, state your business or get the hell out of here." The sheriff was now glaring at him.

Unruffled, David spoke evenly as he retraced the events of the night before, leaving out no details of the grisly evening.

"Jefferson, you say, Thomas Jefferson coerced you into this scheme?" Otto's glare bored into him.

"I wouldn't say *coerced*. I helped him on my own volition," David remarked, sensing the sheriff's dislike for the distinguished Virginian.

"Listen, boy, Mr. Jefferson and his colleagues have caused nothing but trouble since they arrived in my city," declared Otto.

I didn't realize it was your city, David thought to himself as he prepared his rebuttal. "Mr. Jefferson wasn't the one torturing people and threatening to kill them," David replied.

"You said Mr. Jefferson told you that the man committing these so-called crimes was Patrick Rourke, correct?"

David nodded.

"Well, Patrick Rourke is one of Philadelphia's finest citizens, very generous to every charity in town. And yet you say Mr. Jefferson shot one of Philadelphia's finest patrons. I would say that's trouble."

"Look, you say this Patrick Rourke is one your finest citizens. The man I saw was a raving lunatic, threatening to kill two women and an older gentleman. He had already put a ball into the man's arm. And furthermore, the look in his eyes showed me he was enjoying every moment of what was going on. Mr. Jefferson saved those people's lives and deserves to be treated like the hero that he is." David glared at Sheriff Otto, not intimidated by his position in the least.

"Well, Mr. Abernathy, is it? I will initiate an investigation into your charges, and if Mr. Rourke is involved, I assure you, we will not be frightened by his stature." The sheriff's sudden cooperation caught David by surprise. "Please don't misinterpret my reluctance to delve into tough cases. We have to be careful. Many people come in here accusing wealthy citizens of committing all kinds of despicable crimes. Most of the time, these accusations are nothing but fairy

THE SIGNERS

tales. You seem to be more adamant than most. I will get one of my assistants to begin an investigation today. Is there anything else, Mr. Abernathy?"

David couldn't belief the change in the sheriff's attitude. *Perhaps my first impression was wrong.* "Very well" was all he could muster and headed back out into the driving rainstorm.

The back office door swung open soon after David had left.

"You handled him quite well, Sheriff," the lavishly dressed beauty commented as she entered the room.

"Don't worry, Ms. Ames. By the time I finish this investigation, I might just charge Jefferson with attempted murder and breaking and entering. Nothing will happen concerning Mr. Rourke."

"See to it, Sheriff. Our usual donation to your re-election will be doubled this time," Lydia Ames remarked as she gracefully glided out of the room.

Sheriff Silas Otto smiled to himself as he applied the mathematics to his annual payment from Patrick Rourke.

The breakfast and tea had somehow made Cushman feel stronger. The dizziness had disappeared and was replaced by an occasional muscle spasm. Little by little, he was regaining some strength. Not that he was ready to tangle with Rourke's thugs again, but perhaps he could get on his horse and visit Deborah. Sarah Yard had told him about how Red had arrived in the nick of time to save the family. She had told him about Deborah's condition, which had put Ben into a lousy mood. Blaming himself for not staying with her during her escape, Cushman was bound and determined to muster enough strength to visit the Johnson household. At the very least, he had to see Deborah and make sure she was safe from another attack by that lunatic Rourke.

Cushman had spent his breakfast rehashing the events of last night. Many fears continued to plague his thoughts, especially the one involving Deborah. Had Rourke been telling the truth? Was she truly working for him, or was it just one more form of diabolical physiological torture from an evil genius? If she was somehow involved with Rourke, it would explain how she had managed to find where he had been held captive. *Had it all been an act?* If so, she was a pretty good actress. As much as it pained him to admit, he had fallen hard for Deborah. Perhaps *love* was too strong a word, but it was close. He couldn't imagine being away from her laughter, the wonderful smell of her hair, and the electricity he felt every time she touched him. The conflict continued to grow as Ben contemplated every possible explanation. Unfortunately, Rourke's words kept haunting Ben. *"She was working for me the entire time. Your girlfriend set you up this whole time. You were nothing more than a pawn, a very weak one at that."* Could Deborah be guilty of such treachery? Cushman had to find out the truth and, more importantly, what to do if indeed it was the truth.

The doctor gave the four boys final instructions and watched as they hoisted the heavy trunk and began their three-block march to pier number 5, near Penn's Landing. He had made last-minute arrangements with the same Philadelphia banker to sell off his belongings. No doubt the banker would screw him royally, but the alternative was to do nothing. Satisfied that the boys would complete their task, he walked next door to see if he could help speed things along.

"Angus, thank God you're here. Could you look in on the girls?" David Johnson looked haggardly as he directed several workers loading two flatbed wagons.

Dr. Angus Dixon had recently lost his wife and newborn, and the tragic event set in motion events and decisions that had caused his life to spin out of control. Booze and questionable medical practices had cost the doctor most of his friends and associates. David was one of the few who had stood by him while he battled his demons. Recently, however, Dr. Dixon had begun to regain some of his old confidence and seemed to be digging himself out of the doldrums.

Once the doctor put his mind to something, he could be a real bulldog.

Deborah lay sleeping in the middle of the living room. Dr. Dixon didn't want her moved. She looked pale. The bandage wrapped around her head made her look like a pirate. He removed the wrapping and examined her head wound. A two-inch gash ran along the side of her head, from the temple to the ear. It wasn't very deep, perhaps an eighth of an inch. Dr. Dixon had seen far more severe wounds, and people had not even lost consciousness. "It doesn't appear to be severe," he stated cautiously.

"Then why won't she wake up?"

"The human body is a mystery, David. Everybody reacts differently to similar situations. Why does the flu epidemic kill thousands and yet have little or no effect on others? Deborah is young and healthy. She will probably awaken very soon." *Or will lay asleep and wither away from lack of food.*

"So the trip will not affect her outcome." A worried father fretted.

"She needs bed rest. Whether here or at sea will not matter. But at least at sea she will be away from the clutches of Mr. Rourke."

David Johnson shuddered at the mention of his former friend and associate. How could he have been so stupid to be drawn into his circle? Of course, the answer was Lydia Ames. She had been an evil temptress, and David had fallen under her spell. There was only one way to break the spell and save his family: to get as far away from Rourke as possible.

"How about Sarah?" Dr. Dixon asked as they made their way toward her first-floor bedroom.

"I checked on her several times during the night. She remained curled up the entire night. Have you ever seen anything like this, Angus?"

"Yes. When I was a teenager back in London. My friend Jack and I were studying medicine. Every Tuesday, we would venture out to Bedlam and watch the crazies. It was normally a penny to watch the freak show, but on Tuesdays it was free."

"I've never heard of such a thing," an appalled David Johnson responded.

"I know. It sounds cruel, and in reality, it was. It was London's first insane asylum, founded by the sisters of St. Mary's. A regular hospital at first, then they began to accept lunatics. After many centuries, it was turned into a lunatic asylum. It was called Bethlehem Hospital, but most people referred to it as Bedlam."

"Bedlam? The word *bedlam* refers to confusion, out-of-control antics."

"Exactly," countered the doctor. "The word derives from that hospital, and believe me, the definition fits perfectly. Normally, the inmates were chained to the floor or the wall. But some were allowed to roam around the rooms. People would pay a penny to watch them fight and fornicate."

"You're not serious?" an incredulous David Johnson responded.

"Afraid so. People would bring long sticks to prod them, which would enrage the inmates and create an even livelier show. Thousands and thousands of people visited Bedlam every year."

Johnson shook his head in disbelief.

"Not exactly my finest moment as a human being. But while visiting, I remember a number of people who sat in the corners of their rooms, curled up in a ball, like Sarah, and just stare off into the distance. I was always curious about these people. Others would poke them with their sticks, and there was never a reaction. It was as if they had no feelings."

"Did any of them ever recover?"

"I do recall asking Dr. Mason about such people. His theory was that they were shocked into a state of paralysis by witnessing something horrible, similar to Sarah last night. He believed that the only way to recover was to receive a similar shock. And since in their current state that was unlikely to happen, you had to simulate that shock."

"What, have someone murdered in front of their very eyes?" Johnson asked.

"Well, no, but you had to simulate a horrifying experience."

"How on earth could you do such a thing?"

"Dr. Mason suggested you tie the person's hands and feet together then toss them into a lake or river."

"Drown them?" David Johnson looked at his friend in astonishment.

"No, no, but make them think they are drowning, then rescue them before it occurs."

"Sounds barbaric."

"No more barbaric than amputating an arm or leg or forcing blood from a person without any real knowledge that the procedure might do more harm than good."

"Angus, I will not let you do that to Sarah."

"Have no fear, David. The voyage across the ocean may prove the very cure that Sarah needs. But if she hasn't recovered by the time we land, you will need to make a very difficult decision. Either try the shock therapy."

"Or…"

"Or have her admitted to Bedlam."

Ben Cushman's frustration was reaching a boiling point. He had tried walking across the room and only made it halfway before collapsing to the floor. Mrs. Yard was at his arm but couldn't support the heavier Cushman. *It's as if my legs were made of rubber.*

"Give it time, Mr. Cushman, give it time. Dr. Rush promised a full recovery," Sarah Yard kept telling him.

"I don't have time, Mrs. Yard. A madman's on the loose. I have to visit Deborah, to make sure she is safe."

"The police have been alerted. I am sure this Mr. Rourke will be apprehended soon."

"I'm afraid Mr. Rourke's tentacles reach far into powerful circles. I don't know who we can trust."

"Very well, drink some more tea and we'll try again."

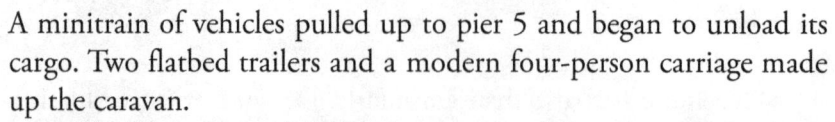

A minitrain of vehicles pulled up to pier 5 and began to unload its cargo. Two flatbed trailers and a modern four-person carriage made up the caravan.

The short powerfully built captain of the ship strode down the gangplank with a wide smile. The downpour had been replaced by sprinkles of rain, but the clouds to the west suggested the worst might not be over.

"David, my good friend, I am so happy you and your family will be sailing with us. It is a great pleasure for me to serve you."

"Captain Medford, thank you for accommodating us with such short notice," replied David Johnson.

"Not a problem at all. Anything for an old friend." The captain laughed.

That and the one thousand pounds I paid you. "I was a bit surprised that with the landing of the Howe brothers imminent, you would not be with the fleet."

"Just between you and I, the fleet will indeed be landing very soon," Medford replied uncomfortably.

"How soon?" David Johnson, the Tory, was still concerned for his country.

"Maybe today, but very soon. As for the role of the *HMS Richmond*, suffice it to say that we have an important mission to complete before we re-engage our traitorous brethren. But enough talk of the war. Will your lovely daughter be joining us on the voyage?"

"Yes, but I'm afraid she has suffered a serious injury, as well as my servant, Sarah. They were involved in some terrible business, I'm afraid."

"What type of terrible business?" Captain Medford's interest was aroused.

"Have you ever had any contact with a merchant by the name of Patrick Rourke?" Johnson's question was not accusatory.

Medford hid his surprise well and answered nonchalantly, "Heard the name before, but never had any contact with him or his ships. Why? How's he involved? Isn't he a Tory, like you?"

David Johnson told a short version of what he knew to be the truth, only leaving out his relationship with Lydia Ames and her manipulation of him and his daughter.

"Sounds like a Shakespearean play," noted Captain Medford, trying to avoid suspicion. Medford, of course, had paid Rourke to carry out the plot against the members of the Continental Congress. The Howe brothers and Colonel Nathan Parker had put him charge of the daring plan.

Ironic that Rourke had used the Johnson family, Medford thought to himself. *So Rourke had failed and then sought revenge on the man responsible for his failure. I probably would have done the same thing. But more importantly, I'm a thousand pounds richer because of his failure.*

Medford was not worried in the least that the plot had failed. The only true reality in war is that chaos will reign, and even the best-laid plans will go awry. The fact that Rourke had come so close to killing so many of the rebel leaders should give comfort to professionals like Colonel Parker. *The Howe brothers will be impressed by the effort,* Medford thought. A silver lining in the failure was that Medford would be able to cover his ass by placing the blame on Rourke. David Johnson would be a perfect witness to Rourke's incompetence. Medford would have preferred that Rourke had succeeded, but he now had the perfect scapegoat. Wars brought opportunities for people who were willing to do those things that polite society looked down upon. It was men like Medford and Colonel Parker, and yes, even Rourke, who would profit the most.

The Howe brothers, Lord North, and even King George would take credit for the final victory and be toasted throughout English society. History books would talk of their steady leadership and clever strategy. But it would be men like Medford and Colonel Parker who would execute the harsh realities needed to win wars. History books wouldn't mention the brutalities necessary to achieve the wonderful end. And if in the meantime they made a little profit for themselves, so be it.

Medford watched as Deborah Johnson, prone on a stretcher, was carried onto the *Richmond*. He had met her twice, once at her father's store and once at City Tavern. She was as beautiful as he remembered, even with a bandage around her head. *What a shame. Hopefully she can recover soon, and—*

"Captain, I pray the payment you received is acceptable," David Johnson whispered quietly.

"Quite sufficient, David. I have moved from my quarters. Your family shall share it. It has four beds, as you requested." Medford looked up to see a middle-aged man with his arm around a young woman, guiding her slowly up the gangplank. The woman was an attractive mulatto, but she was hunched over and staring off into the distance. Her eyes were dull and lifeless, like she was a walking corpse.

Johnson noticed the captain's discomfort and remarked, "She witnessed some terrible things yesterday. She has been in a trancelike state ever since. Captain, I would like you to meet a family friend and doctor, Angus Dixon. He will be watching over the girls during the voyage."

They exchanged pleasantries as Medford continued to supervise the loading of the luggage. "David, are you planning on transporting the carriage?"

"Is it possible?" Looking suspiciously into Medford's eyes, David knew what was coming next.

"Well, it would take a while to secure it on board, and of course, when we make port—"

"How much more, Captain?"

"Oh, I imagine fifty pounds would work." Medford smiled.

"Very well, fifty pounds. Make sure it is secured properly. She's pretty heavy."

Medford smiled and gave the orders to hoist the expensive carriage aboard. "Lieutenant Smith, how long will it take to load that carriage?"

"About one hour, sir, sooner if we can store it under the foredeck," replied the nervous lieutenant. The young officer was still intimidated by the captain. He had just recently been promoted to

THE SIGNERS

second-in-command after the unfortunate drowning of Lieutenant Addison Prescott, who had fallen overboard and was never recovered.

Medford pondered his officer's reply. He was the only one who knew the true contents of the secretive crates stored under the foredeck. It had been under lock and key and constant guard since it was removed from the colonial merchant ship. There was room for the carriage, but it would require the pulley system to lower it down into the forehold. Many eyes would be able to see the stolen crates. Although they couldn't guess the contents, it may cause too much curiosity. "No," replied Medford. "Use the storage under the aft deck, even if it takes longer."

"Yes, sir." And Lieutenant Smith scampered off to oversee the loading of the year-old carriage.

A young Marine nervously approached Medford. Armed with a British musket, complete with bayonet, he and his partner had been guarding the entrance to the gangplank. "Excuse me, sir, there is a man on the dock that wishes to speak with you. He says he represents a friend of yours, something about *Operation Chaos*."

Medford's eyes widened as he gazed at the man pointed out by the Marine. The man was average in height and weight. His clothing suggested upper middle class, along with his posture and bearing. His tricorne hat was soaked from the earlier heavy rains. "Excuse me, David, please go on board." Medford slowly walked toward the newcomer.

"Captain Medford, my name is Albert von Schweinitz. I am a lawyer here in Philadelphia."

More reason to wage war against the colonies. Dirty, filthy Germans fornicating with our lovely English lasses. Another generation of mingling the races and you won't be able to recognize an Englishman anymore. "Yeah, well, how in the hell do you know my name?"

"I represent a mutual colleague, Mr. Patrick Rourke." The lawyer ignored Medford's lack of civility.

Not willingly to affirm any relationship with Rourke, Medford replied, "He's no colleague of mine. I've heard of him, though."

"He said you would say that, Captain Medford. Regardless, he asked me to give you this note. If you read the note in my presence,

I was instructed to give you this box." Von Schweinitz produced a two-by-four-inch box.

Medford was tempted to grab the box and shoot the lawyer. Had it not been for the loading of the Johnson carriage, he probably would have done just that. Slowly he opened the enveloped and produced the letter. Droplets of rain still fell and began to pepper the note, forcing Medford to bend over to protect it.

Dear George,

If you've received this note, then you undoubtedly know that I'm interested in several of your last-minute passengers. I anticipated such a maneuver by Mr. Johnson and was having the docks watched. Imagine my surprise when I was informed that the HMS Richmond was their ship of choice. No matter what they have told you, their treachery against our plan and against the Crown is unassailable. As much as I admire your loyalty to our king and country, I have added a special bonus if you should see fit to the demise of the entire family. I have been told that the sea never gives up its dead. A clever warrior like you should have no problem staging a few accidents. Because my trust in you is firm, I will assume you will follow through if my lawyer does not return with the contents within the box. If this request is unsatisfactory to you, then please instruct my lawyer to return the box to me. There will be no hard feelings on my part if this occurs.

Sincerely
PR

Medford tucked the letter into his pocket, looked up, and stared at the box being extended to him by the filthy-dog lawyer. Without hesitation, he tore open the box. Even the cloudy day could not dim the sparkle emulating from its contents. Staring up at Medford was the golden profile of King George III. Surrounding George's head was printed "George III Dei-Gratia." By the grace of God, George III. The eight-gram gold guinea was first minted in 1761 and had continually held its value. Over thirty coins were crammed into the box. Medford smiled at the German lawyer and winked. As he walked back toward the British warship, he thought about the wonderful opportunities the war with the colonies had brought to him. Tossing the box of coins gently into the air, Medford looked forward to those wonderful opportunities yet to come.

Ben Cushman eased his way out the narrow wooden plank that served as a door on the outhouse in Mrs. Yard's back garden. The five glasses of tea that Sarah had forced him to drink seemed to be helping, although this was his second trip to the outdoor latrine within the last hour. His legs were feeling more like normal, and his strength was slowly returning. Dr. Rush's prediction was proving to be on the mark.

Sarah Yard stood watching from the back patio and smiled as Ben walked steadily back toward her well-kept two-story home. "Looks like Dr. Rush was right. Your strength is returning, Mr. Cushman."

"Only because of your expert nursing care, Sarah. I don't know how to thank you."

"Well, from what Mr. Adams has told me, it is I who should be thanking you for all you have done for the cause of liberty." Her faced beamed like a proud mother.

"You don't happen to have a horse I could borrow?" Cushman still wasn't sure if he could walk the several blocks to Deborah's home.

"You happen to be in luck, Mr. Cushman. Mr. Jefferson told me they have not been able to locate your horse, so he sent one over this morning. It's waiting outside."

Cushman gave Sarah a bear hug that lifted the tiny woman off the floor, and walked slowly toward the front door. He had been injured before but was always able to gauge easily what he could and could not do. This time he had no idea if his legs would hold up, and decided to go slow.

A greater worry than his physical state was the prospective conversation with Deborah. *How will I even bring up the subject? "Well, honey, just before this lunatic Rourke ordered my murder, he admitted that you are one of his many employees. You were with him from the beginning. What are we going to tell the children, that Daddy met Mommy while she was trying to have him killed?"*

Cushman rode slowly. *A million scenarios danced in his head. What if she never wakes up? What if she admits her guilt? Or what if she denies everything?* He continued to torture himself, picturing every conversation, and unfortunately, none of them ended happily. Cushman cursed himself when he realized the best set of circumstances he could come up with was that Deborah remained in a coma. *Ben Cushman, the coward, takes on the French, Indians, and mad assassins but cowers at the thought of a conversation with the woman he thinks he loves.* He turned the corner and could see the Johnson home.

Ben's body tensed as his eye caught the broken window, even though Sarah had told him of Jefferson's colorful entrance. Something seemed amiss, though Ben could not put his finger on it. He instinctively reached for his saddlebag, laden with weapons, only to realize he wasn't riding his own steed.

He drew closer, his uneasy feeling growing greater. In battle, he paid close attention to his instincts, a practice that had allowed him to survive many a tight spot. This was no exception. Dismounting, he decided to walk the remaining fifty yards, paying close attention to his surroundings, as if he were about to walk into a trap. Something was definitely wrong. *The window.* People in David Johnson's position would never have let a broken window remain unrepaired. At least it would be boarded up, let alone having it replaced almost immediately. The heavy rain that had fallen all morning would have done even more damage to the luxurious home.

His pace quickened to match his apprehension. Cushman broke into a jog as he approached the home. Without hesitation, he climbed through the window and entered the home of Deborah Johnson, the woman who had stolen his heart. A quick search of the first floor only heightened his worries. "Hello? Is anybody here? Deborah, Mr. Johnson, is anybody here?"

Cushman struggled up the stairs. He burst into the master bedroom, only to find it unoccupied. Two more bedrooms revealed similar circumstances. Sitting on the edge of the bed, Cushman racked his brain, attempting to decipher a totally unexpected discovery. It suddenly struck him; he bounded from the bed and opened the closet doors. *Empty. But what about the other rooms?* A quick sweep of the other closets revealed similar results. *No clothing.*

So David Johnson, fearing for his daughter's life, moved the entire family overnight. But where? Deborah never talked of an extended family, only her father and her servant, Sarah. Perhaps a summer home along the eastern shores of New Jersey. But Deborah had never talked of another home.

Ben's body stiffened. The sound of broken glass being dragged across the floor startled him. Walking slowly to the top of the stairs, he paused to listen. Sure enough, he heard footsteps, soon followed by another, and still another. Three people. Cushman cursed himself for not bringing a weapon. Walking quickly into the master bedroom, he found what he was looking for at the second-story fireplace. Cushman grabbed an iron poker and worked his way back to the top of the stairs. Deciding to go on the offensive, Ben worked his way along the wall, descending the stairs slowly. The footsteps grew louder; they were now approaching the stairways. Cushman readied himself and jumped the last three stairs to the main floor. A high-pitched scream pierced the air as Cushman came face-to-face with a young girl. She looked to be no older than twelve. Another youngster, this one a boy, stood beside the frightened girl, a small knife held gingerly in his trembling hand, ready to defend her.

"What the hell you screaming about, Jenny? I told you no one is home—"

A third young boy appeared from the kitchen, stopping dead in his tracks upon seeing a strange man armed with an iron rod. The newcomer quickly recovered and spoke slowly. "Look, mister, no one was supposed to be here. We didn't take nothing. We were just showing Jenny the house."

"Okay, you stop screaming." Cushman lowered the poker while pointing at the frightened girl. "And you put that knife away before someone gets hurt." They both quickly obeyed as Cushman took a less-threatening pose. "Now, all of you, sit, over there."

"Please, sir, we meant no harm. Jeremy and Andrew were just showing off a little. I dared them to show me the Johnson home. It was really all my fault. Please don't hurt us."

"Look, Jenny, is it? I'm not going to hurt you or your friends. Now, what were you saying? Why would anyone come into someone's home uninvited? How did you know the Johnson family wouldn't be here?" Cushman asked the question while knowing full well the answer he was about to receive would not be to his liking.

"We weren't gonna take nothing," Jeremy repeated. "Jenny's never been in a real nice house before, and we thought we could show her how rich people live. 'Cause they left."

"Are you talking about David Johnson and his daughter, Deborah?"

"Yea, and Sarah too. She's their nigra servant," replied Jeremy.

"Deborah's so beautiful, and nice too," added Jenny. "So is Sarah. I used to help Sarah clean their stable. Deborah would always say hello to me."

"So you repay their kindness by ransacking their home?"

"No, honest, sir, we were just showing off the house to Jenny." Andrew spoke for the first time. "We made a pact that we wouldn't steal nothin'. Even though we could, we made a pact."

"What do you mean even though you could?" Cushman demanded.

"Well, we could, because they're not comin' back. I heard Dr. Dixon tell my mom." It was Jeremy again.

"They're not coming back? Where did they go?" Cushman was afraid of the answer.

"To England. I heard Dr. Dixon say they were going to England. He said Mr. Johnson was selling his store and reopening one in London. Dr. Dixon went with them because Mr. Johnson needed someone to watch over Deborah and Sarah, 'cause they're both sick or something. The doctor also said something about somebody trying to kill the Johnson family."

Ben's heart began to race as he absorbed Jeremy's words. "You said Deborah was sick. What did you mean?"

"I saw them carry her into their carriage. She was on a stretcher. I thought she was asleep, but Jeremy said she got shot and hadn't awakened yet," Jenny said sadly.

"Mister, are you feeling all right? You don't look so good." Jenny stood and softly asked, "Was she your girlfriend?"

Cushman stared at the young girl and forced a weary smile. "That's a good question, Jenny, that's a good question."

"You're not going to tell on us, mister?" It was Andrew.

"No, but quickly, how long ago did they leave? And do you know from where?" Cushman's voice was growing weaker.

Andrew smiled a big toothless grin and spoke first. "Sure do. Me and Jeremy helped carry the doctor's trunk to the waterfront, and we needed four of us. It was so heavy. Took it to pier number 5, down at Penn's Landing. It was scheduled to leave over an hour ago."

"I don't suppose you notice what ship they boarded?" Cushman asked with renewed hope.

It was Jeremy, this time with the wide grin. "I know the ship. It had thirty-two guns. I counted 'em."

"A warship?" Cushman's voice was incredulous.

"Yes, sir. I talked to one of the Marines guarding the gangplank. He said they were taking on supplies and sailing to London, but they had to wait for a while because they were going to take some ship store owner and his family. I told him it was the Johnson family and Dr. Dixon. The ship, it was the most beautiful thing I've ever seen. I will never forget the *HMS Richmond*."

Cushman bolted up from his chair, and before he left, he turned to the three youngsters. "Next time you try to impress a beautiful young girl, try not to break and enter into a private home. Now, get out of here…and thank you for the information." Cushman winked at the threesome as he hurdled through the broken window in the vain attempt to catch the *HMS Richmond*.

Thomas Jefferson glanced up at the clock hanging on the front wall. It was three o'clock, and the debate was still raging. The two main debaters, John Dickinson and John Adams, had summed up the pros and cons earlier in the day. As far as Jefferson was concerned, they had said everything that needed to be said. Unfortunately, politicians being politicians, they had to speak out, if nothing more to make themselves feel worthy.

Despite his low opinion of politicians and lawyers, Jefferson held every member of the Second Continental Congress in very high esteem. Even those he disagreed with could present their case with clarity and passion. Oh, sure, there were a few arrogant and pompous windbags who loved to hear themselves speak. But unlike any other representative body he had served with, these men had managed to check their own self-interests at the door. No small feat, considering the majority of the delegates were lawyers.

No one could question the patriotism of a John Dickinson, who, despite his opposition to independence, was determined to oppose the king and his power grab. Dickinson stated often that if war came, he would leave the Congress and take an officer's position in the Pennsylvania militia. No, this group of men were united in stopping King George and Parliament from usurping the God-given freedoms from these American colonies. At present, they might disagree with the method, but even that, Jefferson believed, was about to change.

The Reverend John Witherspoon was currently speaking. His accent could never hide the fact that he had moved to the colonies from his native Scotland. A fierce supporter of independence, he used imagery combined with his lyrical Scottish accent to make it seem like he was reading poetry. "This country is not only ripe for independence but also in danger of becoming rotten for lack of it." Jefferson's eyes met Ben Franklin's, and both men smiled at the clever analogy. Franklin's Pennsylvania delegation would hold the key for victory. Jefferson no longer doubted that the resolution would pass and his Declaration of Independence would become the stated course of action. However, if they were to succeed, a unanimous vote would be necessary, and that was going to be difficult. The majority of the Pennsylvania delegates were loyal to Dickinson, despite Franklin's giant presence. New York was also questionable, as was South Carolina. Delaware was in favor, but Jefferson noted that one of the delegates was missing. Caesar Rodney was one of the most outspoken advocates for independence in the Congress, but he was nowhere to be seen. Without Rodney, Delaware was a toss-up.

The Thirteen Colonies would need to present a united front to stand firm against King George III. If the colonies had any chance of persuading France or Spain to become their ally, then they would have to be convinced that the split was permanent and that the Americans would not run back to their mother country at the first sign of adversity. *No, it must be a unanimous vote, somehow, someway,* Jefferson thought to himself. *We will have to convince everybody.*

The four-block ride to the riverfront seemed like an eternity. Cushman urged the horse over the cobblestone streets of Philadelphia with all his skill. Heavy rains had started again, flooding certain portions of the road, making it slippery and very dangerous. Several times, Ben thought his horse would tumble to the ground, only to recover. A lesser-skilled rider would have hit the ground three blocks prior.

The Philadelphia riverfront was a crazy quilt of organization and structure. Some of the piers were new and well-kept, with modern warehouses and loading and unloading equipment. Their naval yards were clearly marked with excellent access roads and protective fences securing the entire complex. Contrasting the rather-modern structures were barely usable piers featuring rotted decking and pylons. Dilapidated warehouses dotted the river scene, with no visible boundaries to determine where one complex started and another began.

Luckily for Cushman, the access road leading to pier number 5 was actually marked with a large wooden sign signaling the beginning of the river complex. There were two piers jotting out perpendicular into the Delaware River. The piers appeared to be about twenty-five yards wide and seventy yards apart, easily capable of securing ocean-going ships on each side. There was only one ship moored at the pier, while another ship was negotiating the Delaware River, about to raise its last sail. From his vantage point he could not read the ship's name, but the ship getting under sail was certainly a British warship. His heart sank as the warship began to slowly move south toward the Atlantic Ocean. Cushman rode hard toward the pier, hoping the ship underway was not the *Richmond*. Empty shipping crates and newly arrived cargo created an artificial barrier between the pier and Cushman's current position, causing him to slow down as he approached. Hope quickly returned when he noticed that the ship tied to the pier had cannons on the deck. *Another warship,* Cushman thought as he approached the barricade of cargo. He negotiated his horse expertly among the large crates. He was about to hail several sailors standing on the pier when he heard a low whistle. The weary Virginian came to a stop and listened closely. *There it was again, definitely a whistle.*

"Cushman, over here, hurry," a familiar voice whispered.

Ben glanced to his right and couldn't believe his eyes. Crouching behind a large crate was none other than Major Jacob Hall. He waved him closer and pointed to a nearby fence where Hall had secured his horse. Cushman did the same and was soon crouching beside the mysterious spy.

"What in the hell are you doing here?" Cushman whispered harshly.

"Just getting my gold back," replied the calm provocateur.

"Gold? What are you talking about?"

"Remember the night of the assassination attempt at City Tavern?"

"Of course. It was just last week." Cushman was starting to lose his patience. He glanced at the ship, under full sail, leaving the pier complex.

THE SIGNERS

"Relax, that's not the *Richmond*. That's the *Jason*, her sister ship. There's the *Richmond*, and that's where your girlfriend is." Hall pointed to the docked ship.

Cushman could only mutter, "But how did you—"

"I was about to explain. Remember when Dr. Franklin wouldn't let me tell you about your brother George? George was a boatswain's mate on one of John Hancock's ships, the *Treasure*. I was on a secret mission to France when we were attacked by the captain of the *Richmond*." Hall pointed toward the ship with bitter disdain. "I can't reveal the entire mission, but I was responsible for a large amount of gold. It was stolen, and I'm sure it's still aboard that ship."

"How did George fit into all this?"

"He saved my life and many others at that time. The British captain tried to murder all the survivors. Your brother helped me arrange an escape. We were lost at sea for several weeks. George and I were the only survivors." Hall paused as both men continued to survey the British warship.

"While we were at sea, we passed the days talking about everything, mostly our families. I reaffirmed our adventures at Fort Duquesne." Hall paused, his eyes looking downward. "George told me about your parents. I haven't had a chance to tell you how sorry I am. He told me about James and you going after *Yellow Snake*. Any luck?"

Ben's shoulders sank as he recalled the horrible murders, but his half-smile also indicated success. "Yes, it was the fuckin' *Snake*. We went into the Ohio Country, five different times. We had a few close encounters, but that devil had nine lives. I finally caught up with him this past winter near the southern shores of Lake Erie. It was quite satisfying ending his life. I'll tell you about it over some beers, hopefully soon."

Hall smiled broadly. He was very familiar with *Yellow Snake* and his French partner, Ignes Caron. "Evil bastard, not unlike this Rourke character," Hall mused out loud. "The best revenge is to be unlike him who performed the injury."

"Since when did you become so philosophical?" Cushman smiled.

"Marcus Aurelius. I read occasionally," Hall protested.

A pulley system was beginning to drop a carriage below the aft deck. Hall continued his tale. "I recently discovered who was responsible for the theft. It was orchestrated by none other than Patrick Rourke. One of Ms. Ames's girls had seduced a bank accountant familiar with the gold shipment. Rourke hired the British captain George Medford to intercept the shipment."

"Perhaps the two were also acting together arranging for the assassination attempts," Cushman pondered out loud.

"My thoughts exactly, and if that's true, how far up into British leadership does this go? It gets even more complicated. I got word this morning that the *Richmond* was in port, but for only a short time. I came by Mrs. Yard's this morning to recruit you to help. She informed me of your condition, so I came here soon after."

"She never told me," replied Cushman.

"I told her not to. Didn't need you coming down here half-dead, trying to help me."

"I'm a fast healer."

"It appears so, but I'm afraid the news gets worse. When I got here, I saw Medford talking to David Johnson. They were carrying Deborah on a stretcher. She appeared unconscious. The servant girl also needed assistance, like she was walking in a trance. A well-dressed gentleman interrupted them, and I saw him give Medford what looked like a box of gold coins."

"Any idea what he wanted?"

"I do now," replied Hall with a smile. "I followed the man back to the access road, and let's just say after some persuasive techniques, he told me everything. He was hired by Rourke to bribe Medford to kill the entire Johnson family while at sea."

"We can't let them leave. We have to get them off the ship!" Cushman stated firmly.

"Yes, of course, but don't forget, I must get the gold back also," countered Hall with equal firmness. "You got any ideas how we can accomplish both?"

Cushman nodded, a smile slowly emerging. "Maybe I do, but you might not like it." Cushman eyed several crates tied together with a sturdy rope. "You got a knife?"

"Of course." Hall nodded. "Just what do you have in mind?"

Cushman quickly cut away a six-foot section of rope and smiled. "I told you, you might not like it."

Thirty miles northeast of Philadelphia sat the small village of Trenton, New Jersey. Situated on the eastern banks of the Delaware River, the small town had a thriving economy. River commerce competed with hundreds of small family farms to make Trenton a vibrant and growing center of economic activity. The village consisted of approximately one hundred quaint homes. It was hard to get lost in the small town that consisted of only two roads, King and Queen Streets. Located in the middle of King Street was the town's only tavern. It was appropriately named the *King Street Tavern*. The early-evening crowd hadn't arrived yet as the two men sat in a corner booth, sipping their ale.

"So he escaped? That's two in a row you've bungled, Rourke." The British Major glared at him.

Rourke returned the look, placing his hand on the pistol. *I ought to put a hole in your head right here and now*, Rourke thought as he squeezed the loaded gun.

"I know what you're thinking: you'd like to kill me. Get in line, Mr. Rourke. Besides, despite your incompetence, my offer still stands, unless, of course, you still can't deliver what I want."

Rourke's temper was at a boiling point; he never had to endure the failures of the past week, and all because of one man, Benjamin Cushman. Next time they met, he wouldn't fool around—just one bullet between the eyes. Because of those failures, Rourke had to put up with the arrogant British officer. "Look, as I told you before, he had help. I was betrayed by one of Lydia's girls. He also had help from Jefferson, Adams, and some of the other delegates."

"The same delegates you were supposed to have done away with, a bunch of politicians and lawyers," Major Hadden Campbell sneered. He wouldn't let up as he continued to glare at Rourke.

"There was someone else, a soldier. I still don't know his name. Look, Boninghausen, or whatever your name is—"

"Stop. I don't want to hear your threats," the British spy interrupted. "What's done is done. Victors in wars rarely win every battle. What's important is to win the last battle. Now, do you have my list or not?" Campbell asked emphatically.

Rourke made a mental note to personally torture and kill the arrogant Brit. "I do." Rourke held up a protective canister. "Not before my money, ten thousand pounds sterling was the figure, I believe."

"That's correct, as long as every member is on the list," replied Campbell.

Rourke glanced away briefly, knowing the list was incomplete and knowing further he didn't have much to bargain with. Sheepishly Rourke came clean. "There are nine names the girls failed to get."

Campbell pondered Rourke's honesty, stroking his chin while staring at the wealthy merchant. "Honesty from you, Rourke. I hadn't expected that. Very well, that's roughly one-sixth of the list. Therefore, I will subtract one-sixth of the payment."

Rourke began to protest, but for one of the first times in his life, he chose to be quiet and accept the verdict.

"That's roughly 1,700, subtracted from 10,000 pounds sterling, for a total of 8,300." Major Campbell produced a small wooden box and counted out Rourke's payment. Rourke handed over the list and began to gather the coins.

Regaining some of his confidence, Rourke smiled. "A pleasure doing business with you, Mr. Boninghausen. If our paths cross again, I might have to wipe that smile off your face, permanently."

"Why, Mr. Rourke, is that any way to talk to your partner? Despite your failures, I have been very impressed by your passion to our cause. You just need a little more experience and perhaps some luck," replied the British major.

The backhanded compliment only served to enrage Rourke even further. "Mr. Boninghausen, the next time we meet will be our last…" Rourke let the threat hang in the air.

"Rourke, before you leave, answer me this: What have you done to the people that betrayed you?"

Rourke stopped in his tracks, unable to leave without at least one boast. "They will be taken care of, the whole family," Rourke replied with a twisted smile.

"How and by whom?" Major Campbell asked slyly.

Patrick Rourke turned to face Boninghausen. "By an old friend of yours, Captain Medford."

"Medford? There's no possible way. He has rejoined the fleet, off New York," Campbell stated with confidence.

"He just left Philadelphia this afternoon. He was paid a handsome fee to exact my revenge." Rourke's mood was beginning to brighten as he watched Boninghausen's astonished face.

"Rourke, are you sure it was the *Richmond*?" Campbell's face betrayed his worry.

"My attorney made the transaction at the dock. It was Medford, and it was the *Richmond*." Rourke happily noticed Boninghausen's discomfort.

So, Campbell thought to himself, *the rumors are true. Medford may indeed have found a treasure. Colonel Parker won't be happy. I'll have to leave immediately to get word to the fleet.* "Rourke, unwittingly you may have just saved the day. I apologize for my harsh comments. Will you return to Philadelphia?"

Rourke was stunned with the British officer's change of demeanor. "I will retreat to Cape May. I have a summer home there. I will wait for the arrival of General Howe and offer my services to him when he arrives in Philadelphia."

"Well, your wait won't be long, and I will tell him of your loyalty to the king," declared the major.

Rourke weighed the sincerity of the British spy, his instincts telling him to be careful. "Perhaps I misjudged you, Boninghausen. Maybe we will do business in the future. I bid you adieu."

Major Hadden Campbell started to calculate how long it would take to ride the sixty-six miles to New York City. The list he had from Rourke could help win the war. The information he just learned about Captain Medford could help him enjoy the aftermath in untold luxury.

"Mr. Jefferson, how much longer do you think? I'm starving to death," the heavyset Benjamin Harrison whispered to his fellow Virginia delegate.

Jefferson smiled and replied, "Perhaps instead of a war with the British, we could challenge the Parliament to a talking contest. I'm sure we could win with very few casualties."

Both men laughed softly as the debate over the Lee Resolution continued. It had been nine straight hours since John Hancock had begun the session. The dark, rainy day had continued throughout most of the debate. It was seven o'clock, and slender lines of sunshine penetrated through the thinning clouds. The storm was subsiding along with the debate. Just one-half hour earlier, Joseph Hewes of North Carolina had bolted up from his chair and proclaimed, "Enough already! You have beaten me into submission. I will abide by it, and God help us." And with that, one more Dickinson ally had fallen.

Finally, no one rose to speak as everyone looked to the president, John Hancock. Hancock wasted no time in striking down his gavel. "If there is no more debate, we will take a fifteen-minute break and return to vote on the motion." In an unusual move, Hancock added, "Mr. Thomson, please take an informal vote during the break."

Suddenly, after nine hours of debate, the delegates were faced with perhaps the greatest vote to be cast in the history of the entire world. The tension began to build as the delegates filtered out into the hallway. Pockets of delegates gathered hastily, seeking information and advice.

Benjamin Franklin, sitting on a bench in the hallway, motioned to John Adams. "Mr. Adams, you did a fine job in there. Congratulations!"

"I hardly think I said anything new or dramatic. It's the same thing I've been saying for the last six weeks." Adams actually sounded humble.

"On the contrary, John, you seemed quite different. There was passion and commitment in your voice like never before," Franklin said with admiration.

"Cousin," Sam Adams interrupted as he came running over, the excitement in his voice unmistakable. "Victory is ours. We have a majority of nine to four." Several other members of the Massachusetts delegation joined the group; their enthusiasm was beginning to spread throughout the hallway.

John Adams looked up to his cousin and replied, "Sam, you know that's not good enough. It must be unanimous." Benjamin Franklin nodded in agreement.

Elbridge Gerry joined the gathering and reported, "Pennsylvania, New York, South Carolina, and Delaware will not vote for independence."

Thomas Jefferson had also joined the group and added, "Delaware is divided. Mr. Read is against, and Mr. McKean is for. Where is Caesar Rodney? He has championed independence for over six months. We must have his vote."

John Adam's shot up from his seat, seeking out Thomas McKean. "Mr. McKean, where in the devil is Mr. Rodney?"

"I'm afraid he is back in Dover, attending to some problems with the Tory government there," replied the harried delegate.

"We must have him here," declared Adams.

"I will send a rider, but—"

"Yes, yes, I know, get him here by tomorrow. Understand?"

"If I have to ride myself, it will get done."

Adams shook his hand as McKean bolted for the front door of the Pennsylvania statehouse.

"Mr. Adams, I was wondering if I might have a word alone with you," the youthful speaker implored.

Adams turned and was shocked to see that it was Edward Rutledge, the leading delegate from South Carolina.

"Why, certainly, Mr. Rutledge. Shall we?" Adams led the Dickinson ally outside to the courtyard, where much of the haggling was done.

They sought out a private bench. The sun was slowly dropping into the west. To the east the storm clouds were still visible. Adams thought, *New York City would be getting a good drenching by now.*

"Mr. Adams, I will get directly to the point. South Carolina is now wavering. I can promise a yes vote," Rutledge said; his Southern drawl was most distinguished.

Adams was shocked. Rutledge had been an outspoken advocate for reconciliation with the king. But like Boston, the city of Charleston had felt the sting of the British Navy. The people of South Carolina were rapidly undergoing a change of heart, and their leaders in the Congress were listening. "Mr. Rutledge, forgive me, but coming from you, I am rather shocked."

"It is true that you and I have disagreed about a great many things this past year. However, I hope you don't hold it against me. We Southerners are very deliberate in our thinking. I have a great desire for independence, but the timing was never right."

"And now…?" Adams asked the gentle Southerner.

"And now the winds are changing, and South Carolina does not want to be a drag on the other colonies—excuse me, states. There is one thing, however."

There's always one thing with politicians. Why can't they just do it because it's the right thing to do? "And that is…?"

"South Carolina will vote yes if you can get a unanimous vote," declared Rutledge.

An astonished Adams replied, "That's all, Mr. Rutledge. You have a deal."

The two stood and shook hands. "You see, Mr. Adams, two gentlemen, one from the North and one from the South, can always come to an agreement. May it always stay that way."

"Hear, hear, Mr. Rutledge." Adams's smile covered his entire face. Emotion overcame the stoic New Englander, and he did something very un-Adams-like: he embraced Rutledge with a huge bear hug. "Hear, hear, Mr. Rutledge."

THE SIGNERS

By the time the two men returned to the assembly room, John Hancock was ready to resume the session. To the surprise of just about everyone in the chamber, Edward Rutledge stood and spoke. "Mr. President, I move that we postpone the final vote until tomorrow. Give us one more night to think about it."

Hancock looked annoyed; they had already spent more time on the issue than he had allowed, and he was about to say so when John Adams rose up. "I second the motion." A chorus of yeas followed.

Hancock reluctantly relented and began to give instructions for tomorrow's vote, with a clear reminder that there would be *no more debate*. "Gentlemen, it has been a long day. This meeting is adjourned—"

A commotion inside the hallway forced Hancock to pause. All eyes in the chamber turned to see what caused the interruption. Several delegates reached for their sidearms as a man barged into the assembly room. He looked like a drowned rat, dripping rainwater and mud with every step. One of the secretaries called out to Hancock. "Mr. President, a rider from General Washington."

The man stopped at the railing. Jefferson noted he was covered in mud so badly one couldn't distinguish between his clothing and his bare skin. His face was red from exhaustion. "Mr. President, please forgive my appearance, but I have come from New York City with an urgent message from General Washington."

Every member of Congress stopped in their tracks. There was much persuasion left to do, and most were eager to do it over dinner. But now, dinner could wait.

A secretary hurriedly delivered the handwritten letter to Hancock. "Mr. Thomson, please help our friend to a change of clothing and a decent meal."

The exhausted rider nodded his thanks, while Hancock opened the envelope and began to read aloud the letter from the commander of the Continental Army.

"Gentlemen, if I may." He proceeded to read it out loud.

Dear President Hancock and members of Congress,

I must inform you that Admiral Howe and the British Navy have arrived off the coast of Staten Island. My men have counted over 150 ships of war. My spies estimate that the number will reach over 400 in several days. We are not far from a major engagement, so I urge you to work quickly on the men and supplies that were requested over three months ago. As I've stated previously, our position is tenuous. Illness continues to plague the Army, and many of our troops' enlistment year will soon expire. I will continue to keep you apprised of our situation.
Sincerely,
General George Washington

The members of the Second Continental Congress stood in silence, absorbing Washington's letter, especially the estimate of over four hundred ships, an armada larger than any in history. It was the wily old Benjamin Franklin who finally broke the silence. "Well, gentlemen, as I'm often fond of saying, we had better hang together, or we shall surely hang separately."

Jefferson noted the somber look on John Dickinson's face as he and his allies whispered together while preparing to leave. Washington's letter could not have arrived at a more opportune time. *Perhaps this will be the catalyst to create the unanimous vote we need,* Jefferson thought as he left the building.

"This is crazy," Major Hall whispered as the two men walked up the pier toward the gangplank of the British warship. Two Marines were helping several dockworkers begin the process of removing the boarding structure.

"If you have a better idea, then now would be a good time," replied Ben Cushman.

"I'm afraid not. I guess 'crazy' is our only option."

Cushman laughed. He had been in many fierce battles. Major Jacob Hall was a rare breed, confident, composed, and focused, all necessary for a superb warrior. The two would need all that and more if they were to succeed with their daring plan.

"What is this?" The British Marine elbowed his fellow soldier upon noticing two strangers approaching their position. The strangers were dressed in civilian clothing, but neither appeared to be armed. What was odd about the two was that one man had his hands tied together in front of his body while the other pulled him along, as if leading a horse to water. The *prisoner* wore a triangular kerchief, which completely covered his face below his eyes. Both Marines retrieved their muskets and leveled them at the new arrivals. "Stop right there," the first Marine ordered. "What is the meaning of this intrusion?"

"I must speak with your captain," Cushman commanded firmly. "It is a matter of utmost importance."

The second Marine responded, "Concerning what? We are about to set sail."

"I can only talk to Captain Medford, but I can assure you he will be pleased that you took the initiative to alert him to our presence. My name is Silas Otto. I am sheriff of Philadelphia, and this prisoner is of great interest to your captain." Cushman was counting on what every subordinate in every army around the world cherished more than anything, praise from their commanding officer.

Indeed, both Marines immediately recalled the pleasant exchange with Medford about an hour early. Medford had personally complimented both Marines after the Philadelphia lawyer had left. The first Marine was still being cautious when he asked, "Why is your prisoner bound, and why the mask?"

"He is bound because he is dangerous, and he has a nasty habit of spitting at me, thus the handkerchief," Cushman replied coolly.

The two Marines huddled, never taking their eyes off the strangers. Finally, the first Marine told the dockworkers to take a break and turned toward the strangers. "Wait here."

Cushman turned to face Hall with raised eyebrows, signaling his surprise. Although his face was covered, he could see Hall's eyes were smiling.

The news of the British fleet anchored off New York spread like wildfire throughout the city. At City Tavern, the news was being used to pressure the moderates to support the Declaration of Independence. Delegates attempting to eat dinner were easy targets for Samuel Adams, who went from table to table, working his political magic. "Don't you ever eat, Sam?" William Hooper of North Carolina asked while trying to carve into his roast duck.

"Not until we beat back those British bastards." Adams laughed while ordering a round of beer for the men seated at the table.

"You think you can bribe us with beer, Sam?" Stephen Hopkins of Rhode Island asked the persuasive New Englander. "I'll take the beer, but you already have my vote."

"That's to make sure you don't change it," replied Adams as he left to work the next table.

Across the room, in a corner booth, fierce negotiations were beginning that would eventually prove to have an incredible domino effect. John Adams, Benjamin Franklin, and Thomas Jefferson were attempting to persuade one of the last holdouts in the call for independence.

James Duane was the main voice for the New York delegation. While Robert Livingston and several others were starting to show signs of moving toward independence, Duane remained a strong supporter of John Dickinson. Duane was son to an Irish immigrant, his mother having died when he was three, and his father when he was thirteen. Orphaned as a young boy, he became a ward of a family friend. He took to books like Thomas Jefferson, and at twen-

THE SIGNERS

ty-one, he was admitted to the New York Bar. At thirty-four he was appointed the state attorney general, one of the youngest in New York State history. A gifted orator, Duane had been a strong second to the effective Dickinson.

"Mr. Duane, the British Navy is not going to want to negotiate. They are there for one purpose and one purpose only, to wage war. It is far too late for reconciliation, and a unanimous declaration will inspire our troops and our cause," John Adams said firmly, but with respect toward the New York delegate.

"James, when this first started, the colonies came together to support their brethren holding out in Boston. But let's face it, none of our lands were being threatened at that time. Well, that has all changed. British warships have attacked Charleston. It is quite clear that New York will be their beachhead. Philadelphia will not be far behind. None of the thirteen are safe, and if we don't stick together, the war will be over very fast. Do you think the king will return the liberties he has already stolen? It doesn't take a genius to realize that the king will place more and harsher regulations upon us. Most men can face adversity, but the true test of character is how a man handles power. The king has certainly failed this test miserably. This is our chance, our one and only chance for freedom," Thomas Jefferson, the shy speaker, said, urging Duane to reconsider his opposition.

"Gentlemen, I am not opposed to independence, but in good conscience, I must exhaust every avenue before going down this bloody path."

"With four hundred warships sitting within sight of New York, how many more avenues must you travel?" replied the witty Franklin.

Duane lowered his head slightly; his shoulders sagged while he absorbed their arguments. It was as if he had made a complicated decision. "I can deliver New York if…"

Here comes the dreaded if. John Adams thought about his earlier conversation with Edward Rutledge.

"If you can deliver Pennsylvania," Duane stated, looking directly at Benjamin Franklin.

Jefferson was the first to reply. "There it is, it all comes down to Pennsylvania and, of course, finding Caesar Rodney."

Adams looked at Franklin. "Where is Mr. Dickinson dining tonight?"

"At home," replied Franklin. "I'll go get my hat and coat."

"We should have set sail hours ago. This had better be good, or I will have both your skins!" Medford barked at the Marine as they made their way onto the pier.

We would have set sail hours ago if you hadn't decided to transport a civilian carriage, the Marine thought but would never think to say out loud.

Medford stared at the odd couple and didn't speak.

Cushman's senses were heightened with keen anticipation; this would be the moment of truth. Desperate to come up with a convincing plan, he thought posing as Sheriff Silas Otto seemed a good idea at that time. Both men were willing to gamble that Medford had never met the Philadelphia lawman but had probably heard of him. They would soon find out if their gamble was successful.

"You are Otto?" Medford barked at Cushman. "Don't look anything like what I've been told about you."

"How is that, sir?"

"I've been told you were quite homely."

"Well, my mother would argue to the contrary," Cushman replied with a hurt look on his face.

"What's this about, Otto? Who is this prisoner you're towing?" Medford grew more and more impatient.

Cushman leaned closer to the British captain and whispered, "This man has made some wild accusations against you, Captain Medford. Something about a large amount of gold and an American merchant ship named the *Treasure*."

The shock on Medford's face was instantaneous. It soon turned red as Medford's mind raced to absorb what he had just heard. "I have no idea what you're talking about!" he bellowed and turned to leave.

"Don't mistake my appearance here, Captain Medford. I didn't come here to blackmail you. I came here as an ally. We share an important friend, Mr. Patrick Rourke. He has said you are one of us. Look at my prisoner." Cushman yanked the handkerchief down, exposing the face of Major Hall.

Medford stared at the bound captive. Recognition came about ten seconds later. Medford couldn't hide his distress and thought back to the confrontation between the two deep in the bowels of the merchant ship *Treasure*. *So the emissary survived,* Medford thought as he contemplated his next move. "Perhaps we should go someplace quieter, Sheriff Otto. Leave the prisoner. My Marines will guard him," the British captain ordered.

"No, I am not letting him out of my sight. Don't worry, he is securely tied. He won't cause any trouble."

"Very well. You two!" Medford barked at the Marines. "Follow us to my cabin. Stand guard outside. If I so much as raise my voice, you enter my cabin and shoot them both."

They took Ben Franklin's roomy carriage the full six miles into what Philadelphians called Germantown. Originally found by Dutch Quakers, it was soon overwhelmed by migrating Germans into Pennsylvania. Since 1688, it was referred to as Germantown. Mary Dickinson's family owned a large mansion on the edge of the neighborhood. While serving with the Second Continental Congress, John Dickinson preferred to stay at his wife's family estate rather than travel back and forth eighty miles from his own mansion, Poplar Hill, located in Kent County, Delaware.

Mary Dickinson opened the door. Standing beside her were two small children.

"Why, Sally Dickinson, I think you've grown six inches since I saw you last." Ben Franklin placed his hand upon the head of the well-dressed five-year-old girl.

"Mr. Franklin, you always say that." Sally Dickinson smiled, revealing the loss of her top two front teeth.

"And you're losing your baby teeth." Franklin laughed.

Mary Dickinson just shook her head as the two children, five-year-old Sally and the seventy-year-old Franklin, went off to view Sally's newest toy. "Mr. Adams, a pleasure, as always," Mary stated lightly.

"Mrs. Dickinson." Adams bowed slightly. "I was unaware you are with child," he declared.

"About two months to go," she stated bravely.

"And how is little Isaac?" Adams asked about the three-year-old boy, clutching at his mother's leg, looking scared and very pale.

Her face furrowed into deep sadness. "I'm afraid he is very sick, Mr. Adams. He hardly eats, and he cries much of the day. It's the same ailment that took Mary from us," she stated, referring to the death of their daughter Mary, who had died the previous year before reaching her first birthday. Her Quaker upbringing allowed her to speak bravely about such a heartbreaking subject. "And how are your children, Mr. Adams? I believe John said you have five."

"Four, Mrs. Dickinson. Like you, I have felt the cruel death of a young child. Our second, Susanna, was only two when she was taken home to the Lord."

"I am sorry, Mr. Adams. I didn't know."

"No apologies necessary, madam. Childhood diseases are a scourge throughout the world. But thank God my other children are doing just fine. Abigail does wonders in my absence. Nabby, our eldest, is ten now, going on twenty."

Mary Dickinson laughed, knowing full well the difficulty developing from a child into womanhood.

"John Quincy will be nine next month. He is more inquisitive and brighter than a child of sixteen. I think he gets his intelligence from his mother. Charles is six and quite a handful. All boy, that one. Thomas is our youngest. He will be four in September and is the apple in Abigail's eyes."

She smiled, obviously enjoying the talk of children. "We will name this one after John," Mary Dickinson declared, rubbing her protruding stomach. "He's already pretty ornery, always kicking in there."

Adams smiled, but he was anxious to get down to business.

Mary Dickinson understood, but before letting Adams pass, she gently grabbed his arm. "Mr. Adams," she said softly yet firmly, "John is a prideful man, and I doubt whether Mr. Franklin and yourself can change his mind."

Adams knew from previous conversations with the Pennsylvania delegate that they shared one thing in common. Both men valued their wives' opinions regarding everything, including the political intrigues and upheaval of the past few years. "Please don't be disgusted with him. He believes in the cause of liberty and speaks very highly of the men leading the charge for independence. He just can't overcome the grief he feels in being part of a body causing young men to march off to war, knowing full well the death and destruction it will bring."

"Let me assure you, Mrs. Dickinson," Adams said while patting her hands, "your husband has no greater admirer than I. He is a man of great principle and passion. I just think on this question he happens to be in the wrong. As far as sending young men off to war, there is not a man in the Congress that doesn't agonize over that very possibility. But make no mistake, hundreds have already died for the cause of freedom, and many more will die at the hands of the British. I believe with all my heart that liberty is a far greater prize than the promised safety of a tyrannical king."

Mary Dickinson nodded her approval and led John Adams into a cozy den, where Ben Franklin had made his way, sitting beside a wigless John Dickinson. He looked much older without his wig, which he always wore when Congress was in session. His short hair was both graying and balding, no doubt a by-product of the stresses faced by the Pennsylvania lawyer.

"Ah, Mr. Adams, I needn't inquire about the reason for your visit. Please sit. May I pour you some wine?" Dickinson preformed his hosting duties, despite the intrusion. Mary Dickinson closed the door, and the three men sat in silence, sipping their wine, as if it would lessen the coming argument.

"John, two of your followers rose up against you today and joined me in the vote for independence." Ben Franklin started the conversation, referring to John Morton and James Wilson, a long-time ally of Dickinson.

"Aye, that is so, Benjamin, but the vote was still six to three," replied the forty-five-year-old third-generation American.

"True, true, but with the Howe brothers sitting off New York City, the others may quickly begin to side with me," suggested Franklin, a fact Dickinson knew all too well.

"Benjamin, you know my feelings on the subject. What kind of man would I be if I changed my mind because the British have arrived? No, this show of force could be just that, a show of force to get us to negotiate before bloodshed. What kind of man would I be if I compromised my beliefs?"

"A man of your principles and honestly should never have to do such a thing," John Adams stated sincerely.

Dickinson looked up at the man from Massachusetts who, hours earlier, had debated with fierce passion against all of Dickinson's positions regarding the subject. "Thank you, John. Coming from you, that means a lot."

Adams nodded.

"But it's far too dangerous to add my voice leading us down this path toward annihilation," continued Dickinson.

"Perhaps there is another way, John. You don't look like yourself. You look pale. Have you been sick lately? Perhaps you may be indisposed tomorrow?" Ben Franklin raised his bushy eyebrows, leaving the question hanging in the air. All three men remained silent, contemplating Franklin's suggestion.

Adams looked at Franklin, his admiration showing enthusiastically on his face. *Brilliant,* Adams thought to himself. *If Dickinson abstains from voting, his principles remain intact but will allow his allies to fend for themselves. Franklin's influence will clearly push the others toward independence. If Pennsylvania votes in the affirmative, then New*

York and South Carolina will surely follow. Now, all we need for a unanimous vote is to find Caesar Rodney.

Ben Cushman breathed a sigh of relief as they entered the captain's quarters aboard the British warship *HMS Richmond*. The first potential flaw in their plan hadn't materialized. It was obvious that Captain George Medford had never met Sheriff Silas Otto. As he pulled Major Hall into the roomy cabin, he was quickly shocked back to reality when he came face-to-face with Deborah Johnson's father, David.

David was first to react as the three men entered the room. "What are you doing here, and why is—"

Cushman marched quickly forward and interrupted the puzzled David Johnson. "David, I didn't expect to see you here," he said, firmly gripping his hand and staring hard into his eyes. "Remember me, Sheriff Silas Otto? I'm a good friend of Patrick Rourke. We've met several times at some of his parties. I'm afraid I got quite drunk at the last one." Cushman raised his eyebrows and gave Johnson a stern look. He turned toward Medford and smiled, repositioning himself between Medford and David Johnson.

"What, what are you talking…?" David Johnson stammered, totally confused at the current circumstances

Returning his glare toward Johnson, Cushman continued, "I'm afraid I'm going to have to catch up with you later. As you can see, I have important business with the captain." Cushman rolled his eyes toward the door and gave Johnson his best *don't-ask-any-more-questions* look. "Please don't go far. I would like to talk with you when I'm done with Captain Medford."

David Johnson's confusion was magnified when he finally recognized Jacob Hall. Before he could open his mouth again, Cushman was gently moving him toward the door. "I won't be long. Please wait." Cushman rolled his eyes once more toward the deck and closed the door behind the dumbfounded shipping mogul.

The *HMS Greyhound* lay anchored within sight of Staten Island. The sixth-rate frigate weighed over five hundred tons and had the honor of being the flagship for the commander of the British forces in North America. It would be his job to teach the unruly mob of colonists a lesson they would never forget. The British had achieved their first goal, intimidation. It was such an impressive sight, over 250 British warships anchored between Sandy Hook, New Jersey, and Staten Island. Surrounding the *Greyhound* were four of the newest ships in the British fleet, *HMS Phoenix, HMS Centurion, HMS Chatham,* and *HMS Asia*. Combined with the *Greyhound*, those five ships alone, with their 236 heavy guns, outnumbered the entire arsenal attempting to defend the city of New York.

"See that light, Colonel? That's the farmhouse you will make your headquarters." General William Howe pointed out as the two men stood along the bulwark.

The light rain made it hard to focus, but after a few seconds, he was able to make out the flickering light in the distance. The ship rolled with each swell. The colonel felt another wave of nausea overtaking his stomach; the same feeling two nights early had caused him to vomit uncontrollably over the railing. "If there are no docks, how will we get our horses ashore?" Colonel Nathan Parker asked the commander of the British invasion force.

"Our Tory friends have been hard at work on Staten Island. Inside our farmer's barn are two flat-bottom barges. They will be rowed out to the ships transporting your horses. Especially designed ramps will allow us to lead them onto the barges," Howe boasted.

Parker nodded in admiration. His doubts about Howe had dissipated some, but he was still suspicious of any general not named Braddock. His mission was both aggressive and necessary in helping quell the rebellion quickly. Parker thought to himself, *If the rebels got another victory like Boston, then they might start to believe they could win. A confident army is a dangerous army, even if it is made up of a bunch of shopkeepers and farmers.* No, his plan to hunt down and kill the colonial leadership was a stroke of genius. The Europeans had begun to wage war with rules, like no targeting officers. *What poppycock! Wars with rules. There would be none of that here. Chopping off the head of the snake will not only save many British soldiers but, in the long run, will also cause fewer rebels to die, since they will give up sooner, especially if the New York operation goes smoothly.* "Well done, General. It seems you have thought of everything. When will I be able to go ashore?"

"How does tomorrow sound?"

"Tomorrow it is. I will send a scout party to our crossing area into New Jersey," replied the handsome colonel.

"How soon will you be ready to begin your ride to Philly?" Howe inquired.

"Three days. In three days we will launch and end this nonsense. Historians will mark that day as the beginning of the end for this silly rebellion."

"You know that I probably won't be able to launch our attack on New York for at least several more weeks," Howe replied just as a beautiful woman dressed in expensive clothes passed both men and went directly into Howe's quarters.

Parker tried not to stare but stealthily admired the woman as she walked by. Of course, everyone aboard the ship knew the rare beauty was Howe's mistress, Elizabeth Loring. Howe had made her husband the head of all British prisons. The relationship among the three was quite scandalous in many people's minds, but Parker admired Howe's gumption. His only reservation about the illicit affair was that Howe seemed overly infatuated and was easily distracted by her charming ways. Parker thought that Howe seemed to be in no hurry to restart the war, and that bothered him.

"As I said before, sir, I will need no reinforcement for this mission, just your permission to begin," Parker replied, shielding his eyes from the steady rain.

Howe smiled and replied, "Very well. Let's join Elizabeth and get out of this rain. A celebratory drink to a historic day. Let's see, three days from now will be July 4. July 4, 1776. Future colonials will live to regret that date in history."

"Hear, hear!" Parker agreed as the two walked quickly toward the captain's quarters.

Captain George Medford was a survivor. His instincts were almost always dead-on. The exchange between Sheriff Otto and David Johnson was very disturbing. His antenna was on high alert, and he almost called in the Marines. Hesitating, he looked at Major Hall and decided to wait, full of confidence in the two Marines stationed outside his door.

"Mr. Anderson, if I remember correctly, how is it that you survived? As I recall, you promised revenge against me. Is this what you had in mind? Not exactly a successful return from the dead. I suppose this time I will have to do it myself." Medford quickly reached into a nearby desk and retrieved a fully loaded revolver. He immediately leveled it at Major Hall's head while glaring at Cushman.

"Go ahead, shoot him. You'll save me the trouble," Cushman remarked casually while pouring a glass of wine from a nearby table. "You don't mind if I have a drink, do you?"

Hall finally spoke. "I'll kill both of you. You'll never get away with—"

Cushman yanked hard on the rope, propelling Hall away from the captain. "See what I have to put up with?" He smiled at Medford. Cushman grabbed the prisoner, threw him into a chair, and slapped him across the face. "Now, be still and keep your mouth closed."

Medford relaxed, still brandishing the gun at Hall. He moved closer and spoke harshly. "Not so cocky, are you, Mr. Anderson? Or whatever your name is. I am going to enjoy your death—"

Medford never saw it coming. The cold, sharp blade of an eight-inch knife was digging into his throat as Cushman pulled the British captain away from Hall. "If you so much as breathe heavily, I will cut your throat from ear to ear. Nod if you understand."

George Medford cursed to himself as he nodded vigorously at Cushman. He considered alerting the Marines, but the pressure from the knife was already beginning to draw blood. *Why had he been so careless?* "Now, place the revolver in my other hand," Cushman said softly.

Hall skillfully threaded the rope through the sailor's loop and was freed instantly. He glared at Cushman and whispered, "A slap, you had to slap me?"

Cushman shrugged his shoulders and smiled.

Medford looked on in disdain at the simple deception and cursed himself a second time. He would bide his time; he had a ship full of Marines and sailors fiercely loyal to him. He would wait for the right time to act.

Cushman led the British officer to the door and whispered, "Order your men in quietly, or you will die instantly. Do this and you might survive."

The knife continued to draw blood as Cushman reinforced his order with more pressure to the throat.

Medford gasped and opened the door. "Men, come in here, now," he ordered softly.

The Marines entered quickly, their muskets pointed toward the floor. What they saw stunned them, but before they could react, both Marines felt a barrel shoved into the back of their necks. "Gentlemen, I am holding two revolvers at the base of your skulls. If you move a muscle or say anything, I will kill you both." The cold-blooded voice of Jacob Hall sent waves of fear throughout their bodies. Neither Marine moved as they looked at their commander; the fear in his eyes told them they had better obey. "Now, lay down your muskets, lie on the floor, and put your hands behind your back."

It took Hall less than two minutes to hogtie the Marines and place linen tablecloths into their mouths. He laid down Medford's revolver and the dinner spoon that he had shoved into the necks of the two Royal Marines. Next, the two Patriots bound and gagged Medford in the same manner. While Hall stripped the uniform off the larger of the two Marines, Cushman opened the door and called out to David Johnson. "Mr. Johnson, please come here. The captain wishes to speak to you." Cushman said it loud enough so that a number of sailors, preparing to cast off, heard the command. David Johnson's confusion worsened as he took in the scene before him.

"What is going on here? I demand you release Captain Medford immediately." David Johnson was used to getting his way and instinctively barked his orders.

"Mr. Johnson, please relax," Cushman demanded. "Major Hall has uncovered a deadly plot against your family. Please hear him out."

Just then, Hall appeared from behind a curtain, fully dressed as a British Marine.

"Mr. Johnson, did you know your benefactor, Captain Medford, met with a representative of Patrick Rourke within the past two hours?" Hall was looking into a mirror, admiring his new uniform, while Medford squirmed and attempted to spit out his gag.

"I saw the captain talking to a well-dressed man. How do you know he represented Rourke? I can't believe these wild accusations!" Johnson demanded, still confused.

"Believe it, Mr. Johnson. Read this letter. I found it in the captain's pocket." Hall handed the letter to David Johnson. Johnson quickly scanned the letter. "Well, this is certainly Patrick's writing, but…" He looked up and was staring at the box of gold coins.

"Found these in the captain's desk. Any further questions?"

"Oh my god, we have to get off this ship!" was all David Johnson could come up with.

"Where is Deborah?" Cushman demanded.

"Deborah still hasn't awoken. She is right there." The confused father pointed toward a mobile cloth screen in the back of the captain's quarters.

Cushman gasped at the sight of the two girls lying motionless on the captain's large bed. He went to Deborah's side and gently laced his fingers among hers. He knelt down and felt a powerful surge of sorrow pass over his entire body. She looked dead, except for her heaving chest. Even in her unconscious state, she looked beautiful.

THE SIGNERS

David Johnson watched Cushman with the intensity of a father attempting to protect his loved ones. Any doubt about Cushman's intentions quickly dissolved as he watched him lovingly caress his daughter's hand. The look in Cushman's eyes proved to the father that this man was no threat to his daughter.

In Major Jacob Hall's business, it was important to understand human emotions and human motivation. He instantly understood the situation and gently called to his colleague, "Ben, come, we must move quickly. I promise we will get them to safety."

Cushman pulled away slowly, knowing his actions in the near future would either save her or kill her. The two men huddled for several moments.

"Mr. Johnson, you are traveling with a doctor. Do you trust him?"

"How did you know? Never mind. Yes, he is a neighbor, and I trust him."

"Good. Find him immediately. Tell him the truth or make up a story, but have him help you get the girls off this ship. Now go."

"But what if they won't let us off? What then?"

"Don't worry, I will take care of that," replied Cushman.

Lieutenant Joshua Smith was worried. The supply stop in Philadelphia was supposed to last for several hours. The admiralty believed that certain ports were no longer safe for British warships. Boston and Charleston were now completely off-limits, as was New York. The Patriots had been attacking British ships in port for well over six months now. Captain Medford had said that they would make port in Philadelphia at night and be gone by morning. But they were delayed when a wealthy family was allowed to book passage back to England. Smith was certain that Captain Medford was receiving a large payment from the family. The delay lengthened when Medford allowed the man's carriage to be loaded aboard ship.

Joshua Smith was only twenty-nine years old, very young for being the second-in-command of a British warship. Of course, he was elevated to the position under unusual circumstances with the unfortunate accident involving Addison Prescott.

Smith's impatience was growing by the moment, and as he approached amidships, he was astonished to see several sailors sitting on the dock. "What is the meaning of this?" Smith barked as he stormed down the gangplank.

One of the sailors managed to mutter, "Sir, Captain Medford pulled the Marines and went into his quarters. The local sheriff seemed to be delivering a prisoner aboard. He told us to stand down."

Smith absorbed the information, which only added to his worries. He decided to approach the captain and made for his quarters.

Hall hadn't taken two steps from the captain's quarters when he heard the command.

"Marine, is Captain Medford in his quarters?" Lieutenant Smith barked the question.

"Yes, sir, says he doesn't want to be disturbed," Hall replied sheepishly, trying to sound like a groveling soldier.

"Who is with him?"

"Local sheriff, sir. He has a prisoner that the captain is very interested in. They are interrogating the prisoner now. That's why he doesn't want to be disturbed. The prisoner has some valuable information." Hall stood in the shade of the poop deck and kept his head low for fear the lieutenant might get suspicious.

"Very well. Carry on." Lieutenant Smith was now even more concerned. If they delayed much longer, they might have to stay another night. Word would spread quickly that a British warship was still in port. Their sister ship, *HMS Jason*, had left hours ago.

Smith decided to risk the wrath of Captain Medford and knocked on the captain's door. He was surprised when a civilian answered and walked out onto the deck with him.

"Hello, Lieutenant," the civilian said brightly, looking at the sailor's uniform. "Captain Medford is busy. He is interrogating a valuable prisoner. Very valuable." Cushman emphasized *very* for effect.

"Just who are you?"

"I'm sorry, Lieutenant. My name is Silas Otto, Sheriff Silas Otto. I have jurisdiction over Philadelphia and am a loyal citizen of King George. And you, sir?"

"Lieutenant Joshua Smith, sir, but I am very worried at the length of our stay here. We are exposed without much protection. We must set sail immediately."

Cushman pondered what the lieutenant said. A possible opportunity, but he would have to alert Hall of the change of plans. Cushman decided to roll the dice. "A wise assessment, Lieutenant. The Philadelphia rabble has become emboldened lately. Why, just a few days ago, the rabble tarred and feathered my colleague the coroner."

"Exactly! A British ship tied to a pier is a tempting target," Smith answered, glad someone shared in his concern.

"I feel responsible for your delay. How can I help you?" Cushman asked, a new plan now formulating.

"This prisoner, is it so necessary to question him here? Can't we set sail or at least anchor somewhere downriver?"

"Well, I suppose. Yes, a great idea! There is one problem, however. You see, Lieutenant, the family you have so graciously accepted to transfer to England has been implicated into the murder of several Loyalist this past evening. They were trying to escape to England to avoid prosecution. Your Captain Medford was duped, and the prisoner I brought aboard is providing that proof as we speak."

"I knew something was wrong with that family!" Smith crowed.

"You have good instincts, Lieutenant," Cushman praised the young sailor. "The two girls, as innocent as they may appear, were part of the murder investigation. Their current condition is only temporary, but it will take some time before my people arrive to carry them on their stretchers."

"Perhaps I can help. I could get some men to carry the girls to the access road, where you could wait for your people," suggested the lieutenant.

Cushman looked up at the rain clouds gathering and laughed. "It would serve the swine to wait outside in the rain. Arrange it, Lieutenant. I will force Mr. Johnson to help bring the girls here to the deck, while you round up some men. Oh, Lieutenant, one more thing. I will need to take Mr. Johnson and his doctor friend also. But I won't need any help with them." Cushman pulled out his knife and showed it to Smith. "They won't cause any problems."

Smith smiled and turned to gather four sailors for the chore of carrying the girls.

Major Jacob Hall had worked his way into the storage room, where he hoped to find the gold. He was still working on a plan to *steal* it back. The room was dim. Two lanterns provided the only light into the spacious storage area. A quick glance around the room proved to be fruitless.

Where would a greedy lunatic hide four trunks of gold? It has to be out of sight, no prying eyes to investigate, he thought, snatching a lantern and taking a closer look at the dingy room. The light from the lantern revealed something he hadn't seen in his initial sweep. *There, in the back.* A four-foot-high door with a large padlock and clasp. A tap on the wall suggested another storage area behind the small door. Hall quickly found a crowbar, set down the lantern, and began to assault the four-inch lock. He had better luck when he was able to pry the clasp from the wall.

Hall poked his head through the door, the lantern in his right hand. Sure enough, there were four trunks. A huge smile gripped his face. He could recognize the wooden crates even in the dark. He had located the stolen gold. Hall pried off one top to make certain Medford hadn't removed the contents. The shimmering golden glow bouncing off the lantern and dancing in the dim light reassured Hall that he had found what he came for. He wasn't prepared for what happened next.

THE SIGNERS

The three men watched as British sailors began to move the two beautiful young women toward the gangplank and down the pier. "Sheriff, we haven't been able to locate Dr. Dixon yet," Lieutenant Smith informed Cushman. David Johnson's look revealed he wasn't ready for the spy game as Cushman continued to play the *sheriff*.

"As soon as we find him, we shall leave and allow you to depart. Captain Medford wanted me to relay his praise on your initiative. He doesn't want to stop interrogating the prisoner but asked me to tell you to begin to move out into the river. He also stated that there may be some evidence on board that will be helpful in prosecuting some of the Patriot swine responsible for last night's murders. He wanted you to stand by with more men, to transport several boxes. I am not exactly sure what he is referring to, but I told him I would relay the order."

"I'm sure I have no idea either, but I will have the men standing by. The longer we stay here, the longer we are exposed to danger."

"I agree. Perhaps I can help locate the missing doctor?" Cushman offered.

"What about him?" Lieutenant Smith pointed toward David Johnson.

"Where will he run, with all your men in the area? But if it will make you feel better, I will tie him up in the captain's quarters."

"Very well, Sheriff." Lieutenant Smith was interrupted in midsentence by the unmistaken echo of a gunshot.

"Stand down, Marine. Just what in the hell are you doing down here?"

Major Jacob Hall was staring down the barrel of a British musket. The Marine behind the gun had his finger on the trigger and a menacing look on his face. "Captain Medford sent me down here to check on the trunks," replied the quick-thinking Hall.

The Marine sneered. "With a crowbar?"

"Well, yes. It seems the captain has misplaced the key." Hall slowly got to his feet, lantern in hand.

"You mean these?" Dangling from the Marine's hands was a set of brass keys.

"Oh, there they are." Hall laughed nervously. His situation was growing more tenuous by the moment.

"I know every Marine on this ship, but I have never seen you."

"Been stationed in and around Philadelphia. Things are getting pretty bad around here. I was just transferred from Trenton to the *Richmond* yesterday." Hall began to slowly swing the lantern back and forth.

The Marine smiled and shouldered his musket. "Not a bad lie. The captain thought someone might come down here, looking for the trunks. That's why I'm here." The Marine didn't hesitate; he leveled his musket at Hall and pulled the trigger.

Hall whipped the lantern toward the Marine the instant he triggered the weapon. The roar of the gunshot echoed in the tight quarters. The musket ball grazed Hall just above the hip, striking mostly fatty tissue. Although not deadly, the pain was immediate and severe. The lantern missed the Marine and landed onto a sack of dried animal feathers and immediately ignited. The Marine was distracted by the instant blaze of fire. Before he could recover, Major Hall attacked, the crowbar leveled directly at the Marine's head. The young Marine was able to blunt the blow with his right forearm. He tumbled to the ground, quickly snatching his musket. Within seconds, he was able to secure his bayonet to the gun. As the two warriors squared off, the fire began to grow.

Ben Cushman knew instantly that Hall was in trouble. He made a quick decision. "Lieutenant, it must be the doctor. Maybe one of your men has him cornered. May I help you?"

Smith was confused. The shot was clearly from a musket, and it had come from below ships. "I must alert the captain." The lieutenant moved toward the cabin door, only to feel the sharp point of a knife stuck into his back.

"Afraid I can't let you do that," Cushman said calmly. "Go through the door, quietly." Cushman motioned for David Johnson. "Get to the girls."

"What about Dr. Dixon?"

"Sorry, every man for himself now" was Cushman's only comment as he closed the door to the captain's quarters. Cushman hurriedly tied the lieutenant to a chair and, like the others, stuffed his mouth with linen. He bolted from the room and headed toward the storage room. Hall's directions were perfect.

Major Jacob Hall was a talented soldier, but he was now in his early forties and showing some age. The twenty-year-old Royal Marine was strong as an ox and extremely quick. He was able to parry every single move made by Hall and his crowbar. The only thing that was in Hall's favor was the smoke and fire that were leveling the playing field by reducing visibility. The fire was starting to reach a very dangerous threat to the ship as more and more storage items began to burn, and some of the ships timbers were starting to catch fire.

Hall's experience told him this fight would be over one way or another in a matter of minutes. He redoubled his effort and began to move in for one final furious attempt to defeat his younger opponent. Hall swung the crowbar with both hands and nearly connected with the Marine's exposed head. His opponent's superior conditioning allowed him to duck just in the nick of time. The momentum of the vicious swing caused Hall to sway off-balance and stumble over a short box. To Hall's horror, he fell flat on his back. The Marine quickly pounced and stood over the fallen American, both hands gripping his rifle, ready to plunge the bayonet downward. Hall kicked violently upward, just missing the Marine's crotch. The Marine smiled. "Nice try, mate, but it is time for you to die." The Marine raised his musket high and had started his downward motion when suddenly he lurched forward and fell over top of Hall. The major scrambled quickly to his feet, stunned to see a knife protruding from between the British Marine's shoulder blades.

At the foot of the stairs, a grinning Ben Cushman called out to his old friend. "There, now we are even."

"Not even close," countered Hall.

Bells began to ring out as the smoke poured from the ship. Every sailor's nightmare is fire at sea, and fire in port was no less frightening. The ship had to be saved at all cost. Almost everything aboard the British warship was combustible, from the ropes to sails to cargo and to the ship itself. Of course, the greatest danger aboard a warship was the fire reaching the gunpowder locker.

Sailors quickly organized into fire brigades. Drills they practiced over and over were now very real. Fire buckets attached to ropes were quickly lowered into the river and hauled on deck. The water was poured into other buckets as lines were formed to transfer the water to the fire. Others wielded boarding axes capable of cutting through walls to attack the fire. Still others carried large canvasses soaked in water in an attempt to smother the fire. The sailors of the *HMS Richmond* began the battle to save their beloved ship.

The fire had spread rapidly, and the smoke was starting to choke Cushman and Hall. "I have to get the gold!" called out Hall as he worked his way toward the four trunks.

"Jacob, listen to me. It's too late. Besides, you and I can't very well carry the gold topside and waltz off the ship."

Hall started to argue but quickly stopped and made his way back toward the steps leading upward. As important as the gold was to the war effort, he was not about to participate in a suicide mission.

"Hurry, we have to get out of here!" called Cushman.

Hall abruptly stopped. "Ben, I've got an idea."

"Why do I suddenly get frightened when you get an idea?" countered Cushman.

"We don't have to take the gold. We have to prevent them from taking it, and we have to keep it from melting."

"Are you thinking we have to…?"

"You're a quick study, Cushman." Hall cut him off. "Hurry, it's located in the next room."

Cushman was already on the move.

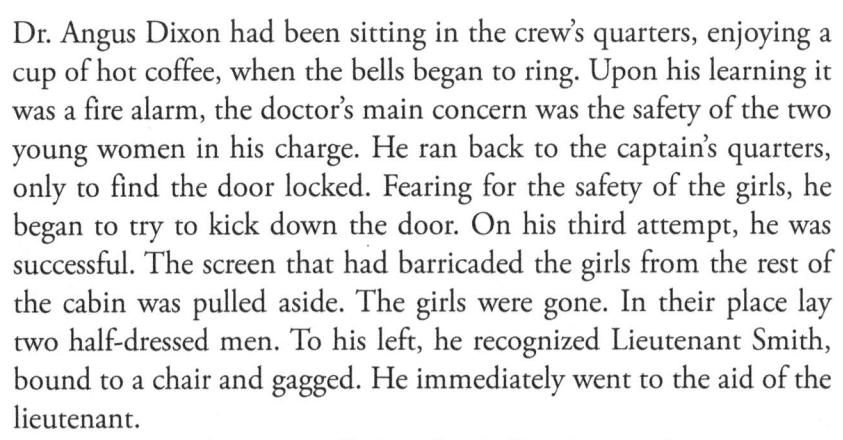

Dr. Angus Dixon had been sitting in the crew's quarters, enjoying a cup of hot coffee, when the bells began to ring. Upon his learning it was a fire alarm, the doctor's main concern was the safety of the two young women in his charge. He ran back to the captain's quarters, only to find the door locked. Fearing for the safety of the girls, he began to try to kick down the door. On his third attempt, he was successful. The screen that had barricaded the girls from the rest of the cabin was pulled aside. The girls were gone. In their place lay two half-dressed men. To his left, he recognized Lieutenant Smith, bound to a chair and gagged. He immediately went to the aid of the lieutenant.

Smith cried out a muffled, "Thanks!" and ran to his captain on the other side of the cabin.

Medford let fly a string of obscenities, some of which Smith had never heard before.

"Untie the Marines!" Medford screamed at the doctor. "Smith, where are those two scoundrels?"

"I don't know, sir. The fire bell has been ringing for over five minutes."

"You think I didn't notice, you idiot?" Medford was on the move, barking orders to the Marines as he yelled at Smith. "Find them, Smith. Find them, or I will personally shoot you. Go, get out of here!"

"Do you think it is far enough below the waterline?" Cushman asked as he extended the makeshift fuse another few feet. He finished untangling the last of the fibers of roping that were used to pad a cannonball into the cannon.

"Should be. If not, the blast should punch a large-enough hole," Hall countered, thinking back to the merchant ship *Treasure*. "Never in a million years did I think I would ever be doing this again." As they continued to prepare the explosives, Hall told Cushman of his escape from the burning *Treasure*.

"She's lit. Let's get out of here!" cried Cushman as the burning fuse began its lethal countdown.

Captain Medford was in a tyrannical rage as he barked orders from the main deck of the *Richmond*. Smoke was now billowing throughout the entire ship as the sailors of the British war vessel were beginning to realize they might be fighting a losing battle with the spreading fire. Medford was scanning the dock when he gazed upon a sight that enraged him even further. David Johnson and four of his men were guiding two stretchers away from the ship. The captain sprinted toward the ship's bow, screaming at the top of his lungs, "Stop them! They have betrayed us, stop them now!"

One of sailors spotted Medford waving at them but couldn't hear over the absolute chaos resulting from the crew fighting the fire. The sailors interpreted his manic gestures for them to return to the ship and help fight the fire. "Sorry, Mr. Johnson. This is as far as the girls go. We have to return to the ship."

David Johnson knew that Medford meant them harm and signaled the sailors his thanks. He quickly grabbed one end of Deborah's stretcher and began running as fast as he could, yelling back to the semiconscious Sarah, "I will be right back, my darling!"

Medford couldn't believe his bad luck. The ship was in chaos as the smoke and fire continued to spread. The four men helping Johnson had joined the others fighting the fire.

"Marine, where is your weapon?" Medford demanded.

"Against the wall, sir," he responded.

"Get it and load it. Now!"

"Yes, sir."

In less than a minute, the Marine returned and handed Medford the musket. "Stay here. I may need you to reload."

The Marine nodded his consent but shivered in fear as he gazed into the eyes of a raving lunatic.

Medford didn't have long to wait as David Johnson soon came into sight, running full speed toward the girl called Sarah. Medford waited patiently as Johnson lifted the front end of the stretcher and began walking it down the pier, away from the ship. He took careful aim and fired.

For a brief second, David Johnson allowed himself to believe he might be able to save his daughters. He had successfully dragged Deborah to a safe haven, off the docks and protected behind some cargo. The ride had been bumpy and hard, but she had seemed to survive it. David even thought he heard her speak, quickly dismissing it to the frantic situation.

He was beginning to pick up speed, dragging Sarah to safety, when he felt the sharp pain. He tried to continue to run, but his right leg would not respond. *Someone had stabbed him in the lower calf,* he thought. But there was no one there. As he staggered out of control, it finally dawned on him: he had been shot. He careened sideways, losing all control, until finally he came crashing hard onto to the wooden pier. The stretcher carrying Sarah came to rest perilously close to the edge of the water. David struggled to reach Sarah before she plunged into the Delaware.

Medford smiled amid the pandemonium and ordered the Marine to reload the musket.

Hall and Cushman reached the main deck and were amazed at the chaos they had created. They were on the starboard side of the ship and needed to get to the opposite side in order to get to the gangplank and to the pier. They were about to make their move when a voice called out.

"Stop where you are!" ordered Lieutenant Joshua Smith. "You two will hang tonight, I promise." Smith held a flintlock revolver in both hands, leveled directly at the two Patriots.

"How can you serve under such a murdering dog?" Hall asked Smith. He glanced toward Cushman, who was holding up his hand and extending all five digits. Both men gripped the ship's railing and readied themselves for the blast. They didn't have to wait the full five seconds.

The explosion rocked the ship like a twenty-foot wave. It teetered inward toward the pier and then rocked back to the starboard side, listing at forty-five degrees. The explosion knocked Lieutenant Smith to the deck, dislodging both guns. Cushman and Hall didn't hesitate; they both dived into the murky dark waters of the Delaware River.

Medford yanked the musket impatiently from the Royal Marine and quickly took aim at David Johnson. "Get another ball ready. I will need it for the girl." Medford smiled and was about to pull the trigger when the deck of the ship violently moved, sweeping him off his feet. He hit the deck hard, his head bouncing roughly off the surface. Captain George Medford lay still as the *HMS Richmond* began to take on water.

David Johnson struggled to remain conscious. He had managed to slow the bleeding, but he was struggling hard to pull Sarah to safety. Half of the stretcher was now hanging over the pier. David knew if he let go, she would plunge into the river. The explosion had startled him, and he wasn't ready when the Richmond careened into the pier, then listed back onto its starboard side. Sarah shifted

THE SIGNERS

with the pier and was now dangling over the side. David held on, but he knew it was only a matter of time. One minute later, Sarah shifted again, and David could only watch as his illegitimate daughter plunged into the Delaware.

Cushman and Hall swam hard toward the shore. They decided to avoid the pier altogether as there would surely be many survivors from the *Richmond*. Hall noticed her first and yelled to Cushman, "Ben, look."

Cushman looked just in time to watch one of the girls plunge from a stretcher into the river. Without saying a word, both men swam as hard as they could toward the pier. Sarah hit the water with a thud and remained on the surface for only a few seconds. She began to sink quickly into the muddy Delaware. Hall arrived first and dived below the water. Cushman waited anxiously, ready to dive as soon as Hall came up for air. Seconds later, Hall surfaced and yelled, "No luck!"

Cushman dived immediately, driving hard to the bottom. Flailing his arms in all directions, he remained on the bottom as long as he could. The frustration was mounting, and the horror of losing Sarah was too much too bear. He swam to the surface, breaking water and gasping for air. "No" was all he could get out.

Hall was on the bottom in no time. Like Cushman, he moved his arms and legs in every direction, hoping for contact. Hall was about to resurface when he thought he touched something suspended in the water. He moved toward the area, rapidly moving his arms. His lungs were burning, but he was determined to probe a little longer. He was soon rewarded when he came face-to-face with the girl. Hall grabbed ahold of her dress and brought her quickly to the surface. Cushman was about to go under again when he saw her pop above the water. It was Sarah. The two men pulled her toward the shallows, and soon they were onshore. Hall began to pound her on the back. Cushman waited for a sign, silently praying for her recovery. Sudden violent coughing alerted them that Sarah was gasping for air. She vomited and began to cough again. Slowly her breathing came back as Hall held her tightly in his arms.

"Sarah, Sarah, can you talk? Sarah." Cushman continued to talk to her while Hall patted her gently on the back.

She sat up slowly, shaking her head as if awakening from a dream. The first thing she saw was a large fireball in the distance. She then focused on Cushman. "Well you must be Mr. Cushman, you're all right, thank God! Deborah will be so happy." Sarah became more aware of her surroundings as she looked around to see who was holding her. "Oh my god, who are you, and where are we?"

Both men laughed. Cushman smiled at Sarah and spoke softly. "Sarah, this is Jacob Hall. He is a good friend. Stay with him while I search for Deborah."

Sarah nodded and smiled at Jacob Hall. "So, Mr. Hall, what do you do for a living?"

Cushman ran toward the pier. A good number of survivors were huddled not far from the *Richmond*. She was listing heavily to starboard and was starting to sink. Hall's plan had worked to perfection. He was about to walk toward the survivors when he heard a noise. Retrieving his knife, he went to investigate. The noise came from behind the crates of cargo where earlier Hall and Cushman had made their plans for retrieving the gold and the girls.

"Hello, is someone there?" The voice was definitely female.

Cushman burst into the open and saw her. She was struggling to stand and leaning on a crate. He went to her quickly, reaching out to catch her. She began to focus, and recognition came immediately. Cushman held her with all his might. The light from the burning *Richmond* sparkled like a thousand fireflies, dancing in her beautiful blue eyes. She gazed lovingly at Cushman, not believing that she was here with him at this very moment. Deborah reached up and caressed his cheeks; she smiled and kissed him with all her passion.

THE SIGNERS

The clock on Sarah Yard's mantel said it was eleven forty-five in the evening. July 1, 1776, was almost complete. "Sarah, I didn't know whom to turn to. I can't thank you enough."

"Nonsense, Mr. Cushman. It is my pleasure to help out a family in need. Mr. Johnson's wound should heal eventually. He is sleeping soundly."

"We will just be across the street if you need anything."

"We will be fine. Come on, girls, let's get you out of those wet clothes." Sarah Yard waved the two young women to follow.

"We'll be right there, Mrs. Yard," replied Deborah Johnson. "Can't we go with you?" Deborah turned to Ben Cushman and gave him a seductive smile.

"Dressed like that? Why, they would kick you out, and probably me, too, for bringing you into their fine establishment." Cushman chuckled, still holding her tight.

"You're soaking wet, and I still work there," Deborah protested mildly.

"Not if you showed up like that," teased Cushman, who received a playful punch in the arm for his comment.

"Will you be back tonight?"

"Yes. Sarah has laid out some blankets in the front parlor. Major Hall and I will sleep there. Don't worry, no one knows you are here, and if by some reason they find you, they'll have to get past us." Cushman waved at Hall, who was busy in conversation with Sarah Johnson.

Deborah leaned into Cushman and sighed. "Oh, Ben, will this nightmare ever end?"

Cushman held her tight and thought how he had almost lost Deborah, and replied, "It already has, my dear, it already has."

City Tavern had been busy the entire night. Political maneuvering was always practiced at the popular tavern, but never so much as tonight. The powerful promise of liberty had won the day as more and more representatives gave their vow to support the vote for independence scheduled tomorrow. The tavern was only now beginning to thin out.

The five men seated around a large table in the tavern room were enjoying a celebratory pint of ale. "A fine day, gentlemen. Here is to tomorrow's vote. May there be some pleasant surprises!" toasted the oldest member of the group.

"Do you really think Mr. Dickinson will withdraw tomorrow?" Thomas Jefferson asked his colleague Benjamin Franklin.

"I believe so, Thomas. He seemed sincere. Wouldn't you agree, John?" Franklin asked John Adams.

Adams nodded in the affirmative as the five men continued to give their predictions of tomorrow's historic vote. Samuel Adams and John Hancock rounded out the fivesome as they all ordered another pint.

The next round arrived quickly, and at the same time, all conversation stopped. The five Patriots stood simultaneously as two familiar faces entered the room. The warriors were drenched from head to toe, and both wore wily smiles of success.

Jefferson ran to meet his best friend. "Ben, Sarah told me you were up and running. She said you went to the Johnson house. How are Deborah and Sarah? And why are you two soaking wet?"

"Both have recovered, and well, it's a long story." Cushman smiled as the five leaders of the American Revolution broke into cheers.

"Come join us, men. You look like you could use a pint," Samuel Adams stated while Hancock slid two chairs into their table.

Hall and Cushman joined the group. "So, Red, how did the vote go today?"

"Postponed till tomorrow, but things look promising," Jefferson responded. The five members of the Continental Congress took turns recalling the day's events, from John Adams's gifted oratory to the conversion with James Duane of New York and Edward Rutledge of South Carolina. Franklin told of their meeting with John Dickinson, and Hancock related the ongoing pursuit to find Caesar Rodney.

"Sounds like a very busy day," Cushman commented.

THE SIGNERS

"So, young Benjamin, while we were busy creating a new nation today, you just lounged around Mrs. Yard's home and courted my Debby?" Franklin laughed in mock jealousy.

"Yes, that's about it." Cushman smiled. Major Hall laughed particularly loud.

"And you, Major Hall," Franklin remarked, "was your day filled with leisure like our friend Cushman's?"

Hall smiled at his friend and patron and slowly answered, "Pretty much the same as Cushman's, although I do have one of those good-news, bad-news scenarios, but it is only for members of the Secret Committee."

Hancock looked at Franklin, both members of the Secret Committee, and shrugged. Franklin nodded his consent. "Go ahead, Major Hall. The Secret Committee was going to report to the entire membership tomorrow. Give us your news."

"Good news first," demanded the always-positive Franklin.

"Very well. With Mr. Cushman's help, we were able to recover the gold."

"What gold?" echoed the three nonmembers of the Secret Committee while Hancock and Franklin cheered and congratulated the two men. A quick review of the events leading up to tonight's recovery of the gold drew unanimous approval of the operation. Even the lawyerly John Adams thought the plan brilliant.

"Ah," Franklin said, interrupting the celebration, "and now the bad news."

"Well," Hall said, hesitating, "we found the gold, but it is at the bottom of the Delaware River."

Chapter 25

Those who expect to reap the blessings of freedom must, like men, undergo the fatigues of supporting it!
—Thomas Paine

Philadelphia and New York City
August 2, 1776

As was his custom, Thomas Jefferson arrived early and decided to welcome the morning sun on one of the many benches situated in the courtyard behind the Pennsylvania statehouse. Philadelphians were busy starting the unusually comfortable Friday morning, unusual in that the air was cool and the humidity nearly nonexistent, indeed a rarity for an August day in Pennsylvania. Many stopped to watch with pride the local Pennsylvania militia drilling on the back lawn. Jefferson marveled at how young some of the soldiers looked. Their eager faces, filled with youthful confidence that bordered on cockiness, masked any fear they might have felt. Jefferson felt a tinge of guilt having helped bring his country to the abyss of war, but he also felt jealous of both their youth and their positive spirit. Hardly an old man, having just turned thirty-three back in April, Jefferson thought about resigning from his seat in the Congress and joining the Virginia militia. He could handle a horse and rifle better than most. He had revealed his thoughts to Ben Franklin earlier in the week, and Franklin had reinforced what Jefferson had instinctively known. "Older men like us send young men to war to fight and die for worthy ideas. It is up to men like us to make sure their sacrifice is not in vain."

The day would be important, but mostly for its symbolism. Today would make it official, but its impact was already being felt around the world. Delegates present today would affix their names to Jefferson's Declaration of Independence. The signers would make it official, thus ensuring two things. One, that the war was no longer a civil conflict between quarreling family members but a war truly for the independence of the Thirteen States of America. And secondly, by signing the declaration, the signers would be ensuring their treason to the Crown. If captured, each and every one of them would face the hangman's noose. With that in mind, copies of the declaration currently in circulation were without the signatures of the members of Congress. Secrecy was still trying to be maintained, but with little success. Many newspapers around the Thirteen States reveled in the courage of the signers and bragged about their local representatives, while mentioning some of the more prominent members of the Second Continental Congress.

Jefferson thought back to the day it all happened and laughed when he recalled the strangest set of circumstances to close out the historic day. The state of Delaware had just three delegates, and one, Caesar Rodney, was missing. During the preliminary vote, the remaining two delegates had been split. Rodney was a strong supporter of independence but had been recalled to Dover in order to help quell a Tory uprising in the state legislature. Caesar Rodney had ridden through the night, changing horses several times. He arrived seconds before John Hancock had ordered the doors closed and for the day's business to begin.

Jefferson recalled the amazing sight of Rodney lurching into the assembly room. It was indeed quite a spectacle as Rodney entered the room, every man knowing the significance of his surprise arrival. Some in Congress had called him a strange character, and the Delaware delegate did little to dispel that notion. Tall and razor-thin, Rodney possessed a long bony hooked nose that made him look like a caricature from a political cartoon. The left side of his face was scarred with terrible pockmarks suffered from a form of skin cancer. Rodney often wore a green silk scarf to hide the hideous markings, adding to his odd appearance. Covered in mud from head to toe and exhausted from the eighty-mile ride through a nightlong thunderstorm, Caesar Rodney appeared both surreal and inspirational.

Jefferson would never forget the look on John Adams's face after viewing the two empty chairs in the Pennsylvania delegation and Rodney's entrance. Adams had been the voice to Jefferson's written words, and words could not describe the look of satisfaction on the Bostonian's face. Standing next to John Adams, his cousin Samuel accepted congratulations from nearby delegates even before the official vote. Sam Adams's tireless work behind the scenes had kept the Congress from falling apart, especially in the earlier years. He was about to see his countrymen vote for independence, an action he had championed for over ten years. Jefferson saw tears creeping down his face as more and more delegates offered their congratulations.

Hancock's gavel had banged the meeting to order, while Caesar Rodney had taken his seat. The vote went as expected: all twelve states voted for independence, with New York abstaining. Jefferson thought about John Adams's quote that *all thirteen* clocks must strike as one. Well, at least twelve had struck as one, while the other remained silent. It was done. The Americans had done the unthinkable; they had broken away from the most powerful country in the world.

The four hundred or so British ships anchored off New York might have something to say about whether the Thirteen American States would ever be able to practice independence, but the die was cast and the revolution was about to enter a new stage.

The July 2 vote for independence had indeed been historic, but the next two days would be excruciating for Jefferson as the Congress worked in whole to begin to edit and cut his Declaration of Independence. Franklin had predicted this would happen, but it hadn't made it any easier. Although Jefferson tried to rise above it, each cut hurt him personally. John Adams, true to his word, fought hard to keep the document unchanged.

Jefferson was mortified when South Carolina and Georgia fought for the lines about slavery and the slave trade to be omitted. Political reality struck home when several Northern states accepted the omission. The North had very few slaves, but their merchants had profited from shipping them throughout the hemisphere. Several other lines were either cut or changed, and Jefferson had been surprised at how each change had upset him.

Ben Franklin had noticed Jefferson's irritation and had tried to soften his disappointment by relating a story about an apprentice hatter striking out on his own and his attempt to include his friends in designing a sign. The friends, of course, would mutilate the young hatter's original design, replacing it with a much different version. Jefferson wasn't sure if Franklin had made up the story or not, but his attempt to assuage Jefferson's displeasure at the editing of the declaration was greatly appreciated.

Mercifully, on July 4 the editing was finished and unanimously approved by the Congress. In the end, the Congress had deleted about one-fourth of Jefferson's original document, but the only major change was the paragraph dealing with slavery. Although Adams was true to his word and fought hard keep the document in its original form, he had to admit that the cuts had actually improved the document without ruining any of the key principles championed by Jefferson.

At the end of the day, Hancock had ordered the five-man declaration committee to supervise the printing of the newly edited document. Robert Livingston had returned to New York, so the remaining four, Roger Sherman, Benjamin Franklin, John Adams, and Jefferson, had sought out the young man who was contracted to do the printing for the Second Continental Congress. An Irish immigrant, twenty-nine-year-old John Dunlap was given the task. A strong supporter of the revolution, he had won the lucrative contract with the Congress over some of the more established printing houses in Philadelphia. The committee arrived at dinnertime, and Dunlap went right to work, setting type and running off close to two hundred broadside sheets. Dunlap listened with admiration as one of the world's most famous printers, Ben Franklin, offered tips throughout the night. The large broadsides were printed on just one side and measured twenty by twelve inches.

Hancock ordered the broadsides sent to all thirteen state capitals, to local newspapers, and to all his generals, especially George Washington. While the Dunlap broadsides were being distributed throughout the country, only two names appeared on the copies, president of the Congress, John Hancock, and the secretary of the Congress,

Charles Thomson. In an attempt to maintain secrecy and avoid the hangman's noose, the delegate's signatures would come another day. Only the delegates knew that Jefferson had written the declaration. Hancock ordered a handsome copy or engrossed copy to be written for the delegates to sign at a later date. Charles Thomson's clerk, Timothy Matlack, was given the task to write the handsome copy.

Reaction around the country was beyond Jefferson's wildest expectation. John Adams had written his wife, Abigail, proclaiming Americans would celebrate July 2 for generations to come with parades, picnics, and fireworks. However, almost the entire nation was rallying around the July 4 completion date.

Jefferson joined Adams and Franklin for the first public reading of the declaration in Philadelphia on Monday, July 8. As the bell tower clock overlooking the statehouse courtyard struck twelve noon, Lieutenant Colonel John Nixon, commander of public safety in Philadelphia, read aloud to a cheering crowd. Thousands listened intently to the majestic words and cheered loudest when the abuses of King George III were listed. Nixon's strong baritone voice gave wings to Jefferson's words, and when he finished, the crowd erupted with applause. The shouting and screaming of approval was so loud that Jefferson couldn't hear the drum corps. Every man emptied his rifle into the air, causing several people to be stung by descending lead balls. Strangers embraced, while young and old danced in the courtyard, creating energy and emotions seldom seen. Many members of Congress strode over to Jefferson to offer a handshake of congratulations. The modest Virginian accepted his fellow delegates' kind words with his normal humility. Adams and Franklin seemed to enjoy his uneasiness.

When the New York provincial government formally adapted the declaration on July 9, citizens went wild in celebration. The state went so far as to release everyone from debtor's prison. In Boston, citizens cheered well into the night, and the taverns remained open to accommodate their merriment. In Virginia, the state legislature ruled that all morning and evening prayer services remove the phrase *"Lord save the king."* And in Baltimore, a crowd of thousands burned King George in effigy.

Some argued that these celebrations would have little effect on the coming war and in fact might bring false hope. But perhaps the most important reaction happened at the epicenter of the revolution. Two miles from the largest armada ever assembled in world history, George Washington ordered the reading of the Declaration of Independence to the troops organizing the defense of New York City. On Tuesday, July 9, soldiers from all Thirteen American States were marched into public square to hear the declaration read aloud. Similar to the reaction in Philadelphia, soldiers and citizens alike enjoyed a riotous celebration. Bands played, people sang patriotic songs, and of course, the taverns stayed open late to accommodate the revelers. According to reports coming from New York, the soldiers and citizens had marched down Broadway to Bowling Green and, using ropes and crowbars, toppled the huge lead statue of King George III perched upon his giant horse. The crowd exploded with joy when the statue tumbled from its base. Later that night, passersby screamed in delight at the sight of George's head impaled atop a long spear outside a nearby tavern. Further reports from New York indicated that the remaining statue was to be melted into bullets, to be returned to the *brains of British soldiers.*

In a letter to the Congress, Washington indicated that he had been displeased with the mob mentality. However, privately, Washington was elated with the turn of events. The Declaration of Independence had given his soldiers something very worthwhile to fight for. Enlistments were skyrocketing, desertions had trickled to a handful, and most importantly, men whose enlistments were completed were beginning to rejoin by the thousands. Morale hadn't been this high since the siege of Boston. John Adams might have summed it all up when he wrote, "We are in the very midst of a revolution, the most complete, unexpected, and remarkable of any in the history of nations."

Jefferson's recollection was broken when a familiar voice called out, "Thomas, you look quite contemplative. What are you daydreaming about?" Benjamin Franklin smiled as he struggled to lower himself beside his friend. Jefferson's offer of a helping hand was waved off as Franklin steadied his cane and gently lowered himself onto the bench.

"Arthritis?" Jefferson asked.

"Perhaps, probably just old age. But don't let anyone fool you, Thomas. Being old beats the alternative." Pausing for a few seconds, Franklin asked his colleague, "It's a beautiful day to commit treason, don't you think?"

Jefferson laughed at his friend. "I couldn't think of a better group of men to cause the king such trouble," he stated while waving his hand toward the gathering crowd.

"Yes, I'm sure the king will raise the bounty on all our heads once he sees our signatures. Not that it has been such a big secret. I received a letter from a friend living in New Jersey. A couple hundred of the king's cavalry were attempting to cross into New Jersey from Staten Island. Seems they had an old map and didn't realize how swampy it was this time of year. Got hung up for a few days, and some of our boys started shooting at them, sending them scurrying back to camp. The rumor is that they were on a secret mission for the king."

"And what might that mission be?" Jefferson asked his fellow delegate.

"To hunt down and kill the members of the Second Continental Congress," suggested the patriarch of the Continental Congress.

"Heading to Philadelphia, eh." Jefferson shrugged off the threat but instinctively knew that it was probably real.

"I suppose they will attempt to succeed where Rourke failed," commented the older statesman.

"Any clues to his whereabouts?"

"Seems to have disappeared from the face of the earth," replied Franklin. "Don't worry, we'll find him."

"Any word on the woman I saw him with? I only got a glimpse of her, but from what I saw, she was stunning. I swear she was the woman we saw at City Tavern talking to Deborah. Ben was introduced to her only as Ms. Lydia."

"Of course, I remember, beautiful black hair and piercing eyes. Her name is Lydia Ames. Some call her Philadelphia's first courtesan. She was one of the many beautiful women who associated with Rourke. Seems she and Rourke have both disappeared."

"I'm a bit surprised you weren't close friends with Mr. Rourke," Jefferson declared with a smile.

"How so?" A surprised Franklin looked with disgust that he would associate with a murderer like Rourke.

"Well, you said he kept the company of beautiful women." Jefferson laughed with delight as Franklin finally recognized Jefferson's jab.

"It's not often you can pull one off on me." Franklin grinned.

Jefferson shook his head in agreement and decided to change the subject. "Did you hear about the British ships moving up the Hudson?"

"Only bits and pieces. What have you learned?"

"Ben got a letter from his brother James. You might recall he is an aide for General Washington. He stated that the two warships and several tenders sailed right by our Brooklyn guns. They never even got off a single shot. Our batteries at Red Hook and Governors Island fired off over 150 rounds, inflicting only minor damage on the *HMS Rose*. The only casualties were six of our own gunners, killed when one of the cannons blew up. Seems they were rather drunk at the time and were careless.

"The warships fired into the town. Women and children were literally dodging cannonballs in the streets of New York City. Needless to say, there was quite a panic. They sailed all the way up to Tarry-Town, where the river widens. Their ships are anchored there now, effectively cutting off any supplies to Washington coming from the north. To make matters even worse, at the end of the day, the *HMS Eagle* was spotted off Long Island. It is the flagship of Admiral Howe. The rest of the fleet can't be far off."

"I see an even bigger problem. If they can get several ships past our guns, what will stop them from sending fifteen or twenty ships, loaded with troops, anywhere up or down the river? They can surround Washington at any time," Franklin concluded.

"True, defending New York is a fool's errand without naval power. We must work to get Congress to withdraw his orders to defend the city," Jefferson stated firmly.

"I'm afraid the political winds will have to blow differently for that to happen. Perhaps our good general will perform like Caesar or Alexander. Historians will write about his genius in defeating superior British forces in and around New York City," Franklin replied hopefully.

"Perhaps so, but remember, Caesar and Alexander both had professional armies. Washington has a bunch of farmers and shopkeepers," Jefferson stated cautiously. "I am still curious as to why Howe continues to dawdle. He has plenty of ships and men to attack General Washington."

"Perhaps he is too busy entertaining his mistress. Rumor is, she is quite stunning. You know, he brought her from Boston, made her husband the head of British prisons."

Jefferson laughed; he was amazed at Franklin's uncanny pipeline of gossip, which always turned out to be true.

Three young boys, barely into their teen years, had been cutting through the courtyard, heading toward Fifth Street. They carried fishing poles, and each had what looked like a bucket of worms. Stopping within twenty yards of the two famous Patriots, the two smaller boys seemed to be challenging their leader. Hitching up his trousers and with a determined look on his face, he began to stride toward the bench.

Jefferson was first to notice the intrusion.

"Excuse me, Mr. Jefferson, Mr. Franklin, might I have a word with you?" The boy was shaking with apprehension as he stood before the two.

"Boy, can't you see you're interrupting important business?" Franklin scowled with his angriest face.

The boy took a step back as if to run; his colleagues took two.

Jefferson smiled and held up his hand. "Boy, are you from Philadelphia?"

"Yes, sir." The boy spoke squeamishly as he continued to shuffle away.

"Then I suppose you've heard of Dr. Franklin's legendary sense of humor?" Jefferson asked softly.

THE SIGNERS

"Yes, I suppose I have." The boy stopped his retreat, but the look of fear remained.

"Well, I believe you've just been subject to one of his pranks. You see, Mr. Franklin's bark is far worse than his bite."

Franklin burst into laughter, as if he were a twelve-year-old. "Sorry, boy, but you should have seen your face." The seventy-year-old continued to laugh as all three boys realized the two famous Patriots were indeed human.

"Come, come," Franklin said, urging the other boys to gather around. "Now, what can we do for three such fine fellows?"

The leader of the group ginned up his courage once more and asked, "Just wanted to thank you both."

"What for?" Franklin asked.

"For standing up and doing what's right!" the smallest of the three yelled.

"Yeah, my dad says it took courage to stand up to the king. He said we're gonna create a brand-new country, a country where no one has to worry about a king takin' away our freedoms!" It was their leader speaking again.

Both men smiled as Franklin poked his cane toward the middle child. "What about you? What do you think?"

The boy hesitated, then spoke softly. "My mom thinks you're all crazy."

Everybody broke into a hearty laugh as the other boys playfully punched their companion. Jefferson took a deep sigh and responded, "You know, boy, your mother is probably right."

The boys stayed for a few more moments, trading fishing stories, speculating on British strategy, and bragging about who was the best marksman among them. Franklin, of course, convinced all that he would hold that title. The boys left, heading for the Delaware River, all three promising to join the Army next year and help win the war. Both men stared at the three youngsters as the gallivanted away from the courtyard.

"The future, Thomas, they are the future. The sacrifices we make today will guarantee a brighter future for our children and grandchildren. This is why we do what we do today," the elder statesman philosophized.

Jefferson shook his head in agreement. "Indeed a great sacrifice will be demanded from all of us, young and old. I do believe generations from now will look back and thank us for those sacrifices. Perhaps the lessons we learn today will spare future generations from the same mistakes that have brought us to this war."

"Perhaps, Thomas, perhaps, but if history has taught us anything, it is that humans have a tendency to do just the opposite." Both men nodded and then waved at yet another interruption.

"Gentlemen, a fine morning for such an important ceremony, don't you think?" It was Samuel Adams, whose grin covered his entire face.

"Good day to you, Sam. Won't you join us on our bench?" Franklin smiled and slid to an end, offering the Massachusetts delegate the middle of the bench.

"Yes, Sam, please sit," encouraged Jefferson.

"Don't mind if I do," replied the fifty-three-year-old retired tax collector. "Thomas, I haven't seen your friend Ben in a few days. Has he left us?"

Jefferson's face turned sorrowful. "Yes, Ben received a letter from his brother James. Seems that their younger brother George has also joined up with Washington." Franklin and Adams nodded their approval as they recalled how George Cushman and Major Jacob Hall had survived the cowardly attack on Hancock's merchant ship *Treasure*.

"Apparently, General Washington heard Ben was in Philadelphia and requested James to write and offer him a commission as one of his officers."

"Very impressive, three Cushman boys with the general," Adams noted.

"And dangerous," added Franklin.

"When did he leave?" inquired Adams.

"Just yesterday, Dr. Rush gave him a clean bill of health."

"Our reluctant Patriot will be a valuable asset to the general," commented Adams.

THE SIGNERS

"Pity the poor British who run into him," added Franklin.

Jefferson smiled; he missed his friend greatly and prayed daily for his safety. "If he didn't encounter any difficulties, he should be with General Washington today or tomorrow."

"Gentlemen, I think it's time," Adams proclaimed, pointing at the sturdy group of men as they began to file into the Pennsylvania statehouse from the courtyard. The three Patriots rose simultaneous and headed toward the back door. They entered into the lobby, past the stairwell leading to the second floor, and into the assembly room. The familiar space had the same table arrangement with the green covers, inkstands, and candles.

Thomas Jefferson was the last to enter, soaking in the significance of this day. Today, they would attach their names to the document he had grown to love. Looking over the delegates, he began to make some observations.

The first thing he noticed was that several of the men who had argued and fought over the declaration during the final week of June and early July were not present. Most noticeably absent was his fellow committeeman Robert Livingston. Also missing was John Dickinson.

Other delegates, who had been absent during the debate, were now back and ready to sign. And still some others who had been there and voted for the declaration were absent today but would be returning soon. Perhaps the most important man missing today was the author of the resolution for independence, fellow Virginian Richard Henry Lee, who was back in Virginia and was scheduled to return in several weeks.

There were also a number of new delegates who were elected to the Congress after July 4. President Hancock had already ruled that they would be allowed to sign the declaration. *Allowed to sign,* Jefferson thought to himself. *With a bounty on every signer, they ought to be given the choice not to sign.* But all eight had already declared a desire to be part of history. Dr. Benjamin Rush, who had helped Ben Cushman recover from his injuries, was one of the eight and a good friend to Jefferson.

Hancock's gavel boomed down at exactly ten o'clock. "Gentlemen, we have much to discuss today, but as all of you know, it is time to sign the Declaration of Independence." Hancock hesitated for a few seconds, then added, "Admiral Howe continues to send peace emissaries to General Washington, and the general continues to tell him that we will take both peace and independence." Hancock placed heavy emphasis on *and independence.*

"God bless ol' George. Next time they send a document, the general ought to shove it up Howe's arse!"

Jefferson couldn't tell which Maryland delegate had shouted out, but the rest of the Congress roared their approval.

"Very colorful," replied Hancock. "On a serious note, gentlemen, I am sure no one would think any ill with anyone who chooses not to attach their signature. All of you have families, and they will certainly be targets of the British. By British law we will all be committing treason." Hancock spanned the assembly room, searching for any last-minute defections, but only saw firm and determined faces staring back at him. "Very well, let us begin." Hancock stood, removing his white wig, something he had never done while Congress was in session.

"Gentleman, it has been an honor and a privilege to serve alongside you these past months. Your unselfish dedication to your country and your constituents has both impressed and humbled me. I may be your president by election, but I hope you will consider me your equal by example."

"Hear, hear!" the members responded with approval of the heartfelt words.

"Mr. Thomson has the new, handsome copy at his table. We will start with the Georgia delegation and move north," declared the president of the Second Continental Congress.

"You first, Mr. Hancock." It was Samuel Adams who called out from the Massachusetts delegation.

"Very well, it will be a great honor," replied Hancock.

Hancock strode from behind his perch as leader of the Congress and proceeded to sign on the center-bottom of the declaration. He was followed by the Georgia delegation.

"Why so large, Mr. Hancock?" Lyman Hall of Georgia asked about the large signature of the president.

THE SIGNERS

"So the king can read my name without his spectacles and may double his reward of five hundred pounds for my head," replied Hancock. The men nodded their approval.

Hancock stood beside the table as each delegate attached their signature to the inspirational document. No one hesitated as the men signed freely.

William Ellery, from Rhode Island, leaned over to Jefferson and observed, "Mr. Jefferson, I look into the faces of these signers and see no fear. A truly remarkable group of Patriots."

"An astute observation, William. I, too, am overwhelmed with the gravity of the situation, yet the calm and determined demeanor of my fellow signers is indeed impressive," replied Jefferson, who, when he got nervous, tended to speak as he wrote.

When it was Jefferson's turn to sign, one of the members called out, "Mr. Jefferson, your words are indeed poetic and will have an impact beyond any of our wildest imaginations. God bless you, sir." And with that he signed his name to the Declaration of Independence. Jefferson quickly turned away, hoping to keep the sight of tears welling in his eyes from the other delegates.

Jefferson lingered near the table as the Middle states gave way to the Northern states. No one said anything more as key members of the Massachusetts delegation began to sign. Jefferson was the first to congratulate John and Samuel Adams, who, like Jefferson, signed in silence but attempted to hide their emotions.

It was the sixty-year-old Stephen Hopkins of Rhode Island, one of the last delegates to sign and second only to Ben Franklin in age, who might have summed up the emotional ceremony when he stated softly before signing, "My hand trembles, but my heart does not."

And then it was over; the members returned to their seats as Hancock continued with the day's business. Thomas Jefferson allowed his mind to wander. He looked around the room at the men who had just signed their names to the document he had produced. Would it be their death warrant or the opening act of a brave, new world?

The End

About the Author

Jim Bollenbacher taught American government and American history for thirty-one years at Midview High School and Sandusky High School, both located in northern Ohio. Recently retired, he coached for forty-one years as a high school assistant and head football coach. He graduated from Hiram College in Ohio, majoring in political science and minoring in history. While at Hiram, he played two years of football and four years of baseball. Jim is a member of the Hiram College Athletic Hall of Fame. He holds a master's degree in education from Ashland University. Jim lives in Huron, Ohio, on the shores of Lake Erie, where he and his wife, Patty, raised four adult children. When not writing historical fiction centering on the American Revolutionary period or attempting to work on his golf game, he, with his wife, spend time playing with their three grandchildren.

Two of his great passions are history and athletics, which inspired him to write historical fiction. He says, "Great movements in history have many things in common, dynamic leadership, unwavering commitment, and stubborn persistence, the same characteristics one gains from athletics. These are the elements that drew me to write about the American Revolutionary period. My hope is that you will be entertained by an adventure story and, in the process, relearn this vital period of American history."